★★★★★★★★★★★★★★★★★★★★★★★★★★★★★★

ALL-AMERICAN
KIDD

★★★★★★★★★★★★★★★★★★★★★★★★★★★★★★

ROB POULIN

GROUP POULAIN

Published by

Group Poulain Publishers
P.O. Box 850015
Braintree, MA 02185

ISBN: 0996796703
ISBN-13: 9780996796705

★★★★★★★★★★★★★★★★★★★★★★★★★★★★★★★★★★★

For Kristen—

who pushed me twice to drive cross-country, alone, for
ideas and inspiration, and met me both times at the end
of the road.

★★★★★★★★★★★★★★★★★★★★★★★★★★★★★★★★★★★

PROLOGUE

★ ★

President Kidd took the official phone call at 3:27 P.M. on a sweltering Tuesday in the middle of May.

Seated behind his desk in the Oval Office, chin to his chest, green eyes studying the threads of his chartreuse necktie, Kidd listened politely to the voice at the other end of the phone. He offered an "Uh-huh" and "Okay," but said nothing else. The call itself was short; it couldn't have lasted more than twenty seconds. Then the voice ended and the line clicked off.

The conversation over, Kidd reached out and placed the receiver in its cradle. His hand was shaking. Every part of him seemed to be shaking—his knees, his shoulder blades, even his liver.

Kidd leaned back in his chair and returned his chin to his chest. He took a deep breath to calm himself, but the breath had little effect; his body was on an anxiety-fed rampage. He felt beads of sweat sprouting on his brow like cabbages in a field. He studied the threads of his necktie again, until he heard—

"Ahem."

Kidd looked up.

At the end of the oval he saw Tom Prudell, his chief of staff; Kidd's longtime adviser was leaning back against the marble mantel of the fireplace at the far side of the room.

At forty-eight, Prudell still had wavy black hair and a young face. He was a large man, considered fat, and he wore horn-rimmed eyeglasses which did nothing to enhance his appearance. In front of his mouth, he was rubbing his thumb and index finger together like a Boy Scout with wooden sticks trying to start a fire. In his right hand he was holding a Dixie cup containing Poland Spring water from a dispenser in the kitchenette.

Most prominent of all, Prudell was staring at Kidd, not kindly. He had curled his top lip, bent his nose and arched his eyebrows. His face appeared to Kidd like a jigsaw puzzle just spilled from its box.

That look told Kidd something very clear: The chief of staff wanted a sign about the contents of the phone call.

Kidd pursed his lips in contemplation. How could he say what he was about to say? No man, not one, had ever had to say it in all of American history. Kidd hesitated. Few words came to him, not even a simple yes. Instead, Kidd nodded sheepishly. It was a nod to affirm what Prudell had been warning him to expect for three weeks: In the matter of his impeachment, Charles Bentley Kidd had been found guilty.

Behind the desk, Kidd looked on as Prudell's top lip went limp, his nose straightened and his eyebrows sank below the rim of his glasses. In the process, the chief of staff's face lost all expression. Prudell stared into his Dixie cup. He mumbled something, raised the edge of the cup to his bottom lip and drained it. Then he did something he never would have done under normal circumstances, not within the working space of the most powerful man on earth: He crumpled the cup, set it on the mantel, and left it there.

Prudell pushed off the mantel, stood straight and adjusted his tan suit coat to smooth its fabric. Like everything else about Prudell, the suit was too large. He wore large shoes, broad shirts, long ties and a gargantuan wrist watch. It was the watch Prudell was looking at now. He had cocked his wrist and was studying its pie-plate face, marking the time.

Ignoring his commander in chief, Prudell stepped forward and waddled out a camouflaged door to his right. The chief of staff pulled the door shut with a lonely thud that brought a pit to Kidd's stomach.

The room fell silent.

Kidd lowered his eyes to the chartreuse threads of his necktie. He wondered where Prudell was going, but at this point, the answer wouldn't be good. He made an attempt to drum his fingers over the chair's armrests, but he summoned little energy to complete the motion. Taking that phone call had been draining enough, but the five sleepless nights preceding it had been debilitating. Now Kidd was experiencing a robust nausea, as if someone had poured liquefied uranium down his throat. All he wanted was to slump in his chair, and stare at his necktie, and remain entirely still.

After a few silent seconds, Kidd noticed how empty the Oval Office could sound. Empty and dead. Even as the outside world was clamoring for its president of six years to be hanged by the testicles he loved to use.

The thought of an American public that hated him devastated Kidd. His eyes began to tear; his sinuses clotted. He broke his gaze from the necktie and tried to shake the moisture away.

You must be strong, Kidd told himself. You have to summon your reserves. You've got to be a man undivided, like Mama used to say. Things will go fast now.

Certain he would never see the inside of the Oval Office again, Kidd made a mental inventory of the surroundings.

He started with the smooth white wall to his left and swept his gaze across the gentle curve of the room, over beautiful sculptures and paintings, across elegant sofas and chairs and cabinetry.

Kidd's damp eyes took in every object, which stirred memories both giddy and chest-swelling. He did not own any of these objects, but they had become a part of Kidd during his administration. Each object, firm and fixed in its place, had borne witness to all the momentous events Kidd had made happen in this room. It was a few of those events (the naked ones, mostly) that those bastards on the Hill were punishing him for now.

A knock at the camouflaged door broke into Kidd's thoughts. The knob twisted. Prudell had returned.

The chief of staff opened the door and stepped into the office. He wasn't alone. Kidd looked on with a sense of dread as four Secret Service agents trailed in behind Prudell.

The agents were not unknown to Kidd. He had known them for years. They were Gary, Brad, Billy and Jay—his regular afternoon detail. They were men he had laughed with, shared stories between and told the occasional dirty joke to. They were men he considered loyal. By the way they were inspecting him now, Kidd felt as beloved as a Pakistani caught taking a piss on a statue of Gandhi.

Then Kidd's dread grew. On the outdoor patio to his right, he heard a cackle.

Turning his head, Kidd saw a group assembling outside. Those gathering were all excited, talking as loudly as a bunch of teenagers ready for a Homecoming pep rally.

Kidd couldn't see much through the window, only bits and pieces of body parts—swaying arms, shifting torsos, a pair of smoking-hot breasts. He wondered whom the body parts belonged to. Especially those breasts.

Kidd didn't have time to ponder. The Secret Service agents surrounded him, taking up positions at each corner of the desk. When they were set, Prudell studied the arrangement and approved it with a nod. He turned and walked five paces to the patio door.

At the door, Prudell rested a hand on the knob. He paused like a magician about to perform a trick, then he reeled back and yanked the door open.

The cackling crowd went quiet.

The chief of staff poked his head into the silence and checked something on the South Lawn. Satisfied, he turned toward Kidd and the agents.

"Mr. President," Prudell said, crinkling his nose as if sniffing a mound of pig shit, "we're ready."

The door swung wide, and Kidd could finally put some faces to the body parts. Waiting for him on the patio were staff members, interns, tour guides, even a chef. Under normal circumstances, these workers would never be allowed to congregate outside the office of the president. But these weren't normal times. This was history. The first instance of a president's getting booted out of office by impeachment, and for a so-called "sex scandal" at that. How could anyone pass up an opportunity to witness that president's departure from the White House up close and personal? There might even be a book deal in it.

Some of the workers craned their necks at Kidd through the rectangular opening, trying to catch a glimpse of the man who allowed them to hit one of history's all-time jackpots.

Kidd took a deep breath. He had expected a crowd, but nothing this big, and definitely not so close to the Oval Office. The moisture in his eyes and nose grew thicker.

Seeing all the workers who had come to witness his death march, Kidd set one goal—to keep from crying. He considered it his dignified obligation to make it out of the Oval Office and over to the waiting helicopter without sobbing in front of everybody. His legacy, if he had a legacy left, demanded it.

It isn't going to be easy, Chuck, Kidd thought. If you're going to make it out dry-eyed, you better do something. Fast!

Kidd tried to rev himself up by remembering past successes. He recalled his first presidential primary campaign, when he had made the other contenders (one of them his current vice president) look like thumb-sucking ninnies through the sheer force of his incomparable good looks. He thought back on the G20 summit in Honolulu, when he had held Japan's feet to the embers over an auto-parts trade issue he knew nothing about. He gushed as he brought forth visions of his international diplomacy in Quito two years earlier, where he brokered his famous peace treaty between Peru and Chile.

These instances were all good times, and great victories. Sufficiently pumped, Kidd pushed away from his desk and stood as tall as his six-foot three-inch frame would allow. With a grand gesture sure to be seen by the people outside his patio door, he stretched his hand forward and flipped the lid on a mahogany humidor which sat on his desktop. Inside the box were not cigars, but a stash of plastic-wrapped, heart-shaped, and now-infamous lollipops, each adorned with a star-spangled ribbon tied around its stem. The lollipops gazed back at him from the Spanish cedar lining.

Kidd put a finger to his chin, then he rummaged through the stash and selected one from the bottom of the pile. To Kidd, it looked like it was being crushed, a feeling he could commiserate with. He slipped off the plastic wrapping and thrust the lollipop into his mouth. Vanilla-cherry poured across his tongue, calming him.

Kidd enjoyed the flavor for a moment, then he rolled the lollipop to his cheek and looked around at the agents and Prudell and the crowd. Everyone seemed stiff and serious, so Kidd did what he always did in uncomfortable situations: He grinned. As usual, he knew the situation was wholly inappropriate for it, but he had never been able to control himself when it came to matters of the smile. He was, after all, a man who had laughed out loud the first time he met his wife's retarded cousin.

With a bulge in his cheek and the grin on his puss, Kidd felt ready to make his departure. He smoothed his tailor-made charcoal suit coat, flattened the necktie against his white dress shirt and swung around the desk. He walked with the Secret Service agents toward the door. When he reached it, Kidd nodded to Prudell, who was holding firmly to the edge of the doorframe.

"Take me out, Tom," Kidd said in an upbeat voice. "Let's get this thing over with the right way, eh?" He slapped Prudell's shoulder with a hollow joviality.

Prudell led the group to the patio and into the soupy heat of the May afternoon. Kidd stopped among the crowd to find and say goodbye to his secretary, a menopausal woman whom Kidd had never once seen smile. With his farewell to her in order, Kidd turned and came face-to-face with a flagstone walkway lined on both sides with more staff—

And more chefs.

The presence of the staff didn't fluster Kidd, but the sight of the chefs did. What is this? Kidd asked himself. Had the whole damn kitchen crew wandered over from the house? He noticed that many of the chefs were grinning, too, their vengeful eyes following him as he started to make his way between them.

Kidd struggled not to let their grins bother him. He stuck out his jaw and kept up his smile. He tongued the lollipop with irreverent indifference. He tried to think of the chefs, wrapped in their bleached smocks, as just another White House colonnade he needed to stroll past. He would not give these idiots one more teaspoon of satisfaction. Deep down, though, he couldn't really blame them for wanting him gone. After all, it was one of their ranks who got him into this mess.

Her name was Amanda Pacheco, a young pastry chef just out of the Commonwealth Culinary Institute in Boston. She was also attractive and vivacious as hell, and in her short time at the White House, she had created many tongue-melting confections for the leader of the free world—rich, succulent concoctions which he had devoured with frequency, and ferocity, and an insatiable desire to always have more. But while Kidd loved the sweets, it was Miss Pacheco he found most irresistible.

Come to think of it, Kidd pondered as he walked away from the kitchen crew and into a gauntlet of gawking underlings, many of them nubile administrative assistants clutching legal folders to perky bosoms, he found most women irresistible. He fluctuated madly between a desire for brunettes, blondes, redheads and raven-haired. Between skin tones of dark chocolate and white cream, with stops along the way for all variations in the middle.

Was that so wrong? Kidd wondered. Could you really fault a man for his love of the scrumptious sex? No! No more than you could fault Eisenhower for loving golf or Nixon for that stupid dog.

Unfortunately, Congress didn't see it that way.

The votes in the Senate hadn't been close, it was made clear to Kidd during his brief phone call a few minutes earlier with that chamber's sergeant at arms. By overwhelming margins, one of them a unanimous one hundred to nothing, Kidd was found guilty on seven counts of making false statements to Congress, five counts of obstruction of justice, and three ridiculous counts of accepting a bribe. He was to leave the Oval Office immediately and cede his duties as leader of the free world to Vice President Russell. There would be no farewell speeches, no packing the suitcase, and no final romps in the Red Room with the *strange du jour*. Just hang up the phone and go. They'd send a U-Haul.

Well, Kidd chuckled, as he eyeballed another delectable assistant in a thigh-high mini, he would have the last laugh yet. They'd be finding condom wrappers around this place for years.

The entourage reached the end of the flagstone path. Across an asphalt driveway, Kidd could see the South Lawn; on it was parked the green-and-white military helicopter known as Marine One. His favorite ride. Kidd felt his concern ease off. He was halfway to his goal and still no tears.

But as Kidd took a step onto the asphalt, he heard a commotion that made his heart stall. He turned sharply to see a horde of network reporters and news crews pressing forward against velvet ropes strung across the driveway. Shutter clacks riddled him like bullets from a Tommy Gun; video cameras rolled. Then each reporter, eager and obnoxious, shouted out a question.

Kidd squeezed the lollipop between his cheek and teeth. What a bunch of knobgobbers. He decided it was better to avoid them. He cut toward the helicopter and did his best Ronald Reagan, pretending not to hear, but hearing every word.

"Did your female distractions lead to the current economic crisis?" yelled CBS's David Towne.

"What about the abandonment by your own party?" blared ABC's Fulton Rey.

"Do you have any plans to see Amanda Pacheco again?" That one came from some twit at the *National Enquirer.*

Kidd sighed. It wasn't always like this, he reminded himself.

He remembered a time when he had loved the White House Press Corps, and its members had loved him more. Back then, such was his power over these nubs that he had dictated their every move. Complain about some vital initiative bogged down in committee, and it would only be a matter of time before reporter after reporter was tearing at the committee's chairman until the poor slouch finally caved. Need a hit piece done on a snarky congressional loud mouth? No problem. They would shut her up, mostly by persuading their primetime news programs to rip into her husband's business dealings. He had taught them well how to sniff out a decaying carcass. Now the vultures he created were coming down to feast—on him.

Kidd had almost made it to the end of the press gaggle when something caught his eye. It was NBC's Susan Fratz. She was pushing out to him against the velvet ropes, her glossy hair curling deliciously in cinnamon spirals, her azure eyes gleaming brighter than the diamonds in her wedding band.

"Mr. President! Mr. President!" she yelled. "When can I have a post-impeachment interview?"

Against his better judgment, Kidd stopped, turned and gave Susan Fratz the once-over.

The sight of this delectable cupcake made his blood simmer; a fluid pulse shot into his Lil' Kidd. Maybe it was the wind, or his keen olfactory sense, but he could smell her intensely—the sultry wafts of sweat mingled with perfume, salon-brand shampoo and high-end skin moisturizer. It was always his sense of smell that weakened Kidd, and today was no exception. His body ached with an overwhelming desire to burrow into every part of this woman. And he wanted to do it right on the South Lawn.

But Kidd played it cool. He tongued his lollipop and said, "You want an interview, Suzy? I'll be staying at my lawyer's cottage in the Hamptons until I can find a place of my own. Why don't you take a ride up?"

Then Kidd lowered his head and stared directly into Susan Fratz's gorgeous azure eyes. His smile became inviting, even salacious. He could already taste her.

"Or maybe," he said, "you'd like it better if I took a ride *down*."

With their eyes locked, the outgoing president grinned wickedly. He just had to. His response to her had been vintage Kidd—the act of saying one thing but meaning something completely different. Especially when that something involved his lips and a woman's privates.

He couldn't blame himself for such duplicity of speech. That skill had become ingrained in him through years of politicking, when he was forced to merge the disparate concepts of indulging his libido while never appearing out of control. Or at least not indictable. On a transcript, his statement to Susan Fratz would seem ordinary, a typical answer to a typical inquiry.

But Kidd knew better, and by the look of disdain spreading across her face, Kidd knew Susan Fratz knew better, too.

Kidd left a disgusted Susan Fratz and stepped with his entourage onto the South Lawn. As he did, the clouds broke, and for the first time since leaving the Oval Office, Kidd was bathed in sunlight, making an already stifling day even hotter as the sun beat his backside.

The Secret Service detail pressed Kidd toward the helicopter, but Kidd forced them to stop.

Out in the open now, away from the gauntlet and the press corps and the many trees towering over the grounds, Kidd could get his first, best view of the White House proper. He turned to his left, squinting through ambient sunlight reflecting off the house's south face, for one final, intimate gaze at the stunning manse that was no longer his home.

He may have been standing close to it, but to Kidd the White House felt as distant as mythical Shangri-La. He would miss her.

And somehow he imagined that this graceful white lady would miss him, too. Unlike many of his predecessors, he sure as hell had brought life to the old dame—with his parties, his pizzazz, his lust for adventure. He had pumped into her a much-needed vibrancy, a flush hue to her pale cheeks, even if those lick-ass congressional hypocrites couldn't appreciate it.

"Ahem."

The voice was Prudell's again. Kidd looked over and saw the chief of staff standing stiffly.

"It's almost quarter to four, sir," Prudell said. "The vice president is waiting to be sworn in at the Capitol."

Kidd nodded. He reached for the chief of staff's clammy hand.

"So long, Tom," Kidd said with a shake.

"Goodbye," Prudell replied curtly.

Kidd started to move toward the chopper, but another inadvisable urge made him turn back.

"Oh, and Tom," Kidd said.

The chief of staff's eyebrows rose.

"Just a word of advice," Kidd said. "Nothing that's national security, you understand. Just something I've wanted to say for a while."

"Uh-huh," Prudell said. His chubby face tightened.

"You're a large man, Tom," Kidd said, "but you look good. You're youthful, you have great hair, and you always smell nice with that body spray you use. But trust me on this one. Spend a few bucks and go for that laser eye surgery. Take those glasses off your face. I don't know if you'll see any better, but with your position of power, you'll be reeling in the ladies. Just like the time we went trout fishing on the Green River in Utah."

Prudell's face froze. Without moving his lips, he replied, "I'm married, sir." Then he paused before adding, "And I didn't catch anything that weekend."

So what? Kidd wanted to ask. To both counts. But, Christ, why bother? Prudell really had been a bad fisherman, but he was the consummate goody-goody, and he always would be. So hopeless.

"And that wife of yours sure is a peach, Tom," Kidd said, trying to smooth the situation. "Give my love to her, will you?" Kidd turned and started for the helicopter again.

"Oh, and Chuck," Prudell yelled after him.

Kidd turned back.

Prudell flattened his eyebrows. "If you wanted to do this the right way, you should have done it three months ago—with

a letter of resignation." The words hung in the soupy air, sus-
pended, then all the Secret Service agents around Kidd began
to snicker.

Although it was ninety-nine degrees outside, and more
humid than a possum's crotch, Kidd felt the air turn ice-cold.
The president lowered his head and swung his chilled body
toward the giant green bug that was Marine One. A thin stream
of snot dripped from his left nostril. He really wanted to bawl.

Don't break, Chucky, Kidd begged himself. The television
cameras are still on you. They're covering you from every angle.
They're sure to see. America would see. Don't break.

Kidd forced his chin up and sucked the snot into his nose.
He shook out his mocha-brown locks that, unlike those of his
predecessors, had never turned gray during his time in office.
With a controlled gait, he pushed himself toward the helicopter
as its wilting blades prepared to cut the air above the South Lawn.

Halfway to the chopper, Kidd tried to think of his friends,
close friends to lean on in such a time of trial.

To his dismay, he realized he didn't have any. He had
acquaintances, sure—more than he knew what to do with. One
of them, his lawyer, who had argued his defense before the Senate, was letting Kidd have a temporary place to live on Long
Island until he could find a more permanent dwelling. But how
would simple acquaintances treat Kidd in the future, now that
he had been removed from office in disgrace? How would they
react to him now that he no longer wielded the power that drew
them to his flesh like mosquitoes on a balmy evening?

And what about his family? Images of them flickered
through Kidd's mind like scenes from a Saturday matinée—

—Images of his mama, Anna Kidd, now deceased. A
woman so proud of her only child that she succumbed to a

bursting heart midway through his first term, and in the process probably got him re-elected with the sympathy vote. Thank God she has already passed, Kidd thought, as he walked toward the helicopter's stairs. Just seeing her little boy in this predicament would have killed her with grief.

—Images of his wife Margaret, known to the world as Peggy but to him, always and forever, as "The Rhino." Almost six feet tall, jarringly aggressive, never wrong or willing to compromise, Margaret Huff Kidd had left her husband months ago, after the full disclosure of his relationship with Amanda Pacheco, to move back to her hometown of Chicago, where she was going to set up some new charity for the retard cousin. Which was ironic, Kidd thought now. The Rhino had never seemed one for charity. His wife, in fact, had never seemed one for sensitivity of any kind, especially toward him. He could only imagine what vulgarities she was hurling at the television as she watched this whole debacle unfold on CNN.

And, finally, he thought of his daughter Annabelle—his single, solitary child—and his heart collapsed.

His daughter Annabelle was his most priceless of jewels— an awkward, auburn-haired, green-eyed girl who had grown taller than her mother to become a beautiful, statuesque woman. He could still remember how she smelled as an infant, alternating between scents of warm formula, stale diapers and no-tear baby shampoo, when his interactions with her had been terrifying for fear that he could hurt her somehow through an act of carelessness. Now Annabelle was close to wrapping up her freshman year at the University of the West in Los Angeles, and the thought that he might be interfering with her studies caused a stab of pain. He knew this process had not been easy on her, but she had stuck by him, even as he denied and delayed, and even after she found out he was speaking "mistruths." Annabelle loved him unconditionally; he was grateful for that. But he still didn't think it wise to tell her about the blonde-brunette sandwich he had made with two of her classmates when she'd brought them home for Thanksgiving last November. There were still some things a daddy needed to keep to himself.

Kidd reached the chopper and noticed the Marine sentry posted at the staircase did not salute him. Kidd let out a sigh, then ascended the stairs. "At least you made it," he whispered to himself. "You got away without crying."

At the top of the staircase, Kidd turned to look at the crowd.

He saw the staff and kitchen help spill onto the asphalt driveway. Most were jockeying for position, cutting in between swooping journalists eager to rip away the juiciest tidbits from the last long walk of Charles Bentley Kidd. Kidd waved. He really wanted to moon everybody.

Kidd slid inside the chopper, followed by one of the Secret Service agents. The Marine sentry entered behind them. He raised the staircase and secured it as Kidd took a seat by the window.

The helicopter blades started up with a wheeze, then rumbled. The whole chopper shook.

In a few minutes, Kidd could feel the bug rising up for its short flight to Andrews Air Force Base, where he would board a private jet to take him to MacArthur Airport on Long Island. With the helicopter in motion, Kidd felt better. His sinuses were drying out and his adrenaline level had lowered. The tears he fought so vigorously to restrain had receded back to their glands.

Kidd fingered the star-spangled stick protruding from his mouth and peeled the lollipop away from his cheek, which left the skin puckered in the shape of a sunken heart. He crunched the last of the special confection, then swallowed the granular bits triumphantly.

"You made it, you wily bastard," he whispered to himself.

But in his moment of victory, Kidd's mind wandered.

What, exactly, had he made it to?

Where was he going to live after his stay in the Hamptons?

What would the future possibly hold for him?

For the first time in twenty-seven years, he held no public office.

For the first time in thirty-one years, he had no home.

For the first time since college, he was alone.

He was a pariah now—to his wife, to his party, to an America that was livid with him. What did the future hold? What could it hold?

Suddenly, Kidd felt his body shake, but it wasn't his knees rattling, or his shoulder blades, or even his liver. It was his stomach.

As the Marine helicopter cut the sky toward Kidd's uncertain destiny, the now ex-president of the United States lurched forward in his seat, heaved, and vomited a putrid layer of vanilla-cherry acid into his lap.

★ ★

PART I
EASTERN LOWLANDS

★ ★

CHAPTER 1

★ ★

It was just after dawn when Kenny Kernick made another attempt to dislodge the lump in his throat. With all the force he could muster, he swallowed hard, twisting his head and scrunching his face, trying to drive the lump down with a steady blow from his esophagus, but the lump was stubborn; it wouldn't move. Discouraged, Kenny swallowed again, grinding against the lump until his neck hurt, but none of that worked either—the lump just sat there, thick and gelatinous.

The lump had been stuck in Kenny's throat for almost three hours. As a boy who prided himself on efficiency and precision, Kenny Kernick could trace the lump's origin back to a specific point in time—the exact moment when Trooper Monk of the Massachusetts State Police poked his head out of a side office and yelled to him as he stood near a vending machine. "Your father's coming up," the cop told Kenny. He threw the boy a trio of quarters, which Kenny fumbled to the floor. "He won't be here for a while. Grab a soda and get comfortable."

But with the knowledge of his father's impending arrival firmly in his mind, Kenny could hardly think of soda, and he definitely couldn't think of comfort.

That Kenny's father was coming to get him may have been a boon for Trooper Monk, who would soon be able to pass Kenny off to someone else, but it unnerved Kenny. Forming from the elements of Kenny's growing anxiety, the lump sprung into his throat like a submerged buoy released from its anchor. With the lump firmly established, Kenny wandered out of the state police barracks and took up position on a hard metal bench at the far end of the building. From there, in the darkness, he could stare down Route 154, to watch the road with diligence for his father's golden Cadillac XTS luxury sedan.

What showed up first wasn't the Cadillac—it was drizzle. Sheets of it. The weather of that mid-October morning was wet, windy and cold. Nothing Kenny Kernick was wearing was a match for any of it.

As a result, Kenny was frozen to his core, shivering through damp khakis and a soaked button-down Oxford. The streaks of water droplets on his coke-bottle glasses made it hard for him to see. And he was sore. With every shudder from the cold, he felt pain in the muscle tissue of his shoulders, thighs and feet, the by-product of having walked for twenty miles along the back roads of Massachusetts with most of his belongings slung around his neck in an overstuffed hockey duffel bag.

But after three miserable hours in the rain, Kenny still hadn't budged an inch off the bench—not to warm himself inside the barracks, not to find food, not even to stretch. Regardless of the soaking cold and the pain, and the gelatinous lump that was lodged at the base of his throat, something terrifying compelled Kenny Kernick to sit on that bench. To sit there, and watch Route 154, and wait for his father.

That something was the announcement he would soon be forced to make. Kenny had some news for his father—some wonderfully embarrassing news that his father, who harbored a violent disdain for any type of embarrassment, was not going to like. Staring at a quiet Route 154, Kenny only hoped he could survive the disclosure. His father was known to bare fangs when he felt threatened, and Kenny had supple flesh.

Kenny winced at the thought of those fangs. He could feel the puncture of his jugular already, the river of blood wrapping around his neck like a silk scarf. His shivers mixed with nervous ticks. How had it come to this? How did things go so wrong so fast? How could one's life change so quickly?

Twenty-four hours ago, the life of Kenny Kernick had been different. At dawn the previous morning, a quiet Friday, Kenny had been asleep in his dorm room just off Harvard Yard. But by a turn of events both fateful in its occurrence and final in its outcome, Harvard now lay behind Kenny in a blackened swath of destruction.

In Harvard's aftermath, Kenny ceded the title of student and instead became something grotesque—a failure. By Friday evening, he was a boy without purpose in the world, a boy left to wander the earth in whatever direction the prevailing winds cast him.

For Kenny, the prevailing winds had not been kind. They blew him on a zigzag journey through Boston, from Beacon Hill to the Fens, then across the Mass Avenue Bridge and out onto Route 2 heading northwest. It was near Lexington, just before three in the morning, that Trooper Monk found Kenny struggling along the shoulder of the road. The boy was so spent that he was dragging his duffel bag behind him like a busted sled. Trooper Monk said he was concerned for Kenny's safety. He wasted no time throwing Kenny into the back of the cruiser, hauling him over to the barracks in Concord, and calling his father in Connecticut. Kenny could only imagine the shock Carl Kernick received when he had taken that phone call from a dead sleep. Ah, well, Kenny thought, there are other shocks to come for the man, and they promise to be much worse.

Reflecting on the night's journey, and how it ended on a cold, wet bench on the outskirts of Boston, Kenny tried to swallow again, but again, swallowing was useless. The lump felt cozy in its environs; it still wouldn't move.

Then something happened to take Kenny's mind off the lump. He heard a sound down the road, a muffled sound at first, but it got louder in a hurry. Its tone was unmistakable: It was the velvet whirr of precision-crafted pistons firing through the morning calm.

Kenny swung his head east, just in time to see a golden Cadillac XTS with Connecticut license plates race out from behind a thicket of trees. The vehicle was careening down the roadway, bounding from side to side between the shoulder and the centerline like a runaway barrel.

The sight of the luxury sedan made Kenny's stomach plummet. He considered offering up a prayer that Carl had actually been killed by a Mack truck and this Cadillac belonged to someone else, but Kenny had never been the prayerful kind. It wouldn't have done him any good anyway, for there was no mistaking the golden vehicle that was getting bigger in Kenny's eyes—Carl Kernick had arrived. Kenny felt the gelatinous lump in his throat turn rock hard.

Anxiously, Kenny looked on as the Cadillac veered to the side of the road. It threw up streams of mud from the shoulder then powered down to a gravel-crunching halt. It never bothered to turn into the driveway which led to the barracks.

From the bench, Kenny could see his father's silhouette in the driver seat. The silhouette wasn't moving. *Why isn't he getting out?* Kenny asked himself. *Why doesn't he help me? I could really use a hand with the duffel bag.*

Instead, Kenny watched his father lift that hand off the steering wheel and drop it below Kenny's line of sight. In a moment the Cadillac's trunk popped open. That's when Kenny got the picture: The amount of help Carl Kernick was in a mood to offer this morning was a big fat diddly-squat.

Honk—Carl pounded on the horn. *Honk, honk, honk, honnnnnnnnnnnnk*—

Kenny tried to steady himself, to gird his loins for the confrontation to come. Sadly, he could no longer feel his loins— they had frozen, too. With the parts of his body that still had sensation, he managed to stand up, reach down, grab the strap of his duffel bag, and drag it for thirty yards over wet grass, to the objection of stiff screaming joints.

With a grunt, Kenny lifted the duffel bag and placed it in the trunk. He latched the auto-closing decklid and walked to the Cadillac's passenger door. When he opened the door, a wall of cigarette smoke made him recoil. He beat a path through it, tumbled into the plush leather of the bucket seat, and yanked the door shut.

In the dim light of the cabin, he looked at his father. His father didn't look back.

The Cadillac peeled out.

Speed was a strange thing in the Cadillac XTS luxury sedan—it never felt like much. Why would it, given the XTS's refined interior and high-horsepower engine? But with trees flying by in a blur and his stomach doing somersaults at every dip in the road, Kenny had a pretty good idea of how fast he was traveling on this dreary Saturday morning—about ninety-five miles per hour, with only the minimal sounds of thumping wiper blades and tires on wet tar to fill his ears.

It didn't take long for the silence to eat at Kenny. He hoped his father might turn the radio on. Maybe Carl could fart. At least the man could say something. Why wasn't he saying anything?

The lump in Kenny's throat tightened.

In one month, Carl Maxwell Kernick would turn forty-nine years old, but for a multi-millionaire, his age was his only modest trait. At five-foot seven, the man could be thoroughly imposing. He was built like an American black bear, with powerful legs, stubby arms, a thick middle, and a big head topped by a short crop of dark brown hair. On his face, a well-trimmed moustache provided foundation for his broad snout. And he was, normally, the talkative sort. From a thin-lipped mouth that resembled a tear in a shopping bag, Carl Kernick frequently let loose opinion after opinion after incessant opinion. More often than not, those opinions were channeled at his scrawny, five-foot four-inch, redheaded son, especially when it came to how that son—his only child—would proceed through life.

But Carl wasn't letting loose those opinions now. He wasn't uttering a peep. Not as they got on the Mass Pike; not as they turned onto Interstate 84 and entered Connecticut; not as they hit the northern approaches to Hartford.

Through it all, Carl Kernick only stared forward, his brown eyes focused squarely on the road, his fingers clawed tightly around the steering wheel. Motionless, except to breathe.

They were crossing the Charter Oak Bridge to the east of downtown Hartford when Carl finally made a move: He dug into the left breast pocket of his cashmere overcoat and pulled out a cell phone. With vicious accuracy, Carl punched up a number on his speed dial, the chirps of the device finally pumping some much-needed noise into the silence. Then the cabin went quiet again.

When the other party picked up, Carl said, "I've got him."

There was more quiet. Kenny figured the other party was his mother, and she was rippling off some frantic question.

"He's fine," Carl shot back. "I just got onto 91. I'll be home in an hour."

More questions.

"No, you can't talk to him. You'll have plenty of time for that when I get home."

Carl punched off the call and thrust the cell phone back into his overcoat, then he reached into the pocket of his Oxford shirt and pulled out a crumpled pack of Parliament Blue cigarettes.

Smoke billowed up as he lit one of the sticks from the Cadillac's cigarette lighter.

Carl snapped the lighter back into its slot and stared at the road again, sucking on the cigarette until his cheeks puckered. He blew the smoke out in a plume and narrowed his eyes. His breathing grew heavier. The nostrils on his snout began to flare rhythmically. With a firm precision that betrayed his proud Germanic roots, Carl reached out and tapped a lick of ash into the Cadillac's tray.

"First thing Monday," he said in a rigid voice, "we're getting right back in this vehicle, driving to Harvard, and straightening this whole mess out. Understand?"

Kenny tucked his hands under his legs; he couldn't help but squirm. "It might be too late for that," the boy replied.

"Really?" Carl asked. "Tell me, why is that, Kenny?" The man took a giant inhale from his Parliament and held the smoke in his lungs, waiting for a satisfactory response.

Kenny said, "Well, I did make it official by turning in my ID card."

Carl crooked his lips, unimpressed.

"And I did receive a letter yesterday confirming I was no longer enrolled."

"Oh, you received a big fat letter saying you were no longer enrolled?" Carl said. He blew the smoke in Kenny's face.

"Yes, sir," Kenny said, coughing.

"It was signed and everything, I imagine," Carl said.

"It was," Kenny said.

"Signed by Alice Snyderman herself," Carl said. "Your freshman dean. In nice black ink."

"Something like that," Kenny muttered. Actually, it was blue ink, and there was a lot more to the story, but he was too busy blinking his smoke-stung eyes to go into detail.

Carl took another drag off the Parliament, then he let the smoke fly immediately in a powerful jet from the corner of his mouth. "Stop being such a dummkopf, Kenny. This is hardly over. What's the first thing I've tried to teach you about the real world?"

Kenny repeated Carl's mantra as if by rote: "Anything can be—"

"Renegotiated," Carl said. "That's right. Thank you for listening to me for a change."

"I just think it's too late for that," Kenny said. He noticed his meager body was sinking deeper into the plush leather beneath him. The seat felt like a casket.

"Kenny," Carl said, "it's time to pull your head out of your hole and smell the daisies. I'm a businessman, am I not? Isn't that what I do every day? Do I not trek into New York City every morning and bust my hump to run an award-winning company?"

Kenny had heard these questions before, and they always confounded him. Technically, his father worked in Larchmont, just north of New York City. And Kernick Handling Systems, Carl's small but successful automation engineering firm, had never won a single award handed out by its trade associations. It had been written up once in *The Automator* magazine over a new technique for optical-pneumatic cranberry sorting, and they had sent Carl a laminated, wall-mounted copy of the article for the KHS office, but never an award. However, challenging Carl Kernick was a difficult game. Kenny had learned early and often to toe the line.

"Yes, sir," he replied.

Carl took another suck from his Parliament. He spoke his next words slowly, like he was talking to a toddler.

"What I'm saying, Kenny, is that when we grown-ups sit down, we can usually come to a consensus. Now on Monday morning, when I call the freshman dean, and I explain to her that you think you made a mistake by asking to leave, and that you've changed your pea-sized little mind, I'm sure she'll see fit to tear up that drop letter. Then I can get you back to your studies like you never missed a day." At the conclusion of his spiel, Carl's voice relaxed. His grand plan must have made the world seem safe again. It was time to blow that notion out of the water.

"Except for one thing," Kenny said.

"What's that?" Carl asked. He drew a last drag off the Parliament, cracked his window, then expelled the butt and the smoke to the passing roadway.

"Dean Snyderman isn't going to take me back," Kenny said.

Carl's eyes narrowed again. "Why not?"

Kenny whistled a breath between clenched teeth. Here was the moment he had been dreading. How to put it? Finally, he just decided to get it over with. The truth would have to come out sooner or later, and in this case, with this man, sooner was preferable to later.

"Because a couple of weeks ago they... sort of... caught me," Kenny said.

"Caught you?" Carl asked.

Kenny nodded.

"Caught you what?" Carl asked. His rigid voice had returned, twice as tough.

"Collecting things," Kenny said. He removed his hands from under his legs and started to fidget with his seatbelt strap.

"Things?" Carl asked. "What things?" His narrow eyes grew curious, his voice leading. "Things like rare coins?"

"No," Kenny said. "Not rare coins."

"Old books, then?"

Kenny said no a second time.

"Rocks?" Carl asked.

"Nope."

"Pez dispensers?"

"Uh-uh."

"Stamps?"

"Wrong."

"Knickknacks?"

"Try again."

"Social Security?"

Kenny shook his head.

"Then in the name of the Savior," Carl fumed, "tell me and tell me now: What were you collecting?"

"Brassières," Kenny said. "Girls' brassières. From the laundry room."

Carl's jaw went slack. At the same time, his eyes twisted at grotesque angles and his foot sunk on the gas pedal, speeding the Cadillac to one hundred seven miles per hour.

Kenny's heart started to race with the vehicle, pounding against his concave chest. The confession had unleashed something monstrous in him, and that monster was raging unfettered. Kenny couldn't hold back his words.

"I took red ones, black ones, lace ones, even big mamas," he cried. "But apparently, these girls notice their stuff is missing. They started to complain. The proctors set up a sting. That's when they busted me, and Dean Snyderman took me before the Ad Board. They must have taken pity on me. I'm short, you know. I got placed on disciplinary probation, and they told me not to do it again. So I didn't."

"You didn't?" Carl asked, more like he was begging.

"No, sir," Kenny said.

"Oh, thank God." Carl breathed a sigh of relief.

"I started collecting their underpants instead."

Carl slammed on the anti-lock brakes. The Cadillac, cruising faster than any vehicle on the road, pulsed to a ferocious stop in the middle lane of the highway. Horns blared from behind, cars swerved to avoid hitting them, but Kenny kept on confessing, the words flying fast and forthright.

"Then the proctors caught me a second time, and Snyderman convened an Ad Board immediately. And the board told me that since I had violated my probation, I was being required to withdraw for disciplinary reasons. No appeals, just gone. *Au revoir*! *Auf Wiedersehen*! *Adiós, amigo*! And I figured, so what? I didn't really want to be at Harvard anyway. I hate the place. So what's the big deal?"

Carl's eyes bulged; his face turned as crimson as a Harvard sweatshirt.

"So two proctors brought me back to my room and made me pack and escorted me through the Yard. And before they let me go, they gave me a formal letter from Dean Snyderman, and the letter said I wasn't allowed into Harvard again until I had been readmitted to good standing." Kenny started to shake his head violently. "But no, no, no, I told the proctors; they didn't have to worry about that. They never had to think about it. It was never going to happen. Because I am never—going—back—to college—again—ever!"

Kenny's shouts reverberated through the cabin, drowning out the screaming traffic and making Carl's face scrunch up like the man had just licked a lemon half. Then as quickly as the noise had risen, glorious quiet fell.

Kenny took a deep breath. When he released it, his body deflated, and he settled back into the plush leather of the Cadillac's passenger seat. Life seemed okay again. The truth was out. The seat didn't even feel like a casket anymore.

The boy looked at his father with a contented smile.

Carl didn't smile back. Instead, his face had progressed to blood red, his mouth was locked into a snarl, and his bulging eyes pulsed with every heartbeat. He slammed down the gas pedal. The Cadillac shot forward like a missile.

But again, Kenny did not feel the speed. And if he had felt it, he wouldn't have cared. He was in his own world now, a world where his father didn't roam. Even as the Cadillac built up g-force, fueled by Carl Kernick's primal rage, the lump in Kenny's throat disappeared.

Carl Kernick didn't say another word all the way home. In renewed silence, father and son flew down central Connecticut's I-91, bore west at New Haven, and merged onto I-95, where they joined a slew of Mack trucks heading south to the Connecticut panhandle.

Twenty minutes later, after playing a harrowing game of vehicular leapfrog with a chemical transport, the Cadillac finally approached its destination—the town of Simondale, an upper-crust bedroom community of big houses and bigger egos snuggled along the Darien-Stamford-Greenwich corridor leading into New York.

Carl took the exit for Simondale, barely slowed, and blew through the stop sign at the end of the off-ramp. He spun the Cadillac to the right, up an oak-lined road where the treetops, still green and full, had yet to reveal any sign of autumn.

The journey to the Kernick home unfolded along a graceful curve of such roads, up and down and over—a steady stream of old-growth white oak trees punctuated by large and lovely New England-style colonial houses that had been built for southern Connecticut's burgeoning rich in the early 1990s.

For newer houses, the colonials were stunning. Kenny would give them that. They had broad hip-roof designs and spectacular 24-pane window settings, and they were frequently glorified in haughty home journals and architectural magazines.

But as amazing as they were, the colonials never meant much to Kenny. He took comfort in the oak trees. Their leaves were the only things that changed in Simondale. Nothing else ever did.

As the Cadillac crested Pheasant Hill, its V8 engine revving high, Kenny caught the first glimpse of his neighborhood below them.

At the base of the hill sat twelve shining, clapboard structures on formidable Hoban Lane, the most expensive street in Simondale. The houses were perfectly aligned in two rows of six, and all of them looked exactly as they had when Kenny first left for Harvard five weeks ago. Then his father cut the Cadillac onto Hoban, and Kenny discovered that something had changed in Simondale—across from his own driveway, someone had erected a guardhouse.

That sight made Kenny do a double take. Irrational, he thought. Nay, comical. Mrs. Croushore must have gone screwy. Kenny closed his eyes and shook his head, half expecting the guardhouse to disappear. But when Kenny opened his eyes again, the small building hadn't gone anywhere.

Instead, Kenny saw a figure in a raincoat standing in its narrow doorway; the figure was keeping an eye on the Cadillac as it roared up the lane. A second man appeared, this one wearing a trench coat. He was African-American, which was a shock given Simondale's lily-white homogeneity.

When the Cadillac pulled farther onto Hoban, Kenny noticed something else. The men at the guardhouse seemed to be buffering a third man, also wearing a trench coat, who was standing in the driveway. But it wasn't the third man who was the focus of concern; it was the guy next to him—a tall, dusty-haired fellow lugging plastic grocery bags from the back of a black Chevy Tahoe SUV.

A new neighbor? Kenny wondered. Apparently, Mrs. Croushore hadn't gone screwy after all. She had moved. Or died.

Kenny gawked at his new neighbor's curious entourage until Carl careened the Cadillac into the Kernicks' driveway. Carl thrust the vehicle into park, jerked the keys from the ignition, and sprang out of the Cadillac, slamming the driver door. At that moment, Kenny saw his mother appear in the mud room connecting their colonial with its garage.

Martha Kernick was a plump-hipped woman who had recently turned forty-seven. She had faint blue eyes, graying red hair, and a creamy skin that rarely showed color. Kenny often contemplated his mother's pale nature. And time and again, he couldn't help but wonder: Was it a result of her Irish genes, or the fact that Carl Kernick shouted at her so often, he pounded the glow right out of her? Either one was a viable hypothesis.

Martha popped her head out from behind the mud room's storm door. In her singsong voice, she asked, "Carl, what's the matter?"

Carl didn't respond. He just grunted something loud and incomprehensible, then he ripped the storm door from Martha's grasp, leapt the mud room steps, and barreled past his wife of twenty-five years before he vanished into the house.

Martha crushed one set of fingers in the other and descended the steps to the driveway. She came upon Kenny as he was opening the passenger door.

As Kenny stepped out of the vehicle, he didn't look at his nervous mother. He didn't even think to hug her. Facing the street again, his eyes moved to the action across it. To the stranger—was it a stranger? This stranger didn't seem so strange.

Then it hit him.

"Is that Charles Bonehead Kidd?" Kenny shouted.

Martha's hand flew to Kenny's mouth, but it was too late—Kidd froze for one brief second as he bent down to place a family pack of toilet tissue on the driveway. Martha pumped up her often-used fake smile. She locked her teeth together, spread her lips, and wrapped an inviting arm around Kenny. When Kidd looked at them, their pose was that of a harmless mother and son.

"We'll talk about it later," she sang without a flinch of her face. She led Kenny to the trunk. When their backs were to Kidd, Martha leaned in close to her boy. "But your father is bull pooh about the whole thing."

Kenny lifted his duffel bag from the trunk, trying to absorb her words and the shock of the neighborhood's new dynamic.

But as Kenny turned toward the house, he could not stifle his curiosity. With as much stealth as he could muster, he tried to steal one last look at the disgraced politician who had taken up residence across the street.

To his surprise, Kidd was still looking at him. Stunned, Kenny tried to avert his gaze, but he wasn't fast enough. The two new neighbors locked glances and held them, like a couple of first-day kindergarteners sizing each other up at the cubbyholes.

Kenny took in Kidd with a detached reality, as if he were seeing the man as he always had, through newspaper photographs.

In person, Kidd was much taller than Kenny realized—at least half a foot taller than Carl. He still had that brilliant facial construction which seemed to mark all men of destiny—the precise alignment of, and perfect interaction between, nose, chin, lips, cheeks, and forehead. But even with those features,

Kidd looked haggard, hardly a figure of stature. The wrinkles in his face cut deep. His light brown hair, once as glossy as a movie star's, had dulled significantly.

But what seemed totally out of place for the date and time was not how Kidd appeared physically, but what he was wearing. For some reason, Kidd had donned his presidential charcoal suit with trademark light green tie, which Kenny found odd because Kidd was almost five months removed from being president, and he had obviously just come back from Wal-Mart.

Kenny and Kidd kept their eyes glued to each other until the moment grew awkward. Then Kidd flinched.

With a grand gesture sure to be seen by Kenny and his mother, the former president reached out and stuck his hand into one of his suit's breast pockets. When the hand emerged, it was holding a red lollipop whose stick was garnished with a red, white and blue bow. Kidd peeled the lollipop from its wrapper, stuck it into his mouth, and flashed Kenny a cocksure smirk.

That's when Kenny laughed.

He remembered the Amanda Pacheco impeachment testimony about her sexual relations with Kidd. Even when read from newsprint, the testimony came across as kinky stuff—intercourse on all manner of furniture, late-night bondage parties, surreptitious sex in an Air Force One luggage rack. But most intriguing, it was filled with food fetishes, particularly an infamous episode dealing with just that kind of lollipop being swirled around Miss Pacheco's naughty parts.

As Kenny's mother led him from the driveway to the mud room, peppering him all the way with questions about why he was no longer at Harvard, it took every ounce of strength Kenny had not to ask a question of his own.

"Hey, Bonehead!" Kenny wanted to shout. "Where's that lollipop been?"

Kenny Kernick had his ideas, but he doubted, as most of America had learned to doubt, that Charles Bentley Kidd would ever tell him the truth.

CHAPTER 2

★ ★

Three weeks after Kenny Kernick returned home, he had the strangest dream.

In it, he was walking through a field of heather, quiet and solitary, when he heard a woman giggle behind him. He turned, expecting to find one of the many Harvard hotties come to torment him over his misdeeds. He was shocked to see his mother instead. Standing ten feet away, Martha Kernick was dressed in a yellow hazmat suit, as if her son were an object of filth. Worse, she was laughing at him over the fact that he had been busted for stealing women's underwear at school. "How crass!" she said, pointing a toilet bowl scrubbing wand at him. Then she giggled again and disappeared. The shock of the event jolted Kenny so hard that he awoke immediately feeling sick to his stomach.

Gathering his senses, he rolled onto his back. He stared at the ceiling, really not seeing it—without his glasses his vision was nothing more than a blend of colors. He reached to his nightstand, grabbed the lenses and pushed them to his face, and closed his eyes until his stomach settled.

Kenny opened his eyes and noticed the sun peeking in through his blinds. It illuminated his room with a ghostly hue, casting soft gold glints off the top row of his bookshelf, the row which held his academic trophies—the math awards, history awards, foreign language awards, science awards—presented to him during his time at Griggson Academy, the rigorous private school where Kenny had placed first in his graduating class.

"A lot of good those trophies or that ranking did me," Kenny lamented as he leaned over the side of the bed and lifted his sweatshirt off the floor. On the way up, he tilted the alarm clock on his nightstand to see the time. The red digital display flashed 1:39 P.M.

And what day was it? Kenny had no idea. Since his ouster from Harvard, the days and nights had all blended together. Today could have been a Tuesday, but really, he didn't care.

Kenny scratched an itchy shin and closed his eyes again, hoping for a return to the field of heather, this time without his mother. Before his mother's appearance, he had felt safe and protected there, a place where he would not be destroyed, devoured or obliterated by a force larger than himself. Kenny had no such luck. The unexpected presence of his mother in the dream had zapped him awake. His mind was already starting to roll.

What had he done since he had been home?

Not much, Kenny concluded. Days were generally spent loafing around the house. Okay, "loafing" probably wasn't the proper term for it—"being bored out of his skull" was a better phrase.

In the Kernick home, one simply did not find much in the way of entertainment. There was one television—an ancient Emerson—which was locked away in a cabinet in Carl's office for the man's private use; a computer on Carl's desk which

Kenny was allowed to touch only for typing papers or to run spreadsheet or presentation programs; some newspapers like the boring New York, Washington and New Haven broadsheets; and very few magazines outside of his mother's home and garden monthlies and his father's trade journals. Kenny's alarm clock didn't even come with a radio.

The Kernick home did have some things in bountiful abundance: books, loads of them; every printed item Carl Kernick could think of to prime his son's pea-sized mind. There were worn paperbacks on the Apollo space program, pre-Roman civilizations, and Thomas Edison. There were lengthy hardcovers about antitrust cases, the plague history of Europe, and every war the U.S. fought from the Revolution through Vietnam.

The *World Book Encyclopedia* was in-house, as were Homer's *Iliad* and *Odyssey*, Cervantes' *Don Quixote* (in Spanish), Balzac's *Cousin Bette* (in French), everything published by F. Scott Fitzgerald (in glorious American English), and a singular nonfiction work by some guy named Dale Carnegie, who had discovered a foolproof way to win friends and influence people.

Accumulated over years, they were more than Kenny could possibly devour. Those books now got Kenny through the toughest part of his existence—the evenings, after Carl Kernick had returned from work and was freely roaming the house. Kenny slunk away to his bedroom without dinner, avoiding his father at all costs.

In the refuge of his bedroom, with the door tightly closed, the up-ended world of Kenny Kernick turned serene. Kenny would crawl into bed, prop his head on a pillow and grab a book.

There he would read for hours. His eyes tracked across printed pages; they veered hypnotically over seemingly ceaseless lines of text until even the letters of the Latin alphabet began to take on an odd hieroglyphic quality. He would read throughout the night, stuffing his brain full of knowledge until dawn. Then, as light began to filter in through the slits in his closed blinds, Kenny would hear his father get ready for work and drive away.

Another darkness passed, Kenny would reassure himself. Another night survived without Carl sinking his fangs into Kenny's delicate flesh. Only then could Kenny sleep.

But for all the awkwardness which permeated the Kernick house since Kenny's humiliating return, Kenny still found himself at peace these days. How could he not be? At least he wasn't at Harvard anymore.

As with everything in Kenny's life, going to Harvard had been Carl's idea. "Trust me, son," Carl stated on the day Kenny received his acceptance letter, "Harvard University will be the defining experience of your life." Kenny believed him—until he got there, took a quick look around, and noticed the coeds. If there was one aspect of college that Kenny had not been prepared for, it was life among girls.

The reason was simple: Girls had not been part of Kenny's social fabric. No family on Hoban Lane had girls; Griggson Academy didn't admit girls. Kenny didn't even have female cousins.

The day he arrived at Harvard, Kenny looked at these feminine wonders—with their style, their beauty, their sense of experience—and he felt pathetic. Later, as the influx of the female population inundated him everywhere on campus, he found himself shying away. Just their mere presence rendered him mute. Kenny wanted nothing more than to hide from girls forever.

But there were some things an eighteen-year-old boy could not hide from, things he dared not speak about, or understand—turbulent, primordial urges deep in him.

Quite simply, Kenny wanted to touch these girls.

He wanted to smell them.

To stroke them.

To bury his nose in their hair.

To lick their toes.

Suck on their necks.

Lose himself in their girlish goodies.

But how could he? The boy just didn't know how. So Kenny Kernick came up with an equation:

$$\Omega = (\infty + \varpi)^n$$

Roughly translated, if he couldn't get close to these girls physically, he would get close to their underwear. It was Kenny's precise and efficient way to handle social impotence. It had seemed like a great equation at the time.

Kenny rolled onto his side and tucked a hand between his head and the pillow. Since his mind was already filled with visions of hot coeds clad in luscious undies, Kenny's stream of consciousness suddenly swung in a related direction. It veered toward a man who also loved girls clad in luscious undies. That man was his new neighbor, the former president Charles Bentley Kidd.

One thing Kenny had expected to see once he learned that Kidd was living across the street was a parade of girls coming and going through Kidd's front door.

The idea wasn't ludicrous. During her testimony before the Joint House-Senate Committee Investigating the Memorial Day Appointments Affair—more commonly known as "Pastrygate"—Amanda Pacheco, knowing she was licked like one of Kidd's red, white and blue bowed lollipops, had provided the committee with a list of the president's conquests as part of her immunity deal. It was a list she had accumulated mentally from the totality of her conversations with Kidd, when he had apparently admitted much to her in the throes of passion. The list was never made public during the investigation, and it never made it to trial in the Senate, but it did end up in the *National Enquirer*. From there it sent shock waves across the world by naming, among Kidd's paramours, movie stars, news reporters, swimsuit models, and even congressmen's wives. Eighty-nine congressmen's wives, to be exact. One a day for almost three months. Like they were vitamins.

Kenny expected that at least one of these former conquests would come to Simondale, or Kidd would go off to meet somebody somewhere, but this didn't happen.

On the contrary, Charles Bentley Kidd never stirred, never went anywhere, and never did anything. Since that Saturday when he and Kenny had locked eyes from opposite sides of Hoban Lane, Kidd's Chevy Tahoe had not left the driveway. The only people who ever moved around Kidd's house were the Secret Service agents, and they only came out for a shift change or to inspect any vehicular or foot traffic moving along the street. To Kenny, it all seemed so strange.

Kenny twisted onto his stomach. His thoughts about Kidd were beginning to lull him to sleep. He closed his eyes and awaited the field of heather. That's when another giggle startled him.

Kenny's eyes flew open. "What the heck?" he asked aloud. Kenny had not been dreaming those giggles after all. The giggles were real and had somehow made it into his dream. The voice of the latest giggle still sounded like his mother's, but that wouldn't make sense. In all his years, Kenny couldn't remember ever hearing his mother giggle. Life with Carl did not afford it. He could tell it was coming from downstairs.

Kenny peeled back the covers. He pulled on slippers and raced across the hardwood floor.

When he opened the bedroom door, Kenny let the giggles (and the pungent aroma of burnt coffee) guide him. He maneuvered his way across the hallway, flopped down the stairs, and scurried into the kitchen.

When he arrived there, he saw his mother sitting at the kitchen table. A coffee mug sat in front of her, but she wasn't paying attention to it. Instead, she was leaning back in her chair, laughing uncontrollably, her face redder and more animated than it had ever looked. The vision shocked him.

Then Kenny looked across the table at her guest, and he got an even bigger shock.

That guest was none other than Charles Bentley Kidd.

The former president of the United States was sitting at the opposite end of the table from Martha Kernick. He was dressed in the same charcoal suit and light green tie he had worn the first day Kenny saw him in the driveway. He palmed a coffee mug emblazoned with the word "Carl," and he was leaning over the table's Formica finish toward Kenny's mother, as if Kenny had interrupted the scoundrel in mid-detail as he regaled Martha with some amusing story from a made-up life. The moment Kidd saw Kenny, he straightened and gave the boy an uncomfortable look.

Martha followed Kidd's eyes. "Oh, Kenny," she said, trying to lean forward in her chair. Before she could stabilize herself, she giggled again and almost fell backwards.

Martha caught her balance and sucked in her laughter. After a few muffled chuckles, she composed herself. As she wiped tears from her eyes, she said, "Kenny, come in here and say hello to Mr. Kidd." She glanced at Kidd glowingly. "Mr. Kidd, this is Kenny, my son." Kenny threw his mother a cutting glare.

Kidd released the coffee mug, rose, and offered Kenny his hand. "We've met," he said. "How are you, Kenny?"

They shook. Kidd's hand was hot from the coffee mug, and it felt like granite.

"Mr. Kidd," Kenny said, nodding with reserve.

"Please, call me Bent," Kidd said. "All my friends call me Bent." He released Kenny's hand and smoothed his charcoal suit.

Kenny studied Kidd curiously as the former president sat again. "I'm sorry," Kenny said. "You want me to call you what?"

"Bent," Kidd said, returning his palm to the coffee mug.

"As in 'crooked'?" Kenny said.

Kidd didn't bat an eye at Kenny's insinuation. "As in 'Bentley,'" he said. "My middle name."

Kenny scrunched his face. Something wasn't adding up here. "I thought all your friends called you Chuck," he said.

Kidd locked his eyes on Kenny and took a sip of coffee. He pursed his lips in thought as he swallowed, seeming to ruminate hard on the question. "Nope, don't think so," he replied with a touch of bravado. He turned to Martha and smiled: "Mrs. Kernick, I have to ask you—"

Kenny cut him off: "I thought even your wife called you Chuck."

"Kenny," Martha barked. "If Mr. Kidd says people call him Bent, people call him Bent. Isn't that right, Bent?"

"That's right, Mrs. Kernick," Kidd said. Then he looked at Kenny with that cocksure smirk. Kidd had won this little battle, and the man knew it.

Martha asked, "More coffee, Bent?"

"I'd love some, Mrs. Kernick."

As Martha rose and walked to the kitchen counter, Kidd focused on the boy. "Kenny," he said, "I have to share something with you. Did you know that your mama here makes the finest cup of coffee I've ever tasted? Better than The Ritz, better than Tavern, even better than that overpaid staff at the other place I used to live. And that's the truth."

As Martha grabbed the carafe from a well-worn coffee maker, she let out a high-octave roar. "Oh, Bent!" she said, her giddy voice scraping the ceiling. On the way back with the carafe, she threw Kenny a skeptical look. "You'll have to pardon my son's—" she said, filling Kidd's mug. But when she looked at Kidd, she stopped talking. Her eyes had locked on him. Before she knew it, she was pouring his mug past the brim and, coffee had spilled onto the table.

"Whoopsie!" she cried, finally breaking her gaze and seeing the mess. "Oh, my! I'm sorry, Bent! What a dummkopf I am!" Martha laughed nervously.

"That's quite all right, Mrs. Kernick," Kidd said. He reached for some paper napkins from a stack on the table and wiped his mug and the spill.

Martha took the soiled napkins with one hand and slapped his wrist with the other. "Now, Bent," she said, "you must stop calling me Mrs. Kernick. I prefer Martha."

"Certainly, Martha," Kidd said. "If you insist."

"I insist," Martha insisted. She threw the napkins into a trash bin under the kitchen sink, then she returned to the table and filled her mug from the carafe. Without incident, this time. When she was done, she sat, sipped, looked at Kidd and said, matter-of-factly, "Now, where were we?"

Kidd smiled, nodding to Kenny. Martha glanced at Kenny again. "Oh, yes, well, as I was saying, Bent, you'll have to forgive Kenny's appearance. He's been sleeping in these days."

Suddenly, Kenny became fervently aware of how he looked. He was wearing ratty sweatpants and a faded Griggson Academy sweatshirt, and his hair was standing straight up. He licked his fingers and tried to flatten a thicket of red spikes.

"That's quite all right," Kidd said, waving him off. "I have a little girl about your age. Trust me when I tell you that I have seen her in some of the most wretched conditions..."

Kidd thumbed the handle of his mug, letting his voice trail off mysteriously. His eyes seemed to grow dim and distant, and it was clear to Kenny that the man had just brought up a topic he didn't relish discussing. Kidd changed the subject. "So, Kenny, your mama here said you used to go to Harvard?"

Kenny nodded uncomfortably. It struck him that Kidd and his mother had been sitting at this round kitchen table that had no corners to keep them separated, and that they'd been alone. Kidd was definitely a man who needed corners, or at least a chaperone. Kenny asked, "Where's the Secret Service?"

Kidd's face melted once more into the cocksure smirk, like he knew what Kenny was thinking. He jutted his jaw forward and scratched at gray whiskers sprouting from his chin.

"Well, let's see," Kidd said. "I imagine most of them are still milling around my house, because they never leave. And the two who walked over with me? They're probably taking a nap on your front lawn." Kidd let out a chuckle. "Honestly though, Kenny, I don't really keep much track of this bunch. My old detail stayed behind after I left Washington, and I got assigned to these yahoos from the Stamford office. I don't even know their names. All I know, and all that makes any difference to me, is that they're prepared to save my ass at a moment's notice, whether they think I'm King Jehovah or a goddamn knobgobber. It's protocol. Isn't that right, Martha?" Kidd winked at her.

Kenny's mother let loose an enormous cackle. She sounded like a turkey.

Kidd went on, directing his words more to Martha than to Kenny. "That's the tough thing about being around these boys, though, about having only them to associate with: They're everywhere, but really they're nowhere, all at the same time. They never talk to me. If I didn't see them with my own eyes, I wouldn't know they existed. I guess that's why they're secret." With that proclamation, Kidd's lower lip seemed to buckle. Kenny couldn't believe it. Was the man trying to drum up a pity party right at Carl Kernick's kitchen table? While using Carl's coffee mug?

Kidd gathered his emotions and looked at the clock on the stovetop. "Well, I'll be a frog catcher," he said, standing abruptly. "I really have been here too long, Mrs. Kernick. I should go."

Kidd slid his mug forward, and Martha jerked from her chair.

"Remember, Bent, it's 'Martha,'" she said.

"You bet, Martha," Kidd said. "Thank you so much for inviting me."

Inviting him?

"Kenny!" Kidd extended his hand. "A pleasure."

Kenny shook, but said nothing.

Martha came around to Kidd's side of the table and patted the ex-president's arm. "We'll have to do it again sometime," she said. Then she hugged him.

A hug! Kenny was stunned. He looked at his mother in disbelief.

Kidd wrapped his arms around Martha's ample waist. "Thank you, Mrs. Kernick," he said.

"Ah—" she corrected.

"Martha," Kidd said.

Martha giggled the loudest yet, her cheeks glowing with fire. Her eyes actually looked like sapphires instead of dull blue stones, and Kenny swore she was wearing lipstick. Who was this woman?

Kidd cupped his hands to his mouth and yelled toward the mud room: "Okay, you numb nuts, I'm coming out! Don't shoot me!" He winked at Martha again. "I love doing that."

In ten seconds, it was over. Kidd sped out of the kitchen, charged through the mud room, and strode down the driveway with his detail flanking him. Kenny and his mother stood at the kitchen table. Neither could move.

Absent of Kidd, the house took on a cathartic air. It was as if a great mass of energy had risen up, gathered force, then spilled out in a rush, leaving behind participants both exhilarated and exhausted. To prove Kenny's point, Martha exhaled a voracious sigh and said, "Well, that was the best guest I ever had."

Kenny twitched his head. "What was that A-hole doing here?" he said.

"Kenny, don't be crass," Martha said. She picked up both coffee mugs and brought them to the kitchen sink. With her back to Kenny, she scrubbed the mugs under the faucet, her plump butt jiggling in houndstooth slacks. "Besides," she added, "I don't know what you mean. Neighbors come over all the time."

"Because you invite them," Kenny said. "You *asked* this person to come over. When Dad finds out Sucky Chucky was here, he's going to flip."

"Well, he's not going to find out, is he?" Martha said, slamming down the faucet knob. Kenny couldn't believe his ears, or the display of emotion.

"Besides," Martha said, collecting herself. She placed the clean mugs upside-down on a drying rack. "The man looked like he could use some company, Kenny. He's all alone in that big house, all cooped up. And that wife of his, abandoning him—don't even get me started on that. I can't believe he still wears a wedding ring."

"Since when do you care about Charles Bentley Kidd?" Kenny asked.

"What makes you think I don't?" Martha asked.

"You voted against him twice," Kenny said.

"Never let politics get in the way of being neighborly, Kenny," Martha replied. She wiped her damp hands with a towel from the counter.

Kenny tried to gather his confused thoughts. This whole experience was blowing his gaskets. He opened his mouth to say something, but before he could speak, a strong knock came from the mud room.

Martha dropped the towel in the sink and hurried to the mud room. Kenny followed.

When they reached the door, they saw Kidd standing outside with his two-man detail behind him. Kidd was squinting through the bristling sunlight of a warm October afternoon, but the Secret Service men weren't—they wore sunglasses. One of them was yawning. Martha threw open the storm door.

"Mr. Kidd," she declared in a maple-sweet tone. "Couldn't tear yourself away from my delicious coffee, could you?"

"Not at all, Martha. I'm hooked," he said, his syrup matching hers. "But I had a thought."

Kidd stepped into the mud room. He towered a foot over Kenny's mother, and his dusty hair almost touched the room's low ceiling. Kidd glanced at Kenny, who was standing beside Martha with arms folded.

"Since Kenny has some time on his hands," Kidd said, "I was wondering if I might occupy him."

"Depends on which part of him you want to occupy," Martha joked. She and Kidd shared a wicked laugh. Kenny felt violated.

"No, seriously," Kidd said. "Now that I've settled in, I could use an administrative assistant. Someone to help with tasks. I could pay him."

Kidd looked at Kenny again, and Kenny felt his shoulders go rigid.

"I don't—" Kenny started to say.

But Martha finished: "He'll do it."

"Oh, Martha, that is wonderful," Kidd said. "You won't regret it." Then he turned toward the door and looked back, eyeing Kenny like he had just purchased the blue-ribbon hog at a county fair. "Tomorrow, then? Let's say ten o'clock?"

"Ten in the *morning*?!" Kenny cried.

"He'll be there, Bent," Martha said. "I'll see to it."

Kidd nodded graciously and left. As Kidd and his entourage walked down the driveway a second time, Kenny looked to his mother with horror in his eyes. What had she just done to him? And why? For her part, the woman merely shrugged. "Sometimes people need help," she said.

But Kenny wasn't sure that, having succumbed to the shallow charms of Charles Bentley Kidd, his mother wasn't really making a statement about herself.

CHAPTER 3

★ ★

At half past nine the next morning, Martha Kernick dragged Kenny out of bed—by the ankles.

Under Martha's prodding, Kenny showered, dressed in khakis and an Oxford, and combed his unruly red hair, then he descended the stairs to find one of Martha's typical breakfasts waiting for him—leathery eggs, blowtorched bacon, and orange juice that tasted like battery acid.

He ate the breakfast as slowly as he could, keeping an eye on his mother as she kept her eyes on the clock.

At three minutes before ten, Kenny ran out of food. He crunched the last of the bacon between his teeth, then he raised his glass and swallowed what was left of the cankerous orange juice. No sooner had he set the empty glass on the table than Martha grabbed him by the arm and yanked him out of the chair.

Martha led Kenny to the mud room.

When they reached the door, Kenny thought his mother might give him some words of encouragement, or a comforting kiss goodbye on the forehead, something to reassure him that everything would be okay before she condemned her only child to Kidd's den of iniquity.

Not this morning.

Using her thick lower body, Martha hip checked Kenny. Kenny crashed through the storm door and stumbled down the steps, scuffing his hands and knees as he spilled out onto the driveway. Behind him the storm door slammed shut.

Shocked and disturbed, Kenny picked himself up. Then something wonderful happened: He felt a sharp twinge in his left ankle from where his foot had hit the pavement. He jiggled the foot lightly; the pain was joyously intense.

Yes! he thought. It's twisted! His mother's wacko behavior had actually been a boon. He turned to look at her through the storm door window, to signal her with clenched teeth that he was so terribly injured she would have to call off the deal. But he was too slow—Martha was gone.

Kenny shook off the pain and resigned himself to his fate. It was time to meet his new master. He looked across the street to the Secret Service guardhouse at the end of Kidd's driveway.

An older, wiry agent was leaning from the doorway of the guardhouse. His eyes were fixed on Kenny. Wearily, Kenny started toward him.

When Kenny reached halfway across Hoban Lane, the agent stepped out of the guardhouse. His eyes narrowed and he shot up a stiff arm. "Stop!" he yelled.

Kenny froze in the middle of the street. He looked at the agent with confusion.

"Arms out!"

Kenny struggled to stifle a laugh. Was this guy kidding?

"Arms out, now!" The agent flung up his own limbs like he was playing a child's game of airplane. Kenny half expected him to start swooping around, sputtering engine noises from his lips. Instead, he nodded to Kenny like someone who had never heard of play. "Do it!"

Terrified, Kenny lifted his arms as the agent gestured.

"Step this way," the man said.

Kenny took five strides forward until he was standing in front of the agent. Stringy and grizzled, the agent stood a head taller than Kenny. His breath smelled of unfiltered cigarettes and provolone cheese. It was so rancid Kenny flinched.

"Hold still," the agent said, unleashing more stench in Kenny's face.

As Kenny held still, the agent patted him down. He tapped Kenny's underarms, his pant pockets, his sore ankle, his crotch.

Kenny jumped.

"I said 'still!'" Kenny complied, trying hard not to move as the agent gave Kenny's genitals a squeeze. When he finished, the agent stood straight and cocked his head toward the house. "Front door only. Got that?"

Kenny nodded with wide eyes.

"Good," the agent said. "Have a ball." Then he swung his attention back to the street with the approach of a pearl-gray Volvo sedan, a vehicle driven by the widowed Mrs. Berkley from three houses up.

Taken aback by the agent's frisk, Kenny continued his shuffle to the front door. He climbed the brick steps to the house, knocked on a reinforced steel entryway and popped the latch. He stepped inside to the foyer and closed the heavy door behind him.

Then... nothing. No greeting, nobody. The place was empty.

Kenny looked at the stairwell in front of him, then he looked left and right into the living and dining areas. Kidd's house had no furnishings—no sofas, no tables, no chairs, no carpets, no hutches or cabinets, not a single wall hanging. Nothing. The rooms were vacant. It appeared like Kidd had never bothered to move in.

This place isn't just vacant, Kenny told himself. It's dead. To Kenny, the house was as lifeless as the raccoon and skunk carcasses he had trudged past on Route 2 during his exodus from Boston. It smelled as bad, too. The air was permeated with the scent of deep, sweaty sleep.

"Mr. Kidd?" Kenny asked. The words echoed back to him from bare walls.

A muffled reply came from the second floor: "Kenny, is that you? I'm upstairs."

Kenny climbed the stairs, his ankle throbbing with every step. When he reached the landing, he turned to the left and walked to the master bedroom, where he assumed Kidd would be. But when he poked his head through the doorway, Kidd wasn't there, nor was anything else. The master bedroom was as barren as downstairs.

"Kenny, where are you?" Kidd shouted. "I'm over here."

Kenny turned back and walked across the hall to the bedroom that corresponded to his own, but it was barren, too. Then he traveled down the hallway and looked into one of the smaller bedrooms, the one which had a view of the backyard.

What he saw there taught him never to assume anything about where Charles Bentley Kidd might be, either physically or mentally.

Kenny found the ex-president seated behind a tan metal desk at the far wall. The desk was probably purchased at Wal-Mart, on clearance.

The room itself was a disaster zone. There were no shades or curtains on the windows, and the full wattage of the sun was blazing in uninhibited. Dust flecked everywhere in the sunlight like sea monkeys in a jar of brine. All around the room stood columns of white cardboard bankers boxes, some columns stacked seven boxes high. Bunched together, they were taking up quantities of floor space, making an already small room feel tomblike.

In one corner of the room, however, Kenny noticed there were no boxes. There was no dresser, either, and no bookshelf like Kenny had in his bedroom, and there was no bed, for that matter. In a tiny space carved out from the tall white stacks of bankers boxes, Kenny saw only a beat-up suitcase and one lonely, aluminum-frame army cot.

That's when Kenny understood. Kidd didn't sleep in the master bedroom. He slept on a cot in this spare room, with nothing but a ragged wool blanket for bedding. The sight of the whole set-up, and what it implied about Kidd's fragile state of mind, made Kenny ill, to the point where he wanted to throw up his mother's awful breakfast.

Kidd finished writing something on a piece of paper, then he threw the pen down and pushed himself back from the desk.

"What do you say, Kenny boy?" he bellowed, jumping out of his chair. "Glad you could make it. Hope I didn't call for you too early." Kidd laughed, joyful yet sinister.

Kenny threw Kidd a raised eyebrow. He noticed that Kidd was once again wearing a suit. Kenny could also smell the powerful scent of musk cologne.

"Nice room," Kenny said, lying.

"Thank you, thank you," Kidd said. He waved his hand with a cavalier flip. "Just something I threw together. Come in here, Kenny. Don't be shy. Come in and sit down and take a load off. So we can talk."

Kenny stepped hesitantly into the room. As Kidd ordered, he looked for a chair, but he couldn't find one. He took a seat on the floor in front of the desk.

"You're limping, son," Kidd said as Kenny sat. "What happened? That jerk-off out front didn't get rough with you, did he?"

Kenny struggled to crisscross his legs. "It's nothing," he said. Although Kenny wanted to mention that he had not enjoyed getting his testicles frisked.

"All right, well, you just let me know," Kidd said. "I told that bastard you were coming, so he should have passed you right through."

"You've got a lot of boxes here," Kenny said, trying to change the subject.

"Oh?" Kidd said. He walked out from behind the desk, scanning the box columns. "Files, Kenny. They're just files. Some documents from Washington. The damn things had just been sitting around until I got them back at the end of the summer."

Kenny twitched his nose. He smelled something funny and it wasn't Kidd's cologne. Something about Kidd's statement seemed deliberately incomplete.

These files had just been sitting around...*in the Special Prosecutor's office.*

He got them back at the end of the summer...*when President Russell pardoned him over Labor Day weekend.*

Kenny suddenly realized that he might be surrounded by the historical documentation from Pastrygate, the most tantalizing political scandal in half a century. The realization made his adrenaline spike, along with his interest in his new job. Maybe, just maybe, there might be something else for the *National Enquirer* stacked up in here.

"Well, you told my mother you needed some administrative assistance," Kenny said. "Why don't I organize them for you?" Kenny tried to keep his newfound glee restrained, even as a Kidd-like smirk tugged at the corners of his lips.

"Oh, these?" Kidd said. "No, these are minor. Nothing constitutional, statutory, or ceremonial. The NARA keeps that stuff. Besides, they're already sealed." Kidd pointed to the line of official government packing tape that secured a nearby box. "No, Kenny," Kidd continued, "I need you for something more special than filing. Something of magnanimous importance. Something you and only you can help me with. You'll be doing a service to me, to your country, and to posterity. Are you up to the challenge?"

Deflated at being shot down with the files, Kenny shrugged.

"I like your spunk, son." Kidd winked at him. "Here's the situation. I've got some stuff I want to do. Stuff that will take me out of the house more. The problem is, whenever I leave, there's nobody in this office." Kidd rubbed his freshly-shaved face, sending more of the musky odor into the air. "Now, I ask you, how does that look? I'm a former leader of the free world, am I not? I need to be reachable at all times, don't I? For counsel? For speaking engagements? Hell, Russell might even call and ask me to be an envoy. And since this office will be otherwise unoccupied when I'm out, I'm going to need someone"—Kidd pointed a suggestive finger at Kenny—"to sit here and do one thing." Kidd clapped his hands together to punctuate each word: "Answer. The. Phone."

Kenny looked at Kidd incredulously. As a rule, Kenny never took well to staid tasks. He needed to move, to read, to research—anything with activity behind it. All he could say was, "You want me to be a receptionist?"

"That is such a wuss-ass term," Kidd said.

"You told my mother you needed an administrative assistant, not a phone boy."

"Technically," Kidd said, "answering the phone is administrative, and you are assisting me by doing it."

Kenny scrunched his face. "I don't know, Mr. Kidd. With all due respect, why don't you just get an answering machine?"

Kidd shook his head. "You're reticent, son. I can tell. But you don't understand. I've been around the block a few times, and there are a lot things I know, and one of them is that people like a voice. They want someone to talk to. It makes them feel good. And the Secret Service won't do it. I asked. There are always two or three agents milling around the property when my detail is with me, keeping the place secure. But they said it 'wasn't their job.' You tell me how someone can take a bullet for you if the situation arises, but they can't go out of their way to pick up a goddamn ringing phone when you're gone. Do you see my dilemma, Kenny? Now look—"

Kidd hurried around to the back of the desk and lifted a Wal-Mart bag off the floor. He began to rifle through the bag as Kenny untangled his legs and stood up.

"I got you one of these," Kidd said, slapping a phone message pad on the desktop. "And some writing utensils, and a stapler, and those yellow stickies. Hey, look at that stockpile. You should be good to go."

"Except for one thing," Kenny said.

"What's that?" Kidd asked.

"Where's the phone?"

Kidd looked around, his eyes searching frantically. There wasn't a telephone anywhere.

"Oh, shit," Kidd said. He scratched his chin. "Well, I'll have to dig one up later. But today, why don't we do a practice run? You sit here."

Kidd pulled Kenny to the other side of the desk and plopped him down in the chair. Even with cushioning, the chair felt hard on Kenny's meatless butt.

"Cool?" Kidd asked.

Kenny nodded indifferently.

"Now just rehearse what you're going to say."

"What do you want me to say?" Kenny asked.

"I don't care, Kenny," Kidd said. "Use your imagination. Just make it professional. Can you do that?"

Kenny nodded.

"I thought so," Kidd said. "Now, if you'll excuse me, I have an appointment to keep. I'll be back later."

Kidd turned and strode out of the room, a ribbon of musk cologne trailing after him.

Kidd's footfalls echoed loudly as he hurried down the hallway and then the staircase. When he was near the mud room, Kenny heard him yell to the Secret Service: "Okay, you assholes, let's boogie!" Then the mud room door thumped shut, vehicle doors slammed, an engine started, and the Tahoe backed out of the driveway. In the distance, Kenny heard the sound of the Chevy's motor fading away; the vehicle was moving toward Pheasant Hill Road.

Kidd's house fell silent again.

Kenny leaned back in the chair. For a lack of anything better to do, he yawned. The time was still early to him, and he was exhausted. He hadn't fallen asleep this morning until Carl left the house at 7:30, which had given Kenny just two hours to snooze before Martha came in and dragged him out of bed. To make matters worse, the temperature in Kidd's office was increasing from the sunlight, baking Kenny into tiredness.

I've only been doing this for a minute, Kenny thought, and I already want to sleep on the job. For peak performance, Kenny decided that he had better occupy his mind, so he started to engage in one of his favorite pastimes—fidgeting. He gripped the metal edge of the desk with his fingers, reared back and gave the desk a shake. The desk looked cheap, and it was; it wobbled like gelatin.

Kenny swung his attention to the desktop, looking for something to play with. On the left corner of the desk, Kidd had placed a wooden cigar box. Kenny tried to pop the lid on it, but the box was locked. On the opposite corner was a banker's lamp, its pull chain still swinging from the shake. Kenny jerked the chain and found the bulb burnt out. Frustrated, he jerked the chain seven more times and flicked it away. Then he glanced down toward the floor and noticed a column of drawers aligned on the desk's right side.

He yanked open the top drawer—empty.

The middle drawer—empty.

The bottom drawer—

Not empty. In fact, there was a girl inside it. A stunning lass with the most brilliant green eyes Kenny had ever seen.

The boy gasped at the sight.

Deep in the lowest drawer of a cheap metal desk, Kenny found Annabelle Kidd staring back at him.

He reached down for the photo, which was encased in a silver frame tarnished with oxidation. He lifted the frame gently and brought the picture to his chest, temporarily blinding himself with an angelic flash as the glass caught sunlight.

When his eyes readjusted, Kenny gazed upon the vision of a goddess.

In the picture, which looked like a high school senior portrait, Annabelle Kidd was sporting long gingerbread hair that curved delicately around her sculpted face. Her skin glowed pink, and she had full, ripe lips the shape of a butterfly. Everything about her—her nose, teeth, chin and cheeks—seemed perfect in size and contour. Then those eyes. They were her most amazing feature. It was as if something were illuminating Annabelle from the inside, lighting up her soul with an emerald conflagration, using her eyes as its beacon. Her image startled him.

Kenny had only seen Annabelle Kidd in newspaper photos. He remembered how odd she looked when she was younger. In her early teens, Kidd's daughter seemed comprised of nothing but awkwardness—her ears too big, her nose too long, her cheeks too gaunt, her hair too short. She had virtually no weight for her frame. Kenny knew she had grown quite tall for a girl, but she had clearly filled out along the way. There was nothing awkward about her now; her parts came together magnificently. And the girl could smile. In the picture she was beaming. It made her appear honest, trustworthy, and warm. Unlike her father, she didn't come across as someone who would take a pee on your head and tell you it was Niagara Falls.

Kenny yawned again. He felt incredibly hot. Maybe it was Annabelle Kidd's smile toasting him; more likely it was the sunlight slowly creeping toward him through the windows. There was no use in fighting his tiredness. It took hold of him, consumed him, and he knew he would soon succumb to its power.

As he returned the picture to the bottom drawer, thoughts swirled in his head of what a gorgeous girl Annabelle Kidd had turned out to be. How odd was it, Kenny pondered, that someone who so much resembled a scoundrel like Kidd could have such a different aura about her. Such a glowing, kind persona.

Another yawn.

Kenny took off his glasses, folded his arms on the desk, and dropped his head into the crook of his elbow.

Within a minute, the crawling rays of sunlight nipped at his shirtsleeves. His breathing deepened, and his eyelids grew as thick as grade-school paste. Three more breaths and he slipped into sleep.

His last thought before snoozing was how nice it would be to dream of Annabelle Kidd. Of walking with her. Of holding her hand. Of kissing those butterfly lips. Instead, a field of heather was waiting for him, and Annabelle Kidd did not frolic in it. But his mother was there. And she was still laughing at him.

CHAPTER 4

★ ★

Kidd returned later that afternoon, appearing flush and freshly-showered. He woke Kenny with a knock on the desk, then proceeded to rave about an amazing health club he had discovered along Route 136 near Darien.

"FitMasters," Kidd said. "They've got everything there. They even have individual television monitors, with cable, for when you're doing your cardio. Some fat neck was watching *9½ Weeks* on The Harlequin Channel. Now that will really get your heart pumping."

With animated hands, the haggard ex-president told Kenny he was so impressed with FitMasters, he had signed up for the no-commitment plan. He had the intention, he said, of getting as healthy as he was back in his presidential days. To that end, after he had signed the contract, he immediately jumped onto an elliptical machine and put in a good workout for the first time in ages. "I sweated like a bull moose, and I flailed at times," Kidd declared, "but honestly, Kenny, at the end I felt like a man renewed."

Kidd looked at his watch. The time was three o'clock. He thanked Kenny for his service and asked the boy to return tomorrow. Kenny didn't want to return tomorrow, but for a reason he could not explain, he agreed. Maybe it was the fact that his mother would make him come back anyway, or maybe it was the sight of that pathetic army cot, but whatever the reason, Kenny found its allure to be undeniable.

"Ten o'clock tomorrow morning," he said. "I'll be here. Anything for you, Mr. Kidd."

On his way down the staircase, accompanied by Kidd, Kenny brought up the subject of the telephone.

Kidd chuckled heartily. "Tomorrow, Young Kernick," he said, doffing a pretend hat, "you shall have your telecommunications device." Then Kidd bowed. It was very strange.

The next day, Kenny arrived at the appointed time to find Kidd holed up in the back bedroom again. This time he wasn't dressed in a suit, but in running pants and a black Jesuit University sweatshirt.

As Kidd promised, the metal desk now sported a telephone. It was shaped like a football. Kenny noticed a label on the thing that stated "Sports Illustrated," but Kidd swore it was a gift from the president of Shangri-La. Nevertheless, the phone worked. Although the "nine" button, worn clean, stuck a little from a buildup of gunk around its edges.

Now equipped with a telephone, Kenny saw his working relationship with Kidd through that day, then another day. And another. And before Kenny knew it, two weeks had passed. October gave way to November. Kenny's beloved white oak leaves turned to rust and fell off the trees. Yet, even with the leaves gone and colder temperatures setting in, Kenny found himself content.

Every morning, Kenny would arrive in Kidd's front yard at ten o'clock sharp.

On the way through security, he would always get frisked by Agent Crotch, as Kenny came to call him. Most of the time the foul-breathed agent would pat down Kenny's testicles, but a few pleasant days he would leave Kenny unmolested.

Kenny would then watch Kidd leave the house in workout clothes at exactly 10:12 A.M.

Then Kenny would take his seat behind the desk.

Then he would look at the picture of Annabelle Kidd in the bottom drawer, and wonder why Kidd didn't place such a beautiful photo of his daughter on the desk.

Then he would always prepare himself to field a legion of phone calls for the former leader of the free world.

Then he would fall asleep. Always. Kenny found it easy to sleep on the job. Because no one ever called Charles Bentley Kidd.

When Kidd returned from the health club exactly five hours later, he told Kenny about how much iron he had pumped and how many pounds he was putting back on. Then he would look at Kenny with expectant eyes. Kenny would deliver the bad news: "No messages, Mr. Kidd."

"Please, call me Bent."

"Well, okay, Bent, but there are still no messages."

Kidd's next reply was always concise, always complete: "Then fuck their souls!"

Even though Kidd found himself condemned to a life of oblivion, the disgraced ex-president was happy now, frequently giddy, and nothing was going to kill his buzz.

And when he came home, this man renewed was often at his mental peak, an overflowing caldron of staggering ideas and insights. One day Kidd stated that he had discovered a cheap way to generate biodiesel from orange peels; the next he claimed to have found the mathematical basis for why crabs walk sideways. He deduced the location of Atlantis in the shower one morning, then figured out how to poke a hole in the space-time continuum by lunch. Kidd was alive, on fire, and unstoppable. No notion or theory was safe from his nimble mind.

Then one day something happened.

On a bitter and rainy morning in mid-November, Kidd suddenly changed.

It occurred a week after Election Day, when Kidd's old party had taken a beating in the congressional races that the New York broadsheet could only describe as biblical.

For some unexplained reason, Kidd returned early from his daily workout. His renewed vigor was gone; his green eyes dead. Even his rich, silky voice stalled at a hush. Preoccupied, he dismissed Kenny with an absent wave then locked the door to his office.

When Kenny descended the staircase, his ears caught an odd noise—something that sounded like a cross between a jackhammer and a horny beagle. It was the sound of sobbing. Kidd's sobbing. Hearing it made Kenny uncomfortable. He hurried out of the house fast.

Outside in the rain, Kenny stood on Kidd's stoop and stared across the street at his own house, its white clapboards streaked with watermarks as if it too had been crying. The vision of the house at this time of day put Kenny out of sorts. He had become so used to his daily routine with Kidd that the early dismissal left him disjointed. He didn't know what to do with himself, but he knew that he didn't want to go home. Unfortunately, he would have to go home sooner or later, before his father returned from work. The last thing Kenny or Martha wanted now was for Carl to discover exactly where Kenny had been spending his afternoons.

The reason for their fear was legitimate: On the landscape of American political demographics, Carl Kernick was what was known to pundits, radio talk show hosts and party poll-sters as a "Kidd Hater." Loosely defined, the term signified someone whose detestation of Charles Bentley Kidd crossed all rational lines. Few pundits could point to a specific incident that had unleashed such a torrent of anger toward the man, but what was known for sure was that Kidd Hatred started up well before Kidd ever became president, and it had only swelled from the ranks of its creators once Kidd's Pastrygate troubles began.

Carl Kernick hadn't waited for the swell of Kidd Hating to reach him; he met it on the ground floor. As early as the morning after Kidd's announcement of his candidacy for president, which he had made at a rally in his hometown of Hawleyville, Ohio, Carl tossed his breakfast plate in disgust as he read about Kidd's speech on the front page of the New Haven daily. From then on, Carl's hatred toward Kidd grew exponentially, with Carl telling anyone who would listen that "this bonehead is going to be the ruination of our country."

For Carl, Pastrygate and its outcome were a time of deep schadenfreude, that malicious satisfaction one feels in the mis-fortunes of others. Kidd was humiliated by a congressional investigation. He was charged with crimes and convicted under Articles of Impeachment. He was removed from office on live television, with the added humiliation of being prohibited from making a farewell address to the nation. On the evening of the impeachment verdict, Carl seemed satisfied. Kidd would soon be a distant memory, one of the many undistinguished presi-dents left to rot in the dumpster of American history. Like Mil-lard Fillmore.

Then Kidd moved in across the street. That was one sick cosmic pill for Carl to swallow.

Always a boy who needed answers, Kenny tried over the past few weeks to understand his father's hatred of Kidd. His initial thoughts turned to the obvious—that on a base level Carl and Kidd represented opposite ends of every spectrum: Order versus Emotion; Integrity versus Appetites; Fastidiousness versus Laissez-faire. Carl was even a self-avowed Animal Hater, while Charles Bentley Kidd had often been called the World's Biggest Lover of Beavers. In a sense, though, it came down to Spirit: Kidd had Spirit in droves, and it exuded from him like the aurora borealis; Carl, by contrast, lived his life through precision and vector—he wouldn't understand Spirit if it crawled up his butt and tap danced on his spleen.

These insights for Kenny were all well and good, and they explained a lot. But recently Kenny had begun to sense another component to Carl's unabashed hatred of Kidd, something which went far beyond the polar differences between these two men. The way Kenny figured it, Carl was just plain jealous.

All his life, Carl Kernick had considered himself to be "The King." In Carl's mind, he was king of his home, of his industry, of his neighborhood, king in every thought and deed. The Kernick name was even derived from the word "king"— the German *könig*, before some impatient moron at Ellis Island phonetically bastardized it. And as king, Carl could be ultra-territorial. He stalked. He charged. He drove out all challengers with a ruthless decisiveness Kenny had never seen in others.

Then one day, into Carl's territory wandered Charles Bentley Kidd. The newcomer spelled trouble for Carl. Kidd was taller than Carl. Kidd was more attractive than Carl. Kidd had gone to a better university than Carl. Kidd was also famous in an infamous sort of way, and he still had charisma to boot. And unlike Carl, Kidd had actually been a king, of sorts.

Like any true predator, Kenny's father did not take lightly Kidd's encroachment onto Hoban Lane. Kenny had learned from his mother that on the evening in September when Carl first heard of Kidd's impending move into the neighborhood, he immediately got everyone on the street to sign a petition against it. When that tactic failed—and worse, made Carl appear weak in the eyes of the neighbors—Kenny's father reasserted his masculinity by taking a meat mallet to the living room walls. Two months later, the spackle marks from their hasty repair were still visible.

Well, tough noogies for Carl, Kenny thought as he stepped off Kidd's stoop and walked toward the street. The boy was glad Kidd had triumphed over his father's irrational opposition. What was more unexpected to Kenny was that he had actually come to enjoy the ex-president's presence across the street. In Kenny's view, Kidd brought vivacity to the neighborhood, a buzz, some type of sassiness which Simondale had so terribly lacked.

But most of all, Kenny believed it was about time that Carl Kernick learned he couldn't get everything he wanted, no matter how loud he shouted or how forcefully he stomped. Kenny had taken the first steps toward proving as much when he got kicked out of Harvard—Carl found himself powerless to do anything about it. Since then the man had been utterly neutered, both in voice and action.

Good, Kenny thought. Snip Carl's testicles off and throw them into that dumpster of history along with President Fillmore. College could go to hell; Kenny was enjoying himself. Together, he and Kidd might actually do the impossible: They might force Carl to keep his mouth shut for the rest of his miserable, grumpy life.

It was a grand idea, to be sure, and one that Kenny reveled in. But little did Kenny know, as he crossed Hoban Lane against a frigid downpour, that it was an idea destined to fail. For while his father may have surrendered the fight to keep Charles Bentley Kidd off Hoban Lane, it would soon be clear to Kenny that the man was not about to make surrender a habit. Especially in fights that involved his son, and the direction life would take him.

CHAPTER 5

★★★★★★★★★★★★★★★★★★★★★★★★★★★★★★★

"Kenny, come down here!"

Kenny was in bed with a book when he heard his father call him. His spine went stiff. For a moment he couldn't breathe. Carl's voice had rolled up the staircase with the destructive force of a tornado.

Kenny quickly closed his book—*Farragut's History of Alaska*—and placed it on the nightstand. Before he could stand, his father yelled again.

"Kenny, get into the family room! Now!"

Kenny hurried out of bed and rushed into the hallway. With every step down the staircase, he felt his legs turn to rubber.

He ran to the family room and saw his father sitting in the high-backed Victorian chair, which Kenny had often thought of as King Carl's throne. Behind the chair stood Martha. Kenny's mother rested one hand on the top edge of the Victorian, and she carried no expression on her face. More unsettling, she appeared to be back to her old pale self.

Carl waved Kenny toward the chair's matching sofa beneath the front windows. "Come in, Kenny, come in," Carl said to him. "Grace us with your glowing presence."

Kenny sat on the sofa. He could hear the ominous patter of rain as it hit the windows to his back. The living room smelled like a newly-lit oil furnace. Facing his father, Kenny searched the room for someplace small to hide—a nook, a cranny, anything. He found none. Every point of escape in this room had been sealed off long ago.

"Make sure you're comfortable," Carl ordered.

Kenny wasn't, and there was no use trying.

Carl studied Kenny for a moment, then he crooked his lips and held them, saying nothing. The pause seemed endless. Kenny wanted to melt into a puddle. Finally, Carl unscrewed his mouth and cocked an eyebrow. "So tell me," he said. "Have you been enjoying your days off?"

Kenny nodded timidly. He had been enjoying them. He couldn't lie about it.

"What have you been doing to keep yourself busy?" Carl asked.

Kenny looked at his mother. This was the question they had been hoping to avoid, and he wanted some guidance on how to answer without invoking the name of Charles Bentley Kidd. Martha didn't guide him. She glanced down at her feet. Kenny was flying solo.

Kenny improvised a response. "Oh, you know, some of this, some of that."

Carl took a dismayed breath. "Kenny, Kenny, Kenny," he said, shaking his head. "Would you like to hear something instructive?"

Not really, Kenny thought, but there was no stopping his father now.

"Every day, I meet and interview candidates for job openings at Kernick Handling Systems," Carl said. "Everybody from vice presidents to administrative assistants to low-level janitors who'll do nothing more than scrub toilets and lay down urinal cakes. And in all my years, in all my days evaluating talent to improve my company, I don't think I have ever hired some dummkopf who said the main body of his work experience consisted of 'some of this, some of that.'"

"But I don't—" Kenny started to say.

Carl leapt from the chair. "No!" he shouted, pointing an index finger at the bridge of Kenny's coke-bottle glasses. "No 'buts!' No 'ifs!' No nothing anymore! I want you to shut up and listen like I'm the voice of God. I have busted my hump for you since the day you were born. I have sacrificed, bled, and poured my guts out to provide you with the kind of opportunities I never had. Never! Ever! And this"—Carl waved the index finger at some unseen foe—"this is how you honor my benevolence? You throw it away on a pair of female undergarments?"

"Eighty-seven," Kenny whispered.

"Excuse me?" Carl said.

Kenny paused to moisten his drying mouth. Martha piped in. "I think he said it was eighty-seven pairs of undergarments, Carl."

Carl turned and threw Martha a corrosive glare. "Well, thank you for clearing that up, dear. But I don't care if it was eighty-seven or eighty-seven thousand. I don't care if they were woven out of gold. I don't care if he peeled them off this year's Miss USA!" Kenny's mother shrunk like a decaying rose.

With Martha defeated, Carl swung toward Kenny, his five-foot nine-inch frame towering over the miniscule boy on the sofa.

"Tell me something, Kenny," Carl said. "Why did I send you to an all-boys high school? Why did I work so diligently to keep you away from girls all these years? Well, I'll tell you why. Because they're distractions. I won't allow you to throw your life away on distractions. And I won't, absolutely will not, allow you to embarrass me. My son is going to be Ivy League educated. He's going to rise to the top of his class. He's going to be considered a success. But most of all, he's going to carry on the Kernick name with honor, integrity and character. Do you hear me?"

Carl paused, his face frozen, then he seemed to relax. He reached backward, felt for the armrests of the Victorian chair and sat again. From his shirt pocket, he pulled out a pack of Parliaments.

"Well, you really screwed up Harvard, didn't you?" Carl said, pulling a cigarette from the pack and sliding it between his lips. He lit the stick with a fluid wave of a lighter and blew the first puff of smoke at the living room ceiling. "We can never show our faces there again, can we?"

Kenny shook his head.

"But we're not giving up, Kenny. I refuse to give up." Carl took another pull off the Parliament and blew the smoke at his son. "So to that end, it's all arranged: At the start of January semester, you're going to Yale."

"Yale?!" Kenny cried.

"That's right, Kenny," Carl said. "Yale. The second-best Ivy League school in the country. And you can thank Mrs. Berkley up the street for it all; it was her late husband's position on the Yale Corporation that got you special dispensation, no questions asked. All they did was look at your achievements from Griggson, and they gave you the benefit of the doubt."

Yale, Kenny tried to cry again, but this time his mouth produced no sound.

"Unfortunately, son," Carl said, "I am done giving you the benefit of the doubt. Your days of dorm life are over. This time around, you'll be a commuter student. I'll drive you up to New Haven in the morning, and I'll pick you up at night. You'll go to your classes, you'll study in the library until I arrive, and you will stay away from everyone. But more important, you will live right here at home, where if you want to get your hands on a pair of female undergarments, they'll have to be your mother's. Nod if you understand me."

Kenny stared at Carl with eyes agog. He didn't move.

"Martha, tell your son to nod," Carl ordered.

"Kenny," Martha said with a ruptured voice, "show your father you'll do what he wants."

But Kenny couldn't nod. He couldn't move his head at all. Any motion from his neck up was impeded by the object that had just crawled into his throat—

A thick, gelatinous lump.

CHAPTER 6

★ ★

As a businessman, Carl Kernick believed in protecting his assets. In his position as President and CEO of Kernick Handling Systems, Carl always carried more insurance than necessary to cover property and loss, he drilled his workers every four months in the latest safety procedures, and the building itself possessed an array of security apparatuses designed to prevent external or internal theft. Carl would invest in anything and everything that could keep from destruction all he had worked so hard to acquire. It was fortunate for Kenny, then, that Carl was also that way as a father. Which is why Kenny had a two-story fire escape ladder under his bed.

"This thing just might save your life someday," Carl said on the afternoon he showed Kenny how to use it. How prophetic those words had become, Kenny thought, as he tiptoed to one of his bedroom's front windows. How prophetic, indeed. Just not in the way King Carl expected.

Kenny silently slid the window open and looked out onto a damp November morning. The time was twenty minutes past one. The bitter rain that had soaked Simondale all day had stopped at midnight. The entire landscape stretching out from Two Hoban Lane glistened as if someone had applied to it a layer of glaze frosting. The whole scene made Kenny hungry with an insatiable desire to get out of Simondale as fast as his legs would take him.

The duffel bag went out the window first. Overloaded with every article of winter clothing Kenny could find, it crushed one of Carl's closely-pruned boxwood shrubs, the sounds of snapping twigs quickly lost into the night.

Next came the ladder. Kenny followed his father's previous instructions to a tee: He placed the hooks around the windowsill; he rolled the chain links to the ground; he jiggled the first step to make sure it was secure. Then he climbed out and scurried down.

As soon as Kenny touched the ground, he lifted his duffel bag from the crushed boxwood, hoisted it over his shoulder, and trudged across the wet lawn, heading toward Pheasant Hill Road.

As he neared the edge of the lawn, Kenny stopped. He turned and looked at the house he would no longer call home.

Except for an illuminated reading lamp in his bedroom, the entire structure was dark; it gave a deceptively peaceful appearance under the subtle glow of street lamps. Kenny wondered if he would ever see this place again. It truly was, he could appreciate now, a magnificent work of colonial-style New England architecture. Too bad the man who owned it was such a magnificent work of modern-day parental A-hole.

Kenny gazed at the house for a few moments, then turned back to the street. Before he could continue with his journey, his eyes locked in on Kidd's house across the lane. It was dark, too, and Kenny felt a pang of guilt.

Was he leaving Mr. Kidd in the lurch?

For some reason, the notion bothered Kenny. He felt loyal to Kidd, though he couldn't explain what Kidd had done to earn his loyalty. The ex-president really was a self-absorbed egomaniac. He decided that at least he could say goodbye, even if he had to wake Kidd up. Kidd deserved that much. Kenny started across the street.

That's when he got steamrolled.

Halfway across Hoban Lane, Kenny was slammed by something solid and debilitating. The boy spun violently, lost his balance, and fell belly-down onto the asphalt. When he came to a stop, the solid object was sitting on his back, keeping him from moving.

Stunned, Kenny tried to turn his head to see what massive force was pinning him to the street. Then he realized he didn't have to. One good whiff of the air told him not what, but who, it was. The object of Kenny's compression had breath that smelled like a provolone-laced cigarette.

"I got him! I got him! I got the little peckerhead!" Agent Crotch yelled.

Within seconds, four other agents surrounded Kenny. All he could see were polished dress shoes and wisps of pant cuffs as they took up position to the left and right of Kenny's tar-licked face. An agent to his left bent down, yanked Kenny's hands out from beneath Agent Crotch and locked a pair of handcuffs around the boy's wrists.

With their perceived threat neutralized, Agent Crotch jerked Kenny to his knees by the shoulder blades. "Little late to be out, ain't it, son?" he asked. The agent's breath was particularly noxious this morning. The smell made Kenny stiffen to the rigidity of a flagpole.

"I just wanted to talk to Mr. Kidd," Kenny squeaked.

"Is that so?" Crotch spewed. He pointed to the duffel bag. "With a full cargo, huh? That's suspicious, I say. That is very goddamn suspicious."

The agents unzipped the duffel and started to pull out his clothes, inspecting then strewing them over the wet road.

Kenny could see his tighty-white Fruit of the Loom briefs shining particularly bright against the dark tar.

The African-American agent said Kenny was clean.

"Not so fast," Crotch replied, cracking his knuckles. Then with loose hands, the stink-breathed agent flexed his fingers, reached around to Kenny's front, and got off an early morning frisk of the boy's cowering genitalia.

Kenny was sitting on his duffel bag near the guardhouse when the lights in Kidd's foyer flashed on. In a few moments, the African-American agent stepped through the front door and called to Kenny with a curled finger.

Kenny climbed off his duffel bag, walked to the front door and entered the house unimpeded.

At night, the interior of Kidd's home was even creepier than it was in the daylight. A lone chandelier illuminated the foyer and cast jagged, angular shadows through the empty living and dining areas.

"He's in his office," the agent told Kenny, then he stepped out of Kidd's house and shut the door behind him, leaving Kenny alone.

Kenny climbed the stairwell to the landing. In the dim light, he fumbled down the hall until he came to Kidd's door. Its hinges creaked as Kenny pushed it open.

"Mr. Kidd?" Kenny called.

"Kenny—" Kidd's voice was labored and torn. "Come in here, Kenny. I want to see you. I want to see your face."

Kenny stepped into the dark room. He ran his hands down the wall to his right until he felt the familiar stub of a switch.

Without thinking, he flipped it. The room exploded in blinding light.

"Whoa! Whoa!" Kidd screamed. He threw his hands to his eyes and crumpled under the glow. "Turn it off, Kenny! Turn it off!"

Kenny threw down the switch. He walked a few feet down the hall and turned on a light in the bathroom.

"Thank Christ," he heard Kidd say. "Now come back in here, Kenny, and take a load off. So we can talk."

Kenny walked back to Kidd's bedroom. In the diffused light, he could see that Kidd was sitting on the cot with his head in his hands. He was still wearing the workout clothes from when Kenny had left him that morning. Worse still, Kidd's eyes were swollen, and his hair jutted in every direction, as if given a workout with gnawing fingers.

"I just came—" Kenny started to say.

"Ssssssh," Kidd replied, touching a finger to his lips. "Do you hear that, Kenny?"

Kenny listened but heard nothing. As usual, Kidd's house was dead silent.

"Hear what?" Kenny asked.

"That," said Kidd. "The sound of nothingness, Kenny. Of vacancy. Of deep, bottomless, vacuum-packed oblivion. Do you know what it means, Kenny? Do you really know?"

Kenny shrugged. "That you need a television?"

"No, Kenny," Kidd said, flashing an annoyed glare. "It means nobody loves me, Kenny. The White House used to have a constant stream of noise—the sound of important activity, of people coming and going, of people who cared for my well-being. But now there are no people, because nobody cares. Nobody even calls anymore." Kidd let out his beagle-like wail.

If there was one thing Kenny didn't like, it was the sound of a grown man crying. The wail made Kenny shudder. "But I thought it didn't matter that nobody called," Kenny said, trying to tune out Kidd's howls while offering some perspective.

"Who told you that?" Kidd asked.

"You did," Kenny said. "You said to F-U-C-K their souls."

"F-U-C-K?" Kidd said. "The word is 'fuck,' Kenny. 'Fuck.' And fuck that. You think I'm that strong?" Kidd pounded his breastbone. "I need people, Kenny. I need their love. I need to love and be loved. And now what have I got? I'll tell you what. I've got jack shit, that's what. My mama's gone. My family's gone. Nobody wants me. I can't even get Russell to send me on a diplomatic mission to some Third World shit hole. I'm a nonentity, Kenny. A pariah. I'm obliterated. I'm a walking friggin' waste of metabolism."

Kidd's eyes unleashed a rage of tears. He threw himself on the cot and curled into the fetal position. In the dim light, Kenny couldn't tell exactly what the former leader of the free world was doing in that position, but with slurping noises filling the room, it sounded like Kidd was sucking his thumb.

It was time to leave, Kenny told himself. "Well, Mr. Kidd," he said. "I wish I could help, but I just came to say goodbye."

Kidd sprung up from the cot. "What do you mean goodbye? You're leaving me, too?"

Kenny nodded.

"But why?" Kidd cried. "Why, Kenny, dammit? Why?"

"Ask my father if you ever meet him," Kenny said. He offered Kidd his hand. "But I can't stay. I have to get out of here before it's too late. It's for the best. You really have to trust me on this one, Mr. Kidd."

The ex-president let out a sigh and lay down again, slapping a forearm over his eyes in despair. "Oh, God," he lamented, "why don't I just take the gas pipe? May I at least ask where you're going?"

"You can ask," Kenny said, "but I don't know."

Kidd sprung from the cot again. "You don't know?" he said. "You mean you're leaving me and I don't get to know why you're leaving me? Christ, Kenny, even my wife told me she was heading back to Chicago. Okay, she used every profanity to do it, but she told me. Because she had a plan, Kenny. You have to have a plan."

Kenny let out a heavy breath. "Well, I've been reading about Alaska lately. It's an amazing place, and it seems like lovely country this time of year."

Kidd wiped his nose with a sleeve from his sweatshirt. "Oh, Alaska's great this time of year," he said, sniffling. "If you don't mind twenty hours of darkness, or your testicles turning to ice."

"I brought warm clothes," Kenny said. "Besides, by the time I get there, it will be crab season. I could work on a boat. Make some good money."

"You want to work on a crab boat?" Kidd said. He shook his head. "Now it's your turn to trust me, Kenny: You'd rather catch a case of the crabs than fish for them."

Kenny was perplexed by the statement, and Kidd noticed. "You have no idea what a case of the crabs is, do you?" he asked.

Kenny looked down at his feet.

"God, Kenny, that's just sad. That is really sad."

Kenny folded his arms defensively. "Anyway, I have to go."

"And how are you planning to get there?" Kidd asked.

"With these." Kenny pointed to his feet. "Look, I can't really get into it, but if I stay here, I'll die. I figure there has to be something better than this"—Kenny waved his arms at lovely Simondale—"out there somewhere. And it sure doesn't involve college."

Kidd's sunken eyes lit up. "I know what you're talking about, Young Kernick. You're talking about a quest." The ex-president jumped from the cot, inspired. Towering over Kenny, he uncurled an index finger and poked it into Kenny's concave chest. "You're leaving for a quest. That's why you don't know where you're going. You're setting out to seek your fortunes and slay your dragons. You're embarking on a journey to learn about yourself."

"Something like that, I guess," Kenny said. "Maybe a little less 'Prince Valiant.'"

Kidd let out another sigh. "I used to know about myself, Kenny. I used to know who I was and who loved me. And let's be honest, everybody loved me." Kidd smirked, but sullenly. "I used to know what I was capable of, like a man should. Then everything I thought about myself turned out to be a joke, all because I screwed a friggin' pastry chef."

Well, her and that truckload of congressmen's wives, Kenny wanted to say. And technically, he had screwed the economy as well. But Kidd seemed down enough; he didn't need to be reminded of the larger picture of his impeachment conviction. Instead, Kenny pointed to the door. "It's getting late, Mr. Kidd. Thanks for everything."

Kenny started to go, but Kidd said, "Before you leave—"

Kenny stopped and turned.

Kidd looked at the boy with moistened eyes, then he walked over to the metal desk and tapped the desktop twice with his knuckles. "There's a photo in the bottom drawer, Kenny. I know you've seen it. It's the picture they took of my daughter last year for her senior portrait. A picture of my precious Annabelle."

Kenny nodded. With the mention of Annabelle Kidd, he was not so eager to leave.

"Do you know the last time I saw Annabelle?" Kidd asked. Kenny shook his head.

"The sad thing is, neither do I. I think it was last Thanksgiving, but I really couldn't tell you. Everything got so crazy at the end, and Annabelle has her own life these days. Now Thanksgiving is coming up again, and she doesn't even call me anymore. Me. Her daddy."

"Maybe she doesn't know where you are," Kenny said.

"Maybe you should shut your trap and let me finish," Kidd said. He brushed the arm of his sweatshirt, trying to wipe away a dried snot streak, then he cleared his throat with a rumbling hack. His voice took on a regal, authoritative tone.

Kidd proclaimed, "A quest is a wonderful idea, Young Kernick. We shall embark."

Kenny looked at Kidd sideways. "What do you mean *we*?"

"Oh, yes," Kidd said. "I'm going with you. We shall travel together, you and I, as knight and squire. We shall use a carriage, of course—a black Chevy Tahoe—because let's face it, a knight does not walk. We shall journey to the farthest reaches of the realm, to a place called Los Angeles—the City of Angels. When we get there, we will celebrate Thanksgiving with my precious Annabelle, then you may continue on your travels to the Northland. We shall seek our fortunes and slay our dragons, and I shall repair my tattered reputation across this great and noble domain, so that my people will love me again. And hey, if I can disrobe a princess or two along the way, all the better. Are you amenable to our journey, Young Kernick?"

Kenny chuckled. Now he knew Kidd was nuts. "You're forgetting one problem, Mr. Kidd. The Secret Service. Don't you think they'd get in the way?"

"The Secret Service," Kidd repeated, slamming down his palms on the desk so hard Kenny could feel the vibration in his own elbows. "You're right, Kenny. You are absolutely right. The Secret Service is a burden. If we're going to get anything out of this quest, we have to do it solo."

"How exactly?" Kenny asked. "You're a pretty kept man."

Kidd put a finger to his chin. After some deliberation, he said, "Kenny, for your last assignment as my administrative assistant, I'm going to need you to perform a special task."

"Let me guess," Kenny said. "Answering the phone?"

"Ha, ha," Kidd said. "You know, you're really quite droll when you don't have that maypole shoved up your ass. No, Kenny, I need you to write. Grab a pen and sit down. You're going to take a letter."

Thirty minutes later, that letter read:

To the United States Department of the Secret Service Stamford, Connecticut, USA

Dear Sirs:

When in the course of human events, it becomes necessary for one Former Leader of the Free World to dissolve the security ties which have connected him with your department, and to reacquaint himself with the peoples of this great nation, as the Laws of Nature and the God of his Mama entitle him, a decent respect to the opinions of mankind requires that he should declare the causes which impel him to the separation:

To state it bluntly, you all suck.

It is the truth. I am not exaggerating. You suck big wad. And I hold these truths to be self-evident, that I am created as equal as the rest of you bastards, and that I have been endowed by my Creator with certain unalienable rights, that among these are Life, Liberty and the Pursuit of Scrumptious Humptious.

That to secure these rights, the Secret Service has to get out of my way.

That whenever the Secret Service gets in my way, I have great injustices inflicted upon me. To wit:

Your agents have refused to speak to me as a normal person, with any kind of compassion or caring, or sincere interest in my daily well-being whatsoever—

Your agents have often called me names behind my back, vicious, humiliating names like "Chucky Poke and Tickle," "The Pastry Licker," and (worst and most foul of all) "President Poon"—

That your agents (especially the class clown with the crew cut) have frequently let loose the most vile of farts when we're in the Tahoe, with stenches so rank that they make my eyes burn like somebody poured lye in them—

And, finally, that one of your agents, that idiot out front, has repeatedly fondled the testicles of my administrative assistant, causing him irreparable mental harm for which years of psychotherapy (and, not to mention, considerable financial remuneration) may be necessary.

I, therefore, do, in the name of me, solemnly publish and declare that I am, effective immediately, Free and Independent from the protections of the United States Secret Service, and that all security ties between us be totally dissolved forthwith; and that as a Free and Independent man, I once again have the full power to walk across the street, shop at a big-box store, get seated in a restaurant, take a piss at a public urinal, and pick up willing, delectable babes in thigh-high minis, all without the overbearing and intrusive presence of you surly motherfuckers.

Now get the hell out of my life!

Sincerely,

Charles B. Kidd

Forty-somethingth President of the United States

The freshly-drafted document was pinched between the fingers of a Secret Service agent Kenny had never seen before. When the agent finished reading it, he looked up at Kidd and crumpled his forehead until it resembled a contour map of the Rocky Mountains. "Are you shitting me?" he asked.

Kidd was seated behind the cheap metal desk, his fingers making a steeple at his lips. Kenny stood behind the former president. It had been Kenny's idea to fashion the termination letter in the manner of the Declaration of Independence, and the boy was beaming with pride. Especially at the part about monetary recompense for Agent Crotch's constant molestations.

Kidd took a firm tone with the agent. "I'm not shitting you in the slightest. I want all of you out of here now. And don't worry about your stuff. I'll send a U-Haul."

The agent glared at Kidd, then he rubbed his face, stretching his mouth like molding clay. "I need to call this in," he said.

"By all means," Kidd said, motioning to the *Sports Illustrated* football phone. "My assistant will punch up the number for you."

"Whoa, whoa, whoa," Kenny said. "I don't work here anymore."

Kidd lifted his hands and shrugged at the agent. "I guess you'll have to dial it yourself, then."

Ten minutes later, after a heated phone conversation peppered with phrases like "Yes, sir" and "That's what it says, sir," the agent hung up the receiver. He folded Kidd's letter twice and tucked it into the breast pocket of his suit coat. His next words effectively terminated all Secret Service protection for Charles Bentley Kidd: "You always were a cocksucker, Chuck." Then the agent wheeled on his heel and left.

"It's 'Bent,' you asshole!" Kidd yelled.

When the agent shut the back door to the house, Kidd turned to Kenny. "Time to pack, Young Kernick."

As the Secret Service pulled up stakes, Kenny helped Kidd jam his possessions into the beat-up suitcase. When Kenny and Kidd stepped through the front door of Kidd's house, the agents were pulling their vehicles onto Hoban Lane in single file. Kenny glanced at Kidd. The ex-president unleashed a cocksure smirk as he watched these Secret Servicemen leave the property as he commanded.

But any cocksureness for Kidd was short-lived when he and Kenny heard another vehicle start up in the driveway. It was the black Chevy Tahoe. Kidd's anticipated mode of transportation westward was departing with the Secret Service. Kidd's smirk disappeared.

"Oh, shit," Kidd said. "I forgot they owned that thing."

Kenny and Kidd watched it turn the corner out of sight. The two journeyers were left alone on the steps, without a vehicle.

"Well, that really fucks us up," Kidd declared.

Kenny remained unaffected. He had planned on walking in the first place. He strolled to his duffel bag, hoisted it over his shoulder, then he turned toward Kidd and motioned to the street. "Let's go," he said.

By the look of disgust contorting Kidd's face, Kenny realized that the lanky ex-president had been serious back in the bedroom—he wasn't about to walk anywhere.

"Then what do you suggest we do?" Kenny asked.

Kidd shook his head in a fluster. He looked crestfallen. Then his eyes caught sight of something, and another cocksure smirk crept to the corners of his mouth. Kenny followed Kidd's gaze to Kenny's own house, and the golden Cadillac XTS. The vehicle was parked neatly in the Kernick driveway. It looked so ripe you could pick it.

"No!" Kenny said.

"Kenny," Kidd said. "Kenny, listen to me—"

Kenny threw his hands to his ears and let out a boisterous "La, la, la, la, la, la, la, la, la!"

Kidd yanked Kenny's hands down and put him in a bear hug, making him face the beautiful piece of American automotive engineering that lay ready for the taking only ninety feet away. Kidd whispered into Kenny's ear, "I'm an old man, you know."

"You're fifty-three!"

"Well, I've got bad knees," Kidd said. "And my prostate gets cranky when I walk. I would never hold up. But that"—Kidd swept one long arm toward the Cadillac—"that is a ride for the quest. For renewal, Kenny. For rebirth."

"You're asking me to steal my father's vehicle," Kenny said.

"In the government," Kidd said, "we never steal. We requisition."

Kenny peeled himself away from Kidd. When he looked into Kidd's eyes, he saw passion. Or was it desperation? Kenny couldn't tell.

The pathetic fool did have a point, though. What *would* Kenny have to fear by taking the vehicle?

Would Carl Kernick really call the police and tell them his only child had stolen the precious Cadillac and disappeared?

Could Carl handle all of Simondale talking about "that troubled boy in the Kernick family?"

Was Carl capable of giving the order to launch a manhunt from here to California?

Kenny thought not.

"Let's requisition it," Kenny said.

"Woo-hoo!" Kidd shouted. He grabbed Kenny by the shoulders and kissed the boy on both cheeks. "May God love you, Young Kernick. Now where are the keys?"

"He keeps them on a hook by the stove," Kenny said, as he wiped Kidd's saliva off his face.

Kidd waved a hand. "Off you go. I'll wait here."

Kenny shook his head and said he wasn't going anywhere. First, he hadn't brought a house key with him, because he never intended to go back. Second, the security system was on, and he didn't know the code. Third, he had only managed to escape from the house in the first place by fleeing on that fire escape ladder still dangling from his bedroom window. And finally, he was not going to climb the ladder again, given that the way down was terrifying.

"You know, Young Kernick, there really is a lot you're afraid of. We'll have to work on that." The ex-president adjusted the elastic waistband on his running pants and slicked back his hair with a wad of spit. "Cover me."

Kidd bolted across the street and scrambled up to the façade of the house, his nylon running pants making a swishing noise with every stride. He threw himself against the clapboards and looked around to make sure no one was watching. Kenny found the whole motion a ridiculous waste of time. As if the sight of a fire escape ladder hanging from an open window in the middle of the night wasn't tip-off enough that something was seriously amiss at the Kernick home.

Kidd grabbed the ladder and began his climb. Within seconds, he had disappeared through Kenny's bedroom window.

For the next five minutes, Kenny chewed every fingernail he had. He was about to start on his toenails when he saw Kidd emerge from the bedroom window and begin his descent. Kenny grabbed his duffel bag and Kidd's suitcase and rushed to meet the ex-president as he reached the bushes.

"Your mama looks so cute when she sleeps," Kidd said, jumping from the ladder.

"Please tell me you didn't wake them up," Kenny said.

"Gee, Kenny, does it look like I woke them up?" Kidd pointed the Cadillac's key tag at the vehicle and thumbed a button—the trunk popped open. Kidd grabbed his suitcase from Kenny.

They ran to the Cadillac and threw their luggage in the trunk. Kidd went to slam the decklid, but Kenny grabbed it.

"Gently," Kenny said. He lowered the decklid until the auto-closing device kicked in.

"Well, I'll be a frog catcher," Kidd said over the soft whirr of the latching motor. "We are journeying in style." He bowed flamboyantly. "Shall we?"

"But of course, sir." Kenny returned Kidd's bow. Then he got a shock when Kidd threw him the keys.

"Oh, no, no, Mr. Kidd," Kenny protested, holding out the keys as if they were a hand grenade with its pin detached. "I can't. I've never driven a vehicle in my life. I don't have a license."

Kidd opened the passenger door and let out a tired sigh. "Young Kernick," he said, "you really must stop this incessant fretting. It bores me. Besides, I haven't driven my own car in fourteen years, and I don't plan to start tonight. Now get in."

Kenny's insides churned at the prospect of driving a vehicle for the first time, but he did as he was told. He got in the Cadillac and shut the door.

"Adjust the seat," Kidd ordered.

Kenny flipped a lever near the floor that glided his small frame up to the steering wheel.

"Set that rear-view mirror."

Kenny grabbed the oblong object and positioned it so he could see out the back window.

"Key in the ignition."

Key in.

"Engage."

Kenny twisted the key and felt a strange but beautiful sensation—that of a motor vehicle starting by his own command.

"Big pedal means 'stop,' thin pedal means 'go.' Don't use both feet—that's bad. Now reach for that knob there, put it on the 'R' and—Holy Christ, stop!" Kidd swung his head around to his house, his eyes alight with fear. "Stop, stop, stop! I almost forgot!"

Without explanation, Kidd jumped from the Cadillac and ran back to his house. Kenny saw the ex-president duck inside the massive colonial and throw on a light. Moments later, Kidd charged across the lane with the cigar box from the desk cradled in his arms.

"I don't go anywhere without this," Kidd said, getting back into the Cadillac. He shut the door, set the box on his lap and pulled out a small brass key from the pocket of his running pants. When Kidd opened the box, Kenny smelled cedar mixed with cherry. In the bottom of the box, he saw four heart-shaped lollipops, each with a red, white and blue bow tied to its stem.

There they are, Kenny thought. Amanda Pacheco Twirlies. Lollipops lodged in the annals of historical infamy. The power of their attraction caused Kenny to reach toward the box, mesmerized. Kidd slapped his hand.

"The first rule of the quest—" Kidd said. "Nobody touches these but me." Kenny watched as Kidd took a lollipop from the case, gently removed its wrapper, and slid the lollipop into his mouth. "It has been so long, sweet Amanda," he whispered. "It's been too long." Kidd leaned back in the passenger seat and seemed to let the lollipop soothe him. Soon he let out another sigh (voracious this time) and turned to Kenny. "What are we waiting for? Drive."

Kenny quickly forgot about the lollipop. Feeling clumsy, anxious and awkward, he put the vehicle in "R" and let the slope of the driveway take him to the street. When the Cadillac appeared to slow, he did what he thought he should do— he gunned the thin pedal. It was a bad choice. The Cadillac raced backward and crashed into the guardhouse at the end of Kidd's driveway. The force of the collision tore the shack from its foundation and scraped it across Kidd's lawn.

"That's okay," Kidd said dismissively. "Too bad that frisky bastard wasn't in it."

Kenny reset the knob for "D" and felt the vehicle creep forward. "This is what they call idle speed," Kidd proclaimed between joyous sucks on his lollipop.

Kenny spun the steering wheel to the left, back onto the street. Slowly, through unsure bursts of gas, Carl Kernick's Cadillac XTS traveled down Hoban Lane, with Carl Kernick still asleep in his bed. Kidd beamed like a proud father at Kenny as he watched the boy take his first steps in the world of vehicular operation.

"Oh, Young Kernick," Kidd said, placing a hand on Kenny's headrest. "There is so much I want to teach you. So much potential I see in you."

Kidd fingered the stick of his lollipop. For the first time since Kenny had met him, the man seemed content. After a quiet moment, Kidd surveyed the road ahead and said, "Now, Kenny, let me tell you about the worst case of the crabs I ever had. And from the most beautiful of women, too. Talk about your ironies."

Seven miles later, well into a spirited story of Kidd's flaming, itchy crotch, the college dropout and the impeached ex-president of the United States left Simondale, Connecticut, on the road to renaissance.

★ ★

PART II
MIDDLE AMERICA

★ ★

CHAPTER 7

★ ★

In the whole span of his brief life, Kenny Kernick had never once crossed the Appalachian Mountains—never by train, not once by bus, he had never even done it by airplane. Yet, here he was, on a crisp November morning exactly six months to the day after he had turned eighteen, traveling for the first time over the Appalachian range somewhere in the middle of central Pennsylvania. To celebrate, he was doing it in grand style—by means of one golden Cadillac XTS that had formerly belonged to a man named Carl Maxwell Kernick.

The reason for Kenny's failure to cross these mountains was neither intentional nor nefarious. It stemmed from the inevitable confluence of two separate but indisputable facts: First, that Carl Kernick was a workaholic; and second, that Carl Kernick was a controlling boor. As a result, Kenny's father never had time for a vacation, and if Carl Kernick didn't have time for a vacation, he sure wasn't going to let his wife and child go anywhere without him.

The problem was, of course, that Carl's actions were bound to have consequences, the major one being that a sustained lack of travel ended up putting a crimp in Kenny's experience of the world. But Kenny's father had an answer for that, as he always seemed to have an answer for everything. By Carl's reckoning, if Kenny couldn't see the world firsthand, then he could see the world through books. Through some twisted logic, Carl Kernick had concluded that book learning for Kenny would turn out to be more instructive, more unbiased, more anything, than tasting, touching, hearing, smelling, and seeing real things.

Well, for Kenny, book learning had turned out to be a big, fat bunch of diddly-squat.

Kenny understood that fact now as the Cadillac climbed and fell through this mountainous terrain along a twisting highway called Interstate 80. Kenny had read about these Appalachians countless times in the volumes of his *World Book Encyclopedia*. But none of it had done them an ounce of justice.

Kenny could now see with his own eyes that these mountains were grand. They lapped the sky with brilliant ridges coated in the colors of autumn, then spread down to a valley floor dotted with farmhouses, barns, and churned pastures. Everything looked so amazingly rustic, like something out of an Andrew Wyeth painting. It was stirring in him a host of brand-new emotions, emotions which felt as strange to Kenny as an oversized pair of boots—feelings of awe, and disbelief, and a touch of power.

Kenny welcomed their advent, these odd sensations of grandeur. He was relieved by them. Because for Kenny, the first few hours after he and Kidd left Simondale had been filled with emotions of other kinds, none of which had been overly pleasant or comforting. In fact, for Kenny, the first few hours out of Simondale had turned into a time of unmitigated terror.

It all had to do with the driving. Kenny just couldn't get the hang of it. Numerous times, he would look down to find he was traveling one hundred miles per hour. Then just as suddenly he would slow to fifty-five, which Kidd wouldn't stand for.

As they had careened through the Bronx on I-95, approaching the George Washington Bridge, Kidd decided that serious action needed to be taken regarding Kenny's driving. For the third time, Kenny had almost swerved the Cadillac into a Mack truck. Then he nearly rear-ended a sedan that was pulled over in the breakdown lane. Kenny was also having trouble dealing with any type of curve in the road, jerking and weaving the Cadillac like he was negotiating a hairpin turn instead of an easy bend. But the final straw for Kidd was when Kenny scraped a concrete construction barrier about a mile before the George Washington. Kidd ordered Kenny off the highway and down the Henry Hudson Parkway, heading due south for New York City. The teacher was about to school the pupil.

For the next three hours, as the sun began its rise over a slumbering America, Kenny cut his driving teeth in Manhattan. It was quite a brutal affair—

"Turn down this street," Kidd yelled.

Or "Change lanes now!"

"Parallel park!"

"Gun it past that bus!"

"Watch out for the hooker crossing the street!"

"Don't let that cab driver honk at you! He's a goddamn foreigner!"

And most important...

"Get us the fuck out of Harlem!"

Kidd was like a drill instructor. The whole experience overloaded Kenny until he wanted to vomit on the Cadillac's dashboard.

When Kidd felt confident that Kenny had mastered the subtle coordination between eyes, hands and feet, he gave Kenny a final exam. He had Kenny pull the Cadillac up to a traffic light at the intersection of West 26th and Tenth Avenue and told the boy, point blank, that he didn't want to stop at another red light for at least fifty blocks. When Kenny asked for clarification, Kidd just gestured up to the newly-changed green and said, "Go!"

Kenny soon discovered what Kidd was talking about. The traffic lights along Tenth Avenue were time-delayed, each one turning green a few seconds after the last. But that nice little piece of city planning didn't ensure a swift run up fifty New York City blocks, because at quarter to seven on a weekday morning, there were plenty of other obstacles to stop the Cadillac—turning vehicles, construction lane closures, pedestrians and buses, double-parked delivery vans, and worst of all, taxi cabs, thick as swarming bees.

Almost as if he were involved in some professional motor race, Kenny shot the Cadillac forward. He sped, swerved, cut in, and jerked out. He laid on the horn. He barked at jaywalkers. He even ran two yellows for extra distance. But most of all, he controlled his vehicle. By the time the Cadillac reached a red on 83rd Street, Kidd was hooting and hollering. "Fifty-six intersections!" he shouted. "Fifty-six!" Then he declared that Kenny was henceforth a seasoned driver, true of dexterity and knowledgeable of the road.

"Now let's chow," Kidd said, slapping his tummy.

They found a Burger King on Broadway just as it was opening. Once inside, Kidd introduced Kenny to something called a Croissan'Wich. The meal was stacked high with egg and sausage and dripped with orange cheese. It looked saturated with more grease than Kenny had ever seen on one food item in his life.

Kenny asked Kidd, "Do I have to eat this?"

"Damn straight," Kidd replied.

Kenny smelled the breakfast sandwich, then he nibbled at it—it seemed good enough. He took a baby bite. By this time, Kidd was getting impatient, so he reached over, pried open Kenny's jaw, and stuffed the Croissan'Wich into Kenny's mouth. As Kenny chewed, his eyes began to glow. He had to admit, while the thing looked like it could drop a horse with heart disease, it was tastier than any of that slop his mother made. At Kidd's prodding, Kenny finished off three more Croissan'Wiches, and two sides of hash browns.

While Kenny was devouring his fourth breakfast sandwich, Kidd reached for a napkin. He borrowed a pen from an elderly woman behind him and began to write on the white spread of paper. As he wrote, he said to Kenny, "What the State of Connecticut never granted you, Young Kernick, I bestow upon you by the power vested in me as a former leader of the free world: one valid and legal driver's license, good in all fifty states, and Hawaii."

Kidd beamed with pride as he handed the marked-up napkin to Kenny. Kenny had to laugh as he looked at the "license." At the place where it indicated restrictions, Kidd had drawn a thick, bold asterisk. Kenny flipped the napkin over to see a matching asterisk on the back, with the note: "Make sure he wears his glasses. Without them, he's as blind as Stevie Wonder."

After breakfast, Kenny and Kidd hopped into the Cadillac, crossed into New Jersey through the Lincoln Tunnel, then bolted toward the Delaware Water Gap, with the sun rising higher behind them.

Now the Cadillac was traveling through majestic Pennsylvania, surrounded in all directions by those magnificent mountains. But increasingly, Kenny began to notice that the Cadillac was becoming surrounded by something else, something not so magnificent—Mack trucks. On Interstate 80, there were more Mack trucks than Kenny had seen on the roadways of Connecticut, New York and New Jersey combined: lines and lines of the brawling beasts, charging in and out, streaming by in a whoosh, chugging up hills and speeding down them, all with mind-boggling magnitudes of horsepower and brawn. They were starting to make Kenny nervous, and when Kenny got nervous, he farted.

Thankfully, Kidd, who according to his termination letter with the Secret Service couldn't stand it when someone farted in a vehicle, was asleep in the passenger seat. Kenny could only guess at what kind of stink Kidd would put up over the Croissan'wich-tainted stench Kenny was emitting. It smelled like burnt rubber.

They were passing Exit 161 for Bellefonte—where Kenny saw a sign for State College—when Kenny thought he was about to find out. From a dead sleep, Kidd sniffed. Whatever he sensed made his eyes fly open, then he shot up like he had been hit in the head with a steel girder.

"Do you smell that?" Kidd asked. He sniffed again.

Kenny felt his gut thrash. The flatulent boy was busted. Fearful of Kidd's wrath, he tried to cover, even as another burnt-rubber expulsion slunk out silently from his butt.

"I think it's from the tires on these Mack trucks," Kenny said.

"Not that," Kidd snapped. "But Jesus, shut off the outside air, will you? It's killing me."

Kenny flipped a switch on the climate control.

"Not that smell, Kenny," Kidd said. "I'm talking about the other smell—the smell between the smell. You catch it? Perfume, shampoo, moisturizing lotion, and a hint of sweat, just for flavor—"

Kidd tested the air again with his nostrils, like a timber wolf prodding his environment for meaty, succulent prey.

"Only one thing smells like that," Kidd said. "Scrumptious humptious. We're near a reservoir of it. Judging by the low-end perfume, I'd say these girls are younger. Where are we?"

Kenny remembered the highway sign for State College a mile back, and he recalled that State College was the home of Penn State University. Fearful of where the Cadillac—and by extension, he—might end up if Kidd knew this fact, Kenny played dumb. "Beats me, Mr. Kidd," he said. "I think there was a sign for Bellefonte a few minutes ago."

"Bellefonte, huh?" Kidd said. "Never heard of it." Then he thumbed at his nose, as if to test its accuracy. "I'll bet there's a college around here. A big one. This nose, Kenny"—Kidd tapped the fleshy protrusion with pride—"never lies. It can smell a woman through a brick wall. The younger she is, the easier it is. That's why I usually pick up the scent around institutions of higher learning, where you've got all those delicious aromas stewing in a pot." Kidd took a long drag of the air. A blissful look spread over his face. "Heaven," he said. "Back when I was in college, Jesuit had just started admitting girls, so there weren't many on campus. Boys today don't realize how lucky they are. Co-education is God's gift to the male olfactory nerve."

Kenny squirmed at the mention of girls. Figuring Kidd was expecting some type of discourse, Kenny stated shyly, "Well, college wasn't really for me, Mr. Kidd, so I couldn't say."

"Listen, Young Kernick," Kidd said. "If we're going to make this quest together, there are a couple of things you need to do. First, stop calling me Mr. Kidd. We've known each other long enough that it's uncomfortable, and a little insulting. And second, crack a goddamn window. Because the smell in here isn't from any Mack truck. It's from your ass. And it reeks to the nostrils of Jesus H. Christ Almighty. Son of a bitch!" Kidd powered down his window and stuck his head into the rushing mountain air. "Goddamn! That stink is going to turn my eyes brown."

"Sorry, Bent," Kenny said.

Kidd pulled his head back in and looked at Kenny. "Did you just call me Bent?"

Kenny nodded.

Kidd tapped Kenny on the side of the head. "Well, that's more like it." After waiting a moment for the smell in the Cadillac to clear, Kidd raised his window. "Now tell me something, Young Kernick, seeing we're friends. I want you to share something with me."

"I'll try," Kenny said.

"Good. It's something I've been wondering about, but I haven't wanted to breach, but here it goes: Why would a bright, articulate, somewhat attractive boy such as you drop out of Harvard? I mean, Harvard is one of the biggest scrumptious humptious reservoirs in the country. Call me crazy, Kenny, but that's stupid."

Kenny shook his head. He had always suspected Kidd's every waking thought involved sexual desires, but now that he was locked into an enclosed space with the man, Kidd's über-libido was on full display. All Kenny could think to say was, "Have you ever been to Harvard?"

"No, never," Kidd said. "I slept with a Harvard professor once, but that was at a G20 summit in Honolulu. She got me out of a trade war with Japan; I got her out of her clothes at the hotel. Why does it matter, though? Would it change my opinion on something?"

Kenny took a deep breath. He felt ill. Too many Croissan'Wiches. "Harvard is not like you think it is, Mr.—"

"Uh-ah," Kidd admonished.

"Bent. Right," Kenny said, scratching his red hair. "Harvard is just different. The girls are different. They're attractive, sure, but they're also smart. And stylish."

Kidd laughed. "Well, of course they're smart and stylish, Kenny—they're Ivy League. What do you want them to be, dumb and skanky?"

Kenny powered the gas to get to the top of a ridge, then he cut the wheel sharply around a crawling Mack truck. From the rear, a horn blared—Kenny had cut off a Volkswagen. The grungy-looking fellow behind the wheel gave Kenny the middle finger.

"You're missing the point, Bent," Kenny snapped.

"How can I be missing the point, Kenny? You're not making a point."

"The point is," Kenny said, "I don't do well with stylish. Or smart, for that matter."

"Then what the hell do you do well with?"

Kenny ground himself into the seat's soft leather. "I do well with anything… not female."

Kidd scrunched his face. "Are you telling me you're a homosexual?"

"Bent!" Kenny yelled.

"Okay, okay. Jesus!" Kidd dusted off his nylon running pants and pulled up the sleeves on the sweatshirt. "So let me get this straight. You dropped out of Harvard because of the girls? Is that what you're saying? Now Kenny, I have got to tell you, that's not just stupid, that's pathetic."

"I didn't drop out," Kenny said, his voice a defiant punch. Then his tone turned triumphant, almost proud, and a tad cocky. "I was *asked* to leave."

"Oh, really," Kidd said. "Why was that?"

Kenny sat taller in the driver seat. "Because," he said, "I got caught stealing."

Kenny watched Kidd's eyes bug out, his head cock sideways, and his mouth wrinkle into a zigzag. To Kenny, the former leader of the free world looked wholly as if his nimble mind could not reconcile an act of thievery with the mousy boy sitting next to him. Kidd shook his head, then he looked out at the Pennsylvania mountainside flying by his window. After a moment, he turned back to Kenny and said, almost hushed, like one prisoner talking to another, "So what was it, dude? Television? Laptop? Some pizza man's Vespa?"

"None of that," Kenny said. "But if you must know, it was underpants. Girls' underpants. Just out of the dryer."

Kidd stared at Kenny blankly for what seemed like forever, then he exploded in laughter.

"It's not funny," Kenny said.

"Oh, no, it is," Kidd said, barely able to control himself.

"Well, you don't have to laugh at me."

"No, trust me, Kenny, I do," Kidd said. He let out a high-pitched wail, then he inhaled a deep, wheezing breath. After a moment, he seemed to settle down. He wiped tears off his cheeks. "Oh, God, that's a peach, Kenny," he said. "A big fuzzy peach. Just tell me something. Why in God's name did you have to steal their underpants? It's been my experience that most women will just give them to you."

Kenny felt his stomach thrash. He wanted to let out another rubber-scorched fart. Instead, he sighed.

Kidd took it from there. "Listen, Young Kernick, while making fun of you brings me immense pleasure, I can see that it troubles you."

"So you apologize for laughing?" Kenny said.

"Hell, no," Kidd said. "But I'm perplexed. Baffled, really, at how a boy like you could do such a thing. I mean, let's face it, you don't seem to be much of a risk-taker. If it weren't for me, you wouldn't even be driving this car."

Kenny stiffened in his seat, and stepped on the gas pedal. The Cadillac, now on a steep downward slope, charged by a Mack truck with Illinois plates. As Kenny stared ahead at the bending road, his bottom lip started to tremble. Then all of a sudden, he unloaded on Kidd: "Well, you know, not everyone is like you, Bent. We're not all six feet tall and look like a movie star."

"For your information," Kidd said, "I'm six-three. And movie stars look like me."

But Kenny's defenses were riled. His words spilled out in a rush. "Yeah, well, those Harvard girls were no shrinking violets, you know. They were strong. They had style. And attitude to match. They looked like they could have eaten me for lunch."

"Oh, Kenny," Kidd said ruefully, "if only you had been so lucky." Kidd ran a hand through his hair. "Look, Kenny," he continued, "I'll accept the fact that you're a genius, but let me tell you something: When it comes to life, you have no clue."

Kenny laid on the horn at a passing Mack truck; it was pinning the Cadillac into the slow lane. At the top of his lungs, he shouted to the driver, "Get out of my way, you insufferable A-hole!"

Kidd lifted Kenny's hand off the horn and placed it on the steering wheel. "Easy, killer," the ex-president said. "You don't want to piss him off with that potty mouth."

There was an awkward silence. Kidd reached to the climate console and turned the outside air back on. "Look, Kenny," he said, "all I'm trying to say is this: The first thing you need to realize about life is that things are rarely as they appear, especially when it comes to women. Don't get caught up in presentation. Presentation means nothing. Smart-looking girls can be stupid; wild-looking girls can be dull. That Harvard professor? She didn't give me a single seductive look during the negotiations, not one hint of attraction to me, then back at the Rostoff, she's handing me her thong. No, when you get right down to it, most women present one way and act completely opposite. They are as full of shit as anybody. And you can quote me on that."

Kenny exhaled deeply, then he ruminated on Kidd's words. Finally, meekly, he asked, "So what do you get caught up in?"

"Ah-ha, see, now you're asking the right questions." Kidd's eyes began to glow. "You want to know what you get caught up in, Kenny? Yourself. If women are presenting you with shit, then you have to have a buffer. It starts with attitude, and confidence. Those are the things that mean something. And you don't have to look very far for proof."

"I don't?" Kenny asked.

"Hell, no," Kidd said. "Take me. You said it yourself—I'm tall and devilishly handsome."

"I don't think those were my exact words," Kenny said.

"Well, they should have been," Kidd said. "But here's the rub. Even if I weren't tall and handsome, I'd still be tall and handsome. Because I act tall and handsome. Do you understand that? Now for the other side of the equation, let's take you."

"Let's take me what?" Kenny said.

"You, Kenny, are short and scrawny. But the fact is, you act short and scrawny, which is your problem. But you also act superior, which, unfortunately, is everybody else's problem."

"I do not act superior," Kenny said.

"Oh, come off it," Kidd said. "You're as big a snob as the girls at Harvard. Worse off, you're more than a snob. You're boring. I mean, insufferably dull, Kenny. That brain of yours has been plied with so much information you never learned how to have any fun. You know what you should ply your brain with sometime? Alcohol. Then we'd see the real Kenny."

Kenny was aghast, his voice a stutter. All he could think to say was, "How dare you, sir."

"How dare I?" Kidd said.

"That's right," Kenny said. "You're acting like a—"

"Like a what?" Kidd asked.

"Like a"—Kenny stumbled—"like an A-hole."

"Oh, no, not that." Kidd grabbed his chest melodramatically, as if he had just been stabbed in the heart by Kenny's censured condemnation. He turned to Kenny and his face lit up with the cocksure smirk. "You think I'm wrong?"

Kenny didn't respond.

"Seriously, Kenny, do you think I'm wrong?"

Kenny could feel his teeth grinding together.

"Then tell me this," Kidd said. "How many foreign languages do you speak?"

Kenny glared at Kidd. "I hardly think that's relevant."

"How many, Kenny? Come on, tell me."

"If it will shut you up," Kenny said, "I speak three: French, Spanish, and German."

"Three," Kidd said, impressed. "Three foreign languages. Not bad. Now tell me something else, Young Kernick, and be truthful: How many girls have you kissed?"

Once again, Kenny didn't respond. The look on his face said it all.

"That's what I thought," Kidd said. "None. You're a smart boy, Kenny, so plot that data on a graph. When you can speak more foreign languages than you've kissed girls, you're definitely in the dull quadrant. And to top it off, you dress like the bastard child of Eddie Bauer and L.L. Bean, you talk like someone out of an F. Scott Fitzgerald novel, and you never swear. Just swear for me once, Kenny. I'm dying to hear it."

"This is ridiculous." Kenny jerked the steering wheel, sending the Cadillac into the passing lane.

"Come on," Kidd implored. "Say 'asshole.' Say 'shit.' Wait, I've got a better idea—say 'fuck' for me, Kenny. Don't spell it like you did this morning in my house—I want you to say it. Put it in your mouth, and chew on it, and savor its flavor. Fuck, fuck, fuck, fuck, fuck, fuck, fuck. Tell me to fuck off. I know you want to. I can see it in your eyes. Say to me, 'I do believe, Mr. Kidd, that you can go fuck yourself with a pogo stick.'"

Kenny stiffened in his seat again. He jutted his jaw and kept his eyes forward. "I will not," the boy said haughtily. "That would be crass."

Kidd leaned across the Cadillac's center console and got right under Kenny's ear. His tone became flat but tough. "Therein lies the lesson, Young Kernick. A few well-placed moments of crass would go a lot further with the ladies than this bullshit Lord Fauntleroy act you pull."

Kidd leaned back in his seat. He yawned like a lion, then tilted his body to the right and let out a prolonged, rumbling fart of his own, right at Kenny. As the rank odor began to waft through his nylon running pants, he said, "Listen to me well, Young Kernick, and take root in what I say. You're using intellectualism as a cover for what you think you don't have—physical stature, or style, or confidence, power, whatever. But the problem is not that you lack these things; it's that you think there's something wrong with you because you lack them. It's all about how you think, Kenny. Thought breeds confidence, and confidence breeds attitude, and no amount of highbrow intellectualism can cover for you if you think you're a piece of shit. So stop acting like an adult and grow up."

Kenny pressed his lips together, taking in Kidd's words. They were strange words, but they seemed to make sense. He asked, "So how do I do that?"

Kidd didn't answer.

"Mr. Kidd?" Kenny asked. "Bent?"

Kenny heard a shuffling snore. He looked over to see Kidd sleeping again, his head crooked into the space between the passenger seat and the doorframe.

Kenny let out another sigh. He didn't want his question to hang in the air like Kidd's fart; he wanted answers. He was a knowledge junkie, and answers provided his fix—the full and complete set of facts to make his disjointed world straight again. And right now, he wanted an answer worse than ever, because he was more than a little frightened.

Kenny scanned the highway in front of him, staring ahead at its twists and turns. He knew that his journey, both of the road and of the spirit, would be more challenging than any academic course he had ever taken. It would be harder than physics, or organic chemistry, and even harder than that ridiculous tensor calculus with continuum mechanics. But looking out at Interstate 80, as it cut through the majestic Appalachians, Kenny knew he was committed to the journey. He wanted to be confident; he wanted to have attitude; he certainly wanted to know what it felt like to kiss a girl. He hadn't driven halfway across the mountains of central Pennsylvania just to find a bunch of diddly-squat on the other side.

Kenny tried to comfort himself in his desire for change, even as a howling pack of Mack trucks surrounded the Cadillac as it began its ascent up another steep and suicidal incline.

CHAPTER 8

★ ★

Two and a half hours later, as the Cadillac approached the Ohio border along I-80, Kenny Kernick ran out of gas, both in the car and in himself.

By Kidd's estimation, Kenny had been awake for over thirty-one hours. With drooping eyelids and his control waning, the boy managed to pull the vehicle into a truck stop on the outskirts of Sharon, the last town in Pennsylvania heading west. After Kidd paid for a fill-up in cash, Kenny drove the Cadillac to the parking lot, climbed into the backseat, and fell asleep. He didn't even take off his glasses.

While Kenny slept, Kidd wandered the parking lot. Given his nap that morning, Kidd wasn't tired, and the brisk air of the afternoon enlivened him. To occupy the time until Kenny woke up, Kidd decided to walk over to the truck stop's main building.

It had been twenty years since Charles Bentley Kidd last set foot in a truck stop, and the years showed. This place looked more like a Wal-Mart, and it housed everything within its walls: a convenience store, a shoe repair shop, a video game arcade, travel and tourism booths, and of most importance to Kidd's stomach, a diner. Kidd rubbed his tummy and started for the diner, but before he got there, he detoured through the convenience store and bought himself a cheap baseball hat as a defense against being noticed. When he drew the hat over his brow, Kidd felt anonymous, just another traveler looking to take a load off.

Kidd sat at the back of the diner, stuffing his face with pancakes and bacon. And with every chew, he berated himself for his plight.

How was it that a man once so proud and accomplished could now feel the need to hide in shame in a rural truck stop at the edge of Pennsylvania? How could he—he, of all people— have fallen that far that fast? How in Christ's name had it ever come to this?

Kidd understood the facts of the scandal known as "Pastrygate." How could he not? He had lived, sweated, shed weight, pulled out his hair, and gone sleepless over them. But ever since he left the White House, Kidd couldn't understand the "Why?" of the scandal. Why, goddammit, why? Why did this happen? Kidd's mind railed constantly in turmoil, incapable of conjoining what he still thought were innocent interactions between him and Amanda Pacheco with the harsh punishment meted out by Congress. Even after six months, the wound still stung. He had once been the most powerful man in the world. Now he was sitting in a lonely diner booth, and the only power he possessed was to butter his blueberry pancakes, because the waitress had forgotten the syrup.

So Charles Bentley Kidd put another slab of butter on his pancakes, and he stuffed his face some more. And as he ate, his insides began to shake.

He was anxious partly from being alone in a public place for the first time in ages. That anxiety didn't come only from being there alone; it came from the fact that for the first time in memory he was partaking of life alone, with no handlers, no assistants, no staff or security. Kidd didn't even have the comfort of knowing that he had come to this diner to make a big speech, or to unveil some initiative in grandiose style from behind a polished podium. Events like those had always relaxed him. Briefly, Kidd regretted dismissing the Secret Service—he would have loved for them to be there, to provide him with an element of gravitas as he stuffed his cheeks with pancakes. They had recently performed a similar function at the Wal-Mart in Simondale, when he had walked through the aisles in fear but still felt a twinge of bravado, if only because he was surrounded by three shorter men with guns. The whole scene had said, "Hey, you gawking dickheads. None of you may have voted for me, but Charles Bentley Kidd is still important."

And yet, Kidd was sitting in this diner alone. He considered dragging Kenny out from the car to make the boy sit with him, but the thought passed quickly. Kenny was exhausted. Better to let the boy rest. Otherwise, he might fall asleep behind the wheel and wrap the Cadillac around a tree on the way through Ohio.

Kidd chewed, then swallowed. The word "Ohio" was lingering in his mind. Once Kenny woke up, Kidd realized, he would cross into Ohio. He would be going home.

With that realization, Kidd's insides convulsed. He leaned forward and tried not to throw up his blueberry pancakes. After a few minutes, the nausea passed.

Why, he wondered, regaining his composure, did going back to Ohio come as a shock to him? Hadn't he thought about it fleetingly in New Jersey, when he calculated that to get to Los Angeles, he might have to pass through his former state at some point? Yes, he had thought about it, but he had also contemplated telling Kenny to go around Ohio, down through Virginia and across Tennessee. The problem was, something wouldn't let him. Something made Kidd tell Kenny to take Interstate 80. Something was calling him. Something he could not ignore.

But what was calling him? Kidd pondered the options.

Was it the land itself, with its rolling hills and tilled plains, its Appalachian plateau and those fertile Great Lakes lowlands? No, it couldn't be the land. Ohio was magnanimous in its diversity, and such a sundry land could never join together to speak to him with a unified voice.

Was it the river then, that thick Ohio River which entered the state near East Liverpool and formed its border south and west until just past Cincinnati? Kidd had been born along the banks of that river and still had its mud caked into his feet. But it was such a preoccupied river, Kidd knew, consumed as it was with the production of electricity and the business of manufacturing. Kidd chastised himself for thinking the voice could be coming from the Ohio. The river wouldn't have time to give him a thought.

Then maybe it was the people. Ohioans were a glorious people—hardworking, reverent, and firm. They had raised Kidd from his childhood in Hawleyville in the southeastern part of the state, then raised him higher during his rise through state politics, making it possible for his stratospheric ascent to the presidency. But like the river, would his fellow Ohioans even have time for him now? Would they deign to give him a thought these days, considering that his stratospheric ascent had turned into a catastrophic fall?

Or perhaps the voice was emanating from a source Kidd really didn't want to contemplate. Perhaps the voice belonged to his mama.

Kidd felt moisture gather in the corners of his eyes. Maybe it *was* his mama calling—beckoning to him as she lay there in a grave on a hillside up from the Ohio River. But why would she need him? She had been gone for almost five years, plenty of time for her spirit to move into the light. Was she all right? Was her gravesite manicured? Did people come to visit her? Was she being taken care of by someone? By anyone?

Kidd went limp with shame. He dropped his fork, slunk back in the booth, and rested his chin on his chest.

How had he let himself neglect the memory of his beloved mama? Why had he not seen fit to put in a continuing order for flowers on her grave? When had he let himself get to the point where he wouldn't even think about her for weeks at a time anymore?

Kidd didn't know the answers to those questions. But now, as he sat just minutes away from the Ohio border, he knew exactly what to do next. He couldn't just skim along I-80 through northern Ohio. No, at this point in his life, at this place, he would have to turn south and go back to Hawleyville, where he would pay his respects to his deceased mama.

That prospect made Kidd sicker. Returning to Hawleyville wouldn't be like eating in a diner at a truck stop. In Hawleyville, he would be recognized. Kidd thought back to the last time he visited Hawleyville. That trip had taken place before his second inauguration, when he and The Rhino made an impromptu appearance at his first school, Turtle Stream Elementary, for a "Thank You, Hawleyville!" rally. Back then, the townsfolk loved him. But what would those same townsfolk think now? Was he still their favorite son? Did they still have pictures of him hanging everywhere? Were they still naming their children "Charles Bentley Whatever," even if they had a girl? Kidd had no idea, and that uncertainty spooked the shit out of him.

Then Kidd's mind flashed with a stroke of brilliance.

His return home didn't have to be difficult, and it didn't have to be uncertain. He could control the situation. He would do that by having an announcement to make once he got there. He would give an important speech to the people of Hawley-ville, complete with news coverage and a podium, and another rally. And for the substance of that speech, he had just come up with a humdinger: He would return to Hawleyville bearing a gift. Not just any gift, but a gift of epic historical importance, something that would change the town forever. He was confi-dent that his townsfolk would love it. Kidd pulled his chin off his chest and congratulated himself. His idea was pure genius. The wily bastard had done it again.

Charged by the idea, Kidd sprung to life. He finished his pancakes, then left the forgetful waitress a huge tip. He tossed the baseball hat in the trash and ran from the building, dashing for the car to shake Kenny awake. Even if the boy was tired, Kidd could not wait. They had to get on the road. The journey to Hawleyville would take at least four hours, and he wanted to be there by sunrise. He had much to do, and the voice was encouraging him to be a man undivided.

When he got to the Cadillac, he saw Kenny sleeping in the backseat. Kidd knocked on the window. Kenny's eyes popped open.

"It's my mama!" Kidd said to the boy. "It's my mama!"

"Who's your mama?" Kenny asked. But before Kidd could offer a reply, Kenny fell asleep again. And this time, he wouldn't wake up.

CHAPTER 9

★ ★

During the 1950s, the city of Stampler was the jewel of West Virginia. Built on an ancient flood plain along the southeastern bank of the Ohio River, near a bend in the waterway where Ohio, West Virginia and Kentucky all converge, Stampler (pop. 60,109) wanted for nothing, at a time when West Virginia was thought of by most Americans to have nothing at all.

The people of Stampler understood the conventional national wisdom, and they took it upon themselves to prove that wisdom wrong. To that end, their city proudly displayed a public transportation system and a big city hall. It lured in national banks and accounting offices and law firms. It built movie theatres, cultural centers, and a playhouse which put on summer shows and winter festivals. It supported French restaurants and European hair salons, furniture stores and musical instrument shops, a daily newspaper and a hospital. And, as its crowning achievement, it was the location for a nationally-renowned university which, year after year, swelled the ranks of professional sports leagues with the finest stock of scholar-athlete that any institution of higher learning could develop.

But of all the shining attributes of Stampler at that time, none was more revered by the community than the man who occupied the pulpit every Sunday morning at the Elm Street Baptist Church. That man's name was Reverend Charles Ray Laudermilk, and not only was he one of the most well-respected and learned men of faith, the author of three books on evangelical theory, wildly popular throughout the border states for the power, amplitude and insightfulness of his preaching, but he was also the keeper of a dark secret. For while he considered himself a man of the cloth, he preferred that cloth to be sheets, and for his body to lie between them while being mounted by the latest female soul in need of spiritual guidance. Especially when he was on the road, and the younger girls came out to hear him preach before finding themselves back in his motel room for an extra-credit ministry session which usually involved the crying out of God's name.

One of the younger girls who crossed Pastor Laudermilk's path during that quiet decade of family, faith and morals was an affable seventeen-year-old named Annabelle Earl. To the rest of Stampler, Annabelle was the cheerful daughter of a railroad machine shop clerk and his homemaker wife. To Pastor Laudermilk, however, she was so much more—at once a stunning angel, and yet a wicked temptress, one who possessed the most amazing platinum locks and liquid green eyes to which he had ever borne witness.

He had known Annabelle Earl since she was a little girl— her parents were longtime members of the church—but over the years the good Pastor Laudermilk had never given her much more than a cursory glance, consumed as he was with matters of riper flesh. Then one summer, he ran into her at a Baptist youth retreat, and her transformation startled him. Gone were the flat body, the oversized teeth and the boyish haircut. In their places had arisen a structure of divine ungodliness: gleaming white incisors, downy hair that tickled her shoulders like the breath of a whisper, and a body formed of the most seditious curves, bowing out at all the proper places against the fabric of the sack dresses she wore.

It didn't take long before Pastor Laudermilk couldn't keep his eyes off Annabelle Earl during Sunday sermon. She bewitched him, possessed him, inhabited him, more than any of the other young women whom he had "ministered" over the years. While preaching, he found himself thinking not of the salvation of his flock, but of how best to separate Miss Annabelle Earl from her undergarments. Many times, he had to extend his sermons because of a gigantic erection bulging at the zipper of his black wool preacher's pants. Once, he kept his congregation enthralled with a fiery message of hell and fury for over three hours while waiting for his throbbing knob to recede, like the waters of the Great Flood had receded for Noah. Many parishioners afterward called it the good Pastor Laudermilk's finest sermon. Annabelle's mother said Jesus must have been with him.

Pastor Laudermilk was an experienced man; he knew well which paths to trod to find the fruits he so desired. Annabelle Earl, however, presented him with a dilemma. She violated his Holy Trinity of qualifications for women with whom he would fornicate. First, she was still in high school, where all of his other conquests had been eighteen or older. Second, she was a member of his congregation, which went against his prohibition never to dip his pen in Elm Street Baptist ink. Third, any indulgences with her would have to occur within a twenty-mile radius of his church, something he had always avoided. But for as much as Annabelle Earl presented such a dilemma, she was impossible to disregard. To Pastor Laudermilk, caught in the glare of those green eyes, seventeen was as good as eighteen. Against his better judgment, he initiated a pursuit.

It was common knowledge in the community that the Earl family had limited financial means, so Pastor Laudermilk extended an offer: He invited Annabelle to work in the church administrative office after school. To his delight, she accepted.

Four days a week, Annabelle would arrive at the church office only to find there wasn't really any work for her to do. What there was, however, was conversation. Annabelle discovered that Pastor Laudermilk could talk a blue streak. He wanted Annabelle to know about the small town he came from in Georgia; he wanted Annabelle to know who he was as a man, deep down, and how vulnerable he could be, especially when he was cuddling a kitty. He told Annabelle that his wife (a materialistic shrew) and his sons (dumb as nails) didn't have the wherewithal or the desire to acknowledge him further than he could provide funds for their fancy clothes or fast cars, and that their lack of interaction, and his wife's standoffishness in general, made him terribly lonely.

While he talked on endlessly, in that same commanding voice that always held the faithful in rapt attention, Annabelle didn't hear much of what the pastor said. She was too busy gazing at him with her wide green eyes. To Annabelle, the Reverend Charles Ray Laudermilk was just plain gorgeous, even for an old man in his forties. He was tall, had wavy mocha hair, and the features of his face combined in perfect harmony. He smelled good, too, like pleasant intensity, which was a first for Annabelle, given that her father always came home from the railroad shop smelling like armpit stink.

More than anything else, he was successful, wildly successful, in everything he did.

It took a week for Annabelle to have a crush on the pastor. It took a month for her to fall in love with him. That's when she started carrying the conversations.

Annabelle started to ask the pastor questions about redemption. The pastor asked her if she was having a crisis of faith. She said no, that it wasn't so much about not believing in Jesus, but that she was having evil thoughts which she couldn't control. She loved Jesus, but she also loved someone else. Since that someone else was visible, and Jesus wasn't, the someone else was beginning to consume her. Which was a bad thing. He was married, with a family. She was scared, she said. She didn't want to burn in eternal damnation.

The good Pastor Laudermilk nodded his head, then he did something completely unexpected. He kissed her. To her surprise, she kissed him back. When their lips parted, his hands moved to her waist and he told Annabelle that she was in the grips of Satan, and the only way to get the devil out of her was for him to do battle with the Bringer of Hellfire on the ground of Satan's choosing. Baptism only went so far, he said, as he lifted her sack dress and slid her cotton dainties to the floor. Even a rededication to Christ wouldn't do the trick, he panted, as he pressed his throbbing knob into the fold of her flaxen triangle. Pumping her eager body against the office's dark wood paneling, he commanded Satan to leave this girl. After fifteen euphoric seconds, he shouted, "Jesus H. Christ on a Radio Flyer!" and stopped thrusting, appearing to think he had done the job. As a blissful Annabelle pulled up her underwear and lowered the sack dress to her knees, the pastor promised her that she would no longer be taunted by the Ruler of Demons, and that the power of his saving salve would protect her from the flames of hell. All it really did was knock her up.

When Annabelle found out she was pregnant, she had a choice to make: She could either stay in Stampler, where all her family, friends and neighbors would condemn her and call her a whore; or she could run away to someplace else, where she could lie to people who might otherwise condemn her and call her a whore.

To Annabelle, the choice was no choice at all. She didn't want to disgrace her family, and she certainly didn't want to destroy the man she loved with a ruinous scandal, the likes of which were sure to make the front pages of countless newspapers throughout the border states. So one Thursday evening in November, she decided to leave town. She told her parents she was going to bed, then she packed a suitcase in silence, and formulated a plan for her new life.

She knew that to be pregnant in a new place, she would have to be married, but to be married with no husband by her side would arouse suspicion. So Annabelle would feign widowhood. Her age wasn't an issue. There were more than a few girls from the rural towns who had gotten married at fourteen and already had broods of children. But to pretend to be a widow, she couldn't remain Annabelle Earl. She would have to change her identity. She needed a new name. She needed a ring.

For the ring, she took a simple gold band from the jewelry box on her mother's dresser. It was the ring which had belonged to her grandmother, but Grandma had died when Annabelle was a child and Annabelle knew that her mother hadn't touched the band in years. Slipping the ring on her finger for the first time, Annabelle found it a little loose, but in the following months, as her weight increased, it would fit just fine.

With the ring in place, it was time for a new identity. She wanted to keep names that meant something to her, and yet, she didn't want to make them obvious. To that end, Annabelle took the names of the objects around her. For a fictitious maiden name she chose "Bunton," because it was the name on the label of her mother's jewelry box. For a married name she chose "Kidd," the maker of her favorite porcelain dolls.

Under Annabelle's plan, if anybody were to ask about her origins (and wherever she ended up, someone was sure to ask), Annabelle would tell them she came from Oxford, West Virginia, in Boone County, just south of Charleston. She decided that her husband, a man named Horace Kidd ("Horace" for the street she'd grown up on), had died in the huge coal-gas explosion which had taken more than one hundred lives of real men only two weeks prior. Everybody in a five-state area was still reading about the explosion at the Nickleton Coal Works; the bodies were too many to account for, the conditions too dangerous to bring them up from the depths of the mine. Given the slack with which the foremen often let in desperate day laborers, many men would go unknown.

By the circumstances of the tragedy, Annabelle felt safe that her story would remain unchallenged, but she also felt a strong current of guilt wash through her. She was using the deaths of others as a way to cover her own sin, and she hated herself for it. Sadly, she didn't think she had much choice. A baby was growing inside her. Time was getting short. She was already beginning to feel nauseated. It was the nausea which terrified her the most, and not because of how sick it made her feel. Annabelle knew that her mother, who had given birth to six children and had thrown up with each pregnancy, would not mistake persistent vomiting for illness.

With a ring on her finger and a suitcase in her grip, Annabelle Earl sneaked out of the house through the kitchen while her family in the living room watched *Dragnet*. For her mother, she left a note by the jewelry box. It read: "I love you all. I won't be back. There's something I have to get out of my system. Never worry. I'll call someday. With Love, Belles."

Annabelle Earl walked across town and over the Cabell County Bridge into Ohio. From there she decided to head north. There were bigger cities up north, she told herself, cities like Youngstown or Akron, or even Cleveland. Places she could hide in.

But Annabelle Earl would never make it to any of those cities. After eight hours of walking along dangerous Route 7, she collapsed from hunger and exhaustion on a bench in a place called Hawleyville. In the darkness, the town around her didn't look like much, but when the sun came up, and the fog lifted, and she could see Hawleyville's gentle charm, she knew she would never leave. A redbrick town with old-growth ash trees lining the streets, Hawleyville was smaller than Stampler by two-thirds, and the place had a really odd smell in the air, like the scent of her father after a heavy night of drinking. But these characteristics only added to the allure. Hawleyville seemed to her a big city rolled into a little package, and she could tell from the morning hubbub, as stores opened and the traffic increased, that the town was rich with energy and civic pride. The people even seemed friendly: Around eight in the morning, a robust old woman in a kerchief found Annabelle on the bench and took her to a nearby diner for breakfast.

"What's your name, child?" the woman asked as Annabelle gulped down scrambled eggs.

"Kidd," Annabelle said. "Anna Kidd. From Oxford, West Virginia."

The old woman eyed the gold band on Annabelle's finger. "You have a ring but you have no man with you."

Annabelle cleared her throat. She didn't relish what she was about to say, but she said it anyway. "I'm recently widowed."

To that revelation, the old woman did something bizarre. She smiled.

"I'm a widow, too," she said, whispering, as if widowhood held an accursed mark. "But not recent. My husband died in the Great War. That's World War One to you young folk."

The old woman took to Annabelle that very morning, even offering her a place to stay while the girl got her affairs in order. On the walk back to the old woman's simple four-room bungalow house on the other side of Rabbit Stream, the Widow O'Dell flapped her arms and pointed excitedly, and told Annabelle that Hawleyville had everything a girl starting fresh would ever need—shoe stores and clothing boutiques, good doctors and great schools, food markets and places to get your dainties. Most important, because it employed half the town, Hawleyville even had a factory that made soap, which explained the peculiar smell in the air.

Like the giant ash trees lining every street in Hawleyville, Annabelle Earl (now known as Anna Kidd) dug her roots into the town, and the roots took. She got a job in the typing pool at the soap factory, eventually landing a position as the secretary to the factory's owner, Herbert R. Tackmann. She rented an apartment in the middle of the downtown, above a store that sold Electrolux vacuum cleaners. She made friends. On more than one occasion, as her tummy began to swell and she could no longer deny her condition, she was asked about the father of her unborn child. To those questions, Annabelle Earl kept up the lie. Horace Kidd was the father of her child. They had been married for less than three weeks when she got pregnant. She loved him deeply. Then he died in that coal-gas explosion in West Virginia, and she needed to get away from the awful place that had taken her man. To Annabelle's surprise, nobody ever doubted her, not even a few months later when she gave birth to a son and not a single member of her family was there to support her—no father, no mother, no siblings, and no dead husband's relatives.

But to Annabelle, holding a new baby boy in her arms, the past hardly seemed to matter anymore. Her name was Anna Kidd now. She had just turned eighteen, and that made her a woman in the eyes of the law. She had responsibilities. She had to provide for this child. And the first thing she wanted to give her son was a chance. She made three vows that day: She would give him a good name; she would give him a good home; and she would give him a good education. The rest, she told herself, would be in God's hands.

Annabelle named her child Charles Kidd—"Charles" for his real father, whom he already resembled, and "Kidd" for his fake daddy, whom she hoped would conceal her baby's identity wherever he went in life.

But while she loved the name Charles Kidd, to Annabelle it seemed incomplete. Her boy needed a middle name, and that name needed to stand out. Annabelle's family had always been poor, with poor middle names like Wayne and Bob. Her son, she determined, would have no middle name like that. He would have a middle name like a leader, like Franklin Delano Roosevelt or William Jennings Bryant. She wanted it to be an English name, for the class and dignity such a name would convey, but try as she might, with her limited life experience, she couldn't think of a single English name she liked. So, again, Annabelle looked to the objects around her for inspiration. She checked the pillow sheets in her hospital room, and the maker of the bassinette beside her bed, but those names were more Eastern European than English. Then she remembered that her boss at the soap factory, Mr. Tackmann, drove a ritzy English car with all the bells and whistles, and certainly one with class. He parked it every day under her window, and she had always loved the looks of it. That car was a Bentley.

"Charles Bentley Kidd," she declared as she tickled the cheek of her swaddled boy. "It's perfect."

How could a name like that not be perfect? she wondered. How could his life from that moment on not be the most blessed life ever? His name was Charles Bentley Kidd. He would be as tall and as handsome and as successful as his real-life daddy. He had been born on the Fourth of July.

These were good omens, she thought.

Whether or not Charles Bentley Kidd realized it, the disgraced former president of the United States was approaching Hawleyville, Ohio, on the exact anniversary of the morning, over five decades ago, that his mother had wandered into town, although he was coming from the opposite direction.

Kidd hadn't thought of his mama much after he and Kenny left the truck stop near Sharon, Pennsylvania. Instead, he was consumed with the brilliant idea, the stunning gift he was coming to Hawleyville to bestow. But as Kenny drove him closer to the town along Route 7, and the road condensed under a morning fog in the Ohio River Valley, Kidd's mind began to fill with the sound of his mama's twanged voice. And the form her voice took was of the story she had told him when he was sixteen about the circumstances of his true parentage.

"It's our little secret," she had whispered, hugging him ferociously. "But it shows you're marked for greatness, Chucky. Because your father, the Reverend Charles Ray Laudermilk, was a great man. He wasn't a miner like our friends and neighbors think. Remember, Chucky, it's our secret."

It had stayed their secret, mother's and son's, to this very day. Even the two people closest to Charles Bentley Kidd— his daughter and The Rhino—did not know the identity of his real father. Kidd had only ever feared its revelation once, when he first announced that he would be running for president after two terms as Ohio's governor. How deeply would the press dig into his background? Should he prepare for his past to be exhumed? The answer came quickly—the press never even put a shovel to Charles Bentley Kidd's fertile earth. From the start, Kidd was their man, and they saw no need to muck him up with irrelevant facts, whatever those facts might be. For Kidd, it paid to have jaw-dropping good looks, a youthful exuberance, and to have been born on the Fourth of July, but it also paid to be the right man in the right place at the right time in a nation's circumstance. The United States under President Molson was heading down a shithole. Given the country's eight percent unemployment rate, and Milquetoast Molson's middling mediocrity of looks, speech and effectiveness, Charles Bentley Kidd figured that he could have been born of a jackal and the press still would have proclaimed him the dashing knight come to save a country that could not save itself.

But now it was seven years later. Milquetoast Molson was long gone, and Kidd had endured a tumultuous administration during which Molson's recession lessened, seemed to disappear long enough to get Kidd re-elected, then blew up shortly into Kidd's second term. The unemployment rate, once as low as five percent for Kidd's re-election victory, had exploded to the high side of twelve before his impeachment. It was not uncommon in Kidd's later term to hear panic filling the talk-radio airwaves and Sunday morning news programs.

And gone, along with the jobs of a nation, the promise of a new tomorrow, and the hope for a revitalized America, was any love for Charles Bentley Kidd. In the wake of Pastrygate, his popularity had been obliterated. It was all too hard to swallow, Kidd thought, when for most of his adult life he had been placed on the gilded pedestal and gazed upon, where the men looking up at him would think, "We just want to *be* him," and the women would think, "We just want to *do* him." How could love disappear that fast?

That was a question Kidd had pondered obsessively during the six months since his removal from office, without a satisfying answer. But as the Cadillac plowed through the quilted fog of this autumn morning, Kidd had a sense that his return to Hawleyville would bring him resolution. He was going back to the one place where a man knew he would be loved; to a place where the people were, he was quite certain, obligated by law to love you. He was going home. To make sure he would find love at home, he had brought his plan, his stunning gift, all worked out and ready to roll, waiting to be embraced by his townsfolk.

By Kidd's calculations, joy would erupt in the streets of Hawleyville when the town heard of his gift. The city council would initiate a weeklong holiday, starting with a rally, and the soap factory would issue a commemorative bar of its trademark facial cleanser just to honor the occasion. There would be a grand parade around Hawleyville's redbrick downtown. School children lining the sidewalks would wave American flags. Confetti would fall like mist from the rooftops. The Hawleyville High School marching band would play "Son of a Preacher Man" but have no idea why they were doing it. There would be singing and laughing, tear-shedding and amazement, and hopefully, lots of sex.

Then the parade would stop at the town common. The mayor would emerge from the VIP car, followed by Kidd. They would make their way to a gazebo surrounded by a crushing throng of Hawleyvillers. A hush would fall over the crowd. The mayor would introduce Kidd. The crowd would explode in cheer. The mayor would raise a hand to quiet them. Then he would unveil a plaque. From the plaque he would read a declaration:

THAT THE GOOD PEOPLE OF HAWLEY-
VILLE, OHIO, do hereby state and affirm that we
have missed Charles Bentley Kidd; that we are glad
he has returned to us; that we thank him for his
gift with immeasurable, unending gratitude; that on
the political and historical fronts we think he got
the shaft, but that his ridiculous impeachment conviction and subsequent removal from office hardly
matter to us, because regardless of what the rest of
this country thinks, he will always and forever be
etched in our minds as that tall, handsome boy of
unlimited promise—the debate team virtuoso, the

glee club soloist, the president of the Future Business Leaders of America and the local 4-H.

PRESENTED TO CHARLES BENTLEY KIDD
by the people of Hawleyville, Ohio, on this whateverth day of November, in the year of our Lord yadda yadda yadda, sis boom bah.

As he imagined the whole hullabaloo, Kidd felt his body shiver with delight. The townsfolk would say those things, wouldn't they? They will celebrate me, right? They have to, don't they? He was, after all, the prodigal son returned.

As powerful as he had once been, Kidd could not divine the answers to those questions. In fact, looking out the windshield of the Cadillac, Charles Bentley Kidd couldn't divine the answers to anything right now, particularly the whereabouts of his hometown.

As usual, there was too much fog.

CHAPTER 10

★★★★★★★★★★★★★★★★★★★★★★★★★★★★★★★★

From experience, Charles Bentley Kidd knew that the thick November fog currently engulfing the Cadillac would not disappear before ten o'clock in the morning. To compensate for the cataract of fog on trips home at this time of year, Kidd had learned to use his eyes like the fingers of a blind man. Through the fog, Kidd would search for five landmarks along the road—"touch points," he called them—as if he were pressing his thumb, then his index finger, then his middle and ring fingers and finally his pinky, so he could, like a man impaired of vision, discern the beauty of Hawleyville, all while having no clear visual means to do so.

The first touch point arrived just after eight in the morning: It was the old Red Pouch Tobacco advertisement which had been painted, decades ago, onto the side of an outlying barn at the farthest reaches of Hawleyville's borders. The barn was dilapidated now, looking as if it might fall apart from gravity alone. The advertisement was faded and jumbled by the crook of misaligned barn slats, but the sight of the ad still whirred in Kidd a burst of joy—he had, at last, taken his first step home.

The Red Pouch advertisement on the old barn heralded the arrival of the second touch point less than a mile later: the transition of two-lane Route 7 into a four-lane highway with divider. The Cadillac crossed this threshold, and Kidd told Kenny to get off at the upcoming exit for North Hawleyville Road.

Along the three-mile stretch of North Hawleyville Road, the touch points increased in frequency and significance. In the old days, this part of town was mostly undeveloped farmland; over the past twenty years, however, it had become a boondoggle of urban sprawl, providing asphalt pasture for the chain stores of the world. Kidd found his touch points nestled in among these recent additions.

First, behind a big-box mart, he saw the metal skeleton of the transmitting tower for WHAW. "The Haw," as it was called, was one of the oldest radio stations in the state, and had broadcast over its airwaves many of Kidd's stellar high school debates, at a long-ago time when local radio stations did that sort of thing. He could still hear its promotional call—"Bee Hee Hee Haw Haw!"—which some marketing manager had pilfered from an episode of *The Flintstones.*

Next, beside a food supercenter, Kidd saw the Blue Bell Motel. But Kidd didn't call it the Blue Bell Motel anymore, even though its name was still clearly emblazoned on its crappy sign. To Kidd, this flea-ridden dump would always be the "Blue Ball Motel," because it was the unfortunate location, one month before his graduation from high school, where he was finally supposed to lose his virginity to a voluptuous, tawny-haired chatterbox named Sally Jean McClean. That was the plan, anyway, until Sally Jean came down with that most insipid of infirmities—her period—just as Kidd was dropping his pants to the floor. Kidd had never again come that close to unlocking the divine secrets of Miss Sally Jean's delectable girlhood. He hadn't even gotten one of her legendary blowjobs out of the deal, she had run home so fast.

A quarter-mile past the Blue Ball, on the opposite side of the road, Kidd saw his final touch point: a Pizza Hut, tucked back from the road and bordering Rabbit Stream. Strangely, it was the only piece of recent development for which Kidd felt any affection. To unknowing Hawleyvillers, especially the teenagers, this brick building was just another place to stuff their faces, but to Kidd it was the former site of the old four-bedroom bungalow house belonging to the Widow O'Dell. The good widow had been like a grandma to him, showering him with love and giving him hours of babysitting, before she died when Kidd was in middle school. The house had stayed abandoned for years, ultimately succumbing to ruin, before an enterprising franchisee from nearby Marietta bought the site and turned it into Hawleyville's first Italian restaurant.

With his five touch points gathered, Kidd felt his heart melt. In the quick rotation of tires, the Cadillac sped over the Rabbit Stream Bridge, past the "Welcome to Hawleyville" sign with its colorful local organization badges, and into Hawleyville proper.

Kidd's mind raced now, burning on the fuel of memory. Kidd pointed in every direction, as he gave Kenny the guided tour of his fog-cloaked hometown—

"Look, Kenny, that's Bixby's Convenience Store. That was where I got my first job.

"Hey, those are the houses where my friends lived—Barry Code and Anson Tomaski. And that's where John Gerber grew up. He lost a testicle in a high school pole vaulting accident. Boy, you should have heard him scream.

"Watch, Kenny, we're coming into the downtown. See all the brick buildings? It's called a redbrick town, Kenny, because everything is made of red bricks."

And on and on. Kidd directed Kenny to drive around the downtown, his eyes bulging with delight, his voice giddy with reverie at what lay beyond every turn. Even though he could only see it through a few feet of fog, he was amazed at how well the downtown looked. Much like it first appeared to his mama on that November morning over fifty years ago, Hawleyville seemed alive, even in the early hours of the day. All along the brick-lined sidewalks, the ash trees were well manicured, and the benches freshly painted. The storefronts were in great shape as well; some were even being remodeled and had newspaper covering the windows—a sign of healthy economic activity. There weren't many cars on the streets, but the morning was still young. Kidd was certain traffic would increase as soon as everyone started off to work.

But what was most important to Kidd was not how Hawleyville looked, but how it smelled. Kidd powered down the Cadillac's window, stuck out his head like a dog enjoying a car ride, and inhaled an intense whiff of his hometown air. There it was. Kidd's keen olfactory sense, usually reserved for women, picked up the smell immediately. Coursing through the streets of Hawleyville, like lifeblood flowing through a body, was the familiar fatty odor of soap. It was Hawleyville's trademark scent, a frothy whip of all the Tackmann Soap Company's best-selling brands—*Frond* facial wash, *Scrub with Pumice* industrial hand cleaner, and *April Spring*, a moisturizing bath bar that smelled of lilacs and was, as far as anyone could tell, completely impervious to having pubic hair stick to it.

Kidd beamed as he took in the air, his green eyes firing, a broad grin stretching. Smelling soap is grand! he thought. Smelling soap means they're selling soap! It was another sign that all was well in Hawleyville despite the recession. Kidd pulled his head back into the car, clenched his fists and raised them to the Cadillac's ceiling. "Thank you, Jesus!" he cried. "Thank you, Jesus H. Christ!" Kidd saw Kenny glance over at him as if he were a goddamn psycho.

Kidd's nimble mind roared into gear. He had finally made it to Hawleyville. It was time to get out word of his plan. But how?

Kidd processed the possibilities—

Newspaper article in the *Hawleyville Bell-Sentinel*? Too slow.

Radio live spot on WHAW? There had been no local programming on "The Haw" since it had become a syndicate for some all-sports mega station in Cincinnati.

Printed flyers tacked to telephone poles? Christ, he wasn't holding a bake sale.

All of these methods were wrong for another reason, too: They might force Kidd to describe his upcoming announcement in detail, and detail was something Kidd wanted to avoid. He wanted mystery for his announcement. A sense of hushed anticipation. He wanted Hawleyvillers to ask, "Why is Chucky Kidd here? What does he want for his town? How can we help him help us?" If it was that type of curiosity Kidd hoped to cultivate, he knew exactly what to do.

"Take a left here, Kenny," He pulled one of his star-spangled lollipops from the humidor, tore off the wrapper, and popped the sugary sucker between his lips. "We're going to see an old friend."

When Kidd spotted the familiar storefront, he ordered Kenny to stop. He threw himself out the door, stood on the sidewalk, and waited as Kenny jammed the car in a slanted slot three spaces down. Kenny stepped out of the Cadillac and looked at the parking meter. "Do you want me to put a quarter in this thing?"

Kidd could only snicker. Such a naïve boy. "Kenny," he replied, "I'm a favorite son."

Kidd led Kenny to the storefront—a hair salon called Mystique, which most people around Hawleyville pronounced as *"miss-STAKE."* Kidd check the hours-of-operation sticker; the salon had opened at 7:30. "It's kismet," Kidd said, slapping Kenny so hard on the shoulder that Kenny almost fell over. Kidd pushed on the glass door; the clonk of a cowbell signaled his glorious arrival.

Mystique was just like Kidd remembered—dark and claustrophobic, with the intense smell of hair-twisting chemicals and incontinent old women. There were women's magazines strewn about the waiting area and dusty plastic plants popping out from dim corners. And if Kidd recalled correctly, hanging on one of Mystique's very walls was a portrait of him from a time when he was "The Most Handsomest Governor in all of these United States." Kidd looked up above the bank of lighted mirrors to where that portrait always hung. It wasn't there today. Probably being reframed, he told himself.

But one thing that was at Mystique was the salon's longtime proprietor, Miss Sally Jean McClean, the voluptuous, tawny-haired chatterbox from Kidd's blue-balled youth. She was Sally Jean Barker now, and she had three grown children, but her marriage to Don Barker had ended six years ago, and the children were all out of the house. Sally Jean recognized Kidd the minute he entered her salon. He saw her staring at him with mouth agape, scissors frozen in one hand, comb locked in the other. Her customer, the dour Mrs. Skent from Langer Road, had frozen too, and was looking up at Kidd through a mop of matted white hair. Two other elderly women, Mrs. Fletcher and Mrs. Brooks, peered out from beneath beehive dryers.

Kidd took a suck on the lollipop, then said, "Sally Jean Barker, how are you, dear friend? It is so good to see you."

Sally Jean didn't budge, not even to affirm that she heard him. Kidd didn't let her reaction fluster him. It was natural. He had seen the same response in women countless times before—Sally Jean Barker was obviously in stifling awe of Kidd's presence. Kidd nodded to the elderly women in the salon. "Ladies."

The ladies made no attempt to nod back. Same cause, Kidd figured.

Kidd gestured with the lollipop to the empty wall space above Mystique's bank of lighted mirrors. "I'm guessing you've sent out my picture for a reframe, huh?" he said. "Well, that was an old picture anyway, Sally Jean. Let's say I get you one of my presidential portraits. I'm much more handsome in those. Kenny—" Kidd snapped his fingers. "Contact the staff back in Simondale and have them send Ms. Barker a presidential portrait. Have them send portraits to each of these beautiful ladies as well. And get Mrs. Skent here a pack of presidential pencils with those big erasers on the ends—she was my calculus teacher, after all."

Kidd didn't look to see if Kenny was following orders. Kenny always followed orders. Carl Kernick had trained him well.

"Look, Sally Jean, let's cut to the chase. I'm in town to make an announcement tonight. It's at 7:30 sharp, in the Turtle Stream Elementary School gymnasium. I want everybody there, Sally Jean—the city council, the school board, the mayor, and every Hawleyviller who still has a pulse. So I guess that excludes Mrs. Brooks here. Ha, ha! Just kidding, Thelma! Look, tell people it's a matter of historical importance. Can you do that?"

Sally Jean didn't answer, but Kidd noticed she was grinding the blades of her scissors together, open and closed, open and closed, slowly. He took that gesture as a response in the affirmative.

"Good, then," he said, sliding the lollipop into his mouth. He nodded to the old women. "Ladies."

With his first mission in Hawleyville complete, Kidd turned to leave the salon. Before he got out the door, an inadvisable urge made him stop. He turned back and looked at Sally Jean again; she was still staring at him with mouth agape. Oh, the stories he had heard of that mouth, told mostly by the boys on the football team. And the basketball team. And half the 4-H club. It was legend in the halls of Hawleyville High that Sally Jean Barker could suck a stone through a swizzle stick. And she still looked stunning. Her long tawny hair was free of gray and blended perfectly with the purple dress that was clinging to her menopause-resilient frame. She looked as delicious as a plum. Kidd wanted to sink his teeth into her right there, just to see which way those plum juices flew.

"Tell me, Sally," Kidd said, taking a slurp on his lollipop, "do you remember the time, back in high school, when you and I walked over to the Blue Bell Motel for my first afternoon delight? If you'll recall, we had *delightus interruptus*, and I didn't even get a consolation prize. But I'll say this, Sally Jean: If you come to my announcement tonight, and hear what I have to say, you'll be so grateful for what I'm about to unveil that you'll want to go back to the Blue Bell and make it up to me. And this time, we'll drive there in a Cadillac. Won't we, Kenny?"

Kenny looked down at the floor, but Kidd knew Kenny agreed with him.

"See you tonight," Kidd said with a wink. Then he pulled on the glass door and stepped outside to the jingle of the cowbell. Kenny followed behind him.

Once outside, Kidd threw his hands into the air and said, "Did you see that performance, Young Kernick? My Christ, the Wily Bastard still has it. What did you think, Kenny?"

"What did I think?" Kenny asked.

"I want to know," Kidd said.

Kenny shook his head. "First of all, what staff back in Simondale are you talking about?"

"It's all a façade, Young Kernick," Kidd said. "If those women think I still have a staff, it helps me keep my aura of importance."

"Second," Kenny said, "how many people are in this town?"

"These days?" Kidd shrugged. "Sixteen thousand."

Kenny hit the keyless entry to the Cadillac. "And you're counting on that lady to tell them all?"

Kidd opened the passenger door. He could only look at Kenny and smile. "On this one, Young Kernick, you'll have to trust me. When I was growing up, Sally Jean Barker didn't just have the most popular mouth in town. She also had the biggest."

Kidd and Kenny settled into the Cadillac. "Where to?" Kenny asked as he started the car.

Kidd touched a finger to his chin. The day was new again, both of the weather and of the spirit. The fog was beginning to lift, the sun was coming through, and he had succeeded in his first task back in Hawleyville. "Just drive," he said buoyantly. "There's so much I want to see. But there's one place I have to go."

Kenny backed the Cadillac out of its parking space, put the car into drive, and sped the golden chariot away from Hawleyville's redbrick downtown, all to Kidd's serenade of where to go and what to do, and to do it quickly. They were on a timeline, after all. 7:30 in the evening would come soon.

By lunch at his daughter's favorite Hawleyville hangout, a fast food joint called BurgerMeister MeisterBurger, Kidd sensed that Sally Jean Barker had done her job. He swore he could hear the murmur of excited voices rising up throughout Hawleyville. The voices were spreading out from the downtown, slipping in all directions toward the town limits like a syrup spill on a kitchen counter. The voices even passed by Kidd and Kenny later in the day as the Cadillac made its way across Turtle Stream Bridge, past the Tackmann Soap Factory, and over to a quiet hillside near the southwestern edge of Hawleyville.

But Kidd didn't linger on the voices for too long. He would deal with them in time. Right now, the former president had something more important to think about as they approached the hillside.

He was directing Kenny to the place where they would find the Tremont Cemetery. He was directing Kenny to the place where they would find his mama.

CHAPTER 11

★★★★★★★★★★★★★★★★★★★★★★★★★★★★★★

As he sat behind the wheel of his Cadillac in the parking lot of the Tremont Cemetery, Kenny Kernick began to feel that spending an entire day in Hawleyville, Ohio, seemed almost as eternal as death itself.

In the morning, as dawn had broken over the Ohio River Valley and a heavy fog hemmed in the Cadillac, Kenny was excited by the prospect of a trip to this town. He wanted to see the streets that Charles Bentley Kidd walked as a youth, to learn about the people who had raised Kidd. More enticing to Kenny was what the town itself was like. Did having a soap factory make Hawleyville the cleanest town in America? The most fragrant? And what about all the ash trees Kidd mentioned? Did they make it the prettiest? As was his way, Kenny had come to Hawleyville seeking answers. By three o'clock in the afternoon, he had gotten those answers. And they weren't pretty.

Hawleyville was a town devoid of life. For all that Kidd had talked up this community, using words like "animated" and "vibrant," Hawleyville, Ohio, was about three breaths away from mortality. That diagnosis came early for Kenny—it happened as soon as the fog lifted. The first thing Kenny noticed as he took an unencumbered view of the place was that half the houses were for sale.

But if the realty signs didn't signal trouble in Hawleyville, the downtown area sent out a Code Blue. For starters, there was no traffic on the streets, vehicular or pedestrian, which Kenny found odd for a Friday morning at work time. Then there were the storefronts—most of them were empty, covered by a patchwork of newspapers taped to windows. Even the ash trees were few and far between. Kidd had told Kenny that the ash trees of Hawleyville were so big and plentiful that Hawleyville's nickname was "The Ash City." Kenny did manage to spot a couple of ashes lining the streets of Hawleyville's downtown, but in the residential neighborhoods, where Kidd had said that the towering trees formed canopies of breathtaking magnificence, there were almost no trees to be seen. In their places, Kenny saw only stumps—swollen, round tabletops which had long ago ripped up the sidewalks with their roots, making the walkways of Hawleyville uneven and choppy.

But for Kenny, the most disappointing aspect of Hawleyville, and the one that really killed his joy, involved the soap factory. Instead of being the purveyor of cleanliness throughout the town, it rose up from its acreage like a soot-covered brick outhouse. The building had a smokestack jutting from its top, intricate piping on its sidewall that resembled a twisted saxophone, and it wasn't fragrant in the least. No, the smell coming out of this factory was rank, like rotting animal fat. It made Kenny want to vomit.

How can anyone live here? Kenny wondered. Why would anyone want to? Based on the realty signs everywhere, it seemed many residents of Hawleyville had come to the same conclusion.

For seven long hours after Kidd and Kenny left the hair salon, Kidd had treated Kenny to Hawleyville's special brand of stink-filled boredom.

They scoured every part of town from the river to a rocky bluff. They drove by more houses of former acquaintances. They looked for the old dirt roads where Kidd used to take girls "necking," whatever the hell that was. They scoped out Kidd's first school, Turtle Stream Elementary, where Kidd would be holding the big announcement he had mentioned to the pretty beautician that morning, just before he sexually harassed her in front of four witnesses, including Kenny. They drove past Kidd's old high school, which was now a nursing home, and his old 4-H club, which had been razed to make a parking lot for a discount liquor store (the only store in Hawleyville that seemed to be doing a solid business). At the edge of the stream named for a turtle, Kidd dipped his hands in the water and rubbed his face; an hour later he did the same thing at the edge of a stream named for a rabbit. Then they sat for what seemed like an interminable amount time on a bench in the town common. Kidd provided running commentary on anything that fluttered, rolled or walked by, which wasn't much, leaving Kidd to delve more deeply into the banal architecture of a redbrick town, and how the buildings were restored in the 1980s during the height of the soap boom, and how redbrick was made, and blah, blah, blah. For the first time in his life, Kenny wanted a good, stiff drink. He had even thought about leaving Kidd on the bench and driving back to the discount liquor store.

Now, after a late lunch at the BurgerMeister MeisterBurger, Kidd had taken the boy to this cemetery on the side of a quiet hill in the southern part of Hawleyville. On this hill, one could overlook Hawleyville below with a disappointing panoramic view, from the soap factory in the south, past the redbrick downtown, all the way up to North Hawleyville Road, with the residential districts wrapping around everything like a decrepit letter C. Charles Bentley Kidd had disappeared almost an hour ago, telling Kenny to leave the Cadillac in the lot and stay there while Kidd attended to some business.

Enough of this ennui, Kenny told himself. It was time to find Kidd and get out of here. Kenny opened his door and stepped out of the Cadillac, then he crossed the parking lot and began to wander down the hills and through the headstones.

After trudging for several minutes down the adjoining curves of the cemetery, through sections filled with illegible white headstones, then weathered gray headstones, Kenny reached the bottom of the hill. This section was filled with black headstones—polished, gleaming, and recently placed. He had not seen Kidd anywhere on the way down. Then something caught his eye.

It, too, was a headstone, but it wasn't black like the others—this one was the color of a rose. It lay in the shade of a willow tree, and seeing it among the dark markers around it was like spotting a flower lei resting gently on a black sand beach. The rose-colored headstone stood out for another reason: It was the place where Kenny finally found Kidd.

Kenny walked slowly toward Kidd. In this isolated part of the cemetery, it was too quiet for Kenny's comfort. The only sounds the boy could hear were the swish of his footsteps across grass, the rustle of wind through the willow, and the distinctive, disturbing howl of Charles Bentley Kidd's sobbing.

Kenny approached Kidd from behind, unseen by the former leader of the free world. Kidd was crouched in front of the headstone with his arms resting on his thighs and his head wilted downward.

Over Kidd's shoulder, Kenny stole a glance at the engraving on the headstone. In block letters was the name "Anna Kidd," and beneath that name were the dates of her life. By the years listed, Kenny calculated that she had been sixty-seven when she died. From a heart attack, if Kenny remembered correctly, halfway through Kidd's first term. Below the dates was a simple epithet: "Mother of a President." The headstone struck Kenny as something quite understated for a woman who had given birth to a man so important in American history, even if that man had been thrown out of office on his ass.

Kenny broke the silence. In a soft voice, he asked, "Why doesn't she have something... bigger?"

"Oh, Kenny," Kidd said, turning to look at the boy. A string of snot clung between his nose and his sweatshirt, and Kidd wiped it away with a fist. "Where did you come from? Why didn't you stay in the parking lot? Did something happen to the Caddy?"

"Yeah," Kenny said. "It died. Of boredom."

Kidd let out a doleful chuckle then dabbed his eyes with a fingertip. His face, swollen at the cheeks, was the color of the headstone.

"She didn't want one," Kidd said. "An obelisk, or a monument. God knows the town wanted to give her one, and I wanted it as well. But she was stubborn, Kenny. She could be so stubborn. She put it in her will that this was the headstone she wanted. And all the power of the presidency couldn't let me change it." Kidd inhaled a stuttered breath. "All the power of the presidency couldn't even let me save her, Kenny. She died so fast. She had never even complained of symptoms, but—"

Kidd's thought went unfinished. He bent forward and flicked an errant weed from the base of his mother's stone. "Mama, this is Kenny. He's my friend. Kenny, this is my mama."

Saying "Nice to meet you" to a plot of earth was too macabre for Kenny. Instead, he nodded to the headstone.

"You would have loved her, Kenny," Kidd said. "She was such a jewel in the rough of the world. She was so beautiful, and warm, and she ate up life like there was never going to be another serving on her plate tomorrow. And she was tough, Kenny. The toughest." Kidd's voice began to creak like a dried-out floorboard. "She took everything this brutal world ever threw at her and molded it to her own designs. I only ever saw her cry once—"

At that point, Kidd lost his composure completely. The ex-president began to howl like the horny beagle. He fell to the grass, forehead down, and let streams of tears flow to the ground.

"Oh, Kenny," Kidd cried. "Oh, precious Young Kernick. Can you keep a secret?" The former president looked up at Kenny with a face so puffed by despair that Kenny could have easily mistaken Kidd for a man twenty pounds heavier.

"You want me to keep a secret?" Kenny asked.

Kidd reached over and grabbed the pleats of Kenny's khakis. He gripped them firmly between his fingers and tugged downward, sharply, with every word. "Promise me," he said. "Swear to me. That what I'm about to tell you will never leave your lips. Ever. Can you make that promise?"

The terror in Kidd's eyes convinced Kenny that what Kidd was about to utter was as serious to him as the Second Coming might be to a Jehovah's Witness. "Yes," Kenny said. "Yes, I can."

Kidd released Kenny's pants and flopped back onto his mother's plot. He sat cross-legged and put his head in his hands. After taking five deep breaths, he looked up at Kenny.

"I am *not* the man the world thinks I am," Kidd said. "Do you understand me, Kenny?"

Kenny shook his head. He had no idea what Kidd was talking about. After the intense coverage of the Pastrygate scandal, with all its microscopic insight, it was hard for Kenny to fathom what possibly could be left for the world to find out about Charles Bentley Kidd. Coverage of the scandal had been so minute, Kenny could state with complete certainty that Kidd had a mole shaped like Idaho on his wank. There were some things a boy just shouldn't know about his travel companion, Kenny thought, and that was one of them.

"One afternoon, Kenny, when I was in my teens, I came home from debating practice and found my mama back from the factory. It wasn't even suppertime, and there she was, sitting at our kitchen table. This is a woman who never missed a day of work unless it was a vacation, and I knew she didn't have any vacation left because she had used it up to take me to Chicago to look at Jesuit. Her back was to me, Kenny, so I called out, 'Mama?' She turned, Kenny, and this rock-hard woman had tears flowing down her cheeks, and her face was pink with heat. It was so odd, Kenny, so awkward to see my mama like that, that I didn't know what to do."

Kidd placed a hand on his mother's headstone and began to rub it with long, tender strokes. His voice became thick with emotion.

"Instead of saying anything to me," Kidd said, "she reached for me, Kenny, and she took my hand into her hand, and she pulled me close to her, and she buried her face into my chest, and she wept, Kenny, for what felt like forever. Finally, after the shock of seeing my mama like that had worn off, I said, 'Mama, what's the matter? Won't you tell me what's the matter?' But she didn't say anything, Kenny. All she did was—and I will never forget this—she just slid forward that morning's copy of the *Hawleyville Bell-Sentinel*. The obituary section."

Kenny felt a chill run up his neck from the cool breeze wisping through the willows. He wrapped his arms around himself and rubbed his biceps for warmth. He so wanted to get out of this place, to leave the cemetery and Hawleyville and this part of Ohio behind for good. But he was caught in Kidd's grip. The man's eyes were aflame with memory.

Kidd asked, "Have you ever had a moment that just changed your life forever, Kenny? A moment when you knew that nothing in your world was ever going to be the same again, no matter how much you tried to put it back together, or how much you prayed that your world had never changed in the first place?"

Yes, Kenny wanted to say. He had experienced a moment like that. It was called getting busted with an armload of stolen women's underpants in a laundry room at Harvard. But Kidd was on a roll. Kenny kept his mouth shut.

"That day," Kidd said, "on paper still splotched with my mama's tears, I read the death notice for a man named Charles Ray Laudermilk. He had been young, Kenny, not a year over sixty, and a Baptist minister of some renown, a father and recently a grandfather, and he had died just down the road in Stampler. After I finished the obituary, I said, 'Mama, who is this man? Did you know him when you were growing up in Oxford? Did he come to preach to you?' All she did was ask me a question, Kenny. She said, 'Who do people say your daddy was?' I said, 'They say what you told me, Mama. That he was a coal miner who died in a big explosion, and that you were so sad by his passing that you left West Virginia forever and never went back.' And Mama said, 'Then tell me, Chucky, what my last name was before I married Mr. Kidd.' I said, 'It was Bunton, Mama. I've known that forever.' And she said, 'No, Chucky, what you've known forever is fiction. Because my daddy's last name was actually Earl. Your daddy's last name was Laudermilk. There never was any Horace Kidd. There wasn't even any Anna Bunton.'"

It may have been from listening to Kidd's story, or it may have been from standing too long, but Kenny legs buckled. He bent down and sat, facing Kidd.

"That's when she told me the whole story, Kenny. About how she had been born Annabelle Earl in Stampler, West Virginia, the oldest of six children. About how she had grown up quiet and pious, never thinking about the carnal pleasures, until she'd gone to work for a good man named Reverend Laudermilk. About how she had fallen in love with him so rightly quick, and how she had been with him in that passionate way, and how they had conceived me against the knotty pine of a church rectory office. About how she'd fled Stampler for fear of a scandal, changing her name and history along the way. How she'd ended up in Hawleyville much by kismet, but was accepted here for her new self. But while it was an interesting story, Kenny, something suddenly hit me. Struck me like a bolt of lightning from the hand of Jesus H. Christ Almighty: I was a bastard, Kenny. I was the bastard son of a preacher man. I started to cry, Kenny. I broke down. My insides were shaking harder than a chain-link fence in an earthquake. Do you know what they did to bastards in those days? Do you know how these God-fearing people treated them? Do you know what low place in society a bastard was destined for? That's when my mama pulled me close, Kenny. She pulled me tight and almost choked me, and she rocked me like she had never rocked me before. And she told me that no, I was not bound for the margins of society. I was bound for greatness. I had greatness in my blood. Charles Ray Laudermilk was a great man. That from that day forward, she was never going to accept anything less than greatness in me. She comforted me, Kenny, and she changed my life. Because from that day until the day she passed, I would never accept anything less than greatness in myself either. And now, Kenny"—Kidd's eyes unleashed fresh tears—"my life has become a disaster, and I need my mama. I need her to pull me tight, and I need her to rock me like I've never been rocked before. I need her comfort. And she can't give it to me, because she's dead."

Kidd collapsed in a heap on the grass and thrashed around, his big feet hitting Kenny with every whine and wail. Finally, Kenny had to stand again for fear of bruising. He stepped back and watched Kidd with a growing sense of empathy. Over the past two weeks, he had become invested in Kidd's life, or what was left of it. He actually cared about this man. And the man needed help. So Kenny Kernick shuffled to his feet, looked at the headstones, and wondered how he could comfort a former leader of the free world. Then he knelt beside the crumpled man and did the only thing he could think of—he slapped Charles Bentley Kidd across the face. Hard.

Kidd snapped up and grabbed his cheek. "What the hell was that for?" he said.

"I don't know," Kenny said. "Didn't your mama ever whack you when you were a child?"

"Jesus, Mary and Joseph," Kidd said. A welt the color of his mama's headstone was beginning to rise on his cheek. "I said comfort, Kenny, not assault! Goddamn, that stings!"

"Well, how did your mama comfort you?" Kenny asked.

"Were you not listening to me?" Kidd said. "She would hug me, Kenny. Then she would tell me everything is going to be all right."

Kenny thought about those prospects. Finally, he said, "Dude, I am not hugging you."

"Then tell me everything's going to be all right," Kidd said. "Please, Kenny." Kidd threw himself on Kenny's feet and wrapped his long, gangly arms around Kenny's calves. His eyes rained tears with torrential force.

Not in his craziest dreams did Kenny Kernick ever anticipate having a former president of the United States sprawled out at his feet in the middle of a cemetery, while the once most-powerful human being on the planet cried like a toddler spanked for eating crayons. For Kenny, the moment should have felt like proof positive that this boy of modest size truly possessed some big clout in the world. But it didn't. To Kenny, all Kidd felt like was a pair of cement shoes.

Kenny exhaled in an upward stream that lifted his flaming red bangs off his forehead. He said, "Why do you frequently have these moments of doubt, Bent? What is it you worry about when you get like this?"

Kidd looked up into the boy's face. "Just tell me these people are still going to love me," he said, with no hint of the cocksure bravado that Kenny had come to expect in Kidd. For the first time, Kenny saw a man who was truly terrified.

"What people?" Kenny asked.

"These people," Kidd said. He waved in the direction of the town. "My people. Hawleyville people."

Kenny looked out at the headstones surrounding Mrs. Kidd's plot. Many of the Hawleyvillers interred here probably loved Charles Bentley Kidd, but like Kidd's mama, they were no longer capable of expressing it, at a time when this sad shell of a man needed it most.

Kenny struggled to say something that would comfort Charles Bentley Kidd, but finding a nugget of comfort in the economic and civic desolation of Hawleyville was no easy task. Finally, Kenny decided to use Kidd's own words for succor.

"What do you have to fret about, Bent?" Kenny said. "On the drive in this morning, you couldn't stop telling me how great the town looked."

"Oh, fuck that," Kidd said. "I was deluding myself. This town looks like shit, Kenny, and that's a fact. There's nobody around. Most of the stores are closed. All the houses are for sale. And what happened to the goddamn trees? All the ash trees are gone. I used to be a politician, remember? I've had the power of positive thinking shoved so far up my ass that all I can taste is a smiley face." The ex-president wiped his eyes futilely. "What the hell am I going to do? I have to stand in front of these people in three hours."

Kenny scratched his head. "If it's any consolation to you, Bent, I can attest to your powers of charm."

"How do you mean?" Kidd asked.

"I mean my mother," Kenny said. "Let's face it, you got yourself a place at my mother's kitchen table for coffee one morning, and my mother hated you."

"Your mama hated me?" Kidd asked.

"My whole neighborhood hated you," Kenny said.

"Your mama didn't act like she hated me," Kidd said.

"Oh, no, she did," Kenny said. "She never voted for you. She never spoke well of you at all. One time during the last election, she even referred to you as a—"

Kidd threw out a palm. "Stop right there. I don't need to know." He glanced around the cemetery, shaking his head. He seemed to be drying up. He eyed Kenny again, a hint of mischief glinting off his pupils. "You really think these people might still love me?"

"What did you tell me right before we went into that beauty salon this morning?" Kenny asked.

Kidd sighed. "I don't know, Young Kernick. This morning was so very long ago. And I'm so very tired."

"You told me you're a favorite son," Kenny said.

Kidd squinted. "A favorite son? Did I say that?"

"You sure did," Kenny said.

Kidd rubbed at the stubble on his chin, his expression turning from a mash of confusion to a ridge of bald determination. "I did say that, didn't I? Yes, I did. And you know what, Young Kernick? I was right. I am a favorite son."

"You're a favorite son," Kenny repeated for pithy emphasis.

"I'm also the most famous son," Kidd said.

"Nobody from here is more famous than you," Kenny said.

Kidd stood and wiped the dirt off his running pants. "I'm a white knight, Kenny. I'm the boy of unlimited promise. I'm the debate team virtuoso and the glee club soloist, the president of the Future Business Leaders of America and the local 4-H."

"I have no idea what you're talking about," Kenny said.

"You don't have to, Kenny," Kidd replied. "You've done your part. Maybe the people of Hawleyville still love me and maybe they don't, but they're sure as hell going to love the gift I brought them. Because it's something only a most-famous son can give. It's one of a kind. I'm bringing it here to save a town that cannot save itself. Thank you for reminding me, Kenny. We must depart."

Kidd kissed the fingertips of his left hand and placed them on top of his mother's headstone. He let them linger for a moment. "Goodbye, Mama," he said.

Then Kidd turned and strode down the row of black headstones like a man revived. "Come on, Kenny!"

Kenny nodded to Mrs. Kidd's headstone then charged after her son. With what seemed to Kenny like a giant's bounds, Kidd effortlessly ascended the three hills of Tremont Cemetery, his head held high, his chin set, his chest swelling with confidence.

By the time Kenny and Kidd got back to the Cadillac, it was half past four in the afternoon. As the sunlight began to wane, they traveled six miles on a winding road to the Turtle Stream Elementary School, where they waited in the far corner of the parking lot until only two vehicles remained—"Janitorial staff," Kidd told Kenny, "setting up for my big announcement." With the coast seemingly clear, Kidd asked Kenny to grab his suitcase from the trunk. Then Kidd led Kenny across the parking lot, through a set of metal doors, and into the school. There, over the next three hours, they would prepare in earnest for the much-anticipated rendezvous between the proud people of Hawleyville, Ohio, and the once-famous, now-infamous man whom those same people used to claim as their own.

CHAPTER 12

★ ★

Kidd told Kenny that he chose the Turtle Stream Elementary School because of its intimate setting, and Kenny could immediately see why. Smaller than the high school by a half and the middle school by a third, everything at Turtle Stream was designed for the perspective and utility of a three- to four-foot-tall child, and a public school child at that. For unlike the private Griggson Academy which Kenny had attended, there was no stand-alone gymnasium at Turtle Stream, nor was there a separate theatre, nor even an individual dining hall. At Turtle Stream, in the manner of budgetary frugality which was so ubiquitous in public education, all three locations had been combined into one common facility in the center of the school—a facility that, while clean and well lit, with a nice stage area at the back wall, betrayed its poorer roots by smelling strongly of curdled milk, overcooked tomato sauce and canned mixed vegetables.

Attached to this "cafegymnatorium," at each corner, was a wing of classrooms. Kidd and Kenny traveled up and down all four wings in search of an unlocked door. "A place to make our base camp," Kidd told Kenny. Finally, in the third grade section, at a room assigned to a Mrs. Cox, they found a doorknob that turned. When Kidd and Kenny stepped in and flicked on the lights, they were inundated by a wall display of big stenciled letters, a horn of plenty and all things turkey—the collage of a class preparing for Thanksgiving.

Kidd took in the collage for a moment, seeming to admire its amateurish charms, then he turned around and told Kenny to pull out the charcoal suit from the suitcase. As Kenny followed Kidd's orders, Kidd overtook the restroom at the back of the class. From behind the restroom door, Kenny heard two plops and some singing; it reminded him that he couldn't remember the last time he had moved his bowels, which were now completely compacted with greasy fast food, especially after all those Croissan'Wiches for breakfast in New York City, and the German Herman from BurgerMeister MeisterBurger for today's lunch.

Kenny heard a toilet flush, then Kidd opened the restroom door, fanning his butt with a copy of the *Weekly Reader.* "You need to smash the deuce, Kenny?" the ex-president asked.

Kenny looked up from his work on Kidd's suit; he was putting the coat and pants on a hanger he had found buried among Kidd's clothes. "Do I need to what?" he asked.

"Smash the deuce," Kidd said. "You know, take a crap? If you do, you'd better go. I've got prep work to get on with."

Euphemisms for one's bowel movements, Kenny thought; that is so completely crass. Kenny declined politely. He could smell Kidd's fumes from across the room. Even if Kenny could manage to "smash the deuce," it was probably best to leave that particular restroom to Kidd at the moment.

"Suit yourself," Kidd said, then he took his suit from Kenny and hung it, along with a wrinkled white dress shirt, on the edge of a paper towel dispenser near the restroom sink. Next Kidd turned on the hot water at the sink to full blast, stripped down to his boxer shorts and gave himself a paper towel bath from forehead to kneecaps. He shaved his facial scruff with a razor from his toiletries bag before strolling out to the classroom in his boxer shorts. He shut the door to the restroom behind him, the water still running hot, and glanced at Kenny. If anyone had seen Kidd in his current state, standing half-naked in a classroom, Kenny was quite certain that Kidd would have been busted on the spot, maybe for breaking and entering, but most likely for potential child molestation.

"Can I ask a question?" Kenny said.

"Oh, that's good, Kenny." Kidd rubbed deodorant into his armpits. "I need to get used to hearing that again. Hit me."

"Maybe I don't need to know," Kenny said, "but what exactly are you announcing tonight?"

"You're right. You don't need to know." Kidd dropped the deodorant into his toiletries bag, then he flexed his muscles like a bodybuilder. "How do I look, Kenny? Check me out."

For someone who had been pumping iron every day for the past two weeks, Kidd seemed remarkably soft. And with a bodybuilder's grimace on his face, he looked particularly stupid.

Kenny said, "I've spent a never-ending day in Ohio with you. I've taken you everywhere you wanted to go. For what it's worth, I think I've earned the right to know what's going on here."

"Listen, Kenny," Kidd said, relaxing his muscles. "I'd love to tell you, I really would. But this"—Kidd tapped his temple with a middle finger—"this is the greatest idea I have ever had. Better than roller derby around the East Wing, better than disco night in the Blue Room, even better than body-shot Sundays on the presidential dining table. So I'd like to keep it to myself as long as possible. To enjoy it." Kidd grabbed the restroom's door handle. "Besides," he said, "it's not like you're going to speak. I just want you to sit behind me and keep your yapper shut. Can you do that?"

Kenny nodded.

"Good," Kidd said, then he pulled open the door to the restroom and disappeared inside.

"Goddammit!" Kenny heard him yell after a few seconds. "What, they can't make the water hot enough in this school to steam press anything? Son of a bitch!"

Kenny could hear Kidd dressing—the rise of a zipper, the fumbling of shoes, the crisp swipes of a hand down worsted wool. After a moment, Kidd threw open the door to the restroom.

"How do I look?" Kidd asked, striking a goofy pose in the doorway.

"Tie," Kenny said, gesturing to Kidd's bare front.

Kidd touched his chest, then said, "Aw, shit, I didn't bring any. Well, this will have to do. What do you think?" Kidd spread out his arms and struck another goofy pose, like a rube's impression of a big city fashion model.

Wrinkly, Kenny wanted to say. In that rumpled suit, you look wrinkly. The coat was a disaster, the pants double-creased, and the shirt was even worse. But Kenny acquiesced. "Hey," he said, "it's your party."

"That it is," Kidd said, flashing his cocksure smirk. "That. It. Is."

The people of Hawleyville began to arrive at the school around 6:30, an hour before Kidd's announcement was scheduled to start.

They trickled into the gymnasium at first, in groups of no more than three, speaking in low tones and whispered voices, as if the empty gymnasium, or even this strange event itself, possessed some quality worthy of reverence. Quickly, these small, independent groups combined in the air of hometown familiarity, gaining mass and form. As time went on, more groups arrived, larger groups, and with greater frequency. The reverent whispers grew into a steady murmur. Space condensed. By 7:20 the gymnasium had exceeded its capacity, the distance between the groups closed, until the rows of folding chairs were pressing together like an accordion's contracted ribs, buttressed on their ends by people who had no choice but to stand.

Kenny and Kidd saw none of these arrivals. But they heard them all.

Kenny and the ex-president had come to the gymnasium at a quarter to six, expecting to do a walk-through for Kidd's entrance. When they got to the gym, they peered through a window in the fire door next to the stage and found that the janitors were still there, about halfway through the process of setting out the folding chairs into two wide columns with a center aisle. Not wanting to make a scene, or to be seen, Kidd decided to scratch the rehearsal. He led Kenny over to the stage door and onto a darkened set for what appeared to be an upcoming student production about the Pilgrims. When Kidd shut the door behind them, the only light Kenny could see came from the thread-like gaps between the stage curtain and the floorboards. In the darkness, the boy fumbled for a wall, took a seat near a paper-mâché Mayflower hull and listened, as the drama of the arrivals played out in his mind in vivid detail.

As time went by, the voices grew from patchy whispers to steady murmur, and Kenny knew Kidd could hear everything he was hearing. He wondered how it was affecting Kidd, knowing that there was a vast quantity of people out in the gym who were all waiting for him to appear, all ready to hang on his every word. Kenny had never spoken to a group of people larger than ten, and never outside of a classroom. He kept glancing over toward Kidd, who was sitting a few feet away from him, and wondering what Kidd was feeling as the murmur grew louder. But the glances were futile if Kenny hoped to glean some notion of Kidd's mindset from his body language—in the darkness behind the stage curtain, all Kenny could make out on Kidd was the white of his dress shirt, the paleness of his handsome face, and an ear. If Kidd was nervous, the darkness was shielding his anxiety well. As far as Kenny could tell, the ex-president wasn't even breathing.

A few minutes later, Kenny heard two fingers snapping.

"Let's go," Kidd said. "It's time."

Kenny peeled himself out of the chair and followed Kidd's silhouette to the stage door.

Back in the stairwell, Kidd stole a furtive peek through the fire door's window. He tensed up. "Jesus H. Christ on a unicycle!" he said. "They forgot the podium!" Kidd huffed for a moment, then he brought both hands to his neck and tried to adjust a tie that wasn't there. "Well, screw them. These people always were a bunch of frog catchers. The announcement must proceed. Come hither, Young Kernick."

Kenny ambled down the stairs and took his place by Kidd's side. The ex-president threw an arm around Kenny and pulled the boy close. He stared at Kenny with a glow of grandiosity that made him look partly like a man of confidence and partly like a senile old grandfather. "Are you ready, Kenny? Let's make history."

With one fluid motion, Kidd released Kenny, reached for the door handle and yanked open the fire door.

That's when the murmur of the crowd stopped cold.

Into this vacuous silence strode Kidd, his swelling chest leading the way. Kenny followed behind him, first focusing on the heels of Kidd's shoes, then looking up at the mass of bodies that filled the gymnasium. What he saw stunned him.

Kidd had said there were thousands of people living in Hawleyville, and it seemed that every single one of them had come to this gymnasium on this night for Kidd's announcement. From wall to wall, both the length and breadth of it, the gymnasium floor was a vast ocean of shapes and colors—fat heads and narrow shoulders; gray overcoats and plaid farmers jackets. Some people were sitting, but most were standing to the back and sides of the chair rows. There were even people crunched together on the lunch counter.

About ten steps into the gymnasium, the silence turned to whispers. Kenny could see heads bobbing together, eyes following his and Kidd's every move, hands cupped to mouths, as this odd duo made its way toward the front of the gym, where an audio system had been set up. Kenny looked at the system. It consisted of a black microphone and receiver connected to two large speakers. The janitors had placed the set-up on a lunch table. As Kidd and Kenny approached the table, the whispers grew louder, and it seemed ominous to Kenny that, in Hawleyville, a lunch table and cheap audio system were about the best this former president was going to get, favorite son or not.

As they reached the microphone, Kidd looked back at Kenny and nodded to the lip of the stage behind them. Kidd's eyes, stern and demanding, told Kenny that it was the place he wanted the boy to stand during the announcement.

Kenny complied. He scurried over to the stage as fast as he could. It was too fast. His right foot reached the stage before the rest of his body and came down with a thud against the bay door. The bay door popped open. Kenny stumbled against the door, knocking it with his knees, his knuckles and his butt before he managed to steady himself and get the bay door closed. When he turned around, the vibrations from the melee were still echoing through the gymnasium, and everyone was staring at him. Including Kidd, who flashed him a quizzical "What the fuck are you doing?" glare.

Kenny's face went flush. The pent-up burgers and break-fast sandwiches in his gut began to loosen. Things got better when the glaring Kidd, his back to the crowd, finally threw Kenny a muted cocksure smirk. Kenny felt sweat break on his forehead, but his tension eased off. He leaned back against the lip of the stage and watched as Kidd turned to the assembled masses. Then the former president picked up the microphone and flicked its mesh knob twice with his middle finger.

Thump, thump! roared out from the speakers. The crowd straightened up. All eyes were on Kidd, and it was clear to Kenny, even with Kidd's back to him, that the man relished this position.

"To everyone who came out tonight," Kidd said to the crowd, "thank you and welcome. Welcome to this historic occasion. I'm glad you're here." He nodded in a variety of directions. "Mayor Dunston, the city council, a pleasure. John and Brenda Gerber. Mike Tilden. Roy Plunk and his fetching bride, Candy. Sally Jean Barker"—Kidd flashed her a succulent smile—"you're the best, Sally Jean. I knew you could do it." Kidd pulled his shoulders back and stood tall, his posture that of a man thoroughly in control. "Good to see you all. Everyone. It's been a long time. Too long."

Then in a rich timbre that filled the hall with the power of a church sermon, he began his announcement.

"Back in May," Kidd said, "as many of you might remember, my tenure as president of this great and noble land came to a close. It was a presidency which experienced many ups and downs over the years, but I think we can all agree that it was also a presidency dedicated consistently to the ideas of freedom, prosperity and opportunity."

Kidd walked toward the center aisle, trailing the long cord of the microphone behind him.

"Now, six months later, we find ourselves at a crossroads of debate," Kidd said. "A debate about how my presidency should ultimately be commemorated. It is only fitting and proper that we do this, since all presidents before me are commemorated in some way. Washington has Mount Vernon. Jefferson has Monticello. There are many birthplaces or boyhood homes out there with plaques on them." He swung around and started walking toward the rows of chairs on his right, working the room with his robust presence.

"And yet," Kidd continued, "with my presidency, we are faced with a few logistical problems, as you, the good people of Hawleyville, well understand. First, we cannot commemorate the place of my birth, because Minot Hospital was torn down twenty-three years ago. Second, we cannot commemorate my childhood home because my mama and I only lived in apartments when I was growing up, and those apartments no longer exist. The first was converted into law offices, and the second was leveled nineteen years ago to make way for a gas—"

Kidd reached the end of length on the microphone cord and snapped it tautly. The cord pulled out from the receiver and cut Kidd off in mid-sentence. He looked down at the microphone and tapped it twice to no effect. Muted chuckles spread through the crowd. Kidd turned toward Kenny, his eyes frantic. Kenny hurried to the lunch table and plugged the cord back into the receiver. A blunt *whomp!* echoed through the gymnasium.

"Station," Kidd said, recovering well and silencing the chuckles. "It was leveled to make a gas station. Long before I even became governor. So that's a bust. Thus, with the place of my birth torn down and my childhood homes no longer in existence, the way I see it, we have only one remaining option for commemoration. That option is something of which many a modern president has availed himself. I'm speaking, of course, about a presidential library."

A grumble rippled through the crowd as the people of Hawleyville got their first taste of Kidd's proposal.

"But if any of you have ever visited a modern presidential library, you can probably testify that those facilities can be quite staid." Kidd glanced over to a section of the crowd which was occupied by a number of gruff, tired men wearing plaid flannel shirts; they looked like a road crew who had recently knocked off from work. "That means 'boring' for all you fellas over here." Kidd grinned at them, but they didn't grin back. Kidd cleared his throat nervously. "Anyway, as I'm sure you're probably all aware, 'staid' doesn't really capture the grandeur of Charles Bentley Kidd. 'Boring' is not a word used to describe me. No, my presidential library needs more to it. It needs pizzazz, some fun, something special to set it apart from all the other presidential libraries that have gone before it. So I hereby announce the following."

Kidd removed a sheet of paper from his shirt pocket, unfolded it and proclaimed:

"The construction, on the tract of farmland where the dilapidated Red Pouch Tobacco barn now stands, of a joint Charles Bentley Kidd Presidential Library and Amusement Park complex, hereafter referred to as 'Chucky World.' It will be the only place in America where you'll be able to view the document that finally brought peace to the nations of Peru and Chile, then go out for a log flume ride. It will be grand, it will be exciting, and there should be a minimum of four roller coasters. Planning will start immediately, actual construction will begin by the summer, and it will be open for business in two years' time. 'Chucky World—Putting the Toy in History!' Or... something like that."

Kidd folded the piece of paper and stuffed it into a pant pocket. "That's my vision," he said. "I'm excited about this, and I'm sure you're excited as well. So let's open it up for questions, shall we?"

Beaming with pride, Kidd lowered his microphone and waited for the queries. But the queries didn't start right away, because the look of shock on the Hawleyvillers' faces took a full minute to clear.

Finally, Mayor Dunston stood. "You know, Chuck," he said in a ham-handed Southern accent (Kenny had noticed that everyone in Hawleyville spoke with this clumsy version of a Southern accent, probably because they were situated close enough to West Virginia and Kentucky to gain dialectal influence but were still considered people of the North), "I have to say, speaking for my constituents here, that I don't particularly think this plan of yours is exactly... well... optimal."

"Optimal?" Kidd asked into the microphone. "That's an interesting comment, Bill. But I don't think I follow you. Why wouldn't it be optimal?"

"Well, Chuck, it's just—" The mayor's thoughts trailed away in a nervous titter. The mayor was at least ten years younger than Kidd, and his unamplified, southern-inflected voice came off as weak against Kidd's flat-accented, microphone-enhanced boom. It was easy to see that the mayor was feeling a little intimidated under Kidd's steady polish.

After a few moments of the mayor's vocal impotence, Kidd took over. "Well, Bill, if you don't have anything further to add, it seems like it's settled."

"Not so fast, Kidd." The twanged voice came from the man whom Kidd had identified as Mike Tilden, a fiftysomething blue-collar type wearing a pair of maroon overalls and a faded baseball hat. He stood as he spoke. "Mayor Dunston may think he speaks for me, but I speak for myself."

Kidd waved an arm toward the man. "Of course, Mike. That's why we call this country a democracy."

Tilden tightened his jaw and looked as if he were about to tell Kidd to take his civics lesson and stick it through his sphincter. But a gentle hand on his back from the woman seated beside him settled the man. He composed himself, then said, "Answer me something, Kidd, seeing you always were the know-it-all in high school: What do I do for a living?"

Kidd smiled. "If I remember correctly, Mike, you work in the soap factory. You oversee the mixers for April Spring."

"Very good," Tilden said. "Now tell me something else: When was the last time I got a paycheck from the Tackmann Soap Company?"

Kidd seemed perplexed by the question. He paused for a moment, then he put a hand to his chest. His tone became overly sincere. "Okay, I think we need to clear up a common misconception here. Yes, I was once the most powerful man in the world, but even then I was not privy to the details of any one person's specific financial situation. Well, not yours anyway, Mike. But I can understand your mistake. I mean, I've seen some FBI stuff on people that would blow your gourd. Let's go drinking sometime and I'll tell you about it." Kidd glanced around at the rest of the crowd. "No more questions? Good."

Tilden shook his head brusquely, his lips as taut as suspension bridge cables. "You're not worming your way out of it that fast, Kidd." He jabbed a finger at the floor. "Two years," he said. "Two long years I haven't gone to work for Tackmann. And do you know why? I'll tell you why. It's because of your recession."

New murmurs of "Damn straight!" and "That's right!" rippled through the crowd.

Kidd let out a nervous catch of breath. "My recession?" he said. "*My* recession? With all due respect, Mike, that recession started well before I took office. If you want to blame anybody, take it up with Milquetoast Molson. He was there before me."

Tilden threw out a hand. "Let me tell you something, Kidd. For all the unemployment we had under President Molson, I worked under President Molson. These people"—Tilden spread his arms to the crowd around him—"worked under President Molson. You know when we stopped working? We stopped when the economy really went to hell because you were too busy porking that pastry chef."

The murmurs that had rippled through the crowd turned into a mighty cheer. Hands clapped together; hoots and hollers rose to the rafters. It was as if a "Hallelujah!" had been spoken in the middle of a church. Kidd could only stand in front of his hometown crowd, stiff as bamboo, and tap his microphone.

"Excuse me, excuse me," Kidd said, his pleas booming over the speakers.

The crowd quieted down enough for Kidd to speak.

"I think we need to clear up another misconception," Kidd said. "Contrary to what Mr. Tilden thinks, Miss Pacheco and I did not 'pork.' There was never any pork involved. It was strictly sugar-based confectionery."

"Are you for real?" The voice came from a short woman near the lunch counter who had to stand on her chair to be seen. She was older, probably sixty-five, but her spunk made her appear much younger and taller. "Who gives a flying leap if it was pork, or sugar, or even those damn lollipops she made for you that you used to twiddle in her hoo-hoo. The fact is, Chucky, that your affair with Amanda Pacheco killed our business."

"They laid off half the factory!" shouted another voice.

"I'm gonna lose my house!" yelled a third.

Someone else shouted, "I had to pull my daughter out of college!" followed by a "Me, too!"

Kidd raised a palm in an attempt to settle the crowd. "Relax, please," he ordered. "Relax. Please, relax." The crowd complied. "Thank you," he said. He took a deep breath. "Now, let's clear up a third misconception. I want you to ask yourselves something, something that will show you how irrationally you're behaving: Even in a recession, what is the one thing that people need to do? Someone? Anyone?"

Nobody answered.

"Okay then, I'll tell you," Kidd said. "They need to shower. They need to wash their hands. They need to scrub their faces. They need cleanliness in all its forms. Staying clean is an essential activity, regardless of economic conditions. Do you understand that? Do you? People buy soap whatever the state of the economy. They don't make it themselves, and they don't go without it. So blaming me for Tackmann's lack of sales is just passive-aggressive bunk. If you want to blame someone, blame your marketing department. They're obviously not pushing the product line effectively."

Suddenly, the man identified as Roy Plunk leapt from his folding chair. "Now you wait a minute," he said. He pointed to his "fetching bride" beside him, who was actually a homely woman. "My wife works in that department."

"Then you know what I mean, Roy," Kidd said. "I've followed Tackmann's marketing campaigns for years; they've always intrigued me. But I have to say, the ads have become old, tired, or just plain unfocused." Kidd put a finger to his chin and crossed his eyes mockingly. "'April Spring—it smells like a fresh morning dew.' I mean, what kind of slogan is that? Do you think a farmer in Topeka gives two shits that his soap smells like dew? He doesn't want it to smell; he wants it to work. Would you like to sell more April Spring? Is that what you want? Then make your marketing campaign target the product's functionality; make the ads tell people how your soap can solve a problem that has plagued bathers since the invention of bath soap." Kidd slapped a hand on his thigh. "'April Spring—your pubes won't stick to it.' There, that's your new slogan."

There was an audible gasp from the crowd. Roy Plunk's mouth dropped to his navel; his ugly wife covered the ears of the young girl sitting next to her. Probably wanting to prevent a riot, the mayor stood again in an attempt to calm the crowd.

"Tell us," he said to Kidd. "Tell us more about this library. Who would pay for it?"

"That's a great question, Mayor." Kidd scratched at his freshly-shaved cheek. "I'm thinking the usual suspects—corporations, private donations, you."

"Us?" shouted one member of the city council.

"Of course, John," Kidd said. "I may be giving you a gift, but it isn't free. You'll need some revitalization of your infrastructure. The Red Pouch barn will have to be torn down. Roads need to be built. Just the log flume ride itself will require significant water-transportation resources not available in Hawleyville at this time."

The city council member rubbed his nose with a thumb. "And where do you expect us to get this money, Chuck?"

Another chorus of "Damn straight!" rippled across the gymnasium. Kenny thought he heard a "You tell him, Councilman!"

The councilman continued, "The soap factory is running at half-capacity. Everybody's moving away. Tax revenues are down. We're broke, Chuck. We're that close to receivership." The councilman held up his thumb and forefinger an inch apart. "We don't even have enough money to replace any of the old ash trees that came down in that ice storm last year. We lost seventy-five percent of them, and now this town is barren. Barren, Chuck. Do you know how hard it is for ice to take down an ash tree? We're cursed. Marietta and Ironton have started calling us 'The Ass City.'"

"I make a motion," declared another city councilman, jumping from his folding chair. "That when we do have revenues again, we use them for replanting ash trees instead of giving one dime to this nonsensical bombasticity known as Chucky World. All in favor?"

Every member of the city council raised a hand, as did all the people in the gymnasium. When everyone lowered their hands, they looked at Kidd, waiting for his next move.

Kidd cleared his throat over the speaker and said, "No one respects the democratic process more than I, but all I have to say is, I think you're acting really stupidly."

The gymnasium erupted in a chorus of boos and catcalls.

Kidd said, "No, you hear me out." His tone had turned harsh. "You come in here and you bitch about revenue and civic pride and jobs. Well, what have I brought you? I've brought you the blueprint for a facility that will create revenue. I've brought you the blueprint for a facility that will elevate your civic pride. 'Hawleyville: Home of Chucky World,' they'll say. Trust me, Marietta will have a serious inferiority complex over this. And Ironton—well, they've always been second-rate to us anyway. But most important, and I stress 'most,' I've brought you the blueprint for a facility that will create jobs. Lots of jobs. More jobs than you can imagine. And this"—Kidd waved his arm at the crowd—"this is the thanks I get?"

"Thanks?" It was the Tilden guy again. He was back on his feet, and he was mad. "You want thanks? I'm a skilled union laborer. Before your recession, I made a respectable living in a respectable job at a respectable factory. Now you think you're bringing me respect by telling me to be a ticket taker at your amusement park?"

"Actually, Mike," Kidd said, taking a moment of contemplation. "I more see you selling the cotton candy."

What happened next to Mike Tilden's face said it all, and set the tone for what was to follow. The proud factory worker's cheeks turned brilliant red, followed by his chin, his brow, and his ears, the red spreading out and down until the man's whole head looked like the front of a fire truck. Even from Kenny's position some feet away, he could see that Tilden had ice blue eyes, because against the red of his face those eyes were shining brighter than high-beam halogen headlights. The man couldn't even speak. That's when Roy Plunk jumped to his feet.

Plunk said, "You've got some nerve coming here, Kidd."

The short woman popped up on her chair again. "It's not nerve. It's arrogance. He always thought he was above everybody else."

Then Sally Jean Barker stood. The pretty beautician was running nervous hands through her dirty-blonde hair. When she spoke, her voice was fragile with emotion. "Mrs. Williamson is right," she said, turning to the crowd. "Do you know what this man did to me today? Do you know? He walked into my salon, told me about tonight, then proceeded to proposition me. Prop-o-sition me! In front of my customers."

"That's the truth," came a voice from the back of the gymnasium. The woman stood, and Kenny could see that it was Mrs. Brooks from the salon, now with a well-coiffed mane of black hair. "I heard him do it, and I was under a dryer."

"I couldn't believe it," Sally Jean Barker continued. "I was so upset. The first thing I did was call my boyfriend. I couldn't work for the rest of the day."

"Yeah, Kidd." A man next to Sally Jean Barker stood up. He was thick-necked and muscular, and stood at least three inches taller than Kidd. He glowered at the former president, to the point where Kenny wondered if Kidd wished he still had Secret Service protection. "You wanna proposition her now?" he said. "Come over here and tell her you wanna take her to the Blue Bell. I dare you."

Then John Gerber stood. The friend from Kidd's youth said, almost contemplatively, "You know, every time I see this guy, he asks me about my missing testicle. Not just sometimes—every time. Brenda always said you were a sex fiend."

"I'll tell you what you are, Kidd." It was Mike Tilden again. His face hadn't cooled, but he had apparently found his voice. "You know what you are?" He turned to the crowd and shouted, "You know what he is? He's a frog catcher."

"A frog catcher! A frog catcher!" repeated the crowd.

"He's pathetic," came one voice.

"He's a liar," came another.

"He's a mess," said a third. "Look at him. He didn't even care about us enough to press his suit."

Then Mrs. Brooks stood again and shouted, "He's a motherfucking, son-of-a-bitch douchebag!" All heads turned to her. "And that ain't easy to say," she added, "cuz I loved his mama."

The crowd went silent. All eyes focused on Kidd, who was standing fence-post rigid in front of the lunch table. He let the crowd stay still for a moment, then he raised the microphone back to his mouth. "I'll now turn over the rest of the questions to my press secretary, Kenny Kernick. Kenny?"

Kidd dropped the microphone onto the lunch table with an echoing *thunk!* and walked back to where Kenny was standing at the lip of the stage. He took up position next to the boy, stood tall and folded his arms.

Kenny looked at Kidd with doe-like eyes. Kidd nodded over to the microphone. "You're up."

Kenny pushed off the stage and walked tenuously toward the lunch table. The walk, although only ten feet or so, seemed endless, every step like one taken with thighs made of sand. Kenny could feel the pent-up fast food in his gut loosening again, dangling precariously at the base of his belly. He felt flushed and sweaty. He wanted to die. He made it to the table, picked up the microphone, brought it to his quivering lips, and looked at the crowd.

So many faces, he thought. So many strange, angry faces.

That's when Kenny felt the bulge of fast food cut loose. It slid through his intestines on a wave of grease and settled with a crash at the base of his back. The force of its slide made his descending colon inflate like a balloon. He stared at the crowd and said the first thing that popped into his head: "I think I have to smash the deuce."

Kenny dropped the microphone, clenched his butt cheeks, and waddled as fast as he could toward the gymnasium's fire door.

"What did he say?" he heard one woman ask. The response came from the mayor: "I believe he said he has to go poop."

But Kenny wasn't stopping to clarify. The mayor had gotten it just fine. Kenny rushed for the fire door, the pressure in his rectum increasing exponentially, his head growing dizzy with abdominal pain. Kidd would have to forge ahead without his press secretary. Kenny's only concern now was making it to a toilet without soiling his tighty-white Fruit of the Looms.

CHAPTER 13

★ ★

The "deuce" that came out of Kenny's butt as he sat on the toilet in Mrs. Cox's classroom didn't just smash its way out—it exploded with the magnitude of a tactical nuclear device.

This is a warning, Kenny realized. It was his body's way of telling him that he couldn't eat all his meals at fast food restaurants. In reality, though, he doubted he could stop. Not at this point. On the road, fast food was easy. Worse still, it was addictive. Worst of all, it was consuming him with a singular vision: to sink his teeth into the perfect burger. And he had not yet found that perfect burger. Until he experienced the end-all, be-all of meat-on-bun, Kenny was certain that his taste for the tallow would continue, whatever his gut's reaction might be.

When the explosion ended and he had cleaned up, Kenny felt relieved but spent. Instead of pulling up his pants, washing his hands, and heading back to the gymnasium, Kenny stayed where he was. He sat on the toilet seat and exhaled a deep breath. He found that the small confines of the restroom suited him. It was quiet in there, vacant, and pleasant. Even though he had his pants around his ankles, and even though the restroom smelled like a sewer, Kenny felt something he hadn't felt since the moment he had started up the Cadillac and backed it out of Carl Kernick's driveway: He felt at peace. With Charles Bentley Kidd occupied for several more minutes, Kenny would finally have some time to himself after a stressful thirty-six hours on the road with a former president. He intended to enjoy the silence. He closed his eyes and focused on the sublime sound of nothing.

That's when he heard the cry.

"Kennyyyyyyyyyyyyyyyyyyyy!"

Kenny cocked an ear toward the door. Was that Bent? Why would Kidd be crying for him? Maybe Kenny was just hearing the start-up wheeze of an exhaust fan on the roof.

"Kennyyyyyyyyyyyyyyyyyyyy!" he heard again. This time there was no mistaking it. It was a voice, the voice belonged to Kidd, and Kidd was in trouble. And if Kidd was in trouble, Kenny was in trouble, too.

A punch of adrenaline slammed Kenny. He leapt off the toilet and pulled up his khakis so fast that he almost caught his wank in the zipper. No time to tuck in his shirt, either. He bolted out to the classroom just in time to see Charles Bentley Kidd rushing into it. The former president looked aghast. He was sweating like a distance runner.

"Jesus, Kenny! They're after me! They're all after me! We've got to hurry!" Kidd lunged forward and grabbed Kenny by the wrist. He started to drag the boy to the classroom's exterior door, a hulking metal rectangle which was painted forest green and had a shining silver sphere for a knob.

"What about your suitcase?" Kenny pleaded, reaching back for the beat-up piece of luggage.

"Fuck it!" Kidd shouted, pulling Kenny to the metal door. He flung it open and pushed Kenny outside—backwards.

Kenny hit the ground palm-first. He felt pain zing up his left arm. Then he looked up, glancing back into the classroom, and all thoughts of pain disappeared—

A mob led by Mike Tilden had burst through the classroom's interior door.

"Holy crap!" Kenny yelled.

The exterior door slammed shut behind Kidd. He grabbed Kenny by the sore wrist and pulled him to his feet. "I don't know how fast you can run!" the ex-president shouted, running away and looking back at Kenny, "but unless you want to hang by your testicles from the soap factory's smokestack, you better run faster than that Canadian sprinter who took steroids!"

Point taken, Kenny charged after Kidd. He hadn't gotten very far before he heard the exterior door to Mrs. Cox's classroom fly open with the pop of metal against rubber door stopper. He looked back to see Mike Tilden and the mob pouring out through the doorframe.

Kenny turned on his burners, which was a shock to him because he never knew he had burners. But the boy discovered he could run fast. Thank God for small feet and young legs, Kenny thought. He was soon passing Kidd, who flashed him a surprised look.

"The Caddy!" Kidd yelled to Kenny, losing ground to the boy as the mob gained ground on him. "That's good! Go start the Caddy!"

Kenny ran like a gazelle across the playground—nearly decapitating himself on the monkey bars—then across a patch of lawn, over the school's main road and into the parking lot. The Cadillac was parked at the far corner of the lot, its exit potentially blocked by what appeared to be every vehicle in Hawleyville, a conglomeration of dented pickup trucks and rusting American-made compacts.

Ten feet from the Cadillac, while he was weaving between a Ford Contour and a Chevy Corsica, Kenny hit the unlock button on his key transmitter. He raced to the Cadillac, yanked open the driver door, and fell into the seat. He started up the Cadillac and was just about to pull out and look for Kidd when Kidd ran between the Contour and the Corsica. The ex-president pulled open the passenger door, threw himself into the Caddy, and slammed the door shut, just as Mike Tilden and company started to weave between the parked vehicles.

"Drive, Kenny!" Kidd yelled. "Drive, drive, drive!"

Kenny jammed the Cadillac into gear and rushed out of the parking space. He managed to speed by Mike Tilden and the mob just as they were about to catch the Caddy. Kenny's vehicle felt smooth, it wouldn't break down, but there was a larger problem brewing: To get out of the Turtle Stream Elementary School complex, one had to drive to the exit for the parking lot then make a one hundred eighty degree loop to the main road, a loop which brought the driver right past the school's front entrance. That loop, and the time it took to navigate it, would allow Mike Tilden and the mob plenty of opportunity to weave back through the parking lot and wait for them a short distance down the road.

But Kenny and Kidd didn't even get that far. Just as they were exiting the parking lot, a second mob, led by Roy Plunk and Sally Jean Barker's gargantuan man-friend, burst out through the main doors of the school and rushed the Cadillac as it was making its one hundred eighty degree turn. Kenny had to stop cold as the mob surrounded the vehicle. They pounded on its roof, shook its struts, and bounced its trunk. Sally Jean Barker's lover jumped on the hood, spread eagle, and cursed at Kidd through the windshield. In a moment, Mike Tilden appeared and started to slam his fists against the passenger window. Both men glowered at Kidd; they barked at him; they made threats to separate his gonads from his torso with a pair of bolt cutters from Mike Tilden's pickup truck.

"Hit the gas, Kenny!" Kidd ordered, as fear made him cower into the soft leather of the passenger seat.

"I can't!" Kenny cried.

"Shake them loose, Kenny!"

"But I might kill somebody, Bent!"

"Either they die or we die!" Kidd said. "And I'm a hell of a lot more important than they are! So punch it!"

Kidd lifted his leg and slammed down Kenny's pedal foot with his own foot. But Kenny countered Kidd's action by hitting the brakes. The opposing forces of acceleration and restraint caused the Cadillac to rumble in place long enough for those Hawleyvillers of lesser intestinal fortitude to step back from the vehicle. But not Mike Tilden and Sally Jean Barker's man. They clung to the Caddy—Sally Jean Barker's man on the hood and Mike Tilden now on the roof—until the vehicle shot forward a hundred feet. When the Cadillac made a turn at the bend in the school's main road, both men finally succumbed to the laws of physics and went spinning off the vehicle by way of centrifugal force.

With the Cadillac free of hindrance and gaining speed, Kenny looked back through the rear-view mirror. Under the orange glow of street lamps, Kenny saw both Tilden and Sally Jean's man get up and continue to run after the Cadillac. Behind them a convoy rolled up, headed by a Ford truck. The driver of the Ford slowed enough for Tilden and Sally Jean's man to hop into the bed, then he resumed the pursuit of the fleeing Cadillac. In his gut, Kenny felt like he had to smash the deuce all over again.

"What did you say to these people?" Kenny demanded.

"I don't know," Kidd said. "I think I may have insulted their sense of fashion. And maybe their use of grammar. And their accents. And definitely a few of their masculinities." Kidd turned around and looked out through the rear window. At the same time, Kenny glanced at the rear-view mirror and saw what Kidd saw—the mob's convoy was growing and gaining.

"What's the top speed on this thing, Kenny?" Kidd yelled.

"I don't know!" Kenny cried.

"Then I suggest you find out!"

With that order from the former commander in chief, Kenny put gas pedal to carpet. In a matter of seconds, the Cadillac shot through the streets of Hawleyville, hit Route 7, turned south, and rolled into the clear darkness of a southeastern Ohio night.

As the Cadillac blew past the Hawleyville city limits sign at one hundred twenty miles per hour on a crisp, clear night, Kenny had the strangest thought. Here he was, a boy who had been raised staunchly Catholic, and yet, at that very moment, he would have sold his soul to the devil himself.

And what would his asking price be for an eternity of damnation? That was easy.

Kenny wanted some fog.

CHAPTER 14

★ ★

By the time the Cadillac came to its next complete stop, Kenny and Kidd were in Cincinnati.

They had driven for two and a half hours straight, blowing through or by every stop sign, red light and slower-moving vehicle, until they had crossed from eastern Ohio to western Ohio along the state's southern Route 32. Along the way, both Kenny and Kidd kept checking the mirrors to see if the Hawleyville mob was catching up to them. It didn't appear to be the case, but Kenny wasn't taking any chances. He kept the gas pedal to the floor and forced himself to forget that the Cadillac XTS came equipped with brakes of any kind.

They arrived in Cincinnati just after ten in the evening, approaching the city along its southern edge, on the roads that bordered the Ohio River. The time was growing late and Kenny was tired, not only from the anxiety of their near-disaster in Hawleyville, but also from his not having slept since one o'clock that morning. He told Kidd he needed to pull over or that Kidd needed to drive, whichever the former leader of the free world preferred. Kidd chose to pull over. Kenny knew he would.

Along Pete Rose Way, they found a quiet side street which climbed fifty yards up a steep incline before terminating in a dead end. The inlet was dark and secluded off the main road; it would provide good cover for the night. Kenny brought the Cadillac to the top of the dead end, turned around in the driveway of a luxury condominium complex (the street's only development) and swung the Cadillac to face outward to Pete Rose Way, just in case he and Kidd needed to make another quick exit. Kenny was hungry, but in the epic fight between hunger and exhaustion, exhaustion won. The boy took the front seat while Kidd stretched out in the back.

When Kenny woke up, the angle of the sun told him that it was probably noon. It was also a Friday, if he remembered correctly. Thanksgiving was still two weeks away. Kenny rubbed his eyes, wondering how, given the events of the past forty-eight hours, he would ever survive those next two weeks. There was still a lot of country left to cover on the road to Los Angeles, and Kidd had already proven a man with a strong penchant for diversions. Last night, one of those diversions had almost gotten Kenny killed. Or at least dangled by his testicles from a lofty height. Fortunately, neither he nor Kidd had come away with any damage.

Kenny sat up. Behind him, Kidd was still sleeping, wheezing melodically. Kenny adjusted his glasses against a sweaty face. Every part of him felt sweaty. The inside of the Cadillac was pressure cooking under the sun. Kenny kicked open his door and stumbled out, the frosty air consuming the moisture on his skin. As he cooled down, he noticed pain in his left hand. He turned the hand to his face. To his surprise, there was damage from last night—the base of his thumb had swollen where his palm hit the pavement when Kidd pushed him out the classroom door, and was a sickish blend of purple and red. Kenny tried to flex the thumb, but it would barely move against the swelling. He walked to the front of the Cadillac and sat against the hood, trying to loosen his thumb without sending jolts up his arm.

In the distance, Kenny could see a yellow steel-arch bridge that reminded him of a McDonald's sign, then the river, and beyond the river, the blue-green hills of Kentucky. He basked in the sun, but his palm was throbbing now, and he put his chin to his chest and closed his eyes. Moments later, Kidd stepped out of the Cadillac and joined him on the hood. Kenny didn't look up.

"Mornin', glory," Kidd said. Kenny could hear him stretching.

"Uh-huh," Kenny said.

"Magnificent view," Kidd said.

"Is it?" Kenny asked. His eyes were still closed.

Kidd said nothing else, but Kenny could tell the silence was bugging him. He became restless—drumming his fingers against the hood, scraping pavement with his shoes, clearing his throat. Finally, Kidd had had enough quiet.

"Speaking of magnificent," he said, "I have to tell you, that was some piece of driving you did last night, and right when we needed it most. First rate. I'd give you the Congressional Medal of Freedom if I could. That turn you made to get us onto Route 32: I thought for sure we were going to take out those gas pumps, but you executed it with grace and aplomb. Quite impressive, Young Kernick."

"Anybody could have done it," Kenny said, looking up now, the pain in his hand causing him to take bursts of breath.

"Trust me, Kenny, that's bullshit." Kidd stepped back and started to do tai chi with a slow, graceful arch of his arms. "My driver in Washington was military-trained, and he couldn't have pulled off those moves. They should hire you."

"Who?" Kenny asked.

"The Secret Service," Kidd said.

Kenny flexed his thumb. "It was no big deal," he told Kidd.

Kidd dropped his arms and stared at Kenny. "What the hell's the matter with you?"

"I don't know." Kenny held up his hand. "Look at that hematoma."

"Hema-what?" Kidd asked.

"Toma," Kenny said. "When damage to the tissue causes a localized collection of blood in the muscle."

"First of all, Kenny," Kidd said, "The rest of us don't call that a hematoma. We call it a bruise. Second—"

"No," Kenny said, interrupting. "A bruise is when blood spreads out under the skin in a thin layer. Also called an ecchymosis. This is definitely a hematoma."

"Here's a word you probably haven't heard before, Kenny— whatever! Second, I'm not talking about that. I'm talking about your attitude. Here I am, spending my precious time trying to build you up with kudos for a job well done, and all you keep doing is shooting yourself down. That's annoying, Young Kernick. It really is."

Kenny cringed. "This is either a tissue strain or a fracture."

Kidd glared at Kenny with the strong scent of frustration. "Kenny, let's get this straight. It wouldn't be a 'tissue strain"— you would have sprained it. It wouldn't be a fracture—you would have broken the fucking thing."

"No, a sprain is a stretching or tear of a ligament in a joint. This is probably—"

"What! Ever!" Kidd said.

"It hurts like Hades nonetheless."

Kidd shook his head, dejected. "No, Kenny," he said. "It hurts like hell. Better yet, it hurts like a cock-knocker. Shut up and trust me on this. If you go around saying you strained some tissue, or you fractured something, and it hurts like Hades, you sound like a cheese ass. Believe me, you do. But if you go around saying you sprained or broke your thumb, and it hurts like a cock-knocker, and don't you want to see this awesome bruise, then you sound like a stud. And I don't care how accurate the terminology is. Most women aren't going to know."

"And why would a woman care?" Kenny asked. He really had no patience for this today.

"Oh, I don't know," Kidd said. "Maybe it's because studs tend to get laid more than cheese asses. You would have found that out if you had stayed in college."

Kenny felt his heart flutter, not with a desire for coitus, but with anxiety over it. He quickly forgot about his hand. Instead, he wished for a laundromat nearby where he could calm himself with some warm, clean female undergarments.

When his mind cleared, Kenny said, "You know, Bent, I don't think this whole getting-women thing is for me."

"Really?" Kidd asked. "And what makes you say that?"

Kenny slid off the Cadillac's hood and stood straight with arms folded. "I just don't think I'm capable of it."

"You don't think you're capable of having sex?" Kidd looked aghast.

"I don't think I'm capable of having an attitude that will lead to sexual intercourse with a woman," Kenny said. "Truth be told, they kind of scare me."

Kidd shook his head a third time, but this time it wasn't with frustration; it was with disdain. Kenny could tell because Kidd pressed his lips together until they resembled a duck's bill.

Kidd looked off in the distance and let out a sigh, then he turned back to Kenny and pointed to the west. "Look over there, Young Kernick."

Kenny followed Kidd's finger down the length of the river. It was pointing at the yellow arch bridge that reminded Kenny of a McDonald's sign.

"I really want a Big Mac," Kenny said.

"Stifle it," Kidd said. "What I want you to see is the distance between the road deck and the river. Now, as crazy as it sounds, one of my old Secret Service guys, Jay Joyce, used to throw himself off road decks even higher than that one. Would just strap a bungee cord around his ankles and leap. He did it all over the world. Anywhere there was a giant chasm, he threw himself into it."

"Sounds like you," Kenny said.

"Ha, ha, ha," Kidd mocked. "You're so comedic. No, Kenny, what it sounds like is attitude. Jay was an extremophile, and extremophiles have attitude in spades. It's a prerequisite. Since the time they were little kids, they've been fearless. Pain does not concern them; the prospect of death is but a drop of rain in the ocean. They are studs. And that's very attractive to women. Fortunately, you don't have to be an extremophile to have attitude. Take me, for example. I was always afraid of heights, Kenny. Would you believe that?"

Kenny nodded. He had seen Kidd's face during the end of the fire ladder climb back in Simondale. The man had appeared a bit pale at the prospect of coming down again, once he'd returned to the window with the keys to the Cadillac, even though he had tried to hide it with bravado.

"No, Kenny," Kidd continued, his dusty hair flapping in a stiff autumn breeze off the Ohio, "I was a chicken shit like you in a lot of ways. But there was one thing I could do that you can't. Do you know what that is, Kenny?"

Kenny shook his head and stiffened up.

"I could always talk to girls," Kidd said. "I never had a problem with it. I could always talk to people in general, in any situation. I was never shy, Kenny. You, on the other hand, might as well put your asshole where your mouth is, because your skills at speaking—public or otherwise—stink to the nostrils of God. You were a goddamn disaster at the announcement last night, and right when I needed you most."

"You said you wanted me to stand back and keep quiet," Kenny said. "I didn't know you were going to call me out. I would have prepared something."

"Have you ever heard of improvisation?" Kidd asked. "Jesus, you almost got us killed."

"You just told me you were trying to build me up."

"Well, that's done. Now it's time for some truth. You choked under pressure, and I find that pathetic."

Kenny glared at Kidd through his coke-bottle glasses. He really wanted to lunge at him and strangle the bastard. Kidd must have sensed it because he rubbed his brow in exasperation, walked over to Kenny and leaned back against the Cadillac's hood.

"Look, Kenny, speaking to people is not difficult. When you're speaking to groups, they tend to connect with you, even if they're hostile. It's that hostility which feeds the connection, and regardless of how mad they get, they're still connected to you and you can still sway them. Well, until one of them comes after you with a folding chair. Then it's pretty much over." Kidd lengthened his legs along the asphalt. "But dealing with girls is no different. Most of them are just looking for someone to connect with. Sometimes you do that by commenting on something about them—something they're wearing; something they're carrying; something you see happen to them. Or sometimes, it's just the location you're in that connects you, or an ordeal you share. I once picked up a woman in a dentist's office. She was sitting across the couch, and when I made a comment about the dentist's reputation for sadism, she laughed. Then I got a crown, she got a filling, and we both got our rocks off in the back of her minivan."

Kidd smiled, remembering fondly his encounter with the woman, then he turned serious and scuffed a shoe against the asphalt. "If a girl is interested in you, Kenny, she'll be very open to almost anything you say to her, as long as the statement is delivered in a confident manner, like you couldn't care less if she ignored you. If she's not interested in you, then she'll probably think you're being creepy by initiating contact with her. But it's trial and error, Kenny. You can't be afraid to fail. You won't know if a girl is waiting for you to talk with her until you talk with her. If she isn't, you move on. Whatever. If she is, she talks back, and from there you can build trust."

"Trust is important that quickly?" Kenny said.

"Oh, trust is the keystone," Kidd said. "If you want a girl to sleep with you, Kenny, she's got to trust you, even if it's in some small way. That's the starting point. No woman really wants to get hurt, even your standard sorority house whore. No, a girl wants to believe in you; she wants to think you're a boy who might screw over all of the other girls he meets, but you'll never do it to her. She wants to trust that you are who you appear to be—that you're not really a serial killer in sheep's clothing, or you're not abusive to animals, or that you don't bitch slap your grandma when nobody's looking. If she trusts you, it only enhances her attraction to you. That seed of trust starts with solid verbal communication."

"Of which you're the master," Kenny said sarcastically.

"Absolutely," Kidd said.

"Smooth as silk," Kenny said.

"I," Kidd said, "could talk the chastity off a nun."

"Like Chucky World?" Kenny said. "Yeah, that was smooth. Why didn't you just offer to make them your personal bum wipers?"

Kidd shot up at Kenny's castigation. He got right in Kenny's face. "Forgive me," he said, "for caring about my hometown. Forgive me for caring about my presidency by wanting to honor it."

"You cared about your presidency?" Kenny asked with a hint of mockery.

"Every day," Kidd said.

"Then why," Kenny asked, "did you throw it away on a pastry chef?" Kenny locked his eyes with Kidd's and held them, waiting for (nay, demanding!) an answer.

That's when Kenny saw something he had never before seen in Kidd: The man's face turned crimson. This smooth talker began to stammer for words.

"Have—have—have you ever *met* my wife?!" Kidd finally sputtered.

"I have never had the pleasure," Kenny said.

"Oh, the pleasure," Kidd said. "The *pleasure*! That pleasure will be all hers, Kenny."

"She can't be that bad," Kenny said. "The press loved her."

"Well, that settles it, doesn't it? If the *press* loved her. You know what I think, Kenny? I think it's time you found out something for yourself, instead of reading about it and reciting it back by rote, like hematomas and sprains versus strains, and ecco-mecco-whatevers. You up for that, genius? Get in the Caddy!"

Kidd strode to the passenger door, threw himself into the vehicle and slammed the door shut. He waited with arms folded until Kenny got in and started the engine.

With a face still aflame, Kidd barked orders that led the Cadillac off the dead-end street, down Pete Rose Way and over to I-74.

For the next five hours, Kidd didn't say much, stuck as he seemed to be on anger toward Kenny. But as day turned to dusk, the crimson in Kidd's face receded and the man went pale, and he began to mutter, "Something I have to do, Kenny. Just something I have to do."

It was clear to Kenny, even in the fading light, that what had started as an act of bravado in Cincinnati over Kenny's standing up for the former first lady had become much more personal for Charles Bentley Kidd.

He was, after all, about to confront The Rhino.

CHAPTER 15

★★★★★★★★★★★★★★★★★★★★★★★★★★★★★★★★

By her junior year in college, Margaret Huff thought herself cursed at love.

In her first two years at Magdalena, a Catholic, women-only school in the Rogers Park section of Chicago, Margaret had dated more than a score of boys. Her lengthy list of failed relationships included Bill, the jock from Wisconsin, who had a nasty habit of doing pushups while they were having sex, and Frank, the pre-med student from Iowa, who always asked her to wash her hands before she touched his genitals because "Germs! Germs are out there, Margaret!" There was Gary the Bookworm, who studied morning, noon and night, and David the Pothead, who had smoked so much marijuana since coming to Chicago that he had forgotten how to read a book. There was Raymond, who liked to fart loudly in public, and Michael, who had an intense fear of crowds. There were Rocco and Curly and Spike (her wild phase) and Matthew and Mark and Luke (her apostle phase). There was Bill the Second and Bill the Third, and even a Three Dollar Bill, who was obviously queer but refused to admit it, until he later became a dancer in a traveling production of *Brigadoon* and fell in love with a makeup artist named Bruce. There were Max and Kevin and Tom, who all came from Indiana, then Mitchell and Ron and Ted, who all hated Indiana. There were boys whose names she could barely remember and boys whose names she would like to forget. And most recently, there was Edgar. None of her boys lasted more than a month, while some, like Edgar, lasted only one night, after he had bragged to her that his name in Old English meant "great spear man," but a quick trip to Thayer Beach had deemed him a two-pump chump with no great spear. Upon reflection, she knew there was a reason Edgar drove a big car.

In addition to their early exits from Margaret's life, her boyfriends had three other traits in common. First, they were all students at Jesuit University, the nearby brother school to Magdalena. Second, they were all older than she was. And finally, and most insidious to young Margaret, they were all, to a fault, absolutely incapable of being controlled, even after she had slept with them. It was that last characteristic which had usually been the deal breaker to any long-term relationship. In Margaret's world, control of her boy (and, by extrapolation, the course and minutiae of the relationship itself) was something she was not going to proceed without.

The ability to exercise control in her life was an obsession to Margaret for one simple reason: Growing up, she had possessed no control of anything.

Margaret Huff had been raised on Josten Avenue in Rogers Park, less than a mile up Sheridan Road from Magdalena College. By fortune's folly, she had been born the ninth and final child to Walter and Dorothy Huff, two God-fearing Irish Catholics who went to Mass three times a week, never ate meat on Fridays, and who had never in their lives thought of using condoms. While her mother stayed at home to care for the children, Margaret's father supported his family as the head accountant for Tosco Foods, maker of YummyKakes, one of the most respected brands of store-bought pastry in the upper Midwest. But being a successful accountant was merely a secondary pursuit to Walter Huff, important to him only because it put food into the mouths of his wife and children. Most important to Walter was fatherhood. To that end he approached being a father like he approached his accounting job—with a strong mathematical mind that valued the rational, that never strayed from a proven path, and that was intolerant of error.

To the outside world, Walter Huff's approach to parenting seemed to work well. While large families were not rare in Rogers Park during the fifties and sixties, what separated the Huff children from their neighbors was the perfection with which they acted and achieved. They never roughhoused, never used foul language, and never got into trouble with the authorities. Their grades were impeccable. The boys, all six of them, were lifeguards on Thayer and Jarvis Beaches during the summers— the models of boyish strength, respect and protection—while the girls (Patricia and Dolores, especially) learned needlecraft and cooking skills. Any casual observer strolling by the Huff's modest four-bedroom house on a warm summer's night might have easily deduced that the family inside was living the prototypical American dream. And to the other members of Margaret's family, it might have been a dream. But to Margaret Huff, her family's repressive dynamic often seemed like a wide-awake nightmare.

From her earliest age, Margaret felt like a high-energy child living in a slow-motion home, and that feeling only got worse when she became a teenager. The hormones bubbling inside her made her want to play, want to run wild and see where the sun came up, want to indulge in her nascent and growing appetite for boys, who were beginning to look at her lengthening figure (five-foot-eight by age thirteen) and straight glossy hair (as dark as crow feathers) with dripping tongues and ogling eyes. But Walter Huff would have none of it. Any hint to him of errant (and thus, immoral) behavior on Margaret's part was nipped in the bud, as it had been nipped in the bud for each of the eight perfect children before her. For Margaret, Walter Huff made it clear that there would be no diversion of course, no slack given, even if she were the youngest child.

Tensions with her father reached a boiling point just after Margaret's fourteenth birthday.

To Margaret, it wasn't hard to see that society was changing. By the time she was ready to enter high school, the hints of a cultural revolution were already scratching at the doors of quiet Rogers Park. Having endured seven years of parochial grammar school at St. Stephen's Parish, she begged her father to let her attend high school at Allister, a public institution where she thought she would be free to pursue her own wants. Her brothers had gone to Allister after all, and they had turned out well. But again, Walter would have none of it. In his mind, it was a very simple proposition. His sons went to Allister, then to Jesuit, where they would study for careers that would allow them to support families. His daughters, since they were not expected to be the breadwinners of their families, would be sent to high school at the Catholic, all-girls Sisters of Mercy. They would then attend Magdalena, where the exceptional education offered by that esteemed women's college would prepare them to be supportive-yet-subservient wives to successful husbands. And during college, every one of his children, boys and girls alike, would live at home to save money. Walter Huff was frugal like that.

"That's the way it's going to be, Margaret," Walter Huff declared as he signed the forms enrolling her at Sisters of Mercy. Margaret wasn't even given the choice not to comply.

So Margaret Huff went to Sisters of Mercy, where the nuns showed no mercy, and she stewed, to the point where she thought her brain would dissolve into broth. Away from home, in those short spans of time when she could avoid the control of her father and the watchful eyes of her mother and neighbors, she began to change. By sixteen, she was smoking Winstons with her friends in the alleyways along Chicago Avenue. By seventeen, she was swearing like a South Side gangster. By eighteen, after she had been sent to Magdalena, she was indulging in the sexual freedoms of the time by sleeping with every boy she dated, some with mildly pleasurable results, but most with a fizzle, like her experience with the Not-So-Great Spear Man.

And through it all, she was becoming bitter and angry. The cultural revolution was in full swing. The country had turned dynamic. Women were making progress in a man's world; more and more, they were competing with their male counterparts for success on a variety of levels. To Margaret's dismay, Jesuit University had even begun to accept women to its College of Arts and Sciences a full three years before her graduation from high school. Some of the first girls to attend Jesuit were former schoolmates from Sisters of Mercy. But when she tried to broach the subject with her father, to convince him to try something new and let her apply to Jesuit, Walter refused to discuss it. He would never allow his youngest child to veer from the course he had plotted out for her, the course which had worked so well with his other children.

So a stifled Margaret Huff exercised control of her life wherever she could, and the most turbulent of these areas involved her unrelenting litany of boyfriends. Margaret could be almost fanatical in her demands, telling them to be someplace at an exact time, or to do something right away, or to use only words and phrases acceptable to her, and not to wear any article of clothing that offended her sense of style. She plotted out their lives, anchored those plans in concrete, and told each of them that this was how it was going to be if they wanted to continue taking pleasure in her tall, raven-haired beauty. But like most college boys, Margaret's boyfriends simply ignored her demands. And like most control-freak women, Margaret Huff dropped them cold. Then she would lament to her friends over how insufferable boys could be. Many times, she would go into a complete state of depression about how she would never find a boy she could handle.

It was on one such occasion, three weeks after the start of her junior year, that Margaret first set eyes on Charles Bentley Kidd.

She had been sitting in a diner on Sheridan Road, chatting with her friend Ellie and nibbling on a ham-and-cheese sandwich, while she told the story of Edgar, whom she had dated at the end of the summer after he had returned early to Jesuit to train for a resident assistant position.

"That's about the only position he can handle," Margaret remarked flippantly to Ellie. "He sure as fuck couldn't handle doggy style."

As Ellie responded with a similar story of unfulfilling sex, Margaret took a long drag off her Winston and noted the jingle of bells from the door of the diner. When she looked up, she found herself gazing upon the lanky figure of a mocha-haired boy as he strode through the door and made his way to the lunch counter.

She was immediately taken with this boy, whoever he was. Ignoring Ellie, she watched him sit at the counter and order a soda. She knew right away that he was not from Chicago. His clothing was rural, at best, and he used the word "soda" instead of "pop." Then there was the dead giveaway: He had the most god-awful Southern accent she had ever heard, an accent that was more like a northerner trying to imitate a southerner.

As the clerk fetched the boy a pop, he looked over at Margaret, and that's when she gave him a test: She held up an index finger and curled it at him to come to her booth. To her surprise he did, without any fuss.

This one has promise, she told herself. But given her past experiences in matters of love, she needed to verify his boyfriend potential on the spot. No more wasting her time with dopes and limp-dicks.

When he got to the booth, Margaret told him to open a bottle of ketchup for her. He did.

She told him to get her a clean ashtray from another table. He did.

She told him to order her a refill on her Fresca, and to pay for it himself. He did.

She told him to sit down and stay a while. He did.

She told him to tell her all about himself. Boy, he did.

As the lanky figure named Chuck sipped on a "soda," he gave Margaret the long and short of his life's story.

She learned that he was a freshman who had come to Jesuit on an academic scholarship, which was really nothing more than a cover to get him on the university's nationally-renowned debate team, of which he was expected to be its star.

She learned that he was from a small town in southeastern Ohio near the Kentucky and West Virginia borders (which explained the noncommittal Southern accent) and that he had grown up among redbrick buildings, lush ash trees, and a river so mighty it infused life into the whole region.

She learned that he had been raised by his mother, a widow who worked for a soap factory, and that this woman had given him a good upbringing and the departing instruction that he was always to be a gentleman, especially to ladies.

She learned that he had come to Jesuit to study philosophy because recent events in his life had led him toward introspection, toward an unquenchable desire to know life's meaning, to know where he fit within the grand plan of the universe.

Then Margaret Huff learned something that made her nether regions quake with want: He told her that he was destined for greatness someday. That someday, people all over the world would know his name. That he would achieve magnanimous things on the stage of human history. He didn't exactly know the path by which he would accomplish greatness, but he was certain that he would accomplish it.

When he was done talking, Margaret took a long drag off her Winston. She studied him for a moment, then she blew the smoke toward the ceiling. "Nice to meet you, Chuck," she said, extending a hand. "I'm your new girlfriend. Now give me a kiss." And he did. It was the beginning of what Margaret Huff considered the perfect relationship.

Charles Bentley Kidd was unlike any boy Margaret Huff had dated. He was taller than she by a good five inches, which made her feel delicate and girlish; he was her equal in attractiveness, which made her feel proud when they walked down the street together; and he was immaculate of dress and grooming, even in that rustic clothing, which made her feel put together herself. He was also a staggering lover, able to make the most out of their quick jaunts to Thayer Beach, where they had to go to have sex, seeing that Margaret lived at home and Chuck lived in a "Catholic triple"—one roommate and the Holy Spirit to keep them apart. But most of all, what Margaret Huff cherished in Charles Bentley Kidd was that he was malleable. When she told him that his rustic clothing had to go, he threw it all into a dumpster and took a trip downtown with her to buy a new wardrobe. When she told him that his rich voice and superb debating skills made him a natural for politics, he dropped his philosophy major and enrolled in political science. When she told him his Southern accent made him sound stupid, he found a course in speech and worked it out of himself. When she told him she wanted an orgasm, he gave her three, even if it was twenty degrees outside and snowing at Thayer Beach, and they hadn't bothered to take off any of their clothing. He would simply find a way to satisfy her. And like everything else she asked of him, he would do it with style, with adroitness, and, most glorious, with no resistance.

Two years after they met, Margaret Huff was finally able to bring some normalcy to her relationship with Charles Bentley Kidd. As soon as she graduated from Magdalena, she moved out of her parents' house. Gone were the jaunts to Thayer Beach; she and Chuck could have sex in a real bed, whenever they wanted. To pay for her new life, she started working at a real estate development firm near the Merchandise Mart. But while she found development fascinating—the art of building something substantial and enduring where nothing had previously existed—she held very little power in her position as secretary to the partners. So she saw to it that she honed her skills as a developer in another way—by directing Charles Bentley Kidd to greatness. He got the grades she demanded, and he participated in the extracurricular activities she found necessary to train him to be a future man of the people. If she didn't like something about the way he acted, she would encourage him to change his behavior, usually with sex, but sometimes with a cuff to the skull. She held firm to the declaration that she would cut him no slack, and in that effort she could be quite cruel at times. But she loved him dearly, enamored as she was with his size, his looks, his verve, and even his classy name. And she assumed, because of the enthusiasm with which he engaged in her demands, that he loved her, too.

So when it came time for her boyfriend's senior year, Margaret Huff decided that she would marry Charles Bentley Kidd after his graduation the following spring. But for Margaret, marrying this northern boy with a southern edge presented a problem. While Chuck had always gotten along well with her family, including her retarded little cousin Jimmy-Jim, who was the only member of the family for whom Margaret felt any real affection, her parents made no bones about the fact that Charles Bentley Kidd wasn't Catholic. Nobody could really tell what religion Chuck practiced. From what Chuck said, his mother didn't go to church, and he was oddly evasive on questions of what church his father had belonged to, before the elder Kidd died in a coal mine explosion a few weeks after Chuck was conceived. Regardless of what Margaret's parents thought, there was one thing Margaret knew for certain: She wanted a big, expensive, Catholic wedding, just to stick it to her tightwad father. To accomplish that feat, Charles Bentley Kidd would have to become a Catholic.

As with everything else involving Margaret, Chuck agreed, and he threw himself into his conversion with more vigor than Margaret ever expected. Already well on his way to graduating *summa cum laude,* he used the last semester of his senior year to learn everything he could about the Catholic faith, to the point where Catholicism became his obsession. He read the entire Bible, old and new testaments, twice. He memorized the list of popes. He completed the requisite coursework handed out by the priest and studied his catechism diligently for extra credit. He made Margaret proud of his efforts, and got laid for it in bulk. And when it came time for the completion of his conversion, he demanded that it be done correctly. He wanted to be baptized, he said, but not in a church. No, Charles Bentley Kidd wanted to be baptized like his newfound savior had been baptized—in a river.

Father Hartley, the priest at Margaret's parish, tried to talk Charles Bentley Kidd out of it, saying that baptism by submersion was neither necessary nor prudent, given the toxicity of the local waterways. But on this matter, Charles Bentley Kidd remained unmoved, and not even Margaret could dissuade him. He would be plunged into a river or nothing else. When Father Hartley refused, Charles Bentley Kidd turned to Father Whitlock, a constantly-inebriated Jesuit who had once been Chuck's math professor. It only took two bottles of Rémy Martin V.S.O.P. to seal the deal. "If you wann-be dunked in a river," the drunk Father Whitlock told Chuck as he inspected the labels on his new alcoholic bounty, "then we're gonna dunkyouina (burp) river."

On a sun-drenched Sunday in April, Charles Bentley Kidd, Margaret Huff and Father Whitlock found a clearing along the banks of the Chicago River, at a canoe put-in in the La Bagh Woods. Charles Bentley Kidd took off his shoes and socks, rolled up his pants, and waded into the swampy filth of the listless Chicago. While Father Whitlock was too drunk to notice the sludge floating around him, Charles Bentley Kidd seemed undaunted by it.

"If Jesus H. Christ is my savior," Charles Bentley Kidd declared, "then I have nothing to fear."

With wobbly hands, Father Whitlock pushed Charles Bentley Kidd's head beneath the surface of the Chicago River and held it there for an eternity. Then, in the name of the Father and of the Son and of the Holy Spirit, Charles Bentley Kidd emerged from the water covered in flotsam, and gasping for air, with a plastic six-pack ring holder dangling from his left ear. As he stood again, he closed his eyes, raised his hands to heaven and in a loud, booming voice that would become the trademark of his political skill, he let out a mighty declaration that he had experienced a vision, that he had seen the face of God Himself, and that he had finally found the enlightenment for which he had so desperately searched over the past few years.

"Halle-fucking-lujah," Margaret replied. "Now get the fuck out of that water before your cock rots off!"

Two weeks after his graduation from Jesuit, Charles Bentley Kidd married Margaret Huff in an afternoon ceremony at St. Stephen's Church. All eight of Margaret's siblings served as bridesmaids or ushers, and even little cousin Jimmy-Jim served as ring bearer, while on Chuck's side, only Anna Kidd attended, traveling up from Ohio. After a weeklong honeymoon to Puerto Rico, the newlyweds settled in Columbus, where Margaret would begin work as a junior associate in the real estate development firm of Nadler and Rossi. There were limitless open spaces on the outskirts of Ohio's capital city, and Margaret Huff intended to fill them all. She would use the salary she earned to support her new husband, as he began work as an assistant to the Ohio Speaker of the House. It was Chuck's first step, she figured, on his rise up the ranks of national politics.

Many times during those first months in Columbus, Margaret Kidd would laugh out loud for no apparent reason, then smile broadly to herself with a glint in her blue eyes. At twenty-four, she was making a great living as a junior real estate developer. She was the possessor of stunning raven-haired looks, an intimidating height of five-foot-ten, brains to the nines, and a brawn which had led her to be the master of her own universe. To top it off, she was the blissful wife to a gorgeous young husband who did whatever she told him to do. Her life was becoming a fairy tale. She felt confident that nothing would ever be out of her control again.

But like most twenty-four-year-old women who believed they were living a fairy tale life of marital bliss, Margaret couldn't have realized then just how wrong she was.

It was a few minutes past 6:30, and dark, when the Cadillac XTS swung off I-90 and headed north on the Dan Ryan Expressway, a bustling, ten-lane road which ran like a concrete vein toward the heart of Chicago.

After three long and somewhat crazy days of travel, Kidd found himself a spent man. His energy was running low, and his emotions felt as fragile as wet toilet paper. Many times on the trip up from Cincinnati, as he thought more and more about Margaret and the past they shared, he didn't know if he wanted to cry over her one minute or lash out at her the next. He was tired—of rejection, of living like a leper, of not feeling connected to anyone other than the mousy boy named Kenny who was currently driving the car.

Which was why Kidd was glad he was coming to this town. For Kidd, Chicago had always been a place for rejuvenation when he felt worn down. A place where he could find invigoration in the smallest detail—the lights of a skyscraper, the honk of a cab horn, or the sound of water lapping against the beaches of Lake Michigan. A place which had beckoned him as a teenager, that had called him away from a small town in Ohio by virtue of its size and energy. A place which had promised a new beginning for a young man whose identity had been shaken to its core a year earlier with the revelation about the true nature of his parentage, but who was then, more than ever, hell-bent on doing great things in the world.

So it was no surprise to him, as the Cadillac roared up the Dan Ryan Expressway and the former president began to set his eyes upon the illuminated, rectangular mishmash of Chicago's night-draped skyline, that his emotions settled. As the skyline grew bigger in his eyes, and the skyscrapers began to climb above him, he knew that he must follow through on the reason he had come to Chicago: He had to tell Margaret, face-to-face, that he was taking Annabelle for Thanksgiving. No discussions about it. He was Annabelle's daddy, and, as such, he would be joining her in Los Angeles for the holiday. Margaret could make other arrangements, regardless of whatever arrangements she had already made.

Through correspondence between their surrogates, Kidd knew that Margaret lived at the intersection of North Kingsbury Street and West Grand Avenue. According to his lawyer, she had purchased two entire floors in some stunning new high-rise. The Secret Service ran their operations out of the bottom floor while Margaret took the top. Kidd never caught the name or exact address of the high-rise. In fact, he didn't know anything more.

Kidd had not communicated directly with his wife since the day in January when she had moved out of the White House with the Secret Service and the Press Corps in tow. Never one to do something quietly, Margaret Kidd had made a flashy show of her departure from Washington. Three days before she left, she threw herself a going-away party at Teaberry's, the poshest restaurant in Georgetown, and invited seventy-five Washington elite to help send her off. On the eve of her departure, she held a farewell press conference in the East Room, in primetime. The next day she exited the grounds in a goddamn helicopter— not Marine One, which Kidd would have gladly lent her, but a private helicopter she had rented herself.

Margaret's last words to Kidd had taken place in the living quarters on the top floor of the White House, just before she exited the mansion for good. As she ordered a box of valuables loaded into the helicopter, she turned to her wilting husband and declared, "I'm going the fuck home. I'm going to set up a charity for Jimmy-Jim. Then I'm going to try and put this whole fucking disaster behind me. Maybe I'll even fuck a Secret Service agent. But let me tell you one thing, Chuck. I hope Congress fucks *you*. I want you to experience humiliation like you've never experienced it before. Do you understand that, you cocksucking motherfucking fuckmonger?"

Then she left.

Well, she can't leave now, Kidd thought. He felt certain he had her trapped. In the lights of the skyscrapers climbing above the city, Kidd's eyes sparkled with glee. Only a few minutes more, Margaret. Then Chucky's back. He couldn't wait to see the look on her Botox-ridden face when she saw him.

The Cadillac pulled over at the intersection of North Kingsbury and West Grand. There were two high-rise complexes at that intersection, both new. Kidd leaned forward, looking up at them through the windshield. He studied them. The structure to the north was shorter, white, and alive with light. The structure to the south was forty-plus stories tall, black as death, and dominating. Just like Margaret. He pointed to the one to the south. "Take us there, Kenny."

Kenny drove over and stopped across the street from the black building. Kidd stepped out of the Cadillac. It was a crisp night in Chicago, and the wind was whipping up a chill.

"Your wife lives here?" Kenny asked, getting out of the Cadillac.

"That's my guess," Kidd said. He turned his collar up against the wind.

Kenny closed his door and surveyed the tower. "Condos in this place must cost a million dollars," he said.

"Actually, Kenny, they cost *millions* of dollars. Everything this close to the river does. But my wife has millions on top of millions. At one time she was the most successful real estate developer in Ohio. So don't worry about her. She's doing fine."

Kidd walked across North Kingsbury, and jaunted over to the semicircular driveway for the Millennium Tower Chicago. Kenny followed behind as Kidd entered the reception lobby and surveyed the area for proof positive that this high-rise was indeed the habitat of The Rhino.

The proof he sought didn't come from the man at the concierge desk; it came from the man seated behind the man at the concierge desk. If there was one thing Kidd could spot easily after the past seven years, it was the look of a Secret Service agent. This guy had it in spades—the crisp suit, the stone face, the eyes like needles sticking into Kidd and Kenny as they traversed the lobby.

The concierge, a diminutive man of Central American features who carried deep lines around his eyes and mouth, spoke first. "May I help you?" he asked. Then he seemed to recognize Kidd. "Um... sir."

"Yes indeed, *amigo*," Kidd said. "I'm looking for Mrs. Margaret Kidd. Could you ring her for me, please?"

The concierge turned to look at the stone-faced Secret Service agent, almost for instructions, then he turned back to Kidd. "I'm sorry, sir. I cannot do that."

"Why?" Kidd asked. He eyed the Secret Service agent, then he looked back at the concierge. "You're not going to tell me she doesn't live here."

The concierge seemed to grind in his shoes. His Spanish accent became thicker with anxiety. "No, Mr. Kidd, she lives here. But she is not here. Not right now."

"Well, that's okay, my good man," Kidd said. "Just tell me where she went and I'll find her."

"Thank you, Reynaldo. I'll handle this." It was the Secret Service agent speaking. The stone-faced man stepped forward and flicked the concierge aside like a gnat. "I'm Agent Morris," he said, his needle eyes piercing Kidd as if the former president were a pin cushion. "How may I assist you?"

"I need to speak to my wife, Agent Morris," Kidd said in a curt, authoritative voice. It usually did the trick with these guys. It reminded them of their lowly place compared with his grand stature. "It's a matter of great importance. Direct me to her, please."

The agent's eyes narrowed. "That information is classified, sir."

"Classified," Kidd repeated.

"Yes, sir."

"As in 'Top Secret.'"

"The highest."

Kidd found himself growing incensed. He began to grind down in his own shoes. "Just so I get this straight," he said to the agent. "I want to speak to my wife, to whom I've been married for thirty-one long, laborious years, and you're telling me that her whereabouts are classified?"

The agent's stone face twitched. "That's correct, sir."

Kidd rapped his knuckles on the countertop, just for punctuation. "Let me tell you something, friend. I have been privy to more classified information than you can fathom. Some of it would turn your brain to pudding. Do you know what really happened at Chernobyl? Do you have any idea how close we've come to intergalactic annihilation? Do you know where Elvis is living right now?"

The agent glared at Kidd. "No, sir, I do not."

"Then I think I can handle the location of my wife." Kidd stood with arms folded and stared at the agent. He was waiting for an answer.

The agent said, "That information, sir, is classified. But if you're unhappy with my assistance, maybe you could take it up with my supervisor."

"Where is he?" Kidd asked.

The agent chuckled. "Well, Mr. Kidd, he prefers things in writing, so a nice letter would do. I hear he's partial to ones that sound like the Gettysburg Address."

Kidd watched as the agent fell into laughter, turned, and walked back to his seat toward the rear of the concierge area. "Four score and seven hours ago," he mocked under his breath, his back to Kidd, "your agent brought forth on me a great indignation..." The agent laughed again, then he sat down on a stool and glared at Kidd with the same stone face and needle eyes as before, like nothing had transpired between them.

Kidd turned and wheeled out of the lobby, with Kenny trailing behind. He fumed all the way back to the car. How dare the Secret Service treat him like that? He was a former leader of the free world, for Christ's sake. "Get in the car, Kenny!" he barked.

"Where are we going?" Kenny asked.

"Shutupanddrivedownthestreet," Kidd said. "We'renotlicked yet."

"I don't know, Bent. You looked pretty licked to me."

"I did, huh?"

"That guy wiped his butt with you. The only thing you're missing is a brown streak down your face."

"Oh really, Einstein? Is that what you think?" Kidd and Kenny slammed their doors at the same time. "I'll tell you something I'm not missing, Kenny. I'm not missing the power of deduction. In fact, I have that power on red alert. Did you see the lines in that concierge's face?"

Kenny affirmed that he had indeed seen those lines.

"There's only one way somebody that young gets lines like that," Kidd said. "Our little *amigo* smokes three packs a day."

Twenty minutes later, the concierge at the Millennium Tower Chicago walked out into the chilly November night. He strolled up to Grand Avenue and walked east for a block and a half, until he was well away from the entrance to the high-rise. Then he stopped, leaned back against the brick façade of an art gallery which was closed for the evening, and pulled out a pack of cigarettes. No sooner had he lighted up in the stiff wind than a golden Cadillac XTS slowly pulled into the empty parking space in front of him.

"*Amigo*," Kidd called from the passenger window. "A word, please?"

The concierge glanced at Kidd suspiciously, blew smoke out of his nose, and looked down the street. Kidd could tell he was still nervous about the Secret Service. Kidd motioned him toward the car.

The concierge took a huge drag off his cigarette then placed it for safekeeping on one of the art gallery's windowsills. When he got to the Cadillac, the small concierge known only as "Reynaldo," who looked to be about forty-five but was probably years younger, slid into the backseat and shut the door. His whole body reeked of stale smoke.

"Mr. Kidd," he replied, when asked again where Mrs. Kidd had gone, "the agent has told you. That information is classified. She is the former first lady."

"Let's not think of it that way, Reynaldo," Kidd said, eyeing him through the mirror on the flip side of the passenger sun visor. "Let's think of it as just another husband asking about just another wife. Does that help?"

"I don't know," Reynaldo said. He glanced around anxiously. "What if they have listening devices? What if I go to jail? I have many children."

Kidd scratched his chin. "That's a salient point, my good friend. I can understand your reticence. But there is a way out.

Why don't you say it in Spanish? They can't bust you if they don't know what you said."

"You speak Spanish?" Reynaldo asked.

"No," Kidd said, "but my friend Kenny does."

Kenny shot up in his seat. "Hey, don't get me involved in this."

"You're already involved in this, Kenny. They're probably running your photo through an FBI database as we speak." Kidd eyed the concierge through the mirror. "So, Rey, what about it?"

The concierge let out a labored breath, sour with nicotine. Kidd could tell he was still reluctant. Time to raise the stakes.

Kidd reached under his seat and brought out the humidor. It pained him to do what he was about to do, but the concierge was resistant and Kidd's urge to confront Margaret was growing stronger. He keyed the lock and opened the humidor to reveal his last three heart-shaped, star-spangled lollipops, fashioned for him by the loving hands of Amanda Pacheco. He held one up. To the concierge he said, "These are my most-prized material possessions, Rey. I have nothing else that brings me greater joy. Help me, and I'll give this one to you."

The concierge laughed. "Mr. Kidd, I have had many lollipops."

Kidd laughed right back at him. "I can guarantee, Reynaldo, that you have never had a lollipop like this. Note the bow, and the heart shape. They are Amanda Pacheco Twirlies—the infamous lollipops of which, by now, you have no doubt heard tell. Bow intact, wrapper unmolested, never licked—a collector's item."

The concierge's eyes grew wide. He leaned back in the seat and beheld the lollipop which was pinched between Kidd's fingers. "No shit?" he asked.

Kidd raised his right hand and said, "One hundred percent, absolutely true." He reached back and waved the lollipop in front of the concierge's wrinkled face. "Think of what you could do with this. Think of the possibilities."

"Could I rub it around my girlfriend's *chocha* like you did to Pacheco?" the concierge asked.

"You could do that," Kidd said, taken aback by the concierge's bluntness. "Or your wife's, since you're wearing a wedding ring."

"My wife doesn't let anything near her *chocha* anymore," Reynaldo said, deflated. "Including me."

"Then I have a better idea," Kidd said. "Instead of rubbing it around anyone's *chocha*, why don't you sell it on eBay in a special auction? Then you'd probably be able to support your mistress, and your wife, and pay for college for each one of your many children. It's that valuable."

"I don't know how to use eBay," the concierge said.

"Then go buy *eBay for Idiots*," Kidd said.

"But nobody will ever believe that it is for true."

"They will if I give you a certificate of authenticity," Kidd said. "Kenny, a pen and some paper please."

Kenny opened the glove compartment. From it he removed a felt-tip pen, but he could find no sheet of paper. Finally, he tore off the back cover to the Cadillac's user manual. He handed both pen and cover to Kidd, who wrote out a statement of verification on its blank white side and signed his official signature with a flourish. When Kidd finished, he held up the certificate and the lollipop for the concierge to inspect.

The concierge hesitated for a moment, then he tugged the confection and its documentation out of Kidd's hands. He inspected both carefully. Seemingly satisfied, the concierge leaned forward to Kenny and rattled off a litany of Spanish that sounded to Kidd like something from a saucy Mexican soap opera. When the concierge was done, he stuck his new booty in a coat pocket, jumped out of the car, and walked back toward the Millennium Tower. He never even made a move to retrieve his waiting cigarette.

Once the concierge was out of sight, Kidd pounced on Kenny. "What did he say?"

Kenny repeated in English what the concierge had told him in Spanish: that Margaret Kidd was hosting a benefit tonight at the Chicago Rostoff Waterside, which was located downtown along the north side of the Chicago River; that the benefit had something to do with Rohm's Palsy, a disease of which Reynaldo had never heard; that it was being sponsored by her new charity and all the hotshots of Chicago society were expected to be there; and that it started at eight, but that Mrs. Kidd and her entourage had left early to pick up some relative in Rogers Park who was escorting her, and who was also to be the guest of honor.

Kidd slapped Kenny on the shoulder. "Perfect, Young Kernick. A job well done. I may have to promote you from administrative assistant to some higher position."

"I thought you already made me your press secretary," Kenny said.

"Yes, well, you failed in that endeavor, Kenny. And blisteringly, I might add. But I can find something else for you, so don't fret. We'll deal with it another day. Tonight I just want you to kick back, relax and enjoy the show. You're in for some real entertainment."

"Why's that?" Kenny asked.

Kidd closed the humidor and locked it. "Because," he said, sliding the humidor under his seat, "you're about to meet someone who will really put the chuckle into you."

"Who?" Kenny asked. "Your wife?"

"No," Kidd said. He looked at Kenny and grinned. "Her retard cousin Jimmy-Jim. Just wait until you see this guy. It's a riot. He wears a hockey helmet. And he shits himself constantly."

Kenny crinkled his face. "Please don't tell me you're making fun of a retarded person."

"I'm not laughing at him, Kenny," Kidd said. "Well, yes I am. But we need to move out. The show's about to begin, and I want a front row seat."

CHAPTER 16

★ ★

Kenny and Kidd entered the Chicago Rostoff Waterside from the brick-paved Riverwalk that bordered the lolling main branch of the Chicago River.

On the ride up the escalator from the Riverwalk level, Kenny and Kidd had been alone—that floor, devoted to meeting rooms and a fitness club, was empty at this time of night, and the Secret Service was nowhere to be seen. But once they got to the Reception level, they were joined by many people for the trip up to the ballroom, and it didn't take Kenny long to see how underdressed both he and Kidd were for Mrs. Kidd's party. All the men in attendance were clad in black tie, while the women wore expensive dresses. Kenny looked down at his khakis and Oxford, dirtied by two days of use, then he looked at Kidd, who was still wearing the rumpled charcoal suit, and he felt his nerves tighten. He and Kidd resembled ruffians. It was no wonder, then, that everybody on the escalator was staring at them. Then Kenny heard the whispers, and he knew—they didn't notice him at all. It was Kidd they were staring at.

True to form, Kidd ignored them. He kept his chin level and his eyes forward. Kenny wondered if Kidd was even cognizant of the stir he was creating. He soon got an answer when Kidd turned to Kenny and flashed his cocksure smirk. "Don't you just love shaking things up, Young Kernick?"

Not really, Kenny wanted to say. Shaking things up only made Kenny want to soil himself.

To the serenade of whispers, Kenny and Kidd stepped off the escalator and onto the third floor of the hotel. In front of them, across the promenade, Kenny could see the double doors to a grand ballroom, and in front of those doors, milling about with cocktail glasses in their hands, a throng of guests about two hundred deep.

Kidd grabbed Kenny by the collar and pulled him through the throng. Kenny heard bits of condemnatory conversation as people recognized Kidd:

"Who does he think he is?"

"No class, that one."

"Peggy will flip."

Feeling overly conspicuous, Kenny was quite happy when they arrived at the doors to the ballroom. Then he looked inside and saw three times as many people.

"Damn," Kenny said above the din. "Your wife can really turn them out."

Kidd scratched his chin and shook his head. "All these people, here for a retard. I never would have believed it. Let's find a table."

Kidd stepped into the ballroom, but was stopped immediately by a young woman wearing librarian's glasses. "Tickets, please," she said. Then the spark of recognition hit her. "Oh, it's you."

"That's right, it's me," Kidd said. He studied the girl. "You know, I remember all my wife's assistants, but I don't recognize you."

The girl clasped her stack of tickets to a flat chest. "I'm Janet," she said. "I joined the foundation last month."

"Oh, the *foundation*," Kidd said in mimicry. "Did you hear that, Kenny? My wife doesn't have a charity; she has a *foundation*." He looked at the girl again. "This is a pretty swank affair, Janet. My wife really dialed up the society. Tell me, how much is the foundation charging for a plate tonight?"

"It's by the table," Janet said. "Fifty thousand per table."

"Fifty thousand?" Kidd repeated. He nodded his head and arched his eyebrows, and Kenny knew he was impressed. Kidd glanced around the ballroom. "Now tell me something else, Janet," he said. "Where's the security? Where's all the Secret Service? I'd at least expect to see a metal detector somewhere."

Janet shook her head forcefully. "Oh, no, no," she said. "There's not much of that for tonight. It's the way Ms. Huff wanted it."

Kidd arched his eyebrows again, but this time he didn't look impressed. "Ms. Huff," he cried. "Ms. *Huff*?"

"Of course," Janet replied. "Ms. Huff has final say on all the arrangements."

Kenny could tell that Kidd was trying hard to keep his composure, but it wasn't working. He had stiffened, and his face was turning a dazzling hue of crimson. Kenny even detected a twitch in Kidd's otherwise rock-solid jaw.

"Well, Janet," Kidd said in a mocking, syrupy tone, "could you please tell Ms. *Huff* that Mr. *Kidd* is here to see her? Would you do that for me, please?"

Janet shook her head again. "I can't leave my zone, Mr. Kidd. I have tickets to take."

"Then I'm going to tell her myself, Janet. Do you mind? Even though I don't have one of those tickets to give you?"

Kidd's face was as red as the rubber kickballs Kenny remembered from his days at Griggson Academy.

"I suppose that's okay," Janet said. "I mean, you were the president and all."

Kidd suddenly smiled through his flaming face. "That's right, Janet," he said. "I was the president once. It's about goddamn time somebody remembered that. Come on, Kenny!"

Kidd grabbed Kenny by the collar and dragged him into the ballroom.

With the lights in the grand ballroom set to a soft amber hue, Kenny doubted that many people could really make out the person of Charles Bentley Kidd from a distance. That was a good thing, because he was on a rant.

"The name Kidd was good enough for her when I was the darling of the nation. The name Kidd was good enough for her when she got fame and prestige for it. How dare she drop my name! Well, let me tell you, Kenny, I'm going to tell that peach a few things. I'm going to tell her good."

Kidd dragged Kenny to a half-filled table in the far corner. Of the eight chairs at the table, five were occupied—two by men and three by women—but none of the empty chairs were being saved. The people at the table all looked to be in their early twenties, like they had sauntered over from some brokerage house or law firm for a company-paid night out. They were all chatting away when Kidd and Kenny arrived. All of them, that was, except for a pretentious dark-eyed blonde with physics-defying straight hair. She was staring off into space with arms folded. When Kidd asked her out of courtesy if the two chairs next to her were spoken for, she waved a hand and turned her head away. Kidd took her gesture as a "No."

"Plant it here, Kenny," Kidd commanded, forcing Kenny to sit down next to the blonde. Just then, a waiter approached and asked if either Kidd or Kenny would like a drink.

"Get the driver here a Coke," Kidd said, "and I'll take a rum punch. Loaded."

"One Coke, one rum punch." The waiter nodded and left.

Kidd looked down at Kenny. "I have to find my wife. Stay here until I get back."

He turned to leave, but Kenny grabbed him, digging his fingers deep into Kidd's forearm, making Kidd wince in pain.

"What?" the former president barked.

Kenny stared up at Kidd, terrified. "You can't leave me here alone. I don't know these people."

Kidd let out a sigh and glanced across the ballroom. The expression in his eyes made it seem as if he were taking true pity on the boy. Then those eyes flashed with an idea. He bent down to Kenny's ear.

"Okay, Young Kernick," Kidd whispered, "you like tests, don't you? You were always good at those. I'd like you to think of this situation as a test. While I'm gone, I want you to talk to one of these fine young ladies here. Take a look at this one sitting next to you."

Kenny swung his fearful eyes to the blonde goddess seated beside him.

"Have you ever seen something like that?" Kidd asked. "Something so perfect of form and function? And that hair." He chuckled softly. "I wonder if her other hair gets that straight."

"What, on her legs?"

"No, not on her legs!" Kidd snapped. "Jesus H. Christ!" He slapped Kenny on the side of the head. "Just remember the strategies we've discussed over the past few days, then chat her up. I'll be right back."

"What strategies?" Kenny asked. But it was too late. Kidd had pulled free from Kenny's grasp and started to cross the ballroom. A few tables away, he turned back to Kenny and made an opening-and-closing motion with his hands, the unofficial international signal for "Start talking, you little bastard."

At that moment, with five unknown people around him—two males, two very attractive females, and one ultra-attractive blonde goddess—Kenny felt his whole world begin to spin. He thought that maybe he would try to speak to one of the other girls, but both were already involved in well-established conversations with the guys.

Should he wait until they were finished? Wouldn't that be better? Didn't they look more approachable than this goddess next to him? What should he do?

Kenny's heart pounded. He was growing moist in his armpits. This blonde girl next to him was so beautiful, and chic. And with her arms folded and her gaze set at the wall, she looked like she couldn't have cared less about anything, especially Kenneth Andrew Kernick, college-dropout pervert from Simondale, Connecticut.

Oh, but how he wanted to talk to her. How he wanted to break the silence between them, if only so he could lean in and smell more fervently the gentle scent of hyacinth wafting from the perfume she must have recently applied to her butter-soft neck.

God, she was a flower and he wanted to pick her.

She was a popsicle and he wanted to lick her.

She was a fruit, and he wanted to squeeze her until she dribbled liquid onto his tongue.

He had to talk to her. He had to know that she knew he existed.

But what to say? And how to do it?

Remember the strategies we've discussed, Kidd told him. But what strategies?

Kenny thought back to that morning in Cincinnati. They had been sitting against the hood of the Cadillac then, looking past the Ohio River into Kentucky, and studying the bridge which resembled a McDonald's sign.

Build trust with them, Kidd had said. Build trust through connection. Start connection with conversation. Start conversation by commenting on something about them—something they're wearing, or something they're carrying. Notice something about them and get talking.

But what to notice about this blonde beauty next to him? Oh, there were so many things: Her eyes were brown; her lips were thick; she had a dimple in her chin. She was also wearing a dress the color of a plum, and she tended to rock her leg as she sat. She was drinking red wine. She liked to keep her arms folded at all times. Then there was that hair, that magnificent straight blonde mane.

You're being cliché, Kenny told himself, as if he could hear Kidd's voice chiding him. This girl is so startling that she has probably been told a million times about the straightness of her hair, and the beauty of her brown eyes, and about her lips, and the dimple in her chin, and her taste in dresses. Nay, Kenny, you need to be special. You need to notice something supremely different about her if you're hoping to make a dent in that armor she wears. Think, boy. Improvise.

That's when the blonde girl next to him unfolded her arms. Without looking at Kenny, she shifted back, reached to her lap, and pulled up a matching plum purse from beneath the lip of the table.

Kenny's eyes followed her motions as she brought the purse to table level, cracked it open, and checked for something inside. But what was she checking for? Maybe the others at the table couldn't see, if they cared at all, as engrossed as they were in conversation, but Kenny could see. From his angle, it was plainly clear.

She was checking for a tampon.

The thing was right there, buttressed against her wallet—a white shaft in the blackness of the purse. She fingered the tampon reassuringly.

The blonde goddess closed the purse and returned it to her lap, then she folded her arms and reset her gaze at the wall. Waiting, Kenny thought. Waiting for him to notice something about her.

Kenny giggled nervously. He folded his own arms, straightened up and cocked his head, like a Don Juan ready to link himself forever to this beautiful girl through a shared experience.

Kenny leaned in toward the blonde goddess. In the most debonair voice he could muster, he said, "Having your period, huh?"

The conversation at the table stopped flat. The others looked at Kenny in astonishment.

The blonde goddess turned her eyes to Kenny. They were such cold eyes, he realized now. So stern. And unrelenting. She crinkled her face at him and parted her thick lips in disgust. Then she unfolded her arms, lifted her glass of red wine off the table, and poured its contents into the crotch of Kenny's khaki pants, until the wine had turned the fabric the color of stale blood. When the glass was empty, she cocked it with a flair, smiled at Kenny, and said in a tone as dry as desert dust, "Hey, look. Now you are, too."

The blonde goddess slammed down her wine glass and erupted from the table. "I don't care how much Riley paid for this table, I'm out of here."

Then she stormed away. Within seconds, her minions at the table had followed her. None of them offered a departing word to Kenny.

Kenny looked down at his crotch. It was stained red in a big splotch. He felt his chest tighten. He wanted to pass out from humiliation. He could barely breathe.

"Sir?" Kenny heard from behind.

It was the waiter; he had returned with two drinks.

The waiter lifted a glass off his tray and placed it in front of Kenny. "Coke for the boy," he said. "For the gentleman, a rum punch." The waiter turned and walked toward another table.

Kenny eyed the Coke, watching a bead of dew trickle down the glass and dissolve into the tablecloth. For Kenny, Coca-Cola was all well and good, but the current situation, with the way he was feeling at that very moment, called for something stronger. Something much more powerful in its ability to soothe.

Then he eyed the rum punch, and his choice of beverage became clear.

He was certain Kidd would understand.

Kidd saw no sign of Margaret among the guests in the ballroom. Nor were there signs of her in the promenade, at the coat check, or even in the service hallways—his typical point of entry via the Secret Service during his days as president. He also couldn't find her in the ladies restroom, which Kidd inspected thoroughly, to the screams of many a scrumptious humptious clad in form-hugging silk or taffeta.

Kidd knew Margaret never to be late for anything. It was one of his wife's traits that had seemed amazing to him at first, in his college days, when he needed that structure to keep him in line as he took his first steps into the larger world. But as time had gone on with her, as years had turned to decades, that promptness (and her fascist zeal for it) began to chew into him like beaver's teeth gnawing on a tree trunk. Kidd found it serendipitous, though, that tonight his wife's irritable promptness would pay dividends. Back in the promenade, as he looked over the heads of the arriving guests to a clock at the far wall, Kidd noticed that the time was a quarter past eight. According to the concierge at Margaret's condo, this event should have started fifteen minutes ago. That meant The Rhino was somewhere in the hotel. He would find her.

Whenever Charles Bentley Kidd was mad, he walked fast and with purpose. He was practically running through the guests, steamrolling them with a reckless disregard for tuxedos or evening wear. He charged across the promenade, down the escalator, and into the hotel's reception hall, a vast rotunda of floral carpeting, check-in counters abuzz with activity, and a brilliant chandelier hanging over it all. And whom should he have found standing directly beneath the chandelier but—

"Margaret."

The word came out of Kidd's mouth with no affection. Instead, he spewed it.

She had been walking in from the main doors, with one Secret Service agent five paces in front of her, one agent five paces behind her, and one next to her. Also next to her, his arm intertwined with hers, was a younger man dressed in a tuxedo and wearing a hockey helmet for cranial protection. The younger man walked with a dragging foot and had a face contorted into a permanent look of childish wonder. He was Margaret's cousin, the retarded Jimmy-Jim.

Upon hearing her name, Margaret looked up from watching Jimmy-Jim's tentative footsteps. She stopped in her tracks. Her entourage, which Kidd could now see included another young assistant he didn't recognize, stopped with her.

"Well, look at what rose from the dead," Margaret said with a disdainful laugh. Her young assistant, whom Kidd found to be quite delectable, laughed with her in typical suck-up fashion.

By this time, the lead Secret Service agent, a hulking man who looked as if he had played defensive end in college, positioned himself directly between Kidd and The Rhino. Without looking back at Margaret, he asked, "Ms. Huff?"

Margaret waved her hand and said, "Oh, he's fine, Mark. You might as well let him through." Then she turned to her assistant and rolled her frigid blue eyes. "I mean, it's not like you can stop him anyway. It's been pretty well documented that Chuck finds the holes in everything. Especially pastry chefs." She led the girl in laughter, and the assistant snorted like a pig, which Kidd found... not delectable.

The agent stepped back and let Kidd pass. When he approached Margaret, she said, "Chuck, you remember my cousin, obviously." She pointed her mouth toward her cousin's ear. "Jimmy-Jim, do you remember that pussy-whoring, cockknob husband of mine?"

Jimmy-Jim managed to nod his hockey-helmeted head, then he let out a piercing "Yeah!" that sounded like the call of a wounded harp seal. Even after all the years spent with Jimmy-Jim and the strange vocalizations he made, Kidd had to struggle to keep from laughing.

"So, what can I do for you, Chuck?" Margaret asked bluntly.

"We need to talk," Kidd said.

"Talk? Hmmm. What on earth would we need to talk about? Hannah—" Margaret snapped her fingers and the assistant, who was lean, tall, and had striking Amerasian features, stepped to her side. "Is there anything I need to talk to Mr. Kidd about?"

Hannah raised a clipboard, scanned it and said no, that Mr. Kidd definitely was not on the agenda.

"Thank you, dear," Margaret said. She rubbed her free hand along Hannah's back. "Isn't she good, Chuck? Mother was Vietnamese, father was a Navy pilot, so she has that Asian sense of organization combined with her father's dedication to discipline. She's smart, too—Magdalena graduate, first in her class. And beautiful. God, look at her. Isn't she gorgeous?" Margaret peeled her hand off Hannah's back, waved a finger at Kidd and whispered tauntingly, "Now don't try to fuck her."

Hannah blushed and said, "We're late, Ms. Huff."

"That we are," Margaret said. "Ever forward. My new motto." She began to lead the entourage ahead, their progress slowed by the impeded gait of the retarded cousin. Kidd followed, walking beside Jimmy-Jim, who was starting to drool down the ridges of his tuxedo shirt.

"Margaret, I'm not kidding," Kidd said. "We have serious issues to discuss."

"How's Connecticut these days?" Margaret asked on the move. "What's the town called? Simonize? Simon Says? Simon-and-Garfunkel?"

"I just want a few minutes of your time," Kidd said.

Margaret took a handkerchief from Hannah and wiped the drool off Jimmy-Jim's chin. "They tell me it's a lovely location. Very upscale."

"Just thirty seconds," Kidd said.

"So how much of my hard-earned money did you spend on your house?"

"You can't just ignore me, Margaret," Kidd said. He swung around Jimmy-Jim in an attempt to get right in Margaret's face. The move raised the eyebrows of the Secret Service and stopped the entourage in its tracks again. A chill hung in the air as The Rhino glared at her husband, and the agents prepared to pounce.

"You know, Chuck," Margaret said with a coat of frost covering her voice. "My friends from the Secret Service don't take kindly to an aggressive move like that, even if the person doing it is my husband. Just because you were stupid enough to dismiss your detail—and, yes, Chuck, I did hear about that—doesn't mean I harbor any such notions. I am still a former first lady. Now you will step back, you will step aside, then you will climb into whatever mode of transportation brought you here and head back to Connecticut. I'm going to let you walk away with a modicum of dignity, even in that piece-of-shit suit. I suggest you take me up on my offer."

As he had done for most of his life, Kidd followed Margaret's instructions. He stepped back, stepped aside, and watched Margaret and her entourage continue through the reception area.

Just after the last agent had passed him, Kidd called out to Margaret's backside: "I'm taking Annabelle for Thanksgiving!"

For the third time, the entourage stopped. Without looking at Kidd, Margaret leaned in toward Hannah. "Take Jimmy-Jim upstairs. I'll meet you on the dais."

Margaret slid her arm out from Jimmy-Jim's and replaced it with Hannah's. Then, as Hannah and Jimmy-Jim moved forward without her, Margaret charged toward Kidd, her eyes never leaving the floor. The Secret Service tried to follow her, but she held up a palm to them. "Not now," she said. "Mr. Kidd and I need some privacy."

When she reached Kidd, she used her palm to grab him. But she didn't grab him by the forearm, or the shirt collar, or even an ear—she grabbed him by the testicles. With one firm grip, and in front of many curious hotel guests who had, by now, recognized the disgraced former president and his wife, she pulled Kidd forward by the nuts and led him in a waddle toward the restrooms, squeezing his genitalia between her unrelenting fingers. The pain was so intense that Kidd twice tried to crumple to the carpet, but Margaret would not allow it.

At the restrooms, Margaret pushed open the door to the ladies room and dragged Kidd in. Unlike upstairs, Kidd was thankful that this ladies room was unoccupied. Margaret threw him into a handicapped stall, sat him down on the toilet, slammed the door behind her, and locked them both in.

Towering over her husband, she got into his face. "Listen to me, you cocksucking, motherfucking little fuck!" she said. "Annabelle is my daughter. Do you understand that? She's mine!"

"I believe I provided the sperm," Kidd said.

"Do you really know that?" Margaret asked. "How do you know that, Chuck? How do you know that I wasn't fucking around on your adulterous fucking ass back then?"

"She looks like me," Kidd said.

Margaret scrunched her face, enraged. "Oh, you always have an answer, don't you? Well, here's an answer for you: There is no fucking way you get Annabelle for Thanksgiving. She's flying here to be with me. We're having dinner with my family. I already bought her the plane ticket. I made it happen, Chuck. Me! I get the reward!"

Margaret pulled away from him and leaned against the stall door. She was breathing heavily, almost hyperventilating. Kidd decided to push his luck.

"Maybe 'Belles will change her mind," he said. Then he goaded her. "Maybe I'll make it happen."

Margaret let out a laugh, an annoying little punch of air that sounded like a boat horn. "Oh, you'll make it happen?"

"Absolutely," said Kidd.

"Give me a fucking break," Margaret said. "You never made anything happen. You just stood there and looked good. I was the fuel for your fire. Without me, you were shit. Who got you that job with Speaker Tomlin, huh?"

Kidd didn't answer. He knew his wife was right.

"Then who made you a state rep?" she asked. "Then who made you a governor? And who the fuck do you think made you the president of the United Fucking States?"

Again, Kidd remained silent.

"What, no snappy little answers this time?" Margaret asked. "Well, let me help you out, Chuck." Margaret pointed a finger at her chest. "You're looking at her, that's who. Me, and my determination, and my high-paying job that got us by while you were earning jack shit for twenty years." Then Margaret swung her finger around and pointed it at Kidd.

"So fuck you, fuck all those congressmen's sluts, fuck your goddamn swimsuit models, fuck those tramp news reporters, and fuck that little whore cream puff girl!"

With that retort, Margaret Huff Kidd unlocked the stall door and charged out of the ladies room.

With her departure, Kidd sat on the toilet for a few minutes, stunned by yet another Rhino attack. He had gotten used to them over the years, but it had been so many months since he had experienced one that he had forgotten how paralyzing they could be. He was tempted to reach down and splash cold toilet water on his face, for refreshment.

What finally got Charles Bentley Kidd moving again was the entrance of two women into the ladies room. Feeling a tad awkward, the former leader of the free world waited until they had settled into their respective stalls and were gabbing back and forth at each other before he opened his stall door and walked out of the restroom.

The snippet of conversation he heard as the restroom door closed didn't make him feel any better.

"Chucky Kidd is looking old these days," one of the women said.

Rest assured, Kidd wanted to tell her. He's feeling old, too.

Once back in the lobby, Kidd saw that Margaret and her entourage were gone. He could hear applause from upstairs.

Kidd took the escalator to the Ballroom level. All the guests had moved out of the promenade and were seated inside the ballroom. Kidd walked across the promenade and stood in the open double doorway to watch the event.

On the dais, Margaret and her cousin were standing toward the back while a speaker introduced her. Kidd stared hard at the speaker. The man seemed familiar. Then Kidd recognized him.

No, it can't be, Kidd thought. But it was. The introductory speaker was Nelson Ridgeway, the goddamn mayor of Chicago.

Well, Kidd thought in defeat, at least someone in the Kidd family got a mayor to speak for them. And at a podium, too.

Kidd's thoughts returned to the introduction just in time to hear Mayor Ridgeway say, "I give you Peggy Huff."

The ballroom erupted in cheers. Kidd watched as Margaret handed the retard off to Hannah, then took her place at the podium. She looked good, Kidd had to admit. She wore a stunning black Beba Prax one-shoulder silk dress with a slit that ran almost the entire length of her thirty-five inch legs, and she wore it well for a woman approaching fifty-six. Her legs still looked fantastic; her black hair, cut short years ago, hadn't grayed a bit; and the Botox injections were keeping her face remarkably free of wrinkles. Even her shape was well maintained, Margaret being such a speed ball that she never slowed down long enough to succumb to that nasty phenomenon known as middle-age spread. No, Margaret's waist was still trim, her breasts still taut, her ass still manageable. But as he looked at her, appreciating her body and her appearance for what it was, it stirred nothing in him—no passions, no desires, no urges. In looking at his wife, Charles Bentley Kidd felt as if he might as well be looking at a bowl of cold soup. The lentil bean kind. With plenty of ham hock.

"Thank you, all," he heard Margaret say over the audio system. He watched as her smile electrified the crowd. "Thank you to Mayor Ridgeway. Thank you to the mayor's staff. And many thanks to all of you, my honored guests, for coming out." Margaret motioned behind her. "You all know my cousin James back there. Since birth, James has been afflicted with Rohm's Palsy, a rare disease that affects one out of every five million babies born in the United States today. While that figure may not seem like a lot, and while some cases aren't as severe as his, all cases of RP are debilitating, and the effects they can have on families, especially when the parents are young, are often disastrous. I know. I watched my aunt and uncle fall to the brink of despair from the pressure of dealing with James, and he was their eleventh child. Imagine what would have happened if he had been their first child. Fortunately, they survived. They dug down into their faith, they relied on their extended family, and they made it through. And James has flourished in his own way over the years, making a rewarding life for himself. Now both of us have come to a crossroads in our lives. It's time for us to give back. And my cousin and I agree that the best way to give back is to take on Rohm's Palsy headfirst. Therefore, it is our goal, through the James Geoffrey Huff Foundation, to not only cure RP once and for all, but until we do, to provide support to families dealing with this tragic condition. And we're not going to stop. We're going to give help to every family that needs it, then we're going to hunt this disease where it lives. We're going to attack it. We're going to grab it by the throat and choke it. Then we're going to finish it off. We're going to make it happen. And tonight, that starts with your generous contributions. Isn't that right, James?"

From the back of the dais, Jimmy-Jim howled another "Yeah!" This time he sounded like that wookie from *Star Wars*.

The crowd erupted in applause. Margaret finished her remarks over their clapping. "So enjoy the festivities. I'll be coming around to thank every one of you, my dear friends, in a personal manner. Thank you."

Margaret stepped away from the podium to more applause, and the room exploded in chatter and movement. Waiters began to bring drinks again; plates of food arrived. A five-piece band near the dais strummed up a cheesy instrumental tune.

Kidd left the doorway and walked through the crowd to the corner where he had left Kenny and the delicious blonde. He wondered if Kenny had managed to speak with her, and if so, if Kenny might have even scored a quickie in the restroom. He could dream for the boy, after all.

When he reached the table, he found his dreams dashed.

Except for Kenny, the table was empty—there was no delicious blonde, no delicious blonde's friends, nobody. Kenny's face was planted into the tablecloth. To one side of his head sat a full serving of Coca-Cola; to the other side an empty rum punch glass.

"Jesus Christ," Kidd said. He peeled Kenny's head up from the table by a mass of red hair. It only took him one look at Kenny's melted face to know that the boy was trashed.

"Hellloooooo," Kenny said like a giggly girl.

"What happened?" Kidd demanded, less angry than stunned.

"Well," Kenny said, slurring. "Shewashere, then shewasgone. And sumhow, I gut red pans." Kenny pointed down to his khakis, which were stained in the crotch with what looked to Kidd like a glassful of Merlot.

"Ohhhhh," Kenny said, "she was sopreddy, Chuckybent. She was sofugginggorgeous. And then the fugging bitch lef me. Fug, fug, fug, fug, fug. An all I wanted ta do was ta hug her an kiss her an stroke her back an lick her hair an smell her toes. I'm soooo sad." Kenny started to tear up. The boy threw his head down onto the table and began to pound the tabletop with his meager fists. "I wan my fuggin' goddess bag. I wan my fuggin' goddess bag." Suddenly he stopped, lifted his head and touched a finger to his two front teeth. Kidd could see terror in the boy's eyes. "Ohmygod, I can't feel my teef," the boy cried, tapping his drunk-numb choppers with the finger. "What happent to my teef?" Kenny dropped his head to the table and resumed his pounding. "I wan my fuggin' teef bag. I wan my fuggin' teef bag."

Kidd let out a dejected harrumph. He wondered how his situation over the past twenty-four hours could possibly get any worse—his flight from Hawleyville; the confrontation with The Rhino downstairs; now he had a drunk companion who definitely needed to work on his tolerance. Oh, what else could happen to make this day completely teeter over into mayhem?

He quickly got his answer.

"Still here, are we?"

It was Margaret again, speaking with that sticky, provoking voice she always used when she was pissed at her husband. She had made her way over to Kidd's table during her thank-you rounds, and like downstairs, she was surrounded by her assistant Hannah and the Secret Service. The retard was nowhere to be seen.

Kidd straightened up and said, "I'm still here, Ms. *Huff*."

Margaret grinned at him with a snide smile, and Kidd knew that she knew that her reversion back to the Huff name had wounded him.

"Tell me something, though," Kidd said. "If you've gone back to your maiden name, why is it I have no recollection of our divorce? How come I'm still wearing this wedding ring?" Kidd held up his ring finger for Margaret to inspect. With his other fingers curled down, it looked oddly as if he was flipping her off.

Margaret studied her husband's finger. "My Christ, you still have your ring," she said. "I must say I'm shocked. I thought you would have lost it up some whore's snatch the minute I left the White House. You are left-handed, after all."

"Knock it off," Kidd said. "Why are you going by 'Margaret Huff'?"

"I can go by whatever fucking name I please," Margaret said. "It's my prerogative as a scorned fucking woman." She eyed Kidd with toxic spite. "But don't worry, Chuck, I'm still your wife, if that's what really matters to you. Because at the heart of our relationship, we're digging down into our faith, and we're relying on family, and we're making it through. All that inspirational bullshit. But most of all, it's because we're Catholic, remember? You converted. And rule number two of being Catholic is 'No divorce.'"

"So what's rule number one?" Kidd asked.

"Being guilt-ridden and miserable," Margaret said. "Which is exactly what I intend to make your twat-hopping ass until death do us part." Margaret turned to Hannah. "Get Janet for me, please." The hot Amerasian assistant spun and made a dash for the ballroom's entrance.

Just then, Kenny raised his head from the table. "Holyshit, Chuckybent, mybrainis... spinning."

Margaret studied the boy, then looked at Kidd. "Chuckybent?" she asked. "Is this a friend of yours?"

Kidd put his arm around Kenny's shoulder, like a proud daddy. With a grin, he said, "This, Margaret, is Kenny Kernick. Kenny is *my* assistant."

Margaret's eyes went wide, then she laughed again with her boat-horn bellow. "Your *assistant?*" she said. "Oh, that's precious."

"What?" Kidd asked. "You're shocked that I have an assistant?"

"I'm not shocked you have an assistant, Chuck," she said. "I'm just shocked your assistant doesn't have two tits and a pussy."

"Oh, come on, Margaret," Kidd said. "You know that's not fair. Look at Tom Prudell. He was my most major assistant, and he didn't have those things either."

"No," Margaret said coldly. "He only procured them for you."

Kidd lifted his arm off Kenny's shoulder, grabbed the boy's head and snapped it toward Margaret. "Kenny, I want you to meet somebody. Say hello to my wife."

The boy squinted through his coke-bottle glasses. His head teetered precariously on his neck as he studied the form of Margaret Kidd. After a few seconds, he looked at Kidd and asked, "Is ziss tha... Rhino?"

Kidd chuckled then looked at Margaret. Her steely eyes told him that the former first lady was not amused. "Actually," he said, trying to defuse the tension, "not twenty minutes ago I also called you a peach."

Margaret's eyes didn't lighten. "Isn't that nice of you."

"Oh, it's nothing," Kidd said. "I really do think you're a peach." Then Kidd flashed Margaret a wicked grin. "Well, the middle of it, anyway."

Margaret's eyes went as cold as a corpse. As she stood in front of him, stiff and silent, Kidd knew that her devious mind was struggling for a reply.

That's when Hannah returned with Janet, the ticket taker from the ballroom's entrance.

"You wanted to see me, Ms. Huff?" Janet asked.

Without taking her eyes off Kidd, Margaret said, "Tell me, Janet, when Mr. Kidd arrived tonight, did he present you with two tickets to this event—one for him, and one for his shitfaced little assistant?" She inspected the table's name card. "I don't believe either one works for Riley Pharmaceuticals. Unless Mr. Kidd is trying out their anti-VD drugs." She cackled.

Janet shuffled her feet. "I'm sorry, Ms. Huff. I didn't know what to do. He just showed up and demanded to see you. He is your husband."

Margaret stopped cackling, then she lifted a hand and rubbed Janet on the back. "There's nothing to be sorry for, Janet. I understand completely. My husband can be very persuasive. You're lucky you still have your skirt at your knees. And truth be told, your letting him in is actually going to bring me a great deal of pleasure." She turned to Kidd. "Because he's a party crasher, and a shabbily-dressed one at that. It's time for you to go, Chuck. Gentlemen"—Margaret Huff snapped her fingers and the Secret Service agents stiffened to attention—"please take Mr. Kidd and his friend away."

The hulking agent stepped forward and asked with some confusion, "You want us to throw them out?"

"I'd like you to throw the little one out," Margaret said, clearing up any doubts. She turned and eyed Kidd with a vixen's menace. "For the big one, though, I want you to throw him... in the river."

"Margaret!" Kidd cried. But it was too late. In the beat of a hummingbird's wings, two well-trained agents grabbed Kidd by both arms and began the struggle to lead him away.

Kidd kicked, Kidd pushed, Kidd squirmed, but it was all for naught—like every other Secret Service agent, these boys were fucking strong.

A murmur rumbled through the ballroom as heads popped up from tables and guests stood. People started to point.

Just then, Kidd saw Kenny go by him. But the boy wasn't walking out under his own power; he was slung fireman's carry over the shoulder of the hulking agent, the boy's flame-haired head bobbing up and down against the agent's backside with every powerful step the agent took.

With a piercing twist to his arm, Kidd was prodded forward. "Goodbye, Mr. Kidd," he heard Margaret chuckle behind him. Then he heard Hannah and Janet chuckle with her.

But there was so much Kidd still wanted to say, so much he wanted to yell—to Margaret, to her assistants, to her guests. But the pain screaming from his shoulder blades made speech of any kind impossible.

What happened next was a blur. The agents dragged Kidd and Kenny from the ballroom, across the promenade, and down the first escalator. Hotel patrons in the main lobby parted before the mayhem and stood stone-straight as the group went by. Kidd swore he heard someone mention Amanda Pacheco. He had an urge to go back, find the culprit, and punch him in the nose.

All the way down the final escalator, Kidd thought of Margaret. How could she do this to him? How could she humiliate him in front of all those people, even the mayor of Chicago? How could she still be that mad at her own husband? What on earth had become of this one-time power couple?

The agents rushed Kenny and Kidd out of the hotel and into the cool autumn air of the Riverwalk. The hulking agent bent forward and placed Kenny against an iron fence that bordered the river. Just then, Kenny vomited on the agent's shoes, causing the agent to curse Kenny out roughly. As the agent wiped off his shoe tops against Kenny's khakis, the two agents holding Kidd lifted the former leader of the free world off his feet. In a moment, Kidd was sideways—one of the agents holding him by the ankles, the other by the wrists. They began to swing him.

"One... two," the agent at his ankles shouted. "Three!"

At the apex of the swing, the agents released Kidd. The ex-president flew over the iron fence like a jumbled marionette. He tumbled through the air and landed with a smack against the water's surface ten feet below. Instantly, he was submerged.

"Chuckybent!" he heard drunk Kenny cry through the muffle of water.

But Kidd made no attempt to answer the boy. He couldn't. The chill of the water had paralyzed him, seeping into his every pore and shrinking his testicles to the size of cashews.

And even if Kidd could have responded to Kenny, he wouldn't have done so. In the blackness of the Chicago River, he was consumed with revelations. He was coming to an understanding. He was finding enlightenment, just as he had found enlightenment in the Chicago River all those years ago during his Catholic baptism.

But this time around, that enlightenment wasn't turning out to be fervent and inspiring. No, this time around was much different. This time, Charles Bentley Kidd's enlightenment was proving to be damn cold.

CHAPTER 17

★ ★

The next morning, Kenny Kernick climbed out of sleep into a realm of senses he did not understand.

Touch—

Against his face he felt the scratchy pile of synthetic carpeting. His back was pressed firmly against foam, his arms and legs tucked into nooks, and he was crumpled into the fetal position.

Taste—

Stale vomit in his mouth. It covered his teeth, tongue and cheeks like a moldy blanket over a wet dog.

Sight—

Blurry, as usual when he awoke. But through the blur he could also see darkness, and beyond it a shaft of gray light. To Kenny, it was as if he were peering through a tunnel.

Smell—

Rubber and plastic, and the organic pungency of mud.

Sound—

Now that was the strange thing. Kenny could accept the input from his other senses, but he didn't believe what was coming into his ears. It was the din of the ocean. The tumble of giant waves rolling rough against land. He was confused. The last thing Kenny remembered, he was in Chicago, and Chicago didn't have an ocean.

Maybe he was still drunk.

Without his glasses, and having no idea where they were, Kenny peeled his face off the synthetic pile, uncurled himself from the fetal position, and rolled onto his back. They were motions he quickly regretted. His head pounded with a sloshy stab; the muscles from his neck to his toes felt as if they were about to rend apart. Fists of gray light beat at his eyes until he thought the orbs were about to implode. He clamped his eyelids tightly, remained motionless, and waited for the collective pain to recede. But one thing became clear to him as he lay completely still: He figured out where he had spent the night. Kenny Kernick had awoken to find himself crammed into the rear floor space of the Cadillac XTS.

It took ten minutes for the pain to recede. Once it was bearable, Kenny reached up and swept his hand across the Cadillac's backseat. The leather was dappled with water, but Kenny didn't remember rain. His glasses weren't there. Kenny began to creep his eyes open, allowing them to adjust to the light. When he could keep them open without pain, he surveyed his surroundings through opaque vision. He finally saw the image of what he thought were his glasses hooked on the backseat's grab handle. He wondered how they had gotten there. He also wondered how he was going to reach for them without causing his body to slip into convulsions. But he had to have them. Kenny took a deep breath, then with a jolt of intense agony, he lunged from the Cadillac's floor, grabbed the glasses off the hook, and tumbled onto the backseat, where he expected the wetness he had previously felt to soak into him, making his pants damp. The strange thing was, his pants were already damp. In fact, every article of clothing he wore was damp. Even his tighty-white Fruit of the Looms.

Kenny put on his glasses and surveyed his surroundings. The interior of the Cadillac was a mess of mud and muck. Kenny himself was covered in a layer of green silt, and his pants had a giant red blotch at his crotch, the remnants of a parting gift from that otherworldly blonde. Charles Bentley Kidd was not in the vehicle.

Where the hell is Kidd? Kenny wondered.

Fuck yet, where am I?

Kenny looked outside and saw that the Cadillac was parked at a place he didn't recognize—in a small, square lot at the end of a dead-end street. On both sides of the street sat long processions of multistoried, brick-faced apartment buildings; they were old but well kept, as if they had been constructed during the prosperity of the 1920s and renovated continually since urban renewal. In the lot with the Cadillac was a vast assortment of fine automobiles, none cheap to own or operate. Kenny realized that the Cadillac had somehow come to rest in a robust city neighborhood. That neighborhood also had something else about it that was robust, and that was the sound of the ocean. Why was Kenny hearing that sound? The neighborhood he was seeing and the sound he was hearing did not mesh. So Kenny turned his head to the left, toward the sound, expecting to be transported to another world, where the city neighborhood would disappear and a boundless ocean might spread out before him. On the contrary, all he saw was a cement retaining wall, and a few feet beyond it, another taller wall made up of boulders. It was on top of that boulder wall where he saw the strangest sight of all—the motionless form of Charles Bentley Kidd. The former president was standing stiff against the wind and facing outward toward the sky like a copper soldier atop a Civil War memorial in some small town's central common.

What the shit is he doing out there? Kenny wondered. The question worried Kenny. One of the few memories the boy had from the previous evening was of Kidd being thrown into a river by the Secret Service, and Kenny, drunk, climbing over a railing and reaching down to help him out of the water. The recovery was made difficult, though, by the fact that the former president didn't seem like he wanted to come out of the water. Kenny remembered yelling at Kidd to take his hand, and Kidd not taking his hand, then Kenny's memories went black. Now he was concerned that Kidd was still in some morose mood, and that he might jump off these rocks and kill himself. What he would be jumping onto, or into, Kenny had no idea, but he was certain that Kidd would meet his end nonetheless. Kenny couldn't let that happen. So he forced himself to turn, twist, and open the rear door with his hematomic hand. In tiny, pain-minimizing increments, he uncoiled himself from the Cadillac and stood up in the damp air.

That's when the nausea hit him.

Pain be damned, Kenny stretched his muscles and ran for the cement retaining wall. He leaned over it and heaved, but nothing came out of his stomach. He heaved again and again— all dry. His body screamed at him to stop, but he couldn't. Finally, the heaves ended and he collapsed against the wall in a spineless heap. Breathless, he looked up, expecting to see Charles Bentley Kidd staring down at him from the top of the boulder wall, giving him one of those now-standard "What the fuck are you doing?" glares. But Charles Bentley Kidd was not flashing Kenny any such glare. The old president was still standing motionless, his arms pressed against his sides, his hair and charcoal suit flapping in the unrelenting wind.

After a few moments, Kenny managed to pull himself up from the cement wall. The nausea did not follow. He made his way over to a set of steps leading down from the wall, descended them, crossed a layer of sand strewn with leaves and trash, and began an ascent up the boulders, placing careful footsteps into the joints created between the rocks.

Kenny stepped onto the peak of the boulder wall. There he beheld a breathtaking vision, one which made everything about the irregularity between the sight and sound of this neighborhood clear to him. The vision was that of Lake Michigan spreading out before him in a wide, churning ocean of fresh water. The lake was so wide and long, in fact, that there was no land visible in the distance. The waves seemed to emanate from some indefinable point on the horizon, whereupon they would build, approach the land in a fury, and crash onto the sand and rock at the base of the wall, creating the ocean sound which had so confused Kenny back in the Cadillac.

Kenny stood in awe of the lake. The ex-president didn't even look at Kenny when the boy took up position next to him—Kidd's eyes remained focused on the lake, his body eerily still. He and Kenny stood there together for what seemed like an eon before Kenny broke the silence.

"That is goddamn one big lake," Kenny said.

Kidd said nothing in reply, nor did he flinch.

"You can't even see the other side," Kenny added. "That's fucky."

Kidd remained silent.

"Where the shit are we, anyway?"

Finally, Kidd moved. He parted his lips and said to his companion, "Where we are, Kenny, is the fulcrum of my life. It's a very special place to me, so when you speak of it, I'd appreciate it if you watched the profanity. There's a time and a place for that, and this isn't it. Besides, your swearing prowess needs some work. It's clunky, Kenny. 'Where the shit?' 'That's fucky?' Who talks like that?"

"Sorry, Bent," Kenny said, looking down at the pathetic red splotch on his khaki pants. Swearing had felt so good last night when he was drunk that he couldn't wait to do it again. But Kidd was correct: Kenny was simply terrible at it. He would have to practice, but not here at this... whatever Kidd called it.

"We're at the what?" Kenny asked.

Kidd looked down at him and shook his head. "At the fulcrum of my life," he said. "The fulcrum, Kenny! Jesus, did all that water get stuck in your ears last night, or did drinking my rum punch kill off your brain cells?"

"Christ, Bent," Kenny said. "I'm just asking. What side of the passenger seat did you get up on this morning?"

"I don't know, Kenny," Kidd said. "I was too busy trying to figure out what side of the floor you were going to get up on."

"What the hell is your problem?" Kenny asked.

"My problem is that you're acting like an interruptive, insensitive moron," Kidd said.

"Oh yeah," Kenny said, "well you're acting like a... goddamn... shit-licking... fuck face!"

Kidd stared at Kenny for a moment, letting the words die down between them. After a few seconds he said, "Now that's better, Young Kernick. A much better sense of flow. And yet, on point. I am acting like a goddamn, shit-licking, fuck face. I'll try to be more aware of that. For your assistance last evening, I should be grateful."

Kenny felt overcome by another burst of nausea. He buckled his legs and sat on the cold rocks.

"If it's any consolation to you, Bent," the boy said, placing his butt into a depression on the boulder beneath him, "I don't remember much about last night. How did you finally get out of the river?"

Kidd let out a chuckle. "The question you should be asking, Young Kernick, is how did *you* get out of the river?"

"How did I get *in* the river?" Kenny asked, suddenly aware of why all his clothes were damp.

"You fell in," Kidd said. "Trying to help me. At first I thought you might enjoy it, then you started screaming, mostly about your glasses." Kidd threw his hands to his face and mocked Kenny in an insulting 'fraidy voice. "'Oh, no, where are my glasses?! I'm going to lose my glasses!'" Kidd shook his head with disdain. "You sounded worse than a five-year-old who can't find his blanket. But it attracted the attention of those runners, so I guess it worked. They pulled us out."

"And we were all right?" Kenny asked.

"We were ay-okay," Kidd said. "A little hurt of pride, and very wet, but we made it back to the Cadillac fine."

"And then you drove us to this place?" Kenny asked.

Kidd let out another chuckle. "Hell, no, Kenny, I didn't drive us here. You did."

Despite his pained body and sense of nausea, Kenny lunged up from his rocky seat. "I drove us here?"

"You sure did," Kidd said.

"Was I drunk?" Kenny asked, his tone turning frantic.

"Completely," Kidd said. "You couldn't walk a straight line let alone drive one."

Kenny summoned all the strength he could muster to yell as loud as he could. "You let me drive drunk?! Are you fucking nuts?!"

"Relax," Kidd said, waving off Kenny's concern. "You handled it like a pro. You only swerved over the centerline three times, and you made every light and stop sign. Although, I think there's a newspaper box on Sheridan that's seen better days—we clobbered that son of a bitch. When you get back to the Caddy, you might want to check its grill for a copy of the *Tribune*. There were papers flying everywhere."

Kenny threw himself down on the rocks. The adrenaline of the moment was serving to soothe his pain and nausea, but he couldn't pry the image of driving while intoxicated from his head. "You are seriously going to get me killed one of these days," he said to Kidd.

"Not killed," Kidd said. "Maybe arrested, but not killed."

"Lovely," Kenny said. "You risked having me sent to jail just so I could take you here to the fullness of your life."

"That's *fulcrum*," Kidd snapped. "Get it together, Kenny. You're really not on your game this morning."

"Yeah, well, I'm hung-over." Kenny put a hand to his stomach. "I feel like somebody threw me into one of my father's pick-and-place machines." He bent forward to prepare for another dry heave, but nothing came. When he sat up, he asked, "What the hell is a fulcrum of one's life anyway?"

Kidd stuck his hands into his pant pockets and gazed out over the lake. His facial expression turned from playful to somber. "It's a hub, Kenny. Like on the wheel of a bicycle. Do you understand that?"

"I'm not really understanding anything right now," Kenny said, releasing a silent fart that somehow relieved his nausea. "Why don't you explain it so I can figure it out?"

Kidd flattened his eyebrows. He didn't look somber now—he looked pissed. He bit his lower lip then said, "It's a center point, Kenny, where all the events of your early life come together, and from where all the subsequent points emanate. Every life has a fulcrum, Young Kernick, so don't give me that snotty attitude you put off so well. In time your life will have one, too, at a location you will look back on with fondness. But my fulcrum has already been established, and it's right here." Kidd tapped his shoe twice. "Right under these rocks."

Kenny looked around at the rocks, and the cement retaining wall, and at the pieces of trash strewn about everywhere—crushed soda cups, beer-can boxes, twisted plastic grocery bags, and even a rusty shopping cart—and he asked, "Why here? This place looks like the neighborhood dump."

Kidd's face turned sour. He raised a hand, and for a moment Kenny thought the ex-president was going to club him for insulting the fulcrum. Instead, Kidd pointed across the lake.

"Over there," he said, "is Ohio, land of my youth. Down there a few blocks"—Kidd pointed south—"is Jesuit University, sight of my education. Back on Josten Avenue"—Kidd pointed a thumb behind them—"well, that's where Margaret grew up. And it's where many of her siblings still live. This is Rogers Park, Kenny—the Far North Side of Chicago. And this—" Kidd spread his hands out over the boulder wall. "This is Thayer Beach. What's left of it anyway. Thayer Beach is where it all came together for me, Kenny. Where the early parts of my life intersected, gathered strength, and set the path for what came after: marriage, and Annabelle, and the governorship of Ohio, and..." Kidd's voice trailed off. "Well, you know."

Yes, Kenny did know. Infamy was what came next for Charles Bentley Kidd, after an unremarkable six-year stint as chief executive of the United States. But Kidd was looking particularly sullen at the moment; Kenny saw no need to remind him of his lowly place in American history. Besides, the impeached president knew it well enough already—he had been living it since the day he was escorted off the White House grounds by the Secret Service. Things didn't get any lower than that. But Kenny had come to prefer a cheerful Kidd to a depressed one, so he changed the subject.

"This used to be a beach?" the boy asked.

"Oh, a thriving beach," Kidd said, taking Kenny's bait and recovering his spirits. "With lifeguards and recreational events, and people from all over the neighborhood coming here on hot days and cool nights. For a boy from the boondoggles of Ohio, it was an amazing sight to see. Even though I didn't grow up here, Thayer Beach became special for me, too. This is where Margaret used to bring me. In our first throes of intimacy."

Kenny felt his nausea return, and his mouth curled into a frown. "Please don't tell me you had sex on this beach."

"Sure did," Kidd stated proudly. "Like randy possums. And I'll tell you something else, Kenny—under these boulders, in these sands, I buried enough used rubbers to make a Goodyear blimp. But it was such a vibrant beach, nonetheless, even without all the sex. I can still smell the corndogs and funnel cakes. I don't know why they rocked it up."

"Maybe you contaminated it with all your sperm," Kenny said.

"Ha, ha," Kidd said. "Apparently, you're still well enough to bless me with your special brand of humor." Kidd gazed down along the length of boulders—it stretched for fifty yards from a beach at the north to a beach at the south, both adjacent beaches still in operation—and he let out a sigh. "Anyway, they usually have their reasons for closing down a place like this—erosion or the like. It was such a thin strip of beach, Kenny, much more narrow than the others, which provided good cover for lovers. But sometimes in the winter, the waves would crash up so high that in the morning, you'd see all the cars here coated over in six inches of ice. Hell, even I got coated in six inches of ice one night going down on Margaret right near that retaining wall. She had to take me to Rosehill Memorial for hypothermia. But I got her off, Kenny. I always got her off." Kidd let out another sigh, deeper this time. "Maybe that was my problem."

Kenny scrunched his face. In a matter of seconds, he and Kidd had gone from discussing beach closures to talking about orgasmic cunnilingus. Kenny was completely confused now, especially at Kidd's lament over repeatedly satisfying a woman he would eventually marry.

"Help me out with something, Bent," Kenny said. "Aren't you the one who always says that bringing pleasure to a woman is a good thing?"

"Of course," Kidd said. "Don't get me wrong, Kenny. I'm the female orgasm's biggest fan. I have no respect for a man who doesn't give a girl her gumdrops. But in certain circumstances, I think such effort creates a false sense of security—that your partner might think you're more into her than you really are."

"Is that the way you felt with The Rhino?" Kenny asked.

"I don't know, Kenny," Kidd said dejectedly. "I never really had a good grasp on how I felt about Margaret; I just went along for the ride. Then, before I blinked my eyes, the ride was over, and I was married to her. It was all so surreal at the time. And once our vows were exchanged, she turned into a different person almost immediately—demanding, nagging, intolerant of error. For two weeks after our wedding, I felt as if someone had hit me upside the head with a shovel."

"You mean during your honeymoon?" Kenny asked.

"Honeymoon," Kidd said, snickering. "It was more like an indoctrination, Kenny. The Rhinofication of Charles Bentley Kidd. It's taken me decades to recover. But during my immersion in the Chicago River last night, something became very clear to me. And it's this—"

Kidd lifted his left hand and with his right hand pulled the wedding ring off its finger. The ring's thin circumference tore loose from the flesh around his knuckle and left behind a harsh white streak of sun-starved skin, indicating to Kenny that the ring had not been removed for some time. Kidd inspected the gold band for a moment, as if he were contemplating swallowing it, then he reared back and flung it into the cresting waters of Lake Michigan. The material symbol of Charles Bentley Kidd's marriage to Margaret Huff landed with a splash, but it was a splash that made no ripples.

"She may be my wife on paper, Kenny," Kidd said, focusing his eyes on the spot where the ring had landed, "and she may someday decide to use my name again, but she's gone. Our life together is over. I think I knew that the day she left the White House, but it didn't truly hit me until last night—how much she's moved past me. Thirty-one years come to an end, and all that's left is animosity, acrimony and acidity."

And Annabelle, Kenny wanted to say. Maybe. Kidd hadn't spoken to his daughter for so long that it was hard to gauge what her reaction would be to his arrival in Los Angeles.

"Goodbye, Margaret," Kidd spoke to the water. "I did not turn out to be a very good husband to you. Maybe someday I'll understand why."

Kidd stuck his hands into his pockets, turned from the wind, and climbed down the boulder wall. Kenny remained seated for a few seconds, preparing himself for the twin bursts of pain and nausea that were sure to accompany his standing upright. He gnashed his teeth and pushed to his feet. His muscles and stomach were still not his friends, so with tentative steps, Kenny climbed down the boulders. He met the former president back at the Cadillac. Kidd had clasped his hands over the roof and was looking back at Lake Michigan.

"You know, Kenny," Kidd said as the boy approached, "another one of my old Secret Service agents, Gary Tyne, told me a story once that I hadn't remembered until now. He said he knew his marriage to his first wife was doomed when the classy restaurant where they had celebrated their engagement got turned into a strip club." Kidd nodded knowingly. "I'll tell you, if I had known that this beach got rocked over, I might have dumped Margaret right then."

Kenny raised an eyebrow. "I doubt that," he said.

"Oh, do you? Why's that, Einstein?"

"Two reasons. First, you loved being president, which you couldn't have done without her, because she gave you cachet."

"And second?" Kidd asked.

"You loved Annabelle," Kenny said. "And you never would have left her."

By the somber look that returned to Kidd's face, Kenny knew he had scored a direct hit. Kenny even saw tears pooling along the rims of Kidd's eyes. Kidd started to flash a contorted smile, then he wagged a finger at Kenny.

"I have to give it to you, Young Kernick. Sometimes that million-dollar mind of yours is right, and you're right. God, I love Annabelle. There's not a word or phrase accurate enough to express the affection a daddy feels for his little girl. When we get to L.A., if she'll still have me, I'll do what I need to do to build up her confidence in me again. I'll show her that from now on I'm going to be the best daddy that a daddy ever was." Kidd dabbed at his eyes with a knuckle. "I love this country, too, Kenny—I love everything about it, even the things that seem bad sometimes. I know people don't believe that, but I do. And I have to believe that America still loves me, that it will forgive me. Hell, it forgave Nixon."

"Nixon had the brains to resign," Kenny said.

Kidd let out a mocking chuckle. "Ha, ha, again, Kenny. You know, Tom Prudell said the same thing to me about three hundred times. He once yelled it at me while he was standing—standing!—on my desk in the Oval Office. But I wasn't going to resign for acting with the authority clearly designated to me by the Constitution. That would be backing down, and Charles Bentley Kidd never backs down. I'm tenacious, a bulldog. Woof!" Kidd actually barked. "And I'm not about to back down now. Somewhere out there, Kenny, is redemption. And I intend to find it. Are you with me?"

"I'm with you, Bent," Kenny said. And he was with him—there were no doubts about that. But Kenny still didn't feel well, even after a good dose of brisk morning air. He spread his lips and tapped at his incisors with an index finger, discovering yet another symptom of leftover drunkenness. "Only, would you mind if we started looking for your redemption later?"

"I guess not," Kidd said.

"That's good," Kenny said. He pulled open the backseat door. "Because I still can't feel my teeth."

Then he slid inside the Cadillac, threw his glasses onto the backseat, and collapsed on the Cadillac's floor, curling himself pleasantly into the fetal position.

By midday, after Kenny was fully sobered and his hangover had slunk away, Kidd ordered the boy to drive him downtown by way of the lake shore.

On the way, Kidd made three pronouncements that were to affect the future of their journey from that moment forward.

First, Kidd said, they would no longer engage in nighttime driving. He wanted to see this great land in its full daylight glory, see it come alive under the sun. He explained that driving at night had been a way for him to hide, from the populace, yes, but mostly from himself, and he didn't want to hide anymore. "Whenever the sun goes down," he told Kenny, "we are to stop in the nearest town, kick back, and grab some shuteye until the day breaks anew."

Which brought Kidd to his second pronouncement: There would be no more sleeping in the Cadillac.

"We've been slipping to the depths of vagrancy lately," Kidd said, "which does nothing to enhance our mentality or our appearances. We need to travel with class and dignity, and waking up in the same clothes as yesterday, with seam marks pressed into our faces from these stupid car seats is neither classy nor dignified."

Kidd then ran his fingers through his hair; they became tangled in river sludge and scalp grease.

"Speaking of appearances," Kidd said, making his third pronouncement, "we look like shit. The clothes you brought with you are fine—a bit on the home-catalog side, but wearable—but after my flight from Hawleyville, I have no clothes. We could both use a shampoo and a haircut as well. So turn here."

Kidd directed Kenny off the lake shore parkway at an exit for Michigan Avenue. When he asked Kenny if the boy was amenable to his proclamations, Kenny looked at him, nodded, then almost ran over a pedestrian in a crosswalk.

They ended up at a C.G. Cashman's department store on Huron, where Kidd picked out more clothes than Kenny could ever imagine. The former president bought ten pairs of dress socks and twelve pairs of boxer shorts, fifteen pairs of dress pants and a whole armload of open-collar broadcloth shirts from Cashman's signature Burwick line. To wear beneath the Burwicks, he purchased nine crewneck undershirts; to wear over them, one black, single-breasted wool trench, which he would jettison in Los Angeles in favor of a lighter-weight suede country coat that he also picked out. He bought two pairs of lace-up shoes—one black and one brown—and two matching belts in size forty-two. He also bought a set of candy-stripe pajamas so he could sleep in comfort. With no shopping carts in the store, Kidd piled his entire booty onto Kenny, then he put the whole wardrobe on his credit card to the tune of four thousand six hundred dollars, not including Chicago's stultifying sales tax. As he signed the receipt, he giggled. "Nothing like spending Margaret Huff's hard-earned cash in style." He told Kenny to take the bags out to the Cadillac and to meet him at the hair salon they had seen a few blocks back on Michigan.

When Kenny arrived at the hair salon, his arms hanging low from the weight of Kidd's seven shopping bags, he found the former president already sitting in the stylist's chair, reading a newspaper, as the stylist clipped and cut. For her part, the attractive young beautician snipping scissors around Kidd's head seemed neither to notice nor care that the man she was standing over was one Charles Bentley Kidd, until recently the most powerful man on the planet. And apparently to Kidd, the Chicago newspapers had neither noticed nor cared either.

"I can't believe this," Kidd said when he saw Kenny approach. He began to jerk the paper from one page to the next. "I get thrown out of Margaret Huff's posh fundraiser by the Secret Service, in front of every high-class snob in Chicago, including the mayor, and there's not one mention of it in the goddamn *Tribune*? Outrageous!"

"Steady, please," the stylist said to Kidd. With her scissors she indicated the next chair over. "You can sit there," she said to Kenny. "Constance will be with you presently."

As Kenny sat down and waited for the arrival of Constance, Kidd looked at him through the mirror and pointed to one of the pages. "They've even got a stupid article in here on Russell's latest catfight with his new treasury secretary. See, who needs a goddamn treasury secretary?" Without shifting his head, Kidd folded the paper in a crunch and threw it to the floor. "I'll tell you, Kenny," he said. "We have really got to start making the news more."

In retrospect, it would have been easy for Kenny to take that statement as Kidd's fourth pronouncement of the morning, an addendum to the other three. Delivered, as it was, so off-the-cuff, and clearly out of frustration by a man suffering from the pangs of obscurity, Kenny didn't think much about it at the time. But as the Cadillac approached, and then crossed, the Mississippi River, taking Kenny onto the other side of America, the boy would soon learn, at no small cost to himself, just how capable Charles Bentley Kidd could be when it came to getting what he wanted.

CHAPTER 18

★ ★

For Kenny and Kidd, the crossing onto the other side of America came at twilight on Saturday night, after more than three hours of driving through a blinding rainstorm on the Illinois plain.

In accordance with Kidd's first proclamation that morning, it was time to call it a day. Just over the Mississippi River, Kidd ordered the Cadillac off the highway at a place called LeClaire, the first town in Iowa along the river. After driving a short distance up Route 67, they found a Happy Traveler Inn, at which they could act upon Kidd's second proclamation—to sleep in real beds.

"We'll lodge here this evening and retire in comfort," Kidd said, pointing to the two-story hotel which sat atop a bluff overlooking the Mississippi. "But not before we have a grand dinner. We've crossed the Mighty Miss, Young Kernick. The East is behind us. The West lies ahead. That calls for celebration."

With few cars in the Happy Traveler's parking lot, it only took Kidd five minutes to secure a room. Once they had settled into their accommodations, Kidd dressed in a pale-blue Burwick shirt and black slacks, while Kenny climbed out of his wine-splotched clothing and put on a fresh ensemble from his duffel bag. Reordered and aligned, they were back in the vehicle within the hour, heading up Route 67 for signs of the town. The river lay to the right, just off the road, but in the darkness of the evening, it was not visible. Kenny could only discern its presence by the sight of street and house lights on its far side, in Illinois, where they seemed to rise up from an expansive black swath.

A few moments later, thoughts of the river gave way to thoughts of the town as Kenny saw a sign that announced, "Welcome to LeClaire. Birthplace of Buffalo Bill."

"I'll be damned," Kidd said, adjusting the lapel of his wool trenchcoat. "I didn't know Buffalo Bill came from Iowa."

"Where did you think he came from?" Kenny asked.

Kidd evened out the lapels and admired his handiwork in the Cadillac's visor mirror. "I thought he came from Buffalo."

But as the Cadillac traveled deeper into LeClaire, it became apparent to Kenny that this small town on the Mississippi was the perfect birthplace for America's most famous cowboy. The town still looked like an Old West haven. From out of nowhere, on both sides of the main street, two rows of western-style architecture formed the basis of LeClaire's downtown. What years ago may have been stores for telegram services, dry-goods shops or gambling halls now housed antiques dealers, insurance agencies and, more important, restaurants.

They parked down by the river, in a dirt lot that serviced the Buffalo Bill Museum. Next to the museum sat a small town esplanade that was dotted with benches and trees. Kenny and Kidd surveyed the esplanade for a moment—long and narrow, it was illuminated in the night like a ball field—then they walked back to the main road and discovered a restaurant called Tawdry Tom's toward the end of a row of stores. The restaurant was part of a three-story brick building that looked more like a former brothel than anyplace fit for dining. But Kidd was drawn to it, partly because it had a big, illuminated American flag on its façade, but mostly because it claimed to be the "Home of the Cowboy Steak." When Kenny asked what the fuck a cowboy steak was, Kidd said, "To me, Kenny, it's fucking dinner."

They were seated in a dining room comprised of picnic tables and wagon-wheel chandeliers. Kidd and Kenny both ordered the Cowboy Steak—a one-inch thick, twenty-eight-ounce Porterhouse that filled a whole plate. The steaks came with cowboy beans, Texas toast, and a salad which patrons drew from the clawfoot bathtub out near the bar. Kenny was ravenous. Given the circumstances of the past twenty-four hours, he had not eaten since he and Kidd stopped at a White Castle just north of Indianapolis at three o'clock the previous day. When the steak arrived, Kenny devoured his with a surgeon's precision, gleaning every fleck of meat from the length of bone, then he agreed to split another one with Kidd. By the time they had finished eating, Kidd and Kenny had each devoured over forty ounces of steak. Kenny's stomach felt as if it were filled with uranium. He doubted he could move. But he was still disappointed when the waitress told him that at Tawdry Tom's, they didn't serve dessert. "There's an Ice Cream Igloo down the street," she said.

But Kenny's desire for dessert was quickly diminished when, upon leaving Tawdry Tom's, he once again fell victim to Kidd's penchant for diversion. As they were walking to the Ice Cream Igloo, Kidd said, "Hold up, Young Kernick. I want to go down to the river." Kidd turned sharply and started to trot along a connector street, back toward the Cadillac, not even waiting for Kenny. He soon disappeared.

Kenny walked back to the Cadillac, which by now was nestled in the parking lot among thirty or so other vehicles, and looked around for Kidd. None of the bright lighting from the town esplanade or in the parking lot helped Kenny find his travel mate. The ex-president had vanished. With Kidd missing, Kenny wanted to sit down on a bench and let his meal settle. He strode onto the esplanade, his feet scuffing along flattened, spotty grass. On the far side of the river, the Illinois town glowed brightly. Kenny took his own diversion and walked toward the lights of the town across the river, but before he knew it, he had to stop. That's when he gasped. Kenny hadn't realized just how close to the river he was. Looking down, he saw the Mississippi right in front of him, only five feet away, silent in its demeanor. The expansive black swath he had seen earlier now spread out before him like a blanket. A long line of retaining rocks was the only denotation that the land had ended and the Mississippi had begun.

From farther down the esplanade, Kidd's voice rifled through the night. "Kenny, come here!" Kenny bet they could hear the former president all the way to Illinois.

Kenny walked downriver, into the area of the esplanade where the benches and trees traded off at intervals. The lighting here was particularly bright, stoked by multiple flood lamps in the esplanade and streetlights from the main road. Regardless, Kidd was still nowhere to be seen.

"Over here, Kenny!" Kidd's voice still rifled, but the former president now sounded as if he were struggling for breath. Kenny was about to ask Kidd exactly where he was when the boy stopped again. In front of him, lying in the flattened grass of the esplanade, he saw Kidd's wool trenchcoat and Burwick shirt. They were followed in succession by his white undershirt, black shoes, socks, belt, slacks and finally, his boxer shorts, all arranged in a curved path that led right to the water's edge.

"Oh, Jesus," Kenny said, following the path of discarded clothing to its logical conclusion—

Sure enough, there he was, churning in the calm, dark swath—the former most powerful man in the world had decided to skinny dip in the Mississippi River. All Kenny could see of him was a head bobbing up and down as Kidd struggled to tread water in the slow-moving current.

"What is it with you and rivers?" Kenny asked.

"I find them redemptive," Kidd said in a decidedly carefree tone. "But if I'm going to take a dip in one, I do it of my own accord. That's a man who controls his destiny."

"I see," Kenny replied, really thinking that if Kidd moved in the wrong direction, the boy would see way too much. Kenny reached down, picked up Kidd's slacks and held them out to him. "Can we go, though? I'd really like some ice cream."

Kidd swam a few yards upriver, his bare ass surfacing, giving Kenny an unwanted look at the former president's milky-white butt cheeks. Kidd sucked in some water and spit it out, as if he were a cherub fountain, then he said, "Seriously, Kenny, we're going to have to give you a lesson in seizing opportunities when they arise. You're very lax in that."

Kenny picked up Kidd's Burwick shirt and the undershirt, then he moved toward the shoes; he was purposely avoiding any contact with Kidd's boxers. "Well, maybe if you had spurned a few opportunities yourself," Kenny said as he stepped gingerly among Kidd's clothing, "you'd still be the president of this nation you claim to love so much."

"Now see, Kenny," Kidd replied tartly, "a derisive comment like that doesn't even bother me right now. And do you know why? Because I'm swimming in the Mississippi River, Kenny. Buck naked. Wait, I'm going to dunk." Kidd plunged beneath the water's surface and soaked his entire head. He shot up with his hair matted back and let out a spraying burst of breath, like a whale. "And I'm cleansed."

"You're missing a sock," Kenny said, plucking the only one he could find off the grass.

Kidd swam back to the shore. He floated ass-up while holding onto the retaining rocks that lined the river, giving Kenny an entire backside profile of the man who used to run the country. Kenny also found the missing sock. It was still tightly wrapped on Kidd's right foot.

"I think you need to join me," Kidd said.

Kenny looked at Kidd with crossed eyes. "With all due respect, Bent, I am not getting in there."

"It's refreshing," Kidd said, his syrupy voice fermenting temptation.

"It's crazy," Kenny shot back. "That water's got to be forty degrees. You'll catch hypothermia."

"I've survived it before," Kidd said, reminding Kenny of the man's hypothermic experience while going down on Margaret Huff at Thayer Beach years ago. "Now strip down and wade in here, Young Kernick. You'll be transformed."

Kenny shook his head: There was simply no winning with this man. The boy looked around at the bright parking lot full of vehicles, and at the busy main road behind him, and at the broad emptiness of this town esplanade, and he felt a chill go through him that was degrees colder than any temperature outside. How could he possibly do what Kidd was asking of him?

But then something sparked in Kenny—an arc of delicious electricity, initiated by the twin pulses of adventure and change, that encouraged him to fight off the chill, and the doubts, and to do what Kidd told him. Kenny followed the arc's course. He took off his coat and pulled his Oxford shirt over his head in one unbuttoned piece. He kicked off his shoes and danced on one leg, then the other, as he removed his socks. He unzipped his fly and undid his belt and pulled his khaki pants down to the grass. His heart skipped when he heard a vehicle fly by on the main road behind him, but the vehicle was soon gone. Then he stood there, under the intense glow of flood lamps, clad only in his underwear. He was nervous, but he had undressed, and it was a gargantuan leap for him to have done so. He looked down at Kidd for a modicum of praise in acknowledgment of such an action. Instead, all Kidd said was, "Tighty-whities?"

Kenny shrugged.

Kidd shook his head. "Whatever. Get 'em off and get in here."

That's when Kenny froze, and not from the outside temperature. He couldn't take the last step to drop his skivvies to the grass. His hands felt like magnets stuck to his thighs; his heart raced like the Cadillac on a rain-free Illinois flat. But he had to do it—he knew he had to execute this final action to ride the arc to its end. He said to Kidd, "Turn around."

"Do what?" Kidd asked.

"I can't get in unless you turn around." Kenny made flapping motions with his arm. "Go swim or something."

But Kenny knew that Kidd smelled blood—its form was the scent of inadequacy that Kenny put off so well and so often. Kidd wouldn't turn around now, of that Kenny was certain. The boy had just thrown chum to the shark. To protect himself against that shark, Kenny crossed his hands in front of his privates.

"What's the big deal?" Kidd asked. "Haven't you been in a locker room before?"

"Of course I've been in a locker room," Kenny said. "I'm not a total nerd."

Kidd raised an eyebrow mockingly, as if to doubt Kenny's opinion of himself, then he seemed to glow with understanding. "Let me guess. In gym class, you were always the one who never took a shower with the others. Even if you were soaked with sweat."

Kenny looked down at the grass. Kidd was right. Kenny had never dared to disrobe in front of the other boys. The bigger boys.

"It's all right," Kidd said, almost fatherly. "Believe it or not, I've been there myself. Take my Lil' Kidd—"

"Your what?" Kenny asked.

"My Lil' Kidd," said Kidd. He was still floating ass-up in the river.

Kenny shook his head again. "Don't tell me you gave your penis a name."

"First of all," Kidd said, "it's not a penis. It's a dick, or a johnson, or a unit. A schlong, a wand, a meat puppet. Anything but a penis. Christ, listening to you talk, Kenny, is like reading the dictionary—you always use big, proper terms for the most banal of things. Like the Cadillac. It's not a *vehicle*, Kenny; you always call it a *vehicle*. Fuck that. It's a car. A car, Kenny. Understand? C-A-R. And my Lil' Kidd isn't a penis—it's a pecker, a rapier, a dazzling diddler of disproportionate delight. Follow me?"

Kenny nodded.

"Secondly, yes, I gave it a name. Out of respect. You're never going to be a man in this world until you learn to respect and value your dick. Otherwise, you'll spend way too much time worrying about it like you're doing here, wasting my night with needless anxiety while this water starts to get cold." Kidd let out a shiver. The motion of his body caused ripples in the flat Mississippi current.

"But I'm really small," Kenny said. "Laughably small."

"Says who? Your schoolmates?" Kidd asked. "Trust me, Kenny, teenage boys are usually idiots. And no, spending all this time with you hasn't changed my opinion on that matter."

"But they had very large dicks, Bent," Kenny said. "Some of them, at least. I didn't compare to that. And they let me know it. They called me Vienna Sausage Kenny and Caterpillar Kernick. It was humiliating."

Kenny noticed another glow of understanding in Kidd's eyes. "And is that why you've shied away from girls during your most virile years?" he asked.

Kenny didn't need to answer. Once again, the truth was obvious. Part of his aversion to girls lay in his lack of physical height, coming in at a paltry five-four, but most of it lay in his perceived lack of manhood. He didn't want to get laughed at by a girl, ever, especially by one he liked. And how could he ever measure up to where that girl had gone before him, when she had probably engaged in coitus with a boy hung like a summer squash?

Kidd let out a sigh. "Well, we're just going to have to settle this issue once and for all. No need to sit in your own stink, as the shrinks like to say. Let's discover the truth."

"And your qualifications are?" Kenny asked, doubtful of Kidd's credentials. Ask the man about the vaginas of the world and he would be a goddamned genius, but penises were a different animal.

"Listen, Kenny. In the course of my life, I've been with enough women who've been with enough men to know how I rank on the size scale."

"And that is?"

"Not germane to our discussion. The point is, I'll know how you rank, too. So drop 'em."

"Drop 'em?"

"Right the fuck now."

Kenny let out a long stream of breath which condensed in the crisp air. With a knot in his belly, he thumbed the elastic waistband of his white Fruit of the Looms, then he jiggled them to the grass. Standing there naked, the mousy boy felt as if a roaring lion would charge down from the other bank of the Mississippi, leap the river in a single bound, and snatch him away between sharp, lusty fangs.

Kidd just lay there ass-up in the river, cocking his head from side to side as he prepared to pronounce what could only be mocking judgment on Kenny's privates.

"Well, it is a bit undersized in its flaccid state," Kidd said. "But it's cold out here, and you're nervous, so we can't really put much stock in that."

"That's pretty much how it looks all the time."

"Huh. But that's not as big as it gets. You do get bigger than that."

"It gets bigger."

"How much?"

"Not that big." Kenny held out a length between his index fingers to indicate the size.

"Really?" Kidd said, a bit stunned by Kenny's revelation. As Kenny feared, Kidd let out a laugh. Kenny was about to reach down for his Fruit of the Looms and yank them back up when Kidd said, "My dear Young Kernick, I don't know what you're worried about. You, my friend, are what is technically known as a 'Grower, Not a Shower.'"

"A what?" Kenny asked.

Kidd explained. "Some guys have large flaccid dicks that don't get much bigger when they get hard—that's a 'Shower.' But you have a small dick that expands—you're a 'Grower.' It's a common affliction among various populations of the Irish, of which I know you to be half. But your erect size is more than fine, Kenny. In fact, it's excellent."

"You think I'm big?" Kenny asked.

"Well, I don't think you could get work in an Amsterdam sex show, if that's what you're asking. Let me tell you, Kenny, some guys are naturally large in both states, and we call them freaks. But for pleasuring the scrumptious humptious, I think you'll more than do the trick. In fact, I think you'll be somewhat in demand on the humpty-bumpty circuit. I doubt any woman has ever seen something that meager blow up that big. You'll be a rock star."

Kenny felt the knot in his gut slip through, as if its tightness had all been part of an illusion in a magic trick. "Then I'm good," Kenny said.

"You're fine."

"Nothing to worry about?"

"I don't think so, Kenny."

"Son of a bitch," Kenny said. "That's eight years of anxiety for nothing. I guess there's only one thing left to do, then."

Kenny stepped back, poised himself, and ran full speed toward the river. He jumped over Kidd and plunged into the chilly Mississippi, his body exploding with an icy mask that made his flaccid penis retreat even more. But Kenny didn't care. He had wasted enough time with such a trivial line of concern. Right now, he wanted to swim. And feel transformed. Just as Charles Bentley Kidd promised he would.

CHAPTER 19

★ ★

Carl Kernick had driven halfway across Pennsylvania when he reached for the fresh pack of Parliaments he had placed in his coat pocket, only to find them missing.

"Dummkopf!" he shouted to the ceiling of his wife's moon-gray Ford Taurus station wagon. He realized instantly where he had actually placed the pack—in a trash receptacle at the Wawa in Bloomsburg. Right after he had paid for gas and the cigarettes with his credit card, removed the Parliaments' outer plastic wrapper, lifted the top foil, and stuck one of the heavenly sticks into his mouth to light it up.

"You can't smoke in here," the clerk had scolded him, as he held out a receipt for the gas and Parliaments.

Carl grunted something mildly crass, then he shifted the pack of cigarettes to his left hand, which was holding the removed plastic wrapper, so he could collect the receipt with his right. Upon cramming the receipt into a pant pocket, he turned and left the store, depositing the crumpled wrapper (along with his new pack of Parliaments) into the trash bin. On top of the rage which had been burning in him for four straight days, Carl now found himself infuriated. He could envision the tattoo-laden counter clerk spying Carl's miscue, walking over to the trash receptacle, fishing out the pack, and enjoying them on Carl's dime.

"Dummkopf, dummkopf, you're such a dummkopf!" Carl shouted, hitting himself on the thigh for punctuation.

But the thing that disturbed Carl the most wasn't the loss of his smokes, or having to stop to buy more—it was the fact that he had thrown them away so mindlessly. What could lead a brilliant man who always operated at the peak of his mental faculties to abandon those faculties so easily? The answer, for Carl, was plain: When he went to throw away the wrapper, he had been thinking of something else—the exact method by which he was going to kill his only child.

The possibilities are endless and real, he had thought, just before the wrapper and the smokes went into the trash. He was still thinking that way a hundred miles later.

Poisoning is always good, he conceived now.

Or stabbing. Or maybe drowning in a shallow puddle, just for irony.

Strangulation by a garrote of chicken wire. Electrocution via light socket. They were both strong options.

In the place of a Parliament to soothe his nerves, Carl started to chew on his fingernails. It was something he hadn't done in forty years, ever since the memorable afternoon when his mother had slapped him violently across the mouth for it. She had warned me not to do it, Carl remembered, but it was her abuse that convinced me.

Now it was Carl Kernick's turn to abuse his child in an effort to make a statement, but this time the abuse would be taken to the point of death. The big question was how? What was the best way? Which method would bring Carl mollifying satisfaction?

Carl's mind briefly went void of ideas, but he didn't worry. Judging from the mileage markers, he had another hour of god-forsaken Pennsylvania left in front of him, and beyond that, Ohio, Indiana, Illinois, Iowa... who knew where Kenny would be when Carl finally caught the boy. He was certain that in the distance between him and his thieving son, he could think of more ideas for expelling Kenny from an earthly existence. So many more.

The possibilities were endless and real. And they were scintillating.

Looking back, Carl Kernick should have known something was amiss in his world the moment he woke up on Wednesday morning. The harbinger of ill winds was Martha—she was still in bed. In the twenty-five years that Carl Kernick had been married to the former Martha McCann, his wife had arisen dutifully before him every weekday to make sure he had an overcooked breakfast waiting for him when he descended the staircase.

But on Wednesday, she snored well past her usual time. When he nudged her with the words "You're still here?" she only growled at him and rolled over to the far edge of the mattress.

It was the wrong side of the bed, Carl guessed.

He got up, showered and shaved anyway, thinking as he performed each function of any potential flaws with the seven automation prototypes currently under testing at Kernick Handling Systems. Coming out of the master bathroom with a towel around his waist, Carl also thought that Martha needed to get up. Before he could roust her, he saw that she was gone. She had even made the bed, though sloppily. He heard a clatter downstairs—the scrape and clang of a frying pan being slid out from a cluster of cookware. That's more like it, he told himself. Everything was rightly tuned, after all.

Soon, however, he heard Martha swear, followed by the sound of the frying pan hitting the floor. She must have dropped it, he had assumed. Upon reflection from halfway across Pennsylvania, though, the frying pan had sounded more flung than dropped.

Carl dressed in crisp, pleated slacks and a pale yellow Oxford. With his shirt properly tucked at the sides of his stocky body, he left the master bedroom to head downstairs. Along his route, he glanced at Kenny's bedroom door and noticed it was ajar. That slight crack between frame and door should have been another warning sign, Carl thought now, but at the time he only deduced that maybe Kenny had gotten up to use the bathroom in the night, probably to vomit. His son had not looked well the evening before, after Carl told him, with the certainty of the immutable laws of physics, that Kenny would be attending Yale University come January.

Let the boy heave his guts out, Carl thought on the way down the stairs. Yale was for his own good. In twenty years, when Kenny was successful like his father, the son would thank him. Finally.

Breakfast that morning was a quiet affair—rubber eggs, burnt toast, carbonized coffee, and something compressed and fibrous that resembled corned beef hash. Not the most delicious meal, but at least he didn't have to make it himself. Martha kept her eyes off Carl the whole time, said nothing, and occupied herself with cleaning dishes. Carl thought about making conversation with her, but he let the moment pass. Whatever was eating at his wife was her problem; she would get over it. Right now, he just wanted a smoke.

Sitting there as his morning Parliament woke him up, he began to feel properly aligned. He took a long drag off his cigarette and smiled. It was going to be a grand day. And lucrative. The boys from Lil' Mary Foods were in town and Carl was planning to blow them away with his proposal: a revolutionary drum conditioning unit, patent pending. Just wait until they got a load of this thing. They would be begging him to take their money. Yes, he thought, as he snuffed out the Parliament on his breakfast plate, stood from the table, and punched in the code to turn off the house security system, it was going to be a great day.

But his outlook turned sour when he went to grab the keys to the Cadillac. They weren't there.

"Martha, where are my keys?" he heard himself ask. It was an inopportune question. Martha turned from her position at the sink, stared at him tartly, and asked how she should know, since he never let her drive the Cadillac in the first place. "You make me drive that stupid Taurus," she said. "I hate that Taurus. You get to drive a big, expensive automobile, and I get a dull, stupid station wagon!" Then she turned her back on him and scrubbed the frying pan.

At that exact moment, Carl Kernick should have realized the world had shifted. In all his years with Martha, she had never talked back to him. She had always, in fact, been the perfect wife—quiet, supportive, obedient. Why then, on that day, had she decided to engage in backtalk? Why had she gotten up late? Why had she uttered curse words when she dropped the frying pan?

"Why don't you check for them in your big Cadillac?" Martha said as she worked a sponge against the frying pan.

"Why would I do that?"

"Maybe you left them in the ignition."

"I never leave anything in the ignition."

But Martha wouldn't budge. "Carl," she stated bluntly. "For the love of Christ, try thinking you're fallible for a change. God knows I know you are." Then she threw the soapy frying pan into the sink, slammed off the water, and walked out of the kitchen in a huff.

My Lord, Carl thought as he watched her go, Martha hadn't just woken up on the wrong side of the bed; she got up on the wrong side of the continent.

"I'll check the vehicle then!" Carl yelled after her.

"You go, big boy!" she yelled from another room.

He picked up his briefcase, then he headed through the mud room door to check his Cadillac for keys.

Only there weren't any keys in the Cadillac. There wasn't even a Cadillac.

Carl's overriding memory of that exact moment was the sound of his briefcase hitting the driveway—a dull thump which held implications far more severe than the soft tone emitted. With mouth agape, Carl did what any normal person would do when he found his prized vehicle missing from its typical spot: He ran to the end of the driveway and scanned up and down the street for it. Maybe he had left it somewhere else; maybe it had slipped into neutral, blown its parking brake and rolled down the lane. Maybe, but no. The Cadillac was gone.

Unfortunately, Carl did see other things, and those other things told him what had happened to his glorious Caddy.

Exhibit A: The guard shack on Charles Bonehead Kidd's lawn had been flipped on its side, as if rammed by a vehicle at uncontrolled speed. Angle of impact and resting place of splintered shack indicated the offending vehicle had come from Carl's driveway.

Exhibit B: As he turned his gaze from Kidd's lawn back to his own driveway, he was struck by the odd sight of a fire-escape ladder dangling from the open window to Kenny's bedroom.

To Carl, A plus B equaled C. In this equation, C stood for Kenny. The little bastard had stolen his car.

First, Carl hyperventilated, but not at the realization that his son had absconded with the Cadillac. No, his anxiety was being stirred by the sight of that ladder hanging from Kenny's bedroom window. All the neighbors could see it. Most of them probably had seen it. What must they be thinking?

That thought made him gasp. He charged into the house, passed Martha in the living room, and bolted up the stairs.

"Carl?" he heard Martha call after him. "Carl, what's the matter?"

But Carl ignored her. He leapt the stairs three at a time and burst through the cracked door to Kenny's room. He found the bed empty and the dresser drawers in shambles. He tripped over a stack of books on Kenny's floor, banged a knee on the desk, and lunged for the ladder's hooks. He managed to pull up the ladder in seven strokes and shut the window in one. His heart calmed with the closing, as if the window's triple-paned glass would keep out the hushed whispers of the neighborhood.

"Carl, is something wrong?" Martha's voice came from the bottom of the stairs. "Is Kenny all right? Is something on fire? Do you want me to call 911?"

"Ummmm—" Carl said, hesitating.

Think quickly, you dummkopf! Quickly, quickly!

He did think quickly. 911 was out of the question. The police would show up, create a big scene when getting out of their vehicles, then linger, making an already mortifying situation even worse. The neighbors would know something was wrong. If that happened, Carl would find himself so utterly embarrassed that he might even have to move—to Guatemala.

"No," Carl shouted to Martha. "Not necessary."

"Well, the Secret Service is across the street. I could go get them if you need help."

"Not necessary!" Carl shouted again, and harshly this time.

"Suit yourself, then," his wife said. "I'm staying out of it."

Oh, but woman, he thought, you can't possibly stay out of this. So Carl went downstairs to the living room and stood in front of Martha, who was reclining on the couch with a magazine. He told his wife that at some point during the night, her son had climbed out of his bedroom window and pilfered the Cadillac. That the boy was missing. That he was probably lying dead in a ditch somewhere because the little dummkopf had tried to drive that powerful vehicle without a license. Nay, without ever having taken driver's education, if Carl might add. But to Carl's horror, Martha didn't panic. Instead, she giggled.

"Oh, Carl, I doubt he's dead," she said. "The police would have shown up here already." Then Martha lengthened her face and her expression turned droll and mocking. "You did tell him he had to go to Yale, Carl. Maybe he took your Cadillac and went up there early. Just to make his daddy proud." With that, she returned her gaze to the magazine, as though she would not give Kenny's whereabouts another thought.

That was four days ago, and Kenny still hadn't returned. In the meantime, Carl had decided to take matters into his own hands.

Maybe he would asphyxiate Kenny with a trash bag.

Maybe a public stoning was in order.

Whatever method Carl Kernick ended up choosing, he would make it count.

In the days following Kenny's disappearance, Martha Kernick remained seemingly unfazed by the questions surrounding her son's well-being. She would go about her business as if nothing had happened, as if Kenny were still at home. She seemed sad during those days, but Carl could tell that her sadness had nothing to do with her missing child.

Carl had a different reaction—several, actually. None felt pleasant.

His first reaction was shock. After canceling his meeting with Lil' Mary Foods on Wednesday morning, he sulked around the house. He could not fathom, simply could not understand, how his son could have driven off with his Cadillac. Carl's life had always run most efficiently on known quantities. Everything had to be in its proper place, and that place had to be predetermined by Carl Kernick. Now Kenny was not in his proper place, and the realization stunned Carl, vitrifying his emotions like grains of sand melted to glass by a lightning strike.

After a morning of shock, Carl decided to bring the element of known quantities back to his situation. To accomplish that task, he would call upon Jasper Thomas.

One of the many standard features on his Cadillac XTS was its anti-theft device, the GeoStar Tracker 1200, which Carl at first had been exuberant over until the salesman told him it required a monthly subscription fee. During the trial period, Carl wanted to make sure the thing actually worked, if he was going to be shelling out his hard-earned cash every month.

Two weeks after he purchased the Cadillac, he parked in a vacant lot in the middle of Stamford and hit the GeoStar call button in his ceiling control panel. "If your product is so great," he asked the voice on the other end of the line, "where is my Cadillac right now?" The young representative, who said his name was J.T., short for Jasper Thomas, clicked a few keys on his keyboard and proclaimed confidently, "It's at Four Thousand Vandermeer Road in Stamford, Connecticut. Next to the QuikLube."

Carl was satisfied. He bought the service and hadn't contacted GeoStar since.

But on Wednesday afternoon, with stealth on his mind, he locked himself into his home office, dialed GeoStar's customer care number, and requested J.T. directly. Then Carl elected to do something he rarely did: He decided to trust a stranger.

He told J.T. that his son had stolen the Cadillac and that J.T. needed to find the boy fast. No, the police didn't need to be called. Yes, the boy was probably fine. Carl didn't want J.T. to do anything that might give Kenny the knowledge that his father was on to him—no initiating a conversation with Kenny through the on-board speaker; no disabling the ignition remotely. All Carl wanted was to know where Kenny was.

"Right on. Not a problem," J.T. said.

Over the phone line, Carl could hear the clack of computer keys. In a few seconds, J.T. said, "Your vehicle is on I-80 in Pennsylvania, currently in Bloomsburg, heading west at sixty-three miles per hour."

"That little dummkopf is in Pennsylvania?" Carl said.

"Pennsylvania," J.T. said. "Going sixty-three miles per hour."

That made no sense to Carl. Why would Kenny need to go to Pennsylvania? Carl stifled his confusion just long enough to thank J.T. with a promise that he would be calling again. "Right on," J.T. replied. "Not a problem."

It wasn't a problem. Over Thursday and Friday, as Carl's emotions ebbed and flowed, Carl would call J.T. hourly during the business day, as he sat behind his desk in the corner office at Kernick Handling Systems and got nothing done.

"He's in Hawleyville, Ohio," J.T. told him on Thursday afternoon.

"He's in Cincinnati now," J.T. said to him on Friday morning. "Wow, this kid gets around."

By Friday afternoon, as Carl's business suffered and his underlings at the company began to whisper openly that something was just not right with Mr. Kernick, two things became painfully clear to Kenny's father: first, that Kenny, who was consistently moving west, would not be coming home anytime soon; and second, that he was, by virtue of his stop in Hawleyville, Ohio, traveling with one Sucky Chucky Kidd. Carl had suspected as much over the past two days but had possessed no proof. It was evident to everyone in the neighborhood that Kidd had pulled up stakes—the lack of Secret Servicemen and a fallen guard shack betrayed as much—but where he had run to was still a mystery. Now Carl knew.

The simultaneous realization that Kenny wouldn't be coming home and that his boy was keeping company with Charles Bentley Kidd was the moment Carl Kernick's rage exploded. It was only made worse later that day when J.T. began calling Carl's office without prompting, telling Carl news of his son's whereabouts like a sports announcer broadcasting a horse race.

"He just turned onto 74 heading toward Indiana... He's at a White Castle outside Indianapolis... He's on 65 North and going strong. My bet is he's on his way to Chi-ca-goooooooo!"

That night, while Martha just smiled at the news of Kenny's run and kept herself sequestered in the living room with a magazine in her lap, Carl paced the hardwood floors of Two Hoban Lane. He was so angry at Kenny that he could no longer eat or sleep. How could the boy do this to his father after all Carl had done for him? How could he trample on a lifetime of Carl's generosity? How could he run off with that scoundrel across the street, the worst president ever, who had almost single-handedly brought the country to its knees? How, how, how?!

Finally, at a few minutes before four in the morning on Saturday, an exhausted Carl sank into the living room's Victorian high-back. His mind in a tailspin, his successful business on hold until who knew when, Carl decided it was time to stop sniveling and find a resolution to this dilemma. He tried to think of past confrontations, of other times when he had felt as out-of-control, vulnerable and helpless as he did now, and how he had dealt with them.

He remembered a situation from years before, when he was first starting up Kernick Handling Systems out of nothing but a few bucks in the bank and his solid reputation as the wunderkind automation engineer at Crestman Korax. He was not a salesman then; he had never been a salesman—he didn't know the ropes of sales. As a result, he found himself supremely anxious over each Kernick Handling proposal, waiting for the phone to ring so that potential clients could tell him the contract was his. But the phone rarely rang. Time would pass. He would wait with his nerves unraveling—waiting for economic absolution, for career glorification, for any job to come his way, however pitiful. All the while, as revenue dried up, the rent on his and Martha's Stamford apartment went unpaid, and his college loans fell dangerously close to default, Carl felt the lining of his stomach tear with ulcers. He knew he would never survive with his own business if he didn't find a way to stop chasing rainbows that had long since faded.

His solution was something he had learned in a Dale Carnegie course: the stop-loss technique. As Dale Carnegie's minions taught it, Carl could reduce entrepreneurial stress and focus his sales efforts more effectively if he merely put a termination point on everything that was disturbing him, just as investors put a stop-loss on holdings' prices to determine when to sell them without losing their shirts, or their minds. The idea was to pick a point and say, "If so and so doesn't get back to me by this date, either way, I'm going to move on to the next proposal." Once Carl put a stop-loss on his potential clients' responses, his mind relaxed. Soon he found himself offering more than one proposal at a time, and in time, Kernick Handling Systems took off to become a multi-million-dollar world leader in specialized automation design. An award-winning leader, Carl reminded himself with a full serving of bravado.

That Saturday morning, Carl decided to apply the stop-loss technique to Kenny. He went up to Kenny's bedroom and lifted the U-V volume of the *World Book Encyclopedia* off Kenny's floor, where he had tripped over it and other volumes on Wednesday morning. He opened the book to the section on the United States and found what he was looking for: a generic road map of the country. The last Carl had heard from J.T., Kenny was heading toward Chicago. Beyond Chicago, Carl stretched a finger along the map's red-and-blue line markers for major highways, and he picked his stop-loss point—

The Mississippi River.

"If you go over the Mississippi," Carl spoke to Kenny in the fiery light of the boy's bedroom, "I'm coming to get you."

Since J.T. wouldn't be working on the weekend, Carl figured he would have to wait until Monday to find out if Kenny had triggered the stop-loss. In the meantime, his rage reduced to a simmer, becoming thick and clumpy, like a paste he could use to hold his mind together. But Carl's timetable was redrawn when his home phone rang on Saturday afternoon. It was J.T. The young man said he had come into work on his day off just to see where Kenny was. When Carl asked him why, J.T. responded, "This is the best show in town, Mr. K. Half of my shift is here placing wagers." He told Carl that Kenny had pounded around Chicago for a while that morning, then made his way south along 55 to pick up I-80 West near Joliet. He was now shooting a straight line for Iowa.

Carl fumed at the news but kept his emotions in check. "Call me when he crosses the Mississippi," Carl told J.T. Then he hung up and started to pack his largest suitcase with several days' clothing.

The phone rang again just after six o'clock in the evening, after the sun had set on Simondale.

"He's crossing your river," J.T. told him. "Oh, he's pulling off in a town called LeClaire. Yes, he seems to be staying there."

"Well done," Carl told J.T., thinking that if the young man ever wanted a job in automation engineering, Carl would offer him something entry-level in a blink. Heck, he would even pay for J.T.'s schooling, if necessary. "Now let me give you a new number, Jasper Thomas," Carl said. "I won't be at the office, or at home, for a while."

The number was for Carl's cell. After J.T. verified it, Carl hung up, put on his coat, grabbed the suitcase and the U-V volume of the *World Book Encyclopedia*, jumped into his wife's Ford Taurus station wagon and headed toward Kenny. He hadn't even bothered to say goodbye to Martha. He hadn't even cared that he was leaving his wife at home without a vehicle. All that mattered was Kenny, and how Carl was going to murder him.

Maybe Carl would dangle Kenny from a highway overpass and wait for a Mack truck to shatter him like a piñata.

Maybe Carl would take off Kenny's glasses and throw him onto the open prairie, where he would be at the mercy of well-sighted wildlife seeking out prey.

Maybe Carl would strap Kenny to the hood of the Cadillac and crash the vehicle into a bridge abutment.

Maybe, maybe, maybe, Carl thought. A man as successful as Carl Kernick wasn't used to so many maybes.

Carl had driven as far as he could that Saturday night before he began to nod off at the wheel.

He ended up in, of all places, Bloomsburg, Pennsylvania, where J.T. had pinpointed Kenny's location just a few days before. Looking for a high-quality hotel, he drove a few miles up Route 11 and a few miles back down, but found nothing to suit his tastes—particularly no Rostoff, the five-star chain with which he had his rewards membership. In the end, Carl opted for a quaint inn near the highway. He consumed the last cigarette from his pack of Parliaments in five ferocious puffs, and nodded off before he had even turned out the lights.

He awoke six hours later feeling remarkably clearheaded. It was probably that clearheadedness, he realized, which had provided fertile soil for the preoccupation that ultimately led to his throwing out the new pack of Parliaments. He would have to stop somewhere for more cigarettes, and he would still have to call Martha to tell her what he was up to. He would also have to contact his vice president at Kernick Handling and order him to put all company decisions on hold for a while, which would cost Carl a fortune in revenue and reputation. But it was a necessary step. All because of Kenny.

An oversized Chevy pickup truck sporting ridiculous naked-lady mud flaps cut off Carl just past the exit for Du Bois, and Carl wanted to lay on the horn. Judging by the size of the truck and the crassness of its mud flaps, Carl stifled his urge and instead yelled, "Dummkopf!" at the top of his lungs.

Hmmmm, Carl thought after his adrenaline receded. Dummkopf. Translation: "Stupid Head." That's not a bad idea. Maybe when Carl found Kenny, he wouldn't kill the boy after all. Maybe he would exact retribution commensurate with what Kenny was acting like: He would make his son a full-fledged dummkopf, courtesy of a few solid whacks to the skull. Sort of like a poor man's lobotomy. Kenny would still be alive, but he would be rendered completely stupid, never to use his brain in pursuit of wants antithetical to Carl's direction again. To accomplish such an undertaking, Carl had the perfect instrument—a hefty tire iron stored under a compartment panel at the back of the Taurus.

It was quick, Carl thought, and not very painful, but it was exquisitely effective. And without a morning cigarette to steel his nerves, it was just the kind of punishment Carl Kernick was in the mood for meting out.

★★★★★★★★★★★★★★★★★★★★★★★★★

PART III
THE DESERT

★★★★★★★★★★★★★★★★★★★★★★★★★

CHAPTER 20

★ ★

Two hours after crossing the Vail Pass in the Rockies, Kenny and Kidd made it to Grand Junction, Colorado, a thriving desert town located a few miles east of the Utah border, at the convergence of the Colorado and Gunnison Rivers.

As Kenny filled up the Cadillac at a station off the highway, Kidd perused the pages of a road atlas he had picked up at the Kum & Go convenience store in North Platte, Nebraska, the town where they had spent the previous night. While laughing over the name "Kum & Go" had brought Kidd immense joy last evening, his expression in studying the atlas this afternoon was more serious. When the gas pump clicked full and Kenny put the nozzle away, Kidd pointed to the Utah map. "It doesn't look like there's jack shit once we cross the border. There's even a stretch of highway that shows no services for a hundred miles. I say we bed down here tonight and make a play for Las Vegas tomorrow morning."

What Kidd said always went, so he and Kenny turned north to journey up the busiest street in town. Within a half mile, they had found a Happy Traveler Inn, their old reliable lodging locale. Heralding their entry into the expansive West, it was an even bigger Happy Traveler than they had stayed at in LeClaire or North Platte.

Kenny parked the Cadillac at a spot in front of the hotel's main entrance while Kidd went in to get a room. The parking lot was quite full for a Monday evening. A brochure Kenny had picked up at the gas station declared Grand Junction the playground of western Colorado—a mesa-strewn land of hiking, rafting, biking, golfing, wine tours, and live theatre. There was even an announcement on the Happy Traveler's welcome sign for an aestheticians' convention starting at the inn tomorrow morning—an aesthetician being, if Kenny remembered correctly from his encyclopedia days, someone who specialized in various types of beauty treatments. Kenny wondered if the convention's attendees were the reason Kidd was taking so long, and if they might have to try another hotel down the street. After a few moments, Kidd walked out of the hotel and slid back into the Cadillac.

"We are lucky bastards, Young Kernick. I got us the last room in Grand Junction. Around the corner. Number four-two-five."

Kenny drove the Cadillac toward the northern end of the building and pulled into a parking space facing Big Melly's, a touristy restaurant located next door to the Happy Traveler.

Kenny struggled out of the car, his every joint creaking from the eight-hour drive from Nebraska. His body was spent from the lighter air pressure up in the Rocky Mountains, which had actually caused him to grow drowsy at several points of climb and fall through that heavenly range. He raised his hands high to stretch, trying to perk up, but what actually perked him up was the peculiar vision he spied farther down the parking lot.

About one hundred feet away, he observed two women staring at Kidd. The former president had gotten out of the car and walked over to a stairwell leading to the upper floors; he was yawning, stretching, scratching himself and waiting, with one heel on the bottom step, for Kenny to fetch the bags from the trunk. The women, who each looked to be in their mid-thirties, were standing next to a purple sports car. By their ambivalent positioning, Kenny couldn't tell if they had just arrived at the hotel and were getting out of the car, or if they were about to leave the hotel and were getting in, but whatever they were doing, it was evident that the sight of Kidd had stopped them cold. They were consumed with him. They would peer over at Kidd, look at each other, smirk, lower their heads, make comments across the roof of the sports car, smirk again, then peer back at Kidd, at which point the process repeated itself. Their eyes seemed aglow with something that Kenny could only think of as mischief. One of the women was a brunette whom Kenny found attractive. She was taller than Kenny, leggy, slim, with luxuriant curly hair and a pretty face. The other woman looked like a troll. As Kenny watched them, the women continued to watch Kidd—looking at him, whispering, waiting to see if he returned their attention.

After a few moments, Kenny walked to the trunk and removed the bags. When he shut the trunk, he asked Kidd, "Are you catching any of this?"

"Any of what?" Kidd asked in the middle of a yawn.

Kenny looked over to the sports car. The women were gone, but the car remained. Kenny hoisted his duffel bag over his shoulder, grabbed the handle on Kidd's new vertical upright suitcase and said, "Never mind."

Their room at the Happy Traveler was bigger than anything they had stayed in yet, with wide beds, a loveseat, comfortable spaces between the furniture, and plenty of amenities for a boy on the road, like a minibar. As was becoming his custom, Kenny took the bed closest to the window. He suspected that windows made him feel safe—a well-placed window having been his only means of escape six nights ago when he needed to flee Simondale in a Carl-induced hurry.

According to Kidd, dinner would come later tonight; the former president wanted a nap first. While he slept, Kenny sat in the loveseat and stared out the window, thinking back on his experiences at the Mississippi, and of the drive across the prairie and through the mountains. He repeated over and over some of the epiphanies he had realized in those places: that he had wasted a vast chunk of his life in worry about things that didn't matter; that nothing had ever been wrong with him, ever; and that Nebraska really smelled awful—like omnipresent cow shit.

But for all his epiphanies over the last two days, Kenny still had doubts.

He heard his inner voice say, "If nothing has ever been wrong with you, dummkopf, then why don't women ever look at *you* with mischief in their eyes? Why don't you inspire girls to such wilds?" As the voice berated him, Kenny found his insides flipping like one of Martha Kernick's cement pancakes.

Kenny spent naptime riding a wave of polar emotions. For stretches at a time, he felt the peace of his newfound confidence. Then, just as quickly, the voice would emerge to tear him up with uncertainty. He found that when he was thinking peaceful thoughts, the voice inside his head sounded like Charles Bentley Kidd's—warm, reassuring, mentoring. But when he experienced doubtful thoughts, the voice took on Carl's stab—mocking, full of contempt, and merciless. There was a war going on inside him, a battle for control of him which had, at opposing ends of the field, two generals—one a former leader of the free world, the other a master of the world as he knew it. Whatever Kidd would try to build up in Kenny by virtue of their journey together, Carl's years of programming would attempt to tear down. In a sense, it was as if Carl wasn't really two thousand miles away. Instead, he was with Kenny all the time, confronting Kidd's influence, sniping at Kenny's growing confidence from treetops, harassing Kenny's pickets, tracking the boy no matter how far Kenny drove, even though the man himself was probably still in Simondale, waiting for his prodigal son to return home with the Cadillac.

"Let the fucker wait," Kenny heard his inner Kidd voice say.

"Get your butt home, dummkopf," Kenny heard the inner Carl voice reply.

Kenny let out a sigh. It was going to be a long battle. And bloody.

Just then, Kenny heard Kidd shift under the covers. Kidd yawned, and his caramel voice boomed across the darkening room. "Jesus H. Christ," the ex-president said. "I just had a dream I was eating banana cream pie off a swimsuit model's midriff. Do you know what that means?"

"Please tell me it doesn't involve your Lil' Kidd," Kenny said.

"It means I'm hotter than a fresh-fucked fox in a forest fire," Kidd said. "When I'm hot, you've got two choices—get me laid or get me some food. Unfortunately, you're not my type, Kenny, so it looks like dinner is on."

"With dessert this time?" Kenny asked, still pissed off about their aborted ice cream mission back in Iowa.

"Yes, Kenny, with dessert this time," Kidd said. "But we better get out of here. My Lil' Kidd is up and he's looking for love."

That's when Kenny's fight or flight response kicked in. "Let's eat," he said, as he leapt off the bed and hurried out the door.

At a corner table in Big Melly's Bar and Grill, Kidd sliced his knife through a Cajun-spiced rib eye, nodded to Kenny's burger and asked, "How's that working for you, Young Kernick?"

Kenny had a full mouth of Big Bleu Bison Burger, Big Melly's signature offering, but bad manners or not, he couldn't stop his euphoric reply: "Oh my fugging Christ!" He rolled his eyes back as the flavor of bleu cheese, rare bison and caramelized onions spread out from his mouth, up to his brain, and down his limbs. He almost wanted to melt into his chair. After he swallowed, he pointed a finger at the bun and said, "That is the goddamned king!" And it was true. The Big Bleu Bison Burger beat anything from the myriad fast food joints along the road west. And Kenny would know. He and Kidd had stopped at them all.

"The Elvis of Burgers?" Kidd asked.

"Elvis, The Beatles, Sinatra, Beethoven, whoever. Life can't get any better than this."

Kidd chuckled dismissively. "Well, Kenny, I'm glad you're enjoying yourself right now. But wait until you get laid. Or at least your first hummer. Then I'm sure you'll re-evaluate."

"What's a hummer?" Kenny asked, taking another bite of his burger. Kidd just shook his head.

Kenny devoured his meal in a matter of minutes, scooping up all the fallen bits of onions and cheese and sucking them off his fingers. Kidd took his time with the rib eye. He had seemed more introspective since that night in the Mississippi River, as if those waters really had transformed him. He had been virtually nonverbal since then, staying quiet across Iowa, Nebraska and Colorado, speaking only when he needed to give direction, check on the status of the driver, or explode with laughter over another approaching Kum & Go sign. Kenny also noticed during dinner that Kidd's brow seemed smooth lately, not furrowed. And Kidd was snapping less, if at all, which was a good thing for Kenny—he hated it when Kidd snapped at him.

When Kidd finished his meal, he sat back and reached for a laminated menu card tucked behind the bottle of ketchup. "Time for dessert," he said, winking at Kenny. But as the former president studied the menu, he failed to notice what Kenny could plainly see with only a cursory glance across the restaurant: At the bar, the two women who had gawked at Kidd in the parking lot were back. Once again, they were staring at him. Unlike this afternoon, they decided to make an approach. They slid off their stools and started to move toward him. First came the taller, more attractive brunette, then the troll. They sauntered across the restaurant with those same glowing eyes and mischievous grins Kenny had seen in the parking lot. Kidd only took notice of them once they had hovered at the edge of the table for a few seconds. Looking up, he cocked his head curiously. All he managed to say was, "Hello."

The attractive brunette pointed her finger at his chest and said, "Oh my God—you're that guy!"

"You're that guy!" the troll mimicked.

The attractive one swung around to her friend. "Tammy, he's that guy!"

"He's totally that guy!" Tammy crowed.

"Okay," Kidd said, dragging the word out with curiosity. He looked perplexed. "What guy would that be?"

"You know," the hot one said. "That guy. Who did that thing." Kenny studied her face. Up close, she was still attractive, but he had been wrong in the parking lot: She wasn't in her mid-thirties at all; he doubted she had even turned twenty-five yet. It was probably all the makeup she was wearing that made her look older. Her face was caked in it.

"If," Kidd said, "by 'that guy who did that thing' you mean the president who got impeached, then yes, that's me."

The hot one and the one named Tammy started to jump up and down, squealing like schoolgirls at recess. "It's him, it's him, it's him!" they shouted. Everyone in the restaurant—and the place was full—turned to look. Kenny wanted to crawl under the table.

The hot one practically jumped into Kidd's lap. "I'm Tammy," she said, "and this is my friend, Tammy. Tammy One and Tammy Two, people call us, so they don't get confused. I'm Tammy One, of course." She sat down in the empty space next to Kidd and anchored herself there like a banged-up yacht.

Kidd stared at the glow in her eyes. It was obvious to Kenny that Charles Bentley Kidd had seen that look on a girl's face before—teeming, eager, ready to satisfy. The former president calmly slipped the laminated menu card back behind the ketchup, then he turned to Kenny and smiled. "Dessert's here," he said.

CHAPTER 21

★ ★

As she sat in the booth next to Kidd, Tammy One popped a stick of chewing gum into her mouth and said in reply to Charles Bentley Kidd's inquiry that she and Tammy Two came from Utah.

To which Tammy Two, who was taking a stick of gum from Tammy One's pack, added, "Salt Lake City, Utah, if you wanna be exact."

To which Tammy One threw Tammy Two an ice-cold stare, put her hand on Kidd's shoulder and said, "Actually, it's *West Valley*, Utah, just to the southwest of Salt Lake City, if you wanna be more exact." Then she snapped her gum at Tammy Two, making the troll jump.

Kenny, for his part, was enthralled: He had never seen a catfight before. But the boy felt quite certain that if he were ever going to witness his first full-blown, knock-down, girl-on-girl brawl, it was going to be right here, as Tammy One and Tammy Two went at it for Kidd's attention.

To Kenny, the irony of the whole situation was that a catfight over Kidd need not happen at all. Having sized up the combatants, starting with his first view of them in the parking lot, Kenny knew that it was no contest over which girl Kidd would pick. In fact, even though the girls continued to address themselves as Tammy One and Tammy Two, Kenny had begun to refer to them in his mind as Hot Tammy and Ugly Tammy. And as Kenny knew full well, Kidd didn't do ugly.

"We're here for the convention," Ugly Tammy said, chomping her gum atrociously. She sounded like a pig at a trough.

"It's more like a conference than a convention," Hot Tammy said, raising her perfectly-streamlined eyebrows in condescension. "It's for NASA."

"NASA?" Kidd said. He looked at them askance. "Are you girls rocket scientists?"

The girls looked at Kidd askance. Ugly Tammy said, "No, NASA—the North American Society of Aestheticians. Tammy and me are part of their panel discussion on hair removal."

"Well, thank God you cleared that up," Kidd said, grinning. He swirled the remnants of a rum punch around the bottom of its glass and seemed to study something in the red liquid's motion, something lascivious. "So you ladies are into hair removal," he said. "I've always been intrigued by ladies who are into hair removal."

Hot Tammy took the lead. "I'm not just into hair removal, Mr. President," she said. "It's my life."

"It's my life, too," Ugly Tammy said defensively.

"But you're into electrolysis, Tammy, and I'm into laser." Hot Tammy eyed Kidd with a hint of revulsion. "Laser is so much better than electrolysis."

"You are so full of it, Tammy," the ugly one said. "At least my clients can have light-colored hair. All your clients have to have dark hair, or the laser won't see the pigment in their follicles. If it doesn't see the pigment, it can't kill the follicle. So forget you if you're blonde. How democratic is that, Mr. President?"

"Sounds pretty discriminatory," Kidd said.

"Most of her clients are bottle blondes anyway," Hot Tammy said.

"And tan," Ugly Tammy added. She jutted her chin toward Kidd. "If her clients get a tan, it confuses the laser and kills the skin pigment instead. Then they get blotchy. I kill the follicle every time, Mr. President. Every single time. Dark hair, light hair, tan or no tan. I am an equal opportunity hair remover."

"Yeah, and a painful one," Hot Tammy said. "When Tammy over there sticks her needle into you, you'll jump a mile. Then you'll have to come back thirty more times to make sure it worked. But when I do it with my laser, all you'll feel is a little snap, like a rubber band hitting your skin. And with my special touch, I'll kill that follicle after five treatments at most. I've been told my approach is as smooth as silk, stunningly effective, and highly satisfactory."

"What a coincidence," Kidd said, grinning again. "I've often heard the same thing said of me. Now how about a round of drinks? Waitress—"

Kidd waved the waitress over and ordered another rum punch, then he asked the Tammies what they would like. Citing religious beliefs, each ordered something called an Arnold Palmer, which Kenny understood to be a concoction of equal parts lemonade and iced tea. It sounded tasty, so Kenny ordered the same.

Once the waitress had departed, Ugly Tammy leaned in toward Kidd and said, "I'm a Mormon, you know, so I can't drink liquor."

"She still drinks liquor sometimes," Hot Tammy said, snapping her gum. "So don't think she's as righteous as she makes herself out to be."

"I'm more righteous than you, Tammy," the ugly one replied. "At least I was born a Mormon." She leaned in toward Kidd again. "When she was little, her family converted. They used to be Methodists."

"I'm aghast," Kidd said to Ugly Tammy. "Not really," he whispered to Hot Tammy.

Then Kenny saw Kidd make his first move with the hot girl: The ex-president set his arm along the ridge of the booth, so that it was almost resting on Hot Tammy's pale shoulders. As not to leave the move unmotivated, Kidd said, "Actually, conversion to a faith is something I know all about. When I was younger, I made a conversion myself. My mama, God rest her soul, she'd been born a Baptist, but then her only child went out and joined the Catholic Church." Kidd lowered his head and laughed quietly to himself, like he was remembering something painful yet poignant. Then he said, "No, converting is not an easy thing to do. For a while you feel very awkward in your new surroundings. I was confused at first, always wondering: Do I stand at this part or do I kneel? Do I shake hands now or do I give out money? Do I have the priest lay the host onto my palm or do I let the bastard actually put it on my tongue? Which I found creepy. No, new religions are very disjointing. Isn't that right, Tammy One?" Kidd looked at the hot girl with supportive, empathetic eyes. Hot Tammy beamed at him, her eyes shooting off electric sparks. To Kenny, she looked as if she might latch onto Kidd's wank right there and never let go.

The waitress returned with the drinks, at which point Kenny saw Kidd make his second move for Hot Tammy: With complete nonchalance, Kidd refused his rum punch, pointed at Hot Tammy, and said, "On second thought, I'd rather have what she's having." The waitress set the Arnold Palmers on the table, grumbled, and went back for Kidd's new order.

Damn, Kenny thought as he watched Hot Tammy beam anew, this guy is better at wooing women than even the national press described. It was the first time Kenny had felt himself to be in the presence of the Kidd of Legend. Now this Kidd of Legend was having an effect on Kenny. With these two psychotic Mormons vying for Kidd's attention, Kenny began to feel invisible. He noticed it first when he inadvertently made eye contact with Hot Tammy. Instead of looking back at him, she looked through him. He also noticed the phenomenon from Ugly Tammy when he questioned her, very tentatively, as to what made up an Arnold Palmer. Instead of answering him, Ugly Tammy directed her response to Kidd, as if the ex-president across from her, who was clearly in the planning stages of removing every article of clothing from her hot friend, actually gave a shit about what someone as homely as Ugly Tammy wanted to put in her mouth.

With Kidd's affections swinging toward Hot Tammy, Ugly Tammy went on the offensive. Kidd touched off the ugly girl's aggression by complimenting Hot Tammy on her perfectly-streamlined eyebrows.

"They weren't always that way," Ugly Tammy said before Hot Tammy could say a word.

"Shut up, Tammy," Hot Tammy said.

"They weren't, and you know it." Ugly Tammy leaned in toward Kidd, her pulverized chewing gum almost falling out of her mouth. "You should have seen her before she came to me for electrolysis. Her eyebrows were bushier than Brooke

Shields'. That's how she even got interested in hair removal in the first place—from me."

"Well, I may have had bushy eyebrows, but at least I had two of them." Hot Tammy brushed an elbow along Kidd's ribcage; Kidd seemed to bristle with delight at the touch. "You know why she got interested in hair removal? She used to have a unibrow. You know, one big eyebrow. Like that character from *Sesame Street*."

Ugly Tammy let out a gasp. "You bitch!"

Hot Tammy jammed another piece of gum in her mouth without removing the first. "Oh, don't even start with me, Tammy," she said with breathy chomps.

"You always thought you were better than me, Tammy," Ugly Tammy said.

"That's because I am better than you," Hot Tammy replied. "I was better at cheering, I was better at baking and sewing, and I am way better at hair removal—laser, electrolysis, or even ripping it out with tweezers. Look at that arm—" Hot Tammy pulled up her shirtsleeve to reveal a lustrous, hair-free forearm; just the sight of it made Kenny want to drool into his Arnold Palmer. "Not a single hair left on it, or the other one, and I did it all myself with my portable laser kit."

Not to be outdone, Ugly Tammy swung a stubby leg onto the tabletop and yanked up her jeans above the calf. Her skin was also lustrous. "Well, look here," she said. "No hair will ever grow back on that either, and I did it all myself, too, with electrolysis."

Hot Tammy let out a grumble and flipped her curly brown locks in disgust. "My lasered legs are even more hairless than that. I believe I saw some strays."

"You didn't see anything because there weren't any strays to see," Ugly Tammy said. She was having a hard time getting her chubby leg back under the table, and the whole booth was shaking for it. "I don't have one single hair on my legs, my arms or even"—Ugly Tammy lifted one arm high; there were sweat stains soaking through her maroon shirt—"under my armpits." She looked at Kidd and asked, "Can she say that?"

Joining the battle, an amused Kidd, who had been grinning through the entire argument, gazed at Hot Tammy and said, "That's a pretty big raise, Tammy One. Can you see it?"

Hot Tammy straightened in her seat and appeared to take a mental inventory. "Well, I don't have any hair on my arms, my legs, or under my pits," she said. "I don't have any strays on my feet, or my toes, or the small of my back." Then she let loose the coup de grâce. "And I don't have any hair, not one single thread—stray or otherwise—on my patch."

Kidd and Kenny looked at each other in confusion. Kidd spoke first what Kenny was already thinking. The ex-president asked, "What's your patch?"

Hot Tammy wiggled her nose like she was a little miffed at Kidd's lack of understanding. She made a triangle with her fingers. "You know, my patch."

Kidd took in her words for a moment, then he exploded in laughter. Hot Tammy, Ugly Tammy and Kenny all sat there looking at him until Kidd finally caught his breath. Then Kidd gazed deeply into Hot Tammy's rich brown eyes, dropped his voice low and said, "Hell, honey, I would love to know your patch. All you have to do is introduce me to it."

Game, set and match. Ugly Tammy slumped back into the booth, and her defeated eyes fell to the half-consumed Arnold Palmer on the table. It was obvious to Kenny that the ugly one couldn't compete with the hot one's bare nether region, and even if she could, it was clear that Charles Bentley Kidd wouldn't want it.

"Whoa," Kidd said, trying to cool the friction between the two Tammies. His brow leaked droplets of sweat, which he wiped with a knuckle. "All this talk about hairless body parts has given a jolt to my Lil' Kidd."

It was the girls' turn to look at each other in confusion. Hot Tammy asked first: "Your Lil' Kidd? What's that?"

You're practically sitting on it, Kenny wanted to answer.

Kidd, however, needed no help from Kenny in responding to any inquiry about his most-valued appendage. He simply nodded to his lap and said, "You know, my Lil' Kidd."

Hot Tammy's eyes lighted up. "Oh, you mean your pee-pee." She leaned over the table toward Ugly Tammy and whispered firmly, like a teacher instructing a student, "He means his pee-pee." Ugly Tammy threw her a scowl. This troll of a girl may have had a face that could curdle milk, but she sure as hell wouldn't be talked down to. Hot Tammy backed away.

Kidd took a swig of his Arnold Palmer. He made a show of the sip, like the drink had tasted much too tart, then he pinched his bottom lip dry of residual moisture. "Some people call it a pee-pee," he said. "Kenny over there likes to call it a penis. I have my own terms for it, but as Kenny will tell you, most of them are crass. As a man of stature, however, I prefer that my member goes by a proper name." Kidd pointed his fingers down to his crotch below the table, as if to showcase his dick like a fine country ham. "Hence, my Lil' Kidd."

"That is so amazing," Hot Tammy said. "I think guys who name their pee-pees are cool. I once dated somebody who called his 'Dr. Strangelove.' By the way it curved to the left, he wasn't wrong."

"That's a solid name," Kidd said. "Mine has a solid name as well, one that I'm happy with. But I'm dying to tell you a secret. Would you like to know a secret? Would you?"

Both Tammies nodded intently. Kenny could only imagine what self-serving statement was going to depart his mouth next. However, instead of frolicking in egoism, Kidd leveled a finger at Kenny. That's when Kenny heard him say, "Nobody beats what this boy calls his."

For someone who had been feeling quite invisible since the Tammies arrived, Kenny felt a deluge of attention rush upon him. Both of the Tammies' heads swung toward him, their eyes burrowing into him, not out of mischief, but with a mix of curiosity and disgust. It was Ugly Tammy's turn to bring voice to the question that was no doubt racing through her friend's mind as well. "What does he call his?" she asked Kidd.

"Why don't you ask him?" Kidd told her.

Ugly Tammy eyed Kenny with another helping of disgust. "Well, what exactly do you call your thing?"

Kenny sat there dumbstruck. He had never in his life given name to his penis, and until two nights ago along the banks of the Mississippi, he hadn't even considered it.

Kidd prodded through Kenny's silence. "Oh, don't be modest, Young Kernick. Answer the lady."

Kenny opened his mouth, but no sound came out. He was stuck on the burs of some unknown sobriquet.

"Fine," Kidd said, "you want to play it that way, then I'll tell them." He turned to the Tammies. "One word—Elvis."

Both girls gasped in unison. Ugly Tammy sucked down her gum.

"Elvis?" Hot Tammy asked.

"Elvis," Ugly Tammy said, coughing up the wad.

Kidd leaned back in the booth, the cocksure smirk spreading across his face. The man was wreaking havoc with these girls' pliant minds, and Kenny could tell that Kidd relished every ounce of his ability to do so.

"Why 'Elvis'?" Hot Tammy asked.

"Think about it," Kidd said. "Elvis was good-looking, but there were a lot of guys who looked better, especially actors. Then there was his voice—great, yes; strong, sure; but he was no Sinatra. And he couldn't write a song to save his life—most of his hits were written for him. And yet, when you put it all together, when you added up the sum of his parts, he was 'The King.'" Then Kidd fixed Ugly Tammy with a determined stare and nodded his head at Kenny. "And so is that boy's pee-pee."

Hot Tammy, who had been taking a sip of her Arnold Palmer, sprayed half of it onto the table.

Kenny looked at Ugly Tammy. The mix of curiosity and disgust on her face was gone. She now eyed Kenny like his dick was a fine country ham.

"Here's what we're going to do," Kidd said. He placed his right arm firmly around Hot Tammy's shoulder and fused her to him. "Tammy One and I are heading back to her room, where I'm going to authorize a presidential inquiry into all this 'bare patch' business."

Hot Tammy let out a voracious giggle. It reminded Kenny of his mother's giggling reactions to Kidd back in Simondale.

"But we're sharing a room," Ugly Tammy said. From the urgent way she spoke, Kenny wondered if the troll wasn't really hoping Kidd might invite her back, too. For a three-way.

Kidd was unmoved by her last-ditch plea. "Not a problem," he said. "Come back with us, grab some sleepwear, then shack up with Kenny. It's a very big room. The great thing is, it will just be you, him and Elvis."

Ugly Tammy seemed to resign herself to her fate. The mention of Elvis even appeared to perk her up. "Well, I guess I could do that, if you want me to."

"While you're there," Kidd said, "feel free to take Elvis out and have him perform for you. From what I've heard—and as a former president, I'm privy to these things—he puts on quite a show."

Ugly Tammy eyed Kenny again, her facial expression vacillating between hunger and rejection. Kenny wondered if she could see the debilitating fear that was coursing through his body at the prospects of what she might decide, and what she might do to him once they were in that room alone.

Ugly Tammy looked at Kidd. "Well, I'm a Mormon, you know, so I can't fuck him."

Kidd said, "Not a problem. I can think of other ways to make Elvis sing. How about—"

Kidd leaned over the table and met Ugly Tammy halfway. He whispered something into her ear, then he pulled back, leaving Ugly Tammy still lurched over the table, pondering the proposition. Finally, she said, "Just that?"

"It would make me immeasurably happy," Kidd said.

"It would?" Ugly Tammy asked, fawning.

"Trust me, you'd be doing society a tremendous service. I think I might even be able to get my successor in the Oval Office to give you the Medal of Honor."

"You could?" Ugly Tammy asked. Her fawn had turned ridiculously sappy.

"Absolutely," Kidd declared.

Ugly Tammy collected herself then said, "Well, I think I'll be fine staying in—what's the short one's name again?"

"Kenny," Kidd told Ugly Tammy.

"Kenny's room," Ugly Tammy said.

"That settles it," Kidd said, pushing Hot Tammy away from his lap in an effort to get up. Both Tammies stood and slung their handbags over their shoulders.

But the issue hadn't been settled for Kenny. As both Tammies walked toward the front of Big Melly's, laughing and chirping to each other in anticipatory excitement, Kenny grabbed Kidd's arm. He squeezed it. Hard.

"But what am I supposed to do?" Kenny asked.

Kidd tapped a finger to his chin and pondered the question. Finally, he said, "Well, when it starts to feel good, try not to cross your eyes too much. They might stay that way."

Then the former leader of the free world pulled out of Kenny's grasp, walked up to Hot Tammy near the bar, grabbed her by the ass, and led her out of the restaurant, as Hot Tammy's joyous cackles rose to the roof beams.

After Kenny watched them turn a corner for the door, he looked at Ugly Tammy. She was standing at the hostess's podium, her eyebrows arched in impatient wait.

"What room are you in?" she asked, as Kenny moved closer to her.

Kenny sputtered out the room number.

"I'll see you in a few minutes," she said. "And you better not fall asleep."

Ugly Tammy turned to leave, and Kenny felt his insides churn. All he could think about was how wrong Kidd had been when Hot Tammy and Ugly Tammy first approached the booth, when Kidd had pronounced them to be dessert. Because the way this misshapen, uncomely girl was looking back at him from the doorframe, Kenny now knew the complete opposite to be true:

Ugly Tammy wasn't his dessert—he was hers.

CHAPTER 22

★ ★

When a knock came at the door to Room 425, Kenny figured he had three options—he could pretend he wasn't there; he could climb out the window as he had done in Simondale; or he could open the door and let the troll in.

The choice was really no choice at all, once Kenny pondered it. Should he elect to ignore the knocks, perhaps hiding under the bed or in the bathtub, Ugly Tammy would simply walk back to her room, procure Kidd's keycard, and return to Room 425 in a mood as foul as her face. If he opted to go out the window, he would have a hard time of it. The window didn't open more than a sliver, and he was four stories up without a fire-escape ladder. There wasn't even a swimming pool below him to break his fall. No, the only choice was to open the door and succumb to whatever molestations Ugly Tammy had in store for him.

Kenny walked to the door and pulled it open. "It's about time," Ugly Tammy said as she wobbled past him carrying her nightclothes and a toiletries bag. "You better not have been playing with yourself. That'll make you go forever, and I'm tired. Where's my bed?"

Kenny pointed to the mattress where Kidd had taken his nap.

"Good enough," she said. "Now put on some music and get into your pajamas. I'll be out in a minute." She took her nightclothes and toiletries bag into the bathroom and shut the door.

On the clock radio near his bed, Kenny found a smooth jazz station at the far end of the dial. He switched off the overhead lighting, leaving his side table lamp to illuminate the room in romantic amber hues. He closed the shades and sat on the edge of his bed facing the bathroom. But when it came to taking off his clothes, Kenny froze. His hands stalled at his shirt buttons; they wouldn't even make an attempt at his belt or shoes. All he could do was sit on the bed, put his hands in his lap, and await Ugly Tammy's re-emergence.

She came out three minutes later wearing a pair of pink flannel pajama bottoms and a white t-shirt which proclaimed in bold black lettering: "There is no excuse for nipple hair— ever!" She stood about Kenny's height and was also a brunette like her attractive friend. But she was wider than Hot Tammy by a factor of two, her face looked like pinched dough, and she had humongous boobs for her body frame. She walked over to Kidd's bed, threw her clothes into a pile in the corner, and sat down facing Kenny. She studied him from his hair to his shoes and shook her head. "Is that what you wear to bed?" she asked Kenny derisively.

"Lately," Kenny said.

"Huh," she said. She unwrapped a new stick of chewing gum and stuck it in her mouth. "Now, let's set some ground rules," she said, chewing piggishly. "I wanna be clear right from the start. First, I'm not doing this for you; I'm doing it for the president. Secondly, don't you dare touch my goodies—not my boobs, not my ass, and especially not my patch. You put any part of your body near my patch, and so help me Jesus I'll bite your thing in half. My patch is reserved exclusively for my husband."

"You're married?" Kenny asked.

"No, I'm not married," Ugly Tammy said. "But I'm a Mormon and I'm almost twenty-five. That's practically an old maid. I intend to find my husband very soon, so I really don't want your grubby little paws dirtying his prize. Got that?"

Kenny said he understood.

"Good," Ugly Tammy said. "And finally—" She dropped Kenny a scathing glare. "Don't you dare blow your filth in my mouth. You hear me? When you're getting close, tap me on the head and I'll finish it by hand, but your filth stays away from me. Do you got that, too?"

Kenny nodded.

"All right," she said, removing her chewing gum and placing it on the nightstand. "Now let's get this over with. The finale to *The Thorn Birds* starts at eight on The Harlequin Channel, and I don't want to miss one second of it." She took a pillow from Kidd's bed and put it on the floor at Kenny's feet. She knelt on the pillow and added, "I love that Richard Chamberlain—now he's a real man. Say, are you gonna stand up or what?"

Stand up? What did she mean by stand up? Kenny always thought sexual activity took place lying down. But he followed her orders, and he was glad he did, because Ugly Tammy immediately grabbed his crotch and started rubbing it, all while expounding on the virtues of some actor named Richard Chamberlain.

"Huh," she said after a few seconds. "Doesn't feel like there's much down here." Kenny doubted there would be. The girl was simply beastly. Kenny didn't think he would ever be able to get Elvis up and working, such was his lack of attraction for this woman.

And yet, something strange began to happen. Regardless of his repulsion to her, Kenny's loins flooded at her progress. Elvis got a little aroused when she undid his belt buckle, then it got entirely aroused when she unzipped his fly and lowered his khakis to the floor.

Kenny tilted his head back and closed his eyes. He felt Ugly Tammy's fingers pry open the fly of his underwear. He heard her make a sarcastic comment about Fruit of the Looms, and that Richard Chamberlain would certainly never wear tighty-whities, because he was dapper. He felt her fingers pinch his erection and slip it through the slit in the fabric, releasing his penis to waggle like a diving board bereft of its cannonballer. Then her sarcasm stopped and he heard her go breathless. "Oh my," she said. "That is one... amazing... Elvis."

"I'm a grower, not a shower, baby!" Kenny said.

But Ugly Tammy was too overcome to comment more. She let her actions speak for her. Her head bowed to Kenny's midsection. Her juicy-fruit breath fell anticipatorily on his stiff, waiting wank. She reached out, grabbed his Elvis like a sugar cone and brought it to her mouth.

That's when Kenny's mind blew a gasket. Elvis's new confines were as warm as crème brûlée, as moist as a Panamanian rain forest, and as soft as chenille. But instead of just bobbing her head up and down on Elvis (like he had always expected it to go on the many occasions when Kenny Kernick had fantasized about receiving fellatio), Ugly Tammy interspersed her bobs with ferocious sucks—sucking the life right out of it, sucking harder than he imagined even a vacuum cleaner would suck. It was stunning. He could feel all the blood in his body being pulled toward his bulging tip, and the sensations it sent out were unlike any he had ever felt in his life, or even thought he could feel. She worked her tongue around Elvis, sucked, bobbed, tongued some more, then sucked again. But that wasn't all this ugly girl had in store. Because as his mind began to teeter toward euphoria, as his eyes started to roll back in his head, first he heard it, then he felt it—she was humming.

Uh-oh. Elvis went into a spasm. With no warning to himself or to Ugly Tammy, Kenny released his semen to the back of her throat.

Kenny heard Ugly Tammy's hum choke off, then she gagged. The girl stiffened, lurched backward and pulled her mouth off Kenny's wank. In trying to extricate herself from the situation, she turned her head away from Elvis just in time to catch Kenny's second discharge in the ear—a clean, powerful shot right into her auditory canal.

"You've gotta be kidding me!" she said, coughing his first semen delivery onto the carpet. Kenny looked down just in time to see her jump off the pillow and run to the bathroom, her flabby body flapping in time with her steps. "That didn't even take five fucking seconds!" he heard her yelling from the vanity. "Oh, and it's all in my ear—you idiot! Didn't we have a deal? Didn't you say you'd tell me when you were going to lose it? I can't believe this!"

But in a dearth of emotion for which Charles Bentley Kidd surely would have been proud, Kenny didn't care. His head was whirling with endorphins; his whole body, standing rigid only moments before, had collapsed back onto the vastness of the bedspread. Kenny could feel Elvis, fruity-smelling and exhausted, panting for sleep. It took all the energy he could muster to tuck Elvis back into its tighty-white canopy, pull up his pants, and zip his fly.

Just then, Ugly Tammy emerged from the bathroom with her toothbrush in her hand. "I deserve that Medal of Honor, and woe to you if you think I don't, buster. You didn't respect me. I've seen better control on a Tourette's patient. Do you think Richard Chamberlain would ever shoot his load into a girl's ear? I think not!" She pointed the toothbrush at him as if it were a butcher knife. "After I'm done getting the taste of you out of my mouth, I'm gonna hop in that shower and try to get your filth out of my ear. Then I'm climbing into bed, watching my *Thorn Birds* finale, and going to sleep. And if you say one more word to me before the sun comes up, so help me Jesus, I'll kick your balls right off your body. Do you hear me?"

But Kenny had tuned her out already. He just lay there, head cocked forward, staring at this fat, angry girl as she ranted and raved and made further caustic remarks about his lack of respectfulness. In fact, maybe it was the endorphins talking, but with his brain bathed in bliss, he actually thought something odd about her as she turned to walk into the bathroom.

He thought for a moment, as warmth overtook him and he drifted off to sleep, that Ugly Tammy was actually kind of hot.

"Why do they call it a blowjob?" Kenny asked Kidd the next afternoon. They had just pulled out of Grand Junction and were heading west along I-70 for the six-hour journey to Las Vegas, their previously determined next stopping point. The day was bright and warm in the Colorado desert, and the Cadillac, to mark such brilliance, had been given a car wash before they left Grand Junction. It was shining keenly in the unencumbered sun.

"Say what?" Kidd said, pulling his mangled head of hair away from the passenger window, and looking at Kenny with swollen, half-closed eyes.

All morning, ever since Kidd had come back from Hot Tammy's room looking like a ravaged scamp, his and Kenny's roles had been reversed. This morning, Kenny had awoken with Ugly Tammy already departed, thus sparing him any additional tirades about misguided ejaculate. A bit embarrassed over the previous evening's events, he nevertheless found himself refreshed and ready to get on the road. Kidd, on the other hand, had to be peeled off the bed he had collapsed on just seconds after his early-morning return. Kenny experienced such difficulty in waking Kidd that they had checked out of the Happy Traveler at the last possible second, and missed breakfast as a result. Thus, Kenny had run into the convenience store attached to the car wash and emerged with two Snickers bars. The fact that he was waving one before Kidd's wobbly head seemed the only reason the former president was even responding to Kenny at such an "unpleasant" time of thirteen minutes past noon.

Kidd reached for the Snickers and tore off the wrapper. "Oh, God," he said as he bit off a third of the candy bar. "They weren't kidding. This shit really does satisfy." His next bite put another third of the bar into his mouth, and he chewed it in slops.

"So why do they call it that?" Kenny asked again. He opened his own candy bar, keeping the steering wheel straight with his knees.

"Call it what?" Kidd asked with a full mouth. "A Snickers?"

"A blowjob," Kenny said. "I mean, it's not like she blew anything. There was no actual blowing of air involved. Not that I could tell."

"What did she do?" Kidd asked, his sleepy eyes now wide with curiosity.

Kenny pursed his lips in thought. Finally, he said, "It's more like she sucked. And I don't mean just a little bit. No, this girl sucked hard. I woke up this morning and Elvis had a black eye."

"A dick hickey," Kidd said knowingly. "You lucky bastard. Did she do anything else?" He was starting to sound like a man who had ordered a set of goods and was probing to make sure those goods had been delivered.

"She sure as hell did," Kenny said. "She started humming. I couldn't make it out entirely, but the first few bars sounded like 'The Battle Hymn of the Republic.' Regardless, it blew my mind. Hey, maybe that's why they call it a blowjob."

Kidd smiled triumphantly. "No, Kenny, that's why they call it a hummer. God, I love it when a woman hums. 'Hail to the Chief' was always my favorite."

"Did Tammy One hum?" Kenny asked.

"Tammy One," Kidd said, putting his head in his hands. "Don't remind me about Tammy One. I should have been so fortunate to even get a hand job out of her."

Kenny scrunched his face at Kidd. "You mean the two of you didn't have sex?"

"Sex?" Kidd cried. "Ha, that girl didn't want sex, Kenny. Oh, she let me see her patch, and it was as bare as a swimsuit model's ass, but looking at it was as close as I got. The second I moved in for a proper introduction, she pulled up her thong and took out her portable laser machine, then she went to work on *my* patch. First she shaved me, then she zapped me. She's opening a boutique that specializes in body hair patterns, and I was her guinea pig." Kidd rubbed his groin. "Christ, if she's as good as she says, for the rest of my life I'm going to have pubic hair in the shape of a presidential star. That's what I get for trying to hump a Mormon."

But Kenny wasn't upset with his Mormon. On the contrary, his morning had been filled only with pleasant memories of Ugly Tammy, even if she had chastised him profusely for the speed, quantity, and unfortunate location of his semen discharge.

Kidd said, "Please tell me you didn't kiss her, though. Did you, Kenny? My God, she was ugly."

Kenny said that he had not managed to kiss Ugly Tammy, nor would she have let him anyway. She clearly wanted to get it over with and watch television.

Kidd laughed, bits of Snickers clinging to his bottom lip. "Well then, when we get to Las Vegas, we ought to see if they have a Ripley's Believe It or Not Museum."

"Why's that?" Kenny asked.

Kidd used a middle finger to wipe the Snickers pieces off his lip. "Because, Kenny," he said, "you're the only person I've ever heard of who got his first hummer from a girl before he got his first kiss. Jesus H. Christ, even I wasn't that pathetic."

Kenny shot Kidd a scalding glare, feeling his insides tighten from Kidd's insult. He wanted to pull the Cadillac over to the side of the road, flip up the automatic locks, and kick Kidd out to the crusty shoulder, where his body would dehydrate, then perish, then be descended upon by scavenger flying creatures. Kenny's anger only grew as he watched Kidd nonchalantly suck the Snickers pieces off his finger like no insult had been spoken between them.

Instead of kicking Kidd out of the car, Kenny settled for a thought: No, he told himself, you weren't that pathetic, Sucky Chucky.

You were worse.

CHAPTER 23

★ ★

It was hard for Kenny to understand now, looking out over barren desert Utah, where so little vegetation grew and so little was expected to grow, just how a man like Charles Bentley Kidd could have come to such a miserable end as president of the United States. For like the gritty, pale earth of the desert, such a small yield was expected from Kidd when he took office, that just a few drops of water on the parched economic landscape would have been regarded by the public as a life-giving downpour. It was unfortunate, then, that the only person in the country who didn't seem to understand this concept was Kidd himself.

Kenny Kernick was halfway through sixth grade when Kidd took the oath of office on a warm, sun-bleached January day almost seven years ago. A television had been set up in Kenny's classroom at Griggson Academy so that all the boys could witness the inaugural process—whereby leadership of the nation was transferred, seamlessly and without armed conflict, from one person to another through the minimal presentation of thirty-five words sworn before the Almighty.

Kenny didn't really focus on Kidd at the moment of oath-taking. Kenny mostly studied the people around Kidd: Chief

Justice Metz who was administering the oath; Mrs. Kidd at her husband's shoulder, looking firm, determined and utterly satisfied; Annabelle Kidd, back then a skinny seventh-grader who had braces and big teeth, and was showing them off proudly with a beaming smile; and in the middle, holding the Bible, Kidd's mother Anna, a vibrant, younger-looking woman who, no one suspected then, would not be alive the next time her son took the same oath.

That was really the point, Kenny realized, reflecting back on the months of testimony and revelations involving Pastrygate: When did fortune begin to turn poor for Charles Bentley Kidd? What started his tumble? Kenny could see the answer as clearly as he could see the knuckled landscape of desert Utah. It was the moment his mother died.

Until that afternoon two years into his first term, old Chuckybent was a semi-competent leader of the free world. He jetted off to all corners of the country, where he gave rousing speeches and promised the citizenry that this recession, although the longest since the Great Depression, would not last. That people would be back to work again. That factories would hum under the spin of output. That disposable incomes would rise like a phoenix. That there was hope—great hope— if only America would follow his course.

The problem was, there wasn't much of a course to follow. For while Kidd seemed messianic when giving speeches, he came across as particularly soft on action once those speeches were done. Details never concerned him, nor did the need to put his signature on any bill sent over to the White House by Congress. He was a president consumed with the ideal, and once he had given voice to that ideal, it was the job of the citizenry to make it happen. Why muck up the People's ability to perform great acts with any further involvement on his part? Why taint their creativity with specifics? Let them succeed by their own accord. As someone born in the 1950s, Kidd was all about the can-do attitude, and he seemed to have an innate distrust of legislative involvement. As long as the nation's industrial output turned positive, which it did for the first time in nine quarters at the end of Kidd's inaugural year, the people of America were willing to ride out his idiosyncrasies. Unemployment wasn't getting any worse, after all, and the average worker had more money in his pocket than he had pocketed under President Molson. And people liked Kidd. He was personable and good-looking, he had come from modest means so he didn't act entitled, and he was a master at making them gaze cheerfully at the skyline of their future, even if they could plainly see storm clouds on the horizon.

Then his mother died.

After Anna Kidd's funeral in Hawleyville, and an appropriate grieving period granted to him by the press, Kidd seemed to rebound. He hopped back on the touring circuit and continued to rally the country toward a brighter economic tomorrow. A year later he was back in Hawleyville to announce his bid for a second term. The country eagerly followed. Why wouldn't they? They didn't see anything outwardly different about Kidd.

But with his mother's passing, something had changed in the man. An ember ignited in him, smoldered in his breast, and grew hotter. In time, the heat it unleashed would turn into a conflagration, consuming all of America in a charred swath of economic destruction. But unlike most conflagrations, which are clearly visible from the heat, smoke and glow they put off, Kidd's fire was a well-kept secret, or so he thought. It would only jump into public view four years later when a pretty girl named Amanda Pacheco came to stand for the *second* time before the Joint House-Senate Committee Investigating the Memorial Day Appointments Affair. Looking nauseated and terrified, she raised her right hand and swore an oath of her own before the Almighty—that the testimony she was about to give *this time around* would be the truth, the whole truth and nothing but the truth.

"So help you God?" the co-chairman of the committee asked. "Again?"

"So help me—" she replied. Then she fainted.

Signs, Kenny thought.

He was looking at a blue sign along the side of the highway which stated bluntly, "No Services on I-70 Next 100 Miles." The only problem for Kenny was that the sign came a few yards after the exit for Green River, the taking of which might have allowed him to use some of those last services—gas, food, beverage, and toilets—that would now be in zero supply as the Cadillac cut deeper into the crust of desert Utah. The sign in this instance came too late for Kenny to do anything about: To get back to the Green River exit, he would have to drive a long stretch of highway to the next exit, turn around, and drive back. Maybe it would have been better for highway planners to put the goddamn sign before the exit to Green River, when having knowledge of the upcoming dearth of facilities might have done him some good. At least he could have taken a piss in a proper restroom.

But Kenny took comfort in knowing that, in a way, he was experiencing exactly what the people of America had experienced with Charles Bentley Kidd: The signs for Kidd had come *after* the most logical point of exit for America's relationship with their president, that exit point being Kidd's re-election.

The first sign that there were problems brewing in the Kidd White House came one week after his second inauguration. Kidd had won re-election in a landslide, garnering sixty percent of the popular vote against a dour-faced pip-squeak named Mitchell Corn, senior three-term senator from Kentucky. What was not clear to Kenny, even at the time, was whether Kidd's overwhelming victory was a result of the People's outright support for Kidd's job performance, which was wanton at best, or their distaste for having a leader named President Corn, which was easy to say but hard not to laugh at. However, Kenny knew that if what had come down the road during the next two years of Kidd's second term had started its journey down that road just a few months earlier, it was clear that America would have surely preferred a president named Corn, even if his running mate was someone named Hole.

One week into his second term, Kidd returned from a state visit to South America and promptly fired the White House's longtime pastry chef—a tireless, jovial Frenchman named Remi LaCouer. The firing caused an uproar among the kitchen staff. Monsieur LaCouer was a twenty-six year veteran of the White House culinary trenches. He was considered a legend in Washington. But Kidd was unrepentant. When asked about it by a curious media, Kidd's press secretary, who looked as confused as everyone else, stated simply that the president wished to bring some down-home, American-style desserts to White House functions instead of the haughty, hard-to-pronounce confections M. LaCouer was known to serve. Instead of Mintet Tea Sorbet there would be strawberry shortcake; in place of Pistachio Chocolate Marquise there would be whoopie pies, a

New England favorite. To bring this folksy flavor to the White House, the president had found the perfect person—a twenty-three-year-old recent graduate of the Commonwealth Culinary Institute in Boston. Her name was Amanda Pacheco.

Like the "No Services" sign just after the exit for Green River, Kidd's firing of a White House icon was subtle. But also like the highway sign, it signaled a vast stretch of trouble for the next hundred miles.

What the public did not know then, but would come to know in lurid detail later, was that Kidd had met Amanda Pacheco the previous July on a campaign stop in Massachusetts. On a rainy Saturday afternoon, he had pulled his entourage into a pastry shop in Boston's North End saying he wanted a quick cream puff. And while that cream puff might have been delicious, what he became smitten with even more was the cream puff making the cream puffs.

And it was easy to see why Kidd took a liking to her. Described by one weekly news magazine during the ensuing scandal as "fairer than her Portuguese surname implies," Amanda Pacheco had curly auburn hair, high cheek bones, and electric blue eyes whose power of allure came through even in the many black-and-white photos of her that would soon be published in newspapers across the world. She also had a lusty young body that looked poised on the verge of curvaceous womanhood. She later testified that as he eyed her behind the counter, Kidd dispatched his chief of staff, Tom Prudell, to fetch her business card. She didn't have one, so she wrote her number in black marker on Mr. Prudell's shirtsleeve. Three weeks later, even though Kidd had Massachusetts sewn up in every poll of the day, he insisted that his campaign return to Boston. It was during the second stop that Amanda Pacheco quit her job in the North End and joined Kidd's entourage as campaign pastry chef.

Once Amanda Pacheco had been ensconced in the White House, with no hope for a turnabout in the fortunes of Monsieur LaCouer, the kitchen staff's fury over the firing went underground and the press moved on to other topics, but new signs of Kidd's lack of focus soon emerged.

In May, government jobless figures came out that shot the national unemployment rate up to seven percent. There was also a spike in inflation and a decrease in first-quarter output, which signaled a return to recession. Kidd's critics in Congress charged that his administration had fudged the numbers before the election—that they had purposely covered up a bleak economic picture in order to secure a second term. But whereas Kidd would have normally answered his accusers, or would have unleashed his loving press on them to dig up whatever dirt they might find, this time he said nothing, leading many Americans who were losing their jobs to believe that perhaps his critics were correct.

Kidd's uncharacteristic solitude grew worse over the summer and into the fall. In the past, Kidd would travel the country to rally the nation with hope for a brighter future; now he rarely left the White House, dispatching instead the vice president, Richard Russell, and even on some occasions his wife Peggy, to handle the chores. And over the next five months, as industrial output slumped, unemployment crept up a percent at a time, and gas prices entered the stratosphere, Kidd transformed himself from commander in chief to partier in chief, hosting more state dinners than any president before him, from countries most Americans needed to google to know even existed.

The festive atmosphere in the White House continued through the winter of Kidd's fifth year. As the economic crisis deepened to a point worse than that seen under Kidd's predecessor, Milquetoast Molson, Mrs. Kidd began to make the rounds of the television news programs. On these shows, where she appeared frail and worn, she would tell Americans what became known as "Peggy-Vision"—that her husband wasn't traveling because he was working so hard to find cures for the ailing economy; that all those state dinners were really missions to enhance trade; and that his quietness about the matter was his way of focusing energy on creative solutions. She even pointed to the fact that her husband spent many a night in the Oval Office as a testament of his commitment to their problems. "The president," she assured, "is hearing your cries for relief. He's hearing them loud and clear."

But contrary to his wife's faith in him, the only cries Charles Bentley Kidd was hearing at that time didn't come from the People, and they sure as hell weren't cries for relief. Instead, they were the sounds of a ripe, gushing, buck-naked pastry chef singing in orgasmic staccato as the leader of the free world had sex with her on the Cabinet Room conference table.

The sign that finally got America's attention came in April of Kidd's sixth year, just after Mrs. Kidd had spent the winter making the rounds of the news channels, Sunday morning talking-head programs, and even *60 Minutes*.

Citing the president's lack of effort on the economy, Kidd's secretary of the treasury resigned, effective immediately.

The resignation came as a shock, even in a time of economic quagmire, and the confirmation of the secretary's successor became a topic of debate on every news program and Internet site across America. Maybe Kidd would pick a Harvard economist or the CEO from some big New York bank. Whoever it was, the People wanted reassurances that the nominee would help their president get his head out of his ass (in hindsight—wrong appendage, wrong orifice) and pull the nation away from the rising stench of the economic crisis.

Kidd's supporters vowed quick action on the confirmation; Kidd's opponents held up the prospect of a filibuster if the nominee didn't meet strict standards. In an evenly divided Senate, the battle promised to be fierce. Citizen, news reporter and senator alike awaited Kidd's choice.

And they waited.

And they waited.

And they waited some more.

By the end of May, Kidd had not floated a single name for treasury secretary. Congress railed at his indecision; op-ed pieces in all the major newspapers chastised him and offered suggestions. Conspiracy theorists on the Internet blogged that Kidd was probably holding out because he didn't want a fight in the Senate. He could easily wait until Congress adjourned for Memorial Day to make a recess appointment—a right granted to every president by Section Two, Clause Three, of the Constitution, whereby Kidd could simply place a person in the position of treasury secretary, and have said person operate in that capacity, even though he or she were unconfirmed by the Senate, until the end of the Congressional session, which would occur the following January.

To its credit, the blogosphere was half-right. When Congress broke for Memorial Day, Charles Bentley Kidd did indeed make a recess appointment. In fact, he made three. Of those, not one was for secretary of the treasury. Nor were they for any position that would operate inside the United States. Most curious of all, none had an appointee over the age of twenty-five.

With a sound as hushed as the swish of pen across parchment, Pastrygate had begun.

On the last day of May, two days before the Senate returned from holiday break, the White House website announced that President Charles Bentley Kidd had recess-appointed Jennifer Smithee, Sarah Muldoon, and Daniella O'Brien to be the United States Ambassadors to Jamaica, the Bahamas and Trinidad and Tobago, respectively.

As the Cadillac sped along a canyon floor in Utah's San Rafael Valley, Kenny reflected on that moment, understanding now just how much of a violation of protocol those recess appointments had been. During the administration of President Reagan, very clear ground rules were established between the White House and the Senate for how to initiate, properly, the touchy process of recess appointments, since the Constitution, as was typically its way, didn't provide any guidance in the matter. The deal struck between President Reagan and the Senate (represented in negotiations by The Honorable Robert C. Byrd of West Virginia) required a president who was considering recess appointments to submit a list to Congress with the names he was considering, and the positions for which he was considering them. If anyone in the Senate objected to a particular potential appointee, that senator would make his or her objection known to the president before the break, thus asking him to remove the offending name from consideration. Over time, the Reagan-Byrd Agreement had become the ironclad method for recess appointments. It was not law, but its legality and constitutionality had never been challenged in the Supreme Court. So by the end of May, when Kidd neglected to provide the Senate with a list of potential nominees for treasury secretary, or for any other open positions as well, most senators believed no appointments were forthcoming and simply left on vacation, preparing to take up the fight come June. And while there was a fight in June after all, that fight was like nothing they expected.

Immediately upon their return, senators from both parties cried foul. They argued that President Kidd had violated the nature of the Reagan-Byrd Agreement, and that he had "shat" (one senator actually used the word on C-Span) on the Constitution of the United States. Matters only got worse when they found out that Jennifer Smithee, Sarah Muldoon, and Daniella O'Brien had ages that ranged from twenty-two to twenty-five.

It was at that point, Kenny reflected now, that the country came unglued, but at the same time started to fixate nightly on the news programs and talking-head channels.

Why was President Kidd appointing three girls just out of college, none of whom had yet to hold a job in the real world, to be ambassadors to small Caribbean island nations? Susan Fratz of NBC even managed to ask Jennifer Smithee that question a week later when she and her camera crew discovered the lanky brunette sunning herself on a beach a few miles outside of Kingston.

"Do you think you were the best choice to be Ambassador to Jamaica?" Susan Fratz asked.

To which Jennifer Smithee reportedly pulled off her sunglasses, threw a scowl at Susan Fratz and said, "The real title is 'Ambassador Extraordinary and Plenipotentiary to Jamaica.' That's 'Extraordinary' and 'Plenipotentiary.' Get it right, bitch!" Then Ambassador Smithee got up, grabbed her beach chair, and stormed off the sand, ending the interview.

While the rest of the nation was wondering aloud about Kidd's connection to the "Caribbean Queens," and editors at the New York and Washington broadsheets were assembling teams to find the link, the crack in the case came from a much smaller newspaper. The man who unraveled the mystery of Pastrygate was only twenty-four years of age himself, and he wasn't even a reporter. His name was Bill Bonifay. His trade—circulation associate at the *Providence Guardian*.

In his telling, Bill Bonifay had gone to Boston University to major in journalism. At some point during his sophomore year, just before dropping out due to a catastrophically-low grade point average, he spent three weeks dating a junior at Boston's Wheelock College named Daniella O'Brien. Daniella O'Brien, if Bill Bonifay remembered correctly (and he was sure he did, given the incredible hotness of the girl in question), had three roommates that year: a brunette named Jennifer, a bleach blonde named Sarah, and a sweet, auburn-haired girl from the Commonwealth Culinary Institute named Amanda. A call by the *Guardian* to the management company of the property confirmed last names. Jennifer Smithee, Sarah Muldoon, Daniella O'Brien and Amanda Pacheco had been roommates in Boston while attending college, although none of them went to the same college.

For his journalistic endeavors in the case, the *Guardian* immediately promoted Bill Bonifay to beat writer for the local minor league baseball affiliate. Charles Bentley Kidd wasn't so lucky—all the *Guardian* did for him was land his ass in a Congressional investigation.

After the *Guardian* article came out, the question both America and Congress were asking shifted from "What is Kidd's relationship to the Caribbean Queens?" to "What is Kidd's relationship with Amanda Pacheco?" The signpost that they had passed and ignored so long ago, when Kidd had replaced Remi LaCouer with the nubile pastry chef, now loomed as large in everyone's memory as one that declared "Bridge Out" for a car that was approaching a chasm.

The press began to dog Amanda Pacheco wherever she went, from her apartment in Arlington, to her health club near the Pentagon, to her Metro ride to the White House. The questions they asked were brutal and withering:

"Are you the president's mistress?"

"What exactly did you have to do to get President Kidd to appoint your friends?"

"Do you know what your ex-boyfriends are saying about you?"

The press corps interviewed former classmates. They went back to her hometown of Cranston, Rhode Island, and found pictures of Amanda Pacheco with short hair, acne, and braces. They showed America what she looked like as an awkward student in middle school and then a stunning senior in high school. They dug up anyone who had ever seen her smoke a cigarette, or possessed firsthand knowledge of a blowjob she had given to a boy in a local garage band. They went through her trash, set up cameras outside her apartment windows, and rang her telephone sixty times an hour trying to entice her to come out and say something (anything, dammit!) to bring clarification to this situation. But Amanda Pacheco never said a word, other than to deny that she had ever engaged in any improper relationship with Charles Bentley Kidd. She kept her head down, her eyes on the ground, and her high-voltage smile tucked away.

For his part, Kidd claimed nothing improper as well. He stepped out of his yearlong silence to deny, categorically, that he had done anything inappropriate. Kidd could be coy, and often charming, but even Kenny, as a high school student, hadn't bought Kidd's defense. It was obvious as the summer wore on that Congress wasn't buying it either, once details of his and Amanda Pacheco's relationship began to emerge. One turning point occurred when a bellhop in Topeka swore on FOX News that, during the campaign, he had seen Amanda Pacheco leaving Kidd's presidential suite in a flushed and sweaty state. When the anchor asked the bellhop what he had done next, the bellhop admitted that he'd gone downstairs to masturbate in a supply closet. "The sight of this amazing girl, with all that sweaty slick on her, looking like she'd just gotten her brains boned out, well, that was too much for me to handle," he told America. Later, he signed a production deal with the Family Values Channel to do an hour-long after-school special entitled "Give Yourself a Hand!" about the benefits of masturbation over premarital sex for today's youth.

With the revelation from the bellhop, Congress acted swiftly to convene a joint House-Senate committee, and implored the president to testify. Kidd refused to show up in person, but he did offer to submit answers to written questions. His answers to those questions proved to be as coy as the ones he was giving to the press. When asked, based on White House logs, why Amanda Pacheco was in the West Wing at this time or that time, Kidd simply stated, "She was giving me her cream-filled goodies." When asked if Kidd had at any time engaged in a sexual relationship with Amanda Pacheco, be it one of digital, oral, or penetrative coitus, Kidd wrote that he didn't have any knowledge of what Miss Pacheco was like *in* bed, but he could say for certain that the young pastry chef sure knew how to make a mean whoopie pie *out* of it.

Next, Congress called Amanda Pacheco, and although she did show up at the hearing, she, too, continued to play tough. In front of a nationwide audience, with the lawyer provided by her mother at her side, the stunning Amanda simply answered "No, sir," to every question asked by the committee that would indicate a sexual link between her and the president, and that she had used that link to gain ambassadorships for her friends. Her testimony lasted only three hours, but everybody in America was talking about it for three weeks. By the time November rolled around, and the terms of ambassadorship were nearing an end for the Caribbean Queens (who had managed to get killer tans, but accomplished precious little on the diplomatic front), Congress's investigation hit a dead end. Nobody was talking.

Everything changed, however, when Amanda Pacheco returned home to Rhode Island just before Thanksgiving. She had resigned her White House position at the beginning of the month, vacated her apartment, and fled the hounding press in the dead of night. Some of the press, she would later say, had followed her Honda as far as the George Washington Bridge before she lost them with a white-knuckled detour through the Bronx.

At home, Amanda Pacheco may have thought she was in the comfort of family, people who would never betray her trust, but she was wrong. One night in December, after enduring all the pressure of the previous months, Amanda Pacheco finally broke down, but to the worst possible person—her mother.

When Amanda Pacheco was done sobbing, confessing the truth, and apologizing for what she had done, she collapsed in an exhausted mass on the weave rug of her bedroom floor. If she had been expecting some motherly succor with her admission, she didn't get any. Instead, Ellen Pacheco picked up the phone and called one of the co-chairs of the joint House-Senate committee—at his vacation home in the Blue Ridge Mountains. That co-chair was none other than Senator Mitchell Corn, Kidd's former opponent for the presidency. Within ten minutes, he had agreed to provide Amanda Pacheco with full immunity if she would return to testify in front of the very committee she had lied to just a few months earlier. Senator Corn told Amanda Pacheco that the offer was fleeting. Her mother was more blunt:

"You tell them what really happened and get on with your life," she reportedly said to her daughter in a fit of rage, "or I tell them and you go to jail for perjury." Then she pulled open a set of blinds and banged on the dining room window that faced a press entourage still entrenched at the end of her driveway. "But. This. Stupid. Game. Ends. Now!"

The game for Amanda Pacheco ended on a dank, sleety afternoon during the first week of January, after a fainting face plant into the witness table.

Once she had been restored to consciousness by the Capitol medical staff, Amanda Pacheco completed her oath. Then she wiggled nervously in her chair and told the committee (and

America) the whole sordid truth about her relationship with the president of the United States.

She had first slept with Charles Bentley Kidd the day he returned to Boston for his second campaign stop in three months. After their initial meeting in the pastry shop, he had called her six times from the campaign trail and twice from the Oval Office. Although it was just to chat, each conversation left her bedazzled—awash in butterflies, girlish delight, and primal desire. Charles Bentley Kidd was to her the most handsome man she had ever seen. All she knew from that first encounter at the pastry shop, where he simply flashed his sweet eyes at her time and again as she filled cream puffs, was that she wanted to follow him to the ends of the earth, and maybe even the stars, if he would have her.

She maintained that their first sexual experience was a complete accident. She met him at his hotel, where Tom Prudell had arranged for a private tasting of her confections in President Kidd's suite. According to Mr. Prudell, it was a job interview. When she arrived, Kidd was so happy to see her that he offered her the campaign pastry chef position right there. When she accepted, Kidd hugged her. Then he kissed her. Then she kissed him back. Then they devoured each other.

During the two-hour "tasting," they made love (or as the junior senator from Illinois kept correcting her: "had sexual congress") on the bathroom floor, in the reclining chair, against a bookshelf, at the base of the minibar refrigerator, and under the desk with the fax machine on it. She described Charles Bentley Kidd as a master lover—gentle of touch, soft of voice, but voracious in all the right places.

"What places were those?" Representative Shoehammer from Oregon demanded to know.

"Basically, my clitoris," she replied, before adding with the doe-eyed innocence of a young pastry chef from Rhode Island, "He always plunges his head down there like he's trying to win a pie-eating contest." The gallery snickered at this statement, and more than a few congressmen coughed with fists to their mouths, but the ironic double entendre didn't seem to register with Amanda Pacheco. She was, after all, in the business of making pies.

They next asked her when she had joined Kidd's campaign, to which she answered, "Immediately," explaining that the "sexual congress" snowballed from there, as she and the president continued their liaisons in secret but enjoyed them no less passionately.

One representative asked how the committee could be certain that she had actually had a sexual relationship with President Kidd. She said that she could describe his private parts from memory, particularly the mole on his penis that looked like one of those states out west ("Idaho," another of Kidd's conquests would later verify).

A committee member asked if she had been the first extramarital sexual liaison the president had engaged in while in office. To this question she replied that she had not been Kidd's first sexual relationship since he had assumed the presidency, but that the committee should just leave her testimony at that.

But the committee couldn't leave her testimony at that. They pushed for more information. They demanded it. They wanted to know with whom the president said he'd had sex since taking office, and they reminded her that her immunity deal was contingent upon telling the full truth.

So Amanda Pacheco told them. With jittery breaths, she said that President Kidd had confessed to her that after his mother died, he had taken up sexual relations with a number of women in an attempt to stem his grief. She wouldn't name names, but from memory she could state that such a list would include many Hollywood actresses, a number of network news reporters (one each from FOX News and CNN), some swimsuit models she had later seen in *Sports Illustrated*, and the MVP of a professional women's basketball league who stood a full eight inches taller than the president and was apparently large in all ways. "Like climbing Mount Kilimanjaro, then falling into a crevasse," Kidd had described his romp with her.

"Is that all?" Representative Widman asked.

"Not quite," Miss Pacheco said. "But I really think you should stop."

"Let us be the judge of when we should stop, Miss Pacheco," Senator Jenkins said.

"You don't want to know," she said.

"I think we do want to know," Senator Jenkins said.

"And this time, name names," Senator Corn added.

So Amanda Pacheco expanded her list, reveling in payback by rattling off a string of monikers that sounded like a roll call of Congress. At one point she even asked that a Congressional directory be brought to her so she could thumb through it and get the names right, or remember any that she might be forgetting.

That's when the committee members began to gasp. One representative asked, "Are you implying, Miss Pacheco, that President Kidd seduced the wives of some members of Congress?"

"I'm not implying anything, Congressman," Amanda Pacheco said. "I'm telling you. Bent—excuse me, President Kidd—told me that in the year before we met, he'd had sex with a bunch of your wives, and he told me who they were."

"But… when?" a two-term senator from Oklahoma asked.

"When what?" Amanda Pacheco said. "When did he tell me who they were, or when did he have sex with them?"

"The sex, the sex!" the same senator said.

"I'm pretty sure it was during all those after-hours coffee talks he used to hold in the Green Room," Amanda Pacheco said. Then she reflected for a moment and added, "I don't think coffee was ever served."

It was at that point that the room erupted in commotion, such chaos that even twelve bangs of Senator Corn's gavel couldn't quell it. With frantic eyes, the committee members lurched back and forth toward each other, seeming to say "Was it my wife?" An open microphone even caught one representative calling Kidd, unequivocally, "that rotten motherfucker." Finally, when order had been restored, Senator Corn asked Amanda Pacheco to retire to an antechamber, where she would be expected to provide a detailed list of President Kidd's conquests—starlets, reporters, models, athletes, and yes, even wives. She obliged. It was this list, meant to be kept private, which was eventually leaked to the *National Enquirer* by an anonymous source. And the first name on the list was the pretty but prudish wife of one Senator Mitchell Corn, with an annotation in Amanda Pacheco's handwriting stating that Kidd had seduced her on the campaign trail with the line, "Mitch may have some corn, Brenda, but I've got the whole cob."

After the medical staff resuscitated Senator Corn, he returned to the committee room with a newfound vengeance, supported by seven congressmen beside and behind him who had also seen their wives' names on Miss Pacheco's list. He directed Amanda Pacheco to tell them about her time in the

White House, and to focus specifically on how her friends came to possess coveted ambassadorships to small island nations.

Amanda Pacheco replied that her time in the White House was a continuation of what had begun on the campaign trail. "He missed me after the election," she said. "He needed to get me there. And I wanted to be there." She described marathon sex sessions in the Oval Office and quickies in the Map Room; naked romps on the Red Room's scroll-arm sofa and doggie-styles in Lincoln's bed. But most of all, she talked about food fetishes: rich, sticky bouts of sex where any confectionary item was fair game—chocolate syrup, cupcake batter, buttercream icing with a hint of Grand Marnier. She even testified that once, in the Oval Office, as Kidd sat behind his desk sucking on one of the special lollipops she had made for him—heart-shaped, with a big American bow tied around the stem—and she sat on the desk straddling him, unclothed from the waist down, she asked him if she had gotten the flavor of the lollipop right. She was not a candy maker, after all, but a pastry chef, and it was her first foray into lollipops. Kidd, she said, grinned at her, then he took the lollipop from his mouth, inserted it into her vagina, twirled it around, stuck it back in his mouth and said, "Now it's perfect." She said he named the maraschino-and-vanilla flavor "Amanda's Cherry." The exact recipe, Kidd insisted, would be a state secret.

But for all the joy Kidd reportedly got from his and Amanda Pacheco's journey into the blissful union of food and fornication, it was ultimately that connection which would topple his presidency.

Nearing the end of her day in front of the committee, after eight grueling hours of testimony, she recounted the night the previous April when she had talked with Kidd, quite off-the-cuff, about the situations of her three former roommates from Boston. It was an innocent topic, she maintained; she only told the president that the economy was so bad in the Northeast that her friends couldn't find jobs, especially for girls who had majored in modern dance, sociology, and horticulture. They had all recently graduated and their résumés were a little thin on experience. She wanted to know if he could help them.

"Anything they want," she said Kidd replied, before he added with a wink, "but it's going to cost you."

Kenny never saw Amanda Pacheco's testimony firsthand. With no television allowed in the Kernick house, and with Kenny's senior year history teacher unwilling to show this side of the presidency to his students, Kenny could only read about the committee's reaction to Miss Pacheco's statement in the newspapers Carl brought home each evening. But even from their staid black newsprint, lifeless on a page, Kenny knew that Miss Pacheco's blasé revelation was the moment each and every congressman on the committee leaned forward in his or her chair, until a dead silence overtook the room.

"Really?" was the first word to follow, from the mouth of Representative Shareece Walters of Florida. "What did he charge you?"

"It was a joke," Amanda Pacheco countered, realizing that on a day in which she had spent eight hours saying everything, she had finally said too much. "It was just a game we played."

"So there were other times that he made you give him things for favors?" Senator Corn asked.

"It was just our way," Amanda Pacheco pleaded. "We were playing. Don't you play with your wife, Senator?" The question, Kenny realized now, might have been more effective had Charles Bentley Kidd not played with Senator Corn's wife.

"The return, Miss Pacheco?" Senator Corn demanded. "What did you give him in return?"

And that's when Amanda Pacheco, a pastry chef from Rhode Island barely two years out of school, drove a dagger into the heart of a presidency. Under oath, she admitted that in exchange for President Kidd's help in finding jobs for her friends, she had smeared herself with honey and let Kidd lick her to a shine.

"And why—" Senator Corn asked, rubbing his sweaty temples after a long day of revelations that would ultimately end his marriage as well, "why did Mr. Kidd give them ambassadorships? To the Caribbean, no less?"

To this question, Amanda Pacheco reportedly shrugged. Then she replied, "I don't know why he made them ambassadors, Senator. All I told him was that they loved the beach."

With the conclusion of Amanda Pacheco's testimony before the Joint House-Senate Committee Investigating the Memorial Day Appointments Affair, which was being referred to as "Pastrygate" by all the leading news outlets, it was clear to everyone in America that Charles Bentley Kidd's presidency was finished.

Within minutes of Amanda Pacheco's departure from the Capitol, cries went out from all corners of the nation for Kidd to resign. The collective anger brewed to a froth in offices, on subway trains, during lines at the grocery checkout, through e-mail, and across social networking websites. Talk radio hosts pilloried him for his previous denials; Hollywood actors interrupted press junkets to sound off on his disgraceful behavior within their industry. FOX News, CNN, and the WNBA had no comment.

One New York City tabloid newspaper, finding a sliver of amusement in the whole situation, headlined its next day's edition with the mocking words "Sexual Congress!" which only served to piss off members of Congress even more. By the weekend, there were bumper stickers on cars from Maine to Monterey Beach which shouted from bold print: "Kidd got laid. I got laid off."

Members of Kidd's inner circle were not immune to the backlash, nor were they supportive of their leader. Kidd's Cabinet began to make the rounds of the Sunday morning news programs, often using phrases like "I don't know how he survives this," before discussing their prospects of working under Vice President Russell. Three of Kidd's top-level advisers, who would not have been welcomed in a Russell Administration, quit on the same day, citing a newfound lack of admiration for their boss as the main cause.

But the biggest blow to Kidd, and the biggest shock to the country, came a week after Amanda Pacheco's testimony, when Kidd's wife left him. In doing so, she became the first first lady ever to separate from her husband while he was in office. True to her style as first lady, Peggy Kidd made her moment in history count. She called in all the news crews she could find to photograph her departure from the White House, then upon landing at O'Hare Airport in a private jet, she descended to a podium on the tarmac and made a grand, expletive-filled announcement that she could no longer accept the philandering of her husband, and that she was leaving him to focus on her life and what was important to her. The only thing she asked in her departure was that the press leave her daughter alone. As for Kidd, she gave them her permission to "roast the cocksucker like a pig on a spit."

For two weeks, Charles Bentley Kidd stayed quiet. It was reported that he didn't come down from his quarters in the house proper, nor did he take meals, or even telephone calls. Press reports stated that the only person authorized to speak with him was Tom Prudell, his chief of staff, and sometimes only by scribbled note. To add another surreal element to the situation, in the third week of January he delivered his annual State of the Union address in writing, a procedure allowed by the Constitution through Article Two, Section Three, but seen by members of Congress and the populace at large as a tacit admission of guilt. Speculation abounded that he was really preparing to resign. Some staff members claimed he could be heard Ωtalking to a portrait of President Nixon that he had taken up to his room. Many Americans wondered in fear if anybody was even running the country.

Then on the Sunday afternoon following the State of the Union delivery, Charles Bentley Kidd emerged from the White House to speak with a group of reporters who were gathering on the South Lawn.

"Will you resign?" they asked him.

"Hell, no," Kidd said. He referred to himself as a patsy, a scapegoat. He stated that the authority to recess appoint was a right granted to him by the Constitution. He called on Congress to level charges against Mitchell Corn on the grounds of treason, for Senator Corn was obviously trying to subvert the results of the last election. He pleaded with the press to highlight his brilliant triumphs in office instead of his tiny failures. He pointed to the fact that the trade deficit had actually shrunk under his leadership, and that he had never once tried to raise taxes. He even reminded them that he was the man who had finally brought peace to the nations of Peru and Chile, although no one save Kidd seemed to know what it was, exactly, that Peru and Chile had been fighting about in the first place. He extolled his trusted press, begged them really, to go forth and give America the good news on Charles Bentley Kidd.

The press did no such thing. By then, their own human natures had begun to consume them. Instead of opting for pieces that would elevate Kidd's standing, they seemed more content to dig up skeletons from his past. They had plenty of skeletons to exhume—in time, more women came forward to say that they had engaged in trysts with Charles Bentley Kidd, some of the romances going back as far as Kidd's days in the Ohio House of Representatives.

In the end, Kenny knew, Congress had no choice but to impeach Kidd. The business of the United States had reached a state of inertia, and it was clear that Kidd was not going to be the one to get the molecules moving again. Using Amanda Pacheco's testimony and Kidd's own notarized responses to the committee's written questions, the members of the House Judiciary Committee voted unanimously to put forth fifteen Articles of Impeachment—seven for obstruction of justice; five for providing false statements to Congress; and three for accepting a bribe. By the sheer volume of charges, Kidd was certain to be found guilty on at least one count, and one guilty verdict was all it would take to remove him from office. That one of Kidd's former conquests was the wife of the current head of the House Judiciary Committee, or that many of the husbands he had cuckolded were the senators who would decide his fate, didn't seem to matter to the country. People wanted Kidd gone, and they phoned and e-mailed their senators and representatives daily to tell them so, until the Capitol's telecommunications lines jammed and its e-mail servers crashed. By the end of March, the full House had passed the Articles of Impeachment and submitted them to the Senate. On May fourteenth, after a three-week trial whose outcome was never in doubt, Kidd was convicted on all counts.

Charles Bentley Kidd, however, remained indignant to the end—never resigning, never apologizing, and never admitting guilt to any degree. Even on his last day in office, he managed to piss people off. "That goddamn lollipop," they would say. Walking out of the Oval Office with that bow-tied lollipop sticking out of his mouth was viewed by most people who saw it as a big "Fuck You!" not only to America but to them personally. These people had voted for him, relied on him, placed great hope and trust in him, that this man named Kidd might, from the day of his first inauguration, do anything—just one thing—to help them. He had the power to help them, after all; they had given it to him. Now they were taking away that power by their right, and he couldn't even have the dignity to respect them for it. "That fucking lollipop."

Absolutely, Kenny thought now. That lollipop was a "Fuck You!" What an asshole Kidd had been! What a douche! Kenny took his eyes off the road and looked at Kidd in the passenger seat. Kidd was just sitting there, staring blankly out the windshield at the flowing pale canyon lands of eastern Utah. Kenny felt his eyes narrow to contemptuous slits. To Kenny, Kidd just looked too content for a man who had caused so much anxiety to so many.

So Kenny Kernick decided right then and there that it was incumbent upon him, given the opportunity of proximity, to exact retribution for the People. He lifted his hand off the steering wheel and made a fist. "My fellow Americans," he whispered, "this one's for you." Then he cocked his arm back, released it like a spring-hinged door, and slammed Charles Bentley Kidd square in the nose.

CHAPTER 24

★ ★

"You bent my friggin' septum!"

Charles Bentley Kidd was using the rear-view mirror to check his nose. His voice nasally, Kidd poked and prodded it, wincing in over-dramatized pain as he cursed Kenny loudly for taking a swing that he never saw coming.

Kenny's punch had not drawn blood. What it had done was instigate a fight in which one short boy and one tall man, locked together in a claustrophobic car cabin, threw fists and palms at each other. The fight raged all the way into the Fishlake National Forest in central Utah. As the Cadillac climbed the mountains, Kenny's and Kidd's blows fell on each other. At one point, the Cadillac, lacking a focused driver, almost swerved off the highway and into a large ravine. There were screams. There were shouts. There were pushes and shoves. F-bombs exploded. Kidd called Kenny a glorified midget. Kenny said that Kidd was a philandering fuck-knob. In the end, the fight had left Charles Bentley Kidd with only a few bruises to go with his bent nose. Unfortunately for Kenny, it had left him with much worse—a pair of cracked coke-bottle glasses.

"You're paying for this," Kidd said, pointing to his nose. He twisted the rear-view mirror back toward Kenny. "If I have to have surgery on this sucker, you're paying for it. And I want some emotional damages out of it, too. Do you know what deviated septum surgery is like?! If you think I'm letting that slide, pal, you're mis-fucking-staken! I'll send you the bill!"

Kenny adjusted the mirror to provide a functional rear view, then said, "Well, buddy, you're paying for my glasses now."

"That was your own damn fault," Kidd said. He rubbed at a welt on his cheek.

"The hell it was," Kenny countered. On this point, Kenny knew he was right. His glasses had not cracked in the heat of battle, as collateral damage from a wayward blow or an over-zealous slug. They had cracked because Charles Bentley Kidd had gone fucking crazy. Kidd had deliberately pulled the glasses off Kenny's face, placed them against the dashboard, and beat them ferociously with his fist, until both lenses shattered into spider webs, all while a blind Kenny fumbled against Kidd to get them back. Out of distraction, Kenny had nearly taken the Cadillac under the wheels of a Mack truck. The car had even scraped a guard rail. When reminded of these points, and that Kidd's action had almost caused their deaths, Kidd relented and agreed to buy Kenny a new pair of glasses when they got to Las Vegas. With that agreement, a truce was declared, although Kenny's anger persisted. Frothing with adrenaline, he still wanted to punch Kidd, and judging from the rigidity of Kidd's lips, he suspected the former president of harboring similar notions.

So it was through cracked eyeglasses that Kenny continued toward Las Vegas, and toward darkness. With such a late start on the day, it was dusk by the time the Cadillac turned off I-70 and onto I-15 South at the Mineral Mountains, and it was fully dark by the time the vehicle crossed the Utah-Arizona border. By then, Kenny had acclimated to the play of headlights on the spidery weave of his lenses. He was not prepared, however, for the sight of Las Vegas ninety minutes later, when it emerged from the vacuous darkness of the desert as an ocean of glowing orange pearls bobbing along the black valley floor. Seeing that brilliant ocean unfold and spread out in the jags of his glasses, Kenny felt as if he might at any moment succumb to vertigo.

As the Cadillac pushed into the city, Kenny's view sank below the ocean's pearl surface, which was made up of the orange street lights that comprised the Las Vegas grid. Now other lights took precedence, and they were everywhere—on billboards, and buildings, and palm trees. The whole city was defined by lights of every size, shape and color. Kenny felt drawn to them like a moth to moonlight, wanting to give in to their beckoning to see "The Showgirls of Space" at the Luna, or Krutchfeld and Marzook's "Call of the Jaguar" at The Mexicale, or to walk under The Fremont Street Experience, whatever that was. There was even a billboard bathed in scintillating purple neon that announced a Virgin Convention taking place in Las Vegas all this week, complete with a Miss Teen Virgin USA Pageant tomorrow night at Nevada State University's Langdon Arena. A bunch of virgins descending on the City of Sin, Kenny told himself, smiling. Somehow, he had made it to the right place.

When the Cadillac approached the junction for I-515, Kidd was bouncing in his seat in wonderment, but not at the lights. Kidd was ogling the hotels. "Maybe we should stay at Main Street Station, or the California, or Golden Gate!" he shouted. This part of Las Vegas looked like a revitalized downtown, and the big bulbs on its casinos' exteriors made those buildings appear retro. Disregarding the lights, the casino buildings themselves were fairly bland and utilitarian, probably built during the bomb-shelter craze of the Eisenhower Administration. Not much to look at, Kenny thought. Then the Cadillac swung around a bend in the highway and the sights quickly changed.

Another set of hotels came into view. Casinos which were larger, newer, and more melodramatic in their designs and themes than those downtown. Each casino was bathed in floodlights, contrasting its shape crisply against the dark sky, and presenting Kenny with a feast for the eyes. Kidd was enjoying the view as well. His enthusiasm toppled over into full-blown euphoria as he told Kenny that these casinos were part of the Las Vegas Strip. He began to rattle off their names as they grew larger in the Cadillac's windshield.

"Circus Circus, and Wynn, and Treasure Island," he said. "And look, there's The Mirage and Caesar's Palace—God, they're regal. And look at that one, Kenny." Kidd motioned to a place called Bellagio. "We should stay there. Bellagio has amazing water fountains. Do you want to stay there and see the water fountains, Kenny? Don't you think we should stay there? Oh, and Paris—look fast!" Kenny jerked his head to the left and caught a glance at the word "Paris" scrolled onto the front of an illuminated hot air balloon; it stood next to a scaled-down version of the Eiffel Tower which was alight in gold. "Have you ever been to Paris, Kenny? Well, here's your chance."

Kidd was on demonstrative fire, just as he had been back in Hawleyville, pointing, regaling, and never stopping for breath. Which was why Kenny was taken aback when Kidd suddenly shut up. Kenny looked over at the former president and saw Kidd's eyes awash with delirium, his tongue shedding saliva.

When Kidd finally spoke, he spoke reverently, lifting his left arm and commanding Kenny to follow its extension to the end.

"Behold, Young Kernick," Kidd said. "That is where we shall stay."

Kenny looked ahead and noticed a resort snuggled between the Bellagio and the Monte Carlo. Its main hotel complex was comprised of five buildings—four shorter structures surrounding one big building in the middle. The four shorter structures were spherical and shaped like lollipops; the big one in the middle was white and took the form of a marshmallow. Connecting the large marshmallow with the smaller lollipops at its corners were terraces and walkways and lattice work, all adorned with giant, illuminated cookies and cupcakes and chocolate bars. The resort was obviously a new construction, which wasn't hard for Kenny to deduce, given the "Grand Opening" announcement that was featured on electric mesh banners slung along the top of the big marshmallow. But the name of the casino was what struck Kenny more than any other feature; it reminded him of a game he used to play with his mother when he was four years old. That game and this casino were both called "CandyLand."

But Kenny couldn't tell if it was the name of the resort which had grabbed Kidd's attention, or if it was the event billboard located beneath the casino's signature sign. In the smooth electric weave of a high-definition display, the billboard proclaimed, "CandyLand Welcomes Delegates to the Virgin Convention—Monday through Thursday." Kidd answered Kenny's question soon enough.

"Candy and virgins!" Kidd said. "Mmmm, Mmmm. I've never had a virgin before. Well, it's time. Let's get a room."

The Cadillac veered off I-15 at Exit 36. Kenny took a left onto Russell Road and took the first left off Russell onto Las

Vegas Boulevard. That's where the dazzle really started. Every sign was electrified—gas station signs, a McDonald's sign, signs for parking lots, then the signature signs for Mandalay Bay, Luna, Luxor, and Excalibur. They played on the eye with their shimmy and roll, an effect which was enhanced for Kenny by the kaleidoscopic cracks in his glasses.

Once the Cadillac crossed Tropicana Avenue, his journey ended. As he approached Harmon Avenue, Kidd indicated a left turn, and Kenny brought them to the drop-off area for the CandyLand Resort and Casino. A spindly valet dressed in khakis and a candy-striped t-shirt signaled for the car to stop. Before Kenny knew it, he was standing outside the Cadillac, his and Kidd's bags were on the curb, and the Cadillac was gone. In his hand, Kenny held a ticket stub that told him to call a certain number when he wanted to get his car back.

"Are you gentlemen checking in?" The question came from a pimply-faced young fellow in a straw-colored business suit. He shook Kidd's hand, then Kenny's, and told them that his name was Bailey, and that he was an official greeter with the CandyLand.

"That depends," Kidd said about a check-in. "Do we need a reservation?"

The greeter shifted in his shoes and replied that the resort was full this week, given the circumstances of its grand opening and the fact that it was currently being inundated with more than fifty virgin entourages, in town for their annual convention. "But I'd be happy to help you find other accommodations, sir, if that's what you'd like."

"What I'd like," Kidd said, "is to stay here. Preferably at the top of that big marshmallow. If it helps our cause, then you should know that my assistant, Kenny, is a virgin. Isn't that right, Kenny? Well, he's still technically one, anyway. I think there's a Mormon in Grand Junction who might disagree. Let's say we sign him up for this convention and get me a room."

"I'm sorry, sir," the greeter said, "but that's logistically impossible. However, if you'd like to enjoy some gaming—"

Kidd cut him off with a raised palm. He said that gaming wasn't what he had in mind. What he did want was for the greeter to put him in touch with the manager. When the greeter said that the manager was very busy tonight dealing with virgins, Kidd pulled rank.

"Do you know who I am?" he asked the greeter.

The conversation between the two men came to a painful halt. Kenny could tell that something was in charge of Kidd now, and it wasn't Kidd's rational brain. Most likely it was his Lil' Kidd wanting to get a hold of a virgin—preferably chocolate-covered.

Kidd struck a profile. "Get a good look at my face, greeter boy. Who do I look like? Think pastry."

The greeter took a step back and studied Kidd. Then he let out a gasp. "Oh my God, I didn't even recognize you. You're Charles Bentley Kidd."

"Exactly," Kidd said. "And who was I?"

"You were the president of the United States," the greeter said.

"How important is a president of the United States, former or otherwise?" Kidd asked, sarcastically.

The greeter replied, "Oh, he's very important, sir. Very important, indeed. I learned that in high school."

"Then you should have also learned in high school," Kidd said, "that a president, former or otherwise, always gets what he wants. That's the way the presidency works. We're special like that. Do you understand me, son?"

"Yes, sir," the greeter said, conceding the point. Kenny was impressed. With three well-targeted questions, and the arsenal of the former presidency behind him, Kidd had beaten the greeter down to a moldable mush. The pimple-faced Bailey was now Charles Bentley Kidd's official bum wiper.

"Then this is what I *don't* want," Kidd said. "I don't want other accommodations. Instead, I want you to go inside, walk past the reservation desk, go to your manager's office, and tell him or her that you have a former president of the United States of America waiting on the curb outside, and that he demands to inaugurate your presidential suite tonight. You have a presidential suite, correct?"

The greeter nodded. "Biggest one in Vegas. The director of the National Abstinence Alliance is staying in it—"

"Uh-ah-ah." Kidd wagged his finger at the greeter to shut the guy up, then pointed that finger toward the resort's entryway. "Inside, manager's office, former president of the United States waiting on the curb. Wants that suite. Got it?"

The greeter crinkled his nose, and Kenny could definitely sense a shift in the guy's tone. The new tone was antiseptic, like he was dealing with something smelly and foul. "What if my manager wants to know which former president?" he asked.

Kidd threw the greeter a cocksure smirk. "Then you tell him it's the one who *loves* candy."

With Kidd's admonishment, the greeter was off through the entryway. An hour later, after Kenny and Kidd had resorted to sitting on their bags, the greeter returned with a small cadre of bellhops dressed like chocolatiers. When Kidd asked him what had taken so long, the greeter said there was some trouble getting accommodations at another casino for the director of the National Abstinence Alliance, and he admitted that the manager was not too happy to bump her, especially for someone like Charles Bentley Kidd. "But I went to bat for you," the greeter said.

"Really?" Kidd asked as the bellhops loaded the bags onto a roller cart. "What did you say?"

"Oh, nothing special," the greeter said. "I just reminded him of what a promotional boon it would be to have the world's most infamous sugar slut staying at Sin City's only candy-themed resort. That's like having Blackbeard stay at Treasure Island, or Caligula at Caesar's Palace." The greeter chuckled proudly, then led Kidd, Kenny and the bellhops into the CandyLand and over to an elevator. Everyone got in the elevator except the greeter. He handed two keycards to the lead bellhop and said, "All the way up, Ramon. Housekeeping should be done."

"You're not coming up to show us around?" Kidd asked.

"Ramon will do that," the greeter said. "Right now, I have another meeting with my manager. Seems he wants to talk about my future here." The greeter removed a sheet of paper from his suit coat's pocket and handed it to Kidd. "By the way, your stay is complimentary. All we require is that you visit the pastry shop at four o'clock every afternoon, stand in the front window, and stuff your face with an assortment of cream puffs. Then you need to walk the floor of the casino for an hour while sucking on our house lollipops. As long as you stuff and suck, you stay. If our contract is amenable to you, sign this paper and hand it to Ramon."

As the elevator doors closed, the greeter flashed Kidd his own brand of cocksure smirk. When the elevator began to rise, Kenny noticed the expression on Kidd's face. It was not one of triumphant glee at getting to stay in the resort he wanted, but more distasteful, as if he had bitten into something unexpectedly tart. Kenny could understand. The greeter, after all, had just compared him to two of history's most despised scoundrels, then he had told Kidd that the former president was required to perform like a circus elephant in order to remain here.

"That boy's a smart one," said Ramon, the lead bellhop. "He's a marketing major at Nevada State University just down the road. Always the angles with him, the angles. You're good for him, though. You probably just got him promoted."

The doors to the elevator spread open on the thirty-sixth floor. Kenny and Kidd stepped out, followed by the bellhops. Everyone walked down a plush hallway until they came to the entrance of the presidential suite. Once inside, two bellhops removed the bags from the cart and placed each in a bedroom while Ramon showed Kenny and Kidd around.

As the greeter had stated, the suite was vast, with fifteen-foot ceilings, thick Oriental rugs, fashionable Louis XIV furnishings, and ornate moldings with lollipops and taffy drops carved into the wood. The suite contained a kitchenette, a small office with fax and laptop, a spacious living room, and two gigantic bedrooms, each with its own private bath which provided a telephone, flat-paneled television and Jacuzzi hot tub. When Ramon raised the drapes to the broad living room window, he revealed a panoramic view of the city looking north, up the Strip toward Paris, The Mirage and Wynn, and toward all those older casinos downtown. It was a breathtaking sight, and Kenny felt himself safely elevated from the ocean of lights below. Although, looking at that ocean now, Kenny couldn't wait to jump in.

But Charles Bentley Kidd didn't appear to notice or care about the view. He signed his contract, handed it to Ramon, and gave the bellhops a tip of two hundred dollars, which elicited much gratitude toward Kidd in both English and Spanish. After the bellhops had shut the door behind them, Kidd stared at the playful nighttime skyline for all of two seconds before announcing that he was going to bed.

As Kidd walked toward his bedroom, Kenny followed the man with mouth agape. "But there's a whole town down there," he said. "A town filled with lights and excitement and... scrumptious humptious."

"Really, Kenny," Kidd said, "I'm not hungry for anything scrumptious right now. Besides, I've got a lot of pastry to eat tomorrow, and in front of a fucking crowd. There's a menu on the table if you're hungry. Get yourself some room service. After all, it's free, right?" Kidd turned to enter the room, then he swung back toward Kenny with deflated eyes. It was clear how much the greeter's flippant attitude had wounded him. "And I'm sorry about breaking your glasses, Young Kernick. We'll get you some new ones in the morning."

Then Kidd stepped into his bedroom and shut the door behind him, a door so massive and heavy that its closure sounded to Kenny as if Kidd were sealing himself into a tomb.

CHAPTER 25

★ ★

What Kidd needed, Kenny decided over a filet mignon dinner in his Jacuzzi, was a way to build some confidence.

Over the past five weeks, Kenny had come to know Kidd, to understand him, and to appreciate him. Kenny was also becoming fiercely loyal to him—to experience a burst of cheer when Kidd found success, and a burst of despair when Kidd was embarrassed. Kenny felt proud of Kidd, much like that of a son who found pride in the minor accomplishments of a lovable drunk father who was always fucking up. In Kenny's eyes, Kidd was worthy of pride because he had made such strides since leaving Simondale. He had come a long way publicly, pulling himself out of oblivion and hatred, to the point where last night in Grand Junction, an attractive woman even approached him, sat with him, and took him back to her hotel room. Regardless of the final outcome, it was a positive experience for Kidd nonetheless. It was a start.

But tonight, Kidd found his fortunes reversed. Tonight, Kidd had suffered the indignity of being compared to a murderous pirate and a crazy Roman emperor, and he had been subjected to these comparisons at the hands of an oppor-

tunistic hotel greeter looking to make an impression with
management. Feeling the pulse of water jets drum pleasantly
into his back, Kenny thought he had a pretty good read on
Kidd's current state of mind. Since the advent of the Pastrygate scandal, and his subsequent removal from office, Kidd
had gotten used to being the butt of everyone's jokes. That
was normal for him these days. He could handle it. But lately
he was finding himself to be the butt of everyone's jokes for
their own personal advancement. Even Hot Tammy—the
hair-removal specialist hadn't wanted Kidd for sex; she had
wanted him for practice.

The way to help Kidd find confidence, Kenny figured, was
to take back initiative. Between Chicago and Grand Junction,
the anger toward Kidd had appeared to subside. Outright hatred
of him had given way to indifference. Most people across the
prairie seemed neither to notice nor care that Kidd was walking among them, and in that void Kidd had started to find his
footing again. Then last night, Hot Tammy set him to a teeter
with her teasing games, and tonight the greeter came along and
knocked him over. It was now up to Kenny to pick Kidd up,
dust him clean, and return him to the path of balance. But how?

A potential answer came to Kenny when he set his empty
dinner plate on the floor, picked up a CandyLand welcome
packet, and began to rifle through it, flicking sheets of glossy,
water-dimpled paper to the tile. One particular brochure caught
his attention. It was strewn with photos of attractive young
ladies, and it contained information regarding Wednesday
night's Miss Teen Virgin USA Pageant. The brochure's information was fairly basic—starting time, venue, ticket prices, and
an announcement that the pageant would be broadcast live and
in primetime on the Family Values Channel—but there was

one piece of information that stood out to Kenny more than any other. It was found under the heading "Celebrity Judges."

Although Kenny was not particularly knowledgeable about celebrities, and could hardly tell one from another, listed on the brochure was a name Kenny did know. It was a name which had appeared in both the New York and Washington broadsheets with stunning regularity over the past six years, especially during Pastrygate, when its possessor was often held up as a shining example of devotion to family and ethical standards in an administration that appeared morally rudderless.

The name was Tom Prudell. The man attached to it had once been the chief of staff to President Charles Bentley Kidd. From what Kenny was reading off the brochure, the former chief of staff was living in Las Vegas.

"Who?" Kidd asked. He was looking up from a plate of chorizo and eggs, which had been delivered to the presidential suite just five minutes earlier by a waiter wearing a giant bonbon on his head.

"Tom Prudell," Kenny said, taking a bite of French toast.

"Why the hell do you want to know about him?" Kidd asked, refusing to utter Prudell's name. "That guy is ancient history. At least to me, anyway."

"I'm curious," Kenny said. "I always have been. Did you know I used to read encyclopedias? For fun?"

Kidd pursed his lips and raised an eyebrow. "I'm shocked," he said.

Kenny threw Kidd a raised eyebrow right back. If there was one thing he had learned over the past five weeks, it was the signals Kidd sent out when he wanted to avoid a subject—curt replies, use of pronouns over proper names, biting sarcasm, and his broad shoulders slowly curling to his chest out of nervous contraction. Kidd was emitting those signals now. Kenny could see that Prudell was a sore spot with Kidd. Kenny lowered his eyebrow and took another tack. "Fine, if you don't want to talk about it. Pass the syrup." His calculated surrender seemed to loosen Kidd's resistance.

"Prudell was a knobgobber," Kidd said. "A certified and first-class gobber of knobs. Is that good enough for you?"

"Humor me," Kenny said. "Whenever you ask me for information, I'm expected to give you something akin to a national security briefing."

"I am a former president," Kidd said. "It goes with the territory."

Kenny said, "Well, Bent, if you ever want to tread that territory again, and garner the respect of a real former president instead of being some outcast in the desert, then maybe you should tell me a few things. Like what kind of person Tom Prudell was."

Kidd eyed Kenny suspiciously, then he took a sip of fresh-squeezed orange juice from a trumpet glass. After the sip, he picked up his knife and fork, wielded them like a master swordsman, and brought a greasy oval of chorizo to his mouth. He held the fork at the edge of his lips and said, "I liked Prudell at first. He was solid, focused, a real organizer. One hell of a team guy, too." Kidd popped the chorizo between his teeth and started to chew.

"Tell me more," Kenny said, a hint of glee sparkling through his shattered eyeglass lenses.

Kidd swallowed the chorizo and folded his shoulders again, twisting in mock pain at Kenny's prodding. "Christ, Kenny, what more is there to tell? When I met him, he was the director of development for some Jesuit college in East Needledick, Michigan. It was the same school he had graduated from fifteen years earlier, and he had never left, that's how staid this guy was. He was a chubby man, with glasses not much thinner than yours, and he wore suits that were too big. In reality, I've rarely seen a bigger cheese ass, but he was damn good at what he did—pulling in the alumni contributions, securing corporate donations, swelling the endowment. I thought he could do the same for me, so I made him the head of my fundraising team."

Kidd lifted a napkin off his lap and used it to wipe his brow, which was beading sweat at the memory of Tom Prudell.

"After I won the election, he came to me and said he was going back to Michigan. I said he was crazy. His talents were being wasted up there. I could offer him bigger things to develop, like my administration. I gave him the position of chief of staff, and in that position, he excelled."

"Then why is he a knobgobber?" Kenny asked. "If he was so good?"

"Because he was too good," Kidd said. "He was a real Catholic, Kenny. He went to Mass every Sunday; he didn't believe in birth control; he gave up stuff for Lent. I mean, the only thing I ever gave up for Lent was Lent. And it all came together to make him one self-righteous ass. Especially at the end. I wanted to stay in office, and he knew that, but all he kept telling me to do was resign. 'Resign, resign, resign!' he said. One time he told me it was God's will that I should resign, and that I had to accept my fate and move on. And when I didn't, when I fought, he started to get really terse with me, and snippy, and he began to piss me off to the point where I had a hard time even looking at him."

Kenny asked, "Why didn't he just jump ship on you like some of your Cabinet members?"

Kidd cocked his head and laughed in a way that accused Kenny of naïveté. "Good Catholic boys don't jump ship, Kenny. You should know that. Would you have left Harvard if you hadn't been pushed out? Or would you have suffered there until you really cracked? And I'm not talking about just stealing women's underpants, Kenny. I'm talking about wearing them."

Kenny shrugged, conceding the point. Kidd was right. Kenny never would have had the guts to leave Harvard if he hadn't been forcibly removed.

Kidd said, "It's as if Catholics fight some internal battle between staunch loyalty and the desire to run, and the loyalty wins, since the Church demands it. But trust me on this fact: Choosing loyalty makes them really mad." Kidd lifted his trumpet glass and took another swig of orange juice, and Kenny could see his fingers tightening around the glass's stem.

"I'll tell you," Kidd said, "the day I left office, Prudell could barely speak to me. He looked so angry, I almost thought his fat head was going to explode. He walked me to the helicopter, acting like a whiny little know-it-all on the schoolyard playground, prancing in front of the cameras, pretending he was in charge." Kidd scrunched his face, cocked his wrists and performed a prissy imitation of Tom Prudell on that last day. When Kidd was done mocking, he chugged the remainder of the orange juice and slammed the glass onto the tabletop, his face aflame.

"Then he up and resigns a week later," Kidd said. "But no, he can't go quietly. He has to appear on the fucking *Today* show to tell Suzie Fratz about how he kept urging me to resign. How he thought what I did was the modern-day equivalent of Judas betraying Jesus H. Christ Almighty. But that he felt it was his God-bound duty to manage the situation to its inevitable conclusion, to keep the country together by making sure the administration didn't tumble into chaos. That interview made him look like a hero. Then he packed up his wife and kids, moved out of Washington, and that was the last I heard of the man. Sanctimonious goody-goody. I'll bet he went back to Michigan."

"You'd be wrong," Kenny said. He reached into his shirt pocket and took out the puckered brochure, now folded into quarters. He undid the folds and slid the brochure across the table. Kidd gave it a cursory glance until he saw what Kenny had found.

"They made him the president of Nevada State University?!" Kidd cried. "That's outrageous! College presidents always have a Ph.D. This guy never got past a bachelor's."

"You never got a degree past a bachelor's, either," Kenny said, "and they made you the president of the United States."

Kidd threw Kenny a withering glare. "Well, I'm just sure Prudell thinks he's the total cock and balls now." Kidd crumpled the brochure and threw it to the floor. Then he slashed at his eggs, cutting them into miniscule pieces that he didn't attempt to eat. "This is a joke, I tell you. Do you hear me, Kenny? A big, fat, goddamn joke."

While Kidd pulverized his breakfast, Kenny took the last bite of his French toast and drank down the remainder of his own orange juice. When he set the glass on the table, he said, "Try not to think of it as a joke, Bent. Try to think of it as a chance."

"A chance for what?" Kidd asked. His eyes appeared despondent.

"To get back into the game," Kenny said. "You said Prudell was a team player at first, and that he had conflicts of loyalty later. Don't you think that even after all the garbage that went down between you, he might still be burdened by that loyalty? I mean, after all, you were the president of the United States once. You were his ultimate boss."

Kidd's eyes seemed to spark with understanding. He studied the pageant brochure and said, "What exactly did you have in mind?"

As Kenny drove Kidd to the campus of Nevada State University on the northwest side of town, he told Kidd exactly what he had in mind. When Kidd heard the idea, he waved his arms, grabbed at his hair, and let out a forceful "Hee-haw!" He told Kenny that the boy was a genius of economy, and that if he still could, he would nominate Kenny for treasury secretary, for never before had so much benefit accrued from such little cost that was Kenny's plan.

"And if the Senate wouldn't confirm you," Kidd declared, "do you know what I'd do, Kenny?"

Kenny looked over and saw the old cocksure smirk stretching wide across Kidd's handsome mug. "What would you do?" he asked Kidd.

"I'd recess appoint you," Kidd said. "Just to fuck with them." Then Kidd burst into laughter.

He's back, Kenny thought, as he watched Kidd try to dance a jig in the front seat of the Cadillac. Kenny felt like dancing a jig himself. The old Charles Bentley Kidd was back—the man of self-absorption; of irrational confidence; the Charles Bentley Kidd who would not quit, ever.

The world, Kenny realized, was such a better place for it.

CHAPTER 26

★ ★

When the Cadillac swung onto Nevada State University Boulevard on Wednesday morning, Charles Bentley Kidd felt the butterflies take flight in his stomach.

Butterflies were nothing new to Kidd. He had experienced their fluttering all his life, and hidden the effects well. Under normal circumstances, Kidd could usually deduce their cause, but it was tough reading himself this morning. He had awoken in a bearish mood, having stared at the ceiling for most of the evening in depressed shock over being manhandled, insulted, and used by a collegiate punk with career advancement on his mind. Then just as quickly, he found himself in a state of euphoria over breakfast, as Kenny revealed the plan to get Charles Bentley Kidd noticed again, and nationally. But now, somewhere along the drive from the CandyLand to the Nevada State campus, his euphoria had subsided. Now he was feeling butterflies, and he couldn't tell if they were butterflies of excitement or anxiety. He had reasons for both emotions.

The excitement would be easy to understand. Kenny's plan, after all, was brilliant in its simplicity—Kidd would approach Tom Prudell and ask him to relinquish his position as pageant judge to his former boss. In executing such a move, Prudell was to wait until an hour before the pageant began, then call in sick, claiming to have something abundantly contagious, like pneumonic plague. When the director of the pageant fretted over how to replace him at such a late time, Prudell would propose Kidd's name and tell the director that the former president was (surprise, surprise) currently staying at the CandyLand. At which point Prudell would certainly experience resistance, especially for a teenage virgin pageant, and especially with its broadcast taking place on a cable channel known for wholesomeness. But Kenny, the little genius, had planned for that, too.

"If she balks," Kenny said, "then Prudell reminds her that Nevada State University is a co-sponsor of the event, and its host, and that having you as a judge would mean the world to him—and by extension, to the university."

"What if she balks at that?" Kidd asked.

"Then he bribes her," Kenny said. "He promises to get the pageant into the Convention Center next year. I looked it up on the Internet in our suite—they tried to get in there this time around but were rejected. You can see why they wanted it. The Convention Center has a lot more seats, more amenities, and much more prestige than Langdon Arena. The Miss Teen Virgin USA Pageant will hit the big time in there, and they know it. It's Prudell's job to tell them he can make it happen."

Kenny said that securing the judgeship from Prudell had a seventy-two percent chance of success, based on the calculations the boy had run on paper. Kenny had also calculated that once on the panel of judges, Kidd's upside hit the roof. The pageant was going to be broadcast live on the Family Values Channel, with four rebroadcasts in the next week leading up to Thanksgiving. Thus, the event had nationwide coverage, ratings potential, and repetition, three factors that were a boon to Kidd's public image make-over. "At least that's what I think," Kenny said. "I'm pretty sure I read about public relations theory in a book somewhere."

As Kenny described, when the country tuned in to the broadcast, it would be shocked to see Kidd again, especially on that channel and for that particular brand of competition. But over the course of the pageant, as Kidd studied the contestants, applauded politely, punched his scores into the computer, and, of the utmost importance, kept his fly zipped and his tongue in his mouth, the country would begin to see Kidd differently—not as someone totally inept in his job, or who had betrayed them, but as a person of authority who was performing a function with a degree of class and decorum. To viewers, the wholesomeness of the event would rub off on Kidd. In their minds, he would be redefined, even if that redefinition lasted only for an instant before they once again reverted to thinking of him with his face plunged between the legs of a moaning pastry chef.

"But hey, that's one valuable instant," Kenny said.

But for all of Kenny's confidence, Kidd still harbored doubts. As a former commander in chief, Kidd knew that every plan, no matter how well conceived, always had a potential flaw in its design—something that was as unpredictable as the flight path of a common house fly, and in the end was usually fatal. In this case, that potential flaw started with Tom Prudell.

"I don't know if he'll play along," Kidd told Kenny.

"Why's that?" Kenny asked.

"There are many reasons for trepidation," Kidd said, not intrepidly.

First, they were about to drop in on a man with whom Kidd had shared cold final words. "The coldest," said Kidd. "I think I insulted him, then he definitely insulted me." Second, they were going to ask for a favor. "Prudell's not big on doing favors for anyone. He's a lot more self-absorbed than the press made him out to be." Which led to the third issue.

A self-absorbed Tom Prudell was now in a position of power over Charles Bentley Kidd. Not only was Prudell the leader of a large university, but he was also someone who had the authority to say yes or no to Kidd's request. The long-time dynamic between Kidd and Prudell, where Kidd served as order giver and Prudell as order taker, had reversed completely, with Prudell now on top, all three hundred pounds of him.

When the welcome sign for Nevada State University came into view through the Cadillac's windshield, Kidd knew that this reversal of dynamic was the reason his stomach swarmed with butterflies. As they passed the welcome sign and entered the campus, Kidd wanted to throw up his chorizo and eggs. Instead, he held his gut in check and let off a string of nervous farts that sounded like the muted pops from a twist of bubble wrap.

By the time the car's interior began to stink, Kenny had unrolled the window to flag down a landscaper who was mowing a median strip. The boy asked the landscaper for directions to the president's office. The landscaper choked off the motor, approached the Cadillac and said that they needed to go to the Grant-Sawyer Building, then he pointed a finger zigzag to indicate the way. The blue exhaust emanating from the mower was so strong and noxious that it immediately overpowered any flatulent stench, and Kidd was glad for it.

Directions taken, Kenny put the Cadillac in drive, but it was Kidd's farts that accelerated. He tried to calm his guts by occupying his mind with the scenery. All around campus there were concrete and brick-faced buildings that exuded the south-western flare of recent construction. There were lush grounds which were comprised mainly of broad-leafed desert grass, low brush, bright flowers, and palm trees, all cut, pruned and main-tained to precision by more landscapers (they were everywhere) than even the White House employed. Then there were the variations in automobiles that were parked in the campus lots, models which ranged from luxury German SUV to low-end Asian import (Korean or Japanese—Kidd never could tell the difference).

But mostly, Kidd just looked at the coeds.

In his nervousness, with a world of doubt before him and his farts shooting off like small-arms fire, the former president hadn't given a single thought to his Lil' Kidd. But the girls on this campus were inspiring—young and taut and delicious. True scrumptious humptious. Most of them sported synthetic blonde hair and lean, glow-skinned bod-ies which had yet to experience the detriments of a slowing metabolism or dermal weathering. They all wore tight cloth-ing (short shorts or low-rider jeans with spaghetti-strapped tops or cropped t-shirts) and flip-flops that slapped happily against their exposed heels. Some of them were even wear-ing pajamas, which Kidd found smoking hot. Ogling them, the former president felt his gas let up, and he experienced a fluid pulse in his Lil' Kidd. Not good, he told himself. He closed his eyes tightly and struggled to cast the coeds from his mind. The last thing he needed now was a woody. He would never be able to get out of the car.

Kenny parked the Cadillac in the lot outside a monotonous three-story structure. Shutting off the car, he pointed to the building and said, "That's Grant-Sawyer." Kidd eyed it through the windshield. The building had all the style of a chain hotel, but its hollow appearance made it no less daunting. It was, after all, the den of Tom Prudell.

Kidd steeled himself and climbed out of the Cadillac. He discharged one last burst of intestinal pressure to the wind, then slammed his door and followed Kenny toward the building's entrance. With every step he took, he felt less sure of his mission and more unsure of himself.

"But Prudell doesn't know I'm coming," he said.

"Did Hawleyville know you were coming?" Kenny asked. "Did The Rhino? Does Annabelle?"

"Maybe he's not here," Kidd said. "Maybe he's busy. Maybe we should call first and make an appointment. Yeah, that's what we'll do. We'll make an appointment, Kenny. Let's get back in the car and hit a strip club. If I remember correctly, Pussy Galore's does a great Lap Dance Lunch."

Kidd began to shuffle in a sidestep, heading away from the building's entrance toward a fire hydrant near some shrubs. Kenny turned around and grabbed Kidd by the shoulders before the former president could get away. Kidd stopped. Kenny shifted Kidd's body to face his. "I'm only going to tell you this once," the boy said. Then Kenny slapped Kidd hard across the face. Kidd recoiled from the pain—an electric sensation that rattled his molars. But before he could protest, Kenny said, "Does that bring some clarity to the situation?"

"Absolutely," Kidd said, rubbing his jaw.

"Good," said Kenny. He continued walking, with Kidd following behind. When they reached the entrance, Kenny turned and smiled at Kidd. Then out of nowhere the boy slapped him in the face again.

"What the!" Kidd cried. "Was that for more clarity?"

"No," Kenny said. "I just felt like it." He held open the door and ushered Kidd through.

The interior of the Grant-Sawyer Building smelled like plastic plants, dry carpeting and sun-baked rubber, with a hint of photocopier ink for added bouquet.

That he was even thinking of such benign smells told Kidd that Kenny's slaps had done the trick. They had released his mind from a labyrinth of doubts and reminded him that he was once the most powerful man in the entire world, and that, in that capacity, Tom Prudell had been his lackey. Kidd tried to think of himself as a father figure who was now checking in after a long absence to see where his least-favorite son had ended up in life. With such thoughts, Kidd once again took the lead. After searching out Prudell's name on a directory board, he and Kenny rode an elevator to the third floor, where they soon came upon the door to the president's office.

"Knock, knock," Kidd said as he opened the door, not really knocking but merely poking his head through in the fashion of someone who knows they have a right to intrude.

On the other side of the door, Kidd saw a bare workspace—white-painted drywall with minimal hangings, blanched carpet, style-free furniture, and more plastic plants. Even the girl at the reception desk was bare in her appearance. She was attractive in an Oklahoma sort of way. She seemed to be wearing bargain basement makeup on a tired face, and her thick brown hair was pulled up into an oily ponytail, like she had just stumbled out of bed even though the time was approaching noon. She was maybe twenty years of age, and she smelled like cheap perfume, which Kidd homed in on the minute he walked through the door. From behind her desk, she stared at Kidd blankly and snapped her chewing gum. Then she mumbled something which sounded vaguely like "Yeah?"

Kidd asked for Tom Prudell. The receptionist told Kidd that Prudell was in his office, but he was with somebody, then she pointed to a closed door behind her and said that he would probably be in there for a while. Kidd remained undeterred. He informed her that Tom Prudell would surely cut short his current obligation to meet with the man standing before her. To which the receptionist said, and clearly this time, "I don't think so."

"Humor me," Kidd said. He picked up the receiver to her telephone and held it out to her. "Tell him his old boss is here to see him."

The receptionist huffed, took the phone and buzzed Prudell's line. After a few seconds, she said, "Tommy, somebody's here to see you. He says he's your old boss." Another few seconds passed before she looked at Kidd and said, "He wants to know which one."

Kidd grinned at her. "Tell him it's the biggest boss he ever had. Charles Bentley Kidd."

"He says he's Charles Bentley Kidd," the receptionist spoke into the phone.

From beyond the door behind her, a great clatter arose, as if an object had fallen or been thrown. It was accompanied by a piggish squeal, then the scuffle of hurried shuffling.

The shuffling ceased, and the receptionist said, "No, he's standing in front of my desk. He's with some boy. And the boy has really bad glasses." She paused, then said, "Fine!" and jammed the receiver in its cradle. "Tommy said have a seat." Then she looked down at an *Entertainment Weekly* on her desk and paid them no more attention.

They waited ten minutes before Prudell opened the door to his office. When he emerged, he escorted from the room a lanky coed with hair the color of redwood bark. The student was dressed in pink sweats and a white halter. Kidd caught Prudell's conversation with the girl in mid-sentence as the pair stepped through the doorframe and into the reception area. "So that's all, Tina. Keep up what you've started and I'm sure you'll get another 'A' soon enough."

"But will I graduate with honors, Tommy?" Tina asked. She sounded like an eight-year-old begging her father for a ride on the horse at K-Mart.

"Oh, you sure will," Prudell told her, his words flowing like molasses. He winked at her and said, "I can see you graduating *magna cum laude*."

Now, if there was one area in which Charles Bentley Kidd considered himself the undisputed master, it was the art of sexual innuendo through subtle inflection. He had done it so many times in his life, and so well, that he could tell instantly when the art was being practiced by another. Prudell had placed fleeting emphasis on the word "*cum*," and he hadn't said it with its regular pronunciation—"koom"—which Prudell surely would know given his years spent working in post-secondary education. No, the man had said "kum." In hearing that pronunciation and the emphasis placed on it, Kidd's mind ran off its tracks.

That can't be right, Kidd told himself. This is Tom Prudell, the Emperor of Goody-Goody Land. Kidd began to doubt his mental processes, to question his power of perception. He decided that he must have let his own sex-charged brain apply improper meaning where there probably was no meaning. But his conclusion was proven false when Tina giggled in the same piggish tone he had heard a few minutes earlier. That's when Kidd knew she had heard the mispronunciation and emphasis, too. She slapped Prudell playfully on the arm.

"Bye, Tommy," she said. Kidd watched Tina saunter from the reception office, her matching hot-pink flip-flops slapping heels all the way. When she was completely out of sight and the door had shut behind her, Kidd turned back and stared at his former holier-than-thou chief of staff. Prudell was basking in the afterglow of the departed coed. He let out a contented sigh, arching his eyebrows and turning his eyes upward as if he were attempting to find a wayward semen shot on the ceiling. He finally gathered himself, looked at his former boss and said, "Charles Bentley Kidd, what the hell are you doing here?"

Kidd could barely reply. He jiggled his head slightly and parted his lips, so that he must have looked like one of those people he remembered from his childhood—the kind who had been born so slow of mind and dull of spirit that they had no more ambition in life than to go down to the river each day and catch frogs. The man standing in front of Kidd was so alien, so out of sync with Kidd's memory of the chief of staff he had said goodbye to on the White House lawn only six months ago, that Kidd's communicative abilities froze cold in their stream.

The difference in Prudell wasn't so much physical, Kidd noticed. He was still chubby, still short, and he still wore suits a size too large. No, the difference in Prudell was mostly in his attitude. He seemed less sniveling and more fortified, a man who walked like a leader, even in an oversized suit. There was something else about him, too. Something Kidd hadn't seen right away but noticed immediately when Prudell tried to smooth down the thick black hair at his temples—his former chief of staff was no longer wearing horn-rimmed eyeglasses. In fact, he wasn't wearing eyeglasses at all.

Prudell spread his arms in inquiry, until he resembled a broad stage curtain. "Why so quiet, Chuck?" he asked. "Some jealous husband cut your tongue out?" Prudell grinned, and the receptionist let out a snorting chuckle over her magazine. That's when Kidd's brain loosened. Prudell's grin was making him angry. It was the same grin that Kidd was famous for. Some described the grin as arrogant, others called it mocking, but Kidd called it his own, and Prudell had plagiarized it.

"I was wondering if we could talk about something, Tom." Kidd's tone was frank.

Prudell eyed Kidd skeptically. "You're in the middle of the desert, Chuck. How did you get here? Where's the Secret Service?"

Kidd could only motion to Prudell's office. "Can we chat in there?"

Prudell's eyes softened. He seemed to regard Kidd as a curiosity instead of a threat. He waved off the office and said, "Not in there, Chuck. Why don't we walk and talk? See my new home." Prudell turned to his receptionist. "Frannie, could you reschedule my next appointment for three o'clock? I'm taking Chucky and his little friend here on a tour." The receptionist looked up from her magazine, turned to her computer monitor, and picked up the receiver to her telephone.

Prudell said to Kidd, "Let's go." He strode forward and led Kidd and Kenny toward the main door of the reception office. As Kidd made his way out the door, he took a look back at the receptionist. She was speaking into the phone to someone named Darla.

"President Prudell," she said, "would like to do you at three o'clock. And I should remind you that your appointment with him is strictly B.Y.O.P. If you want him to use protection, you must supply it yourself."

Before the look of shock on Kidd's face could register back at the receptionist, the main door to the office closed behind him.

Under a brilliant November sun, Prudell directed Kidd and Kenny around the Nevada State University campus.

During the tour, Prudell was a flurry of words, motions and tones. He pointed out two half-finished buildings being constructed for the biology department, and a recently-completed complex which would house the expanded physical therapy school. He squawked proudly about the fundraising initiatives he had championed to swell the endowment, and cavalierly mentioned how he had ordered a complete overhaul of the library system. He even pontificated on the installation of a new state-of-the-art wireless broadcast array for Internet, one that would cover a two-mile radius around the campus, would provide free web access for the school's neighbors, and would become the envy of every other university community outreach program in the country.

And as he talked, Kidd noticed a peculiar habit: Prudell tended to end every example of his campus successes with the mention of a female student. The two new biology buildings, Prudell said, would be much valued by Sally and Suzie and Jasmine, who were all pre-med majors. The new physical therapy school would bring in more girls like Kelly and Valerie and Jess, who were true assets to the university—wink, wink. The development office, Prudell noted, was headed by an incompetent cad named Chad Hurlbert, but Hurlbert had a work-study assistant there on Mondays and Thursdays who had proven to be a big help to Prudell's fundraising drive. She also had the thinnest lips he had ever seen on a girl. "And I'm not talking about the ones on her face," he said, unleashing another plagiarized grin.

The air under the sun was growing warmer, and Prudell was struggling with the heat; he was panting and lumbering and cocking his head, as if to relieve a buildup of temperature along his collar. Every so often, Prudell would pinch his fingers, move them to his temples, and grapple for nothing, clearly trying to reset out of habit eyeglasses that were no longer there. Near a manicured lawn which acted as a common to three dormitory halls, Prudell rubbed his neck and pulled his corpulent frame up to a concrete retaining wall. He slouched against the wall and motioned for Kidd and Kenny to do the same.

A few moments of silence passed, marked in time only by the rhythm of Prudell's labored breathing. Across the common, Kidd noticed a lanky Asian beauty sauntering away from one of the halls. She wore a brown drawcord skirt, the ends of which snapped tauntingly with each of her steps, and all Kidd could think was that she walked like a Slinky went down stairs. He wanted to follow and slink up beside her. Just the sight of her made his core spin.

Prudell must have seen Kidd eyeing the girl, because the former chief of staff assumed a defensive posture. "Look all you want around here, Chuck," he said, "but don't touch. Especially that one. She's part of The A-Team."

"The A-Team?" Kidd asked. He took his eyes off the girl and put them on Prudell, confused. "Like Mr. T?"

"No, not like fucking Mr. T," Prudell snapped. "Unless I'm the 'Mr. T.'" Then he got an excited, pent-up look on his face, as if his whole blubbery body were about to explode with a secret he could no longer contain. Leaning into Kidd he said, "And I have to tell you, Chuck, that one there is the best piece of poonalicious I've ever had. Tight in all the right places." He flashed that stupid grin again.

But Kidd couldn't grin back; he was too stunned by Prudell's comment. He stared blankly at the fat man, trying to get a grip on his former underling's newfound personality. All he could think to ask was, "Poonalicious? Is that like scrumptious humptious?"

"Good Christ, Chuck," Prudell said. "What is it with you and comparisons? Scrumptious humptious was always your thing. Poonalicious is my thing. And it's no comparison."

"I see," Kidd said, not really seeing much at all. In the absence of a further explanation, Kidd nodded knowingly, quickly making up something to placate his former chief of staff, who was clearly in a mood of one-upmanship. "Well, Japanese girls," he said, "they always were my favorites, too."

"She's *Korean*!" Prudell snapped. "Christ, don't ever mistake a Korean for a Japanese—they hate that!" The former chief of staff snickered. "But you always sucked when it came to foreign relations, Chuck, so I guess I'll have to pardon you. Oh, wait, Russell already did that. My bad." Prudell laughed, gawking at the delicious Asian beauty as she walked down the path. Kidd could hear him breathing harder with every sway of her Slinky saunter. When she turned a corner, Prudell shifted his eyes skyward, avoiding Kidd's gaze.

Kidd ran a set of tense fingers through his hair. Throughout the tour, Prudell had yet to make anything but fleeting eye contact with him. Even when Prudell lowered his eyes from the sky, the former chief of staff didn't bother to look at Kidd. Instead, he glanced off to his right. Kidd followed the line of sight and discovered that Prudell had homed in on a peach-haired girl who was walking on a path between two of the dormitories.

Hoping to change the direction of the discourse, Kidd cleared his throat and said, "I need to ask you a favor, Tom. That's why I'm here."

"Poon... a... licious," Prudell replied. He was still watching the peach-haired girl. "Did I mention this place is a veritable rainbow of it?"

"I know we didn't exactly part on the best of terms," Kidd said, ignoring him.

But Prudell ignored him right back. "Red-haired, brown-haired, black- and blonde-haired, even shaved poonalicious." Prudell turned to Kenny and tapped the boy on the arm. "You know what shaved is good for, don't you, son?"

Kenny shook his head.

Prudell said, "There's never any disappointment that the carpet doesn't match the drapes." Prudell barked like an obese hyena.

Kidd looked down at Kenny and could see from the twisted expression on the boy's face that he was confused over how Prudell's talk of a woman's nether region had anything to do with actual floor coverings and window treatments.

Kidd flattened a palm and waved it back and forth, indicating to Kenny that they would discuss it later. Kidd pulled out the crumpled brochure and started to smooth it against his pant leg. "Tom, if I may digress, we saw that you're listed as—"

Prudell cut him off. "Can I tell you something, Chuck? Just between former acquaintances? I'm not going to stop until I've had every piece of poonalicious on this campus. So help me, Chuck, I'm not. And as you probably remember, I'm always a man of my word."

Kidd crumpled the brochure in the cup of his hand. He could take no more of this idiot's musings. He stared at Prudell, who was staring with beady, obsessed eyes at the peach-haired girl, and asked, "Tom, what the hell has happened to you?"

Prudell took his gaze off the peach-haired girl and, for the first time, met Kidd's eyes. He looked like a junkie coming down from a high. Then he stared ahead again and seemed to consider the question sincerely. After a few moments, he said, "God, I don't really know, Chuck. Maybe it was the Lasik."

"I don't follow," Kidd said.

"Lasik!" Prudell snapped. "That laser eye surgery you told me to get right before you disappeared into the helicopter! Well, I got it, Chuck. I got it just before I came here. I decided I was going to try and put your stench behind me by starting fresh with a new look. The ophthalmologist who performed it was the deacon at my church."

Kidd said, "Tom, that was something spoken in the uneasiness of the moment. It was hotter than hell that day. I was embarrassed. The cameras were on us constantly. I just needed something lighthearted to say to look like I wasn't about to lose my soup, which I was. I pretty much forgot about it once I got airborne."

"Well, I didn't forget about it," Prudell said. He rubbed the back of his neck. "It cost me some coin, which was rough because I was unemployed, but it was so easy—in and out in two hours. It was actually nice to be able to see in the shower for a change, and not fumble for my glasses in the morning, or keep pushing them back up my nose. Or break them." He eyed Kenny. "Other than that, I didn't think anything of it either. I just enjoyed the vision."

"Then what happened?" Kidd asked, more like a demand.

"I don't know," Prudell said. "It's strange. Nothing seemed very different in me, and nothing seemed out of sorts, until one day, a month after I arrived here, a student came to see me about a poor grade she was getting in a course she needed for her major. A cute Latina girl, wearing the perkiest little skirt you ever saw. She said the professor wouldn't let her retake an exam she'd missed, and that was that. I knew my reputation as a hardliner on matters of protocol had preceded me here, so when I told her there was nothing I could do, to me it was the end of the discussion. But not to her. Oh, no! Not at all! Because do you know what she did, Chuck?"

Kidd shook his head.

Prudell leaned in close to Kidd and lowered his voice. "I'll tell you what she did. She got out of her chair and climbed onto my desk. Then she spread her legs before me and hiked her skirt to her tummy. And my Christ, she wasn't wearing anything underneath. Nothing. There was just this brown tangle looking back at me. No, fuck that! It was taunting me. Then she winks and says, 'I'll make you a deal, Mr. President. If you get me an 'A,' I'll give you an 'F.' And you don't look like the type who's ever gotten a really good 'F' before. Have you, Mr. President?' I was stunned. I really had to think—had I ever gotten a good 'F' before? Ever? In my life? No, Chuck, I hadn't. I got a 'C' once in Renaissance Literature, but I had never gotten a good 'F.' And

I really wanted an 'F,' Chuck. I've been such a good boy all my life, haven't I? Couldn't I fail just once? So I did what any man would do—I got 'F'd.' Oh, God, it was the most amazing experience. And now I'm hooked. I haven't stopped getting 'F'd' since, and not just from her. The girls here are all over me. They all want to give me an 'F,' too. And that's when they become part of The A-Team—if you give Tommy Prudell an 'F,' you get an 'A.' It's a little hard to swing. The end of the trimester is coming up and I have to pay off, but Frannie and I have access to the registrar's server. For her help, Frannie is graduating first in her class. No, I have to say, you didn't get many things right when you were president, Chuck—you were a king fuck-up if ever I saw one—but on the issue of eye surgery, you were balls-on correct: Have it and you will reel them in. And boy, do I! Congratulations!" Prudell slapped Kidd on the back.

"Ah, thank you," Kidd said uncomfortably. Then he asked, "But what about your wife, Tom? You love her. You're devoted. Helen's a real peach."

Prudell snorted. "Oh, Chuck, are you going to pull that crap on me? You of all people? Let me tell you something about Helen—she couldn't find my pecker if it were attached to her body. So you can forget about getting a good 'F.' All that woman is capable of handing out is an 'A,' for 'absolutely not tonight.'"

"I'm sorry, Tom," Kidd said. "I had no idea." The strange thing to Kidd was that he actually did feel sorry for the state of Prudell's marriage.

Prudell made slits of his eyelids. "With all due respect, Chuck, take your pity and shove it up your ass. I don't need it." He pointed off in the direction of the Grant-Sawyer Building. "Remember that redhead you saw coming out of my office a few minutes ago? Tina?"

Kidd nodded sheepishly. Prudell's anger always made him uneasy.

"Well, when Frannie buzzed to tell me you were here," Prudell said, "she was riding me reverse cowgirl. I practically bucked her through the window to get up for the call, which I think has put a kink in my neck." Prudell cocked his head again and rubbed his neck, and Kidd realized the motion had nothing to do with a buildup of temperature along the man's collar; it had to do with the buildup of temperature in his libido. "But here's the best part, Chuck," Prudell added. "I didn't even have to ask her for reverse cowgirl. She just came in, dropped her sweats, turned around and straddled me. Then she rode me like a mechanical bull." Prudell began to pound a fist against the concrete retaining wall, punctuating his points. "That's what my life is like now, Chuck. Do you hear me? That's how big I am. That's how much power I wield. I'm not your little spanking boy anymore. I'm not the guy who has to go out and find you a piece of strange and lie about it to Congress. You don't slap my head and tell me to clean up after you. Now I get the girls! Now I'm the man! Now I'm the one they fawn over and frolic to—once, twice, three times a day! Then I get cleaned up after! Follow me?! So take your pity, Chuck, and do me a favor: Go fuck yourself with it! Hard!"

His rant over, Prudell collapsed against the retaining wall in exhaustion. Again Kidd was stunned, particularly at the vitriol his former chief of staff had leveled at him. Kidd stuttered for meaningful words, but all he could manage to say was, "I just had no idea."

Prudell went to adjust his eyeglasses, but he let his hand flit off to the side when he realized they weren't there. "You know, Chuck," he said, "I'd tell you how to have an idea, but I don't think you'd listen to me. You never did. That's why I'm where I am and you're where you are." Prudell folded his arms. His admonishment now seemed complete, causing his prickly defensiveness to deflate, and for the first time since meeting with him, Kidd thought he looked like the old Tom—the brilliant man Kidd had brought into the presidential fold; the loyal soldier he had elevated to Cabinet-level rank on his last day so Prudell could get a pay raise; the confidante he had always admired.

After a few moments of awkward silence, Prudell smoothed the front curls of his shiny black hair. "Now, to what do I owe the pleasure of your visit?" he asked, setting his coiffure just right. "Only two things can get Charles Bentley Kidd lathered up enough to come looking for you: Either you *know* a woman he wants, or you *are* a woman he wants. Since I have a penis, it must be the former."

Kidd felt his shoulders sag. Was this what people thought of him? Even close acquaintances like Prudell? Did he really come across as that selfish and self-absorbed? If so, it was pathetic, and it made Kidd want to run back to the Cadillac and hide in the trunk. Instead, he steadied himself by quietly pressing out the crumples in the brochure. When the brochure was flat, he showed its contents to Prudell. "My assistant Kenny noticed that you're going to be a celebrity judge at the Miss Teen Virgin USA Pageant tonight."

Prudell glanced at the brochure and nodded. "Yeah, we're a sponsor. So what? Don't tell me you think I'm mixing Church and State, because I've already had that argument with Carson City. As long as the event isn't religiously based, it falls under the guidelines of high school abstinence education."

Kidd held up a hand. "Not at all, Tom," he said. "I understand how these things work. No, the reason I'm asking is more personal."

"Personal," Prudell said. "Personal how?"

"All right, I'm just going to drop it on the table," Kidd said. "I want you to give up your judging spot to me."

Prudell stared at Kidd quizzically. "You want me to what?"

"Just like I said, Tom," Kidd replied. "There are no more deceptions between us. I'm coming at you straight. I want you to step aside so that I can judge this pageant tonight."

Prudell scrutinized his old boss for a moment, his breath caught on an aborted phrase, then he started to roll with laughter. "Christ, Chuck," he said, "I have to hand it to you, you almost had me there! No, seriously, why are you here? It can't be over a pageant full of virgins. Do you need some strange? Is that what you're looking for? Because I can hook you up with the Shanley Twins. One's a physical therapy major, one's a speech therapy major. When they're done with you, you won't be able to walk or talk."

Kidd looked Prudell straight in the eye and fixed the fat man's gaze on his own. Kidd didn't want twins. Well, not right now. At this moment, all he wanted was the judgeship. He hoped his serious expression conveyed that point to Prudell.

Prudell studied Kidd's face. Kidd knew he had gotten his point across when the fat man stopped laughing. "Well you can't have it!" he said bitterly.

"Just hear me out," Kidd said.

"No!" Prudell said. "My Tommy Boy's been hard about this pageant since the day they signed the contract. Do you know how many strings I had to pull to get the grant money for this?"

"Tommy Boy?" Kidd asked. "Is that like my—"

"Like your what?" Prudell asked sharply.

"Never mind," Kidd said. Prudell's one-upmanship apparently knew no bounds, even when it came to penis names. "Look, Tom," Kidd said, "I admire your support for high school abstinence, but—"

"This isn't about supporting abstinence," Prudell said. "I couldn't care less about abstinence."

"Then what is it about?" Kidd asked.

"What do you think it's about?" Prudell asked. "You, of all people. It's about recruiting."

"Recruiting?" Kidd said.

"Jesus, Chuck," Prudell said. "Has the clap finally migrated to your brain? Of course recruiting. I'm going to survey the field, pick out the hottest virgins, and give those girls full scholarships to NSU. Young, clean, never-touched virgins. That's like a drink of cold mountain spring water in this godforsaken desert. They can be the dumbest virgins on the planet for all I care, but after they get here, they're all going to get an 'A.' So fat fucking chance!"

Disgruntled, Kidd tried more pleading, but Prudell held his ground. When it became obvious that Prudell would not cede his spot to Kidd, thus condemning Kenny's brilliant plan to failure, Kidd called upon his only remaining option: nuclear supplication. In the process, he did something he had never done before, not even on the day he proposed to Margaret Huff in his dorm room at Jesuit University—he got down on one knee.

A genuflected Kidd took Prudell's ham hock fists into his palms, then he unleashed his arsenal. "I'm going to be frank with you, Tom, and more honest than I've ever been—I need to judge this pageant tonight. I need it like I've never needed anything else. You can't imagine what my life has been like since I left the White House. It's been awful, Tom. I need to get some respect back. And just like the old days, I need you to make it happen for me." Then, as a final plea, he bowed his head into Prudell's stomach, wrapped his arms around Prudell's wide ass, and gave the former chief of staff exactly what he had been searching out during their entire conversation—one-upmanship. With Prudell the one who was up.

"I know you're bigger than me, Tom, and smarter than me, and much more attractive to the ladies. I'm nothing compared to you. Never was. If I had only listened to you, I might not be in the position I'm in today—lower than a tick sucking on a three-legged poodle." Kidd raised his head and looked into Prudell's curious eyes. "But I need this, Tom. I need to get back in the game. Not a big score, just a showing. This pageant will do that for me—it has national coverage, a primetime slot, a wholesome image. It's a way for me to get my name out there again, to reconnect. I'm not going for the girls, Tom, I promise. I'm going for the publicity. I throw myself on your mercy, Mr. President. I know I don't deserve it, but you're the only one who has the power to lift me up again. Please help me, Tom. Please."

Kidd returned his head to Prudell's stomach. With a line of sight directed to the ground, he stared at Prudell's shoes as the brown loafers shifted against the concrete walkway. He could only wonder what kind of scene it made to all the students who were walking by, watching what looked to be a former president of the United States preparing to fellate their current university president right on a dormitory common. Hell, even in Vegas, that was fucked up.

"Christ, get off," Prudell said, pushing Kidd away. "Anyone from the school newspaper takes a picture of us like that and I might never get another 'F' here again." Kidd stood and leaned against the retaining wall, staring off at a dormitory as he awaited Prudell's response.

It took a full minute before that response came. "Chucky, Chucky, Chucky," he said, releasing a tired burst of breath, "what am I going to do with you, huh?" Kidd thought it best to let the question slide. After a few seconds of reflection and calculation, Prudell said, "You know I don't have an advanced degree."

Kidd lied with mock shock. "No, Tom, I had no idea. You always seemed like you did."

"Well, I don't," Prudell said. "And I don't particularly have the desire to get one, either. Not with my heavy extracurricular schedule. I'm sure you understand."

Kidd understood. If Prudell truly was having sex with three coeds a day, then he would have little energy left to pursue a master's, let alone a Ph.D.

"The only reason NSU hired me," Prudell said, "was because of the way I handled you. They said if I could keep your White House together, I was just the man they needed to whip this school into shape. It was a mess when I got here in August—budget problems, construction in jeopardy, crap landscaping."

"You've done a tremendous job," Kidd said in sugary but sincere admiration.

"Pretty soon, though, I'm going to get tired of this place," Prudell said. "The poonalicious here is good, but it's low-end. Intelligence-wise, some of these girls are as thick as posts. There's no culture to them, either. And they smoke a lot. God, I hate that. Especially when they reek of it."

Kidd nodded knowingly. Where the hell was this going? Prudell was sounding like a goddamn fool.

"So I'm thinking," Prudell said. "If I help you get back on top, then you're going to help me get out of here. And I'm not talking about just moving over to some other state system. I'm talking about the big time. The top of the collegiate food chain. The end-all-be-all of post-secondary education. Do you understand, Chuck?"

"Let me guess," Kidd said. "Harvard."

"Very good," Prudell said. "Apparently, the clap hasn't affected your brain."

"I've never had the clap, Tom. Crabs, yes, but never the clap."

"Well, I've had neither," Prudell said. "I don't plan to. What I do plan on is upward mobility. So let's say I help you tonight. Hypothetically. Then what are you going to do for me? Well, I'll tell you: You're going to use your influence as a respectable former president of the United States to set me up at Harvard, even without a Ph.D. Then I'll tell you what I'm going to do. I'm going to kick back, send out some lures, and reel myself in a whole new A-Team. Hell, from time to time, maybe I'll even run the place. That's the way I see it, Chuck. Is that the way you see it?"

Kidd couldn't help but smile. It had taken some effort, but Prudell had finally bent to his will. That he had no idea how he would ever get Prudell into Harvard didn't stop him from saying, "Absolutely, Tom. It's the least I could do." Then to raise the stakes, to get Prudell hooked into the bargain on such a primal level that the fat bastard wouldn't change his mind and back out at the last minute, Kidd pointed at Kenny. "My assistant here went to Harvard. I'm sure he could help you as well."

"Really?" Prudell asked. He eyed Kenny. "You went to Harvard?"

"He was a legend there," Kidd said. "You wouldn't believe the number of girls' underpants this boy got into."

"No kidding," Prudell said. He eyed Kenny again as if he were trying to make eye contact through the boy's shattered glasses. "Personally, I think underpants are a hindrance. How was it in the Ivy League?"

Kenny, who had remained quiet during the entire exchange, didn't miss a beat. He may have been inexperienced when it came to matters of sex, but he was making strides every day in the art of fucking with people's heads. Young Kernick took off his glasses, stared Prudell right in the eye and stated, unequivocally, "You think that Korean girl was something? Wait until you experience a Pakistani violinist who's so smart, she doesn't need your 'A,' but she's giving you an 'F' anyway. Just for fun."

Prudell's eyes rolled to the back of his head. "High-class, intelligent, cultured poonalicious," he said, salivating at its possibilities. He went limp at the prospect and slid sideways against the wall, only catching himself right before he fell supine onto the concrete. When he pulled himself up, he eyed Kidd conspiratorially. "You know, Mr. President," he said, rubbing his stomach with a grimace, "I feel like I'm coming down with something. Do I look like I'm coming down with something?"

On the way back to the parking lot, Kidd put his arm around Kenny. A burst of pride rippled through him. It was Kenny who had come up with the idea to get Kidd back in the game. It was Kenny who had forced Kidd to walk into the Grant-Sawyer Building when Kidd only wanted to run away. It was Kenny who had intuited what Kidd needed him to say to hook Prudell like a poon-obsessed sturgeon—Kidd doubted that Kenny had ever talked to a Pakistani girl in his life. But Kenny Kernick had not let Kidd fail. Kidd began to feel that Kenny would never let him fail, ever again.

Kidd wanted to tell Kenny these things, wanted to share with Kenny the full range of emotions he was experiencing at that very moment. There were so many words to say.

Instead, Kidd pulled Kenny close and shook him with a tight hug. Then he said, "Like the son I never had, Kenny. Like the son I never had."

He hoped the boy would take it as a compliment.

CHAPTER 27

★ ★

At 6:23 on Wednesday evening, the phone rang in the Candy-Land presidential suite.

On the other end of the line was Sandy Butters, executive producer for the Miss Teen Virgin USA Pageant. In a harried voice, she told Kenny that she needed to speak with Charles Bentley Kidd immediately. She asked if he was there and stated again that the matter was of great importance. Kenny asked her to hold, then he walked over to Kidd's bedroom and knocked on the door.

Kidd had returned to the suite only twenty minutes earlier, exhausted and expanded after satisfying his first day's obligation to the CandyLand. He had stumbled through the main door of the suite, clutched his stomach, puffed out his cheeks, and claimed that he had eaten way too many cream puffs, and that the lollipops they made at the CandyLand tasted like the crack of a gravedigger's ass. But he also said that, all in all, people left him alone, preferring to gawk, point and snicker rather than approach, and that their distance had made the obligation manageable. "I didn't even get heckled once," Kidd said, before he ambled into his bedroom and collapsed in a Bordeaux wing chair to relax.

When Kidd didn't respond to the knocks, Kenny assumed it was because Kidd was deep in thought. Instead, he pushed open the door and found Kidd lying face down on the oriental rug, naked except for his boxer shorts, and drooling a puddle of saliva into the low-pile fibers.

"Bent," Kenny yelled repeatedly. But Kidd wouldn't reply. Finally, Kenny walked over and kicked the former president in the ribs.

Kidd shot up and flung his head around, spit flying from the corners of his mouth. "What the?!" Kidd cried. "Who, what?" Kenny held the phone out to him.

"The Miss Teen Virgin USA Pageant is on the line for you."

Kidd rubbed his face and took the phone. He cleared his throat, then said in a deep, rich baritone, "This is Charles Bentley Kidd. How may I help you?"

Sandy Butters must have gone off to Kidd, because Kidd didn't say another word for two entire minutes. From the receiver, Kenny could hear squawks and pitches that sounded like birdcall, but he could not hear specific words. When the birdcall ceased, Kidd said, "I'm sorry to hear that, Ms. Butters."

Then silence.

"He did, did he?" Kidd said. "Well, isn't that nice of Tom. I'm flattered."

Silence yet again.

"Yes, I understand the NAA has its reservations. No, I'd love to help out. Certainly. I had nothing planned for this evening."

Kenny could hear the squawking start again. It ended on an uptick, like a question.

"Yes, I do have a suit with me," Kidd said. "Oh, and you'll send a car, too? How thoughtful. In the Langdon Arena. Backstage. See you then."

Kidd hung up and grinned at Kenny. "It seems Tom Prudell has taken ill. Around lunchtime, he apparently contracted something nasty."

"God," Kenny said, "I hope it wasn't Tina."

Kidd smirked, then he pushed himself off the rug, stood straight and stretched. "Anyway, we're in. Now please tell me my suit is back from housekeeping."

The suit had been returned an hour ago—Kidd's rumpled charcoal suit, last worn in Chicago the night he got thrown into a river, looking as crisp as the day it came off the sewing machine of the White House tailor. It took Kidd ten minutes to shower, twenty minutes to shave, primp and coif, and five minutes to put on the suit, which was now matched with a white Burwick shirt from C.G. Cashman's and a new green necktie from Marzipan, a clothing boutique located on the mercantile level of the CandyLand. While Kidd was putting on the suit, Kenny showered, tossed his hair, and threw on his new pair of glasses. On the way back from the NSU campus that afternoon, Kidd had more than delivered on his promise to replace the lenses he had smashed back in Utah: At a LensFitters on Sahara Drive, Kidd had bought Kenny the Cadillac of eyewear—a set of rimless titanium frames, complete with aspheric lenses so thin that the boy hardly knew he was wearing glasses at all, even with his pathetic eyesight. Gone were the days of coke-bottles—these glasses were professional, stylish, and most important, they complimented his face. Kenny looked in the mirror and admired what he saw staring back. He looked like a man now. Or at least a boy on the cusp of manhood. Which was good enough for him.

When Kenny and Kidd walked out the main entrance of the CandyLand, a valet informed Kidd that a car was waiting to take him to the Miss Teen Virgin USA Pageant. A driver appeared beside a black stretch limousine and held open the rear door. The driver said nothing during the next half-hour as the limo made its way through heavy evening traffic to the NSU campus. He deposited them in front of Langdon Arena, whereupon he informed Kidd that he would be waiting around the corner to take them back to the CandyLand when the pageant was over.

Kenny followed Kidd to the doors of the arena. They walked through a lobby where family and supporters of the contestants were milling about, then headed straight into the auditorium, which was much smaller than Kenny expected. There couldn't have been more than a thousand seats in the place, including the balcony. With a half-hour to go before the pageant, those seats were only partially occupied. The main flurry of activity came from the Family Values Channel production crew, which was checking cameras, lights and microphones, and securing stage cables with heavy black tape. Kidd stepped over a metal equipment box, walked onto the stage and strode to the wings.

He approached a girl wearing a head set and asked her for Sandy Butters. The girl held up a finger and disappeared into a dark corner of the wings. She returned a few moments later with a fresh-faced young woman who was carrying a clipboard. The woman extended a hand.

"Charles Bentley Kidd," she said. "I'm Sandy Butters. Thank you for coming. Follow me, please."

Sandy Butters turned and led Kidd and Kenny into the catacombs behind the stage. Kenny figured they were heading toward a dressing room, where Kidd's face would be made ready for primetime television. Instead, they ended up in an office. It was occupied by a plump, middle-aged woman who was chewing intently on the earpiece of her eyeglasses. From the very first glance at her, Kenny could tell that this woman had few limits to her energy, optimism or enthusiasm, and it made him a little nervous.

"I'll leave you three alone," Sandy Butters said, before pulling the door shut and sealing Kidd and Kenny off with the woman. In addition to her redolent girth, she had piercing gray eyes and straw-colored hair, and she wore a mustard-yellow pant suit that did nothing to compliment her weight.

The woman removed the earpiece from her mouth and stared at Kidd for a moment. A wry smile crept across her face. Finally, she said, "So this is the man who had me removed from the CandyLand presidential suite." She extended a meaty hand and Kidd took it. "I'm Lucille McIntosh, director of the National Abstinence Alliance."

"Yes," Kidd said, shaking her hand meekly. "I apologize for that, Ms. McIntosh. I didn't think I would actually have to meet you."

Lucille McIntosh smiled wryly again. "Honesty," she said. "That's encouraging. When you occupied the White House, you weren't known much for your honesty, were you, Mr. Kidd?"

Kidd seemed to take the question as rhetorical. He offered no reply.

Lucille McIntosh said, "That's okay, Mr. Kidd, I'm not here to judge. What I am here to do is put on the best pageant I can with the resources I have. It appears that what I have is you. There are only five judges in this competition, Mr. Kidd. Los-

ing one of them looks very bad, especially on national television. Do you understand?"

Kidd nodded. "I appreciate the opportunity."

"I appreciate your appreciation," said Lucille McIntosh.
"Now let's have some more honesty, shall we? Have a seat, both
of you." She put her glasses on and sat behind her desk, then she
clasped her fingers at her chin and stared at Kidd suspiciously.
"I love sex, Mr. Kidd, did you know that? Some people think
I'm a prude because of my work, but they're wrong. I love sex
as much as anyone. My husband and I have it three times a
week, at least. Heck, we were married in Vegas twenty years
ago, when it was nothing like it is today. But I believe that sex
is best within the structure of a marriage, and that's what the
NAA seeks to encourage in high school students. To that end,
you're not a very good role model for our cause, are you?"

Kidd shrugged. "If it's any consolation to you, Ms. McIntosh, I married the first woman I slept with. I just didn't marry
the last one. Or any in the middle."

"As I said, I'm not here to judge you, Mr. Kidd." Lucille
McIntosh leaned back in her chair and flashed Kidd another
smile—not wry this time, but calculating. "I never give up on
anybody, either, especially the fallen. We've had teenage girls
come to us with a lot of mileage on them, some since the age of
ten, but they've reclaimed their virginity and started fresh. No
one is beneath us; no situation is too dire. I'm always up for the
fight, which is why we came to Vegas this year. I wanted to put
our girls in the hottest part of the kiln, to harden their youthful
clay into sturdy ceramic. Does that make sense to you?"

"It does," said Kidd. "More than you know."

"But I never give up on an adult, either," Lucille McIntosh
said. "Especially if that adult can help me. Just yesterday I hired

an Elvis impersonator known for his bawdy humor to come and do a show for our girls. He cleaned up his act and was a great hit. Okay, he left with one of the waitresses, but that wasn't the point—holding the girls' attention was." She studied Kidd with a glint in her gray eyes. "Now it's your turn to help me, Mr. Kidd. Because as of right now, you're the most fallen man in America. You're going to be my set piece, my latest challenge—and in the process, you're going to hold our audience's attention. I'm going to show the world how much the NAA has mellowed you, even if it is all bunk. You're going to sit in your seat, perform your judging duties to the best of your ability, smile and wave when necessary, keep your penis in your pants and never, not once, leer at any of our contestants. Tonight you follow the five-second rule—no more than five seconds of view before you shift your head to look elsewhere. Actually, in your case, I think I'm going to make it two seconds. Can you live with that, Mr. Kidd?"

Kidd nodded sheepishly.

"You may think," Lucille McIntosh said, "that this is going to be a walk under the cherry blossoms for you, Mr. Kidd, but I can assure you that if you think that way, then you've never fully appreciated a beauty pageant. This isn't about young girls in bikinis or curve-hugging evening wear. It's about putting yourself out there to be judged by everyone who's watching, and many times to be laughed at, or even talked about by your peers endlessly once you get home. Many of these girls will be ridiculed, especially because they're committed virgins. Most of them have been working with pageant coaches since the summer to try to minimize mistakes. If I remember correctly, Mr. Kidd, you had the summer off. Am I right?"

Again, Kidd nodded sheepishly. Kenny was impressed. Even The Rhino hadn't handled Kidd so effectively.

Lucille McIntosh took off her glasses and began to chew on an earpiece once more. After a few gnaws, she said, "More honesty?"

"Certainly," said Kidd.

"We only called you because Tom Prudell asked us to," Lucille McIntosh said. "As you can attest, Mr. Prudell is a fine, upstanding man who managed to get this convention in Las Vegas when nobody else would take it. He's a committed educator, and a strong advocate for abstinence. He only has our girls' best interests at heart. He's even promised scholarships for some of the contestants. Can you believe that?"

Kenny stifled a laugh. He wondered what Kidd was thinking, being dressed down at the expense of Tom Prudell, a man who had openly bragged about using the pageant as a recruiting ground for future A-Teamers.

"Mr. Prudell was committed to this event," Lucille McIntosh said. "I need to know if you're committed to it as well. Or are you going to get halfway through it and decide you'd rather be doing something else? Or someone else?"

Kidd raised his right hand and said, "Ms. McIntosh, I promise to preserve, protect and defend the integrity of your competition. So help me God."

Kidd lowered his hand and waited for Lucille McIntosh's response. After two gnaws on her eyeglasses, she said, "Well, I certainly hope so. Otherwise, I'll be getting impeached." She popped her glasses back on and pointed to the door. "Makeup takes fifteen minutes. Your boy can have a seat in the auditorium."

By ten minutes to eight, Langdon Arena had filled to capacity as parents and spectators filtered in from the lobby and took their seats. By five minutes to eight, the Family Values Channel production crew was in place and the lights were fixed on the stage.

Kenny made his way up the far left aisle of the balcony and took a seat in the last row. Two rows in front of him was the supporting contingent for the contestant from Wisconsin. They were all wearing buttons extolling that "Virgins are Sexy!" and one of them had a sign at her feet—the mother, Kenny surmised—which proclaimed: "Michelle Is Saving Her First Kiss For Her Wedding Day!" Although he found such a sentiment depressing, Kenny could relate. The way he was going, that same fate might befall him, even if he were getting hummers from troll Mormons on the side.

At 7:55, Kidd's big moment arrived, when he was escorted by Sandy Butters from the wings, down the left-hand steps of the stage and over to the judges' table. Four other celebrity judges walked in front of him. The first celebrity judge was a man in a dark suit who had the demeanor of a used car salesman; the second was an older Indian woman wrapped in a sari. The third judge was tall, African-American, and under the lights he glittered from an excess of gold jewelry on his neck and fingers. The fourth judge Kenny could barely see—she was a pert blonde in a black dress, and from a distance she looked like a dwarf. At first, their entrance stirred applause from the audience, but then Kenny heard it as Kidd reached the bottom of the stage steps: The comments started. Audible gasps and questionings. In front of him, Kenny heard the mother from the Wisconsin contingent say, "Is that Chucky Kidd?" To which a man, probably her husband, replied, "Can't be. The Secret Service would have been all over us."

"I think it is," a grandmotherly woman said.

"Really?" the husband asked. He reflected. "Goodness, I hope they handed out chastity belts."

The crowd only stopped its rumbling speculation when the stage came alive with light. Techno music started up, and a public address announcer took over the ceremonies: "Live from Las Vegas, Nevada!" he boomed. "It's the Fourth Annual Miss Teen Virgin USA Pageant! Now entering the stage, please welcome our contestants—all of them virgins, and all of them committed to the principle of abstinence before marriage!"

That's when the music turned loud and a string of girls emerged from both sides of the stage, dancing clumsily and mouthing the words to a prerecorded theme song about virginity.

"We are virgins. Virginity is awesome.
No one takes our flower 'til it's right for them to pick it.
We are virgins. Virginity is awesome.
If anybody laughs at us, we tell them to go stick it."

All the girls seemed attractive, but there weren't that many of them, maybe twenty-five in all. Glancing at the television monitors hanging on the sides of the stage for the benefit of the attendees, Kenny found out why by looking at their sashes. Unlike a regular beauty pageant, where the contestants represented individual states, the girls in this competition represented regions. There were Miss New England and Miss Mid-Atlantic, Miss Northern Rocky Mountains and Miss Alaska and Hawaii, who was definitely from Alaska and not Hawaii, given her pasty appearance. The lack of contestants was quite telling, Kenny thought. It appeared from this sampling that there just weren't that many virgin teenagers left in America.

Midway through the song, the introductions began, with each girl stepping to the center of the stage, striking a pose, and shouting out who she was to the audience.

"Lisa Roy, sixteen, Miss New England!" a pretty raven-haired girl yelled. "And my boyfriend's a virgin, too!" Cheers erupted from the crowd.

"Mendy Tate, eighteen, Miss Southern Southeast!" came the introduction from an olive-skinned beauty. "A lot of my friends followed my example and reclaimed their virginity!" More cheers.

"Joanne Castigan, seventeen, Miss Texarkana!" This girl was hot but rugged. "They say everything is bigger in Texas, and so is the commitment to abstinence!" The place went nuts.

Then a homely brunette stepped to the center of the stage and announced, "Sally Pittsbaker, nineteen, Miss Upper Great Lakes! Never. Even. Been. Kissed!" The Wisconsin contingent in front of Kenny roared; the mother held up her sign. Kenny just shook his head. Until then, the sign had seemed ironic. Now it just seemed prescient. Miss Upper Great Lakes probably wasn't going to be kissed before her wedding day, unless somebody put a paper bag over her head and cut out a hole for her lips.

After the introductions, the girls finished their song-and-dance number and stepped into prearranged places on the stage. A creamier type of music swelled and the P.A. announcer boomed, "Introducing your host for this evening's festivities. You remember him from his role as Little Ray Ray on the Emmy-winning television show *Martin's Clan*. Now he's all grown up and can be seen daily playing Jerry Jensen on the Family Value Channel's new daytime drama, *Independence, Idaho.* Please welcome, committed re-virgin, Buck Thomas."

The crowd erupted in applause as Buck Thomas walked to the center of the stage. The host was around thirty years old, with perfect teeth and a full head of curly blonde hair. He smiled to the crowd, said his thanks, welcomed the audience on television, and made a short and well-received speech about abstinence. Then he announced that, based on the judges' scoring during the opening number, the field of twenty-five would now be whittled down to twelve. He was handed a list of the chosen contestants, and as he read off the names, each girl stepped forward, music exploding and smiles flashing, to take a new position toward the front of the stage. After all twelve names were read, Kenny saw the Wisconsin contingent deflate—Miss Upper Great Lakes was not among the semifinalists.

The lights dimmed and the girls, both advancers and rejects, were ushered off the stage. The crowd quieted and Kenny felt his stomach tense. He saw a cameraman emerge from the wings and walk down to the judges' table. He wondered if this was Kidd's big moment, his re-emergence into the national spotlight. When the judges' table was illuminated, Kenny knew for sure—Kidd's time had come.

The host said, "Now, you've just seen which girls advanced to the semifinal round, but you're probably wondering who made those decisions. We've assembled quite a team of judges for you this evening. So without further ado, let's meet them."

The cameraman pointed to the first judge in the dark suit, and a red light flashed on the camera. The first judge's face filled the in-house television screen.

"From Atlanta, Georgia, the founder and chairman of Family Values Programming, the parent company of the Family Values Channel, which is broadcasting our pageant tonight to a worldwide audience. Please welcome Herb Townsend."

Herb Townsend waved to the crowd with a crooked arm. The audience applauded lightly, then the cameraman moved over to a position in front of the Indian woman who was wrapped in a sari.

"You know her best as the wife of the world's most famous sitar player, but she's also a former model, an actress in India's Bollywood films for three decades, and now a tireless campaigner for abstinence education in her home country, where she's fighting to stop the spread of AIDS in that ancient land. Please welcome, direct from Mumbai, Jayaprada Shenoy."

As the crowd clapped, Jayaprada Shenoy smiled at the camera and waved delicately with a cupped hand.

The camera shifted to the African-American gentleman with the gold jewelry. "He's a five-time Grammy nominee and two-time R&B Entertainer of the Year. He's also the man who penned our sassy opening theme song tonight, so please give it up for multi-platinum recording artist Lew Kools."

The crowd cheered Lew Kools the most yet. He flashed a brilliant, perfect smile, held up his hand and made a peace sign with his fingers.

The camera then moved down to the next judge—the short blonde in the black dress. Unlike the first judge, her head was not massive in the screen, and unlike the Indian judge, who had been weathered by age, this woman was drop-dead hot. Young and vivacious, she was smiling and waving before the host even began his spiel, and the crowd loved her immediately. Kenny could barely hear the introduction over the crowd, but it didn't matter. He could have just stared at her all night, so easily did his eyes melt into the perfect construct of her face—high cheekbones, pert nose, eyes like wildfire, and a forehead you could hang a Monet on. Forget that blonde in Chicago, Kenny thought. This girl was a true goddess.

"You remember her feats of daring," the host shouted over the crowd, "in the Summer Olympics in Prague, when, at age sixteen, she finished her floor exercise on a broken foot to win the women's all-around gold medal in gymnastics. Since then, she's become something of a cultural icon. She's spunky, she's loveable, and—and this is the shocker—she's already twenty-three years old. From Amarillo, Texas, please welcome Darby Duvall."

So that's Darby Duvall, Kenny thought. He had read her name off the brochure the previous evening, and he remembered hearing about her Olympic accomplishments when he was eleven, but he had never seen what she looked like before. She came as advertised. Darby Duvall stood on her chair and waved to the crowd, radiating warmth and aura, and the crowd ate it up. Kenny, for his part, couldn't take his eyes off her, especially in that black form-hugging dress. But she was very small. Kenny doubted that she was even five feet tall.

Darby Duvall settled down, and Kenny felt his chest tighten with nervous anticipation—the cameraman was moving over to Kidd. When Kidd's face flashed on the screen, Langdon Arena went dead quiet. Kenny wanted to crawl under his seat, such was his embarrassment for Kidd, but he remained anchored to his chair, clutching his hair, waiting to see how Kidd's introduction played out. He had to be strong for Kidd. If no one else was going to clap for the former president, Kenny Kernick sure as hell would.

"And finally," the host began, his practiced voice supplanting the silence, "he was twice elected to the nation's highest office, serving as our country's chief executive for over six years. He was also a successful two-term governor of Ohio. He's with us tonight filling in for his good friend, the former chief of staff and current president of Nevada State University, Tom Prudell, who took ill this afternoon. We're thankful he could join us on such short notice. It really is an honor to have him here. Please welcome former president of the United States, Charles Bentley Kidd."

Kenny squirmed at the introduction, and his shoulders pinched to his ears in expectation of large objects, or at least boos, being hurled at Kidd from the audience. But nothing flew from the seats. The audience simply began to clap. Not a strong clap, and not a clap like any of the other judges got, but a clap nonetheless. Kenny relaxed his shoulders and looked at Kidd.

The former president had risen halfway out of his seat and was waving modestly to the crowd. Then he did something Kenny thought amazing—he tightened his lips and nodded his chin to the audience in a gesture of thanks. There was no cocksure smirk on his face, no grandiosity, pompousness or self-absorption exuding off his manner. He seemed truly grateful to the crowd for their nice token of welcome.

Kidd sat and adjusted his chair, and the competition started again, with the host sending the pageant to its first commercial break on the promise of a swimsuit competition for the twelve semifinalists when they returned.

Kenny watched Kidd through the entire commercial break. Even from a distance, Kenny could tell from his body language that Kidd was relaxed and content, so much so that he was chatting up Darby Duvall next to him, who was laughing and touching Kidd's shoulder every time she made a statement. Kenny had to admit, the man looked happy.

And why shouldn't he be happy? Kenny thought. An "honor"—the host had actually used the word "honor" in discussing Kidd. It was an honor for them to have him here. Then the audience had given applause.

Two hours later, after Mendy Tate, Miss Southern Southeast, had been crowned Miss Teen Virgin USA and the crowd had dispersed, Kenny found Kidd backstage. Once again, he was chatting up Darby Duvall. Kenny kept his distance and waited for Kidd to finish the conversation. After a few minutes, Darby Duvall, who stood no taller than Kidd's chest, grabbed the former president's hand, flashed him a vivacious smile, and bid him farewell. Something about the way she took her leave of him—the glint in her eyes, the lingering of their hands—told Kenny that hers was not a permanent farewell. Not by a long shot.

On the limo drive back to the CandyLand, Kenny told Kidd that it was a night for celebration. They should go out for dinner and walk around town, sucking up the sights and soaking in the dazzle. Then at midnight, they would get a bottle of champagne, go over to Bellagio, wait for those fountains to start up, and toast Kidd's triumphant return to the national stage, regardless of what the ratings or reviews for the pageant turned out to be.

Kidd smiled graciously but declined. "I'm meeting Darby Duvall for dinner and some after-hours entertainment," he said. "I didn't know you'd want to celebrate, and she asked me out, not vice versa. I have just enough time to go back to the room, call for reservations, and freshen up."

"Oh," said Kenny. "Well, that's all right. We can celebrate tomorrow."

"Can we, Kenny? Do you mind?" asked Kidd.

"Not at all," Kenny said. And he really didn't mind. He was just glad that Kidd finally seemed at peace with himself. Since leaving Langdon Arena, the former president had a visible spring in his step, and he walked a little taller. And the soft glow in his eyes told tale of a man who liked who he was again, who had come back to the fold after months of self-loathing. As the limo swung onto Tropicana Avenue, Kenny turned to Kidd and asked, "This is the best you've felt in a long time, isn't it, Bent?"

Charles Bentley Kidd smiled, but he didn't answer. He didn't have to, because Kenny already knew. The boy had been around Kidd long enough to comprehend that the former president hadn't felt this proud, or this confident, or this secure, since the day, two Junes ago, when the whole country awoke to discover that some journalist at the tiny *Washington Courier* had made a new addition to the American lexicon—the word "Pastrygate."

CHAPTER 28

★ ★

The first call Kidd placed when he got back to the presidential suite was to Haiku, a trendy sushi bar on Tropicana Avenue where the Asian servers were world-renowned for improvising poems to their patrons on the spot.

The idea to eat there had come from Darby Duvall: During the final commercial break in the pageant, the one-time Olympic gold medalist leaned over, touched Kidd's arm determinedly, and told him that she wanted to forgo the stuffy Miss Teen Virgin USA Coronation Party. Instead, she preferred a night on the town with him, starting with sushi at Haiku and stretching on from there until who knew when. Although Kidd was feeling worn down after a full day of activities, it took him all of three nanoseconds to accept her invitation. He agreed to pick her up at the Luna at 10:30, with reservations at the restaurant set for an hour later. With the time approaching 10:15, and the Luna a four-casino walk down the Strip, Kidd thanked the hostess at Haiku for giving him a table on such late notice, hung up the phone, and went into the bathroom to reorganize himself for an adventurous evening.

Darby Duvall didn't look anything like Kidd remembered from his first meeting with the gymnast almost seven years ago. She had come to the White House then as a sixteen-year-old—flat-chested, short-haired, and puny—to be honored for her gold-medal performance. She was still puny, at least of height, but the rest of her was all woman now. In that black dress, her thighs had looked like they could crack lobster claws.

Why does she want a night out with a geezer like me? Kidd wondered as he plucked some errant nose hairs. *She's so young, and I'm so... not young.* Regardless, he took off his shirt, washed his face and armpits with cold water, and reapplied his deodorant.

And what is her connection to the National Abstinence Alliance? he wondered. *Was Darby Duvall a virgin? A committed re-virgin? Did she even care about abstinence?* To support that she did, Kidd realized that he had never once heard Darby Duvall's name linked to a boyfriend. Just in case she didn't, he pulled down his pants and washed his crotch, for freshness.

Once he had reassembled himself, he slid on his wrist watch, stuffed his wallet in a breast pocket, and went to stand in front of the full-length mirror hanging off the back of his bedroom door. He smoothed down the flaps of his suit coat and admired the figure he saw looking back at him. Here he was, midway through his fifty-third year, and he was about to hit Las Vegas with a firecracker twentysomething fabulous girl. There would be paparazzi, no doubt, given Darby Duvall's iconic status. They would be whispered about and gawked at as they walked the Strip. They could easily get into the best clubs, and get the choicest VIP rooms. Somewhere along the line, they might even be able to swing seats for the late performance of

Krutchfeld and Marzook's world-famous jaguar show at The Mexicale. This town was big and bright and ripe. All he and Darby Duvall needed to do was to step out into its glow and let the lights guide them.

Kidd slapped some cologne on his face and walked to the door of the bedroom suite. He made one final check of his assemblage. He was ready to rock. Then he strode into the living room to say goodbye to Kenny, and his enthusiasm collapsed.

He found the boy sitting on the couch, flipping around the television channels. It wasn't that Kenny looked depressed to see Kidd going out. He just looked bored.

"What are you going to do tonight?" Kidd asked, feeling a burst of guilt at abandoning the friend who had given him so much that day.

"I don't know," Kenny said. "This television stuff is wild; no wonder my father never let me watch it. You can catch anything on here. They have a lot of something called pay-per-view. Did you know you can get pornography on it? Pornography. Naked women. Having sex. No worries, Bent. I'll be fine."

But Kidd didn't want Kenny to be fine—he wanted the boy to be happy. "It's such an amazing town," Kidd said. "Why don't you go out and have some fun? You don't need to watch porn, Kenny—there's more real-life scrumptious humptious out there than a boy could shake a stick at. This is Vegas, baby! And the stick you're shaking is Elvis himself!"

Kenny shrugged. "Elvis is fine. I'm fine. The only scrumptious humptious you need to worry about is your own."

"My guess is I'm going out with a virgin," Kidd said. "Scrumptious humptious is probably off the menu. I'm going to share a nice evening with a gorgeous young woman, maybe give her a kiss goodnight, then I'm coming home."

"Sounds fun," Kenny said. Then he turned his attention back to the television and started rifling through the 10:30 broadcast menu for the CandyLand's instructional videos on gaming.

Kidd patted his breast pocket and said, "I think I forgot my wallet." He turned and walked back into his bedroom, knowing full well that he hadn't forgotten anything. He sat on the edge of his bed, then he put his head in his hands and let the guilt consume him. It was such an inscrutable emotion, guilt. He had felt none of it when exercising extramarital infidelities. If anything, engaging in forbidden sex had made him feel alive and emboldened. And yet, here he was, suffused with anxiety over leaving a boy alone in a hotel room for just a few hours.

Kenny would have more fun with her, Kidd heard a voice in his head say. You've been around that block before—the pretty girl on your arm, enjoying her company. It means nothing to you. But Young Kernick would eat it up.

That he would, Kidd decided. He took off his suit coat, walked into the bathroom and sat on the toilet. For effect in what he was about to do, he reached to the sink. With a quick twist of the lever, Kidd turned on the faucet and flicked a few drops of water on his forehead. Then he summoned his courage and his best acting skills and yelled, "Kenny, come here! I need you!"

It took the boy but seconds to reach the bathroom. He arrived to find Kidd clutching his stomach and putting on a damn good show.

"Oh, Kenny," Kidd said. "I suddenly feel like hell."

"What is it?" Kenny asked.

"I don't know," Kidd said. "Probably something wrong with those cream puffs I ate. Maybe they were rancid. But it's killing me, Kenny! Killing me! My entire intestinal tract feels like liquid metal. I think I'm going to vomit."

"Is there anything I can do?" Kenny asked.

"Call the concierge desk and have them send up some Pepto, will you?"

"Right now?" Kenny asked. "But you have to leave. You're going to be late to pick up Darby Duvall."

"Just do it, Kenny! Please?!"

Kenny turned and ran to the phone in Kidd's bedroom. As he spoke with the concierge, Kidd shimmied down to face the toilet, then he raised the lid and did something he had never done in his life—he plunged a finger into his throat to make himself throw up. Vomit erupted from his gut. It hurt like hell, but it had motivation. Kenny was a person who needed to see proof of something before he believed it. He would never leave the suite without proof. Kidd was manufacturing that proof by regurgitation, and now that the vomit was flowing freely, the proof kept coming.

He heaved and vomited again as Kenny stepped into the bathroom.

"Oh, God, Kenny! I feel terrible! Is the concierge sending somebody up?"

"They're on their way," Kenny said, putting a hand to his nose. The bathroom had begun to smell putrid, the effect of salivated pastry churned in hot acid for more than six hours.

Kidd released another explosion into the toilet bowl, then he slumped back and wiped his mouth with a shirtsleeve, leaving behind a pink streak against white broadcloth. "I'm toast," he told Kenny. "I'm down and out. What am I going to do? Darby Duvall is expecting me to pick her up in ten minutes."

"Where's her number?" Kenny asked. "I'll call and cancel for you."

Kidd tried to shake his head, but he could only manage to thrust his face back into the bowl and let out a garbled "Noooooo!" as more vomit shot forth from his gaping maw. When his vomiting ceased, he looked up at Kenny with weary eyes and said, "You remember Darby Duvall, Kenny—she's a national treasure. I can't cancel on her."

"Why not?" Kenny asked.

"I'll give you a bunch of reasons," Kidd said. "Going through with the floor exercise after she broke her foot on the vault. Landing all those somersaults, smiling through the pain, refusing to be carried off the mat at the end even though she could barely walk, all while the crowd is giving her a thunderous ovation. Then standing on the medal platform without crutches or even a temporary cast—square-jawed and dry-eyed and belting out the National Anthem, and telling reporters later that she didn't use crutches or a cast on the platform because they were signs of weakness, and no American should ever accept a gold medal with signs of weakness because it sends the wrong message to the world. I mean, Jesus! That chick has balls bigger than King Kong! No, you don't stand up a girl like Darby Duvall, Kenny. If you do, she's the type to make sure the media knows about it. I can't leave her hanging. It will ruin all my good press from tonight. Help me."

Kidd tried to rise, but went limp. Kenny grabbed his arm, lifted him, and waited until he had steadied himself on both legs before letting go.

"Feeling better?" Kenny asked.

"Actually," Kidd said, "I think I just shit myself. Out, Kenny! Out, out!"

Kidd pushed Kenny out of the bathroom and shut the door. For effect, he forced a fart from his ass.

"I'm calling Darby Duvall and telling her!" Kenny said through the door. "I'm telling her, Bent! She'll understand!"

"No, Kenny, don't you dare!" Kidd said.

"Then what do you want me to do?!" Kenny said.

"There's only one thing to do, Kenny. One thing to save face." Kidd let loose another fart. This one stunk like hell. He hoped Kenny could smell it on the other side of the door, just to get the boy out of the bedroom.

"Give me her room number," Kenny said. "I'll have the CandyLand send her flowers."

"I don't want you to send her flowers, Kenny," Kidd said. "I want you to send yourself."

There was silence from beyond the door. Then,"You want me to what?"

"You must be my squire, Young Kernick. My second. You must go in my stead. Present her with my regrets, then offer yourself as her escort. If she accepts you, take her to dinner and then to a show or a movie or whatever she wants. Give her a good time. Then people will speak well of both our names." Another hellacious fart ushered forth from his bowels. Now Kidd really was nauseated.

"But I don't have any money," Kenny said.

"Look in my suit coat," Kidd bellowed, trying to sound like a man about to go down with a sinking ship. "There's a bunch of hundred dollar bills in my wallet. If you need more, take my bank card. My PIN number is sixty-nine sixty-nine. Don't laugh. I swear to God that's the one the bank gave me."

A loud blast exploded from Kidd's ass, sending a gush of diarrhea into his boxer shorts. He had started something he couldn't stop, but it was all for a good end. "She's at the Luna, Kenny!" he yelled. "At the Tranquility Lounge! Waiting for me at the bar!"

"If that's what you want me to do," Kenny said.

"It's an executive order," Kidd said. "Now stop screwing around and get out of here. Hurry, Kenny. Huuuuuuurrrrrrrrry!"

Kidd knew Kenny had taken the bait when the main door to the suite slammed. Kidd took off his clothes, cleaned himself up and threw a towel around his waist, then he walked out of the bathroom and checked his wallet. Kenny had pulled it out of the suit coat and taken all the money in it, along with the ATM card. The boy had more than enough funds to show Darby Duvall a proper night on the town.

But would she accept him? Kidd wondered, as he began to dress in the candy-striped pajamas he had purchased in Chicago. And if she did accept him, would Kenny be able to keep up with her? It wasn't hard to tell that, virgin or not, Darby Duvall possessed immense energy. Hell, at the pageant she had actually stood on her chair and waved to the crowd. Would a woman like that even want to be seen with Kenny Kernick? If so, what if she killed him with overactivity? Kidd had just thrown Kenny out into the world alone, and a world of celebrity at that. As Kidd buttoned the front of his candy-striped pajamas, he only hoped that the boy would survive. Somebody still had to drive Kidd to Los Angeles, after all.

CHAPTER 29

★ ★

Kenny was already seven minutes late to meet Darby Duvall when he ran up to the main entrance of the Luna Resort and Casino—a mammoth, off-white, spherical hotel which, with its rooms' windows creating craters in the façade and black paint applied to its exterior in splotchy pools, really did resemble the moon.

A bellhop dressed in the cold silvers of a lunar landscape opened a door for Kenny. Walking into the foyer, Kenny followed the posted signs for the Tranquility Lounge. He walked briskly in the lounge's direction, making with every step a mental inventory of his appearance. Did he look good? Was he put together? How did he smell? In the desert, stinky sweat did not seem to be a problem. Even after his sprint from the Candy-Land, he was as dry as dust. But his hair was a mess from the stiff wind out on the Strip, and his clothes were untucked and shifted. As he hurried to the lounge, he stopped intermittently to smooth his locks and adjust his clothes until, looking at his reflection in the silver edge of an ATM machine, he had created an image he found presentable to Darby Duvall.

Figuring he was as put together as he was going to get, Kenny walked into the lounge and surveyed the area. It was a dark lounge, with a long bar bathed in scant blue neon and several tables placed in mock crater pits. At the center of the bar, he saw Darby Duvall.

The sight of her made Kenny stall. The former Olympic gold medalist was sitting tall and straight in a plush captain's chair, her legs crossed at the thighs, as she sipped a green concoction out of a large-mouthed glass. She was no longer wearing the elegant black dress she had donned for the Miss Teen Virgin USA Pageant. She had changed out of that garment in favor of a tight, spaghetti-strapped pink slip dress with pink slingback sandals.

Kenny stood silent for a moment, taking her in. She struck an amazing figure. He felt an overwhelming urge to run to her—to run right up, jump in her lap, and roam his eager hands over the rayon of her dress, hoping that from touch his brain could discern the mysteries of what lay underneath. But he stifled the urge. Really, he had no choice. Darby Duvall was probably still a virgin. Bent had said so himself. Kenny trusted the judgment of a man who had made a professional life out of knowing such things. Why else would she have committed herself to the Miss Teen Virgin USA Pageant, and thus the National Abstinence Alliance, if she weren't a virgin? Either way, Kenny realized it was a moot point. Physically, Darby Duvall was built like a miniature German Panzer. Virgin or not, one wrong hand on her and he would probably get his fingers blown off.

"Miss Duvall?" Kenny said upon approaching her.

Darby Duvall turned to him, eyed him curiously, then said with a muted Southern accent, "That's sweet of you to recognize me, but if you want an autograph, I only do those on Mondays." She offered him a dismissive half-smile. "Plus, I'm expecting someone."

Kenny cleared his throat. "I think you're expecting me," he said.

Darby Duvall leveled a set of startling brown eyes at Kenny, and her curiosity turned to cold irritation. "Listen, little one," she said. "That's the lamest pick-up line I've ever heard. Right up there with 'I'm hung like a pommel horse.' Seriously, run back to the school bus. It's leaving." She flapped her hand at him to go.

"First," Kenny said, annoyed, "you are waiting for me, because I'm here at the behest of Charles Bentley Kidd. Second, you have some effrontery calling me 'little one' when you yourself are, what"—Kenny sized her up from the heels of her sandals to the top of her soft blonde hair—"four-foot-ten?"

The irritation in Darby Duvall's eyes softened. A smile played at the corners of her lips.

"At the behest of," she said, repeating Kenny. "Effrontery," she mocked. She reached for the fat-mouthed glass holding the green concoction and held it aloft with a tight pinch of its stem, almost as a toast. "Well, it looks like Mr. Kidd has sent me a smart one." She raised the glass to her lips, sipped, and swallowed hard. With a middle finger, she wiped the corner of her lips to contour her lipstick. "And just so you know," she added, "I'm four-foot-nine and three-quarters, if you want to get technical about it. And I can already tell that you're the type who likes to get technical about everything."

"You have discerned correctly," Kenny said.

"Oh, 'discern'—I like that." She chuckled under her breath, again mocking Kenny. "Then let's get technical. Give me your specifications."

"My what?" Kenny asked. He had become lost in her corded neckline, where the cream of her skin met one of the pink spaghetti straps.

"Your specifications," she repeated, in a tone that told Kenny she didn't like to repeat anything. "What's your name?"

Kenny stated his name in its entirety.

"Kenneth Andrew What?" she asked.

"Kernick," Kenny said. "From the German *könig*, meaning 'king.' But 'Kernick' is how it appears on my birth certificate."

"Wow," Darby Duvall said, mocking again. "So much information. Do you know what 'Duvall' means too?"

"I believe it means 'of the valley,' Kenny said. "In French."

"Damn," Darby Duvall said. "You are a smarty. Now who are you?"

Kenny thought for a moment. "Let's just say I'm Mr. Kidd's new chief of staff."

"Really?" Darby Duvall asked suspiciously. "And how'd you get that job?"

"Through proximity," Kenny said.

"Sounds complicated," she said. "But then again, I like complicated. I always got more points for complicated. So where is Mr. Kidd? Does the bastard know he's late?" She lifted her fat-mouthed glass for another sip of green concoction.

"He's fully aware of the situation," Kenny said. "But as we speak, he's losing his lunch back at the CandyLand. He could be pulling an all-nighter in the bathroom. He sends his apologies. He thinks he got some bad pastry."

"Bad pastry, huh?" she said. "Sounds like he's rehashing old excuses. Well, it better have been bad pastry—those things better have been smothered in salmonella if he's going to stand me up." She threw out her hands in exasperation. "This is just a joy, isn't it? Another Duvall Margarita, Carlos. Heavy on the Cointreau. My date's stuck in a bathroom all night, so I'm going to be stuck at this bar all night."

"Duvall Margarita, coming up," the bartender said.

Darby Duvall leaned in toward Kenny's face as the bartender shook up another vat of her eponymous cocktail. "You take a good look at this dress, little one," she said. She used a hand to highlight some of its curvier, clingier points. "Then you go back and tell your boss what he missed. Then maybe he can do something else in the bathroom all night." She used the same hand to make a masturbating motion.

Kenny took a breath and gulped uncomfortably. "Actually, Ms. Duvall, Mr. Kidd asked me to take you out. If you'll have me." With the completion of his words, his heart started to race. He stood there peg-legged, waiting for her reaction.

Darby Duvall's response came in the form of a laugh thrown to the ceiling. When she was done, she snapped her head back to Kenny so that her straight blonde locks swung like a pendulum. Her brown eyes came alive, bemused.

"Did you hear that, Carlos?" she asked. "The little one wants to take me out." Carlos, a slender man with a shy smile, pursed his lips and placed a new margarita on the bar, then he stepped away. It was clear that he wanted no part of the situation.

Darby Duvall picked up the glass, raised it to chin level and looked off toward some distant part of the lounge. She shook her head. "A girl expects a cowboy and all she gets is the rodeo clown. Damn shame."

Darby Duvall put the glass to her lips and took five strong gulps of the margarita.

"Yummy," she said, putting the glass down. She looked back at Kenny and gave him the once-over. "So you're here to take me out, hey? Well, you do have nice blue eyes. And I like that red hair—always my favorite. And, most important, you're smart. Did you at least get reservations at Haiku?"

Kenny nodded. "We're scheduled to eat there in forty-five minutes."

Darby Duvall shook her head. "Not with you dressed like that, we're not. Not at that restaurant. Not with me. I may be from the scrubs of Texas, honey, but I sure as hell demand style."

Kenny looked down at his clothes, grappling at his Oxford like a robbery victim searching for gunshot wounds. He felt his legs stiffen.

Darby Duvall grabbed a pink bead purse off the bar, snapped it open, and dug out a cell phone. Within seconds she had punched up a number and was waiting for an answer.

"Lilly, it's Darby Duvall," she said when the other party picked up. Her brown eyes locked on Kenny. "I'm sending someone to you." A pause. "Then drop it! This is an emergency. Assemble a team. You'll see why."

She snapped off the call without saying goodbye.

"Up on the mezzanine," she said, sliding her cell phone into the purse, "there's a boutique called Tycho. Lilly is waiting for you. Don't miss the bus."

"Tycho," Kenny repeated. He chuckled.

"What's so funny?" Darby Duvall asked. She was back to taking sips from her margarita.

Kenny shrugged and said, "Tycho is the name of the most stunning crater on the moon. The one at the bottom with all the silver streaks spreading out from it. The name made me laugh, that's all. It seems the Luna people did their homework."

Darby Duvall leveled her brown eyes at Kenny. "Okay, little one, let's get something clear. There's smart, and there's annoying. When you come back, make sure you're just smart."

Once again, she flapped her hand at him to go, and this time, Kenny went.

Twenty minutes later, when Kenny returned to the Tranquility Lounge, Darby Duvall's impatient eyes widened at the sight of him.

Lilly and her team had affected a complete transformation. They had cast Kenny's Oxford and khakis to an incinerator, and adorned him in black flat-front twill pants, black squared-toe loafers with matching ribbed socks, a black plaque belt, and a lightweight leather jacket, also in black. Black, black, and more black. Modeling himself in a triple mirror, Kenny had felt like an undertaker. The only splashes of color on him came from the belt buckle, the jacket zipper, and the shirt—a stretch poplin, open collar, which Lilly had picked out in flat gray. They had been so thorough, they even insisted he give up his tighty-white Fruit of the Looms for a nice pair of boxer shorts. Kenny took their advice.

With her legs still crossed at the thigh and the margarita glass jutting off from one of her hands, she watched Kenny as he came through the door and strode toward her. When he had walked to within five feet of her, she held up a palm as a gesture for him to stop. Kenny halted.

"Give me a spin," she said.

He spun.

When he came around to face her again, Darby Duvall offered no verbal approval of Lilly's handiwork. Instead, she let a sly smile pull at the corners of her lips, then she pumped her eyebrows once. By her actions, Kenny thought he could read her mind. She was thinking, "Yummy."

"You want a drink before we go?" she asked. "The desert can punish you with dehydration. Even when it's cool outside."

Kenny declined politely.

"Suit yourself." She finished her Duvall Margarita in a long, steady sip, then slid the glass forward and jumped off the captain's chair. When the soles of her pink slingback sandals hit the floor, Kenny heard a loud smack, the sound of dense leather slapping tile.

"Carlos," Darby Duvall said, "the little one here is taking me out. Don't wait up." She grabbed her purse, grabbed Kenny's hand, and yanked him out of the Tranquility Lounge.

Little did Kenny know, as he was being dragged from the Luna by the tugging arm of Darby Duvall, that the smacking sound he heard as those sandals hit the floor might as well have been the crack of a starter pistol. For tiny Darby Duvall wasn't just good at gymnastics, Kenny realized—she was also good at distance running. Tonight, Kenny would be her pacer. As the starting line of the Luna faded behind them and the track of Las Vegas Boulevard stretched out long in their path, they were already a streak of color against the dizzying nighttime dazzle.

CHAPTER 30

★ ★

She pushed him hard that night, stopping once for food, and allowing many drinks, but rarely giving him time to catch his breath or thoughts.

For Kenny, dinner at Haiku was a blur, an endless consumption of colorful sushi and tart Duvall Margaritas, punctuated frequently by the heat from wasabi rising up to his sinuses when Darby Duvall made him pile a dollop of the green condiment onto a piece of raw fish, just for fun. "The more the better, little one," she said. "Eat it." He did, until his nasal cavity became an oven. Then there were the improvised haikus for which the restaurant was famous—it seemed to Kenny that every server in the place wanted to come over to Darby Duvall's table and offer a poem to their celebrity guest.

First, he heard:

Lithe beauty of Prague
How hard you spin and tumble—
Without falling down

Then:

On the podium
You looked so young a flower:
Now a woman blooms

And finally,

Gorgeous golden girl,
Will you marry me tonight?
I'm not rich but hung

Whereupon Darby Duvall learned that the Asian waiter's first name was indeed Hung, even though the Americanized servers called him Rich, which Darby Duvall found so amusing that she snorted her fresh margarita all over a plate of maguro nigiri. When she finally tired of the attention, she asked them to offer a poem to Kenny. What he got was:

How can such flawed stone
Find strength to sit so close to
Sculpted perfection?

Kenny barely had time to contest the slight before another slab of wasabi-laden fish was thrust upon him by the hands of Darby Duvall, and his sinuses exploded anew.

After dinner, Kenny's night turned from blur to smudge. As if to test her companion's strength, Darby Duvall made Kenny take her on the roller coaster at New York New York over and over again. When he didn't throw up after eleven rides, she eyed him admiringly then took him downstairs for drinks and singing at the piano bar. At the behest of the crowd, Darby Duvall hopped up next to the pianist and belted out a professional-sounding version of some song called "Friends in Low Places." Not to be outdone, Kenny tried to one-up her by climbing onstage and offering "99 Red Balloons" in German, a song his teacher at Griggson Academy had made him and his fellow Deutsch students sing ad nauseam to help them learn the language. Although sung somewhat off-key, the German accent was perfect, and his performance elicited a standing ovation from the crowd. It also put another glint in Darby Duvall's warming gaze.

But any opportunity he might have had to use his date's increasing affections for a first kiss had to be delayed. Darby Duvall wouldn't stop for anything. Following their time at the piano bar, gambling ensued at several casinos along the Strip. She powered through Charles Bentley Kidd's money on the five-dollar slots, the roulette wheel, and craps, until Kenny had to disappear briefly to get more bills from an ATM at The Mexicale. He returned to find Darby Duvall at the blackjack table, a huge pile of chips in front of her and a crowd gathering around. When she cashed out with a hefty payday, she handed the money to Kenny and said, "Now take me dancing."

Which he did, at a string of the best nightclubs in Vegas. No waiting line was too long for them. They were simply ushered into any club Darby Duvall desired by burly bouncers who sought no proof that her escort was at least twenty-one. Trust, it seemed, came with Darby Duvall's image. By that time, the paparazzi were following them. Pack-mentality photographers snapped their photos as they exited Cream and entered Hysteria. Their cab over to Fusion was followed by a horde of reporters, each of whom asked Darby Duvall the name of her date as she got out of the taxi.

"It's Kenny Kernel," she yelled. The reporters wrote it down. Flustered by all the attention, Kenny didn't have the wherewithal to correct her.

At Fusion, alcohol flowed in the darkness of the broad dance floor and their cozy VIP room. At first, Kenny couldn't feel his teeth. Later, he couldn't feel his toes. But he sure as hell could feel Darby Duvall's thigh touching his as they sat, drank, and held court with the Golden Girl's many admirers. Fans had photos taken with their icon, minus her escort. She signed autographs while she danced, even though it wasn't a Monday. Kenny's head spun to the pounding music. He was sure he had lost most of his bodily fluids to perspiration, but in the dryness of the desert and with his senses dulled by liquor, such a loss could not be accurately quantified. He wondered if the night would ever end, not that he wanted it to. Finally, after hours of incessant motion and innumerable margaritas, Darby Duvall pulled Kenny close to her and shouted over the roar of the music, "I've hit a wall. Take me back to the Luna." Her breath was sweet with liquor. Her fingers felt like rose petals tickling his ribs.

They caught a cab outside the nightclub. On the way down Las Vegas Boulevard, back toward Darby Duvall's hotel, Kenny asked the cab driver for the time.

"Twelve past four," the driver responded. Kenny could hardly believe it. There had still been a line of people in front of Fusion, all of them clamoring to get in.

The cab pulled into the valet area for the Luna, seemingly not followed by the paparazzi, and Darby Duvall got out while Kenny paid the cabbie a ten dollar fare plus tip. He found Darby Duvall waiting for him on the curb as the cab pulled away. She was holding her bead purse in front of her like she was preparing to say goodbye. Instead, she did something she hadn't done in several hours, not since Kenny first met her in the Tranquility Lounge—she asked him a question. "Would you like to come up?"

Kenny wanted to reply in the affirmative, but his tongue was thick with alcohol and his brain was stunned by shock. Was Darby Duvall really inviting him back to her room? Perhaps he had heard incorrectly. Any doubts he may have harbored over her intentions were put to rest when Darby Duvall, maybe intoxicated but still not a girl prone to waiting, snapped, "Well, do you?!" Kenny tried to speak again, but couldn't. Finally, he just held out his hand and let her take it.

The walk to the elevators was the slowest they had walked all evening. Darby Duvall was spent, and Kenny was glad for it. It gave him time to impress her with his Einsteinian brilliance.

"Did you know," he said, "that the word 'Luna' is the actual name for the moon? People forget that. Just like they forget that the proper name for the sun is 'Sol.' Strange, huh?"

"Did you know," he continued as they passed by a security guard and Darby Duvall held out her keycard for identification, "that if you stood in the sunlight on the moon, the temperature would be two hundred seventy-three degrees Fahrenheit, but if you stepped into a shadow—just a little shadow—that temperature would drop to minus two-forty-four in a snap? There's no atmosphere up there to regulate heat. It's bizarre."

"Did you know—" he said as they stepped into the elevator. But Darby Duvall stopped his new line of thought.

"I'll tell you what I know," she said, pushing her wavering body against Kenny's. "I know that you are a smart one, Kenny Kernel."

"Kernick," Kenny said. "It's Kernick."

But Darby Duvall was on a margarita-enhanced roll. She couldn't have cared less if his name was Kenny Kernick, Kenny Kernel, or Kenny Crap-Lapper. "I like smart ones," she said. "I never got to college myself—the demands of being a national treasure take up too much time. University of Texas would have been my choice. In Austin. But I like smart ones. The smart ones like to get things right. They like to please. They don't settle for incomplete work. And you"—Darby Duvall pointed at him with a wiggling finger—"are the smartest one I've seen yet. You're geniusical."

"I am?" Kenny asked. Her compliment took him aback. He realized that at some point along the journey from Connecticut, he had stopped thinking of himself as preternaturally smart (his father's view) and started thinking of himself as just another person.

"The smartest one ever," Darby Duvall said. "And trust me, I've known a lot of boys, Kernel." Darby Duvall let out a spraying raspberry. "But don't tell the Nabsinal Abshonence Alliance. They still think I'm a virgin."

"You're not a virgin?" Kenny asked in disbelief, as the elevator approached Darby Duvall's floor.

Darby Duvall laughed. "Oh, Kernel," she said, "I've been dimpled more times than a golf ball. I can't get enough sex. It's my jock side—I've got a lot of tessosserone in my perky little bod. But people still think of me as that sixteen-year-old girl, so I let them. It's worth a fortune."

But I'm a virgin, Kenny wanted to say as the elevator doors opened. Instead, his voice froze. Here he thought he was spending a nice evening with a wild virgin, but now he realized that he was about to enter the den of a wolf in lamb's clothing. What had he gotten himself into? How would he ever come out alive?

Darby Duvall grabbed his hand and led him onto her floor. Kenny could barely walk, his forward progress not impeded by frozen legs or an anxious gut, but by Elvis, who was up and alert and ready for fun.

"Oh my," Darby Duvall said when she saw the bulge at the front of Kenny's pants. "Is he looking at me?"

"I guess so," Kenny said.

"Good," Darby Duvall said. "I love attention."

When Kenny stepped through the door to Darby Duvall's junior suite, he noticed that the room smelled earthy and intense, much like Darby Duvall herself. Not that Kenny had time to contemplate such scents, or his amazing attraction to them. For no sooner had Darby Duvall shut the door behind Kenny than she thrust herself upon him, kissing him with liquor-laced tongue missiles, groping his butt, and rubbing her firm body into all of his soft places.

She pushed him backward as they entangled, thrusting him against a side table. Sounds of heavy breathing and vacated lip locks filled the room. They stumbled over the side table, then a sofa. She knocked him into an armoire, then threw him onto a desk. At one point, she bit his neck so hard he almost screamed. Finally, she pulled away and stared at him, her breath coursing in and out of her. With Kenny's neck stinging from bites, he understood fully that his elevator assessment of her hadn't been an exaggeration—this girl truly was a wolf, and she was ravenous.

She stood there, lupine, hunched and panting, and Kenny had no idea what his next move should be. Should he start to disrobe? Should he try to disrobe her? Should he put some ointment on his neck? But it was Darby Duvall who answered any questions. Before Kenny could affect a course of action, she reached down, grabbed the hem of her pink slip dress with both hands, and pulled the garment off her body in one fluid motion. To Kenny's shock, she wasn't wearing a single article of clothing underneath. With the exception of the slingback sandals that were still secured to her feet, she stood before him as nude as a Greek statuette, an enticing strip of straw-colored hair winking at him from her loins.

"You've been wondering all night, haven't you?" she asked with a predatory glint in her eyes. "Wondering if I'm a natural blonde."

Kenny shrugged. He hadn't, but why contradict her?

"Most boys assume I'm really a brunette," she said. "Because of my brown eyes—they're misleading. Now you know. The carpet matches the drapes."

Carpet matches the drapes, Kenny thought, finally understanding the meaning behind Prudell's cryptic statement that morning. So Darby Duvall was a true blonde. For some reason, he found that notion incredibly exhilarating. But all he could manage to say in his inebriation was, "My carpet matches my drapes, too."

"Does it?" Darby Duvall said with a laugh. "So you're funny, and smart, and you can sing in German. I imagine that's a combination that gets you laid like floor tile."

"You'd be surprised," Kenny said with a decided nonchalance.

Darby Duvall spun her dress around in a circle, her eyes still locked on her prey. "You like being smart, don't you, Kenny?" she asked, whirling the dress like a medieval mace.

"Actually, it's been more of a curse," Kenny said. He was crouching back against the desk in an effort to protect Elvis from a wayward dress snap.

"I don't believe that for one second," Darby Duvall said. Her Texas accent, which had grown thicker throughout the evening in direct proportion to the quantity of Duvall Margaritas she had consumed, now came out in a full-force drawl. "I think y'all thrive on it," she said. "I think it makes you feel good. Tell me, what were some of your favorite subjects in school? I'll bet you had a lot of them."

"Oh, you know," Kenny said. "Math. History."

"Math, history," Darby Duvall mocked. She whipped Kenny on the chest with her dress, stinging him. "B-O-R-I-N-G," she said. "Technical, Kenny. I want technical. I used to get scored on technicality—that was *my* curse. No room for artistry at all. What kind of math?"

"I don't know," Kenny said. "Tensor Calculus was always fun."

"Oh, that's a good one," Darby Duvall said. "I have no clue what it is, but way to go. And what kind of history?"

"All kinds," Kenny said, trying to placate this luscious huntress before the dress found his softer tissue. "Early Egyptian. Ancient Rome. The Middle Ages. At one point I was particularly drawn to Napoleon."

"Well, you are short," Darby Duvall said.

"Right back at you, Duvall," Kenny said. He waited for a blow to fall from the dress, but instead of hitting him for his insolence, Darby Duvall grinned. They were playing the same game, Kenny realized, and she was enjoying it.

"But what was your *favorite* history?" Darby Duvall asked. "Don't tell me it's all that foreign crap."

"It wasn't," Kenny said, replying honestly. "It was modern American."

"Modern American," Darby Duvall said. "That's better."

"It's my passion," Kenny said. "Everything from the Roaring Twenties to the space program."

"The space program?" Darby Duvall asked. "Is that why you know so much about the moon?"

"I've read tons of books on it," Kenny said.

"I love the moon," Darby Duvall said. "That's *my* passion. It's why I stay at the Luna every time I come to Vegas. Plus, I was born in late June, so I'm a Cancer. Do you know what they call Cancers, Kernel?"

Kenny shrugged. Astrology, as an unscientific discipline, was never one of his interests.

"They call us 'moon children,'" said Darby Duvall. "Because we're blessed by her. I'll bet you didn't know this, but on the night I won my gold medal, there was a full moon over Prague—the brightest there'd been in two hundred years. Did you know that, Kernel? The moon was with me that night, spreading fortune on me. I could feel her in every move I made. My foot hurt like a bitch, but she soothed me."

Darby Duvall pressed herself into Kenny, her naked body melting against him at all the right spots. He could smell the earthiness of her perfume tickling at his nose, but he could also smell something else—the sharp, sweaty scent of his own fear. What he didn't know is if that scent would repulse Darby Duvall, or turn her on. He got his answer quickly.

"Tell me about the moon, Kenny," Darby Duvall implored, chewing on his earlobe. "It makes me so ready. Tell me."

Kenny tingled at the touch of her teeth on his ear. "What more is there to say?" he replied, twisting with apprehension as her lips moved down to his neck and he waited for a bite. "It's just a coagulated mass of rock that we see at night."

"Oh, it's more than that," Darby Duvall said, licking his neck instead of biting it. "Come on, genius. Tell me about the moon."

Kenny didn't want to tell her about the moon. He wanted to get his clothes off and get on top of her. "Darby, this isn't the time," he said.

"Why not?" Darby Duvall asked. She pulled away from him. "Y'all think I'm too stupid to appreciate it? Do you think I'm just a dumb-ass jock because I never went to college?" She raised the limp dress in her hand to a precarious height above her head. "Tell me about the moon, Kernel. I want to hear about the moon."

"Seriously, Darby," Kenny said. "Can't we just—"

Whack! Kenny felt the sting of fabric against his skull. Darby Duvall's dress struck him so hard that he fell off the desk.

Darby Duvall looked down at Kenny on the carpet and laughed. Kenny rubbed his temple and crawled backward in an effort to get to his feet, but Darby Duvall pursued him.

"You want to get busy, then give me some facts," the gymnast said. "Get smart on me, Kernel! Right now!"

Searching desperately for answers, Kenny said, "The moon only shows one face because its revolution period around the earth is the same as its rotation period around itself!"

Whack! Kenny felt his left thigh burn. "No shit, Kernel," Darby Duvall said. "I can learn that in any encyclopedia. I want something smarter." She straddled Kenny's legs as he fumbled toward the sofa.

"The dark spots on the moon are actually solidified pools of lava!" Kenny cried. "Created when asteroids punctured the crust and lava leaked out. They look gray to us, but up there, they're as black as fresh asphalt!" He reached for the edge of the sofa.

"Interesting," Darby Duvall said. She smacked his extended arm. "Smarter!"

Kenny pulled himself onto the sofa. "The moon is really egg-shaped, not round," he said, trying to claw his way across the upholstery. "When we look up at it from earth, we're actually looking at the pointy end. That's why the crater Tycho seems so distorted!"

"Tycho again, huh?" Darby Duvall said. "Sounds like you're rehashing old information, genius. That'll cost you." She snapped the dress on Kenny's ass, making him yelp. Kenny climbed over the sofa and landed on the floor behind it, sending a jolt through his alcohol-numbed arms. He jumped to his feet in time to see Darby Duvall coming over the sofa, the dress spinning menacingly in her hand. Kenny kept his eyes locked to her, even while he stepped backward and reached his hands out to gauge the distance to the nearest wall.

"Smarter," Darby Duvall said. "I want smarter."

Kenny's eyes went wide at the sight of Darby Duvall aiming the dress right at Elvis. He crept back to a closet door and felt the doorknob at his fingertips. He was running out of ground, and he was too frightened to make a dash for the bedroom, where he could hide in the bathroom until Darby Duvall wanted to have sex peacefully. He pressed his back against the closet door. His flight had come to an end. He watched Darby Duvall raise the dress high for a kill shot on his genitals. This time, no amount of protection would deflect her blow. Kenny closed his eyes, dug into the corners of his memory, and cried out the nearest piece of lunar information he could find—"The moon won't be with us forever!"

No blow fell. After a few seconds, Kenny opened his eyes and saw that Darby Duvall's face had turned ashen. "What do you mean?" she asked.

Kenny talked in a rush, lest the dress suddenly drop on his gonads. "Every day the moon uses some of the earth's rotational energy to propel itself farther out into orbit. This time next year, the moon will be an inch and a half more distant from us."

Darby Duvall seemed visibly stunned. She cocked her head at Kenny, her lips parted in silent confusion.

Kenny charged through the void. "Scientists estimate that when the moon was formed, it was only fourteen thousand miles away from the earth. The earth spun really fast and the days were short, and the moon occupied a huge portion of the night sky. But the moon pulled away—now it's two hundred and fifty thousand miles from the earth. But pulling away wasn't a bad thing. The farther away it got, the more rotational energy it stole from us. The earth's spin slowed, making days longer and the rotation of the earth more stable, to the point where we pretty much spin on the same angle of axis now, meaning north stays north and south stays south. Environments stabilized. Stabilized environments meant life could form."

"But life is good," Darby Duvall said.

"But things are changing, Darby," Kenny said, rambling on. "As the moon continues to pull away, our days will get longer. Imagine a day that lasts a month, and then two months. But that's hardly the worst of it. The really bad part is that the farther out the moon goes, the more unstable the earth's rotation will become. The earth will wobble. It will jiggle, Darby. North will become west; south will become east. The tropics will become the North Pole, then they'll go back to being the tropics. Climates on earth will be turned upside down with regularity, and nothing will be able to survive. Nothing, Darby! Not one goddamn thing!" Kenny threw up a hand to shield himself from a dress smack unleashed out of incredulity.

But Darby Duvall didn't strike. Instead, she threw the dress to the floor. "Well, that sucks," she said.

Kenny lowered his hand. "It's orbital mechanics," he said to her, calmly now. "It's just physics. Nobody can do anything about it."

"So what you're telling me," Darby Duvall said, "is that one day you could be swimming in the sweltering heat and the next day you could be freezing your ass off at the bottom of a glacier?"

"Something like that," Kenny said.

"Sounds like the end of the world, Kernel," Darby Duvall said.

"It will be, Duvall," Kenny said.

Darby Duvall cocked her head and let out a sigh. She looked at Kenny matter-of-factly, like a woman resigned to her fate. "Well, you know what people do when it's the end of the world."

"What's that?" Kenny asked. Truly, he did not know.

Darby Duvall grinned at him as if he shouldn't have needed to ask. "Why, they fuck their brains out, of course."

Before Kenny could blink, she had pulled him away from the closet door, thrown him to the floor, and taken his pants down. She studied his boxer shorts approvingly and yanked them off without comment. Then she removed a condom from a hidden pocket in the hem of her discarded dress, and in seconds, a stiff Elvis was sheathed in latex. Kenny didn't exactly know what to do next, but Darby Duvall took care of that for him: She climbed up his waist and straddled him, and all he wanted to do was obey her every command.

In an instant, she was pushing him toward a finish line marked only by a chorus of grunts, a tightening of loins, and a catch of breath. This girl didn't take long to get where she was going; she was actually getting there much faster than he, the alcohol and his hummer from two nights ago stemming his speed. As she neared her end, Kenny could only marvel at her. Darby Duvall had said she loved the moon—that it was her passion, and that as a Cancer, it was part of her. But to Kenny, she was so much more than a moon child. To Kenny, charging along the delightful track of her womanhood, Darby Duvall felt like she came straight from heaven.

CHAPTER 31

★ ★

Outside Carl Kernick's hotel window in Dillon, Colorado, jutting from a mountain which rose above a pine grove, there sat a rock formation of curious size and shape.

Many times over the past two days, as he lay in bed and dealt with the paralyzing pain that was shooting through neck and back, Carl had positioned his head to look out the window. At first, as the memory of his accident was fresh, and the medications prescribed to him by the doctors were still sending his mind through a loop, Carl had only focused on the window itself—its glass was dirty, which indicated that this hotel was purely low-rent, nothing akin to a Rostoff. But as the medications wore off and his heart began to slow after the trauma of his accident, Carl accepted his accommodations and let his eyes search beyond the window. First he had spied a single flagpole, rising up seemingly out of nowhere, from which the American and Colorado pennants snapped in the wind. Then he had spotted signage for an establishment called Kum & Go, which Carl assumed was a strip club. Later he had noticed the grove of pine trees beyond the Kum & Go sign, and then, farther up, the mountain above the pines. Finally, his eyes had settled on the rock formation protruding from the mountain.

Throughout the night, Carl lay in bed with his head turned toward the window, his mind fully engaged in contemplation of the jutting rocks, even though he could not see them in the darkness. Carl had often heard from Kernick Handling clients who lived in Colorado that the rock formations in the Rockies were given names, but Carl had no idea what the name of this craggy structure might be. He had studied it at all times throughout the previous day—in the morning as he nibbled on a plain bagel brought to him by the local visiting nurse association; in the afternoon as he lifted himself out of bed with all the speed of a Panamanian tree sloth to take a bathroom break; and at dusk, before the sun fell behind the formation and cast its shape into amorphous darkness. Finally, after a full night spent in quiet contemplation, Carl had come up with a moniker for the jag. As the sun rose on Thursday in a red-crusted dawn, he began to call it "The Evil Wizard," for it appeared to Carl to be a hooded figure clad in a robe, sitting with its knees pressed to its chest, its face obscured by shadow. This wizard, thought Carl, has no use for good. This wizard corrupts and leads astray. It sends children to their dooms with promises of candy. This wizard was, in essence, the tool of the devil.

"How appropriate," Carl muttered, keeping his eyes on the stony sorcerer as it grew animate in the morning sun. "How absolutely fitting."

On Monday, Carl had raced through the Great Plains, fueled by the rage he harbored toward his son and bolstered in his charge with the realization that Kenny was close enough to be caught. According to J.T., who had worked straight through the weekend, Kenny had left Iowa on Sunday morning, spent Sunday night in North Platte, Nebraska, and by Monday afternoon had made it to the Rockies, where he had taken an early pit stop in a town called Grand Junction. Kenny and Kidd were traveling hearty distances, to be sure, but they were still only driving eight hours or so per day. If Carl could close the gap between him and Kenny with one giant push, if he could put himself in, say, Grand Junction by Tuesday night, he would be in perfect position on Wednesday morning to spring himself at Kenny regardless of what direction the little thief went next. Kenny, after all, was running out of room to maneuver, and fast. The boy couldn't go to Mexico (no driver's license or passport) and he couldn't swim. Kenny's day of reckoning would take place, Carl was certain, somewhere in the Southwest by Wednesday evening. Maybe Carl would even drown Kenny in the Pacific Ocean—he had made sure to add that option to his list.

But if Carl had listened to what his clients said about the rock formations in Colorado, he had neglected to consider fully the implications of what they told him about the air pressure out there—specifically, that there wasn't any. Carl left Lincoln, Nebraska, before dawn on Tuesday. He zoomed across the Colorado grasslands by mid-morning and barreled past Denver and into the Rockies just after noon. If Carl had been using his smarts, he would have realized that the difference in elevation between Lincoln and the Rocky Mountains was considerable, especially when climbed in one six-hour period, and especially for someone who wasn't used to altitude changes. But Carl wasn't using his smarts; he was using his anger. He launched himself into the Rockies along I-70 with a singular vision in his head—the approaching doom of his only child.

By the exit for Lewson, Carl was feeling sleepy, even after a jolt of nicotine from his new pack of Parliaments. By the Loveland Pass, he began to feel drunk, his hands and feet lagging in response to mental commands. By Silverthorne, he had passed out behind the wheel. He was awoken only by the sound of something metal scraping against a guardrail. He shot his eyes open, let out a scream at the sight of his Ford Taurus sending out sparks of fury against the galvanized rail, then he threw the vehicle back into the right-hand lane— directly into the path of an approaching Mack truck.

Carl heard the truck's horn blare, then he pissed himself. To make matters worse, he cut the wheel over to the passing lane, where he was met by a Chrysler Pacifica coming up on the left of the Mack truck. In his terror, Carl could only think of going back to the place whence he had come. He floored the Ford and swerved in front of the Mack truck again. Its horn blared a second time. He rapidly approached the rear end of a Hyundai in front of him. Lacking an adequate response to the Hyundai, he hit the brakes, but when he did so, he found his arms making a turn to the left that his brain hadn't ordered. The Chrysler Pacifica screamed and swerved. Carl wrenched the steering wheel to the right with brakes still applied. It was an unfortunate move. The Taurus spun backwards. The Mack truck behind it came into Carl's forward view. That's when Carl shat himself. Then the vehicle careened off the roadway and onto the shoulder. The last thing Carl felt before the Taurus went airborne was a fierce buck as its tail end clipped the knob of the next guardrail. The Taurus flipped and there was silence, followed by the horrifying sound of metallic crunch as the vehicle landed upside down in a ditch. Hanging in his seat belt harness, with the roof pressed against his forehead, Carl could still hear the roar of traffic up on I-70. After a few minutes, he heard the cacophonous wail of emergency sirens, which told him he wasn't dead. When the EMTs pulled him out of the vehicle, the pain in his back and neck was so intense that he wished he were.

After the accident, the doctors at the Reservoir Medical Center in Dillon told Carl that he had suffered a concussion and a bad case of whiplash. They also told him that he was very lucky, which only served to piss Carl off—luck played no role in Carl's life; he made his own fortunes. Regardless, on doctor's orders, he would have to spend at least one night at the hospital for observation, and maybe more, depending on his rate of recovery.

On Tuesday evening, the dummkopfs at the tow lot told Carl by phone that the Taurus was totaled, and that he would have to purchase or rent another vehicle if he ever wanted to leave Dillon, Colorado.

On Wednesday morning, the doctors told Carl that he wouldn't be able to leave Dillon anytime soon. His concussion was improving, but the whiplash would do him in for a while, particularly since Carl could barely move without agony. He could not, however, stay at the hospital; they needed the room. The medical center set him up at a two-star hotel behind the center of town, gave him Percocet to start off and Tylenol with codeine as a step down, and arranged to have a visiting nurse association look in on him every few hours. One of the nurses who came later that day asked Carl if it was true that during a car crash, your whole life flashed before your eyes. Always someone to possess an answer, Carl suddenly found that he was unable to reply. During the terror of the crash that had landed him upside down in a ditch, a life had indeed flashed before Carl Kernick's eyes. But that life had not been his own. It had been his son's.

Where, in vehicular mid-flight, Carl should have seen his own graduation from high school, he only saw Kenny's birth. When, as the roof of the vehicle smashed into the dirt, Carl should have remembered the first time he kissed Martha, he only remembered Kenny working on a science project. He relived every blink of Kenny's eyes, every sniffle, every question the boy had ever asked, every "Yes, sir" and "How do I...?" And at the end of the crash, when Carl should have seen his own death, he saw nothing, but he felt his rush of anger toward Kenny dissolve.

Kenny had always been a good boy, Carl remembered, and he had always obeyed his father. If Carl said, "Read this book on the economic legacy of the Smoot-Hawley Tariff Act," Kenny would read it. If Carl said, "Recite to me the Declaration of Independence, and get it out in under three minutes," Kenny would recite it with time to spare. If Carl said, "Eat your mother's crappy casserole, and look happy about it," Kenny even did that, too. Except for one indiscretion at Harvard involving the pilfering of women's underwear, the boy was sound. Okay, it was more like seventy-five indiscretions of underwear pilfering, but the quantity no longer held weight with Carl. Kenny was a good kid. This flight west was not his fault.

Then whose fault was it? Carl wondered.

Looking out the window at the rock formation on Thursday morning, Carl discovered the answer. But the seeds for that answer had begun to germinate in Carl's mind many miles before the Rockies. They had actually been planted in him at a hotel along I-80, just south of Chicago. In the rarefied Colorado air, those seeds were coming to maturity. And fast.

Back in Chicago, Carl had awoken on Monday morning to find a newspaper outside his hotel room door. It was the *Chicago Herald*, a tabloid which carried the reputation for being notoriously dramatic. Carl picked it up, threw it onto his nightstand, and began his morning routine. He had set his sights on reaching Nebraska by dusk.

Carl had not slept well that night. He blamed his brain. It simply wouldn't stop. It spun with thoughts of how he would kill Kenny, but it also spun with other thoughts—thoughts that, when put together, made no sense to him.

Like... how was Kenny driving anywhere? The boy didn't know how to drive. Carl had purposely not taught him how to drive so Kenny wouldn't die in a car accident. It must be Kidd who's driving.

But... how could Kidd drive if the Secret Service was with them? The Secret Service went everywhere with a former president. They would never allow Kidd to drive himself.

Then... if the Secret Service were driving, why did they need to steal Carl's Cadillac? Would the Secret Service condone theft? After all, they had that Chevy Tahoe at their disposal, and they used it at Kidd's request.

The thoughts whirred round and round all night, bouncing off walls of incongruity and contradiction. Nothing made sense to Carl. No question could find purchase in the slightest hint of an answer.

Until he read the *Chicago Herald* over breakfast.

That's when he found his answers on the gossip page, under the headline "What else was Peggy supposed to do?" The blurb read:

Yes, that was former president Charles Bentley Kidd getting eighty-sixed from his estranged wife Peggy Huff's charity event on Friday night.

According to our spies who were at the Rostoff Waterside for the swank shindig, Kidd arrived sans Secret Service but in the company of a short, young, redheaded boy, whom he identified only as "Kenny, my assistant." While "Kenny" proceeded to ply himself with liquor, scruffy-looking Chuck exchanged heated words with our homegirl Peggy, first in the lobby of the Waterside, and later in the ballroom, where all eyes (including the Mayor's) were reportedly glued to the brouhaha. We don't know what Chuck said to Peggy, but whatever it was, it was enough to get Amanda Pacheco's old flame dragged out of the ballroom by his shoulder blades, along with his inebriated companion. Many onlookers were expecting Kidd's Secret Service detail to suddenly appear, thus creating what probably would have been quite the intra-agency rumble, but sources have revealed that Kidd terminated his protection from the Secret Service early Wednesday morning. The former president was last seen in the passenger seat of a late-model Cadillac as his "assistant" drove him north on Michigan Avenue.

Reached for comment last night, Hannah Hoffstetter, Peggy's hottie spokesgal, said, "Ms. Huff was really shaken up by the whole thing. She can't help it. She thinks Mr. Kidd is a regular [expletive deleted]."

So that's how it is, Carl thought. No Secret Service. Just Kidd calling the shots. And not only was Kenny driving, but he was also drinking. In public. And getting drunk. Carl left Chicago wanting to kill Kenny more than ever. The boy was only half a Middle America away. Carl's time for retribution would not be far off.

Then the elevation climbed, the air got thin, the Taurus made an upside-down plunge into a ditch, and Kenny's life flashed before Carl's eyes. And Carl was left, in his muscular agony, to stare out the window at a distant rock formation on the side of a mountain. In it he saw that wizard. And he understood.

It wasn't Kenny who was to blame for what had happened. This whole mess was Kidd's fault. Carl didn't have one clue about how the two of them had become acquainted, but he did understand what was happening between them. They were traveling alone. Trending westward toward heaven knew what. And Kidd was Kenny's wizard. Kidd had cast a spell on the boy. He had waved his magic wand, uttered an ancient chant, and put Kenny's mind under his control. He was leading Carl's only child by sorcery down a jaded path, and as much as Kenny might be enjoying that path, the direction it followed could only end in doom. Now Kidd had taken Kenny to Las Vegas, the city of ultimate debauchery. Carl only hoped that he could catch Kenny in time, before Kidd turned the boy into a wart-covered toad. And genital warts, at that.

"Just hang on, Kenny," Carl spoke to the window, as he watched the sun gleam sharply off some mica in the rocky wizard's hood. "Your father is coming to save you."

In a few minutes, after the clock struck eight, another visiting nurse would arrive at Carl's door to check on him. In a few hours, as the codeine-laced Tylenol kicked in, he would fall asleep. In a few days, he would feel well enough to pull himself out of bed, rent a vehicle, and leave Colorado for points west.

But before he left, Carl Kernick would make one important stop on the way out of town—at the nearest bookstore. Once there, he would straggle up to the occult aisle, run his finger along some spines, and only stop that finger when he located the right book. And how would he know it was the right book? Well, that was easy.

It would be the one that told him, concisely and thoroughly, the best way to destroy a wizard.

★ ★

PART IV
CITY OF ANGELS

★ ★

CHAPTER 32

★ ★

Driving through the Mojave Desert on a brilliant Friday afternoon, Kenny Kernick looked at the mountains around him—imposing, serrated, scrub-scoured peaks—and he thought, Hell, I could pound them flat with one blow from my palm.

Driving through the Mojave Desert on that brilliant Friday, Kenny looked out over the valleys between those mountains—so long and flat that they stretched for miles—and he thought, I bet I could leap those gaps in a single jump.

Driving through the Mojave Desert on Friday, Kenny watched countless Mack trucks rumble beside him on the way west to Los Angeles—screaming at him from their wheel wells, trying to push him around with their brawn, making the driving tough—but he didn't care. Where once such Mack trucks scared him beyond imagination, his only thought now was, big fucking whoop!

On the day he left Las Vegas, Kenny Kernick felt unconquerable—taller than the Stratosphere Tower, stronger than any jaguar in that Krutchfeld and Marzook show. His eyesight, although technically poor, had the sharpness of the strobe light shooting off the top of the Luxor; his legs, although skinny, could hold up the full weight of the Luna moon.

On this day, nothing could stop Kenny Kernick. He was speeding down I-15 at ninety-six miles per hour, heading like a rocket for Los Angeles, and who cared if there was a police cruiser up ahead? He was weaving in and out of traffic, cutting off those Mack trucks for a change, and he didn't give two shits. For the first time in his life, Kenny Kernick believed he had right and authority and entitlement in the world. For the first time in his life, Kenny Kernick felt like a man. And this change from boy to adult had swept over him so subtly that he almost didn't realize it was happening.

After having sexual congress with Darby Duvall six times in the early morning, stopping only when they ran out of condoms, Kenny had taken a shower, dressed and bid Darby Duvall farewell as she headed off to the airport. He stayed behind in her room to give her an inconspicuous lead, then he left the hotel alone and glided back to the CandyLand, immune to all concepts of time and distance. He was stuck in the sensations of the previous night—of tingling loins, fingertips through hair, stomach against stomach, and the mind-mashing scent of Darby Duvall's dewy skin. Apparently, something could make you sweat in the desert, and it was called coital bliss.

Back at the presidential suite, Kenny found Kidd curled into the fetal position on his bed, which Kenny took to mean that Kidd was still fighting off the effects of food poisoning. Kenny shut the door to Kidd's bedroom and grabbed a bagel from a tray on the counter. As he chewed the bagel, he stood at the window overlooking the Las Vegas skyline and scanned the vastness of the city in daylight. Not knowing when he and Kidd might head for Los Angeles, he had only one thought—

I'm going to eat this town up.

Which he did, for twenty-two hours straight, right after he finished the bagel.

When Kenny finally stumbled back to the CandyLand on Friday morning, he found Kidd waiting for him in the living room of the presidential suite. Kenny's traveling companion had his arms folded, and there was disdain consuming his face. Kenny wanted to tell Kidd not only about his previous night on the town, but about the whole raucous evening with Darby Duvall. When he started to bring up the subject, Kidd cut him off with a raised hand.

"We need to be out of here in twenty minutes. I'm not going through another day of pastry gorging." Kidd pointed to a row of shopping bags from Tycho that were lined up near the sofa, bags which contained the new wardrobe he and Lilly had picked out at lunch the day before—more pants, short-sleeve shirts, additional loafers, belts and jackets. "Assemble your stuff and get the car."

Kenny put his new clothes in his duffel bag. He left the duffel for the bellhop and took an elevator down to the lobby. He grabbed the Cadillac from the valet, tipped the driver a twenty, and met Kidd at the main entrance.

"Where to?" Kenny asked, trying to lighten Kidd's mood.

"We're going to Los Angeles," Kidd replied, sliding into the Cadillac and slamming the door. He didn't say another word for one hundred miles.

In Kidd's silence, Kenny's mouth filled the gap. With every push of the gas pedal along the flat, dusty highway leading out of Las Vegas, Kenny felt his verbal motor roar. At first, he trickled out only minor information about his night with Darby Duvall, but by the cross into California, he was blabbing, without filter, about the gymnast's most intimate details. With every revelation, Kenny would glance sideways at Kidd and flash a set of teeth, expecting the former president to return his grin in a bond of male camaraderie. But Kidd never smiled back. Instead, he rolled his eyes.

They were passing through Baker when Kenny started to discuss the sexual positions he and Darby Duvall had tried. By the town of Harvard, he was rating each one on a star scale, but he noticed Kidd still wasn't playing along. Kidd was looking out the window, clearly tuning Kenny out. But Kenny gabbed on, rattling off the curvature calculations he had made of Darby's perfect ass, while really watching the mountains and the valleys and thinking of how easily they could be conquered, just as Darby Duvall had been easily conquered.

Finally, when Kenny began a thoughtful dissertation of Darby Duvall's intense screams during reverse cowgirl vis-à-vis her panting moans in oral, Kidd exploded.

"Jesus H. Christ, Kenny!" the ex-president shouted. "Will you shut up?!"

Silence overtook the Cadillac. Kidd was glaring at Kenny and baring his own teeth, but not in a grin. Where Kenny had expected an eager playmate on this afternoon, he got a warring animal.

Kenny sucked the air of the desert between his teeth. "But I thought—"

"Oh, I know what you thought," Kidd said. "I've been listening to what you thought for two friggin' hours. I almost feel like it was me who had rampant sex with Darby Duvall."

"You wish," Kenny said. The words came out in a whisper, and Kenny wondered if Kidd heard them over the roar of tires on bleached asphalt. When he got no reply, he figured that

Kidd hadn't heard, and he didn't care to push the matter. Kenny smiled smugly and returned his eyes to the flat stretch of road along a valley floor. It was yet another valley he could traverse in a single jump. Weren't they all now?

But Kidd wasn't done. He squared himself toward Kenny and said, "I'm just going to give you some constructive criticism here, Young Kernick: Do you know how you sound when you talk like that? Do you know how you come off? Like a neophyte, that's how. Like somebody with no résumé. Like someone who has never been there before. And do you know how that plays, Kenny? It plays crass."

Kenny pushed the Cadillac up to one hundred to pass a meandering Mack truck with Nebraska plates. When the Cadillac cleared the truck cab, Kenny said to Kidd, "Correct me if I'm wrong here, Bent, but *you're* lecturing *me* on the crassness of sex talk?"

"All I'm saying, Kenny, is that if you want to tell me about your little dalliance from Wednesday night—"

"Little dalliance?" Kenny snapped. "It wasn't any little dalliance. It was sex with a world-famous gymnast. She did things to me that were so complicated, technically, that I gave her perfect tens across the board."

"My point," Kidd said, "is that all you need to convey to me are some benign details, if anything. I don't need the blow-by-blow. And you shouldn't be giving it."

Shouldn't be giving it? Kenny thought. Who the hell was this guy to be telling Kenny the shoulds and shouldn'ts of anything, especially in matters of carnal escapades? Years of Kidd's sex life were on display in the Congressional Record, for Christ's sake, including his penchant for sucking raspberry sauce out of cleavage using nothing but his curled tongue.

"You know what I think?" Kenny said, at a particular moment when the Cadillac's cabin fell eerily quiet. Kenny looked at Kidd sideways again, but this time his look conveyed mocking disparagement. He phrased his next words carefully, making sure to enunciate every syllable. "I... think... you're... just... jealous."

Kidd's eyes went ice-cold. That got his attention, Kenny thought.

"You think I'm jealous?" Kidd asked, returning Kenny's mocking disparagement with a dose of his own. "And why would that be?"

"There's no shame in it," Kenny said.

"Shame in what?" Kidd demanded. "Jealousy?"

"Not jealousy, Bent," Kenny said. "In abstinence. Sexual forbearance. The blue-balled life. You can't stand it because I'm the one getting laid, and you're not."

Kidd let out a chuckle and folded his arms. "Really," he said. "And tell me, Einstein—what makes you think I haven't gotten laid?"

"Because I know you haven't gotten laid," Kenny said. "Zero, zip, nothing. You've become a stranger to the poon. You stayed in bed all day yesterday. You were too sick to take out Darby Duvall the night before, thus throwing her to me, where I know she had a good time. You got put off by the Mormon in Colorado. You couldn't get a girl to look your way after Chicago. In Ohio, they treated you like they would have rather cut off your Lil' Kidd than let you use it. And in Simondale—well, in Simondale, nobody ever came to your door. No one. Even my mother could tell you were lonely. Why do you think she invited you to coffee that morning? So don't take it out on me just because your molars are floating in pent-up semen. I'm not the one who made you the biggest laughingstock in America."

The Cadillac hummed on. Kidd shook his head and let out a long, labored sigh. *He knows I'm right*, Kenny thought. But instead of conceding defeat, Kidd said, "You really think you've got it all figured out, don't you, Kenny?"

Kenny kept his eyes on the road and his mouth closed. He had spoken his piece. His silence, however, only seemed to spur Kidd on. The former president's face began to percolate with seditious glee.

"What would you say," Kidd said, "if I told you that I *was* getting laid in Simondale?"

"I'd say prostitutes from Stamford don't count," Kenny said.

"Ha, ha, ha," Kidd laughed. "You've become quite the comedian since I removed those encyclopedias from your ass. No, really, Kenny, if you want to push the issue, let's push it. Let's get honest."

"Then get honest," Kenny said, growing tired of Kidd's coy roundabout.

"When we were in Simondale," Kidd said, "I was getting laid. Quite a bit, actually, and well. But it wasn't from prostitutes, Kenny. I've never had to pay for sex in my life, regardless of what those monkey fucks in Congress said."

Kenny snorted dismissively. "Yeah, then who was it?"

Kidd paused. The man let off another labored sigh before Kenny heard him say, almost surreally, "It was your mama."

The next sensation Kenny felt was something akin to running headlong into a concrete wall. His foot flew to the brake pedal and he slammed it hard. The Cadillac, decelerating from one hundred miles per hour on anti-lock pads, bucked to a stop in only a matter of yards, but it was still in the passing lane of the highway. A Mack truck came wobbling by them on the right, horn blaring, the driver trying to steady his rig after a quick cut from behind. Then another Mack truck. Then an SUV. Then more cars than Kenny could count or catalog. Horns blasted, all aimed at the Cadillac which was stopped dead in the high-speed lane of a major U.S. highway.

But Kenny didn't care. All he could do was look at Kidd with a mouth jacked wide.

"What?!" Kenny demanded.

"Get off the road!" Kidd said.

"What?!" Kenny asked again. Another Mack truck flew by, its horn condensing then stretching under the Doppler Effect. The wash from the truck rocked the Cadillac.

Kidd grabbed the steering wheel. "Kenny, you're going to get us killed! Move onto the shoulder!"

Kenny stared at the steering wheel. He could hear what Kidd was saying, but he couldn't make sense of the words.

"Aw, shit," Kidd said. Kenny saw him kick his leg into the driver well, then he felt Kidd's foot slide his own foot off the brake pedal. Kidd clutched the steering wheel, pressed his foot hard on the gas and jerked the Cadillac forward. Kidd turned his head to check the road behind them. Another Mack truck roared by, almost clipping the front bumper. In the empty space behind the truck, Kidd gunned the Cadillac over the main lane of highway and stopped it on the shoulder. He lifted his foot off the gas and slammed down on the brake. The Cadillac bucked again as Kidd jammed the car into park and turned off the ignition.

Kenny tried to speak, but the words got caught in his throat. The only thing he managed to say was, "When?"

Kidd said, "When do you think, Kenny? When you came to work for me, that's when. Where do you think I went every day?"

Kenny grabbed Kidd by the lapels of his coat and shook him. "You told me you were going to the gym."

"I was going to your house," Kidd said.

Kenny shook Kidd harder. "You told me you were pumping iron!"

"I was pumping your mama!" Kidd cried.

Kenny released Kidd's lapel and gasped for breath. He felt as if desert dust were coalescing in his throat, choking him. "You lied to me," he said. "My own mother lied to me."

Kidd smoothed out his lapel and eyed Kenny thoughtfully. "Don't think of them as lies, Kenny. Think of them as mistruths."

"How would you like to think of my fist in your face?" Kenny asked. "Or would you prefer a foot up your ass?"

Kidd said, "Your mother never meant to deceive you, Kenny. It just happened. Over coffee that morning, I felt a connection to her. I was drawn to her. But I didn't plan to get you out of the house so I could sleep with her. I really did want you to work for me."

"Then what happened?" Kenny asked.

"I don't know," Kidd said. "It all went so fast. That afternoon, right after she said you'd take the position, the Secret Service brought me a note from her. In it, she thanked me for coming to coffee and invited me over the next day as well. But this time, she wanted me to enter your house by the bulkhead in the backyard. So you came to my house, and I left, and the Secret Service drove me around the corner, and then we all got out and marched through the trees to your backyard, where I found the bulkhead wide open. I went inside and made my way upstairs to the kitchen, and that's when I saw your mama. She was standing at the counter fixing coffee, and when she turned around, I just thought she was the sexiest woman I had ever set eyes on."

"Sexy?" Kenny said. "My mother is shaped like a pear."

"True," Kidd said. "But she's the juiciest pear I've ever enjoyed. We are talking 'dribble down your chin' juicy."

Kenny closed his eyes and shook his head, trying to cast out the vision Kidd had just placed in his mind. "I can't believe I'm hearing this," he said. "This is terrible."

"But it wasn't terrible," Kidd said. "That's what I'm trying to tell you, Kenny. Your mother was a godsend to me. She brought me back to life. She lit me up again. Just when I thought no woman would want me, I found someone who couldn't get enough of me. I mean, insatiable. I'm surprised you couldn't hear her screaming from my house."

"Enough!" Kenny yelled. He planted his face into the steering wheel. "Why did you ever move into our neighborhood? Of all the places you could have lived, why there? They tried to stop you, you know—my father and the others. They said you would ruin everything, and I thought they were crazy. Now I find out you've gone and turned my mother into a whore."

"Oh, Kenny, don't think of your mother that way." Kidd tried to place a hand on Kenny's shoulder, but Kenny jerked away. "One thing you'll learn when you get older, Kenny, is that so much of what you see when you look at married people is not reality. When you're married, everyone tends to think the best of you—that your life is rosy; that you've achieved harmonious bliss; that there's an unconquerable love between you; and that you're faithful. And the only reason they think that way is because you have a piece of metal wrapped around an insignificant finger. That's it. Call it Pollyanna, call it irrational optimism, but it's a natural human inclination to think the best of married couples. And it's all bullshit. Look at me. The whole country thought my marriage to Margaret was the stuff of fairy tales—college sweethearts; married for thirty years; parents of a beautiful daughter." Kidd sighed, then shrugged, a moment of defeat. "What can I say? Let me ask you this, though, before you sully your mother's name: Do you know the last time she and your father had sex?"

"Of course not," Kenny said.

"Well, Kenny, neither did she," Kidd said. "But she put on a good face, even to you."

"Then why are you here?" Kenny asked. "Why did you leave her back in Simondale, if she wants you so much?"

Kidd bit his lower lip. Kenny thought he saw tears in the man's eyes. "I didn't leave your mama," he said. "She left me."

Kenny lifted his head off the steering wheel. The highway was vacant. There were no other cars or trucks in sight, either northbound or southbound. A fluff of wind blew over the Cadillac's hood.

Kidd let out a stuttered breath. "The day we left Simondale, remember how I came back to my house early?"

How could Kenny forget that day? Kidd was a wreck when he returned to the house. On the way down the stairs, Kenny had even heard him crying like a horny beagle. Then that night, when Kenny had gone back to say goodbye to Kidd, he had found the man in a state of despair. Given his own problems, like the prospect of being locked up at Yale for the next four years, Kenny never pondered the root causes of Kidd's depression. He had only considered the topical ones which Kidd had provided to Kenny right then and there, like the fact that no one loved him. Now Kenny was experiencing a moment of burning insight as he came to understand that the person Kidd was feeling most rejected by that night was not his wife or his daughter or even his once-adoring populace. No, the rejection which had triggered Kidd's meltdown came from Kenny's mother.

"She said she couldn't carry on like that anymore," Kidd said. "That she couldn't lie to your father, even if he was an inattentive husband. She told me that I had brought her back to life, too, and that I had taken her places she had never known, but in the end, she wanted her old life back, if only so she wouldn't feel guilty. I think it pained her to end it, I know it did, but then she kissed me goodbye and I left. And that night, you showed up on my door and offered me a quest."

"Actually, you invited yourself," Kenny said. "I would have been content just to go to Alaska."

Kidd put his hand on Kenny's shoulder, and this time Kenny didn't jerk away.

"Please don't be mad at me, Kenny," Kidd said. "I can't stand it when you're mad at me. Just know that I didn't use your mama, that my feelings for her were genuine. Trust me on that, please."

"Did you love her?" Kenny asked. His glare should have told Kidd that he expected an honest response.

Kidd paused. "No, I didn't. And I don't think I would have. But the attraction I felt for her was overpowering. We came to each other at a time of great emptiness for both of us, and in that vacuum, Kenny, such powerful emotions can explode. So don't think ill of your mama. Not over this. She's a good woman. Now start the car, please, and let's go. Los Angeles is only two hours away. You'll feel better once we're driving again."

But even after he had started the Cadillac, put it into drive, and gotten back onto I-15 traveling south at a steady, slower speed, Kenny didn't know what to feel. His high-flying emotions from that morning were gone. In their absence, he felt raw. It had only taken a matter of seconds, but under the external pressure of Kidd's revelation, the balloon of his manhood had popped and blustered away. It was now only a gutted and torn piece of red rubber left lying on the desert floor, where, under the arid elements, it would not decompose for another ten thousand years.

Or maybe this is manhood, Kenny thought, as the Cadillac climbed a pass between two approaching mountains—mountains which suddenly didn't look so destructible.

Maybe manhood was about seeing the dirt in life, about turning over rocks until you found the worms, if only for truth's sake.

Maybe manhood was about understanding something, accepting it and moving on, whatever the circumstances.

Suddenly, as the road stretched on to Los Angeles, Kenny felt overcome with exhaustion from his two crazy nights in Vegas—a creeping yawn from the back of his throat; eyelids that demanded closure; a pit in his stomach through which he could fall forever. For the first time in a long time, Kenny didn't want answers. He didn't demand to know at that instant what manhood really encompassed. All he wanted was to put the Cadillac on cruise control, crawl into the backseat, and curl up like a pupa in a chrysalis—sleeping, metamorphosing, hiding, until the world felt safe to flutter in.

CHAPTER 33

★ ★

To Charles Bentley Kidd, the immediate future could not have seemed more bleak.

Staring through the windshield at the scattered Los Angeles skyline, as the Cadillac volleyed among thickening afternoon traffic on the 10, Kidd felt his insides twist and turn with the highway's directional convulsions. Although he had not eaten a heavy meal in days, he was growing nauseated. His hands were moist, his throat dry. Gas was leaking out of him from both directions. Yet Kidd could not bring himself to put an end to his suffering with a simple phrase: "Turn this fucking car around, Kenny, and take me back to Connecticut. I can't do it!" Instead, as the Cadillac forged on, pushing through the congealed mush of the Los Angeles rush, all Kidd found himself thinking about was the one thing causing his trauma—his impending reunion with Annabelle, the daughter he hadn't seen since Christmas. Unlike the powerful and confident leader he had once been, Charles Bentley Kidd, on this day, was a man utterly devoid of courage. A man so scared by the prospect of having to look into his precious offspring's emerald eyes—and

to utter even the most benign of greetings to her—that he now
stood on the brink of internal calamity.

Such fear had not descended upon Kidd acutely. He hadn't
found his body in a state of open revolt only with the sight
of the L.A. skyline. On the contrary, Kidd's nerves had been
wreaking havoc with him for two days. They had started their
twitter on Wednesday night, just after he had willingly given up
his date with Darby Duvall. He could barely sleep that night,
tossing and rolling, turning and staring, grappling at bed sheets
or wrapping his arms around a clump of pillows. On Thursday,
he stayed in bed all day, cowering in the fetal position, locked
in dread, knowing it was time to leave Las Vegas but too terrified to do it. Finally, on Friday, when he had gathered enough
strength to crawl out of bed, put on some clothes, and set himself on the road to Annabelle, he found he had no tolerance for
bullshit, as Kenny had discovered only a couple of hours ago.

It was this edginess, and not any sadistic desire to hurt
the boy, which had made Kidd divulge to Kenny, back in the
desert, the true nature of his relationship with Martha Kernick.
In a calmer state, Kidd would have kept the revelation to himself, even with Kenny's inaccurate bombastic declarations that
Kidd was jealous of Kenny's sexual conquests because Kidd
himself was enduring forced abstinence. But the anxiety in
Kidd had prevailed. Now Kidd had revealed to Kenny that the
boy's mother was an adulteress, and Kenny had gone quiet, not
saying a single word since that argument. Young Kernick was
simply staring at the road, his face wiped clean of expression,
executing only the driving directions Kidd issued to him. That
reaction just made Kidd more fretful. If Kenny Kernick could
go stoic over the only affair his mother had ever had in her
life, and one that until today had been kept entirely secret, how

would Annabelle Kidd act when standing face-to-face again with the father who had cheated on her mother innumerable times and in the most public ways?

How will she respond to seeing me? Kidd wondered as he fought off another gassy stab to his intestines. The possibilities were terrifying. Especially the ones involving bloodshed.

In the end, Kidd concluded, it was impossible for him to predict Annabelle's reaction. His daughter had changed so much since she'd gone to college that she was now a puzzle to him. About the only thing Kidd knew for sure, at that moment, was that the intersection of the 10 and the 405 was fast approaching, and his options had run out. It was time to be a man. He told Kenny to turn north onto the 405. Silently, Kenny obliged.

The Cadillac crawled on the 405 for three miles until Kidd directed Kenny onto Soltavega Boulevard, just north of Wilshire. The main gate for the University of the West sat four stoplights down. On the way through the gate, Kidd realized he didn't know the name of Annabelle's dorm for this year. Even if he did know it, he doubted he could find the place. He had been to the university only once, during Annabelle's relentless college scouting trip. And given the hotness of Southern California coeds, he hadn't really paid attention.

"I don't know where we are," Kidd said, craning his neck to take a gander at the campus through the Cadillac's windshield. He pointed to a flap-haired student carrying a backpack just up the road. "Let's talk to him."

As the Cadillac pulled to the side of the road, Kidd rolled down the window. The flap-haired student, who, with his black vest, white dress shirt and black tie, could have easily passed for a member of the sixties rock band The Kinks, turned when the Caddy glided up beside him. For a moment, he stared at Kidd,

obviously trying to place the man before him in some remembered historical context.

Kidd said, "Excuse me, lad, but could you tell me where I
might find Annabelle Kidd's dormitory?"

The student snapped his fingers. "I knew it!" He snapped
them again, this time at Kidd's face. "I knew it, I knew it! You're
Chucky Kidd! You're the old president! I knew you looked like
someone I knew!"

Kidd smiled at the recognition, forgiving its informality. It
had been such a long, dry trip from Connecticut—with people
reviling him in some places, ignoring him in others, or worse,
referring to him only as "that guy," as the Mormon Tammies
had done—that Kidd was glad for any morsel of properly-
applied celebrity, even if its execution did seem disrespectful
to him as an elder. Kidd asked again if the lad knew where
Annabelle lived.

"Shit yeah," the student said. "Everybody knows where
Annabelle Kidd lives." He raised a finger and pointed in the
distance to a small rise of land covered with squat brick-faced
buildings. "She's in Sycamore Hall. Right up there."

Kidd thanked him, raised the window and motioned for
Kenny to drive away, comfortable in the knowledge that he
knew how to find his daughter. But on the journey up to Sycamore Hall, Kidd had a disturbing thought—was the fact that
"everybody" knew where Annabelle lived a good thing or not?
Did it speak to his daughter's popularity as a vibrant member
of the academic community, or did it mean she was the campus pumping station? It was a well-known truism that girls
who had problems with their daddies often took that frustration out in a multiplicity of sex partners. Was Annabelle
that type of girl? Again, Kidd didn't know. An incident with

her boyfriend in Switzerland last March had shown that she definitely wasn't a virgin anymore, but Kidd tried to be open-minded. Whatever his daughter's sexual status, the best he could do was pray that she at least played it safe and choosy, giving herself only to those boys who were solid of character, free of disease, and firm in commitment. She was his little girl, after all, and no man wanted to see his little girl hurt by predatory male lust.

"We're here," Kenny said. The boy ratcheted the Cadillac into park. Kidd snapped out of his thoughts to find the Caddy stopped in front of a compound of buildings identified by a granite lawn slab as the Branson Housing Complex. Sycamore Hall, as marked in chiseled stone above its entrance, sat at the far end of a quad. Kidd took a deep breath. His hand froze at the latch for his seat belt. He suddenly wished he had instructed Kenny to drive the car off the end of the Santa Monica Pier. "Can we get this over with?" Kenny said, eyeing Kidd's hesitancy. Kenny was already standing outside the car. Kidd's trembling hand pushed the button on the seat belt. He opened his door.

They were let into Sycamore Hall by an Asian girl with blonde hair. She told them that Annabelle Kidd lived in Room 412, then she accompanied them to the appropriate floor to let them in through the card-access security lock. Once on the floor, Kidd hugged the wall as he walked down the hallway. The corridor smelled of all things soft about girls—potpourri and perfume, facial soap and moisturizing cream. But the smells didn't trigger in him a burst of lust, as was usually the case when he caught the scent of femininity. Today they triggered in him the fervor of protectiveness. He was a daddy in the lair of his daughter. He was a father in the lair of all daughters. Woe to the boy who, flushed with post-coital bliss, might step out of one of these rooms in a jumble of reassembled clothing.

They approached Room 412. I've found her, Kidd celebrated inwardly. He knocked, three loud raps. No one came to the door. He knocked again. Nothing. He placed his ear to the door. There were no sounds from inside. "Aw, shit!" Kidd said.

He and Kenny walked out to the quad and sat on a bench. Kidd felt himself deflate against the wooden slats to his back. He had geared up for a moment which didn't materialize, revved his engine for a race that was postponed. Now the adrenaline coursing through him bled out into the surrounding landscape.

"You know, Kenny," Kidd said, after a moment of listening to the breeze rustle through some palm trees, "maybe we should just hop back into the car and keep going. I'll drive north with you, to Alaska, like you planned. We can join up with one of those crab boats you talked about. We'll pull up the traps and work the lines—really get the salt into us. It's a seasonal occupation, of course, but the season is fast approaching, and we don't want to miss it. What do you say?"

Kenny, who was stretched out from the bench with his legs and arms crossed, let out a cynical sigh.

"Just think of it, Kenny," Kidd said, feeling influential, "we could hide from the world for years. When the crabbing is done, we'll get jobs on another type of fishing vessel, or a container ship bound for Asia. Or better yet, we could get our own boat. We'd work ungodly hours that would test our mental and physical limits. We'd turn lean from the chore—so cut and buff that we'd look like different people. We could grow beards." Kidd surveyed Kenny's baby-soft cheek. "Well, I could grow a beard, anyway. Maybe the folks up there would even sprout a legend about us—that we were two of the most fearless seafarers in the Pacific Northwest, and that we died in the drink. That we went out one day to gather up the biggest herring catch in history and were never seen again, lost in a massive swell that took you first, then me. We'd become ghosts, the specters Aleutian parents warned their children about when they didn't behave. 'Act right,' they'd say, 'or Old Chucky the Salt will get you, and that little Kenny, too.' Oh, we'd be famous. No, we'd be bigger than famous—we'd be folklore." Kidd followed Kenny's lead and stretched out from the bench. He crossed his legs, then his arms, and lost himself in a contented sigh. "Imagine that, Young Kernick. Imagine—"

"Daddy?"

Kidd turned to see Annabelle standing on the walkway. His daughter was frozen in place as if she had just witnessed Lazarus' emergence from the tomb. Although Kidd had finally found his little girl, and should have taken great joy in that fact, the sight of Annabelle came as a shock to him. For while, in an ideal sense, she appeared to be the same old 'Belles, she was at the same time jarringly different.

In her White House days, Annabelle had always donned refined clothing, but the first thing Kidd noticed about her was that she was wearing leisurely pink yoga pants and a white tank top. The yoga pants were too tight for Kidd's liking, and the tank top didn't come down over her midriff at all, revealing in the fleshy zone of her navel area a gleaming silver belly-button ring that was obviously the end-product of some drunken night out. She also toted a heavy book bag over her shoulder and wore flat-soled wicker sandals, a combination wholly impractical for walking long distances over such a spread out, hilly campus. Her statuesque body was thinner than he remembered (not eating enough), and her shoulders and face more freckled

(too much sun). Her once-auburn hair, pulled back into a long
ponytail, had streaks of blonde in it, no doubt with the assistance of toxic, bleaching chemicals that would, in time, Kidd
was certain, render her completely bald. He only hoped that
when she pulled off her designer sunglasses, her eyes were still
green. That they hadn't gone gray from the stress of the study,
or turned black after the application of some faulty mascara. Or
that she wasn't wearing tinted contact lenses which colored her
eyes purple, just so she would stand out in this city that worshiped megalomaniacal stand-outs.

"Daddy?" she said again, pulling off her sunglasses and
cocking her head at him. Kidd breathed a sigh of relief—her
eyes were still green.

Kidd rose slowly from the bench and stood to face her. He
didn't raise his arms to her as a beckoning—he wouldn't. He was
a man being judged, and he would not interfere with her judgment by calling to her under the white flag of some paternal writ
of affection. He stood stone still, arms at his sides, body facing
her full on, in a pose of vulnerability. She could kick him, punch
him, spit on him, or throw that meaty book bag into his groin—
he would not defend himself. He inhaled a breath, clenched his
jaw, and waited for her reaction.

Annabelle tightened her grip on the bag and walked up to
him. As she came within striking distance, she made a move
with her bag that Kidd, for an instant, thought was a rear-back.
But she didn't hit him. Instead, she dropped the bag to the
ground, lifted her arms, and wrapped them around his neck.

"Hi, Daddy," she whispered, as she pressed her cheek into
his jaw. "God, I've missed you."

Kidd lifted his arms. He placed his hands on her back and
pressed his fingers into the flesh of her ribs. He raised his lips

and kissed her on the forehead. She smelled of shampoo and facial cleanser—fresh smells for a fresh-faced girl. He noticed that there wasn't a hint of perfume on her, and why did that surprise him? Annabelle never wore perfume. She didn't have to. She always smelled good enough on her own.

"I've come a long way, 'Belles," Kidd said, holding his daughter tightly.

"So I understand," said Annabelle. "I've been hearing stories about you for the past week." She released him and waited for him to release her. When he did, she took a step backward and caught her breath with a hand to her chest.

"What have you heard?" Kidd asked her.

"What haven't I heard is the better question," Annabelle said. "You've been quite the traveler lately, haven't you? Things have been hitting me from all sides. Remember Tracy, Jana and Cindy from grammar school?"

"Vaguely," Kidd said. He wasn't being disingenuous. If they were prepubescent friends of Annabelle, Kidd had no idea.

"Well, they're not so vague on you," Annabelle said. "Each of them called me last Friday with a strange story about how you had shown up in Hawleyville the night before to make some silly announcement."

"Silly, huh?" Kidd asked. "Is that what they said?"

"They also told me you got run out of town by a mob. Apparently, coverage of it hit the ten o'clock news from Cincinnati to Cleveland, and all of Ohio was laughing at you. Including Jana, who called you a dork."

"Lovely," Kidd said.

"But that's hardly the whole of it," Annabelle said, not really listening to him. "Then Mom phoned me over the weekend to curse out your name because it seems you crashed her charity gala for Cousin James. According to her, you put up a big, embarrassing stink in front of all of Chicago society, to the point where she had to have the Secret Service remove you. Then on Tuesday, Sarah e-mailed me a link for the newspaper website in Grand Junction, Colorado—she's from Grand Junction—which stated that you'd been spotted in town leaving a restaurant with a tall brunette, which I have to say didn't surprise me. But yesterday, people were coming over to me and telling me that somehow you ended up as a judge for the Miss Teen Virgin USA Pageant in Las Vegas on Wednesday night. Which I have to say"—Annabelle crooked her lips, searching from the corners of her eyes for the best turn of phrase—"*did* surprise me."

Holy Jesus, Kidd thought, this girl is better at intelligence gathering than most of the spooks in the CIA. But he loved her rants, her unimpeded energy. He had missed that charm of hers. How her rants could spill out, overwhelm, then terminate in a flash, leaving a listener breathless. He noticed she was looking at him with anticipatory eyes, waiting for acknowledgment of her thorough summation.

"Guilty as charged," Kidd said. "All of it is true—Hawleyville, Grand Junction, Las Vegas. Even Chicago. Except for that Secret Service part—your mother didn't have me removed; she had me assaulted. If you don't believe me, ask Kenny here—"

Kidd turned to his right to point to Kenny on the bench, but Kenny was standing next to him already, which Kidd found out when he poked Kenny in the glasses with a knuckle. Kenny didn't notice. The boy was eyeing Annabelle with diligent calculation, like a leopard might eye a young giraffe. It was a look that made Kidd uncomfortable. Kenny practically had spittle dripping from his chin.

"Oh, Daddy, relax. It really doesn't matter." Annabelle tapped Kidd's arm as an indication to let her condemnation go. Then she held out her hand to Kenny. "Hi, I'm Annabelle Kidd. You must be the mysterious companion I've heard about. My mother described you as 'that shitfaced little assistant,' but I assume you have a real name."

"His name is—" Kidd started to say. But Kenny cut him off.

"I'm Ken," Kenny said. "Ken Kernick. From Connecticut." Kenny took Annabelle's hand and gave it a firm shake. Kidd was pretty sure the boy's eyes never left his daughter's.

"Nice to meet you, Ken Kernick from Connecticut," Annabelle said.

"And yes, I was shitfaced," Kenny said. "My apologies to your mother the next time you speak with her. I didn't mean to add further embarrassment to the situation. That rum punch just got away from me."

"Oh, I know the feeling," Annabelle said. She laughed, and Kenny laughed with her, their eyes flashing between each other like fireflies dancing in a hayfield after dusk. Kidd felt his jealous impulses start to brew—Kenny and his daughter had just shared a moment of common experience; they had connected. Something was amiss. Kidd could feel it. This boy was not the Kenny he had known before today. It wasn't even the Kenny who had gotten out of the car five minutes ago.

Annabelle tapped her father again. "So what are you doing here?"

"Your mother didn't tell you?" Kidd sat with her on the bench, Annabelle positioning her bag as a buffer between them. Kidd expected Kenny to return to the bench as well, but Kenny remained standing, hovering over Kidd and Annabelle with his arms folded, as if he were continuing to size up the girl. Kidd's eyes narrowed as he watched Kenny sway and grin, sway and grin, the boy never removing his gaze from Annabelle. There was something in that look of Kenny's, something troubling, and Kidd intuitively knew what it was—lust.

"Honestly, Daddy, I couldn't always follow her," Annabelle said, bringing the conversation back to the subject of Margaret Huff. "All that swearing. She sounded like she was speaking in tongues."

But Kidd's attention was firmly locked on Kenny. The boy glowed at Annabelle and wouldn't stop. His smile was contorted into a zigzag. With that goofy smirk on his puss, and the glossy, overcome gaze in his eyes, he looked like Jimmy-Jim. Kidd just wanted to slap a hockey helmet on his head and send him on his retarded way.

"Hellooooo, Daddy." Kidd glanced away from Kenny to see his daughter awaiting some response.

Kidd cleared his throat and smoothed the fabric of his jacket, then he turned to Annabelle and told her of his plan to share Thanksgiving with her. He made sure not to beg, but he said that he would take her anywhere she wanted to go, any restaurant from San Diego to Seattle, if that's what she desired. Then he awaited her response.

"But I've made other plans," she said.

"Other plans?" Kidd asked. "What other plans? Don't tell me you're going to Chicago to see your mother."

"No," Annabelle said. "She bought me a ticket, but I need a break from her. She's too intense these days. I'm spending the holiday with Nicki and Petra. Do you remember them?"

Nicki and Petra, Kidd thought. Now there were two of Annabelle's friends that he *did* remember. But Kidd referred to them by other names—Night and Day. It had been Night and Day who had made up the bread ends of the blonde-brunette sandwich he had partaken of at the White House last Thanksgiving, providing him with one of the craziest experiences of his life. He had never known teenage girls could be so wild. And since then, he'd hardly been able to forget.

"We're driving up to Petra's parents' place in San Mateo," Annabelle was saying. "We're leaving on Tuesday night. I couldn't go home this year anyway. There are too many things going on."

"I'm sorry to hear that, 'Belles," Kidd said, his plan ruined. "I was hoping we could spend some time together. Thanksgiving has always been special for us."

"Not a lot I can do, Daddy," she said.

"Could I at least get some time with you?" Kidd asked. "What are you doing tonight?"

"Tonight's booked, Daddy," Annabelle said. "I have volleyball practice in an hour, then I'm studying for Monday."

"Maybe sometime this weekend, then."

Annabelle shook her head. "Tomorrow's a mess. More studying for Monday, then more volleyball practice."

"What about Sunday?" Kidd asked in desperation. But Annabelle shook her head once more.

"Volleyball in the morning, then studying for Monday," she said conclusively.

"First of all," Kidd said, annoyed now, "when the hell did you start playing volleyball? And secondly, what's so important about Monday?"

"First of all," his daughter answered him, jutting out her chin and protruding her full pale-pink lips as she spoke (it was her special way of enunciating, and it had always frightened Kidd a little for the stern confidence it conveyed), "I joined the volleyball team this year. I took it up last year in the intramural league, which you should know because I mentioned that I was doing it when I was home for Thanksgiving with Nicki and Petra. Apparently, I was good enough that my friends encouraged me to try out for the real team, which I did, not realizing how much time it would consume. Monday is a big game—we're one win away from clinching the conference, and if we clinch, we get an automatic bid to the NCAAs. But the game is against USC, and they're right behind us in the standings. They're defending national champions. My coach is new, so she's stressed, thus we're stressed. We want this. Our program has sucked for decades. Do you follow me?"

Kidd felt his shoulders drop, ashamed that he had been too busy staring at Nicki's pie-round breasts and Petra's über-tight buttocks that weekend to listen to his daughter tell of her new sport, or of her burgeoning life in Los Angeles, for that matter.

"To answer your second inquiry, Daddy, on Monday I also have my psych stats test. I don't particularly understand stats right now, and the worst thing is, the test is comprehensive. It covers chapters one through fourteen, which at this point is like taking a final. The whole course is really frustrating, and I feel like I'm about to fail. I need you to understand. This is not a good week at all."

Yes, Kidd thought, I should have known. Internally, he scolded himself. Why had he not realized that Annabelle's life would most certainly be different from the way he remembered it, since so much time had passed between their encounters? Why hadn't he recalled from his own schooling at Jesuit that the week before Thanksgiving was always rife with exams? Why didn't he ever stop to consider how frustrated he would have been if his mama had shown up in Chicago on the Friday before a holiday and demanded to spend time with her son? He understood now that he should have stayed clear of Annabelle. He was adding his own weight to her pile.

"It's okay, 'Belles," he said.

"Is it?" she asked, her green eyes suddenly repentant. "Do you understand?"

"Of course I do," Kidd told her. He wanted to leave.

That's when he heard Kenny say, "Unless—"

Both Kidd and Annabelle looked up at Kenny, who was still standing in front of the bench. For a moment, each of them just sat there, waiting for Kenny to say more, but Kenny seemed to be turning something over in his brain. Kidd finally broke the silence by asking, "Unless what?"

Kenny directed his response to Annabelle. "Psych stats. That's psychology statistics, correct?"

Kidd could feel his face pinching into an annoyed scowl. He hoped Annabelle would blow off the question and start talking about something else, like the thick Santa Ana wind that was beginning to give Kidd a sinus headache. Instead, he heard her say, "That's right. Psychology. That's my major."

Kenny rubbed his bare chin in what Kidd thought was a disingenuous show of contemplation. The boy said: "Statistics is just another form of math. I've taken a lot of math in my day, from Trigonometry and Analysis, right up through Tensor Calc. I've had math ad nauseam. In fact, I excelled at it."

"In college?" Annabelle asked.

"In high school," Kenny said. "It was my father's idea. But I aced every course. Teachers always told me I had a math brain, and that's why I was good at science and languages and stuff. Mathematical people understand how to put things together and take things apart. I imagine statistics is kind of the same thing—in-depth questions, putting things together and taking things apart, all done by extracting numbers from presented scenarios."

"It is," Annabelle said. "That's exactly what it's like."

"But you're more of a verbal thinker," Kenny said. "It's difficult for you to see the numbers through the words."

"I'm totally verbal. I'm a reader and writer. I don't do math well, especially if I have to dig for it." Annabelle pressed her hand to her chest. "Oh my, you know what I'm going through. He knows, Daddy."

Kidd shrugged, gazing off to lose himself in the gentle sway of a distant palm.

"Here's my thought," Kenny said. The boy pointed at Kidd. "Before practice tomorrow, if you spend the day with Bent—"

"Who's Bent?" Annabelle asked.

Kidd raised his hand sheepishly. His daughter had never heard that moniker for him, particularly since it was the pet name bestowed on him by Amanda Pacheco in the post-orgasmic aftermath of a liaison against the Oval Office mini fridge. "Ahhh, Bent," Amanda had sighed, still wrapping her arms and legs around him, and the name stuck—the pastry chef would call him nothing else. He had loved his new name so much that after she was gone, Kidd found himself wanting to be called Bent by anyone who was willing, just to be reminded of his Sweet Amanda and how alive she had made him feel. Kenny had actually been correct in the kitchen that morning back in Simondale—everybody referred to Charles Bentley Kidd as Chuck, including The Rhino. But Kidd had wanted a new start, and he had needed old memories, and telling Kenny and Martha to call him Bent had given him both. Better if

Annabelle didn't know the whole sordid story. He lowered his hand.

Annabelle eyed him suspiciously anyway. "Bent?" she asked her daddy. Kidd shrugged again.

"Tomorrow," Kenny said, bringing Annabelle's eyes back to him, "if you spend the day with your father—putting off your studies—then I can spend Sunday with you."

"Going over stats," Annabelle said.

"Absolutely," Kenny said.

"But you've never taken stats before," Annabelle said. She seemed incredulous.

"That's not a problem," Kenny said.

"How is that not a problem?" Annabelle asked. "I think it would be a big problem."

"Not if I learn it," Kenny said.

Annabelle threw him a look of wide-eyed disbelief. "You're going to learn statistics?"

"Do you have the text book?"

"Oh, you bet I do." Annabelle tapped her leather book bag.

"Then, yes, I'll learn it," Kenny said.

"By Sunday," Annabelle said.

"Probably by Saturday night," Kenny said.

Annabelle shook her head. "Wait a minute, hold on. You're telling me, Ken Kernick from Connecticut, that you're going to learn a whole semester's worth of statistics in a day, so much so that you'll be able to help me pass?"

"I'm not only going to help you pass," Kenny said, "You'll ace the thing. Guaranteed."

"Guaranteed?" Annabelle said.

"But you're going to have to let me do something in exchange," Kenny said.

"What's that?" Annabelle asked.

Oh no, Kidd thought.

His fears were realized when Kenny lowered his head and got a subtly-salacious grin on his face, a grin for which Kidd, under any other circumstances and with any other girl, would have been proud. But not here, and not with this girl, and not with the words that came out of Kenny's mouth next.

"You're going to have to let me drill you."

Annabelle raised her soft auburn eyebrows, as if she were well aware that Kenny had just propositioned her. She seemed to hold her breath as she replied: "You want to drill me, Ken?"

"Hard and heavy," Kenny said.

"That is the best way," Annabelle said.

"And nonstop," Kenny said. "Until you feel satisfied with the material."

Annabelle raised her eyebrows higher. "I like feeling satisfied."

Jesus H. Christ on a pogo stick! Kidd wanted to scream. Hello! Your father is sitting right here!

"I have confidence," Kenny said, "that after one session with me, you'll feel like your world just got rocked."

Annabelle stared at Kenny with a look of bewildered amusement on her face.

"Your stats world, that is," Kenny said. His grin turned from salacious to trusting.

Annabelle held her breath for a moment, then she let out a voracious laugh. "Oh, Daddy, where did you find this guy? He's a stitch. Is it true, Daddy? Is he that smart?"

"He's smart, all right. I'll give him that," Kidd said. The boy was so fucking smart, apparently, that he had been memorizing Kidd's playbook all the way across America. He sure as hell had picked a fine time to turn his gathered knowledge loose—on Kidd's own daughter. What was the world coming to? The way Kidd felt about Kenny, as if Kenny were a son to him, this whole interplay smacked of incest.

Kenny asked, "What do you say, Bent? Sound like a plan to you?"

The choice was briefly tempting for Kidd. He would get some time with his child, but in return he would have to give her over to this aspiring Casanova for almost a full day. He wanted the time with Annabelle desperately, but he just couldn't do it. There was no telling how many articles of clothing Kenny might attempt to remove from his precious daughter by Sunday night. He might even offer Annabelle a game of Strip Statistics—"Get this answer wrong, and I get your underwear." No, he could not allow it. Not as a daddy.

Kidd countered, "There's a bit of a problem, though, isn't there, Kenny? Logistically-speaking."

"What's that, Bent?" Kenny asked.

"It's called Alaska." Kidd flung out a finger to the north. "You were supposed to drop me off then head there, remember? To get a job crab fishing?"

"Oh, come on, Bent," Kenny said. "You know how hard that life is. It's brutal." Then the boy leaned in toward Annabelle and unleashed another grin. "Trust me," he said to her, "you'd rather have a case of the crabs than fish for them."

Annabelle let out a second voracious laugh. "Oh, that's funny!"

No, that's mine! Kidd wanted to yell. Now Kenny was stealing his lines.

"Anyway, I'll be in town for a while," Kenny told Annabelle. "So I'm all yours on Sunday if you want to have some time with your father tomorrow."

Annabelle gave her father the once-over. Kidd could tell she was pondering just how much time she wanted to spend with the man who had humiliated her and her mother on a stunningly international level. Her drawn-out scrutiny made Kidd queasy.

Finally, she said, "Yeah, okay, we can do that. You can have me tomorrow, Daddy, before my evening volleyball practice, and Ken can have me all day Sunday. Where I'll get—what did you say, Ken—drilled?"

"Intensely," Kenny said.

"What if I'd rather have Sunday with you?" Kidd asked. "It is the Lord's Day, after all. When was the last time we went to church together?"

"Ken gets Sunday, Daddy," Annabelle said tersely. "That's the plan. Either you live with it or not."

Kidd turned on Kenny. He could feel the bile churning in his gut. "And what's all this 'Ken' crap?" he asked. Kidd turned to his daughter. "His name is Kenny." Kidd wheeled back to the boy. "Everybody calls you Kenny."

Kenny directed his retort to Annabelle. "Your father has called me Kenny from the first time we met, and I've never wanted to correct him. Respect your elders, you know?"

"That makes sense," Annabelle said.

"Oh, that is such a load, Kernick." Kidd could feel the bile rising to his throat. "Even your mother calls you Kenny."

"My *mother*—" Kenny seemed to chew on the word, and Kidd understood instantly that he had broached a really bad subject at an even worse time. God only knew what images of a naked Martha and a bare-assed Kidd, intertwined in orgasmic frolic, were flashing through Kenny's mind at that moment, and how much those thoughts were influencing, in that very same head, the images of a naked Annabelle and a bare-assed Kenny intertwined in a similar fashion. It all led Kidd to wonder: Was Kenny really hot for Annabelle? Or was he flirting with her just to get even with Kidd for the former president's thorough humping of Martha Kernick? Either way, Kenny was flirting with Annabelle, and the flirt smelled sourly of pursuit.

"Daddy," Annabelle said. "If Ken says his name is Ken, then his name is Ken. Isn't that right, Ken?"

"Absolutely, Annabelle," Kenny said. Then Kenny looked directly at Kidd, and his face erupted into that salacious grin. That's when Kidd understood something else instantly. That the interplay to which he was bearing witness was no mere petulant flirtation or retributive pursuit—it was a full-on declaration of war. The battleground would be Los Angeles. The spoils would be Annabelle—Kidd for her heart, Kenny for her body. This first battle had gone to Young Kernick (he would get his study session, and he would get to be called 'Ken'), but there would be more battles to come. Kidd had just committed to putting up with Kenny for at least two more days, and in war, even a single day could bring decisive reversals of fortune. Kidd felt his whole body tighten. He was already girding himself for combat.

"All I need," Kenny said, "is your stats book. Can you study off notes tonight?"

"Here you go," Annabelle said. She pulled a thick tome out of her leather book bag; it was one of about five texts stuffed within, along with some notebooks. "And yes, I can study off notes tonight. I have plenty of them." Annabelle checked her watch. "Now, I really have to go. I need to get ready for practice."

"Let me walk you to the door," Kenny said.

Kidd rolled his eyes. "Kenny," he said, "the door's right there. She doesn't need an escort."

"I'd like an escort," Annabelle said. She stood, lifting the bag off the bench, and Kidd stood with her.

"Let me get your other books," Kenny said. "That bag looks heavy."

Kidd rolled his eyes again. "Kenny," he said, "she can get her own bag. She's not an invalid. Look at her. She's almost six feet tall. What are you? Five-five?"

"I'm five-four," Kenny said, with no hint of embarrassment over his meager proportions.

"Daddy," Annabelle said, and curtly this time. "If a guy wants to carry my books, he carries my books. It doesn't matter how tall he is or how tall I am. Understand?"

Kidd nodded sheepishly, then he stepped back and watched Kenny heave the heavy leather case over his anemic shoulder. As they all walked to the dorm, with Kenny and Annabelle leading the way and Kidd lagging behind, Kidd heard Kenny ask Annabelle an odd question: "Is this a Sadrine Gravos bag?"

"It is, "Annabelle said to him, looking shocked. "How did you know that? Most guys wouldn't know that at all. She doesn't put any labels on her work."

"That's actually how I knew," Kenny said. "There was a woman in front of me at Tycho yesterday; she bought one. She was raving about it."

"She made a great choice," Annabelle said. "They tell me..."

But Kidd didn't hear another word. He sauntered behind and walked peacefully, watching the two of them (one a majestically tall girl, the other a pissant little runt) stride side by side in animated chatter. In his mind, he complimented Kenny for the boy's skill. Kenny had taken another page out of Kidd's playbook: He had commented with interest on something about Annabelle—this time her Sadrine Gravos bag, or whatever the hell it was called. It was sad for Kidd, then, after all this time on their journey together, over all the miles of mountains and fields and deserts and rivers, after the bond he and Kenny had built, that Kidd would now have to lay Kenny waste over something as silly as a girl.

CHAPTER 34

★ ★

That Friday night, after the initial glow of meeting Annabelle Kidd had subsided, his brain had simmered down from its jolly high, and he'd spent considerable time perusing Annabelle's statistics textbook in preparation for his tutoring session with her on Sunday, Kenny found himself lying on a pullout sofa in Room 819 of the Mendelssohn Hotel, unable to sleep.

Kenny and Kidd had come to the Mendelssohn after saying goodbye to Annabelle. In silence, they drove to Santa Monica, where Kidd had a favorite hotel from his junket days as an Ohio state representative. He guided Kenny off the 10 at Fifth Street and through a series of turns that landed them on Santa Monica's palm-lined Ocean Avenue. Out in the distance to the west, Kenny could see the shimmering expanse of the Pacific Ocean as it churned in flame-tinged whitecaps against a descending sun. In a matter of seconds, before Kenny even had a chance to contemplate fully his first sighting of those legendary waters, the Cadillac came upon the Mendelssohn. The hotel was a thin, elegant structure, only eight stories tall, with a robin's egg blue façade that stunted downward into a peach-and-white striped awning. Unlike the amorphous Pacific, the

Mendelssohn carried a distinct style: It was cut in the block-and-groove Art Deco lines popular before the Second World War. Kidd ordered Kenny to park in an empty street space, then he stepped out of the Cadillac, strode up to the veranda, and entered the hotel. Ten minutes later, he returned with two keycards to an ocean-view suite on the top floor.

Excellent, Kenny thought, as he walked through the Mendelssohn's ornate lobby. We're getting another suite. I'll have my own bedroom again.

Wrong, he discovered when he walked through the door to Room 819. The Mendelssohn's ocean-view suites only had one bedroom, and Kidd stated bluntly that he was taking it. Kenny could have the pullout sofa bed in the sitting room.

Without saying goodnight, Kidd retired to his bedroom soon after settling into the suite. After a few minutes, through the closed door, Kenny heard him speaking to someone on the telephone. He gave the party on the other end of the line his name and the Mendelssohn's address before confirming a noon appointment and hanging up. Soon there was a rustle of sheets, a thump of body against bed, and dead silence.

With Kidd retired, Kenny sat down on the sofa and kicked off his loafers. Turning on the television for a distraction, he was overcome by an irrepressible yawn. He simply couldn't remember a time when he had felt so completely spent on so many levels. Physically, he was tired from the day's drive. Emotionally, he was exhausted from the revelation that Kidd had taken to boning his mother for the past few weeks. But most of all, he was utterly drained, emotionally and physically, from his own intense experiences of the previous two evenings—his night out with Darby Duvall, then his own day and night on the town, where, under the cachet of having been Darby Duvall's escort the previous evening, and recognized for it, he had eaten, shopped, gamed, drank, and danced all night with girls who kept grabbing his ass and calling him "Darby's boy." About the only sensations Kenny could feel at the moment were joy at meeting Annabelle Kidd and hunger. It was just six o'clock, but Kenny decided to forgo a trip to a restaurant. He ordered room service instead.

Thirty minutes later, he had made a quick meal of stuffed pork loin, dry mashed potatoes and some yellow vegetable he vaguely identified as summer squash. Between bites, he kept his eyes glued to the television. One of the cable channels was showing a Mexican soap opera called *Picante*, and it didn't take Kenny long to notice that its actresses were some of the most goddamn fantastic-looking women he had ever seen. He finished *Picante*, delightfully, then tuned into *En Sueños* at seven, followed by *Nina y Juan* at eight, sucking up every ounce of the gorgeous Latina parade until he could take no more of irrational love triangles, stilted dialogue, and those melodramatic close-ups put to overbearing swells of synthesized music. He turned off the television at nine and picked up the stats book. Opening it, he found unexpected pleasure in the smell of its glossy pages. Kenny went over the material for two hours until his eyelids began to droop, then he closed the book and set it down on the carpet. Expecting sleep to follow quickly, he twisted the knob on the table lamp and plunged the room into darkness.

That was when his mind, free of external stimuli to distract it, started to wander.

First, a pleasant image of his mother popped into his head. She was standing at the kitchen sink, a white apron tied around her waist, as she washed dishes under a meek stream of water.

He was viewing her from the front when he saw a set of hands approach her waist to untie the apron. But Kenny knew they weren't Carl's hands, which were tough and scarred from years of tinkering with automation prototypes made of sheet metal. No, these hands were smooth. They were idle. They were the hands of a man who had never worked a real goddamn job in his life. They belonged to Charles Bentley Kidd. Kenny felt despair as Martha turned to face their bearer, then he watched in horror as Kidd's hands slipped the apron over Martha's head, dropped the garment to the floor and roamed up her blouse, unleashing her meager bosoms with a calculated series of flicked buttons. Before Kenny could blink a mental eye, he saw Charles Bentley Kidd and Martha Kernick entwined in nakedness on the breakfast table, humping and grunting, thrusting and grinding, until the whole table came crashing down.

Oh, how he begged for the thoughts to cease, but they only charged out and scattered to the corners of his brain like cockroaches caught in the light. With every thought that infested him, his body thrashed against the sheets and his anger inflamed him to night sweats. He longed for the clean cold peace that could only come by smashing his head against a blunt, unforgiving surface.

How could his mother have cheated on his father? How could she have given in, so swiftly and thoroughly, to the seductions of Charles Bonehead Kidd, the most notorious philanderer in United States history? More than anything, how the hell could Martha Kernick have lied to her only child? Lied to me, Kenny reminded himself, just to get me out of the house so she could act upon her wanton lust.

Kenny's thoughts splintered with all the things he wanted to say to his mother, and yet he had no idea what he would say the next time they spoke. What did you say to someone who had betrayed you? Who had treated you as if you were stupid? Who had used you? As he tossed and turned in the lumpy pullout bed, Kenny rehearsed in his mind the answers to those questions, laying out a script for a diatribe to his mother then imagining her response. He mentally played out the whole scenario, handcrafting reams of dialogue, envisioning himself the unchallenged victor in any verbal confrontation. When he got to the end, he started all over again, swapping weak lines for stronger ones, turning up the punch of the delivery, and investing fully in the emotion of the future moment, until he found himself, in the present tense, clutching at his bed sheets with clammy hands.

Kenny kicked out his legs and sat on the edge of the bed. Moisture clung to his skin, and he felt as if he might throw up his supper at any moment. He took in deep, cooling breaths and concentrated on not concentrating at all, on clearing his mind. A blank mind is a good thing, Kenny reminded himself. Such was another piece of Carl Kernick's fatherly wisdom.

Kenny decided he couldn't stay in bed. He couldn't even stay in the suite. He needed to walk, to stretch, to move—to give activity to his restless dwelling. He reached to the end table for the wrist watch he had purchased at Tycho the afternoon before. Its fancy digital readout told him that the time was midnight, an early hour by Kenny's new standards. He got up from the bed and walked over to the room's ocean-view window. From there, he saw a black expanse of nothingness lapping in breakers at the edge of a bone-white strip of sand. "The Pacific," Kenny whispered to himself. He wanted to touch it.

Kenny put on his clothes and left the room, taking the stairs down to the lobby instead of using the elevator. Outside, the Santa Monica air was lively and crisp, but Kenny decided he didn't need a jacket, nor did he want to go back to the suite to get one. He crossed Ocean Avenue and walked south along its adjacent park until he came to a set of steps leading down the side of a cliff. The cliff, which separated the beachfront from the city, was lofty and jagged, and with no light illuminating the steps, Kenny chose to lean against a retaining wall and wait in the wind until his eyes adjusted to the dark conditions.

When he could see the shape and direction of the steps, he descended them carefully until he came to a concrete footbridge that spanned the Pacific Coast Highway. Kenny traversed the footbridge and took another set of steps down to the road. He walked along a flat expanse of parking lot and crossed a bike trail. Finally, he reached sand. That's when he slipped off his loafers, removed his black socks, and let the silky grains of mica spread between his toes.

Kenny walked the depth of the beach, the rumble of ocean growing louder in his ears. The sand was pockmarked with the use of the day, like a cratered moonscape. Closer to the water, trash barrels formed a dotted line between sea and land, and lifeguard stations stood at intervals of several yards. Not far to his left, Kenny saw the Santa Monica Pier ablaze in colored lights and incessant motion from amusement rides and carnival games. To his right, the beach stretched onward, seemingly endless in its expanse, hugged by the cliff, until it faded into a smudge of night.

Kenny walked briskly over the sand, expecting to find the beach devoid of people so late in the evening, but it wasn't. Even in the darkness, he could see some people snuggling under blankets, others playing night volleyball or soccer, and still others walking hand-in-hand along the foamy edge where the ocean crawled up to the shore. More than what Kenny could see, however, was what he heard so keenly in the night—the harmonic roll of the ocean, the caw of seagulls, screams from the riders on the pier, the cheers of the volleyball and soccer players, and a man telling his girlfriend that he would be more than willing to pay for an abortion. About the only thing Kenny couldn't hear was English. Everyone on this beach spoke another language: Spanish mostly; Russian occasionally, and many Asian variants as well. Kenny hadn't realized that by coming all the way across America, he would arrive at the Pacific only to feel like a foreigner.

The descent from dry beach to ocean water was fairly steep. A wave broke just offshore. Kenny watched as it rode up on him, crashed coldly and violently between his toes and soaked him to the cuffs of his pants, then he felt a strong undertow pull on him as the water slid down to the ocean again. The whole episode lasted only a matter of seconds, but to Kenny, it seemed as if the motion of the water was impacting his entire life, and he smiled. He had driven (which in itself was a most unexpected development) over three thousand miles, through fourteen states and three time zones, across intense landscape shifts of hill and plain and mountain and desert, to put his feet into the Pacific Ocean on this night. He had overcome much on his journey, surmounted innumerable obstacles both mental and physical, and left a lot of his old self behind in towns whose names he probably wouldn't remember. The Pacific was his perfect reward, and gave him his greatest hope.

The feeling of hopefulness soothed Kenny, and emboldened him. He let other waves crash to his feet then edged farther out into the water. A wave came in and soaked him to his knees. He didn't care.

With his mind at ease from its previous turmoil, Kenny thought of his mother again. He didn't want to be angry with her. Anger felt toxic to him. Instead, Kenny wanted to understand his mother's actions, he wanted to accept them, then he wanted to move on. Besides, he had better things to think about tonight, like his budding attraction for Annabelle Kidd. God, how that girl had stirred him with her beauty, and kept him aglow for hours. Wouldn't he rather be spending his time fantasizing about her naked flesh pressed against his than his mother's pressed against Charles Fucknut Kidd's? Damn right.

Kenny stood languorously in the water, longing for the worldview he had possessed a mere twenty-four hours prior, when images of his mother *in flagrante delicto* were foreign to him. He longed for the time when he had assumed his parents were asexual. Under that assumption, Kenny had come to think of them as pristine and flawless.

The voice in his head (the one which sounded remarkably like his father's) screamed at him: "You're a sucker, Kenny! A dupe! Your mother has gone and made a whore of herself. Everybody is going to know about her and that bonehead. It will probably end up on the front page of the *Enquirer*. Try handling that one, dummkopf!"

That was the fear which penetrated Kenny the most, and was the greatest fuel for his fire. Just to think of it: Who knew how many neighbors had seen Kidd sneaking in and out of the bulkhead? All it would take was one yabber-gabber, and the breadth of Simondale, and then the world, would be wise to his mother's bawdy wickedness. Those who knew her would agree that, contrary to years of evidence supporting her piety, Martha

Kernick had turned out to be a slut after all. And not only was she a slut, but she was the worst kind of slut—the kind that gave it up for the rich, the powerful, or the just plain stupidly famous. If Kenny was her child, what would those neighbors think of him? Wouldn't they start to look down on Kenny as well? After all, didn't people judge you by the character and actions of your parents? If your father was the local ax murderer, how long was it going to be before people started eyeballing you in a similar light, just because you had received half your genes from him? And if your mother was a wretched, disgusting cockwhore who loved to ride the knob of a former president simply because he had once been the most powerful man in the world, then by extrapolation, weren't you a wretched, disgusting son of a cockwhore?

Kenny felt a chill shiver through him and he looked down. He had become so caught up in his thoughts that he completely failed to notice the pattern of the tide. The water was rising, and his pants were soaked to his crotch.

What does the problem with my mother come down to? Kenny wondered. This time the voice in his head didn't sound like Carl's. It sounded like his own. But his own as an assured, confident man, and not some scared little boy.

"What does it come down to?" Kenny said, echoing his soothing, adult tone.

Feeling vulnerable, he answered inwardly. Feeling helpless and small and weak. Feeling once again as if, at any moment and by any circumstance, I could be destroyed, devoured or obliterated. It was a remarkably discouraging realization, and yet, Kenny felt strangely liberated by its honesty. For the first time, he was isolating the seed thoughts which continually caused his anxiety and anger, and ultimately, his low self-opinion. Getting to these seed thoughts was a boon. If he could find them, he could dig them up and toss them to the sand, where they would never take root in him again.

The night was growing quiet, the wind stronger. A wave crashed on Kenny and soaked him to his navel, making him even colder. He looked over to a large flock of seagulls clustered nearby. Strangely, they seemed impervious to their surroundings: They were just standing in the sand, absorbing the elements, and they didn't appear to be overly concerned about any of nature's battles, like the wind, the chill, the water, or how they were going to find their next meals.

How can I be like them? Kenny wanted to know. How can I just live in this world, this disturbing new world of post-infidelity humiliation, with my head held high and my feathers hardly ruffled? How can I understand the circumstances that impose themselves on my life, accept those circumstances, then move on? Imperviously. Like the gulls.

At that moment, Kenny saw a flutter of rising motion. The seagulls were flapping wildly to the sky. Somebody in silhouette was running through the flock, terrifying the birds, all while letting off wicked, delusional laughter. The seagulls had bolted from the intruder and were flying out over the ocean. Kenny watched the gulls as they turned left in one singular crest. There had to be more than a hundred of them in total, their white bellies hurtling through the night like a barrage of snowballs.

Kenny dropped his jaw in amazement. He was speechless at the sight. The seagulls followed their bank left, then made a sharp turn back and flew en masse right over Kenny, ten feet above his head. It was a display of true natural grandeur.

"Holy shit," Kenny started to say. But before he could finish, the shit found him.

Splat!

A milky stream of seagull excrement hit Kenny in the face. Kenny threw back his head as if it had taken a bullet, then his head recoiled forward and he felt a warm, milky lump in his mouth. An errant drop of bird crap had landed on his tongue. It tasted like hell—bitter and clammy. Kenny choked on the lump, gathered it up with his tongue, and spit it into a retreating wave. He continued to gather and spit for another minute, watching wisps of white-tinted saliva slip back into the ocean like billows of dispersing smoke. He bent over, cupped his hand and washed the last vestiges of feces out of his mouth with seawater.

But when Kenny turned around to see where the seagulls had flown, he wasn't cringing at what they had done to him. On the contrary, he had a grin on his face. Kenny had said he wanted to be like those birds. Now they had accepted him. They had taken him into their flock—baptized him really—in the form of the seagull shit that was lodged in gobs on his hair, forehead and nose, and even on one whole lens of his new eyeglasses. From this moment forward, he was one of them.

Kenny's confidence returned. Thoughts of his mother abandoned him. He left the water behind and walked back across the beach. He used the concrete footbridge to cross the Pacific Coast Highway and surmounted the high cliff along the same dark steps. Then Kenny walked through the park, bounded over Ocean Avenue, and entered the lobby of the Mendelssohn Hotel. His face was covered in bird shit and his pants and shirt were soaked with seawater, which caused the concierge, bellboys and hotel guests to stare at him queerly, but Kenny Kernick did not give one rat's ass. He kept his chin high—impeccably, unflappably. He was living a carefree life now, an impervious existence; the birds had shown him so. He took the elevator up to his floor and entered the suite in the dark, then he tore off his soiled clothes and threw them into the corner next to the pullout sofa.

And finally, he climbed into bed with the bird shit still on him. In the course of a few breaths, he began to fall asleep—his anger soothed, his hope bright, with his thoughts now turning to the looming luminosity of Annabelle Kidd, and his desire to get to know every single part of her.

CHAPTER 35

★ ★

Kidd awoke on Saturday morning with a gasping bodily jerk, the physical result of some surreal blow to his ribcage by a barbed piece of medieval weaponry.

He had been dreaming of a battle between Kenny and him. In the real world, their war had started out discreetly enough—Kenny's lingering presence around Annabelle yesterday afternoon; the boy's predatory looks at her as he beheld Annabelle's unparalleled beauty; words of sexual innuendo exchanged between them; and finally, Kenny's steely glares at Kidd, beckoning the former commander in chief to the fight. But in Kidd's dream that morning, the restrained nature of their conflict had come to a fast end. The battle was joined by both parties, its intensity swiftly accelerating beyond the possibilities of physics or biology.

In the dream, they began by arguing over Annabelle. Kidd told Kenny to stay away from his daughter; Kenny told Kidd to go fuck himself—in nine different languages. Then Kenny made the mistake of adding, "And I can't wait to steal her underpants. Or better yet, maybe she'll just give them to me," which really cooked Kidd's calzone, since Kenny was once again stealing his lines. The argument grew heated. Firm voices turned to shouts; shouts turned to fisticuffs. Blood was drawn. At one point, Kidd threw Kenny off the top of the Mendelssohn and watched him splat on Ocean Avenue, arms and legs akimbo like some beat-up Howdy Doody doll. But when Kidd turned around to go back to the suite, Kenny was standing behind him again like the Risen Jesus. Except Jesus never wielded a machete. Kenny swung the long metal blade madly, going for a gut slash. Kidd ducked; he covered. He pulled a Roman trident from his wallet and stuck Kenny in the thigh. That's when Kenny got really pissed off. The machete turned into a medieval mace—its head the size of a pumpkin; its points as long as shark teeth; the chain that held it ample enough to reach to the moon. Kidd could find no place to hide. He huddled in a corner of the roof near the air conditioning units and watched as Kenny spun the mace in a rage. The mace flew out and struck Kidd's ribs at astronomical speed. The blow should have cut right through Kidd; it should have caused him terrific pain. Instead, he jerked awake—gasping, sweating, his head in a daze. To gather his senses, he looked at the digital clock on his nightstand. The time was only seven in the morning. He had gotten, by his estimate, little more than three hours of sleep.

Kidd tossed in bed for several more minutes, but by 7:20, he had decided that the problem of returning to sleep was caused by being in the same suite with Kenny Kernick. Charles Bentley Kidd simply could not tolerate another few hours in close quarters with the boy, as he waited for the limo service he had called last evening to pick him up sometime before noon.

Kidd made the executive decision to get up. He threw the covers off his legs and stretched them to the floor, the pain in his knees acting as a sharp reminder that he was, at last, getting old. He showered quickly and shaved at his bathroom sink between a wiped patch of foggy mirror. His shaving strokes were smooth and calculated. He was taking great care not to slice his face with the disposable razor he had picked up at the Kum & Go in Nebraska. He did not want his time with Annabelle to be marred by bloody cuts of any kind, particularly by small ones on his face that might betray deeper ones on the face of their relationship.

But as he shaved, Kidd thought back on his visit to the Kum & Go. Oh, how he and Kenny had gone nutty with laughter at the sight of those convenience store signs towering above I-80 all through the Midwest. Every sign had a rectangular red background with white-piped lettering, and they reached so high and were so startling in their simple verbiage that they could not be missed, even by the most distracted driver. By the time he and Kenny were ready to call it a day in North Platte, they just had to stop at one. They filled up the Cadillac at the pumps, bought toiletries and other necessities in the store, and giggled the whole time they were doing it, to the point where the cashier asked them to leave. Yes, he and Kenny had made many a joke about the Kum & Go on their trip across the prairie, but now the joking with Kenny was over. As if to punctuate the finality of their friendship, at that very moment, Kidd's hand slipped, and the disposable razor cut a lengthy crimson line across the front of his chin.

"Aw, shit," Kidd said, wiping the blood away to survey the damage. "Now I'm going to look like Harrison Ford." In Kidd's view, with his own movie-star good looks, such a comparison would be an insult.

It took Kidd a half-hour to stem the bleeding with tissues. Once it had stopped, he dressed in light chinos and a mauve

Burwick shirt, then he walked over to the window to look for signs of weather. The sky appeared gray and flat over the ocean, not necessarily portending rain but not offering any hope of sunshine, either. He opted for a jacket, grabbing the suede country coat on his way out of the bedroom. Before he left the suite, he stopped at the side of the sitting room sofa to eye his nemesis.

Kenny was sleeping on the pullout, in boxer shorts no less, which Kidd found startling—apparently, Kenny's tighty-whitie days were history. Kidd didn't know exactly what the boy had gotten himself into after Kidd had gone to bed last night, but whatever it was, it must have been one hell of an odd situation. Kenny's clothing was piled into the corner near the sofa, in a pool of damp carpet, and the whole room stunk of seaweed. But strangest of all, the boy had a crust of bird shit—Yes, Kidd thought, that is bird shit—all over his head, from his nose to his brow to his Howdy Doody hair. Even his glasses on the end table were caked in bird shit. Kidd just shook his head and left the suite. On the way out, however, he had to stifle an urge to add more shit to Kenny's face. Preferably of the human variety, and from Kidd's own bowels.

Kidd spent the next few hours on the veranda of the Mendelssohn, under the peach-and-white striped awning that offered excellent shadows for Kidd to find anonymity from the hustle on Ocean Avenue. He sipped on a glass of freshly-squeezed orange juice, nibbled on toast lathered in chocolate hazelnut spread, dabbed at his chin with a tissue, and glanced intermittently at the various sections in the Saturday edition of the *Los Angeles Post-Tribune*. Unlike the old days, Kidd's name no longer stood out on the front page. That honor now belonged to Richard Russell, Forty-somethingth-plus-one President of the USA. There were several articles on Kidd's former lackey in the paper on this Saturday: One story detailed how Russell was dealing with a budget impasse between his office and the Congress; another discussed his attempts to broker a trade deal between the United States and some miniscule African country that Kidd had never heard of.

As he perused the paper, however, Kidd ultimately did end up discovering his name in print. It was in the lifestyles section, on page three, and without even reading the article, he knew by its placement under a gossip banner that the news it contained would not bring him joy.

He forged through it anyway. Beneath the headline "New Kidd in Town," whose authorship was attributed to some insignificant claptrap journalist, Kidd read:

> Maybe Charles Bentley Kidd thinks that winning California twice during his presidential bids means we're all still dying for him to visit us. But does that sentiment apply to his own daughter?
>
> The former Beltway Booty Machine sure found out the hard way yesterday when he showed up unannounced on the campus of the University of the West. Kidd was spotted by several students as he milled about the grounds and rode around in a Cadillac with East Coast plates. And he wasn't alone. With him was his new chief of staff, since identified by the *Las Vegas Mercury* as Carey Kernel. My spies report that Lucky Chucky appeared lost and forlorn, and that he was definitely searching for his little girl, whom he was eventually seen chatting up on the quad between the Tree Dorms.

Sad for Chucky, though: My spies also report that Annabelle did not look happy to see her dabbling dad. She seemed much more enchanted by the presence of the redheaded assistant, who, I can confirm, is the same person seen escorting Olympic Golden Girl Darby Duvall to a host of clubs on the Strip in Vegas two nights ago—

Kidd's mouth dropped. Inserted there, to his surprise, was a goddamn photo of Kenny and Darby Duvall striding hand-in-hand out of a nightclub in Vegas. They both looked bombed.

—What transpired between Duvall and Kernel is still a matter of rampant speculation on the celebrity websites, after Kernel was seen taking the virginal Duvall up to her suite on Wednesday and not emerging until late Thursday morning, once Darby had already departed Las Vegas for a fertilizer trade show in Boise. Now Kernel is in Los Angeles (my spies have him and his boss at the Mendelssohn in Santa Monica), and he's sharing time with the former first daughter. It's well known around campus that Miss Kidd is available. She ended her relationship with upperclassman Peter Standish during her father's pastry problems, and she hasn't been linked to any boyfriends since. In fact, one source told me she's been turning down dates.

Could this be Annabelle Kidd's grand reawakening? Could there be a romance brewing between her and the dashing Carey Kernel? Could there at least be a fling? Stay tuned.

Could there be a romance?! Kidd railed. Could there at least be a fling?! Stay fucking tuned?! Outrageous! He crumpled the lifestyles section and threw it onto the sidewalk, where it almost hit a passing poodle. The dog's owner scowled at Kidd, but Kidd ignored her. His morning mood was growing worse. He pushed forward his glass of orange juice and folded his arms in defiance of (or was it annoyance over?) the article. He wished now that he had never walked back to the Kernick's doorway to ask Martha if Kenny was available for work. Inasmuch as Kidd had enjoyed Martha Kernick within every nook and cranny of her Hoban Lane home, he was certain that their romance could have blossomed without dispatching Kenny to Kidd's house every morning. He and Martha could have procured hotel rooms in New Haven; they could have pitched a tent at the beach; or they might have met secretly in some wooded acreage near the Merritt Parkway, to do it on the backseat of the Chevy Tahoe while the Secret Service took a long walk around a thin oak tree. All of these options had been viable, such was the undeniable magnetism of their attraction. Kenny was just an ancillary component, like an appendix.

Kidd was back to dabbing his chin when a black Lincoln Town Car pulled up in front of the Mendelssohn. The engine choked off and the driver door opened, revealing a solidly-built man in a dark suit. Kidd could tell from the man's demeanor (glancing around, looking eager to please) that his limo had arrived. Kidd checked his wrist watch—it was almost noon. Kidd had become so lost in thought that the morning had charged by. He stood, and as he did, the limo driver's eyes locked on him. Then the driver's face exploded in a smile of recognition.

"Christ, man, are you really *the* Charles Bentley Kidd?" the driver asked.

Kidd smiled as he walked down the steps to meet the Lincoln.

The limo driver (a young Latino gentleman of about twenty-eight who Kidd would soon learn was named Miguel Torres) clenched his hands together with unbridled delight. "I can't believe this, man!" he said, beaming. "I voted for you twice! Two times! *Dos!* You hear that? You were the first president I ever voted for!" Then Miguel's eyes narrowed. "I just got one question for you, though."

Oh no, Kidd thought. Here it comes. You could never truly outrun your past. Kidd felt certain that he was about to be slammed with some inquiry on the delicacies of the Pastrygate scandal, or about what Amanda Pacheco was really like between the sheets—or at least on the Cabinet Room conference table.

"Ask away," Kidd told the driver with an air of resignation, pausing before he slid into the backseat of the Lincoln. The driver eyed Kidd suspiciously. Kidd assumed the question was going to be a whopper.

"How come you gave that virgin from North Carolina a perfect ten in the swimsuit competition? Her legs were flabbier than a beefsteak from Tito's."

God bless Los Angeles, Kidd thought, grinning again as he settled into the plush leather of the Town Car while the driver shut the door. In this city, it was always style over substance, celebrity over scandal. The past was dead to these people; you were only as big as what you did next. Forgiveness and forward thinking were the tools of their trade, and Kidd welcomed it.

"First stop?" the driver asked when he started the Lincoln.

"The University of the West," Kidd told him with a flame of renewed hope. Maybe Los Angeles had been working its forgiving magic on Annabelle all along. Maybe she had already moved forward from the pain and humiliation heaped upon her over the past year. Maybe all she would interrogate him about on this day was why her father had bestowed a dazzling score on a fleshy-legged strawberry-blonde in the swimsuit competition of the Miss Teen Virgin USA Pageant.

What would I tell her? Kidd wondered. The truth? That it was out of pity for a young woman who, while somewhat lacking in bodily perfection, looked like she had a good soul? Or would he lie to Annabelle and say that the girl in question actually did have great legs, but the television cameras must have added a few phantom pounds?

He decided, in the end, that the truth was the best course of action. It was certainly the most forward-thinking. And if his answer to Annabelle didn't satisfy her enough, or if she thought it was stupid, Kidd was quite certain now that his daughter would forgive him.

CHAPTER 36

★ ★

The clock on her desk struck 12:01 when Annabelle Kidd finally slipped on a pair of sandals for the trek outside to meet her father.

All morning, as she killed time before her father's expected midday arrival, Annabelle had indulged in the opposite of the obligatory. She had not gone over psychology stats or any other pressing end-of-term coursework. She hadn't reviewed game plans for Monday's volleyball match against USC. She hadn't gone on Facebook to check out the latest roommate dramas. On this morning, Annabelle Kidd hadn't even taken a shower. What she had done was dote on herself. She got up, brushed her teeth, pulled her hair into a ponytail, and dressed in everything but the thick-heeled Sloane sandals that would raise her height to a towering six-foot-one, then she removed the latest half-read novel from her Sadrine Gravos bag. Reclining on the couch in front of the windows, she cracked the book and delved joyfully into the sassy, gore-soaked world (for some reason, murder intrigued her these days) of Detroit-based detective Malachi Mums and his seedy band of indispensable sidekicks.

The reason for her sudden disdain of the obligatory was simple: As the daughter of an American president, Annabelle Kidd had become overly familiar with the concept of "Hurry Up and Wait." Dress quickly for the State of the Union, 'Belles, then sit for an hour before the limo pulls up to take you to the Capitol. Be ready to meet your father's helicopter on the South Lawn, sweet pea, so go play in the Vermeil Room. Smile brightly, Annabelle, but not yet. Look alive for the cameras, dear girl, later. You're needed in makeup at eight for a post-nomination speech stage gathering at eleven. Oh, and dinner at six? Never. Not with her father, who was once referred to as "The Human Rain Delay" by a press sick of standing around before his news conferences started. Annabelle had almost passed out from hunger on several occasions while waiting for him to get his butt into the dining room so the family could eat. No, Charles Bentley Kidd wasn't just a human rain delay; he was the human Rube Goldberg machine—accomplishing by twisted and complex means that which could be done so simply.

Thus, Annabelle Kidd decided on this renewed day of awaiting her father's arrival that she wasn't going to wait for him at all. She was going to honor her desires by reading mind-less gumshoe fluff all morning until the clock struck twelve. Only then would she put on her sandals, walk out to the curb in front of Sycamore Hall and see if he was there. If he wasn't, then the man was out of luck—Annabelle would turn around, walk back into the dorm and devote her afternoon to herself, even if her prodigal father appeared later with an apology. Annabelle would never wait for Charles Bentley Kidd again. Especially not in light of what her daddy was often doing with his time while she and her mother waited.

So Annabelle found herself mildly surprised when she exited Sycamore Hall and saw her father waiting for *her*. He was standing on the curb across the quad, in front of a black Lincoln Town Car, and he was fidgeting with something near his jaw line. The fidgeting was distracting him so completely that he didn't even notice Annabelle's approach. As she crossed the quad, she saw his fingers working a bloody tissue against a gash below his lips, which led her to ask him, when he finally spotted her and they made eye contact, "What happened to your chin?"

"War wound," her father replied glibly, patting the gash delicately before crumpling the tissue in his palm. He turned to the Lincoln, opened the rear door and said, "After you, young lady."

"Well, it looks like hell," Annabelle said, getting off one parting shot on him while still in the power position of standing. "I think you need some Neosporin. If that thing gets infected, your face is going to swell up wider than a pizza."

Her father ignored the remarks as he slid in beside her, and that lack of response angered Annabelle. He shut the door and settled back into the leather seat, then he gripped Annabelle's knee with his left hand, sending a discomforting chill through her body.

"It's good to see you, 'Belles," he said, and she could see that he was sincere in his emotions. But such sincerity did little to soothe her uneasiness over that hand on her knee. It was a hand which had gotten caught in many cookie jars recently, dirtied by the crumbs of illicit pleasures. She had hugged him yesterday and been fine with it, since the hug occurred through her initiative, but she hadn't asked for him to touch her now, and she didn't care for it. "You look so pretty today," her father added. "All grown up. And beautiful. It's hard to believe you're mine."

Annabelle squirmed to encourage the hand off her knee, then she adjusted her pink Capri pants against the seat—getting into the car had given her a wedgie. "Well, I have to be yours, don't I, Daddy?" she said, finally coaxing a wad of underwear from the crack of her butt. "I look just like you."

"I suppose you're right, 'Belles," her father said. And she knew he had taken her point: Mom would never have cheated on you, Daddy, even if she could be the quintessential pain in the ass.

"Where to?" the driver asked, turning around in his seat. He tipped a fictitious hat to Annabelle. "Miss Kidd—"

"Hi," she replied. He was a handsome man, Latino, well cut and confident. "Call me Annabelle," she said.

"Sounds good," the driver said. He started the car.

Kidd put a hand on the ridge of the front seat. "Actually, Miguel, call her 'Miss Kidd.'"

The driver shrugged at Annabelle. "He's the boss."

"Daddy, stop being such a dork," Annabelle said.

"Daddies are allowed to be dorks," her father said, touching Annabelle's hand with his own, and sending another uncomfortable chill through her entire body.

It was serendipitous, then, that the robust scent of the Town Car's fresh leather reminded Annabelle of all the limousines she had ridden in during her life—from her childhood years spent in Columbus to the later, adolescent years in Washington, D.C. While the twelve years in Ohio had been relatively quiet when it came to the press, the following six as first daughter had been a chore, with constant demands to look here and smile there, even after she had been forced into braces. The headgear phase alone was a notorious bitch. Progressing from awkward teen to proportioned young woman with the whole world watching had often made her want to leap off the Truman Balcony and not get up. It was a wonder that she had ever gotten out of puberty alive.

But she had always been able to take comfort in the leathery smell of a black limousine. With its dark, enclosed space and tinted windows, it was a sanctuary, a safe haven from the requirements of a girl whom the entire country thought of as their own. She had treasured the smell of a limo, until now. Now the scent of warm leather wasn't calming her nerves or reminding her of refuge; now that scent was triggering in her the memory of scandal. Of running away from Washington. Of crying with her face pressed against the backseat. Of hiding from hordes of photographers who wanted to capture, from the moist sheen in her eyes, what it felt like to have a father embroiled in controversy on the grandest stage. Of wishing that the whole world would just leave her alone forever. No, on this day, the smell of the leather didn't make Annabelle happy—it made her want to vomit.

"Where are we going?" she asked her father. He had spoken little since the Lincoln turned north onto the 101.

"Santa Barbara," he said. "I thought we'd grab some lunch, then head over the mountains for a tour of wine country. I hear El Tocón has a lot of vineyards. That's what Miguel says, anyway."

The driver named Miguel shifted his eyes to the rear-view mirror. "That's right, boss. Many good wine places. Beautiful country."

"But I'm not legal, Daddy," Annabelle said.

"Nonsense," Kidd said. "You're with me. They'll serve you. It's just wine."

"But I have practice tonight," she said.

"It'll be out of your system by the time we get back," Kidd said.

"And that's a lot of driving," Annabelle said. Her desire to vomit was growing stronger. She cracked a window, then thought better of it and asked Miguel if he minded, since the air conditioning was on.

"That's fine, Miss Kidd." Miguel twisted a switch up front and the ventilated air ceased. He used his switch to lower Annabelle's window, halfway, as if he could sense that she might try to end this whole charade by jumping from a moving vehicle.

Annabelle turned her face toward the window and soaked in the salty smell from the ocean breeze. Her father said to her, "We can turn around, 'Belles, if that's what you want." He was back to patting his chin with the tissue, which was now more torn-up than a West Wing copy of the *Washington Courier's* "Pastrygate Primer Edition."

"No, Daddy, it's all right," she said. But a trip to El Tocón and back was a long time to be in a car with her father, to be immersed in this noxious leathery smell, even with lunch thrown in for a distraction. She tried to remember the last time she had ridden with him for such a stretch. She couldn't recall when.

Another thing that was uncomfortable for her, apart from the smell of the car, was that chin. Her father's attention to it was driving Annabelle crazy. In Ventura, she asked Miguel to pull off the 101 and find them a pharmacy, or at least a Wal-Mart. Instead, he brought them to a Tito's Supermarket. "I'll be right back," Annabelle said, hopping out of the Lincoln. While Kidd stayed in the car, Annabelle went into the store and bought a tube of Neosporin, some gauze and a roll of surgical tape, paying cash under the wide eyes of the checkout lady. Another mute but pithy moment of recognition, Annabelle thought, grabbing her change and the bag. It had been happening like this ever since her father had gotten booted from the White House: People everywhere would look at her, part their lips, but nothing would come out of their mouths. Then they would lower their heads sorrowfully, like they (and not she) were the ones who had been humiliated by an international sex scandal. Of course, there were the occasional jackasses, especially at keg parties off campus. During the Congressional hearings, Peter had gotten into many a scrape defending her honor against fat-necked jocks and loud-mouthed troublemakers. But she had loved him for it, more than she had ever loved anybody in her life, until she had to tell him one day that she couldn't put him through the wringer any longer, and that they needed to break up. Perhaps it was the bruises that constantly spotted his arms, or the fact that his grades were taking a similar beating, but whatever her reason, Annabelle knew she had made the right decision. This time, Peter didn't put up a fight.

Back in the Lincoln, Annabelle used a pinky to swab Neosporin on her father's chin, then she covered the anointed gash with a two-inch wide patch of gauze. To keep the gauze secure, she placed a strip of tape from one ear to the other.

"There," she said, wiping the ointment off her finger with a sheet of gauze. "How's that?"

Her father glanced into the rear-view mirror and grunted. She had to admit, he looked ridiculous. Then again, her father had survived many months of looking ridiculous. This time wouldn't kill him either.

The Lincoln drove on to Santa Barbara. To deflect her nausea, Annabelle tried to make fluffy conversation, but her father only answered in clipped sentences as he stared out the window at the passing mountains. Soon they were sharing the ride in silence. The lack of conversation annoyed Annabelle, and it must have gotten to Miguel as well, because by Carpinteria he had turned on the radio, even though Santa Barbara was just a few miles away.

What do I really want this man to say to me? Annabelle asked herself.

She decided that there wasn't anything her father could say, not at this point. The Pastrygate scandal had dissected Charles Bentley Kidd's life so completely that Annabelle now believed she knew her father better than he could ever amend with diatribes and excuses. She had no desire to look backward. The moment Chief Justice Raycroft's gavel came down on the impeachment verdict, Annabelle Kidd gave up on the past. Her childhood, her adolescence, her high school years, the loving daily interactions with her parents—they were all part of a time spent in fiction. Instead of dwelling on those fantasy days, she dwelled on herself. She cast aside all but her closest friends, keeping only those whom she trusted implicitly, like Sarah, Nicki and Petra. She took up volleyball, gaining new, truer friendships through the team, since her teammates had all met her after her father's fall from grace. She changed her major from English to psychology so she might better understand herself and her crazy parents, and she might understand people better in general. She began to study yoga, to party less, and to eat healthily. In a moment of fractiousness, she got a belly button ring on her front and a tattoo on the small of her back. She also tended to avoid guys these days, at least when it came to dating them, and especially when it came to intimacy. She studied hard and played volleyball harder, and she found in time that it was easy to love herself singularly, with a full heart and a forgiving manner, even when she felt embarrassed by her actions or incompetent in her abilities. Annabelle realized she was strong. She realized she was beautiful the way she was, flaws and all.

Such realizations, though, however good for her soul, didn't dismiss in Annabelle's mind what her father had done. No woman, no matter how abrasive, deserved to go through what her mother had endured over the past year. And no daughter deserved such a degree of humiliation at all. Annabelle didn't know what her father could do to make it up to her, to stoke the diminished flame of trust and affection between them. She did know, however, that it would take a hell of a lot more than lunch in Santa Barbara and a trip to wine country, even if they were swank places, as the restaurant, a sparkling cabana on the water, soon appeared to be. And even if Annabelle, when getting out of the Lincoln at the valet area, spied the latest Hollywood heartthrob as he emerged from his Maserati with a leggy blonde who looked wholly implanted.

"Nice restaurant," Annabelle said, gazing from the A-list clientele to the roofline of the elegant cabana. Unlike the Hollywood heartthrob and his stringy companion, the cabana looked as if it were still standing up in this world the way God had made it.

"My pleasure," said her father. "Miguel recommended the place. Very trendy." He put an arm around his daughter and led her down a set of steps toward the waterfront entrance, where they walked directly behind the movie star and his impossibly-blonde groupie.

And while her father's physical contact didn't make her nervous this time, it did make her wonder—

—Was Daddy really enjoying this stroll with his daughter, or was he lost in the brick-tight ass of the blonde in front of them?

—Did he like having his arm around his little girl, or would he prefer to lick buttercream icing out of real-life Malibu Barbie's exposed navel?

—Was the prospect of sitting down to lunch with 'Belles enough for him, or was he already dreaming of having toilet-stall sex with this synthetic star tagger, while both Annabelle and the Hollywood heartthrob sipped imported Italian water at their respective tables?

—Who is he thinking of right now? she asked herself bluntly. Me, or that?

As sad as it seemed to her, Annabelle could not be sure anymore.

CHAPTER 37

★★★★★★★★★★★★★★★★★★★★★★★★★★★★★★★★★

Annabelle took a bite from her spinach salad, chewed in thought, swallowed, then asked her father the one question he had been hoping to avoid during their special lunch together: "So what's Ken up to this afternoon?"

Kidd swallowed a bit of his own salad, a Caesar with Dungeness crab, then he lifted the linen napkin off his lap and dabbed a splotch of dressing from the corner of his mouth. "Don't know, 'Belles," he said, returning the napkin to his lap. "I imagine he's studying that course of yours, but you can never really tell with Kenny. He's often prone to—how would you say it?—distractions."

Annabelle took a sip of water from her glass and set it down in the exact spot from where it had been raised. She fidgeted with the outside of the glass, using her thumb and forefinger to make precise streaks in the condensation. Heretofore, Kidd's special lunch with his daughter, like his ride with her from Los Angeles, had been extremely nonverbal. Annabelle availed herself of several distractions as well, like fingering the glass's dewy side, or compressing her bread into dense square blocks before she popped them into her mouth.

"So tell me, Daddy," she said, keeping her eyes on her fingers as they mowed a streak down the glass, "how are things? What have you been up to since... you know?"

Kidd pressed down on the surgical tape near his right ear. He was beginning to sweat and the tape felt loose. The gash along his chin was stinging like a bastard, and he wondered how much the pain was causing him to grimace. He also wondered if Annabelle might be taking that grimace as a sign of Kidd's discomfort with her inquiry into her daddy's recent life experiences. Which, in part, it was.

How can I possibly answer her? Kidd wondered. Could he tell her about his exile on Long Island for four months, where he never once left his lawyer's guest bungalow, even though the summer in the Hamptons had been meteorologically perfect? Could he tell her about how that same attorney, an acquaintance of his for years, had finally told him to get lost? Could he entertain her with a story about his move to Simondale, Connecticut, and *why* he had moved there? That there was a precinct in Simondale—Number Four—that was the one precinct in all of the United States in which Charles Bentley Kidd had not received a single vote for president—twice—and that Hoban Lane was situated at the dead center of that precinct. That he had chosen to place himself in the middle of such anti-Kidd sentiment so that he could live among people he knew hated him. That he had to offer double the asking price for the house to get that Croushore woman to sell to him. That he would use his time in Simondale to do penance for his sins against America. But that instead of doing penance, he ended up scrumptiously humping the married woman across the street. And that he had fled Simondale after the woman dumped him, and in the process had taken her only child along for the ride. Did he really want to tell Annabelle these things? He thought not.

Instead, he said, "Life's been really crazy, 'Belles. 'Insane' is a better word for it. Nobody has ever been in my position before, you understand. No one in the history of the country. So it's—"

He stopped short when he saw Annabelle raise a cold eyebrow to him. He knew what she was thinking: Don't cry to me about where you've found yourself, Charles Bentley Kidd. Nobody forced you to bang everything but the pots and pans when you were in the White House.

Kidd pursed his lips and took successive bites from his Caesar salad, until finally, Annabelle lowered her condemnatory eyebrow.

Annabelle used her fork to pick through the remainder of her spinach greens, apparently finding nothing she wanted to eat. "I'm curious, though," she said. "How did you end up with Ken?"

Kenny again? Kidd thought. Jesus H. Cracker Jack! Did his daughter have a case of Pipsqueak on the Brain? Kidd reached for his glass of water and took a long sip, the icy stream cooling his throat. He smacked his lips and tried to devise a response to her inquiry which could not be impugned.

"Well, Kenny lived across the street," Kidd said. "And he was back from college, and I needed an assistant, so he came to work for me."

"And that's it?" Annabelle said.

"That's it." Kidd took another sip of water, and Annabelle stared at him curiously. She seemed to be eyeing her father for the deeper cause to his and Kenny's relationship, like she was no longer accepting what he said at face value. Returning her stare, Kidd felt a twinge of remorse flow through him, saddened by the thought that his daughter might be searching for hidden passageways behind her father's carefully camouflaged walls.

"Huh," she said. Then matter-of-factly: "So you both, one day, just decided to drive across the country."

"To see you," Kidd said.

"And Ken was fine with that?"

"He wanted to go to Alaska," Kidd said. "No matter what he told you yesterday, that was his plan. Besides, it's not like he had anything else to do. He really is a pent-up boy."

"And what happened to the Secret Service?" Annabelle asked.

Kidd blew on his fist and flicked his fingers out. "Dust in the wind, 'Belles. Didn't need them anyway. They were cramping my style."

"Your *style*?" Annabelle asked, clearly searching her father's façade for more passageways. But Kidd was saved by the waiter, who brought their entrees on steaming plates—pan-fried Oregon petrale sole for Kidd and mesquite-grilled Mexican tiger prawns for Annabelle, each served with sides of haricots verts and horseradish-crusted mashed potatoes. When the conversation settled again, Annabelle had moved on.

"Well, he seems nice."

"Who?" Kidd asked, knowing damn well who.

"Ken," Annabelle said. "I liked what I saw of him. He looks genuine."

It was with those words that Kidd felt a new battle begin to unfold. What a one-sided battle it would be. Kenny was nowhere near the field—the boy could not defend himself.

"Genuine?" Kidd asked, taking a piping-hot bite of sole. He spoke with his mouth full. "Does he really? Well, that's interesting."

"Sure," Annabelle said. She was cutting her Mexican tiger prawns into little pieces. "Why is it interesting?"

Kidd swallowed thoughtfully. "Well, not everybody is how they look, 'Belles," he said.

Annabelle threw him another raised eyebrow. "Oh, I know that, don't I, Daddy?"

Kidd shied away from her eyebrow. "What I'm saying, Annabelle, is that I've known Kenny a lot longer than you have. I've seen him at his best, and I've seen him at his worst. I can tell you with certainty that the boy has some particular issues."

That description made Annabelle edge forward in her seat, a spark of intrigue flashing behind her emerald green irises. "Like what?" she asked.

Kidd took another bite of sole, savoring a hint of ginger in its sauce. "Well, I know for sure that any woman who would sleep with him now would probably want to wear a wetsuit. He whored his ass all over Las Vegas."

"As opposed to whoring your ass all over the White House?" his daughter asked. "Or Ohio, for that matter?"

"That's not what I'm saying, Annabelle." Kidd reached for his water and took a gulp this time, emptying the glass. He snapped his fingers. "Waiter!" he called, pointing to the glass. The waiter called for the water boy.

Kidd wiped his brow with the linen napkin and said, "Regardless of what you think of my situations, Annabelle, at least I was safe. There are more condom wrappers still lying around that White House than there are trash bags to put them in."

"You must be very proud," Annabelle said, clearly not meaning it. She started to make a shape out of her mashed potatoes.

"Pride isn't the point, Annabelle," Kidd said. The water boy came over and filled his glass to the rim. Kidd took another large gulp and set the glass down forcefully, spilling half the water on the tablecloth. "The point is, Kenny has no regard for his safety, or anyone else's. He drives like a maniac—speeding, swerving, taunting tractor-trailers to cut him off. Several times, I wanted to throw myself out of the car, just to get away."

"I know the feeling," Annabelle said.

Kidd did his best to ignore her jab, plowing on. "He drinks crazy amounts of liquor, too, Annabelle. Then he'll do things like taunt women or get behind the wheel. Do you know he drove drunk from the Rostoff in Chicago all the way up to Rogers Park? Blasted off his ass? Almost killed a pedestrian on Sheridan and everything. I ordered him to let me drive, but he threatened to gouge my eyes out. And I like my eyes."

"Does he have any tattoos?" Annabelle asked.

"Three, I think. Maybe four. Probably got them off an infected needle."

"Four tattoos," Annabelle said. "That's wild. Where are they?" Her mashed potatoes took on a rectangular form with curved edges.

"I don't know, and you shouldn't care," Kidd said. He rubbed the back of his neck. Sweat was coating him. "Trust me, Annabelle. When it comes to girls, he's the worst."

"How so?" she asked.

"He used one girl from Utah for fellatio," Kidd said. "Then he kicked her out of the hotel room. Just blew his ju-ju at her and told her to leave. And it was her room. Poor Mormon, she was distraught."

"Maybe she didn't swallow," Annabelle said. "That pisses a lot of guys off."

Oh, did I really need to hear that? Kidd thought, but he forged ahead. "Then, when we got to Las Vegas, he went sex crazy. Yesterday morning I woke up to find him missing. He'd spent the night God-knows-where doing God-knows-what with God-knows-whom. Then the night before, he was banging Darby Duvall."

"Darby Duvall?" Annabelle said.

"Darby Duvall," Kidd said. "You thought she was a virgin? Not after Kenny. Now she's the new Madonna."

"Darby Duvall," Annabelle repeated. "That's wild. When I met her at the White House, she seemed so innocent."

"Doesn't any of this gross you out?" Kidd asked, trying to lead the answer.

Annabelle thought about it for a moment, then she shook her head. "Honestly, Daddy, it kind of impresses me."

"*Impresses* you?" Kidd asked.

"So Ken got busy with Darby Duvall," Annabelle said.

"'Got busy'?" Kidd asked. "Is that how the young are referring to it these days?"

"We refer to it a lot of ways," Annabelle said. "Depending on intensity and position."

Now *that* is something I did not need to hear, Kidd thought.

"Wow, Darby Duvall," Annabelle said. "She's famous, you know. She's more than famous. She's an icon."

"Kenny used her up and spit her out," Kidd said. "Shows you how much he cares about famous girls."

"Even so," Annabelle said, "from what I've read about her, she wouldn't just give herself to anybody. If she slept with Ken, and was willing to risk her image over it, then he's got something in him."

Kidd stifled an urge to vomit his petrale sole into his lap. What the hell was his daughter doing, standing up for Kenny Kernick? She had only met the little runt twenty hours ago. God, was she crazy?

Kidd decided that his one-sided battle now tilted in Kenny's favor. It was time to pull out some heavy artillery and lay waste to the field in totality.

Kidd put down his fork, loaded his verbal guns, and leaned forward over the table to get a better trajectory on his target.

"I'll tell you what Kenny's got in him, Annabelle. It's called sociopathy. He's nuts."

"Sociopaths aren't nuts, Daddy," Annabelle said. "It's a personality disorder, not insanity."

Kidd felt his blood froth. The first shell had landed short. He reloaded.

"Well, he's got that personality disorder in spades," Kidd said. "Do you know why I could hire him, Annabelle? Do you know why he wasn't in college? An eighteen-year-old boy? In the middle of October?"

Annabelle yawned, then she tweaked her mashed potatoes. "You said it yourself, Daddy: Ken's brilliant."

"Brilliant, for sure," Kidd said. "A brilliant criminal. The kid's a thief, Annabelle. A sick, perverted deviant. He was kicked out of Harvard, you know. For stealing. Do you know what he was stealing?"

Finally, Annabelle stopped playing with her food and looked up at her father. Her eyes had lost their defiance.

"What did he steal?" she asked.

"Underpants," Kidd said, watching his shells finally make a parabola toward their mark. "Loads and loads of coed underpants. Every shape, color and size. He scoured the laundry rooms of Harvard to swipe those things. When they caught him, they gave him the boot. You should see it, the whole neighborhood in Simondale is laughing over this. His parents are mortified. That's why they sent him to me. His mother didn't want him in the house. She was afraid he would steal her underwear, too."

"Wow," said Annabelle, clearly shaken. "That's bizarre."

"It's more than bizarre, Annabelle," Kidd said. "It's a deal breaker."

"I see what you mean," Annabelle said. "I never would have guessed."

"So you understand how you can be wrong about people," Kidd said. "Just from one interaction." He was watching Annabelle carefully, desperately waiting for an explosion from his target.

"I do, Daddy," Annabelle said. "Yes, I do. Stealing underwear. That is so... weird."

Boom! Kidd thought. A direct, devastating and conclusive hit. The battle was over; the enemy was vanquished. If Kidd wanted to find Kenny on a menu, he would look for the little bastard under "toast." But it was all in a day's work. And there was still time for dessert.

Kidd said, "So I guess you won't be studying with him tomorrow."

Annabelle resumed playing with her food. "I have to study with him, Daddy. I need his help. I really don't get statistics and I'm out of time. It was part of our deal, remember?"

Kidd ran his tongue along the ridge of his lower teeth. That answer was not the one he wanted. But it was a temporary setback. He could adapt.

"Just promise me one thing, then," he said.

"What's that?" Annabelle asked.

"Don't study in your room," Kidd said. "Take him to neutral ground. Otherwise, on Monday morning, when you get out of the shower, you're likely to find you have no underwear to put on."

Annabelle rested her fork on the table and stared into her father's eyes. She pursed her lips, like she always did when she was thinking. "Okay, Daddy," she said. "Neutral ground. No studying in my room."

"You'll be cautious around him?" Kidd asked.

"I promise," Annabelle said.

"Good enough for me," Kidd said. But it really wasn't.

The waiter came over to take Kidd's plate. Then he moved to Annabelle's side and hesitated.

"Still working on that, Miss Kidd?"

Annabelle sat back. "No, I'm done. Thank you."

Kidd looked at Annabelle's plate as it was being lifted off the table. Annabelle had not taken a single bite of anything; the plate still held cut blocks of tiger prawns, a pristine row of haricot verts, and to the side, a flattened mass of mashed potatoes. As her plate was whisked by him, however, something troubled Kidd. It wasn't the physical evidence of his daughter's lack of eating that concerned him so much as it was the sight of those mashed potatoes she had been playing with. The irregular white pile had been rearranged by Annabelle through the course of the meal to resemble a giant hand, with an extended middle finger pointing right at Kidd. His daughter, surreptitiously, had managed to flip her father the bird.

Kidd felt wet at the back of his neck. He wiped his nape with the linen napkin, then tossed the napkin into his lap.

The waiter returned and placed a small, leather-bound menu on the edge of the table, then he turned and walked away.

Kidd perused the menu's offerings, running a finger down its list of fine pastry delights.

"Dessert?" Kidd asked, tapping the section for cream-filled goodies.

"No," said Annabelle, raising that accusatory eyebrow conclusively.

CHAPTER 38

★ ★

At quarter to eleven on Sunday morning, Annabelle Kidd came running down the pathway that led to Sycamore Hall with a gym bag slung over her shoulder. Even from a distance, Kenny could see that she was awash in sweat, reddened from head to toe, and completely drained by the morning's volleyball practice. Such an image was not a good sign, given the mental calisthenics Kenny planned to put her through shortly.

"Ken, I'm sorry!" she yelled from several yards away.

Kenny was sitting on Sycamore Hall's stoop, thumbing through Annabelle's statistics textbook for the fifth time since Friday night. He had spent all of Saturday reviewing it and felt he had a damn good hold on the secrets it contained. He fully expected to give Annabelle Kidd the drilling of her life.

But she had been late returning from practice, which he had discovered when nobody came down to meet him at ten, or 10:15, or 10:30 for that matter. Figuring Annabelle had gotten tied up at the field house, Kenny sat on the stoop and waited. The morning was pleasant enough, with high clouds adding a curl of cream to the abundant blue sky. It was warm as well. Kenny had never realized how clement the weather could be in November until he had come west. It felt like May in New England here, with all the hope that May conveyed, instead of the portents of gloom which November typically signaled in the Northeast for another long, dark winter. At more than one point that morning, Kenny looked down at the shirt he was wearing—lightweight polyester, short-sleeved, and a size too large—and he laughed. Such a summery shirt in the depths of autumn. Life was good in Los Angeles, even if Annabelle was making him wait.

Kenny closed the book and stood up as Annabelle approached. "It's fine," he told her.

"I'm sorry, really. We screwed up our last play and my coach got fantastically pissed." Annabelle extended a sweaty hand and Kenny took it. As they shook, Kenny had to stifle an urge to turn her hand over and lick the back of it, from the ridge of her knuckles all the way up to her glistening shoulder. "I hope you haven't been too bored sitting here."

"No worries," Kenny said. "I'm ready when you are."

"I have to take a shower first," she said.

No! Kenny wanted to cry. He wanted her to study with him just like that, so he could soak up her sweaty pheromonal goodness all day long. Instead, he found himself saying, "That's fine. I can wait in your room if you'd like. I'll get everything set up."

That's when Annabelle got a strange look on her face, as if something Kenny proposed was repugnant to her. "No, that's okay," she said cautiously. She glanced around, pursing her lips in thought. Then she pointed. "There's a building about a quarter of a mile down the road called Squires Hall. If you go up to the fifth floor, there are always some classrooms left open. Set up in one of those, and I'll meet you there in twenty minutes."

Kenny returned her odd look with one of his own. There was something amiss in her face, something uncertain. "Are you sure?" he asked. He had hoped to see the lair where stunning Annabelle Kidd made her home. Most of all, he wanted to smell its mixture of perfume, shampoo and soapy accents, the scents of true feminine beauty.

"I'm positive," Annabelle said. "I'll meet you there in twenty, then we'll get to work."

She turned and walked to the dormitory's door, which she unlocked with a keycard. She pulled the door open, then looked back at Kenny. "Besides," she said, "Sarah is probably still asleep. That girl parties hard on Saturday night."

She slipped past the door and into the shadows of the hallway, leaving Kenny to doubt, just from the hesitant inflection in Annabelle's parting words, whether roommate Sarah was even around this weekend at all.

On the fifth floor of Squires Hall, Kenny found a classroom that appeared—from the half-erased chalk markings of graphs, curves and formulas—as if it had last been used for an economics course on labor theory.

This is the perfect set-up, Kenny thought. The room was bright from fluorescent overheads as well as ample sunlight streaming in through the windows. There was a broad instructor's table at the front of the class that was large enough for both Annabelle and him to spread out on. There were also plenty of chalkboards, and Kenny had spied candy and soda machines around the corner. Kenny set the textbook on the instructor's table, grabbed an eraser, and removed the last vestiges of economics from the boards. Today the room would be saturated with psychology statistics. He doubted that any of the five black monoliths would remain untouched by day's end, and he relished the energy that was about to be unleashed in such a confined space.

Annabelle showed up twenty minutes later. Gone was her volleyball outfit; in its place she wore low-rider jeans and a green camisole that electrified her emerald eyes. Her hair—gingerbread with blonde highlights—was pulled back into a ponytail and still wet. She was also out of breath. "Well, how's that for crazy?" she said when she greeted Kenny.

"Welcome to the caldron," Kenny told her.

"I had a class in here once," Annabelle said. "In my old major."

"Did you ace it?" Kenny asked as Annabelle placed her Sadrine Gravos bag, now many books lighter, on the instructor's table.

"I did not," she answered. "I was a bit distracted back then."

"Well, then was then," Kenny said. "It's a new day, with fresh challenges. So let's attack them forthwith, shall we?"

"Where do you want to start?" Annabelle said with a hint of exasperation.

"Where else?" Kenny said. "At the beginning." He cracked the statistics book and ordered Annabelle to prepare a fresh sheet of paper.

They started at the beginning. As Annabelle sat on the other side of the table, thumbing the eraser of her pencil, Kenny stood at the chalkboard and reviewed for her the basics of stats implementation—levels of measurement; continuous versus discreet measures; real limits and significant figures; and rounding. The great thing about Annabelle's textbook was its abundance of practice questions at the end of each chapter. In high school, Kenny had discovered that the only true way to learn a math-based subject was to answer those questions on your own. It was something few students ever did, opting instead for the minimal exercises their teachers assigned. But on this day, given Annabelle's anxiety over her grasp of statistics, Kenny decided that those practice problems needed to be figured, and each on its own sheet of paper, which would give Annabelle plenty of space to err. When Annabelle asked which specific problems Kenny wanted done, and he replied, "All of them," Annabelle looked as if she might throw up.

Together, they calculated the answers for every question at the end of chapters one and two. It took time. She made several mistakes. Even Kenny made mistakes. But ultimately, with the help of a lot of chalk, they figured things out. Eventually they moved on, plowing through the material and the practice problems. In chapters three and four, they covered measures of central tendency. In chapter five, they studied standard deviation and something called eyeball-estimation. By chapter six, they were into frequency distributions; by seven, the Central Limit Theorem. Chapters eight and nine saw point estimation, confidence intervals, and hypothesis testing.

Through it all, Kenny kept Annabelle focused on the practice questions at the end of each chapter. He made her work out every problem to its correct conclusion, even if it took five tries. She went through page after page of paper; eraser shavings peppered the desktop. When she wore her first pencil down to a nub, she reached into her bag, pulled out a new one, sharpened it at a machine in the corner, and went at the questions again, until she wore that pencil down, too. When she was stumped, she stepped up to the chalkboard and worked out the answers

ALL-AMERICAN KIDD

with Kenny—prodding, calculating, using precise motions of her hands to visualize, manually, the relationships between numbers. Kenny, for his part, consumed an entire box of chalk. Dust coated his lungs, making him cough in lengthy spurts. His fingertips were streaked with white, as were his yellow shirt and flaming red hair. He was pretty sure he had been running nervous fingers across his scalp all afternoon. Combined with the sweat pouring out of him in the hot classroom, the chalk made his hair feel as pasty as uncured mortar.

Yet Kenny pushed Annabelle forward. At times he was not kind. Some observers might have called him a taskmaster, but he considered himself thorough. Until finally, halfway through the practice questions on inferences about means of single samples, Annabelle rolled her eyes and dropped her head to the table. For a few moments, she didn't move, appearing to be down for the count. As Kenny waited for her to come around, he glanced out a window and noticed that, at some point, the sun had set. Curious, he looked at his watch. It was 7:30. They had gone at statistics for eight hours straight, with no breaks for food, no trips to the restrooms, and no clue as to what was going on around them.

"I can't do this anymore," Annabelle mumbled against the tabletop.

"We're not done," Kenny told her.

"I don't care," she said. "My head feels like a funnel filled to its brim. Anything you dump into it now is just going to flow over."

"Maybe you need a candy bar to get you through," Kenny said.

Annabelle sat up and looked at Kenny. While the droop to her face and body signaled exhaustion, her emerald eyes were aglow with fire.

"What I need," Annabelle said, "is real food." She threw her pencil onto a sheet of paper and folded her arms in defiance. "Ken," she said, "how would you like to sink your teeth into the best hamburger you've ever tasted in your life?"

Hamburgers, Kenny thought, the word sounding foreign to him. When was the last time he had eaten one? Kenny pursed his lips, reflecting deliciously on Big Melly's stunning Big Bleu Bison Burger in Grand Junction, the last instance of his tongue finding joyful communion with ground meat. But Annabelle was proposing a tall order: Big Melly's Big Bleu had been the most amazing burger ever—it had actually been the burger which had driven him away from burgers with its perfection—and Kenny doubted it could be topped. "I don't know," he said, "I have high standards in these matters. Are you sure you can back that up?"

Annabelle dismissed Kenny's concern with a vexed glare. "I may not have a clue about statistics, Ken, but there's one area in which I'm an expert by now, and that's the psychology of the male appetite. Come with me," she said, standing up. "It's my turn to teach you something."

CHAPTER 39

★ ★

"I've eaten a lot of these in my day," Ken Kernick was saying, as he took his third bite from the Over-Easy Burger that Annabelle had ordered for him. He chewed the bite religiously, and his eyelids fluttered as if he had just received a shot of morphine into his veins. "But *that*"—he held up the burger ceremonially—"that is the *goddamn* king!"

Annabelle had taken Ken to a bar called Slobberchops, only a short walk up Soltavega from campus. Mostly known as a dive drinking hole, Slobberchops offered one item on its menu that had become legend to the students of the University of the West—the Over-Easy Burger. Its ingredients seemed an awkward combination—a thick half-pound patty of ground beef topped with cheddar cheese, bacon, red onions, lettuce, tomato, pickles and the pièce de résistance, a fried egg with its yolk still running. When she first arrived at West, Annabelle avoided the burger, telling her friends that its composition sounded disturbing. Then she tried it one night after an evening of seditious inebriation. To Annabelle, it was a cure-all, like having steak and eggs on a whole-wheat bun, especially when dipped in A1 sauce, as she encouraged Ken to do liberally. It appeared that Ken thought of the Over-Easy Burger the same way. He couldn't stop moaning as he chewed, rolling his eyes, extolling its virtues, sucking egg yolk off his fingers.

"I'm glad you like it," Annabelle said. She sunk her teeth into her own burger and let the yolk run over her tongue.

"It's just what I needed," Ken said. "Last night, I had stuffed pork loin, and in Vegas I ate filet mignon and sushi. It's time I got back to my fast food roots. God, how I've missed grease."

Annabelle took a sip of Diet Coke and sat back, eyeing Ken curiously. It was hard for her to reconcile the way he carried himself with the things her father had told her about him. He seemed so pleasant by nature, so incapable of nastiness or thievery. Why would he have ever had to steal underwear? He was not unattractive. Ken was small, sure, but he had gorgeous red hair and eyes the color of glacial ice. He dressed like a million dollars, too. Today, on a leisurely weekend, he was wearing a short-sleeve designer shirt with tan dress slacks, instead of the faded jeans and t-shirt most college-age guys wore. And he smiled a lot, which Annabelle loved. So many guys didn't smile, especially when you were out at parties with them. They just stood in a corner or near the keg, trying to come off as all serious, thinking they looked cool and tough. While such a disposition may have been tough, it certainly wasn't cool. Even Peter hadn't smiled very often. It had been her ex-love's one fault in an otherwise flawless presentation.

"I played a game on the road," Ken told her, his Over-Easy half devoured. "Every time we came into a new town, I sought out a restaurant I hadn't been to before. It was quite intriguing, really." Ken licked a dollop of yolk off his knuckle.

"Did you ever make it to a BurgerMeister MeisterBurger?" Annabelle asked.

"I did," Ken said. "In Hawleyville, Ohio, of all places."

Annabelle felt a wave of nostalgia flow over her. Burger-Meister MeisterBurger had always been her favorite place to eat when she was growing up. The chain, which could only be found in the Buckeye State, had been named for some character on a Christmas special from the seventies, and the name stuck, particularly among a younger crowd reared on television. In the afternoon hours, when the middle and high schools emptied, the place was packed with hungry students. BurgerMeister MeisterBurger was legend for anyone from Ohio, and during her first year in Los Angeles, Annabelle had often pined for one of their hearty German Hermans with onions and pickles, just to be reminded of home. The only problem was, since none of her classmates came from Ohio, nobody had any idea what the hell she was talking about. Then, out of nowhere, arrived Ken Kernick. He understood. He had actually been to a BurgerMeister MeisterBurger, and in her father's hometown, at that.

She mentioned the German Herman and asked Ken what he thought of it.

Ken munched on a French fry, swallowed, then said: "It was a very wet burger."

"Wet," Annabelle said. "That's interesting. How do you mean?" She had never heard a burger so described. But Ken Kernick seemed to use a lot of expressions or descriptions that were unique, as if he were just becoming comfortable with projecting his voice out into the world.

"You know, wet," Ken said. "All that drippy grease."

"That's the best part," Annabelle said. "You didn't like it?"

"No, I loved it," Ken said. "Don't get me wrong. I prefer them wet. Better than dry."

"Spoken like a true male," Annabelle said, and Ken blushed, making his glacial blue eyes show even cooler. To relieve his embarrassment, Annabelle added with a giggle, "Oh, Ken, I know what you meant."

But she was having a hard time figuring this guy out. Her father said Ken Kernick was Satan to all things female, and yet here he was, blushing over something as subtle as playful food innuendo. It didn't add up.

"How do you think we're doing?" she asked him, lifting a French fry off her plate and twirling it in a dollop of ketchup.

"With what?" Ken asked. "With my meal? I'm almost done. But you've hardly touched yours."

"With stats," Annabelle said. "This stuff scares the hell out of me."

Ken bit into the last of his Over-Easy Burger, chewed in contemplation, and wiped his mouth with a napkin. Then he dropped the napkin to the table and said, "See, I don't understand that mentality."

"What mentality?" Annabelle said.

"The mentality of fear," Ken said.

"Well, I understand it," Annabelle said. "Statistics is the basis of experimental psychology. If I don't get it down, I don't know how much of a future I have in the field. And that's where I want my future." She tried to scold Ken with a steely glare. "We're not all geniuses, Ken. We can't all learn something overnight and teach it the next day."

Ken let her cool off by taking a long sip of soda. When he set the glass down, he said, "I don't think of myself as a genius."

"Then what's your secret?" Annabelle asked.

"I don't really have a secret," Ken said.

"Everybody has a secret, Ken," Annabelle said, knowing more of his than he realized. Her eyes were boring into him, searching, but still she could find no hint of the devil in this person. "Everybody has a method is what I mean," she said. "My method is not to fail. I don't care how I get there, but I do not want to fail. So what's your method?"

Ken stayed quiet for a moment, reflecting. He parted his lips slightly to signal an answer, then closed them again without saying a word. After a few moments, he shook his head. "I think you're going about this all wrong."

"How so?" Annabelle asked. "I was a fairly good student until this semester. It's just that statistics means so much, and that puts pressure on me. I've been trying for an 'A' in it, but I keep ending up near the bottom. And my focus on it has affected my other grades as well."

"That's the difference between us," Ken said. "I never try for any grade."

"Then how do you study?" Annabelle asked, annoyed now. "And how do you come off so smart? Because I have to tell you, Ken, you may not think you're a genius, but what I just saw in that classroom for the past eight hours told me that you're either a monumental genius or a monumental charlatan. And nobody can fake statistics. Math is the great revealer. Either you get the answer right or you get it wrong."

Ken looked down at the vinyl tablecloth, seeming to contemplate Annabelle's challenge. After a few moments, he smiled knowingly.

"Okay, you want my secret?" he said, leaning forward over his empty plate. "Here it is. I never go into a test thinking I'm going to shoot for this grade or that grade. It's useless, because it puts the focus on the result. Instead, I try to focus on the process."

"The process," Annabelle said. "Like we're doing today. With the practice questions."

"Exactly," Ken said. "My father works in automation engineering, so the benefits of process have always been drilled into me. All through school, I studied something concretely via question and answer to the point where I believed, in my deepest depths, that I was going to walk into the classroom the next day and rip the shit out of that test. It may have taken me an hour to reach that feeling or it may have taken me fifteen hours, but regardless, when I got that test in front of me, I knew I was going to tear it up. I became a student consumed—full of adrenaline and appetite. Nothing could stop me. That's what focusing on the process is about, see? It's studying smarter, which allows you to compartmentalize your other subjects so they don't take a hit as well. If you do that, if you focus on one task at a time, step by step, answering these questions until the process of answering them is ingrained in you, the results will take care of themselves." Ken popped another fry into his mouth and chewed with a grin.

He is one confident dude, Annabelle told herself, and she admired him for it.

"So you want me to rip the shit out of my test," Annabelle said.

"I want you to *feel* like you're going to rip the shit out of it," Ken said. "Whether you do or don't isn't the point. The point is to cover all the ground, to block every exit, to leave no place for that little fucker to hide. You control the test, not vice versa. Do you think you can do that?"

Annabelle laughed. "Oh, I'll try. You know I will."

"That's all you can do," Ken said.

Annabelle fidgeted with another fry, using it to poke at a piece of bacon sticking out from her partially-eaten burger. "Are you up for another question?" she asked.

"Shoot," Ken told her, taking a healthy gulp of soda.

"Why aren't you in college?" Annabelle asked him. "My father said you started the year at Harvard."

Annabelle watched Ken's confident expression dissipate. She knew she was trapping him, but she didn't care. She wanted to see if he would tell her the truth. She was tired of the lies men told, from her father's "I didn't do it," to Peter's "I can handle it." If Ken really were the devil her father made him sound like, his next words would be steeped in fiction, and any respect she may have had for him on a personal level would dissipate as well.

"It's a long story," Ken said. "And not a particularly flattering one."

"Then start at the beginning," Annabelle said. "Stories always come off better when you start at the beginning."

"The beginning?" Ken asked, a bit reticently.

"And don't clean it up," she said.

Annabelle watched as Ken ran a palm over his forehead. He sucked in a deep breath and expelled it with a whistle. Then she listened as he started at the beginning and didn't clean it up.

He told her of how he had been raised in staid Simondale, Connecticut, the only child of a self-made millionaire from Stamford who had decided, in his newly-acquired wealth, to lock down his family among thick oak groves and hilly seclusion, safe from the messy interferences of the Stamford working class from which he had originated. He told her of how he had grown up the smallest boy on a street of boys, and how roughhousing or any type of play with them had been forbidden once Ken returned home at age five with a skinned knee that required (gasp!) a slight application of spray-on Bactine. He had been sheltered all his life, he said. And while he had recently come to understand that his parents only wanted the best for him, he had also come to see how their well-intentioned prohibitions frequently courted hidden disasters.

"With girls?" Annabelle asked.

"Particularly," Ken said.

He told her of how his parents, mostly the father (who sounded to Annabelle like a text-book narcissistic personality), drove Ken to achieve greatness of the mind but didn't place much emphasis on his achievements with the opposite sex, be those achievements something as innocent as playing in a sandbox together. As a result, Ken said, he grew up terrified of girls. The worst part was, it was a fear he believed at the time to be normal, because his father seemed to harbor the same fear somewhere inside himself. Ken told Annabelle that his father never even seemed comfortable around his mother, so how was Ken ever supposed to feel comfortable around a girl who wasn't his mother?

"They call it transference," Annabelle stated clinically.

"Well, I call it fucking insanity," Ken said. "But it gets crazier. Because at the worst possible time, my parents made the worst possible decision. Just as I was reaching adolescence, they elected to keep me at Griggson Academy. It was a private, all-boys, kindergarten-through-twelve school, and while it did everything to foster my academic pursuits, it did nothing to build my confidence. In hindsight, I would have been better off if they'd switched me to Simondale High. I would have graduated first in my class either way, but the daily interactions with girls that would have been forced on me might have greatly enhanced my social skills, and saved me a lot of grief in the future."

"Like what?" Annabelle asked.

"Like Harvard," Ken said.

That's when Ken took another deep breath and told her the truth. He explained how he had been required to withdraw from Harvard for stealing female underpants. As Annabelle listened intently to Ken's confession, she mentally christened the whole affair "Pantygate," and she chuckled under her breath as Ken described the first time he lifted a black Victoria's Secret thong from a dryer in the bowels of some dorm. She realized that Ken could see her laughing, and that her reaction made him stop talking.

"I'm sorry," she said. "Please, continue."

"I looked at these girls," Ken said. "They weren't even girls anymore. They were women. I had skipped the whole 'girl' phase, that time when my awkwardness and their awkwardness would have at least balanced out. Instead, all I was left with was my awkwardness, which never seemed to go away. On a daily basis, I found myself face-to-face with these stunning creatures—with their well-developed bodies and their spectacular hair, and the smells they gave off from perfumes and soaps and shampoos. I couldn't ignore them. I wanted them all. But I didn't know what to do. I mean, look at me." Ken ran his hands from his head to his waist. "The way I saw it, I was short and scrawny. I just figured, who would want me?"

"Darby Duvall wanted you," Annabelle said.

"Oh, you know about that, huh?" Ken said. "Yeah, that's right, she did. Six times."

Ken and Annabelle shared a laugh, and Annabelle threw a fry at him. It bounced off his forehead.

"And that's the point," Ken said, picking the fry off the table and eating it. "I never had confidence in myself. Never accepted myself. Once I started accepting myself, I changed. I'm not proud of what happened at Harvard, but I learned from it. And if you asked me what I'd do differently, if I could go back and do it all over again, I'd say that I would walk up to the girl who owned the black thong and ask her to go to a movie with me, rejection be damned. But I would leave her thong in the dryer."

There was silence at the table. From across the room, Annabelle could hear a mumble of chatter, the sounds of a hockey game on television, and the clinking of forks on plates. Annabelle smiled at Ken. He was the picture of frazzle. Their study session had gotten so intense that afternoon, and Ken had run his hands through his hair so many times, that his red locks were coated white from chalk dust and standing straight up. She wanted to lick her fingers and clean off the dust for him, or at least to smooth down some of the flightier strands. Instead, she reached out for Ken's hand, which was resting on the table. She grasped the hand affectionately.

"Thank you, Ken," she said.

"For what?" Ken said.

She squeezed her fingers into his. "For showing me that there are still people in this world who aren't afraid of being honest."

Ken returned her squeeze and glanced downward. He was blushing again. There's no devil in this guy at all, Annabelle concluded. All Annabelle could see in Ken Kernick was the humility of the recently fallen.

They walked back to Squires Hall in silence, their heels casting rubber thuds against the dry asphalt of a warm Los

Angeles night. They returned to their stuffy room on the fifth floor, picked up chalk, book and paper, and resumed where they had left off.

They finished chapter ten by 9:30 and covered eleven by 10:15. They plowed through chapter twelve by one and chapters thirteen and fourteen by three. And just at the point where Annabelle Kidd knew she had finally figured out statistics, just at the moment when she felt in her soul that she could rip the shit out of any test on the subject, she glanced up and saw that Ken was gone. Then she leaned forward over the table and discovered that Ken really hadn't gone anywhere. He was sitting below the blackboard, asleep against the wall, a half-used piece of chalk gripped in his right hand. His mouth was hanging open and spittle had already formed at the corner of his lips. He had apparently been asleep for some time; Annabelle hadn't noticed.

She smiled affectionately at Ken and sat back. She returned her eyes to the marked-up sheet of paper in front of her—it was covered in a language that until this morning would have seemed as foreign to her as hieroglyphics, but now she understood. She pressed on, finishing the practice questions at the end of fourteen, then returning to the troublesome questions at the end of other chapters. This time, she solved those questions with speed and accuracy.

She didn't know what time she finished studying, or even if she finished at all. All she knew was that she didn't go back to her room that night. Somehow, at some point, she put down the pencil and placed her head against the sheet of paper. Closing her eyes, she cast herself into a dream world filled with means and deviations, intervals and theorems, variances and eyeball-estimations. She saw their structures clearly, and their solutions at once. But most of all, when they had disappeared into the ether of her subconscious after getting a thorough solving, all she was left with was a penetrating vision of success.

CHAPTER 40

★ ★

On the same day that Kenny was drilling Annabelle in the minutiae of psychology statistics, Annabelle's father found himself on the receiving end of his own psychology lesson.

Unlike the previous morning, when Kidd had departed the suite early for his afternoon with Annabelle, the former president stayed in bed on Sunday until he heard Kenny leave the suite to head over to the University of the West. With Kenny gone, Kidd sprung from bed. The time was 9:30. For the past two hours he had been rolling between the sheets with unbridled glee. An excitement had descended upon him after waking up, a freshness and hope that he could only attribute to his victory from the day before, when he had eviscerated Annabelle's opinion of Kenneth Andrew Kernick with the simple revelation that Kenny had once been the vaunted "Panty Thief of Harvard Yard." The victory made Kidd feel like a winner again; it made him feel strong. Now that he was up and about, he wanted to channel that energy into something active. He decided to go for a run. It would be a victory lap, so to speak, along the broad, palm-lined avenues of Santa Monica. Maybe he would even attract a cheering crowd.

Kidd hit the Third Street Promenade around the corner for a new running outfit, then returned to the Mendelssohn to change. He bolted the suite and caught an elevator down to the lobby, stretching his calves, quads and hamstrings against the elevator walls.

Kidd started his run in the park across the street from the Mendelssohn. He ran at a quick pace at first, feeling vivacious against a steady ocean breeze. His legs were loose; his stride graceful. He calculated that at worst he might do a six-minute mile, which was a better time than in his college days. In the breeze, with the motion, under the sun, he felt happy and free. He said hello to bicyclists, rollerbladers and other runners coming toward him. He took deep inhales of the salt air and expelled them out triumphantly, fueling his muscles like coals to a blast furnace. He wanted to wave at the cars going by, to shout out, "Look here, you knobgobbers, it's Charles Bentley Kidd! I vanquished that punk Kenny! I'm unconquerable!" Kidd looked ahead down the park—the path seemed to continue on forever, an Eden of trail and palm and lush grass. If it did continue on forever, Kidd was certain that he would continue on forever. Nothing could stop him.

Except for abdominal cramps, he discovered. And being completely winded. And a heartbeat that threatened to punch a hole through his chest. By the time he had run a single mile, Charles Bentley Kidd teetered on the edge of physical collapse.

"Gotta stop, gotta stop, gotta stop," he chided himself, but his momentum kept him going. In his perpetual motion, sweat began to sting his eyes. His throat felt as if it had been scraped by steel wool. Even his gums were throbbing. He was pretty certain that to anyone watching him at that very moment, he looked like a marionette being dragged along on its strings by the hand of a frolicking toddler. Somehow he managed to slow his pace to a trot, then a walk. His chest heaved. He wanted to throw up. He thought about giving in to the pain in his side and contracting into the fetal position right there on the path. Instead, he looked to his left and found a bench on a patch of grass. He stumbled over to it and tried to sit down, but the pain in his abdomen was too intense. In the end, he settled for a stilted shuffle around the bench, leaning on it at times, stretching his muscles when his body allowed, trying to regroup.

As he hovered around the bench, Kidd thought back to those weeks in Simondale, when he had uttered mistruths to Kenny about working out. Kidd's deception had been so deep at the time that the former president had actually gone through the trouble of putting on all his gym clothes for departure and, upon return, telling Kenny false stories of how much he had lifted and how many minutes he had spent on the cardio machine. Panting, wheezing, feeling like a knotted length of rope, Kidd actually wished he had gone to the gym on those days, instead of pumping Kenny's mama. Okay, *in addition* to pumping Kenny's mama. But he wished that he had at least made some true effort to get back into shape during his time in Simondale, other than banging Martha Kernick against kitchen cabinets and shower tile, and in her guest bedroom. Kidd considered his current condition an embarrassment. When he was president, he could run a mile in eight minutes and twelve seconds, not a bad time for a fiftysomething-year-old guy who ate as many sweets as he did. Today, however, the mile was running him.

Kidd leaned against the bench, catching his breath. In time, his pain receded. With his body refreshed, Kidd knew he wanted to continue running, but he also knew that he didn't want to stay on Ocean Avenue—its flat, endless expanse of park tempted him too much to lay caution aside and charge forward at full pace. If he took that tack again, he was certain he would drop dead. So Kidd looked down the tributaries of Ocean Avenue for more hospitable terrain. Up one of its adjacent streets, Kidd saw a neighborhood of quiet bungalow houses and wide concrete sidewalks. The former president felt confident that by making himself negotiate intersections and corners, he would keep his pace under control. Resolute in his new plan, he crossed Ocean Avenue at a limping saunter.

Even with a slower pace, however, it didn't take Kidd long to realize that his body still couldn't handle the toil. By his third intersection, the man was spent again, the stitch in his side tightening anew. Around the next corner, Kidd spied a Little League baseball field sitting empty under the Sunday sky. Flapping disjointedly, he managed to trudge over to it, intent on making a last-ditch run for its aluminum spectator stands. But he couldn't get to the stands. He simply had nothing left. So he stopped short to lean against a cyclone fence. "Good enough," he panted, putting his back into the fence. He pinched the stitch in his side until the pinch caused more pain than the cramp. He stretched his legs, wiped the sweat from his eyes, and took deep breaths. Then he pushed off the fence and turned around, expecting to distract his mind with the verdant vision of a well-groomed California ball field.

Instead, he noticed a church.

The large marble structure stood on the other side of the ballpark, its bell tower rising like a divine protector above field, houses and trees. Such was the church's boldness of appearance in this homogenous neighborhood that it seemed to Kidd as if it had been carved from a single piece of marble. The sign attached to the façade was modest, but it was legible even from Kidd's vantage point. It stated simply: "First Baptist Church of Santa Monica—Where Everyone is Welcome."

Kidd felt his body loosen and the pain disappear. He walked along the periphery of the baseball field and strolled numbly down one street and then another and then another, in a square, his eyes never veering from the ivory glow of the church's marble casing as it shone brilliantly in the morning sun. When he finally stood across the street from the church, he jaywalked over the road, skipped the curb and made his way up the First Baptist steps, taking them two at a time.

The main door to the church was closed, but it wasn't locked. Kidd gave a tug on the handle. As the door swung open, its hinges creaked.

The former president found himself stepping into a foyer, but to Kidd, he might as well have been stepping into a time machine. Once inside, Kidd felt the sensation of standing fifty-four years earlier in the Elm Street Baptist Church back in Stampler, West Virginia. This is the kind of place where my real daddy would have preached, Kidd told himself as he walked through the foyer and took a service program off a table. He strode confidently down the aisle, inspecting each nuance of the church and noting its corresponding differences with a Catholic tradition.

The interior of this church was austere compared with the ornate houses of worship he had attended after his conversion to Catholicism. Those places (the brooding St. Stephen's in Chicago; the haughty Our Lady of Good Counsel in Columbus) had always terrified the shit out of Kidd, even though he hadn't come to the faith until his early twenties, thus avoiding the mandatory anxious childhood which most Catholics seemed to experience. Every Catholic church he had ever been in, no matter where it was located, looked the same to Kidd: There was an air of impending, catastrophic doom hanging down from the rafters, like the whole church might collapse on itself out of sheer guilt. The giant Suffering Jesus statues above the altars didn't lighten the mood any, nor did the Stations of the Cross that lined church walls. Even the priests couldn't be counted on for consolation; they always appeared dour and burdened to Kidd, which he suspected to be the unforgiving legacy of never receiving a healthy lay, or at least not one they could brag about. No, in every direction that he had ever glanced in a Catholic church, in every dark corner in which he had sought solace for, and understanding of, his place in the world, Charles Bentley Kidd had only found unworthiness.

But this church was different. First Baptist felt alive inside. The walls were bright; they seemed to swell out with joy rather than languish in the abyss of unachievable expectations. It didn't hurt that there was not a single stained-glass window in the place, allowing a flood of sunlight to stream in from the east. As he walked down the aisle, the carpet's rich red hue made Kidd feel as if he were promenading along a bed of rose petals. He looked ahead to the chancel and noticed that it was constructed simply: On one side, it had a lectern for preaching; on the other, a set of risers for the choir and some chairs for the ministry; at the back, there was a basic altar on which sat a small cross of gold. Down from the chancel, near an exit door, Kidd saw a baby grand piano, polished to a gleam. The sight of the piano shocked Kidd. All he could remember from Catholic churches were organs. He even had a memory of Margaret telling him on the day they first met about how she had taken organ lessons as a girl, and he remembered how dull that had made her seem. Then, of course, she screwed his brains out on Thayer Beach, and he realized he had been wrong in such a snap judgment—Margaret Huff, it appeared, was quite skilled when it came to playing organs of all types.

Kidd took a seat in an empty pew toward the front, settling gloriously into its thick bench cushion, which was another non-Catholic touch of comfort. He ran his eyes over the interior of the church once more, then he let out a satisfied breath and glanced down at the program he had picked up in the foyer. It had the day's date on it, followed again by that heavenly word—"Welcome!" For the first time in his life, Kidd felt like a church actually meant it.

"May I help you?" The voice, husky and firm, came from behind Kidd. He turned and saw an African-American gentleman coming toward him. The gentleman wore a suit but no tie. His knees wobbled as if they were busted, yet he appeared relatively young, perhaps mid-forties. He was thick in the waist, but he wasn't fat, and as he came closer, Kidd noticed that he possessed thick hair, a trimmed moustache and, oddly enough, only one hand—the gentleman's right forearm terminated in a stump.

The gentleman walked to the end of the pew and stopped. He studied the white man who was sitting in this church, sweaty and frazzled, dressed only in exercise clothes, and for a moment, his eyes flickered with a spark of recognition. But the gentleman just continued to scrutinize Kidd, awaiting some response to his question.

Kidd shrugged and stumbled to speak. He pointed back to the door. "I was out for a run."

"You don't say," said the man, eyeing Kidd's choice of Sunday clothing.

"I hope I'm not trespassing," Kidd added with a hint of appeasement.

"Trespassing?" the man said. He laughed then clicked his tongue. "Not at all," he said. "It's pretty hard to trespass in a church."

"Well, I'm glad for that," Kidd said, thinking that he had already been thrown out of enough places on this trip. He didn't want to get thrown out of a church now.

"As for running," the man said, "I can't say I blame you. It is a beautiful day to take in the Lord's creation. It rained here all last week, did you know that?"

"I did not," said Kidd.

"Oh, torrents," the man said, keeping his eyes on Kidd. "I'm from Michigan originally, so I've been through it all— rain, snow, sleet, hail, even tornadoes. But you should see what happens in this city when one drop of water hits the ground. You'd think the world was coming to an end. Every newscast goes to live storm coverage. The freeways are useless. Some people won't even go outside." The man looked at the chancel. "I love the rain myself. Love to walk in it and get soaked to the skin. It makes me feel like I'm cleansing my soul all over again. You ever do something like that?"

Kidd shook his head. He didn't particularly care for rain, mostly because it messed up his hair. He told the man that he was one of those people who would rather stay inside.

The man laughed with a robust baritone. "Well, you should come out of that shell sometime. It might do wonders for you." He held out his left hand. "The name is Stubbs. Harland Stubbs. I'm the pastor here at First Baptist."

Kidd took Harland Stubbs's hand and shook it. "Nice to meet you, Reverend," he said. "I'm Charles Bentley Kidd."

"I knew that," said Stubbs. "I didn't at first, it took me a second, but then I did. May I sit down?"

Kidd slid along the pew to make room for the pastor. Reverend Stubbs flopped clumsily into the vacated space and let out a sigh. "It's my knees," he said as he got comfortable against the cushion. "It's never pleasant for me to stand too long. But I'm not ready for replacement surgery. Not yet. My wife Tabitha thinks I'm acting like a coward."

"So you're married," Kidd said.

"Nineteen years," the pastor said, without a single whiff of staleness.

"Any children?" Kidd asked.

"Oh, plenty," the pastor said. "Trying to keep up with them has wrecked my knees even more." He flexed his right leg and cringed.

"Then how do you do it here?" Kidd asked.

"Do what?" the pastor asked.

"I don't know," Kidd said. "How do you make it down the aisle at the start of each service? Or keep the place running? Or attend to your parishioners when they need you? How do you minister, if you can barely move?"

"Everything takes creativity," the pastor said. "And time. Preaching is the toughest part, though. Standing up there." He leaned in toward Kidd and touched his hand to Kidd's thigh. "I hate to admit this, but sometimes when I'm speaking the Word, I'm really praying in my mind that I don't take a tumble in front of the congregation."

"Have you ever?" Kidd asked.

"Not yet," the pastor said. "The Lord's been merciful that way. Just another link in His long chain of benevolence to me. But I can't preach every week, not anymore."

"So what do you do?" Kidd said.

"What do you think I do?" the pastor said. "This is America. There's always someone in the congregation who wants to spout off about something. So a couple of Sundays a month, I let them. Like a guest lecturer in college, so to speak."

"A guest lecturer," Kidd said. He laughed. "I'll tell you, Reverend, you don't see that in every church. At least not twice a month."

"True," the pastor said. "But this is a Calvinist-based faith. We can be a little looser about some things."

"I see that," Kidd said, nodding to the wide, bare wall above the altar. "I mean, where's the great big Jesus? I've never been in a church that didn't have a great big Jesus staring down at me from some towering cross."

"We don't bother with that in the Baptist faith," Reverend Stubbs said. He clicked his tongue again. Kidd couldn't tell if he was playing with a set of dentures or simply snapping the tongue against the roof of his mouth. He looked much too young for false teeth. Then again, the Reverend Stubbs also looked much too young for creaky knees and a missing hand. "Here we like to celebrate the Risen Jesus," the pastor was saying. "It focuses us more on the hope of the Resurrection than on the suffering that got him there. That's why you won't see any Stations of the Cross, either." Kidd noticed that Reverend Stubbs was gazing at his church as a proud father might behold a first-born child.

Kidd said, "But you put cushions in your pews. And you don't even have kneelers. And where the hell are your confessionals?"

Reverend Stubbs chuckled and shook his head. "Let me tell you a few things, Mr. President. First, the cushions are for comfort—do you really think the Lord wants you to suffer, especially when it comes to worship? Second, we don't kneel in this church, we sing." Stubbs used his stumpy arm to point to the piano near the corner. "Darn good songs, too—powerful and uplifting. You should hear us. As for confession, well, you and I can talk about things for counsel, but when it comes to forgiveness, that's between you and God. Nobody else has anything to do with it."

The reverend must have read perplexity on Kidd's face, because he suddenly changed his demeanor to that of a gentle guide.

"Look here," he said, almost in a whisper. "It's real easy. We pray, we learn, we sing. Sometimes we break bread. About the only thing we don't do is use one of those baptismal pools under the chancel floor like some of our sister churches. This structure is too old. Any time we need to baptize someone, I have to pull out an old clawfoot bathtub from the back and have it brought down front. It can get a little messy. But I've never been a big fan of pools under the floor, either—it's too hard for the congregation to see what's happening. Can I tell you, though? Do you know what I'd install if I had the money?"

"What's that?" Kidd asked.

Stubbs pointed to the bare wall at the back of the chancel. "Right there, above the altar, I'd put in a dunk tank baptistery."

"A dunk tank?" Kidd said incredulously. "Like at a carnival?"

"Not that kind," Reverend Stubbs said. "This one would be more like an elevated aquarium, but instead of fish to look at, you'd have baptisms. It'd be twelve feet wide and eight feet tall, with steps leading down on one side and up on the other, waist deep with water. There'd be a piece of glass where that wall is so the congregation could bear witness from these very seats. Then I'd slip on a pair of hip waders and get in there. I'd have my baptizees come down into the water, and that's when I'd dunk them. Hard, too. Really put a good dose of the Holy Spirit into their souls." But the pastor threw up his hand dejectedly. "Unfortunately, it's nothing but a dream. Do you know how much contractors charge to build something like that?" He mentioned a figure to Kidd.

"Wow," Kidd said. "I can see your reticence."

"Reticence has little to do with it," Reverend Stubbs said. "Getting my parishioners to pledge is the bigger problem. Getting parishioners at all is even worse. We're at half capacity, except on holidays. But creating a flock starts with baptizing, and I think people around here would rather have that done in a dunk tank than in an old clawfoot bathtub. It's definitely more Hollywood."

"I was dunked," Kidd told him. "I preferred it that way."

The reverend folded his arms and gave Kidd a skeptical once-over. "Is that so?" he said. "Maybe I'm remembering incorrectly, but I thought you were Catholic."

"I converted to Catholicism," Kidd said.

"I see," the pastor said. "May I ask from what?"

Kidd shrugged. "From nothing."

"I see," the pastor said again, this time letting out a sigh. "Being raised without faith—that can be a tough road for the young."

"To be honest with you, Reverend," Kidd said, "I never really gave it much thought. My mama, God rest her soul, never wanted to go to church when I was little; she seemed saddened by the prospect. Finally, I learned why, but religion still never took much root in me. I was more of a philosophy guy."

"So what happened?" the reverend asked.

"I met my wife," Kidd told him bluntly. "You remember my wife."

"I do," said the reverend. "She always came across as a forthright woman."

"In my wife's case, looks were never deceiving," Kidd said with a snide crook of his lips. "One day she tells me, 'You're going to marry me, Charles Bentley Kidd, and I won't marry anybody who's not Catholic.' So that was that. I was baptized in a river in Chicago, by an old Jesuit priest who'd been my math professor freshman year. After the ceremony, we gave him a stash of Rémy Martin for the effort, but I don't think I ever saw him again. We always wondered if his superiors had learned of what he'd done and retired him to a home."

"I see," the Reverend Stubbs said, nodding solemnly. "Well, the Catholics do things their own way, but it doesn't mean it's the wrong way. Your old priest got you there, and that's all that matters."

"True," Kidd said. "But what's 'there'?"

"What do you mean?" asked the pastor.

It was Kidd's turn to fold his arms. He felt like a philosophy student at Jesuit again, the free-thinking freshman, before that flame of curiosity was roundly snuffed out by Margaret at her insistence on a political science major. "What I'm saying is, I haven't really felt much connection to the Catholic Church since my conversion. Being Catholic has always seemed like a small pair of shoes that I've tried to cram myself into. If anything, since high school, I've felt more connected to the Baptist faith."

"Is that so?" Reverend Stubbs said, a bit taken aback. "And why's that?"

"Oh, my daddy was a Baptist preacher," Kidd said. Then, before he could take another breath, the magnitude of what he had just spoken so nonchalantly hit him, freezing him in his seat. In thirty-seven years, Charles Bentley Kidd had only told one person the truth about his true parentage—Kenny Kernick—and then only recently, when he was a mental mess beside his mama's grave in Hawleyville. He had kept the secret from his wife, his daughter, his friends and foes, and in the end, from the American public at large because nobody would love a bastard. Before long, the lie felt more real than the truth—he actually thought of himself as that dead coal miner's son. But here in this church, under a casual flow of discourse, with no mental anxiety troubling him at all, it had just bubbled out. To a stranger. Why did he feel so scared? Why was he sorry he had said it? It was the truth, after all.

He looked at the pastor, hoping Reverend Stubbs hadn't registered the statement. But the pastor was sitting upright, with his head cocked at such an odd angle that Kidd knew his words had not fallen on deaf ears. "Is *that* so?" Reverend Stubbs said. He used his hand to scratch the knob of his chin. "Now I *definitely* would have remembered that. I thought your father was a miner who died before you were born?"

Kidd let out a sigh and shook his head. He said to the pastor: "There are a lot of things people think about me that aren't true, Reverend. Things I could have set straight early on if I had only said more. But—" He let the statement dangle, swaying precariously on an invisible thread that was tethered between pastor and fallen president. Kidd wasn't ready to say more.

The pastor pursed his lips and nodded. He seemed to understand Kidd's reluctance to go further. He patted Kidd on the thigh and said, "There's only one thing I can tell you, Mr.

President, and it's that we all have scars. Look at me." He held up his stumped arm. "You think I got this way from a war, or from getting hurt in an industrial accident? If only I had been so lucky. No, I got like this in the saddle of a Kawasaki motorcycle, drunk out of my skull one morning, before I hit a pothole doing seventy and rolled for forty yards. Somewhere on that road, I left my hand. I'm lucky I kept my knees. Once I could move again, I decided to get sober."

"And to find God?" Kidd asked.

"The Lord came later," the pastor said, smiling at the memory. "I still wasn't ready for Him. For some people, it takes longer. My wife says I'm a stubborn old ass."

Kidd chuckled and returned the pastor's pat of the thigh. "Well, most people think I'm just an ass in general, Reverend Stubbs, so you've got that on me."

"Oh, I don't think that's true," the reverend said. "Maybe people just think you've lost your way. Maybe they're just waiting for you to find it again."

Kidd shook his head. "I spent a week and a half driving out here from Connecticut, Reverend. If I haven't found my way yet, I doubt I'm going to."

"Maybe that was the old way," Stubbs said. "Maybe what you need is a new path."

"Maybe so, Reverend," Kidd said. "Maybe so." He tightened his jaw to stifle a yawn. He was starting to feel tired. The agonizing high of his aborted run was wearing off, and he became acutely aware that he stank. "I should be going," he told the pastor.

Kidd stood and helped Reverend Stubbs to his wobbly knees. Stubbs grabbed Kidd's arm for balance, then he led Kidd out to the aisle.

"It was a pleasure speaking with you," the pastor said as he walked Kidd to the foyer. Kidd kept a hand at Stubbs's back to keep the reverend vertical. For a man so young, Harland Stubbs walked very old.

"Maybe we'll see you again real soon," Stubbs was saying. "We have a service coming up at 11:30. Maybe you'd want to catch that. Maybe you could stop in."

Kidd laughed. "You know, Reverend, you have a lot of 'maybes' in you."

"I suppose that's true," the pastor said. "But you've got to understand, Mr. President, that 'maybe' is all we're guaranteed in this world. Maybe it will rain and maybe it won't. Maybe that pretty girl will fall in love with me or maybe she'll never know who I am. Maybe I'll get cancer and die young or maybe I'll live to be a hundred years old. 'Maybe' is the Lord's way of keeping us on our toes. The trick is to love your life, whatever happens. Even if what happens is bad, like getting fired because of a sex scandal."

"Or getting flung off a motorcycle in a drunken stupor," Kidd added.

"Ain't that the truth," Stubbs said soberly. He brought Kidd through the foyer and over to the main door. Then he placed his hand on the door's push plate and offered his stump to Kidd. "It was nice to meet you, Mr. President," he said. "I must admit, you're a better man than I thought you were."

Kidd reached for Stubbs's stump and shook it. The former president's eyes, and his grip, lingered on the arm for a moment, as if he were inspecting something. Stubbs noticed the look. "What is it?" he asked.

Kidd said, "Doesn't it seem odd to you, Reverend, that your last name is Stubbs, and here you went out and got into a motorcycle accident that left you with, well, a stub for an arm?"

Stubbs clicked his tongue, pondering. "Sort of like cosmic predetermination? The name begets the destiny?"

"Exactly," Kidd said.

"I suppose so," Stubbs said. "But it's funny you say that." With his hand, the pastor pushed the door open, casting Kidd into the bright sunlight of a warming Sunday morning.

"What's funny?" Kidd asked as he stepped out onto the marble stairs and turned back toward Stubbs, shielding his eyes from the blinding rays.

Stubbs said, "Because, President Kidd, I always thought the same thing about you."

Before Kidd could take Stubbs's comment any which way, the pastor winked at him and smiled, then the church door closed.

CHAPTER 41

★ ★

The sound of snapping fingers—it grew louder in Kenny's ears, pulling him out of darkness, until he opened his eyes and saw a pencil-necked man peering down at him from above.

"Young man," the pencil neck would say, then he would snap his fingers at Kenny's face and say it again. "Young man."

The sight of Kenny's eyes coming open backed the pencil neck away. He looked down at Kenny, cocked his head, and seemed to be awaiting some reply. But Kenny was in no mood to reply. He didn't even know where he was. Who was this guy snapping fingers in his face? Why was his back killing him? And what time was it? Hell, what day was it?

"Are you all right?" the pencil neck asked.

Kenny could only growl in return. His mouth felt as tanned as the leather. Kenny ran his tongue over his teeth, blinked his eyes, then he looked up at the man and asked, "Huh?"

The pencil neck said, "You're in my classroom. We're about to study trigonometry. Why are you sleeping on the floor?"

Classroom? Kenny thought. Sleeping on what? What the hell is this guy talking about? Kenny pushed himself up. His sore back slid against a wall until his head hit a hard metal beam. Kenny looked up and noticed a tray for chalk, then a chalkboard. "Classroom," he mumbled. "Aw, shit."

Kenny stood up and saw, over the instructor's desk, a sea of students staring at him from their seats. It appeared to Kenny that each student had walked in, noticed him lying there, but waited for the professor—this pencil-necked man with snappy fingers—to arrive so he could deal with the issue. A few hefty students in the back, clearly the jocks, were snickering.

"There's something in your collar," the professor said. He brushed his hand along his neckline for guidance. Kenny looked down. There was a sheet of paper tucked into his shirt like a bib. He removed the paper and unfolded it. Inside, written in flowing dark pencil lead, was a message from Annabelle. It read:

Ken—

I tried to wake you. I can't wait anymore. I have to go back to my room, shower, then run to Cass Hall for the test at noon. Thanks for all your help. You don't know how much I appreciate it. I'll let you know how I do.

Hearts, Annabelle

Kenny tucked the note into his shirt pocket. His tired mind was suddenly invigorated by the thought of Annabelle Kidd stepping naked into the shower. Kenny envisioned every square inch of her wet body, from her slick gingerbread hair to the ruby-colored nails at the ends of her toes. The image did more for him than a jolt of coffee. It even woke up Elvis.

"Ahem."

Kenny glanced to his left. The professor was staring at him with crossed arms and a stern expression. "Will you be joining us?" he asked. "Or do you have somewhere to go?"

"My apologies," Kenny said. He strode past the professor and made his way to the classroom door, all to a serenade of whispers and snickers, particularly from the jocks. As he left the room, he heard the professor say, "Now that we've evicted the squatters, let us turn to page——" But the professor's voice was drowned out by a roar of laughter.

It was right at that moment, listening to the laughter created at his expense, that Kenny had a fresh thought—Whatever! So what if people were laughing at him? So what if he had just been embarrassed in front of an entire class of trigonometry students? As a college course, trigonometry was for morons anyway. So what if he looked like hell and felt worse? Overnight, Kenny realized, it was as if his pale Irish-Saxon skin had grown an outer layer of impervious seagull feathers. He didn't care about those students or their pencil-necked professor. He didn't care that he had fallen asleep on the floor of a classroom. He didn't care what any of them thought, jocks included.

Kenny looked at his watch as he made his way down the staircase to the first floor. It was a few minutes before noon. Annabelle would be at Cass Hall, gearing up for the test of her life. He whispered to her a curt pep talk—"Remember to feel like you're going to rip the shit out of it, Annabelle!"—then he crashed through an exit door and stepped into cascading sunlight. It was another warm, beautiful day in Southern California, but Kenny couldn't wait to find the Cadillac and get back to the hotel. He was ready to step into a shower of his own.

Kenny parked the Cadillac at a subterranean garage near the corner of Broadway and Ocean Avenue, then he came streetside and walked a hundred yards to the Mendelssohn, his back finally loosening from the night spent on a classroom floor.

As Kenny entered the Mendelssohn, everything seemed normal. He bellowed a hearty "Good morning!" to the bellboy. He waved a friendly hand at the woman manning the reception desk. The elevator car was even waiting for him when he pushed the "up" button. But when Kenny got off the elevator at the eighth floor, he discovered that something was terribly amiss the Mendelssohn.

His keycard didn't work. Kenny tried the card every which way. He inserted it slowly then whipped it out. He jammed it in and dragged it out. But the door wouldn't unlock. Abandoning the card, he jiggled the handle and wailed against the kick plate with his foot. He pounded on the door until his hand ached. Kidd was either not in the room or not willing to open up.

Kenny took the elevator down to the lobby and made harried strides to the reception desk. The woman was gone. In her place Kenny found an overly-coiffed, impeccably-groomed pretty boy of about twenty-five, someone who was obviously biding his time at the Mendelssohn until a movie offer came through. As Kenny approached in a huff, the pretty boy looked up at him and narrowed his blue eyes.

"May I help you?" he asked.

Kenny slapped his keycard on the counter. "This doesn't work."

"That's not good," the pretty boy said. He lifted the card, inspected its front and back, and asked Kenny for the room number. He punched Kenny's reply into a computer. Then, after a few seconds, he blinked twice at the screen and said, "This is interesting."

"What's interesting?" Kenny demanded. Kenny didn't want interesting. He wanted a shower.

The pretty boy said, "You've been staying with former president Kidd."

"That's correct," Kenny said.

The actor-cum-desk clerk pointed a finger at the computer screen and told Kenny, "It says here that Mr. Kidd has changed the status of his suite to single occupancy."

"Single occupancy," Kenny said. "What does that mean?"

"It means Mr. Kidd has requested to occupy his room alone," the pretty boy said.

"Alone?" Kenny cried.

"That's correct," the pretty boy said.

"You mean he kicked me out?!" Kenny shouted. His voice shot across the lobby and into the restaurant, where several diners looked toward the reception desk.

"Well, let's see," the clerk said, inspecting the screen. "Are you Mr. Kenny Kernick?"

"I am," Kenny said.

"Then yes," the pretty boy said, "Mr. Kidd kicked you out."

Kenny's jaw dropped. All he could manage to say was, "What-huh?"

"There's a note here that says your belongings are in the storage closet, and I'm to have them brought to you." The clerk tapped his hand on a ringer, sending a forceful, metallic ding through the lobby. The bellhop to whom Kenny had so cheerfully offered morning salutations appeared.

"Jason," the pretty boy said, "please bring Mr. Kernick's belongings from the storage closet." Jason, who was tall, scrawny and a little too compliant for Kenny's tastes, nodded and disappeared through a door behind the desk. The clerk turned back to Kenny and raised his streamlined eyebrows. "Do you need me to fetch you a cab, sir?"

"No, I don't need you to fetch me a cab," Kenny said. "I need you to fetch me a room."

"You'd like another room?" the pretty boy asked.

"No, I'd like *my* room," Kenny said. "The one I earned by driving Charles Bentley Kidd's fucking ass all the way across this country."

"There's no need for language, sir," the pretty boy said. He looked so perfectly assembled that Kenny wanted to punch him in the nose just to see some blood mess up that crisp shirt.

"What there's no need for," Kenny said, "is this bullshit. Kidd and I are like that." Kenny flashed the pretty boy two intertwined fingers. "And you're telling me he just decided to throw me out? Why would he do something so rash?"

"I'm not a mind reader, Mr. Kernick," the pretty boy said. "What I can tell you is that his name is on the account and he made the request at a quarter to ten this morning. And we must abide by it. It's a legal issue, you understand." The pretty boy hit a button on the computer and Kenny watched Kidd's information disappear. "Now, if you have a major credit card, I'll be happy to get you a new room. Do you have a major credit card?"

In the two weeks since leaving Simondale, Kenny had rarely been forced to think about money. Kidd had provided for every necessity and want. Thinking about it now, all Kenny knew of his financial picture was that he had approximately one hundred and fifty dollars of cash left over from his nights out in Vegas. He certainly didn't have a major credit card. He told the pretty boy as much.

The pretty boy frowned, but Kenny could see that it was an insincere gesture. "Then until you work out this issue with Mr. Kidd," he said, "you're no longer a guest at the Mendelssohn. I recommend you take your belongings and search for accommodations elsewhere. There's a Happy Traveler Inn by the pier, if you don't mind fruit-fly infestations and the smell of stale urine."

Jason the Bellhop emerged from the doorway behind the reception desk. He was lugging Kenny's bulging hockey duffel bag. The pretty boy waved a hand at Kenny as if instructing him to take the bag and get lost.

But Kenny held his ground. He planted his feet, folded his arms, and glared at the pretty boy. "I'm not going anywhere," he said.

The pretty boy glared back at Kenny, folded his own arms and said, "Now *that* is interesting." Then he glanced at the bellhop and flashed a conspiratorial smile.

For such a scrawny boy, Jason the Bellhop was incredibly strong. Kenny still couldn't understand how Jason managed to carry the heavy hockey duffel bag under one arm while lugging Kenny under the other. In a blur of motion, Kenny and his belongings were whisked through the Mendelssohn, across its veranda and down the steps, where they were dropped onto the sidewalk from a height of two feet. The duffel bag landed with a soft thud, but Kenny wasn't as lucky. He hit the concrete so hard his glasses flew off. He spent a full minute searching the sidewalk for them before he changed course and found them in the street, just below the curb. When he popped them back on,

Jason the Bellhop was gone, but a group of diners had gathered at one of the restaurant's front windows, their heads piled into the frame like a display of honeydew melons at the local Stop 'N Pick. Except honeydew melons were inanimate, but these people—they were laughing at him.

Kenny pressed the gas pedal to the floor and sped the Cadillac through brisk Los Angeles traffic as he headed up the 405. He wasn't going to take Sucky Chucky's betrayal lying down, so he decided to enlist the help of the only person who could understand his plight—Annabelle.

He remembered that she was taking her test in Cass Hall. Once on campus, Kenny asked for directions from a security guard, then he found his way to the hall after getting lost twice. The streets of the campus were fairly quiet, giving Kenny an indication that noon classes had not yet let out. He rolled the Cadillac up to the curb across from Cass's main entrance, then he jammed the vehicle into park and waited.

Seven minutes later, students began to trickle out of the hall. A few minutes after that, the trickle became a deluge. Kenny stepped out of the Cadillac and paced the length of the vehicle as he scanned the crowd for any sign of Annabelle. Not knowing what she was wearing made the task more difficult—he just couldn't pick her out, especially among a mass of students who all dressed and looked the same. Maybe she had taken a back exit; maybe he should just go to her dorm. Kenny didn't know what to do, and his anxiety was starting to mess with him. At one point, he had to stifle an urge to run around the car in circles like a confused dog chasing its tail.

When the flow of students had dwindled to a trickle and Kenny was about to depart, he finally saw her. Annabelle sauntered out of Cass Hall by the side of another man—an incredibly handsome dude, Kenny had to admit, but not a pretty boy at all. He looked fairly down-to-earth. He was well built, had curly black hair, and was dark of complexion. To Kenny, this guy looked like a Greek god, and Annabelle appeared happy with him. She jostled him at comments he made and often tapped his arm to convey a point. Kenny wanted to drive away. He at least wanted to hide in the Cadillac and wait until Annabelle and her beau passed by without noticing him. But as he made his move to open the car door, Annabelle saw him. She smiled an even broader smile than she had flashed at her Greek god, then she bid the beau adieu and ran to Kenny. When she got to him, she wrapped her arms around him and squeezed hard.

"I did it! I did it! I did it!" she yelled, jumping up and down. "I did what you said—I tore that test apart! Ripped it up! Made it my bitch! Thank you, Ken! Thank you!"

She pulled back but took his hand into her own, and all Kenny could think was, God, this girl is beautiful. Her gingerbread hair, pulled into a ponytail, seemed ready to eat, and her green eyes sparkled against the midday sun like emerald fire. He couldn't help but smile at her joy. "That's the Kernick Guarantee," he said. "Thankfully, I don't have to pay it off by making me your bitch." Although Kenny would have made himself Annabelle Kidd's bitch in a millisecond, and gladly.

She slapped him playfully. "Oh, Ken," she said. Then she looked at him strangely. "But what are you doing here?"

"Why?" he asked. He suddenly felt like an intruder. "Was I interrupting something? I didn't take you away from your boyfriend, did I?" Kenny motioned toward the departing Greek god.

Annabelle glanced in the direction Kenny indicated. "My boyfriend?" she said. She looked back at Kenny and laughed. "You mean Andre? Oh no, Ken, he's not my boyfriend. He's not any other girl's boyfriend, either. He's gay."

"Oh, he's gay," Kenny said. A sense of relief enveloped him.

"You get that a lot around here," Annabelle said. "Incredibly good-looking, incredibly sweet, incredibly smart, and incredibly not interested. Well, maybe he'd be interested in you. Andre loves red hair." Annabelle giggled. "So what's going on? I'm sorry I had to leave you on that floor, but you were out."

"It's your father," Kenny said.

Kenny watched as Annabelle's playful demeanor evaporated. Her mouth crooked, and there was an ever-so-slight tightening of the cords in her neck. Clearly, she was bracing for impact. Kenny imagined she must have braced for impact a lot over the past two years, whenever her father became the topic of conversation.

"What did he do now?" she asked.

Kenny told her what Charles Bentley Kidd had done.

Annabelle's eyes went wide, then narrowed menacingly as Annabelle pursed her lips. Her face took on a fearsome appearance, much like Kenny had witnessed on Margaret Huff back in Chicago, when the former first lady had been forced to deal with the reviled husband who had just crashed her Retard Party.

But Annabelle didn't go nutty like her mother had done. She didn't lay down a bedrock of vulgarities, nor did she search for a security detail to sic on her father's ass. Instead, she held out her hand, palm-up, and said calmly, "Give me your keys."

Before Kenny knew it, they were back in the Cadillac and racing toward Santa Monica on the 405. With Annabelle driving.

"Does he have a cell phone?" she asked Kenny. The Cadillac cut sharply around a Mack truck, throwing Kenny into the passenger window. Kenny reached up and grabbed the strap handle above his head—Annabelle Kidd drove like a maniac.

"I never saw one," Kenny said, holding on for his life as Annabelle overtook a pack of motorcycles and cut in among them, scattering the bikes to all lanes as she turned off the 405 and onto the 10.

"Figures," she said. "That would make it too easy for him to get caught at things. If he'd had a cell phone when he was president, do you think he could have screwed around like he did? My mother would have nailed him to a tree the first time out. Brace yourself—" Annabelle took the curve to the 10 at a speed Kenny estimated to be eighty-six miles per hour. He had to estimate, because at some point, he closed his eyes out of terror. The turn made his stomach fly into his throat. He thought he heard the tires squeal. Or was it his bowels?

"Well, we're going to get to the bottom of this," Annabelle said. With a flat stretch of the 10 ahead of her, she roared the Cadillac onward. Pretty soon they were doing one hundred.

"It's that exit there," Kenny said, pointing to the Fifth Street turnoff.

"Got it," Annabelle said. She slammed on the brakes and glided off the freeway. Then she made a rolling right at the stop sign and charged toward Colorado Avenue.

"I usually take Broadway," Kenny said to her, indicating the next road down.

"Not today," Annabelle said. "There are always too many people at that Third Street Promenade, and I'm really in the mood to hit the first asshole who pisses me off."

Annabelle turned down Colorado Avenue and raced forward as if she might just plunge the car into the Pacific Ocean. At the last second, she made a right onto Ocean Avenue and Kenny felt his internal organs flatten with the arc. They ran a red light at the intersection of Broadway, and the Mendelssohn soon appeared on the right. Annabelle pulled into a fire lane in front of the building and threw the Caddy into park. As she and Kenny emerged from the vehicle, Jason the Bellhop charged down the steps. "You can't park that car here, ma'am," he said.

"Shove it," Annabelle told him. "Follow me, Ken."

She charged up the steps, across the veranda and into the Mendelssohn's lobby. When Kenny finally caught up with her, she was already engaged in a heated discussion with the pretty boy.

"Where is he?" Annabelle was demanding.

"I told you, Miss Kidd, I don't know," the pretty boy said. "Your father left hours ago. A driver picked him up." To Kenny, this little prick seemed more subservient with a fiery Annabelle Kidd in his face.

"Ring him, please," Annabelle said.

"But Miss Kidd, he's not here," the pretty boy said.

Annabelle glared at him. "Ring—his—room!" she ordered.

The pretty boy picked up the receiver and punched in a number. All three of them—Annabelle, Kenny, the pretty boy—waited as the call went through. Jason the Bellhop ambled in from outside and leaned back behind the reception desk.

"I'm just getting voice mail," the pretty boy said.

"Give it to me." Annabelle snapped the receiver out of his hands and put it to her ear. "Daddy, this is your daughter," she said when the voice mail began to record. "I'm very disappointed in you, Daddy. Do you hear me? You've left Ken in the lurch. After all he's done for you, and for me, how could you do that? I want to speak with you, Daddy. Understand? I want to speak with you immediately. So you better call me back." Annabelle left Kidd her phone number. "You call me right away, Daddy. Or so help me—you don't have the Secret Service to protect you anymore." Annabelle threw the receiver back to the pretty boy. "Slam it down," she said. The pretty boy didn't even ask for clarification; he slammed the receiver into its slot.

"Now, my friend here needs a room," Annabelle said.

The pretty boy appeared genuinely terrified. Even tall, scrawny Jason was stooping under the pressure of Annabelle Kidd's tremendous five-foot eleven-inch force. The pretty boy cowered then said, "I offered your friend a room, Miss Kidd, but he didn't have a credit card."

"Oh, a credit card is all it takes?" she said. Annabelle reached into her Sadrine Gravos bag and pulled out a wallet. "Then we'll use mine."

That's when Kenny stopped her, putting his hand on her forearm and guiding the wallet down. "Annabelle, this place is six hundred dollars a night," he said.

"Six-fifty," the pretty boy corrected.

"I don't care," Annabelle said to Kenny, struggling to pull out her credit card.

"I do care," Kenny said. "I'll be fine, really. Trust me. Besides, your father and I didn't even sleep in a hotel room until we got to the Mississippi River."

"You're not sleeping in your car, Ken," Annabelle said. "Not in Los Angeles. You'll wake up with a gun in your face."

The pretty boy piped in, "There's a Happy Traveler—"

"Shush!" Annabelle told him, and he shushed.

Annabelle lowered her wallet. She looked across the lobby and out through the main doors, toward the distant ocean, then she let out a harried sigh. When she turned back, she eyed Kenny thoughtfully, as if she were calculating a plan. Finally, she said to the pretty boy, "Ring my father's room again, please."

The pretty boy picked up the receiver and dialed the number for Room 819. He handed the phone to Annabelle.

Annabelle waited for the voice mail to pick up. When it did, she said, "Daddy, I forgot to mention: If you're looking for Ken directly, you can use that number I just gave you. He'll be staying with me." Then she reached over the counter and slammed the phone down herself. "Let's go, Ken," she said. "There's a lot to do, and I have a game to prepare for."

Kenny wished he could remember what happened next, but the only sensation he recalled was that of walking on a cloud. Soon they were back in the Cadillac and speeding toward the University of the West. Annabelle was caught up in an endless diatribe about obtaining a visitor parking pass, putting Kenny's car in the appropriate lot, getting his stuff up to her room, making her next class, then going to the field house to warm up for the game that evening between West and USC, and how inconsiderate her father was, and how she should have expected it, given his stellar history. Kenny tried to follow her rant, but he became distracted by something stirring in his pants. Frequently along the return trip to campus, Kenny had to squirm in the passenger seat to hide what was fast becoming an embarrassing secret—at the prospect of spending the night in Annabelle's dorm room, his Elvis had come alive. The little bugger had pulsed awake, shaken off his sleep and stretched. He was now stepping up to the microphone, which in this case was Kenny's zipper.

"You're being quiet," Annabelle said to Kenny at some point along the 405, once she had taken a breather from her rant.

Kenny laughed uncomfortably. It was true. Ever since they had left the Mendelssohn, he hadn't uttered a peep. But Elvis—oh, boy—Elvis was singing.

CHAPTER 42

★ ★

The drive back to the Mendelssohn found Kidd in a famously contented mood.

The former president had spent the entire day in Long Beach—a bustling city on the south coast which was so close to Los Angeles by geography, yet a million miles different in style, temperament and design. The idea to go there had come from Miguel the limo driver, a recommendation made off-the-cuff when he picked up Kidd at ten o'clock in the morning just after Kidd had ordered the staff at the Mendelssohn to change his room status to a single. Kenny, not returned from his evening with Annabelle, would not be returning at all. To celebrate, Kidd was hitting the road, and like wine country, he was once again heading to a place of Miguel's suggestion.

The first stop on the limo driver's tour was the RMS Queen Mary, a thirties-era luxury liner, now a floating hotel and museum, which was permanently docked at the tip of Queensway Bay and open to the public from ten in the morning to six at night. Although Kidd had seen many cruise ships in his day, and had even spent time on one years ago for a vacation, he couldn't help but marvel at the long sight of this Queen when the Lincoln pulled into the parking lot—its black hull as elegant as an evening dress on a classy grand dame; its shimmering white decks like pearls around the lady's neck; the triple red-and-black smokestacks a perfect hat for her silver locks. He paid his admission fee and used the self-guided tour to view the ship from bow to stern, meandering through the sparse Monday morning crowd and drawing only an occasional glance. He surveyed the sickbay and engine rooms, the radio facilities and children's play area, the wheelhouse and the officers' quarters. And while he enjoyed every exhibition for the rich history it offered, it was what Kidd saw when he came to the bow of the Queen that really rocked his boat.

While other tourists milled about the bow's starboard side, where they looked northeast toward stunning views of downtown Long Beach, Kidd found himself gravitating to the port side of the ship, facing southwest. There Kidd noticed, beyond the parking lot and the highway and a grove of palm trees swaying gently in the morning wind, the Port of Long Beach, a vast expanse of colorful cargo containers, graceful loading cranes and a fleet of commercial shipping vessels, some of those ships stacked six containers high above their gunnels.

Kidd stood at the bow to watch the controlled, precise movements of the loading cranes. There were more ships in port than the former president could count, and more containers around the yard than that. The gathered image before him was a blur of color from the varied markings of the containers, and it all reminded Kidd of one of those Magic Eye posters that Tom Prudell had tried to get him to stare at during a period of levity in the early days of the administration. Back then, Kidd had stared at that stupid poster for four minutes until the three-dimensional image of a Formula One racecar stood out from the print. But as Kidd stared at this view, at the vibrant inter-play of crane, container, and ship, the image that came to the front of his vision this time wasn't a racecar—it was a big fat dollar sign. Kidd was witnessing with his very own eyes the fluidity of commerce. To Kidd, such activity in this port on a simple Monday morning showed him that the United States' economy was moving again. That people were working. That consumers were buying. That the drenching rains of economic misfortune which had soaked the better part of his administra-tion were dissipating. The realization brought a grin to Kidd's face. Maybe someday, he thought, years from now, as econo-mists started to look back at when the recession officially ended and when the growth officially began, they would find it had all taken place during the last months of *his* time in office. Maybe they would even admit the fact that Charles Bentley Kidd, ne'er-do-well fuck-up extraordinaire, King of Distraction, the Pastry Licker, had actually bequeathed to the American people upon his departure from the presidency a long-awaited eco-nomic expansion.

But Kidd's day was hardly over after such comforting morn-ing revelations. His positive mood only increased later when Miguel drove him from the Queen Mary to Second Street, a vivacious area of boutiques, galleries and restaurants. Economic activity here was roaring as well. Shoppers flitted in and out of storefronts. Eateries were packed with boisterous afternoon crowds. Kidd even watched a stuffy gent in seersucker pants walk out of a gallery with the ugliest oil painting Kidd had ever seen. Kidd himself took in the offerings at several boutiques and galleries, contemplating gifts for Annabelle, some artwork for the house in Simondale (or whatever house he ended up liv-ing in next; he was no longer sure he wanted to return to Connecticut). He even bought himself an engraved gold money clip to celebrate the country's renascent economic fortunes. Finally, around dinnertime, he and Miguel straggled over to a Mexican restaurant which was managed by one of Miguel's cousins.

They drank margaritas at the bar, these opposites—one a white-bread former president, tall, handsome, and college-educated, with hair like lamb's wool; the other a struggling limo driver, short and rugged, Latino, a city-worn guy with features that had weathered early. They feasted on nachos and red enchiladas and spicy carnitas, then they ate their fill of rib eye steak stuffed with spinach, onions, mushrooms, jalapeños and mozzarella cheese. When they were sated on entrees, they ordered bananas with caramel for dessert and more margaritas to wash them down. And that's when Kidd learned all about Miguel Torres.

Kidd's limo driver was only twenty-seven years old, and yet he could already boast of having four children at home in Inglewood, although he wore no wedding ring. "An oversight," Miguel said. He and his wife had been contemplating divorce when she'd gotten pregnant with their fourth child, and after the birth a lawyer told him that if he ever wanted to see his paycheck again, he would be best served to stay married to the lovely Rosa for at least the next eighteen years. He told Kidd that his parents had come to the United States from Mexico when he was three years old, and that this country was the only country he could remember. He worked long days in the livery business, but three nights a week he went to a local university to earn his degree in physician assistance—a "glorified nurse," as Miguel called it, but he was fine with that; he had no plans to be a limo driver forever. His extended family was large by U.S. standards. He had seven brothers and two sisters, and more nieces, nephews, uncles, aunts and cousins than he could keep track of. He had even done a four-year stint in the United States Army after high school, attaining the rank of sergeant, and that for a short time Kidd had actually been his commander in chief. He boasted with pride that it was the G.I. Bill that was paying for his studies. He said that although he was not born in the United States, he considered himself one-hundred percent Uncle Sam and would have died for his country if he had been required to do so, but that he still valued his Mexican heritage immensely. "Being Mexican," he said to Kidd with a glint in his eyes, "is like being a rainbow on a gray day. We have a passion for life, a flavor. It shows in everything we do."

"I can see that," Kidd said. The former president wasn't lying. Everything about this restaurant spoke to a love of life— color exploded off the walls; the merengue music was layered and peppy; the food tasted more flavorful than anything Kidd had ever eaten; and best of all, the margaritas were strong. All seven of them.

When finally they departed the restaurant at ten o'clock, Miguel stood rock-solid sober, but Kidd was toasted. He suspected now, as he sat in the warm backseat of the Lincoln Town Car and watched the highway lights pulse by like strobes, that the abundance of alcohol coursing through his system was the major contributing factor to his present contented mood. But it was more than the alcohol that was making him happy, and it was more than the exciting day, and all the sights he had seen, and the gifts he had bought, and the food he'd eaten. His mood also had to do with Kenny.

Young Kernick was finally gone, never to return. Kidd had expelled the boy from the Mendelssohn, vanquished him to homelessness, and he knew Kenny well enough by now to know that Young Kernick could not recover from such a blow. Sure, Kenny had gotten stronger over the past two weeks, and sure, the runt had grown up some, but at his core he was still Kenny Kernick—a paper tiger when it came to fights in the jungle. In one stunning attack, Kidd had napalmed Kenny's meager ass. Now Kenny would be forced to haul his charred carcass out of town on the nearest low road.

"You know what I like, Miguel?" Kidd asked, trying to cover the fact that he could barely speak.

Miguel looked into the rear-view mirror. "What's that, Mr. President?"

"I like this car," Kidd said, slurring. "I like the Sissy of Los Angeles. And I like you, Miguel. You're a quality innaviggu... innavishu... innavidual. How'd you like to come and work for me? I'm looking for a new sheef of stash. Old one—gone. New one—you. Was'say?"

"Chief of staff, huh?" Miguel said. "Well, that is an honor, Mr. President. Can I think about it?" The limo driver seemed sincere in his interest.

"Think about it all you wan'," Kidd said. "No hurry. All the time in the world now. Bye, Kenny." Kidd flapped a wrist at the artificially-illuminated landscape of strip malls, parking lots and car dealerships. "Bye, bye, bye. Have fun catchin' crabs."

Kidd didn't know if he fell asleep next, but in the blink of consciousness, Miguel's Lincoln was pulling up to the Mendelssohn. As he stepped out of the car, Kidd felt his head roll on a painful swell. His buzz was wearing off.

Miguel came around to the door and helped Kidd steady himself. "Pick you up tomorrow, Mr. President?" he asked, buttressing Kidd's shoulder with a palm.

Kidd held his forehead in the tips of his fingers. Even Miguel's gentle voice struck his skull like the blow from a pile driver. Kidd grunted affirmatively, then said, "I'll call you in the morning."

"Sounds good, Mr. President." Miguel released his one-time commander in chief to the vagaries of gravity. "But if you get my voice mail, hang up and try again, okay? Once I get into bed, I'm a heavy sleeper." Behind Kidd, Miguel slammed the door, triggering another wave of pain along the tumid seams of Kidd's brain. Then the chauffeur added: "Just so you know, I had fun today."

Kidd turned and managed to toss him a smile. "I as well, Miguel," he said. "Excellent choices." Kidd's tone of voice suggested that those choices were simply the first in a long line of stellar decisions Miguel would be making for him in the future, once he had accepted Kidd's offer to become chief of staff.

Kidd watched Miguel drive off, then he turned and stumbled up the steps to the Mendelssohn. He walked through the lobby with bleary eyes and a perceptible sway, and he didn't even register in his mind that someone from the front desk was calling out to him—"Mr. Kidd! Mr. Kidd!"—until he was in the elevator and on his way up to the eighth floor.

Whatever they need can wait until tomorrow, Kidd told himself. He just wanted to get back to the suite and restore his sobriety.

On the eighth floor, he slid the keycard into the door lock, popped the handle and entered his room to a wall of darkness. He flipped up the light switch closest to the door, casting the sitting room into fluorescence. As he walked through the sitting room, Kidd took comfort in the sight of a pullout sofa not pulled out, the mark of his newfound singlehood. All he desired now was the flat expanse of bed followed by all-consuming sleep. But as he turned the corner to his bedroom, he noticed something strange—the bedroom door was closed, and a light was on behind it. Even though he was still somewhat frothed on alcohol, Kidd clearly remembered leaving the door open that morning, and he knew the maid wouldn't have left the light on, or even used it. She cleaned during the day, and the day had been bright.

But maybe she did leave it on, he thought. She had come in, cleaned up, changed the sheets, replaced the towels, left the light on, and closed the door behind her. No big deal. Then Kidd heard a clatter from behind the door—the sharp punch of metal hitting ceramic—and he knew an intruder was in his bedroom.

The first suspect was Kenny. The runt had gotten back into the suite, and maybe he was rummaging through Kidd's belongings in search of money. Such was the life of crime and destitution which Kidd now expected from his former protégé. The runt would have to be dealt with severely, Kidd realized. He must be taught a lesson. Nobody would blame a former president for giving an intruder the smackdown, even if that former president were the loathsome Charles Bentley Kidd. He reached for the closest object of demolition—a heavy brass jar lamp from the table near the couch. He ripped the cord from the socket and held the brass base like a football, in preparation to smash it against Kenny's hard, incorrigible head.

Kidd sneaked up to the door and listened silently, but he heard nothing. He gripped the door handle and twisted it slightly until he felt the latch click. Time to pounce, he told himself.

Kidd flung the door open. "Ah-ha!" he cried, staring at the bed, expecting to find Kenny sitting on the mattress and thumbing through Kidd's stash of bills. But what he found wasn't Kenny at all. What he found wasn't even male.

There, in Kidd's bed, lay Annabelle's friends Night and Day, looking as delicious as the last time he had seen them, just one year ago, when they had departed the White House with Annabelle on the Sunday after Thanksgiving. On this night, however, in this bed, the only thing each had departed was her clothing: Both were as naked as *Playboy* playmates. The girls had thrown the bedspread over a chair and were slinking on the bed sheets, their legs, torsos and arms intertwined like two cats ready to toy with Kidd's mouse. "Hi, Chucky!" they said in unison. Kidd dropped the lamp to the floor and heard the bulb break.

He went to say something, but all he could manage was an incomprehensible stutter. Suddenly his mouth felt dry, and his loins alive.

"What's the matter, Mr. President?" Day asked. "Aren't you happy to see us?"

Oh, Charles Bentley Kidd was so happy to see them. How could he not be? At the first sight of these girls in his bed, Kidd had become flush with the memory of their inaugural encounter last year—

Night, over dinner that Saturday, asking if she and Day could sleep in the Lincoln Bedroom just once before they left. Kidd obliging, but warning that the Lincoln Bedroom was notoriously haunted. Day giggling, saying that if Mr. Lincoln showed up, they'd show him a thing or two. Kidd taking that statement as a complete come-on, even though he doubted any impartial observer in the room thought of it that way, including Margaret.

Kidd saying goodnight to Annabelle and the girls later in the evening, then trying to sleep, but the massive throb of his Lil' Kidd keeping him awake. Telling Margaret he was going down to get himself some warm milk. Margaret not even bothering to reply. Kidd getting lost on the way to the kitchen and finding himself at the door to the Lincoln Bedroom. Knocking. The door opening. Night standing there in her sweatpants. Day saying, "We hoped you'd come." Night pulling him into the room. His clothes flying off. Their clothes flying off. Making a sandwich. Going back for seconds. And thirds. Finally, at five in the morning, stumbling out of the Lincoln Bedroom. Fetching his warm milk. Walking over to the Map Room. Falling asleep as he looked over some of Prudell's memos. Waking up to shouts by Margaret to come out and say goodbye to Annabelle and her friends. Hiding any lingering evidence from the night before with a quick shower. Bidding Annabelle adieu with a promise to see her and the girls on campus soon. Night winking at him in approval of the idea. Day furtively grabbing his ass on the way out to the north portico.

No, he wasn't just happy to see them. He was fucking elated.

With no ability to offer a verbal response, Kidd let his eyes flow over every part of their exposed bodies. Night was tall and trim and had locks the color of licorice sticks; Day was shorter and more compact, with hair like a Norwegian porn star. He couldn't deny it: He wanted to slide between these girls right then and there, like a prime slice of honey-baked ham. Apparently his Lil' Kidd was having similar thoughts, because Old Chucky Bent suddenly realized that his penis was pointing at them.

"Well at least somebody's glad to see us," Night said, eyeing the bulge in Kidd's pants.

They were on him in an instant, these tigresses, like predators to a hint of blood. They tore at him, ravaged him, filled his ears with such graphic descriptions of what they were going to do to him—and for him—that even Kidd blushed. Kidd's shoes and socks ended up on the sitting room floor, his shirt and pants flew to the toilet, then his boxer shorts disappeared as if part of a magic trick. In communal nakedness, as they wrapped themselves around and over each other, Kidd could smell their bodies, taste their skin, and those sensations unleashed in him the most base desires for penetration and thrust. All he needed was a sign to act on those desires, an indication that the time had come to "get busy," to use Annabelle's words from Saturday's lunch. He got that sign when Day climbed up onto his back like a cowgirl to his bronco while Night lay out before him. It was sandwich time. All he had to do was bring out the meat.

And get busy.

To use Annabelle's words.

Annabelle, Kidd thought. Oh, Good Lord, Annabelle!

Kidd's reaction to the thought of his daughter was automatic and involuntary. Before he knew it, he had bucked Day off his back, pulled up from between Night's legs and backpedaled to an empty corner of the room, his hands making a feeble attempt to cover his erect Lil' Kidd. He heard himself saying, "Whoa, whoa, whoa!"

"Chucky, what's the matter?" one of them asked.

What the hell is the matter? Kidd wondered. He didn't know. He should have been laying down some Miracle Whip by now. Instead, he was standing in the corner of the room with his dick in his hands, while two naked, willing females stared at him from the bed.

"But you're girls," he gasped, finding his answer. "You're just girls."

Day looked at him fiercely. "We were girls last year, too, Chucky. Even younger ones."

"That didn't stop you from getting busy with us back then, did it?" Night said.

"I thought you liked our sandwich," Day said.

She was so right. Kidd loved their sandwich. He wanted more of it. But the image of Annabelle played through his head. Night and Day were his daughter's age. They were children in adult bodies. He wouldn't want any man of his years seducing Annabelle. Christ, he didn't even want Kenny Kernick seducing Annabelle. Kidd couldn't imagine how he would ever explain to the fathers of these girls that he had discovered (and worse, partaken of) their most precious secrets.

"I think you have to go," Kidd said. He reached for the bedspread on the chair and tossed it over them.

"What are you talking about?" Night said.

"I need you both to leave," Kidd said. "It's not you, it's me. I have to be alone."

Day kicked the bedspread off her body. "I'm not going anywhere," she said. "I'm ready to explode here."

Night said, "Either I get laid, Chucky, or I get nasty. You know the old saying—Hell hath no fury like a woman who doesn't come."

"Trust me," Kidd said, "I was married to Margaret Huff once. Nobody understands that better than I."

Kidd gathered up their street clothes, which had been stuffed under the bed, and placed them at their feet. The girls were glaring at him, flushed and sweaty. It was not a look of love.

"Listen," Kidd said, trying his best to appease. "My former chief of staff is probably floating around here somewhere. His name is Kenny Kernick. He's short, and skinny, with red hair, but he's got a solid pecker and a sex drive that could drink you under the table. Find him and you'll make the king of all sandwiches. I promise."

Day let off a dismissive snort. "Yeah, like that's gonna happen."

"You'll love him," Kidd said, pointing toward the window with an extended thumb. "He drives a Cadillac. His father's rich. A real catch. I only kicked him out a few hours ago. He couldn't have gotten very far."

"You can say that again, Chucky," Night said.

"We know who he is," Day said.

"And where he is," Night said.

"Okay," Kidd said, confused over these girls' up-to-date intelligence. "So where is he?"

"He's staying with Annabelle," Night said.

"With Annabelle?!" Kidd cried. Suddenly, Kidd felt as if a cold, wet hand had slapped him across the face, Aqua-Velva style.

"With Annabelle," Day said, punctuating both words for maximum effect.

Kidd wanted to collapse from shock. Instead, he managed to say, "Oh, please tell me you're joking."

"There's no joke about it, Chucky," Night said.

"No joke at all," Day said.

"He's practically living with her," Night said.

"She's devoted to him already," Day said.

"So much so," Night said, "that she refuses to leave him alone, especially after all he's done for her."

"It's so bad," Day said, "that she called me this afternoon to back out of our Thanksgiving trip, even though I told her she could bring him along."

"But the dorms are locked up from Wednesday to Friday," Night said. "The university wants everybody out."

"So they're going to drive up to wine country near Santa Barbara tomorrow night," Day said, "and get a room at a bed and breakfast for a few days. A little getaway before her volleyball games this weekend. To clear her mind, I'm guessing. And her pipes."

But it was Night who delivered the coup de grâce, a stinging surge that went right to Kidd's gut: "So if anyone is going to be getting busy with Ken Kernick, Chucky—tonight or at any time in the near future—it's *your* daughter. And while she's a generous friend, she doesn't share dicks. I know. One time I asked her if I could bang Peter, and she declined. I actually had to wait until they broke up to have sex with him."

Day slapped Night on the shoulder. "You did not!"

"I did so," Night said.

"You're such a slut," Day said.

Night pushed her away. "Oh, I am so not a slut compared to you, Petra. Peter told me he screwed you the afternoon before. In a classroom at Squires, even."

"Oh, he did not tell you that!" Day cried.

"Oh, he did tell me that," Night said.

"I guess I'm busted," Day said.

"You're busted," Night said.

"Okay then," Day giggled. "We're both sluts."

"Fine," Night said conclusively. Then she turned her eyes back to Kidd, who was clenching his dick in his palm out of pure anger at the evening's revelations. "So Chucky," Night said, bringing Kidd back to the issue at hand, "are we all gonna do the dew or what?"

Do the dew? Kidd thought. Where did kids today come up with these silly sex euphemisms? But Kidd's anger was starting to boil in him, and he didn't reply to her inquiry. He couldn't gather the focus or the words. He simply turned, walked into the bathroom, and shut the door behind him. He waited until he heard Night and Day dress, curse him and depart the suite, then he hopped into the tub and cooled off his anger, and his libido, with a lengthy, intemperate shower.

What surprised him most about the girls' revelation was that this war with Kenny was still on. That Young Kernick hadn't been vanquished after all. That in Kidd's absence as he toured Long Beach, Kenny had crawled out from beneath a shattered bunker and set his limping forces upon a new, ballsier path of conquest—cohabitation with Annabelle. Kidd still remained confident of a victorious outcome. In his historical opinion, what had occurred in the war today was nothing more than a shifting of the front line five miles east, from the streets of Santa Monica to the campus of the University of the West. Kenny was still weak, and he still lacked the tactfulness of an experienced commander like Kidd. This war would go on briefly. The outcome was not in doubt.

By the time Kidd emerged from the shower, it was midnight. Darkness had long settled over the battlefield. That didn't matter to Kidd. He had some reconnaissance to perform, and the night would only make the task easier. But first, the former president required mobility. He needed transport. To that end, there was only one means. It was time to recall Miguel Torres to the Mendelssohn. Kidd's only hope was that he could catch his future chief of staff before the limo driver climbed into bed.

CHAPTER 43

★ ★

While Annabelle Kidd was tall for a woman, she was short for a volleyball player.

Yet, to Kenny's surprise, this undersized outside hitter, who could have easily come off as over-matched by her taller opponents, dominated the hardcourt—diving to the floor to dig out spikes, charging to the net to stuff shots, and bounding to the air to launch stinging attacks. And when she attacked the ball, she shed her graceful every day persona and took on the demeanor of the snarling University of the West Mountain Lion which emblazoned the front of her ocean-blue uniform. She growled as she slammed the ball to the opposing side, causing many reddened forearms, mumbled curses, or, in most cases, a nonreturnable ball. In the end, she did what all mountain lions ended up doing: She tore her opponents to shreds; she made them bleed rivers of terror; she ended their will to resist.

As a volleyball player, Annabelle Kidd was nothing short of spectacular. For all the talk Annabelle had given Kenny that she was too small for her position (where she would have liked to have been at least three inches taller, she said), she was a one-woman demolition machine, leading her team to a three-sets-to-one victory over the defending national champions. Irrespective of the final score, it was a grinding battle between the squads, made more difficult by a slew of early mistakes on the part of West that cost them the first set, nineteen to thirty. The Mountain Lions, spurred on by a vocal, rousing Annabelle, rallied strong after that, but the Trojans kept each set close, matching volley for volley, kill for kill, point for point, until midway through the fourth set when Annabelle went on a rampage. With her last shot—an explosive blast into the face of the Trojans' setter (a "six-pack," some West fan near Kenny called it)—the crowd erupted and the team mobbed Annabelle at mid-court. The sixteen-member squad jumped up and down and screamed, while the students from the stands came to the floor to join the celebration. The atmosphere was amazing for Kenny to watch. In a span of ninety minutes, the University of the West had humiliated its archrival, won its first-ever Pac-10 volleyball title, and made it to the NCAA tournament. More important, the program had instantly transformed from perennial doormat to emerging powerhouse, shedding decades of fetid volleyball history. Annabelle had been the spark for it all. Kenny even heard chatter in the stands that after this game, which saw her record her seventh straight double-double of kills and digs, Annabelle Kidd would surely make *Sports Illustrated's* "Faces in the Crowd" section. Kenny agreed. Maybe, as a prize, they would even send her a telephone shaped like a football.

After the game, Annabelle was surrounded by the press. Scribes from the print media stuck digital recorders to her lips to gather in every word, while videographers from the local television stations pointed cameras at her. For a quote in a newspaper, Annabelle would do just fine, but for the television spots she looked a mess. The gingerbread hair at her temples was matted and damp, other strands had worked out from their ponytail and were flying askew like kinked piano wire, and her cheeks had turned purple during the game. She was speaking in heavy breaths and sweat teemed from her skin. Regardless of such a tussled appearance, Kenny thought Annabelle had never looked sexier—her body flush with victory; her pores exuding pheromones to scintillate the senses; a woman extremely lick-worthy, even if that lick came off her elbow. Kenny wondered if high school boys at home, watching the eleven o'clock news just before they went to bed, would see her in this condition and think the same. If they would dream of her, develop crushes on her that would last for years, and would want to come to the University of the West just to trod the same ground as she. The thought made Kenny jealous. Then Annabelle reminded him of his new, special place with her, a place which trounced that of some enamored high school boy, when she looked up from the reporters and found him in the stands. Flashing her emerald eyes, she tossed him an exuberant smile and wiggled her fingers at him as if to say, "Hi, Ken!" Kenny felt his heart thump.

To his disappointment, Annabelle showered at the field house. She changed into street clothes and met Kenny in the stands about forty minutes after the game. While the stimulating scent of Annabelle's sweat was a sad loss, Kenny enjoyed the buoyant, citrus fragrance of her shampoo, which he could smell intensely in the wind as the two walked through a breezy Southern California evening. They were heading to Slobberchops, where Annabelle's teammates were gathering for their title-clinching celebration.

At Slobberchops, Kenny met a slew of beautiful athletes. There was Woo-Woo from Oklahoma—a middle blocker with flowing blonde hair who stood six-foot-six and looked like she could crush Kenny in her palm, and who, Annabelle whispered to him admiringly, was up for the Chase Award for excellence in inner-city volunteerism. There was Powder from Idaho— six-foot-two, an avid snowboarder with granola flair, who only came to Los Angeles, she said, for the volleyball scholarship. "Otherwise," she yelled at Kenny between chugs from her cup of beer, "you can take this whole self-absorbed town and stick it." There was Ro from South Central who was studying pre-med, and Val from Bakersfield who worked summers fixing transmissions on Mack trucks. There were Shawna and Campbell, Gwen and Nicole; there were Steph and Mallory, and Vicky and Nants. Then there was Tuggy, short for Thugasni, a five-foot-one freshman setter of Malaysian ethnicity who owed her place on the team to quick feet, accurate ball handling, and her ability to jump higher than most six-footers. With the exception of Tuggy, every woman on West's volleyball squad was taller than Kenny. They gave him the impression, as he weaved among them to get more food or drink, that he was walking through a forest of imposing sequoias, such was his eye-level view of their elongated trunks. In the recent past, a similar experience might have made Kenny feel miniscule, overwhelmed or vulnerable— a boy who was less than he could be—but tonight that notion didn't seem to matter to him. He had an appreciation of these women for their height, but he also felt the nascent rumblings of appreciating himself for his own height, however modest. By the end of the evening, after tilting his head upward time and again to meet their eyes, he chuckled inwardly as he was overcome with a feeling, not of pain in his neck, but that he had finally decided to like himself, irrespective of his shortcomings.

Kenny and Annabelle walked back to her dorm in peaceful silence. Perhaps Annabelle was still reflecting on her team's win, but Kenny was reflecting on the wind. It blew warm and stiff from the south, striking his face and tickling his ears, playing games with him. Its frolicking demeanor was so unlike the wind that had almost frozen him solid at the state police barracks in Massachusetts a month ago. That wind had foretold a time of struggle ahead, and for the most part, it had been correct, especially in Kenny's dealings with Carl. This wind, however, was not a harbinger at all—it was a beacon. It was guiding Kenny toward a bright future which was only now beginning to take shape in his mind—visions of goals he wanted to achieve, and the place he wanted to live.

When Kenny and Annabelle approached her room, Annabelle's phone chirped.

"Sarah flew home tonight," she said, reading a text. "Looks like we've got the whole place to ourselves." She grinned coyly, then fingered the combination on the lock and pushed the door open.

Her room smelled like a mixture of potpourri, fabric softener and soft soaps. Even though Kenny had partaken of this alluring mix of scents earlier in the day, when he and Annabelle had popped in that afternoon to drop off his duffel bag, he could now stand back and enjoy the smell for all the femininity it conveyed. He had missed this aspect of college life in his brief time at Harvard—the smell of a girl's room, and how the scent was as unique to her as a fingerprint. Once again, Kenny wished that he had dared to make the acquaintance of at least one girl at Harvard instead of swiping her drawers. Within him all the time lay the ability for such a bold action. He just hadn't known how to summon it.

Kenny took off his jacket, draped it over Sarah's desk chair, and flopped down onto the sofa that would be his bed for the night. He couldn't help but gaze at Annabelle as she tossed her Sadrine Gravos bag on her desk, slipped off her sandals and walked to her dresser, from which she pulled a white t-shirt and a pair of black yoga pants.

"I'll be right back," she said.

"Where are you going?" Kenny asked.

"To the bathroom." Annabelle held up the fresh clothing. "I want to get out of these jeans."

"You can change here," Kenny said.

Annabelle grinned at him. "Oh, you'd like that, wouldn't you, Ken? I'll be right back." She closed the door behind her.

Annabelle's absence left Kenny with time to survey the room. A set of bunk beds was pressed against one cinderblock wall; against the other wall was the desk belonging to the elusive Sarah—it was a disaster zone of scattered books, notepads, pencils, and unframed photos of her in punk regalia with some guy who had a chain connecting his nose to his earlobe. Annabelle's desk faced the footboards of the bunks and was immaculate. The only item out of alignment on it was the bag she'd just set down. The room had a mini fridge and an iPod dock near Sarah's desk, and a coffee table in front of the couch, but there was no television, even though the room had plenty of space for one. Kenny wondered if the lack of a TV might be the residual effect of Charles Bentley Kidd's downfall, when Annabelle would have been unable to tune in to a single channel without hearing some report, commentary or joke made at her family's expense.

When Annabelle returned, she was wearing her yoga pants and the t-shirt. She had also let down her gingerbread hair, the sight of which, falling onto her shoulders, made Kenny purr inwardly. She opened the closet door and stuffed the street clothes into a laundry basket, then she looked at Kenny and studied him as he sat on the sofa. She must have thought he looked bored because she said, "I'm sorry there's not much in the way of entertainment in here. There's a TV in the common room, if you want to watch something."

"I don't need a TV," Kenny said.

Annabelle raised an eyebrow at him and smiled. "Wow," she said. "I think you're the first guy I've ever heard say that. You don't need a nightly dose of *SportsCenter* to fall asleep?"

Kenny shook his head. He had no idea what *SportsCenter* was, but he didn't feel the need to explain. Instead, he said, "Usually, I just need a book."

"A book?" Annabelle said. She crossed the room and lifted a small tin off her desk. She opened it with a twist, dug in a flexed pinky and applied a smudge of balm to her lips.

"Most of my life has been spent in books," Kenny said.

"There are worse places to spend your life," Annabelle said. She set the capped tin on the desk and picked up a comb. Rubbing her lips together, she moved to the couch, sat opposite Kenny and tucked her legs under her. She started to work her long gingerbread hair with the comb, soothing out the knots. "I love books, too," she said. "I think I've devoured three a week since the age of five, although college has slowed that rate significantly. So tell me, what are you into? Who do you read?"

"What I'm into and who I read are two different things," Kenny said. He coughed uncomfortably. "I've mostly followed my father's curriculum—heavy nonfiction; overwritten classics. But if I had to say I was into anything, it would be my encyclopedias. He never made me read those, yet they were my trusty sidekicks, always available when I needed answers. And I like answers."

"Encyclopedias, huh?" Annabelle said. She rested the comb on the coffee table and pulled her hair into a ponytail. "Well, that explains it."

"What does it explain?" Kenny asked.

Annabelle tightened an band around her ponytail, then she dropped her hands to her lap and looked at Kenny in wide-eyed admiration. "What it explains, Ken, is why you're the smartest guy I've ever met. In my life. Hands down. I have to say, I think you really are a genius."

Kenny blushed, then he laughed. Her praise had caught him completely off guard.

Annabelle looked at him queerly. "What's the matter?" she asked. "I can't be the only one who has ever called you a genius."

Kenny sucked in his laughter. "I've been called a genius before," he said. "I've even been called 'geniusical.' But you're the only person who has ever called me a 'guy.' Most people still think of me as a boy. I love it every time you call me that."

"I see," said Annabelle. She slapped his knee playfully. "Well, just so you know, you're all guy to me, baby."

There was a long, pleasant silence between them. The scent of Annabelle's shampoo joined the air, and Kenny gazed at her anew. Annabelle Kidd was one of the most beautiful women he had ever seen. Her stunning visage and lanky body electrified him. And somehow, here he was, sitting beside her on her couch, in her dorm room, at her college. The unexpected craziness of the situation was enough to make Kenny let down his inhibitions. He leaned in toward Annabelle and kissed her.

Annabelle seemed taken aback at first, but she quickly became a willing participant. Her lips, freshly coated with balm, felt as soft as velvet, and they glided against his lips with gentleness and forethought. It became clear to Kenny that Annabelle Kidd wasn't merely reacting to his advances—she was kissing him back.

After thirty seconds, their lips unlocked with a sucking sound. Kenny left his head close to hers, sizing up the moment. It wasn't his first kiss ever. That had come via a Darby Duvall liquor-laced tongue missile. But this was his first tender kiss, with heartfelt emotion, and from the perfect girl. Under those conditions, he had expected to feel his universe explode in dazzle. At the very least, he expected some soulful connection. Instead he felt... nothing. It was a nice kiss, for sure, technically sound, but it came off like kissing his sister, if he had ever had one. Kenny opened his eyes and saw Annabelle contemplating the kiss as well. She looked at him, and in her look—a deflated smile—it was obvious that Annabelle felt the same way. As if to confirm her findings, she cupped a palm around his head, pulled him close and kissed him again with a long, solid lip lock. When she pulled back, she pronounced judgment on any future physical relationship between them with a curious "Huh."

They sat back together on the couch. "I'm glad I met you, Ken," Annabelle said, squeezing his thigh. "I'm glad you're here. You really are a breath of fresh air."

"I appreciate that," Kenny said.

Annabelle got off the couch and turned on some music from an iPod propped in the dock. Spare guitar tunes soon flitted about the room. Annabelle walked to her closet, pulled down a pillow and blanket for Kenny, and tossed them to him. While Kenny set up the couch as a makeshift bed, Annabelle grabbed a book from her bag.

"I have some reading for tomorrow," she said, walking back to the couch. "I usually study here. Mind if I join you?"

Although he had just settled into his bedding, Kenny sat up and held open the blanket, allowing Annabelle to climb onto the opposite side of the couch, facing him. Wrapping the blanket around her, she cracked open the book and began to read. Kenny followed her lead, reaching for a German Philosophy text on her desk and flipping it to a spirited summation of the works of Gottfried Leibniz, the eternal philosophical optimist. Both he and Annabelle read for a while, their legs growing steadily intertwined beneath the covers, but more and more they found themselves putting their books down for bursts of conversation. Before long, they weren't reading at all. They were chatting—about every possible topic under the sun, with passion and compassion, into the wee hours of the morning.

And to Kenny, this platonic interplay, free of desire or expectation, with a beautiful woman beside him, well, as Leibniz himself would have said, it was the best of all possible worlds.

CHAPTER 44

★ ★

The lights stayed on all night—that occurrence Charles Bentley Kidd verified with his own eyes.

On the Tuesday morning before Thanksgiving, as dawn broke in a shade of weepy gray over the campus of the University of the West, a one-time president of the United States found himself squatting in mud behind a row of waist-high hopseed bushes just off the campus's main road. He had been there for over four hours, as he studied a single illuminated window on the backside of Sycamore Hall, the window he best calculated from memory to be the location of his daughter's dorm room. He was cold from the wind, cramped from crouching low behind the bushes, and damp from the bouts of early-morning drizzle which had easily penetrated his dress slacks and cotton Burwick. But he was determined to see his reconnaissance through. At least he wasn't hungry—Miguel, who was squatting beside him, had done some intelligence gathering during his stint in the army; the logistics were old hat to him. To that effect, the limo driver had brought along a pair of high-powered binoculars, and more important, a handful of higher-powered energy bars. "You don't want a rumbling stomach when you're scoping out the Ivans," Miguel told him, handing over a cache of bars with an admonishment to keep their unwrapping quiet. Kidd concurred with Miguel's statement, although he wondered why such a young veteran was still using archaic Cold War terminology.

It could have been worse, this being wet, cramped, cold, and constantly having to duck behind the bushes when an automobile came up the road, lest someone call campus security. But the lights to Annabelle's room had stayed on all night, and that fact warmed Kidd more than any bits of nutritional sustenance. Given his sightline from the bushes, a mere hundred feet away and forty-five degrees down from the window, all Kidd could see, even with the binoculars, was a swath of room leading up to the ceiling. He had spied no sign of Annabelle or Kenny. He could only deduce that they were home, because at one point around three in the morning, a pillow had flown from one end of the window to the other, as if it had been thrown. Kidd didn't know what significance a flying pillow held, but the lights had stayed on and that's what mattered. As far as Kidd could tell, Kenny had not gotten Annabelle in the sack. He had not fondled her in the darkness. He hadn't violated her with that stupidly named penis. It was a comforting conclusion. He didn't even want to contemplate the plentitude of holes it contained. Then he just might have to vomit in these very bushes.

When dawn broke and the lights were still on, Kidd felt a wave of relief wash over him, not merely for the fact that the constant stream of illumination in Annabelle's room most likely indicated that she and Kenny had not engaged in coitus, but also for the fact that he could now go home to the Mendelssohn. He and Miguel gathered up their belongings, ducked behind the bushes, and crawled back to the parking lot where they had stowed the Lincoln Town Car.

During the ride to Santa Monica, Miguel peered into the rear-view mirror. He eyed Kidd like a schoolmaster scrutinizing a recalcitrant student. "Tell me what we learned tonight, boss," he said.

"I'm too tired," Kidd said. The former president had stretched out across the backseat and didn't want to answer questions. He just wanted to close his eyes.

"Good recon means better repetition," Miguel said. "What did we learn?"

Kidd let out a sigh. He sat up so he could better see the limo driver's expectant eyes in the rear-view, then he ran a hand through his damp hair. "That Kenny—" he said.

"Not Kenny," Miguel said. "The target."

"That the target," Kidd said, "has his vehicle parked in Lot Seven."

It was an invaluable piece of information, Kidd had to admit. Under Miguel's direction, the first order of business that night had been to find the Cadillac. They searched five lots at slow speed until they finally came upon it a quarter mile from Annabelle's dorm. It was parked in a middle section of spaces and had an orange visitor tag dangling from its rear-view mirror. Although Kidd had never noted the Cadillac's exact license plate number, he was able to verify that it was Kenny's car by virtue of the many scrapes along its bumpers and side panels, blatant testaments to Kenny's earlier crap-ass driving.

"Near what building?" Miguel asked.

"Something named Squires," Kidd said, then he yawned.

"What's the significance of Lot Seven?" Miguel asked.

"It's a visitor lot."

"And what's the significance of that, boss?"

"It means that the Cadillac will probably be in that lot as long as Kenny—"

"The target—" Miguel said.

"The target—" Kidd said, "stays on campus. So it will be easy for us to find him without having to sit in front of the dorm, where we might be spotted."

"That's great, boss," Miguel said. "Excellent job." He veered the Lincoln to the on-ramp for the Santa Monica Freeway, also known as "the 10." The Mendelssohn was only minutes away, but Miguel forged on with his follow-up. "And what did we learn from our recon of the premises?"

"That Ken—" Kidd caught himself. "That the target is most likely in-house."

"Why?" Miguel asked.

Kidd remembered the pillow and mentioned how it had flown across the window.

"Indicating?" Miguel asked.

"Playfulness," Kidd said, although it was only a guess. The pillow hadn't been thrown so that someone would grab it and use it. It had been thrown like someone was trying to hit the other person over something said. Perhaps a snide comment.

"What else did you notice?" Miguel asked with a full mouth. He was chewing on one of the energy bars. True to his previous admonishment, Miguel had kept its unwrapping completely silent.

"That the lights stayed on all night," Kidd said.

"Indicating?" Miguel asked.

"They weren't *in flagrante*," Kidd said. Another warm feeling descended upon him.

Miguel swallowed the last of his energy bar, then he glanced at Kidd once more through the rear-view mirror. "Unfortunately, I see two problems with that conclusion."

"What's that?" Kidd asked reluctantly.

"First," Miguel said, "the Daisy could have attacked the target when he walked through the door, tearing his clothes off and bumping uglies with him right on the floor, or maybe even a desk, thus never turning on the lights until well after the act had been consummated."

Kidd felt his stomach go sour. "By 'The Daisy,'" he asked curtly, "do you mean my daughter?" But Miguel wasn't finished.

"Or she could be one kinky chiquita, boss," Miguel said. "The kind who likes to bump with the lights full on. My wife is like that. Let me tell you, it's hot, boss, hot! At least until they get stretch marks."

"Are we at the Mendelssohn yet?" Kidd asked, with no small hint of revulsion. He flopped back to his original position across the leather. His head was spinning.

"Getting off the freeway." Miguel took the exit for Fifth Street.

They pulled up to the Mendelssohn just before seven in the morning. Miguel parked in front of the hotel and got out of the Lincoln to attend to Kidd's door, but Kidd was already standing on the curb by the time Miguel arrived.

"You want me to come in, Mr. President?" Miguel asked. "Give you some security? Stay on call?"

Kidd shook his head. "Stay on call," he said, "but you don't have to come in. I'll be fine. I'll ring you in Inglewood if I need something."

"Okay, boss." Miguel shut the car door behind Kidd. "What's the plan for tomorrow?"

Kidd held up his hand as an indication for Miguel to slow down. "Don't know yet," he said. "Have to sleep on it."

"Well, remember what I told you about my cousin Enrique," Miguel said.

Kidd nodded, then he waved goodbye and walked into the Mendelssohn. Maybe it was because he was bone-tired, but Miguel had mentioned so many cousins during the course of their surveillance that Kidd had no idea what the hell the limo driver was talking about.

The eighth floor came just in time for Charles Bentley Kidd. He was about to fall asleep in the elevator.

Kidd stepped off the lift and made his way down the hall to the suite. Like the previous evening, he slid the keycard into the lock and opened the door. Also like the previous evening, as he stepped into his room, he heard noises. Something had shuffled in the general direction of his bedroom, indicating once more that an intruder had been startled by Kidd's arrival.

Kidd's first thought was Night and Day; they had sneaked in again. "You've got to be kidding me," he muttered. Couldn't these girls take "No" for an answer? Were they really so obsessed with him that they had to come back for another helping of rejection? Weren't there plenty of boys on campus to "get busy" with? No, this latest round of breaking and entering just wouldn't do. And this time when he kicked them out, he would be conclusively firm about their lack of future prospects. Maybe he would even claim that two days in Los Angeles had turned him gay.

Kidd walked over to the door of his bedroom. It was closed. "Come on out, girls," he shouted. Then he threw the door open.

What he found in his bedroom wasn't Night and Day. What he found wasn't even female. Kneeling beside Kidd's bed, rifling through Kidd's suitcase, was a short, stocky gentleman. He had a ragged moustache, fierce eyes, and a large head topped with gnarly brown hair. He was also wearing a neck brace, which Kidd found odd. The man was too well dressed to be a vagrant from the beach. What he was looking for in the suitcase, Kidd had no idea.

"Who the hell are you?" Kidd asked.

The gentleman stood awkwardly. He couldn't have been five-foot-nine, and from the way he was slouching, Kidd guessed that he was in severe pain from whatever incident had left him with the neck brace. But the man's weakened appearance was a ruse—his eyes and voice still carried ferocity. "You think this is funny?" the man asked.

"What?" Kidd asked. "Get the hell out of here. I'm calling security." Kidd made a move for the phone on the nightstand, but before he could reach it, the man lunged, picked it up and ripped it out of the wall, then he threw it at Kidd. The phone hit the former president in the chest.

"Oh my Christ!" Kidd said, gasping. "That hurt like a knobgobber!"

"You think this is funny?" the man asked again, but Kidd was too concerned with his chest pain to answer. In the strange irrationality of the moment, he was beginning to feel like Dan Rather when the former newsman got pummeled on Park Avenue by the guy shouting, "Kenneth, what is the frequency?" Kidd had always gotten a hearty laugh over that incident, but now that something similar was happening to him, he didn't feel so jovial.

"Look," Kidd said, grimacing from the blow to his chest, "I don't know who you are, but—"

"But what?" the man asked. He picked up the table lamp, tore the cord from the socket and threw that at Kidd as well. This time, Kidd didn't have to flinch. The man's stiffness impacted the throw and the lamp skidded across the rug. But the man kept on shouting: "Are you going to have me arrested? Deported? Are you going to make me disappear? What are you going to do, Mr. Kidd?" He picked up Kidd's suitcase and flung it forward. It struck Kidd in the legs.

"Goddammit!" Kidd shouted, flexing his left knee. "Listen, you peckerhead, I don't know what you're—"

"You think this is funny, don't you?!" the man yelled. He was coming at Kidd, menacingly, walking like a Frankenstein creation. "You think you just got the best of me, huh?!" His approach made Kidd backpedal into the sitting room, but the man lunged forward and caught the former leader of the free world by the shirt buttons. That's when the bearish man wiggled a finger at Kidd's face, looked sternly into his eyes and chanted, "*Abba de da, bah wenga! Abba de da, bah wenga!*"

"What the hell is that?" Kidd asked. "Yiddish?"

But the man kept on wiggling and chanting. "*Abba de da, bah wenga!*" he said more desperately. "*Abba de da, bah wenga! Abba de da, bah—*" Suddenly, the man stopped. He released Kidd's shirt, removed a book from his back pocket and inspected it. "I should have known this junk wouldn't work. Aw, frig it." He dropped the book to the floor, but before Kidd could glance at its cover, the man began to cuff Kidd in the head with everything he had. Kidd was in too much pain from the kink in his knee and the bruise on his chest to defend himself.

"You steal my neighborhood!" the man said. "Then you steal my vehicle! Then you steal my child! And you think you can get away with it?! Well, I've got news for you, Kidd, you're not the only one who wields power in this world! Did you really think I wouldn't catch up with you?! Are you really that much of a dummkopf?!"

By this time, Kidd had taken several whacks to the ears. He stumbled backwards on his pained knee and landed ass-down against the sofa. He stared with terror in his eyes as the man leaned over him, and suddenly, everything became clear to Charles Bentley Kidd. "Oh my God!" he cried. "You're Carl Kernick!"

"Very good, Bonehead," Kenny's father said. Then he raised his right hand and made a fist, priming the paw for a strike. Kidd gritted his teeth. His jaw would be at the mercy of this man's bearish strength. But before he attacked, Carl Kernick had one final question for Charles Bentley Kidd. It was delivered more as a threat than an inquiry:

"Now," he said, "where—is—my—boy?!"

CHAPTER 45

★ ★

In the end, it was a muscle spasm that saved Kidd from any further attack by Carl Kernick. Just as Kidd was about to tell Carl where Kenny was, Carl's back seized. Before Kidd could say a word, Carl cringed, arched backward and dropped to the floor, where he flopped on the carpet like a hooked fish thrown to the planks of a motor boat.

Always a man sympathetic to another's pain, Kidd climbed off the couch and knelt by Carl's side. "What can I do for you?" Kidd asked.

Carl grabbed Kidd by the collar. "P-p-pills," he said, gasping. "My pills. In my coat."

Kidd found Carl's cashmere coat in the bedroom and removed a vial of prescription Tylenol from the pocket. When he returned to the sitting room, Carl was leaning up against the couch and breathing shallowly. Carl grabbed the orange vial from Kidd, popped off the childproof cap, and tilted a Tylenol into his hand. He didn't need water, he said. He threw the tablet into his mouth and swallowed it whole.

For the next hour, Carl sat back against the couch and basked in the spreading relief of the Tylenol's codeine punch.

Kidd offered to order breakfast from Trala, the restaurant downstairs, but Carl said he didn't want breakfast, declining with a surly "No" Kidd's every offer of eggs, croissants, freshly-baked muffins, yogurt, fruit, cheese, bacon, potato soufflé, coffee, orange juice, or even toast. When Kidd asked him why he would pass up such a feast, especially since it was on Kidd's dime, Carl held up the orange vial of pills. "It's these Tylenol," he said. "I've been on them for a week. Stupid things left me constipated. I haven't wanted to eat in three days. Do you know what it's like to be constipated for days on end? I'll bet you don't." Then Carl snorted, his broad nose flaring its nostrils. "At least there's no pain with them."

No pain, sure, and apparently there wasn't any verbal on-off switch with them, either. For unlike Kenny, who could stay stubbornly silent under most circumstances, Carl Kernick never shut up. The thin lips of his mouth flapped more incessantly than a frayed flag in a hurricane. Kidd had hoped that by having Carl as his captive audience (stuck, as Old Kernick now was, against the front of the couch), Kidd could sit there with Kenny's father and gain the man's confidence. Perhaps he could even indenture Carl to him. By Kidd's logic, whom did you trust more than a person who had assisted you in a desperate time of need? And whom did you want to return a favor for even more than that? It was all a matter of *quid pro quo*. Kidd might need Carl someday. Someday in the near future, in fact. Someday like tonight. Because Kidd now had a plan germinating in his head, a plan to get rid of Kenny once and forever. All he had to do was think it out.

But Kidd could barely think at all around this man. Carl's voice was too penetrating. Old Kernick seemed supremely impressed with his own opinions and experiences, which he described to Kidd without the least bit of urging. Kidd discovered that everything in Carl Kernick's world was the biggest, the greatest, the most potent, and the most challenging. If Kidd hadn't known that Carl Kernick was a successful automation engineer, he would have guessed that the man sold cars, such was the distracting power of his hyperbole. During the rare times when Kidd managed to speak a word or two, he noticed that Carl would stare off blankly, wait until Kidd finished, then throw at Kidd a heavy barrage of counterpoint, somehow always managing to bring the topic of conversation back to himself. It was under these auspices that Kidd filled out the complete picture of how Kenny's father had come to intrude upon him in Room 819 of the Mendelssohn Hotel.

He said he had driven all night from Colorado to Los Angeles, a distance Carl estimated to be over one thousand miles. He told Kidd he had been tracking the Cadillac cross-country by way of a GeoStar GPS service. By early last week, he was hot on their heels, about a day out from catching them in Las Vegas, when he found himself the unwitting victim of a terrible vehicular accident in the Rockies. Hence, the neck brace. The doctors in the town of Dillon ordered him to lay up for two weeks while his whiplash healed properly. They had even prescribed the Tylenol to help him deal with the pain. But Carl Kernick boasted that he wasn't a man who laid up (and considering Martha Kernick's ravenous sexual appetites toward Kidd, boy, didn't Kidd know it). Carl called himself a doer, a mover. "I don't even stop long enough to sit on the john," he said. Thus, he had made a vow in the hotel room in Dillon that as soon as he could manage, he would get back on the road. He simply had to track down Kenny, if only to save his son from the wizard. Given the strange chant Carl had uttered at him during their previous confrontation, and the peculiar book on ancient spellbinding which Carl had dropped to the floor, the former president understood clearly that he was the wizard.

The Tylenol, Carl told Kidd, was a godsend, but its codeine fix caused him tremendous dizziness and some hallucinations. Therefore, he could not drive with any codeine in his system. For two days, Carl cut back on his dosage in order to gauge his pain. By yesterday morning, he could move well enough without Tylenol to hit the road. By yesterday evening, after making several phone calls, he had been able to rent a Dodge Stratus from the Hertz in Breckenridge. Although, truth be told, a Dodge was nothing he was accustomed to driving.

At which point, Carl brought up the Cadillac.

"How dare you steal my vehicle," he said to Kidd.

Kidd's breakfast had arrived during Carl's rant, and Kidd had a mouthful of omelet, but he shook his head vigorously. As soon as he swallowed, he said, "That was Kenny's idea."

"You expect me to believe that?" Carl said. "My son can't even tie his own shoes."

"He doesn't have to anymore," Kidd said. "He wears loafers now."

"Loafers," Carl repeated with disdain, as if his son's preference for shoes without laces indicated some sort of tendency toward sloth.

"And a leather jacket," Kidd added.

"Lovely," Carl said. He eyed Kidd coldly. "You still haven't told me where he is. The last few tracks I had on my vehicle showed it bouncing between Santa Monica and the University of the West. Why is Kenny spending time there? My son is terrified of colleges."

Kidd nibbled on a bit of potato soufflé. The time had come to set a trap for Kenny's bearish father. All through breakfast, during the microscopic breaks in Carl's rant, Kidd had been nurturing the plan to rid himself of Kenny. A slow grower at first, the plan had sprouted up magnificently once Kidd remembered who the hell Miguel's cousin Enrique was and what Miguel had been saying about him—that he worked as a level-three patrolman with the Los Angeles Police Department. Under that nugget of fertilizer, the plan bloomed, and its flowers smelled horrible, like mordant, fleshy decay, just the type of scent to attract a bear. Although Kidd felt confident that he could execute the plan without Kenny's father, he knew it would go easier if Carl were on-board. Time for Kidd to lure in the bear, but not too fast. He didn't want Carl to discover the trap and flee.

"Oh, my daughter goes there," Kidd said with calculated nonchalance. He let the words hang in the air, thick as Ohio fog, then he watched as Carl's shoulders tightened at the implication.

Maybe it was just coincidence, but the man sniffed. "What does that have to do with anything?"

"Nothing much, I guess," Kidd said. He paused for effect. "Just that they're sleeping together."

"They're what?!" Carl shouted. Snap! The trap closed tight around the bear's leg, and he was caught. The next order of business was for Kidd to defeat his prey's will to resist the capture.

"Sleeping together," Kidd said. "You know, banging, bumping, getting busy. They're humping each other blue, Carl. I'm surprised they can still walk."

Carl tried to yell something. Instead, he choked on his tongue. To Kidd, it was as if the bear were thrashing hopelessly against the teeth of the trap. When Carl recovered enough to speak, the fight in him was gone. Tired, beaten, all he could manage to squeak out was, "They're having intercourse?"

Kidd wiped his mouth with a napkin. He decided that Carl's submission still needed some reinforcement. "They're not just having intercourse, Carl," Kidd said. "They're letting it all hang out."

"Like what?" Carl asked.

Like what indeed? Kidd wondered. To complete Carl's capture, whatever Kidd invented would have to be remarkably intense—freaky-deaky type stuff. To that end, the former president dug up something from his gubernatorial days back in Columbus, when he had briefly indulged his libido in a dominatrix named Suzy the Subduer. To borrow from Miguel's colorful language, Suzy had been one kinky chiquita herself, although she was Polish by ethnicity. But she would do. Kidd told Carl, "Like they can't keep the ball gags and nipple clamps away from each other, that's what."

Carl's eyes bulged. "Sadomasochism?"

"Multiple partners, too," Kidd said.

"Threesomes?!" Carl cried.

"I wish it stopped at three," Kidd said. "I think they're up to five now. But who am I to tell you, Carl? Your GeoStar must have shown Kenny in West Hollywood yesterday. What did you think he was doing there? West Hollywood is godless."

Carl began to gnaw on his fingernails. "Oh, this is not good," he mumbled. "This is definitely not good. His mother's going to die."

"His mother?" Kidd asked. The ex-president's mind flashed bright with the beautiful vision of a red-haired woman.

"My wife Martha," Carl said dismissively. "I doubt you've met her. She can be maddeningly shy."

Kidd suppressed a grin, then he said just as dismissively, "We've bumped into each other a few times."

Carl rubbed his forehead. During the conversation, his face had turned a robust shade of maroon, and he began to flex his fingers as if he were dying to hold something between them. "Do you have a cigarette?" he asked Kidd. "I haven't had a cigarette in a week. I think I need a cigarette."

"I'm out," Kidd told Carl.

"Maybe they have some down in the lobby," Carl said. He tried to push up from the carpet. Before he could rise, Kidd placed a hand on his shoulder and directed the man back to the floor.

"Lest you forget," Kidd said, "you're in California. You can't smoke anywhere in this state."

Carl Kernick appeared crestfallen. "That's a shame," he said. "I was in such a hurry to get here, I should have stopped back in Vegas to buy some. In Dillon, I couldn't leave the hotel room. I went through the pack I had rather quickly."

"I understand," Kidd said. "You've endured a lot of physical, and emotional, distress lately."

"You have no idea," Carl said. He ran a trembling hand through his gnarled brown hair. "I've been worried sick over Kenny since he left. His mother thinks it's just teenage acting-out, but she doesn't understand. Things can happen to him out there. He's not equipped."

This time Kidd grinned openly. "Oh, things are happening to him out there, Carl, and Kenny's proving to be quite equipped."

"We have to stop him," Carl said. "I have to come up with a plan. I have to do something."

Kidd raised a palm at Carl, cutting short the man's initiative. "Forgive me, Mr. Kernick," he said, "but only one of us in this room has ever been a commander in chief. I think it's best to let me handle the situation."

Carl bristled at Kidd's suggestion. It was easy for Kidd to see that before him lay a man who did not relish the thought of relinquishing power, and Carl's tone only enhanced such an assumption. "Then you'd better have a plan ready to go, Bonehead."

"Oh, I have a plan," Kidd said. At which point he leaned forward in his chair and presented that plan to Carl Kernick.

It was a bold idea, to be sure, and a dirty one, but it would be highly effective—dealings with law enforcement usually were. Miguel's cousin Enrique would play the central role, with Kidd and Miguel, and perhaps Carl, providing support. As the originator of the idea, Kidd was obviously on-board, and he was certain that Miguel (and by extension, Enrique) would follow. But what about Carl? Kidd had stirred Carl's stew with tales of Kenny and Annabelle engaging in sexual funk, but what Kidd was asking Carl to do would result in a harsh turn for the man's only child, something the boy would not soon forget. Was Carl up to the task? Could Carl put Kenny in jeopardy for the cause of the greater good? Did the father have the stones to condemn the son?

From his supine position against the couch, Carl listened patiently. During Kidd's description of harsh treatment, not a single part of Carl's body moved, nor did his face flinch—Old Kernick retained a blank expression, revealing no hint to Kidd of what he might be thinking of this daring, brutal undertaking.

When Kidd finished with the details, Carl remained motionless. He's not buying into it, Kidd concluded. It's too much to ask.

That's when Carl Kernick sat up, pain or no pain. He twisted his shoulders and loosened his torso, then he rubbed a hand over his mouth. The rub changed the whole air of Carl's appearance—the blank expression gave way to narrow eyes, tight lips, and a clenched jaw. Carl Kernick looked like a bear consumed with the taste of human flesh. "What time do we start?" he asked Kidd.

Kidd raised a glass of orange juice to Carl in agreement. "Recon begins at 3:30 this afternoon," he said. "From there, we go when they go."

"Great," Carl said. He checked his wrist watch. "That gives me seven hours. Now if you'll excuse me, I'm exhausted." Kenny's father turned on his heel, walked into Kidd's bedroom and shut the door.

As a matter of protocol, it was a bit of an asshole move—Old Kernick should have at least asked Kidd for permission to use his bed. But Kidd couldn't get mad. In fact, he couldn't stop smiling. He had never expected it, nor was it anything he ever might have planned, but just like that, Kenny's father—Kidd's antithesis of style, manner, appearance and appetite—was turning out to be the best ally in war that a president could ever want.

CHAPTER 46

★ ★

Seven hours for Carl Kernick passed fleetingly in a sleep devoid of dreams. Barely had he settled into bed and closed his eyes than he felt the weight of a hand on his forearm. The hand jostled, but Carl refused to acknowledge it. Then the hand jostled harder and Carl tumbled out of blackness. He opened his eyes, looked up, and saw the face of Charles Bentley Kidd peering down at him. He felt deeply exhausted and thoroughly violated by Kidd's intrusion, and because of those feelings, he found himself in a particularly foul mood.

"What do you want?" Carl said.

"Time to go," Kidd said. "Miguel is downstairs."

But Carl didn't believe him. "I just got into bed a few minutes ago," he said. "Check your watch." Carl tried to roll over, away from Kidd, but his neck brace prevented it. Instead, he pulled a pillow onto his face—it smelled of his own sweat.

Kidd removed the pillow and tossed it to the floor. "Check *your* watch," Sucky Chucky said. "I've been listening to your damn snoring all day. You sound like a clogged vacuum cleaner. Miguel is downstairs. So get up."

That's when Carl felt the blankets fly off his body and two hands shimmy between his back and the sheets. The next thing he knew, he was tumbling in a rotated force of motion. When the rotation ended, his face was pressed against the carpet, and he was experiencing electric pain through his neck. It became clear to Carl Kernick that Charles Bentley Kidd was not a man of mercy—the bastard had actually flipped a cripple out of bed.

Carl peeled himself off the carpet. The Tylenol had worn off, but given the circumstances, he had neither the time nor the ability to take another dose. Sucky Chucky's plan, though no masterpiece by Carl's standards, was subtly effective, even if it had been conceived by a bonehead like Kidd. In addition, it would require Carl, when he was needed, to have all of his mental faculties about him. As a business leader and a genius automation engineer, Carl Kernick knew the importance of making all parts work together for a common purpose. Slips of the tongue would not be tolerated tonight. Carl could not appear distracted or in any way cloudy of judgment. If he did, the plan might fail. If the plan failed, Kenny could get off lightly. If Kenny got off lightly, well, Carl didn't even want to think about that. He had to get Kenny home. He had to get his boy back to the Ivy League. He had to set that little dummkopf on a proper road to success.

Looking around the room, trying to gather his senses, Carl didn't think he had time to shower. Kidd insisted that he at least shave, brush his teeth, wet down his frazzled hair and dress in his best clothing. "You have to look like the respectable businessman that you are," Kidd told him. "It will have more effect. Lose the neck brace if you can. Do you have a suit?"

Carl didn't know about taking off the neck brace, but he did have a suit. In the garment pocket of his suitcase, out in the Dodge Stratus, was the Brooks Brothers backup he carried with him at all times in case of emergencies. Carl described the vehicle to Kidd, told him it was parked on the bottom level of a garage on the corner, and threw him the keys. Kidd went to fetch the suitcase while Carl flossed.

When Kidd returned with the suitcase, Carl was waiting for him on the couch. The neck brace was gone, and he was sitting stiffly on the edge of the cushion, dressed only in a white button-down shirt, black socks, and his Fruit of the Loom briefs. Kidd brought him the suitcase and Carl dressed. As they were about to depart, Kidd reached for Carl's burgundy tie, unknotted it, and pulled it off.

"This is the West Coast, Carl," Kidd said. "You'll get more respect if you just go with the shirt."

"But I always wear ties with suits," Carl said.

Kidd balled up the tie and tossed it into the suitcase. "Well, it looks like you always wear button-down shirts with suits, too, but I didn't call you out for that fashion faux pas, did I? Now go." Kidd pushed Carl toward the door.

The driver was surly when Carl and Kidd walked out to the street. "So this is the man who keeps me waiting," he said to Kidd, but his eyes were focused squarely on Carl. Carl and the driver were about the same height, but the driver was more rugged, a force to be reckoned with in any clash, physical or verbal. Carl decided it was in the best interest of self-preservation to look away.

Kidd climbed into the back of a Lincoln Town Car ahead of Carl. Carl waited for Kidd to seat himself, then he did his best to settle into the vehicle, but his neck screamed with pain.

Again, he made the driver wait as he took his time getting into the backseat. When he was finally positioned for minimal torment, the driver rolled his eyes and slammed the door. In a matter of moments, they were off, peeled tires screeching north along Ocean Avenue.

They arrived at the campus of the University of the West by twenty past three. At such a late time on a day of departure, the visitor lot where Kenny was keeping the XTS was half empty for the Thanksgiving holiday. For a moment, Carl feared that Kenny might have departed with the earlier crowd, but when they turned the corner into the lot, Carl spied in the distance the comforting shape of the Cadillac's rear end. As they got closer to his beloved vehicle, however, his comfort turned to shock.

"What the hell happened to my bumper?" he shouted at Kidd.

"Hey, don't blame me," Kidd said. "Your son is a piss-poor driver."

"Maybe that's because he doesn't have a license," Carl said.

"Sure he does," Kidd said. "I granted him one back in New York City. And let me tell you, Carl, I took him through a driver's ed course better than anything he could have gotten in Simondale. Before we arrived in Manhattan, he was running over guard shacks and swerving on the highway. After Manhattan, he didn't hit one single thing." Then Kidd scratched his chin and added, "Okay, maybe that newspaper box in Chicago when he was drunk, but that's all."

Carl felt himself shouting "Drunk?!" but the only sound that emanated from his throat was a gasp. As he had suspected from the *Chicago Herald* article, not only was Kenny driving without a license, but he had been doing it while intoxicated.

Carl's insides spun from the confirmation. Kenny was in deeper danger from Kidd's influence than Carl had ever imagined. Rampant alcohol consumption, sadomasochistic sexual deviance, flaunting the law every time he got behind the wheel of the Cadillac. Carl hoped Kenny got his butt out here soon. The quicker he could get his son home and scrub the scum of loose living off the boy, the quicker Carl could put Kenny's life—and more important, his own life—back in peaceful order.

"I don't even want to know about Las Vegas," Carl said, trying to sound resigned to Kenny's disrepute.

"You sure as hell don't," Kidd chuckled.

But Kenny didn't come to the parking lot soon. In fact, if the driver found himself surly over Carl's delay, then he really must have gotten ticked about Kenny's. Darkness fell without any sign of the boy, and Carl found himself anxious the whole time. In the absence of a cigarette to suck on, Carl had returned to fingernail biting as a means of relaxation. He gnawed on the ends of his fingers incessantly during the insufferable wait, to the point where he had chewed up the skin. Finally, around half past six in the evening, after a three hour wait, a figure came walking toward the Cadillac.

"There he is," Kidd whispered. "That's Kenny."

But Carl didn't see Kenny at all. He only saw some student. "Where?" Carl asked.

"Right there," Kidd said, pointing to the student. That's when Carl's jaw unhinged. The figure before him couldn't be Kenny. The student approaching the Cadillac didn't look or move anything like Kenny.

But to Carl's shock, it was Kenny. Even under the dimness of street lamps, that fact could not be denied. His son was wearing pressed slacks, dark loafers and a short-sleeve shirt, untucked. The shirt was either yellow or pale blue, and was clearly made of unnatural fibers. The boy's red hair appeared spiked, not pressed flat as usual, and his glasses were thin and narrow. Carl gasped at the transformation. Kenny appeared fashionable. Even his movements came off differently—they were crisp and self-assured. He walked with a stride, with his back straight, his shoulders spread and his head high, and when he held out his hand to pop the locks on the Cadillac with the transmitter, the motion was fluid and commanding, not mousy and fearful. Carl gawked at his son as Kenny approached the driver door. "That's my boy?" he asked Kidd.

"He's alone," Kidd said to the driver. "Get ready to follow."

"You got it, boss," the driver replied. Once Kenny had settled into the Cadillac, the man named Miguel started the Lincoln but kept the headlights off.

The Cadillac's lights flicked on and the vehicle backed out of its space. Miguel allowed Kenny an unsuspicious lead, then he pursued. He turned out of the parking lot at a different exit than Kenny had taken and followed the Cadillac at a distance of fifty yards.

"He's heading toward the dorm," Kidd said.

"I got him, boss," the driver said.

"What happened to my son?" Carl asked.

Kidd turned his face to Carl but never took his eyes off the moving Cadillac. "Vegas, baby," Kidd said. "It was Vegas."

Carl watched as Kenny drove the Cadillac to the front of a dormitory complex. His son parked on the street, got out of the vehicle, and disappeared down a path. The driver slid the Lincoln in front of another dormitory and idled the vehicle with lights off. Again they would wait, this time not as long. Within four minutes, Kenny was back. He was dragging behind him

a piece of flower-patterned roller luggage and a matching toiletries case, both of which he placed in the Cadillac's trunk. A
tall girl sidled up to Kenny—it was Kidd's vixen daughter. Carl
could tell from the motion of her silhouette that she was fearless and confident, just the type to lead his son into the world
of aberrant sex acts.

Kenny and Annabelle slipped into the Cadillac. Kenny
pulled the vehicle onto the street and turned at a nearby corner,
heading for the campus gates. The limo driver punched up the
Lincoln's headlights and renewed his pursuit, again at an unsuspicious distance. At the same time, he dialed a number on his
cell phone. In a moment he was speaking into the mouthpiece
on a hands-free headset.

"The target is heading toward Soltavega," the limo driver
said. There was a pause. "No, I'm not mistaken, Enrique.
They're turning onto Soltavega right now, toward the 405. I
have them in view."

The Lincoln also turned onto Soltavega, revealing Carl's
precious Cadillac twenty yards ahead in moderate traffic.

"Late-model XTS," the limo driver said. "Bronze in color."

"Gold," Carl said. "That color is gold."

"Did I ask you?" the limo driver snapped. Then back to the
phone: "Connecticut plates, tag number—" He read the Caddy's license plate twice, using military designations for the letters. Another pause. "Well, you better hurry, Enrique. They'll
be on the freeway in two minutes. Sooner rather than not sooner
would be nice." The driver pressed off the call. "Now we pray,"
he said to his passengers. "If you're accustomed to seeking the
intervention of any special saints or blessed-virgin-type figures,
this might be a good time."

The Cadillac passed through one set of traffic signals, then another, and another. Up ahead, there was nothing to slow Kenny down, not even rush hour. A sign for the 405 appeared over the road. If the limo driver's cousin didn't arrive on the scene soon, Kenny would get onto the highway and disappear into a dark swamp of traffic, speed and city limits. Another sign indicating a quarter-mile approach to the 405 came into view, but there was no hint of Enrique. The plan seemed doomed. Carl chewed on the nail of his ring finger until he tasted blood. He might have to find another way to get Kenny home. Maybe the Lincoln could run the Cadillac into a ditch near Ventura, then he could drag Kenny from the Cadillac by the boy's tongue. But there had to be some option. Christ, Carl hated getting so close and failing.

Then, like a rush of metallic wind, a Los Angeles Police Department cruiser flew by the Lincoln and took up position directly behind the Cadillac. Pulsing blue lights pierced the night.

"We got him!" Kidd yelled. He let out an ear-shattering whoop and threw his hands into the air. "We got him! We got the runt!"

By "runt," Carl assumed Kidd was talking about Kenny. Strangely though, contrary to his fatherly protectiveness, and juxtaposed to his natural inclination to despise the bottom-feeding politician with whom he found himself aligned, Carl Kernick had to agree: Kenny was a runt, and it was time to do what nature usually did to runts—remove them from the litter.

CHAPTER 47

★★★★★★★★★★★★★★★★★★★★★★★★★★★★★★★★

At first, Kenny didn't believe the flashing blue lights were meant for him. He pulled over to the right lane, attempting to allow the police car to pass on his left, but instead of passing, the cruiser swung to his tail.

"I think he wants you to pull over," Annabelle said.

"That's strange," Kenny said. But what he was really thinking was, "Oh, shit," as he suddenly remembered that he didn't possess a driver's license.

"Just pull over," Annabelle said. "You don't want to mess with these guys." She pointed to a stretch of sidewalk in front of a Circle K. "Right there."

Kenny pulled the Cadillac to the side of the road, in front of the Circle K as Annabelle directed. He put the car in park, but left the engine running.

"Turn off the car, Ken," Annabelle told him. "Or they'll think you plan to run."

Kenny wanted to run. His heart was running already, banging against his sternum like a caged raccoon. He wanted the Caddy to join it. After all, now would be a good time to resume his trek to Alaska for a stint of crab fishing. But his rational sense kept him cool; it convinced him to listen to Annabelle. He shut off the car.

"Maybe you just have a tail light out," Annabelle said. "Most of the time they only give you a warning for that."

"Hope so," Kenny said. He was watching through the rearview mirror as a stocky, dark-skinned police officer stepped out of the cruiser. The officer clicked on a flashlight and walked toward the Cadillac with the swinging gait of a medieval battering ram. Kenny wanted to throw up.

The officer knocked on the driver window with two thick knuckles, but he kept his body in the protective cover of the Cadillac's center post. Kenny tried to roll down the window, but with the engine off, the glass wouldn't move. Kenny twisted the key on the XTS just enough to trigger the power.

"Evening, officer," he said as the window came down. "How may I help you?"

"License and registration," the officer said.

"Do I have a tail light out?" Kenny asked. "If so, I'll get that fixed right away." Kenny's armpits started to puddle with fear.

"License and registration," the officer repeated, this time tapping his knuckles against the center post.

Kenny turned to Annabelle. "Where would one find a registration?" he asked.

Annabelle looked at him with crossed eyes. She popped open the glove box and rummaged through it until she found a plastic folder. Inside the plastic folder was a sheet of paper. She handed the sheet to Kenny. "Your registration," she said.

Kenny handed it to the officer, who inspected its contents under the beam of the flashlight. "And the license," he said.

Kenny stalled. It was a noticeable stall, and the officer noticed it. Kenny squirmed in his seat. Annabelle was growing impatient. "Ken, show him your license," she said.

Kenny looked at her, smiled anxiously, then he reached down and opened the ashtray. From it he pulled a tattered, soot-covered napkin. He handed the napkin to the officer.

"What is that?" Annabelle asked. Kenny just shrugged.

The officer took the napkin. He unfolded it and turned it over in his hand under the beam of light, perusing the blue-inked print on its front and a colorful trademark logo on the back. Then he said, "I asked for your license."

"That is my license," Kenny told him.

"It's a Burger King napkin," the officer said.

"What's the old saying?" Kenny asked. "'One man's napkin is another man's driver's license'?" Kenny tried to laugh. "Something like that anyway. I'm sure you've heard it."

"Where did you get this?" the officer asked.

"That would be Charles Bentley Kidd," Kenny said. "Former president of the United States? One-time leader of the free world? See his signature there?" Kenny pointed to a scrawl of ink which indicated Kidd's authority. "You can be certain it's valid, officer. The president stated to me, unequivocally, that this thing is good in all fifty states."

"All fifty states, huh?" the officer said.

"And Hawaii," Kenny said, finally managing a laugh, hoping the officer would play along.

But the officer scrutinized the napkin—and Kenny—harshly. "So you're saying that you don't have a valid driver's license."

"Not on me, no," Kenny said.

"Do you have a driver's license at all?" the officer asked.

Kenny contemplated the question, considered his options, then shrugged in the negative. "I'm a really good driver, though."

The officer, however, didn't seem to care what kind of driver Kenny Kernick might be. He stepped back from the center post and ordered Kenny out of the car.

Kenny looked at Annabelle, who was clearly confused. "What's going on?" she asked. But Kenny just held up a finger, an indication for her to sit tight. He stepped out of the Cadillac.

"Turn around and face the vehicle," the officer said. "Place your hands on the roof where I can see them."

Kenny did as he was told. He faced the Cadillac and placed his hands on the roof.

"Are you Carl Kernick?" the officer asked him.

"No, sir, I'm Kenny Kernick. Carl is my father."

"Do you have any weapons on you?" asked the officer. Kenny felt rugged hands patting down his body. From his experiences with the Secret Service in Simondale, Kenny prepared to have his crotch frisked.

"No weapons, sir," Kenny said.

"In the vehicle?"

"No, sir." Over the car's roof, Kenny could see a group of gawkers gathering at the entrance to the Circle K. They were staring at him, making comments to each other. Kenny wanted to shrivel like a raisin and die.

The officer said, "You say Carl Kernick is your father?"

"Yes, sir," Kenny said.

"Does your father know you drive his vehicle without a license?" the officer asked.

Kenny was about to reply that he was sure his father did know (because Carl liked to think he knew everything) when the boy heard a familiar but strangely out-of-place voice to his right. The voice said, "Maybe you should ask the father that question."

Kenny turned his head and discovered why the intonation sounded so familiar. In the process, he got the shock of his life—Carl Kernick was standing between the Cadillac and the police cruiser.

"Dad?" Kenny said.

"Shut up, Kenny," Carl said. Oddly, he was standing in a rigid, twisted pose. Odder still, he was wearing a suit without a tie, something Kenny had never seen him do.

"Dad," Kenny pleaded, "Tell him—"

"I told you to shut up, Kenny," Carl said. "Now shut up." Carl approached the officer with more of a lurch than a stride. But it was the approach that counted.

Phew, Kenny thought. He's going to do the talking and get me out of this. Kenny was never so glad to see his father. He actually contemplated taking back all the unpleasant things he had thought about him since leaving Simondale.

The officer asked, "Are you Carl Kernick?"

"I am," Carl said.

"Is this your vehicle?" the officer asked.

"It is," Carl said. "I paid sixty-seven thousand dollars for it last winter. It's my pride and joy." Kenny watched as Carl ran a warm, loving palm along the Cadillac's decklid.

The officer asked, "Did you know your son was operating this vehicle without a driver's license?"

Thank God, Kenny thought. He'll save my ass. Kenny assumed Carl would give the officer some realistic-sounding bullshit, and the officer would let Kenny off with a warning. Maybe Carl would even bribe the guy. But something had to happen. Carl Kernick would never embarrass himself in front of law enforcement by admitting to the criminality of a wayward son. Carl just didn't have it in him.

Kenny's father cleared his throat, which Kenny took as a good sign—Carl was using a delaying tactic to come up with an effective lie, or an acceptable bribe figure. But when Carl spoke, no lie or money offer issued forth. On the contrary, Carl stated, "Not only did I *not* know that my son was driving without a license, but this vehicle is stolen."

"Stolen?" Kenny gasped.

Carl began to point at the trunk of the Cadillac. "This vehicle was taken from my yard, three thousand miles away, without my permission. My son is a felon. He's a thief. I want him arrested."

"Dad!" Kenny screamed. "You're shitting me, right?"

"Oh, Kenny," Carl Kernick said, "I have not yet begun to shit you."

The police officer had apparently heard all he needed to hear. Strong hands twisted Kenny's arms behind his back, then Kenny heard a stream of clicks and felt cold metal against his wrists. The next thing he knew, he was handcuffed.

That's when Annabelle opened her door and climbed out of the car. "What the hell is going on here?" she asked. She eyed the officer. "What are you doing to him?"

"Get back in the car," the officer said to her. He pulled Kenny away from the Cadillac and placed him face-down on the pavement. The stubble of asphalt pressed divots into Kenny's baby-soft cheeks.

But Annabelle was already making her way around the back end of the Caddy. "I asked you what you're doing!" she yelled at the officer. At the trunk, she found Carl blocking her with his stout body. Annabelle glared at Carl. "Get out of my way," she said.

The officer pointed at her in warning. "Miss, I'm going to tell you for the last time: Get back in the car or you're coming with him."

"For what?" Annabelle asked.

"Disorderly conduct to start," the officer said. "Then we can tack stuff on."

"It's all right, Annabelle," Kenny shouted. "Get back in the car." From his place on the pavement, he saw two other figures approaching the scene from behind the cruiser. At first, he thought they might be back-up patrolmen for the officer, but he soon recognized the taller of the two, with that confident saunter and the perfect head of hair—it was Charles Bentley Kidd. The other man—short and swarthy, with a build much like the police officer's—Kenny had never set eyes on before.

Kidd's caramel voice oozed through the night: "Annabelle, listen to him. Get in the car." That's when Annabelle swung around and saw her father.

"Daddy!" she cried. "Help us! This man is arresting Ken!"

Kidd pursed his lips, wrinkled his nose, and surveyed the situation as if he were smelling raw sewage. Then he stated definitively, "I have no problem with that."

"What?" Annabelle said. She shook her head. "What are you talking about, Daddy?"

"Kenny's a criminal, 'Belles," Kidd said, approaching her. "I tried to warn you, remember? That story about the underwear? Now it's automobiles. What's next—serial killings? No, 'Belles, it's high time they nipped this little Ted Bundy in the bud."

But it was clear, even to an incapacitated Kenny, that Annabelle Kidd wasn't swallowing any of her father's pap. "You did this, Daddy," she said to him. "You did it." She got into her father's face and beat him in the chest with her fists. "I know you did this! Stop it now!"

"I don't know what you're talking about, 'Belles," Kidd said. He was struggling to restrain Annabelle's flailing fists, and not having much luck at it.

"Annabelle, get back in the car!" Kenny shouted.

The officer left Kenny face-down on the pavement and made a move toward Annabelle. "Miss, get away from the president!" he ordered. "Step away or you're looking at an assault charge!"

"That won't be necessary, officer," Kidd said, waving him off. "We've had enough negative publicity in this family already. Miguel?"

Kidd turned around and nodded to the short man. The man nodded back, then he grabbed Annabelle around the waist and hoisted her over his shoulder, fireman-style. It was no easy feat, given that Annabelle was taller than he. Kenny looked on as he carried her back to a black Lincoln Town Car, with Annabelle kicking and hitting him all the way.

"I'll bail you out, Ken!" she was yelling. "Just hold on! I'll come and get you!" Then the man bent down and Annabelle disappeared into the back of the Lincoln.

With Annabelle shuttered, the scene on the street turned eerily quiet under the flickering blue police lights. Kidd took a contented breath, smirked cocksuredly, and nodded to the officer. "Carry on," he said. Then he walked back to the Lincoln and opened the rear door. Kenny could hear Annabelle's yells emanating from within. "You jackass!" she was shouting. "Let me out of here! Get me out of this car!" Kenny couldn't tell if she was addressing her exhortations to the short man or to her father—"jackass" could have applied to both. Either way, Kidd slipped into the backseat and shut the door, cutting off Annabelle's voice. The Lincoln started up, pulled away from the curb, and sped off down Soltavega Boulevard. Kenny finally lost sight of the vehicle when it turned onto the entry ramp for the 405 South.

Free of any further distractions, the officer descended on his prostrate perpetrator.

"Kenny Kernick," he said, pulling Kenny up from the pavement with an awkward jerk that unleashed torment through Kenny's shoulder blades. "You're under arrest for car theft. You have the right to remain silent. Anything you say can be used against you in a court of law. Do you understand that?"

"I do," Kenny said to the officer. But he still had something to say to his father. "Carl," he asked, "is there anything *you'd* like to say?" Like telling him this is all a farce? Kenny was imploring his father. Like telling him to let me go?

"There is something," Kenny's father replied. He addressed his statement to the officer. "When can I get my vehicle back?"

Twenty minutes later, after providing the officer with the requisite proof of identification, Carl Kernick was once again behind the wheel of his beloved Cadillac XTS. Where Carl was driving off to as he pulled away from the curb along Soltavega Boulevard, Kenny didn't know. And truth be told, his father's destination didn't much matter. Not at this point. Because Kenny knew quite well where he himself was driving off to—or where he was being driven off to, as the current situation stood, by Officer Enrique Torres of the Los Angeles Police Department.

Kenny was on his way to jail.

CHAPTER 48

★ ★

Annabelle Kidd pulled at the bedroom doorknob until she tore away the nail from her right middle finger. It began to bleed, seeping out from the tear to coat her pink nail polish in crimson, but she would not stop pulling. She couldn't stop. Whatever way her father and that jackass driver were keeping the door secured from the outside, there had to be some mechanism to jerk it open. If only she pulled hard enough. But each time she tried, the door slipped toward her merely a fraction, then it snapped back.

Rope, she thought. Clearly, they had tied a rope to the outside knob and secured its opposite end to something very immobile. Like the living room couch. While the jackass was sitting on it.

Annabelle pummeled the door. "Let me out of here right now, jackass!"

The reply came back garbled, as if she had caught Jackass mid-nosh from a bucket of KFC: "I told you to shut up, you spoiled brat!" Annabelle could hear a television blaring in the background. Given the din of rapid Spanish dialogue and melodramatic orchestral swells, she suspected that Jackass was watching a Mexican soap opera.

For over an hour, Annabelle had heard nothing but Jackass's voice and the soap opera sounds. She was fairly certain that her father had left the suite, but she didn't know where he had gone. What was clear was that Annabelle was locked in a bedroom at the Mendelssohn Hotel in Santa Monica, that the telephone and other objects had been removed prior to her arrival, and that Jackass was the one guarding her. The absurdity of it all was making her lose her cool.

"I want out of here!" Annabelle yelled. She pulled on the knob again, trying to get the door ajar enough for her to slip out, but it wouldn't budge. From the living room, she heard Jackass laughing.

"Nice try, little girl," he said, "but you're stuck. Just accept it and go to bed."

"Where's my father?" she shouted. "I want to speak to my father."

Jackass stuffed his mouth and said, "Mr. President doesn't want to speak to you, does he? If he did, he'd be speaking."

"You tell him to get back here and answer me." Annabelle whacked the door with a palm.

"I'm telling you to shut the hell up!" Jackass replied. "You're making me miss half of *Picante*."

"Boo-fucking-hoo!" Annabelle yelled.

"Keep it up," Jackass shouted to her, "and I'm going to come in there with this rope and tie you to the bed. You think your father would mind? I'm his new chief of staff. He's given me full authority to handle this situation. So knock off your *mierda* or I'll handle it!" As if to emphasize the point that he wanted no more peeps from her, he turned up the volume on the television.

Annabelle sat on the edge of the bed and tried to soothe her anger. She was letting passion supplant rationality. She needed to gather herself. The first step in that process was dealing with the fingernail that was throbbing like hell.

She inspected her hand to find the finger dripping with blood. The nail was torn away one-quarter inch down from the tip and three-quarters across—not a pretty sight. There was blood on the door, doorknob, carpet, and on her pants. If she didn't tend to the finger immediately, it might get infected, and if it got infected, it might hurt her play in the tournament. As someone who had worked so hard to retool her friendships in the wake of Pastrygate, Annabelle could not fathom the possibility of letting her teammates down at such a crucial time because of some stupidly-acquired injury.

Annabelle huffed and pushed off the bed. In the bathroom, she blasted the water to hot and stuck her finger under the stream.

"Holy shit!" she cried, jerking her finger away. The water temperature coming from the hot setting was scalding. She reset the faucet knob and dipped her pinky in the flow at regular intervals to test the temperature. When the temperature finally reached a comfortable level, Annabelle washed the blood from her nail, scrubbed the tear with soap and wrapped the nailhead in a face cloth, applying pressure.

She walked back to the door and knocked on it twice with her elbow. "Do you at least have a Band-Aid?" she asked. The only response she got from Jackass was more volume on the TV.

Annabelle sat on the corner of the bed. She couldn't stay here. Ken was probably being processed at a branch of the LAPD, and he would need bail. She wanted to help him. He had been shafted by her father, and she knew it.

But Annabelle was in no position to help Ken, even if she could get out of this room. In her confusion, she had stepped out of the Cadillac without taking her Sadrine Gravos bag. That bag held her life. At the least, it held her cell phone and wallet, which were the two means she could use to spring Ken from bondage. She suspected Ken's car was currently sitting at an impound lot, but given the way the whole rotten situation had unfolded, she couldn't be certain where the Cadillac had ended up. It might even be on its way to Mexico by now, stolen by some local gangbanger before a tow truck could get over to Soltavega to transport it.

But if Annabelle could spring herself from her own bondage in the Mendelssohn, she would at least have hope. If she remained in this room, there was no hope. Her father had been very thorough. Upon arriving at the hotel, he had actually left Annabelle in the Lincoln Town Car while he came up to the room to prepare it. He must have also paid off a bellhop to let them in through the service entrance, because once her father returned to the Lincoln, she was taken, hinged over Jackass's shoulder, up a back elevator that smelled of rotten garbage. Once inside the bedroom, she found the phone missing and all heavy objects removed, objects she could have used to break a window or pound a hole through the plaster to get herself into the hallway. Apparently, her father had banked on the break-a-window theory—he had taken the sheets, blanket and bedspread off the bed as well. Annabelle would not be making an escape rope on this night unless she was going to weave it from her own hair. Even though she had much of it, her hair would only get her down about three feet.

"What to do?" she mumbled. And whom to call if she could get out?

It was at that moment that Annabelle thought of Peter. Not of calling him—she hadn't spoken with Peter since the beginning of the new school year, mostly to allow her heart to mend, but also because he had started dating a girl on the swimming team the first week of the semester, and Annabelle still couldn't bear to hear if he was happy with her. She knew she shouldn't wish ill upon people, and she knew she still loved him, but she kind of hoped Peter was miserable, especially since his new girlfriend was just another Southern California bleach blonde, complete with dyed eyebrows. Thankfully, the campus of the University of the West was large enough that she rarely had to see Peter and his new Barbie Doll, if ever.

But at this moment, Peter could be of use to her. Not for what he could do in the present, but for what he had done in the past.

Eight months earlier, just as the Congressional hearings in Washington were wrapping up, Peter had decided that Annabelle needed a break from the strain of her father's circumstances, which were exacting such a toll on her that she wasn't eating, sleeping or studying. He waited until spring recess in March, then he took her to Switzerland.

The distraction did Annabelle good. She loved skiing the thick-powdered slopes of St. Moritz, and at night, she loved taking hot tubs, getting busy with Peter, then ordering room service, where they would dine in bathrobes while gathering sustenance for another round of passion. It was all so romantic, like she and the love of her life were newlyweds.

And if they had stuck to that routine, everything might have been fine. But on the last night in St. Moritz, Peter insisted on going out for dinner. The image that struck Annabelle now was that of the dress shirt Peter intended to wear with his dinner jacket. It came out of the suitcase wrinkled. When he looked for an iron in the closet, he found nothing but empty shelves. Upon calling the front desk, he discovered that the hotel didn't put irons in rooms because of the fire hazard they presented in the hands of distracted guests. He was then informed that if he wanted his shirt pressed, he would have to wait until the next morning, when the maid could do it for him, or he could come downstairs and do it himself. The concierge would be more than happy to set up a place for him under the hotel staff's careful watch.

Peter declined both offers. Instead, he took his shirt into the bathroom, hung it on a door hook, then he turned on the shower to its hottest setting. The water at that hotel was scalding as well. Closing the door to the bathroom, he told Annabelle that the shirt would be steamed in plenty of time for reservations, which Peter had made at the ritziest restaurant in town. While they were waiting, he said he intended for them to bid a proper farewell to Switzerland, then he tore off her clothes and proceeded to ravage her eager body like it had never been ravaged before.

There was only one problem: The steam rising from the shower faucet was so hot that it set off the fire alarm in the hotel. Annabelle and Peter never heard any siren. The first inkling they got that something was wrong came when the Secret Service broke down their door. They were naked, and in the middle of the act, but that didn't matter to the Secret Service. They pulled the couple off the bed and took them down to the street wrapped only in bed sheets. It was there, as they waited in the cold while the Secret Service brought forward a secure vehicle, that somebody snapped a photo of them. The photo made it onto the news and celebrity websites, and into the morning editions of all the American newspapers as well, with corresponding stories about how Annabelle Kidd, while on spring break, had found herself part of a minor international incident resulting from a sex act with her boyfriend. The incident didn't look good for Annabelle, and she suspected it hadn't looked good for her father, either—he was removed from office a mere two months later. In her heart, she felt that the whole fiasco was the last straw for Peter, too. Three days after returning from Europe, his mood had turned so sour that she had been forced to cut him loose.

The shower, Annabelle now thought, returning her focus to the Mendelssohn, and to her current predicament. The shower is my only hope. I have to do what Peter did. I have to set off the fire alarm. There were problems with her plan, though. The water in the Mendelssohn was scalding, sure, but was it hot enough to trip a fire alarm? Did an American hotel even have the same alarm system as a European one?

She decided that she had nothing to lose by trying. If her plan failed, she would simply be stuck in the bedroom for as long as her father deemed it necessary to imprison her. But if it worked, she could at least find someone to help Ken.

Annabelle pushed off the bed and walked to the door. The Mexican soap opera was still blaring at high volume from the living room. Against its noise, Annabelle grabbed the doorknob and pushed in the lock mechanism, securing the door from her side.

"Let's see how you deal with the fire department, Jackass," she whispered.

She went into the bathroom and turned on the shower, swinging the control knob all the way to the left. The water coming out of the shower head felt hotter than that which had scalded her finger at the sink. White billows of steam filled the air in a matter of seconds. The heat gathered quickly, scorching Annabelle's cheeks and ears. Annabelle left the bathroom and closed the door behind her.

She sat on the edge of the bed and waited. Her finger was injured, and her palms, wrists and forearms were sore from pounding on the door, but her legs felt in peak condition. They were ready to spring should the opportunity arise.

Out of her right ear she could hear the shower roaring behind the bathroom door. From straight ahead, she could hear Jackass's laughter. He had apparently turned the soap opera in favor of some raunchy Telemundo sitcom.

Laugh it up, Jackass, Annabelle thought. Laugh as much as you can. Because once I get out of here, you'll be crying.

Charles Bentley Kidd had just dug his fork into a slab of cheesecake when the fire alarm in Trala went off. Instead of popping a hunk of the delectable confection into his mouth, Kidd looked around the restaurant. His fellow diners had also taken note of the shrill siren, but nobody moved, not even the bartender, who continued to pour a martini.

Then came a cry from the Mendelssohn's lobby: "Everybody out!"

Kidd removed the napkin from his lap and wrapped his hands around the dessert plate—he would leave, but the cheesecake was coming with him. He lifted the plate, stuck the fork into his mouth and strode out of the restaurant, where he joined a slithering mass of hotel guests exiting the lobby.

"This way, people! This way!" The orders came from the bellhop, who was standing on the sidewalk and using his long arms to guide the guests into a safety zone near the curb. Kidd trudged across the veranda and down the steps, then he took up position at the front of the evacuees, where he ate his cheesecake and waited for the moment when Miguel would emerge from the hotel with Annabelle somehow secured to his body. Or better yet, maybe they would just stay up in the room and ride out the alarm. Kidd had been through enough fire alarms at hotels to know that most of them were false. He looked up to inspect the Mendelssohn against the dark Santa Monica night—off its façade and in its windows he saw no hint of an orange glow that would come from a fire somewhere in the building. What was more encouraging, when he sniffed, all he smelled was delicious cheesecake, not smoke.

Fire trucks soon arrived and firefighters entered the building clad in full gear. More horns blared from down Ocean Avenue—police cruisers. Kidd's concern intensified—maybe it wasn't a false alarm. He contemplated calling the room to tell Miguel that it was okay to bring Annabelle down, but he had to abandon that idea once he remembered that he had removed all the phones from the suite so Annabelle couldn't get her hands on an outside line.

Three more minutes, he thought. Three more minutes, then I'll go in after them. He opted to idle away the time by finishing the cheesecake. It was certainly delicious, silky on the tongue and rich of flavor, but it wasn't nearly as good as the cheesecake Amanda Pacheco used to make. In fact, in a sobering moment of epiphany, Kidd realized that nothing had been as good for him—not cheesecake, not food, not smells, or tastes, or sounds, or sights, not even life itself—since the day he had lost her.

One minute passed, then another. Kidd's nerves started to fray. Should I go in? he wondered. Finish your dessert, his brain ordered.

Kidd popped the penultimate forkful of cheesecake into his mouth, then he almost spit it out in shock at what he saw charging down the steps of the hotel—it was Annabelle, and she was running like a greyhound sprung from a starting gate. Kidd thanked Christ that she appeared unharmed, but she was alone—Miguel wasn't anywhere around her.

What the hell is going on? Kidd wondered. As Annabelle leapt to the sidewalk, Kidd dropped his plate and lunged forward, hoping to catch her. The plate shattered on the ground.

"Annabelle, stop!" Kidd shouted as he reached for her. But Charles Bentley Kidd found himself not fleet enough for his young, athletic daughter. She sped by him—Kidd couldn't tell if she hadn't seen him, or if she was just ignoring him—and ran at top flight down Ocean Avenue. From Kidd's viewpoint, she soon became a wisp of motion wavering into the streetscape.

"Was that Annabelle Kidd?" a female voice behind him asked.

"Could have been," a male voice said. "I heard that her dipshit father was staying on the eighth floor."

Kidd was about to turn around and tell the gentleman exactly which orifice he could shove his commentary into when Miguel came stumbling out of the hotel. He was walking with a limp and grabbing at his crotch like a four-year-old boy who had to go pee.

"Boss, boss!" Miguel cried. He lurched down the steps and fell into Kidd's arms.

"What in Christ's name is going on here?" Kidd asked.

"I think she managed to set off the fire alarm, boss," Miguel said, wheezing. "But I didn't fall for it. I stayed on the couch. She can't move the rope if I'm on the couch."

"So what happened?" Kidd asked.

"Management arrived," Miguel said. "Looking to protect you. But I still wouldn't get off the couch, boss—I'm loyal like that. They kept pounding on the door. Finally, they came in with two firemen. *They* pulled me off the couch. The minute I got pulled, your daughter yanked on the knob and slid the door wide enough to squeeze out. It was a heavy couch, boss, but she still did it."

Kidd was apoplectic. "So what happened to you?"

Miguel crumpled over and fell to the ground. It was easy for Kidd to see that his new chief of staff was suffering. "She came at me, boss," Miguel said. "Then she nailed me right in the *cojones*. With her feet. I mean, that chiquita reared back like she was kicking a field goal. Thank the Blessed Virgin I already have four kids—I think my nuts are busted. Oh, it hurts, boss. Make it stop."

Kidd knew there was nothing he could offer Miguel except time—a few minutes for the pain in his abdomen to subside, a few days for the residual soreness in his testicles to fade. If Miguel was lucky, he wouldn't ejaculate blood over the next week and a half.

Kidd left his writhing chief of staff on the curb and walked a few yards down the street. Annabelle had disappeared into the night, and where she had run to he didn't have the foggiest. But in that moment, when he should have been angry with her, or at least annoyed, and when he should have run after her to catch her again, he felt only pride.

He had locked his daughter in a bedroom by means of a rope tied from the doorknob to the pull-out sofa, with a rugged limo driver providing anchorage. She had no phone at her disposal, no bedding, no heavy objects, and no possible means of escape, and yet she had gotten out. And she had done it in the most spectacular fashion, with lots of lights, hordes of cops and firefighters, and ridiculous mayhem. The whole event was even sure to make the papers tomorrow.

Miguel could talk all he wanted about his *cojones*. Kidd was now certain that Annabelle had bigger *cojones* than both Miguel and her father combined.

And right at that moment, he just wanted to hug her for it.

CHAPTER 49

★★★★★★★★★★★★★★★★★★★★★★★★★★★★★★★★

That same night, on the opposite side of the continent from Santa Monica, Martha Kernick was just settling into the bubbling warmth of her new whirlpool bathtub when she thought she heard a knock at her front door.

Startled, Martha turned off the pulsing jets with a push of her toes. She let the water settle and cocked her head for a better listen. There it was—knock, knock, knock. They were quick, spare taps, as if they were coming from the knuckles of a lithe woman.

Who can that possibly be? Martha wondered. The time was almost midnight on Tuesday. It was raining outside, and tree limbs had been falling in the wind all day. What dummkopf would possibly want to call on her now?

Martha elected to stay in the tub. Given the circumstances, she considered it too risky to investigate. Not because Carl was gone, and had been gone for over a week, but because of what Martha had done *since* Carl had been gone. Quite simply, in her cantankerous husband's glorious absence, Martha Kernick had become a whore. Not a whore in a physical sense—she had only slept with two men in her life, and both of them had fled from her within days of each other—but a whore to the plastic. To credit cards. Several of them, actually, all in Carl's name. And the pleasure they were bringing her was better than any other sensation she had ever known.

To wit, Martha Kernick had made a number of expensive purchases lately. There was the ten-jet whirlpool tub for the master bathroom, the very tub in which she now reclined. There were the three high-definition televisions—a small one for the kitchen, a big one for the master bedroom, and the biggest one she could find for Carl's office downstairs, which, after she broke open the locked cabinet with an ax and had it and the old Emerson inside it hauled away, she now considered a family den. There were several pieces of new furniture, including a kitchen dinette set, two sofas, and a king-sized foam-mattress bed which was luxurious in its comfort. She had also purchased a whole new wardrobe from Saks in Stamford, some jewelry from Tiffany in Greenwich, and a complete fitness center for the basement, to help her get thinner.

Then there was her most gigantic purchase of all. It was currently parked in the driveway in full view of anyone who drove by—a brand new, burnt-orange Porsche Magnet V8 SUV, complete with power everything, satellite radio, heated seats, four-wheel drive, and the coveted GeoStar 5900 navigation system, so that Martha never got lost again. Unlike her other purchases, the Porsche hadn't gone on a credit card. The only thing required of Martha to drive it off the lot three days ago was a lump-sum payment of ninety-two thousand dollars, cut in the form of a certified check. If, when Carl finally returned home, his eyes popped out of his head at the sight of his wife's credit card bills, the sight of that Porsche and its accompanying reduction in their money market account balance would certainly give him a massive coronary.

Ah, well, she thought. He's the one who left town with my vehicle and hasn't bothered to call home since. Let him suffer.

As a result of her spending spree, there had been a flurry of activity in the Kernick home in recent days. Craftsmen, plumbers, delivery people, the cable guy—all had come and gone in a whirlwind of muddy boots, crass language, and butt crack. And they had left her home smelling joyously of change—of sawdust and caulking, fresh rubber and glue, new plastic and torn-open cardboard boxes. All of these service or delivery people, she was certain, had been given ample opportunity to inspect the growing inventory of Two Hoban Lane. Simply put, Martha now reeked of wealth, as if she had inherited a late husband's fortune, and she could not be sure that the knocks on the door, inasmuch as they sounded like the product of a small woman's fist, weren't really the set up for a robbery. Martha powered the jets again, closed her eyes, and slipped into a Calgon moment.

But the knocks didn't stop—they actually grew louder and more forceful. More desperate, Martha considered. Shutting off the jets for a second time, she got out of the tub, dried herself with a plush new bath towel, and draped a silk kimono around her body. She stepped into the bedroom and listened again. The knocks were thicker, maybe from a flat palm. Unless she did something, they might go on all night. So Martha cinched her kimono tightly and headed for the safest place she could think of to investigate the situation—the bedroom window overlooking the front of the house.

Peering out through the rain-speckled glass, she could only see the wet walkway of flagstone leading to the road. The angle was not sufficient to give her a view of the front steps. She unhooked the window locks and slid the glass up.

"Who's there?" Martha called into the night.

The knocking ceased. Someone leaned back from the front steps and glanced up at the window. It was a woman. Her hair was set high in wide pink curlers and she was wearing a housecoat. Martha saw that the woman was Mrs. Berkley, who lived a few houses up on Hoban Lane. The widow of Connecticut's most famous heart surgeon, she had lost her husband a decade ago only to find that she had more fun without him. She was now a world traveler, especially for holidays. Martha was a bit shocked that Mrs. Berkley hadn't left already to spend Thanksgiving in some exotic locale, where hunky Hispanic cabana boys would mix mojitos for her and massage her toes.

"Janelle?" Martha called.

"Oh, Martha, I'm so sorry to disturb you like this." Mrs. Berkley's breathing was rapid, as if she had sprinted over to the Kernick home.

"I'm coming down," Martha said. "Hold on." She went to close the window, but Janelle Berkley stopped her.

"Martha, we don't have time," the neighbor said. "I need you to come with me."

Martha felt her stomach rise into her throat. Was something wrong? Was Mrs. Berkley feeling ill? The woman lived a high-paced lifestyle after all, and she lived alone. "Are you okay?" Martha asked.

"No, it's not like that," Janelle Berkley said. "But it's the strangest thing. There's a phone call for you at my house."

A phone call? Martha was starting to wonder if the heat from the whirlpool wasn't making her hallucinate. "I don't understand," said Martha.

"Neither do I," said Janelle Berkley, "but she says she's Annabelle Kidd. She's calling from the West Coast. I thought it was a joke, but she insists she's the real thing."

Even without seeing herself in a mirror, Martha Kernick could tell that her blue eyes had lighted up. "Annabelle Kidd," she said. "That's Bent's daughter."

"Who's Bent?" Mrs. Berkley asked.

But Martha didn't have time to answer. "Be right down," she said. She shut the window and ran into the hallway, then she bounded down the stairs, her ample frame jiggling with every step. Without overcoat or umbrella, or even changing out of her kimono, she charged through the front door and into the rain.

"I'll take that call," she told Janelle Berkley.

She was happy to, so happy that she didn't bother to keep her recent purchases safe from thieves by locking her front door on the way out. Halfway up the street, in fact, Martha Kernick realized that she had left the front door wide open.

No sooner had Annabelle Kidd turned the corner from Ocean Avenue onto Broadway than she found her hope at getting free from the Mendelssohn tempered by reality.

The time was just after eight in the evening. It was dark outside and turning chilly, with a stiff breeze gaining. She had no coat or other sufficient outerwear that would allow her to spend the night on the street. Worse yet, she was penniless, without a cell phone, and without friends, all of whom had left earlier in the day for points homeward. To make matters the worst of all, the friend she had grown closest to over the past few days—a person whom she would now rely on in the most trying of situations—was probably in the process of having his belt and shoes taken away from him.

There was, however, one thing Annabelle knew she carried at her disposal, and that was her fame, as burdensome as that fame had become over the years. It was a vicious truism of Annabelle's existence that people never failed to recognize her wherever she went. In Hollywood she had actually found herself more famous than many of the movie stars she often met at social functions. Oscar winners, action heroes, dramatic doyennes, the latest preteen ingénue—it didn't matter. Being part of the acting trade in Los Angeles made you cliché, even for A-listers. But being the daughter of the most powerful man in the world, even if he was an embarrassing philanderer who had ended up shaming himself, his family and his country, and even if he was the only man in United States history ever expelled from the presidency by impeachment, well, that equaled pure gold. There was only one Annabelle Kidd anywhere on the planet, and people she didn't know loved to remind her of that fact by coming up to her and engaging in idle banter, usually about things as bland as the weather. So sure was Annabelle of her star power that she knew if she were to walk into a bar arm-in-arm with the most recent *People* Sexiest Man Alive, Annabelle Kidd would be asked for her autograph first.

That star power would be Annabelle's currency tonight. If she could spend that currency, whom would she contact? As she made her way down a quiet Broadway, heading toward the Third Street Promenade, Annabelle narrowed her choices to two: She could call her mother, who would find a way to emasculate Charles Bentley Kidd all the way from Chicago; or she could bypass her father and find a way to emasculate Carl Kernick. It was Carl who held the cards in this little game—all the power, especially if he pressed charges against his son.

But how could Annabelle emasculate Carl Kernick? There was only one option—she would call Ken's mom.

The process by which Annabelle Kidd found Martha Kernick involved a good helping of twenty-first century college student know-how—she used the Internet. With star power surrounding her, Annabelle walked into a sushi bar at the Third Street Promenade, signed sixteen autographs, shook more hands, took some hugs, then asked the restaurant manager if she could use the establishment's broadband connection and telephone. He obliged, but he insisted that she have her picture taken with him, and she had to promise to come back to sign it after it was printed and framed. Given the circumstances, it was a promise Annabelle would gladly keep.

Sitting down at a computer in the back office, Annabelle remembered that Ken lived on Hoban Lane in Simondale, Connecticut. She used a white-pages search engine to scan for Kernicks on such a street, but she had no luck. Annabelle suspected that Ken's phone number was unlisted, a good bet given the rampant paranoia clearly evident in Ken's father. But what about neighbors? Surely one of them might know the Kernick's phone number. Annabelle removed Ken's surname from the search parameters, clicked the find button, and prayed for a hit. She got one, but only one—the listing for a man called Arthur Berkley, M.D., who lived at Nine Hoban Lane. He would have to do, anger or no anger over a phone call later than eleven o'clock East Coast time on a weeknight. Annabelle picked up the restaurant manager's phone and dialed. It took four rings until someone answered.

The person who said "Hello?" was a woman, probably the doctor's wife, and she seemed a bit put out by the interruption at such a late hour. Annabelle apologized for the disturbance but pleaded her case—she needed to speak to Mrs. Kernick immediately. Did this woman know the phone number?

The woman didn't know Mrs. Kernick's phone number, and she resisted when Annabelle begged her to run over to the Kernick house in what Mrs. Berkley described as "inclement weather," but Annabelle finally prevailed by telling Mrs. Berkley that she was the daughter of former president Charles Bentley Kidd, and that the phone call was urgent. Star power won out again. Annabelle waited on the line, listening to dead air, while the woman left the house and presumably walked down the street to fetch Ken's mom.

After fifteen minutes, Annabelle heard a thud on the other end of the line, then chatter, then a rush of air as someone approached to pick up the receiver.

"This is Martha Kernick." The voice was as soft as silk, and irresistible. God, she sounds just like a female Ken, Annabelle thought. One of the first things Annabelle had liked about Ken was the supple timbre with which he spoke.

"Mrs. Kernick," Annabelle said, "I'm so sorry to bother you, but it's an emergency."

"That's all right, dear," Mrs. Kernick said. "But is your father okay?"

Annabelle was taken aback. "Ah, yes, he's fine," she said. And in that instant, Annabelle knew that her father and Ken's mom had had an affair. Annabelle pulled the receiver away from her ear, then she closed her eyes and shook her head. Did Charles Bentley Kidd's hound-doggedness have no end? Could Annabelle ever travel down any path without discovering some patch of ground on which her father had not spread his scent? She doubted it. But tonight was no time to get on her knees and inspect the terrain at close range. She put the receiver back to her ear.

"No, Mrs. Kernick," she said. "It's about Ken."

"*My* Ken?" Mrs. Kernick asked. "Kenny?" There was dead silence from the other end of the phone. Annabelle suspected that Mrs. Kernick's mind had turned its attention from images of some fleeting passion with Charles Bentley Kidd to images of what was really important in her life—her son. Given that she was taking an urgent phone call at midnight, Annabelle could only assume that the images this woman was seeing must have been terrifying.

Mrs. Kernick stammered. "Is... is he okay?" There was a hitch of helplessness to her voice.

"He's okay, Mrs. Kernick," Annabelle said. "He's not physically hurt or anything like that."

A sigh came over Annabelle's earpiece. "Oh, thank God," Mrs. Kernick said. "Thank God, thank God."

"But he's gotten himself into trouble," Annabelle said.

"But he's healthy," Mrs. Kernick said.

"His danger is of a legal nature," Annabelle said. "He's been arrested."

"He's in jail?" Ken's mom asked.

"Probably in processing right now," Annabelle said.

"Well, what in God's name happened?" Mrs. Kernick asked.

"It wasn't his fault," Annabelle told her. "He was just minding his own business. We were heading up to El Tocón for the holiday—that's wine country around here. We were going to have a nice time. I really like your son, Mrs. Kernick. He's such a gentleman, and so honest and respectful. You did such a good job raising him."

Now it was Mrs. Kernick's turn to be taken aback. "Thank you, dear," she said, clearly stumbling for words. "He was an easy boy to raise. He never gave me any trouble."

"He wasn't giving anybody trouble tonight either, Mrs. Kernick," Annabelle said. "Believe me on that. But somebody decided to get in his way."

"Who would want to get in Kenny's way?" Mrs. Kernick asked.

Annabelle held her breath. With her next words she knew she was about to launch a family war that would stretch the length of the continent. She did not relish doing it, but found the unpleasant business supremely necessary—Ken needed her to do it. Finally, she let out a sigh and forged on. "It was your husband," Annabelle said.

There was more dead silence on the other end of the phone, but Annabelle could sense that this silence wasn't born of fear for Ken's safety—it was born of anger. Mrs. Kernick was putting together the pieces of a vast puzzle, pieces which reached back long before Annabelle Kidd came onto the scene, and of which she only had a partial view.

"Where is he?" Mrs. Kernick asked. Her soft voice had turned to stone.

"Who?" Annabelle asked. "Ken, or your husband?"

"Where there's one, dear, you'll soon find the other." Annabelle heard Mrs. Kernick ask Mrs. Berkley for a pad of paper. "Let's start with Kenny."

Annabelle shook her head. "I don't know where they've taken him, Mrs. Kernick. He's probably at the station closest to the University of the West."

"Where is that?" Mrs. Kernick asked.

"In Westwood," Annabelle said. "It's part of Los Angeles."

Annabelle heard the scratch of ballpoint pen against paper. When it stopped, Mrs. Kernick said, "All right, dear, I want you to tell me exactly what happened. Don't mince it—give me the facts. Go back to when you first met my son."

Annabelle took a deep breath and related the whole story of her involvement with Ken Kernick. In telling his mother about it, Annabelle felt warm at the memories. Ken had been an unexpected shining light in a life that was growing cold from a lack of male involvement. That they had kissed and felt nothing from it didn't diminish Ken's presence in her life. He had, in such a short time, become dear to her, and having no desire to sleep with him—nor him with her—only made that endearment more precious.

"You're good for Kenny," Mrs. Kernick said when Annabelle finished the tale.

"I'm sorry, Mrs. Kernick?" Annabelle said.

"I'm glad he found you," Mrs. Kernick said. "That's all."

The feeling is mutual, Annabelle thought. "So are you going to call the jail and get him out?" she asked.

"It's going to take more than that," Mrs. Kernick said. "You've met my husband."

"I didn't really get a chance to talk to him," Annabelle said.

Mrs. Kernick sighed. "Trust me, dear, you didn't miss much. He's not all that fucking exciting." She giggled. "Oh my, did I just curse? Well, isn't that crass. Here's something else that's crass—it's high time my husband got a cocksucking bitch slap."

"So what do we do?" Annabelle asked.

Mrs. Kernick said, "What we do is find a hotel I can call."

Annabelle shook her head. What was Ken's mom talking about? "I'm sorry, Mrs. Kernick," she said, "but I don't understand."

"The first thing you need to understand, Annabelle, is that my name is Martha. Please call me that."

"Okay, Martha. I will." Annabelle smiled. She liked this woman. "What's the second thing?"

"That I want you to find a hotel I can call," Martha said, "then I want you to stay there tonight and get some sleep."

"Why is that?" Annabelle asked.

Martha set her voice in stone again. "Because I'm going to pick you up in the morning."

Annabelle pinched her face in confusion. She was completely stymied. "But how are you going to do that?" she asked.

"Such is the easy part, Annabelle," Martha said. Then she let off a deliciously sinister laugh. "I'll just use my twit husband's credit card."

CHAPTER 50

★ ★

That Tuesday evening before Thanksgiving turned out to be the longest night of Kenny's life.

Arriving at the processing facility in the care of Officer Torres, Kenny expected to be interviewed, fingerprinted, and stood up for a mug shot. None of it happened. Instead, Kenny was taken to a bare anteroom, where he was ordered by Officer Torres to place his valuables in a manila envelope. After Kenny complied, Officer Torres grabbed Kenny's forearm and ushered the boy from the anteroom into a holding area set off behind a thick retaining door. The time was roughly seven o'clock. The entire holding area smelled of urine, vomit, and feces, which had been scattered about by detainees too intoxicated, or too rebellious, to use the stainless steel toilet near the wall.

Kenny's first cellmates on that Tuesday evening were a yuppie who looked as if he had been busted for drunk driving, a Middle Eastern man who constantly stared at the floor, and a young Asian gangbanger who glared at Kenny. Between the noxious smells and the ire burning in the Asian's eyes, Kenny didn't give himself much of a chance to avoid asphyxiation or homicide. Things turned particularly troublesome an hour into his detainment when the Asian strode over to Kenny, hacked up a wad of phlegm and spit it into Kenny's face, hitting him in the cheek. Why the Asian would do such a thing, Kenny had no idea, but it scared the hell out of him. He figured that if he wiped the spit off, the Asian would probably beat him to death. So Kenny left it where it was and felt it oozing toward his chin.

The Asian was the first to leave the cell, which allowed Kenny to wipe the phlegm off his face. Next went the yuppie and then the Middle Eastern man. But Kenny would get no respite on this night, no moment alone. Each time someone walked out, somebody new walked in. As the hours crawled into the later evening, the levels of harassment and intimidation only increased.

In the course of one night, Kenny was yelled at in several foreign languages (none of which he spoke), pushed to the floor by a street thug who wanted Kenny's bench seat, kicked in both shins, robbed of his leather jacket, and stood over by a homeless man who undid his fly and whipped out his penis, ready to use Kenny as the toilet bowl until Kenny jumped away from the stream. He was the target of growls, curses and shoves, of scratches, body slams and severe vocal castigations. And that was before the bikers showed up.

The bikers were the worst.

Kenny was fairly certain that the arrival of tattooed men with goatees never boded well for harmonious coexistence in any place on earth, especially a jail cell. Detained for their part in a bar brawl, which they announced the moment the officer left the holding area, they made a fast inventory of their cellmates, black eyes searching among the seven faces already behind bars for the smallest, the weakest, the easiest to devour.

Giving a thorough scan, they apparently decided on Kenny. The bikers set upon him like wolves to a wounded lamb.

"Hey, faggot!" they shouted. "Look at the little faggot!" Or "Ain't you dressed pretty. I bet you got that sticky stuff in your hair, too, don't you?" Or "Why you in here, queer bait? Selling ass in West Hollywood?" To each inquiry, Kenny tried to avoid an answer. With each avoidance, the larger of the two bikers, a man of gray teeth, would cuff Kenny upside the head and shout, "What's the matter, you home-ay-sexual? Left your tongue in your fag lover's mouth?" Then the bikers would laugh and Kenny would be moved to offer some response. If the response wasn't what they wanted to hear, the big biker would cuff him again. It went on and on. The other members of the cell smartly stayed out of it.

But the bikers' intimidation didn't stop at verbal harassment or the occasional blow to the skull. They rousted Kenny from bench to bench. They picked him up and threw him back and forth, telling him they were playing a game of dwarf tossing. They hid his glasses and made him find them, one time putting them in the underwear of another cellmate, until Kenny practically had to molest the guy to retrieve them. They flipped him to see how he reacted to gravity and spun him around to watch him stagger. At one unfortunate point, the smaller of the two bikers, who was still a big man of approximately six-foot-two, told Kenny to pay homage to his mother in Kansas by kissing the tattoo devoted to her on the biker's right butt cheek. When Kenny refused, the biker threw him into the bars then farted in his face as he lay splayed out on the floor.

"That's what you get for dishonoring my mama!" the biker yelled at Kenny. Then he grabbed Kenny by the hair, dragged him across the cell and pressed his face into the pile of shit in the corner. Kenny resisted just enough to turn his head so that the shit didn't get him in the mouth, nose or glasses, but from the jaw to the ear. The bikers laughed. They insisted everybody else laugh with them. Kenny felt his blood run cold. His night of terror seemed to have no end.

Hours after they arrived, the bikers were called out from the cell. Their parting shots to Kenny were words of warning.

"If I ever see you on the street, faggot," the big one said, "it's gonna be a bad day for your in-tess-tynes. You hear me?" He made a gesture like he was slicing with a Bowie knife. The bikers both guffawed. The hideous sound of their laughter rung in Kenny's ears until well after they were gone.

With the bikers removed, the cell turned quiet, but there was still a palpable tension between the five remaining detainees. None of them bothered Kenny, but one of them insisted on talking to himself, engaging in independent arguments and ordering himself to perform bizarre tasks, like standing in the middle of the cell on one leg. Kenny could get no respite. The thought of sleep consumed him, but he was too jacked up on adrenaline to fade. One by one, the four other cellmates were called, until Kenny, by attrition, was the only person left. For a moment, he had the glorious thought that new arrivals would not be joining him. The flow from earlier in the evening had seemed to dry up. He reclined on a bench and closed his eyes. Sleep would be a long time coming, but at least he had solitude.

Then he heard the retaining door open. By now, he didn't even bother to look up.

"Why is it," a familiar voice asked, "that every time I find you these days, you're at a police station?"

Kenny turned his head and saw his father standing outside the cell. Behind him lurked Officer Torres, who was jingling a set of keys. Carl Kernick turned to Officer Torres and said, "We'd like a few minutes alone." Officer Torres nodded at Carl, then he walked away, shutting the retaining door behind him and locking Kenny into the holding area with his father, although Carl and his son were still separated by the steel bars.

Kenny studied Carl. His father had changed clothing from the previous evening. He was wearing khaki pants and a polo shirt. He also seemed unrested, and his neck was encased in a foam brace. If Carl was injured, it would explain why he had appeared so stiff last night. Carl struggled to lift his arms into a fold, then he let out a huff. The man looked like he could use a cigarette.

Kenny sat up. "What happened to your neck?"

Carl scowled at him. "Do you really think my neck is your biggest concern, Kenny?"

Kenny shrugged. "Just thought I'd ask." There was an awkward silence between them. Kenny glanced around the cell, taking note of its emptiness. "Could you at least tell me what time it is?"

Carl eyed Kenny suspiciously, then he cocked his wrist and held it up to his face. "It's seven past noon," he said.

"Noon?" Kenny gasped. He shook his head, stunned. It had indeed been a long night—seventeen hours, to be exact. "That's crazy," he said to his father. "It's so hard to gauge time in here. I thought it was maybe just after breakfast. But noon." Kenny looked at Carl. "Don't you think that's crazy?"

"Crazy?" Carl huffed. "I'll tell you what I think is crazy, Kenny. What's crazy is what's happening to my son."

"Why, whatever do you mean?" Kenny asked with decided nonchalance, knowing full well that he was posing the question to his father from behind steel bars.

"Don't be a dummkopf, Kenny," Carl said. "This is hardly the time for it. Have you seen what this place has done to you? You look like shit."

Kenny chuckled under his breath, remembering the dried cake of feces coating his face. "Well, if it's any consolation to you," he said, "I smell like it, too."

"You think this is funny?" Carl barked. He stormed to the bars and glowered at his son. "You think I find this amusing?"

Kenny looked away. He never enjoyed his father's anger, and he particularly didn't enjoy it now.

"Let me explain something to you, Kenny. The only reason you haven't been booked yet is through my good graces. Did you know that?"

Kenny said nothing.

"Oh, it's the truth," Carl said. "There's a bunch of police officers out there just waiting to bring you up on charges. But they want a statement from me first."

"So why don't you give it to them?" Kenny asked.

"For some stupid reason, I still have hope for you," Carl said. "You've spent the past two weeks under the spell of a wizard, Kenny, a man of loose moral fiber. I'm willing to forgive your transgressions for that reason. But I am not playing games with you anymore. I swear to the depths of hell, I am done with this insanity. Do you understand me?"

"Charles Bentley Kidd didn't make me do anything," Kenny said. "Everybody has self-determination. It just takes some people longer to find it."

"That's the mind control talking," Carl said. "See, Kenny, he's cast a spell over you."

Kenny asked, "Was it Charles Bentley Kidd's mind control that made me steal underwear at Harvard?"

Carl's silence conceded the point.

"Do you know why I stole underwear at Harvard?" Kenny asked. "Do you have any idea?"

Again, Carl remained silent.

"Then until you do," Kenny said, "you don't know anything."

"I'll tell you what I know, Kenny," Carl said. "I know that you're on a bad road, son—a road that's leading to your complete destruction. We can argue about how you got there, but there's no arguing about how you're getting off—you're coming home with me. Today. No questions asked. Understand? We're leaving in the Cadillac as soon as you're released. That will give us a week together for me to explain to you the folly of your ways. And in a year, when you're settled in at Yale and back on the path to success, this will all be a fading memory."

But I don't want this to be a fading memory, Kenny thought. I want to remember these experiences for the rest of my life. I want to revel in them. I want to feel like I've felt during the past two weeks for every remaining day of my existence. Why can't you understand that?

Kenny wanted to tell Carl these things—more so, he wanted to scream them. He wanted to stand on the bench and stomp and yell. He wanted to wave his fists and shout like an old-time revivalist. He wanted to make Carl hear his voice. But he was hindered. There was something lodged in his throat, and its presence was rendering him mute.

That something was a thick, gelatinous lump.

Seeing Kenny offer no resistance, Carl said, "Then it's agreed. I'll go talk to the officers and tell them I made a mistake." He turned to leave.

Carl was about to knock on the retaining door when Kenny found a hint of voice. From somewhere deep within him, softer than a whisper, he managed to say, "What... if?"

Carl turned back to scrutinize Kenny, clearly hesitant. "What did you just say?" he asked.

Kenny swallowed repeatedly, fighting the lump, trying to get his voice to launch. "What... if?" he asked. "What if... I... said...?"

"Honestly, Kenny, I don't know what you're trying to say," Carl said. "And I don't much care."

Kenny twisted his throat. It was no use. The lump wouldn't move. But he spoke anyway, his voice going around the lump like rapids around a submerged boulder. "What if I said, 'No'?"

"Excuse me?" Carl said.

"No," Kenny said.

"No what?" Carl asked.

"My answer," Kenny said, "is no."

"You're saying no?" Carl asked.

Kenny managed a nod.

"No?!" Carl shouted.

Kenny managed a bigger nod.

Carl shook his head, then he walked back to the bars and eyed Kenny coldly. "Don't be stupid, Kenny."

Kenny gathered all his might and swallowed hard, so hard that he strained his jaw muscles. Gloriously, the lump jarred loose. Where it flowed off to he didn't know, but his voice was unleashed. Kenny took a moment to restore its strength, then he said, "Why do you always call me stupid?"

"I do not always call you stupid," Carl said.

"Sure you do," Kenny said. "You do it coyly by calling me a dummkopf—a dumb head—but its effect is no less potent. So let's say I act like a supreme dummkopf and decline your offer. What then?"

Carl's pupils tightened, he pressed his lips flat, and an ursine scowl spread across his face—it was the terrifying look which had intimidated Kenny so many times before. Combined with Carl's rage, it could be completely convincing. Carl squeezed into the bars and pointed a stubby, nicotine-stained finger at his son.

"All right," he huffed. "You still want to play games, I'll tell you what. I walk out of this room and I say to those officers out there that you absolutely meant to steal my vehicle. That there's no doubt in my mind about it. That you did it with malice aforethought. Do you know what they'll do then, Kenny? They'll pull you out of here, interrogate you, fingerprint you, strip search you, and take your picture. They'll book you, Kenny. Then they'll contact the district attorney's office, where the fun will really start. You'll be arraigned, and given your recent history, I'll make sure the judge thinks you're a flight risk, so you can forget bail. You'll sit in a jail cell for months, then you'll go to trial. With my testimony, you'll be convicted. Then you'll spend at least a year—a year, Kenny!—in prison for a felony. If you think that a night in this hellhole was no picnic—and by the look of you, I'm guessing it wasn't—then just wait until you get locked up with the boys doing big time. Your name will no longer be Kenny—it will be Kendra. That's what will happen to you, my son. I swear to God. Now, do you still feel like being a dummkopf?"

Carl glared at him, his breathing stunted by rage. Kenny gave the man a moment to collect himself, to let his words settle down, then he looked at Carl with genuine sincerity and said, "Yeah, I do."

"Excuse me?" said Carl. He cupped a hand to his ear. "I don't think I heard you correctly."

"You heard me fine," Kenny said. "Now for the first time, I want you to *listen* to me. You want to go out there and sell me down the river, then do it. Knock on that door and get the process started. But stop wasting my life."

Carl's face went pale. "Jesus Christ, Kenny! Do you think I'm kidding?"

"With all due respect," Kenny said, "I don't give a flying fuck if you're kidding."

Carl gasped at Kenny's use of the four-letter word.

"Oh, you didn't know I drop f-bombs?" Kenny asked. "Well, here's some more. I'm tired of fucking dealing with you, Carl. So get the fuck out of here. Tell them whatever you fucking want. Then don't feel the need to darken my detention cell again with your cocksucking motherfucking presence. Do you hear me?" He waved Carl off.

With Kenny's diatribe over, Carl's jaw came unhinged. It seemed to Kenny an eternity before the man shook off his shock and pointed toward the door. "Fine then, you crass little runt, I'm going right now!"

"I'm watching you right now," Kenny said. "In fact, I'm pissed off you're still here."

"I'm going!" Carl said.

"Go!" Kenny said.

"Right now!" Carl said.

"Just get the fuck out of here!" Kenny said. Then he reclined on the bench and stared at the ceiling. End of conversation.

"Fine!" Carl barked. He straightened up, turned toward the door and took one step forward. But he stopped short. That's when all the hot air seemed to abandon his balloon. He lowered his head, which must have caused him considerable pain given his injury, and when he looked up again, Kenny saw something in his brash father's eyes that he had never seen before—fear.

"Kenny," the man said, "be reasonable. You have no idea what you're getting yourself into."

"Bullshit," Kenny said, sitting up. "That is utter fucking bullshit. In the last seventeen hours, I've been spit on, taunted, punched, kicked, intimidated, tossed back and forth, and had my face pressed into a pile of shit. I think I know exactly what I'm getting myself into."

"Then how can you continue with this charade?" Carl asked. His wide brown eyes fixed on Kenny, waiting for a response.

But Kenny didn't answer. Not because he didn't have an answer, but because the answer he did have—and one in which he felt truly confident—had come from a place that Carl Kernick could never fathom.

It came from his spirit.

CHAPTER 51

★ ★

Kenny Kernick might have been raised a Catholic, but he rarely believed in God anymore. Unlike many people who grew up with a religion only to abandon that religion's tenets as adults, however, Kenny's skepticism wasn't an acquired fad of the newly emancipated. The doubts stormed in early for Young Kernick. They overtook him in his first catechism classes, where he found the teachings about Jesus a bit hard to swallow. Born of a virgin? Miracles with wine and lepers? Rising from death? Huh?

Instead of dwelling on these irregularities, Kenny had plunged into his encyclopedias at age six and emerged years later with a trenchant belief in the immutable calculations of science over any mysteries of faith. And since the Catholic Church didn't stress a notion of the divine apart from Jesus, Kenny put God on the back burner of his mind. To Kenny, God was an amorphous concept, not a structured influence. An observer of path, not a paver of it.

Then one Monday morning, as he rolled out of Nebraska and into Colorado with a snoozing Charles Bentley Kidd by his side, Kenny hit the Rocky Mountains, and his belief in the Almighty turned headlong.

In the Rockies, Kenny was confronted with the worst driving experience of his journey. Steep grades of incline and descent gave way to crazy curves which cut around mountains in tight arcs. Heavy traffic, already traveling en masse at imprudent speeds, was made more dangerous by a raging snowstorm. Mack trucks showed no mercy; they assaulted passing motorists with barrages of slush and mud from their tires. The whole thing was mayhem. But for all of the Rockies' perils, nothing was as bad for Kenny as the altitude.

Within twenty minutes of entering the Rockies, Kenny had altitude asphyxiation—he was unable to breathe and feeling drunk, and he was quite certain that at any moment, he was going to drive the Cadillac off a curve or ram it into the side of a cliff. Instead, his demise came less dramatically. As he climbed toward ten thousand feet, his oxygen supply dwindled and he entered a swirling tunnel. A sign on the highway stated that he was coming into the Eisenhower Tunnel, but to Kenny, it was the Tunnel of Death, and out of its tiled walls, he saw all the relatives he had only ever heard stories about from his mother and father as they stepped from the ether and waved him forward into the light, which was glowing in a point at the end of the road surface. Following his deceased relatives' lead, Kenny pressed into the light and re-emerged back in the mountains. But it was a different kind of mountains Kenny found on the other side of the tunnel—a heavenly kind. The snowstorm was gone. Blue sky shone above a line of marbled peaks. Pine trees stood tall and wore cloaks of fresh snow, an angelic choir singing praises to God. But what God? God, to Kenny, didn't exist. And even if He did exist, He certainly wouldn't concern Himself with matters of humanity, especially when it came to someone as insignificant as Kenny Kernick. Or would He? As was his wont, Kenny wanted answers.

He got his answers near Breckenridge, when he rounded a sharp bend in the highway and saw, high above the road and directly in front of him, a rock formation of the most heinous angles and shapes. The formation formed a face, but it was a face of unimaginable ugliness, cut of warped igneous tumors and unhealed limestone scars, of deeply eroded pits and nauseating asymmetry. But to Kenny, even in its ugliness, this face in the rocks was the most divine structure he had ever seen. It was glorious, magnificent—he couldn't take his eyes off it. That's when he understood: Something this ugly could only be the face of God; something this heinous could only be divine. God did exist after all. And apparently, God cared, because as Kenny approached Him, gazing up in wonder through the windshield, the face in the rock parted its craggy lips and spoke.

"If you've made it this far, Kenny," His voice said, "then you have proven the folly of your thoughts. You are not here to be destroyed, devoured or obliterated, but to attack life with passion. You are not here to be reduced by failure, but to learn from it. Suffer no anxiety, Young Kernick. No one—not one single person—will ever knock you down in this world. You may have setbacks and you may struggle, but you will never, ever, find yourself beaten."

And for the first time in his life, as the Cadillac cut over the Vail Pass and on toward Grand Junction, and as his senses returned to him in the falling altitude, Kenneth Andrew Kernick believed something, not scientifically, but spiritually.

"No one—not one single person—will ever knock you down in this world. You may have setbacks and you may struggle, but you will never, ever, find yourself beaten."

Those words, spoken to Kenny by an inanimate geological formation in the Rocky Mountains, were taking root in Kenny's head as he dug in his heels against his father.

No one would knock him down in this world any longer, of that Kenny Kernick felt certain. His father could try, as he was trying now, as he watched his son squirm in a jail cell and threatened to send him off to a worse place if Kenny didn't acquiesce to his demands. Carl had been playing this game with his son, in one form or another, almost every day of Kenny's life. But today was different. At the moment of greatest danger to his future well-being, Kenny believed that the time had arrived to put an end to Carl's manipulative paternal bullying.

Kenny said to his father, "What I'm telling you is to go and do what you think you have to do, and then to leave me alone. I'll be fine."

"You won't be fine, Kenny," Carl said, clenching his meaty paws around the bars. "It will be the end of you."

"I doubt that," Kenny said.

"Oh, you do, huh?" Carl let out a dismissive snort.

"The difference between us," Kenny said, "is that I'm not looking for perfection. You seek perfection in everything, Dad—in your work, in your finances, and worst of all, in your family. In the process, you've sucked the life out of your wife, and you've come close to doing it to me. I'm not some machine you can design to pump detergent into bottles with a zero spillage rate."

Carl lowered his head. "I never thought of you as a machine, Kenny."

"But you acted like it," Kenny said. "And unlike one of your machines, I'm ready to fail, in the worst way. I'm ready to go out into the world and get my ass handed to me, just to see what I'm made of. If getting put away for car theft is the first step in that process, so be it—I've made my choices. Whatever the outcome, I'll survive. After all, I'm impervious. Like the seagulls."

"Like the what?" Carl asked. "What are you talking about?"

"Did I mention I've seen God?" Kenny said. "You should see Him, too, Dad. He's one ugly motherfucker."

Carl threw his son a twisted look. "Kenny, I think you're going crazy."

"Actually, I'm being quite sane," Kenny said, freezing his father with an icy stare. "And the first component to my sanity is this—I would rather go off to a real prison than spend another day in a prison of your making. I prefer self-determination, wherever it leads. You abhor self-determination unless it's your own. In the process, you've created a wife and son who hate you."

"You hate me, Kenny?" Carl asked. He seemed on the verge of tears.

Kenny said nothing.

"But sons are supposed to love their fathers, no matter what," Carl said. "You're supposed to love me, Kenny."

"Maybe so," Kenny said. "But I don't have to like you. You can change that right now, though. You can support me in what I want. Otherwise, prison or no prison, I'm gone."

Carl took his hands off the bars and rubbed his face. His eyes were moist, and it was easy to tell that he was at the end of his rope. "Oh, Kenny, you're going to be the death of me."

"Actually, I think those Parliaments are going to be the death of you," Kenny said. "I have nothing to do with it."

"I haven't had a cigarette in days," Carl said. "I've been thinking I might quit."

"Mom will be overjoyed," Kenny said. "Now the house won't smell like an ashtray. Maybe she'll even kiss you again."

Carl let out a guilty chuckle. He stared down at his shoes for a moment then looked up. When he did, his eyes were clear, and Kenny heard him ask a question that Carl had never asked Kenny in eighteen years. "So what do you want?"

Kenny caught his breath, such was the shock of hearing those five simple words. He took a moment to gather together the collection of ideas that had been floating around his head since he had arrived in Los Angeles.

"First off," Kenny told his father, "I want to go to the University of the West."

"But that's a second-tier school," Carl said.

"You went to a second-tier school," Kenny said. "No, more like a fourth-tier. Western Connecticut State, remember? You did quite well for yourself."

"But, Kenny," Carl said, "you're Ivy League."

"No, Dad," Kenny said, "you're Ivy League. Or you thought of yourself that way. But I want to be here. West is my destiny."

"You just want to stay in Los Angeles because you're engaging in sexual relations with that Annabelle," Carl said. "See, this is what I always worried about with you, Kenny—making a decision based on a girl."

"I'm doing what with Annabelle?" Kenny asked. "Who told you that?" The image of Charles Bentley Kidd flashed through Kenny's mind. "Forget it. I know who told you that."

"So it's true," Carl said.

"Whatever is happening between Annabelle and me is between Annabelle and me," Kenny said. "But you should thank her, Dad, because she's given me some direction in my life. She's shown me what's possible out here, how someone can transform and start anew. Which is why my second request is for you to buy me a condo in Santa Monica."

"Santa Monica?" Carl said. "Now I know you're crazy. Condos in Santa Monica must cost a million dollars."

"Actually, Dad, they cost millions of dollars," Kenny said. "But you can afford it. Easily. Think of it as an early college graduation present."

"That's a little out of my price range for a graduation present," Carl said.

"When it comes to me and Mom, everything is out of your price range," Kenny said. "Including a high school graduation gift, which you never got me." Kenny folded his arms and turned his head. "Ah, well, maybe you'd rather see me in a coed dorm on campus." Kenny turned back and flashed Carl a sly smile. "Think of all the underwear I could dig into."

"Still with the underwear?" Carl asked.

"Do you really want to find out?" Kenny said.

Carl let out a sigh. "I don't know, Kenny. Why can't you just come home?"

"This is my home," Kenny said.

"How can you say that?" Carl asked. "You've been here less than a week."

"Because home is the place you miss," Kenny said. "And of all the places I've been, I would miss Santa Monica the most. I can do it on my own, you know. I can emancipate and use college loans. That's an option. But I'm asking you to work with me instead of against me."

Carl crinkled his face. He clearly wasn't relishing this line of conversation. "You'd get your college degree?" he asked.

"I'll probably do it in three years," Kenny said.

Carl made a pyramid with his fingers and put them to his lips. He seemed to be considering Kenny's offer. After a few moments, he asked meekly, "Maybe someday you could do graduate work at an Ivy League school?"

Kenny smiled. "I could do that. Maybe. If that's what's right for me. But I won't force it on myself, if that's what you're asking."

Carl shook his head. He was out of options and he knew it. "Well then, Kenny, I guess you have a deal." Carl extended a hand through the bars, ready to shake. But Kenny hesitated.

"There's just one last thing," Kenny said.

"What's that?" Carl asked.

Kenny flashed Carl one of Charles Bentley Kidd's cocksure smirks. "I want the Cadillac."

Carl's eyelids flickered, but before he could offer a reply, there was a burst of noise from the outside hall. Muffled, it sounded as if a woman was yelling at someone. Both Kenny and his father turned toward the door. Kenny made out the words, "You take me to him right now!" There was a jingle of keys. The door crawled open. The yelling became focused and louder.

"And don't you even think about charging him with anything!" the voice was shouting. To his utter shock, Kenny saw his mother step into the holding area. She was followed by Annabelle and Officer Torres.

"Kenny!" his mother screamed upon seeing him. "Ken!" Annabelle shouted. They rushed the bars.

"Are you all right?" his mother asked.

"They didn't hurt you, did they, Ken?" Annabelle said.

"I'm fine, really," Kenny said.

"God, this place smells awful," Annabelle said.

"You're all bruised, Kenny," his mother said. "What's that brown stuff on the side of your head? Is that dried blood?"

"No, Mom," Kenny said, "that's shit. This is a tough place."

Martha gasped. "I don't want you in here another minute."

Carl stepped up to Martha and grabbed her by the shoulders. "Martha, calm down," he said. "It's all right."

Martha turned toward Carl. Kenny watched as his mother's blue eyes went aflame.

"I was just getting him out," Carl told her. "We had a little negotiation, Kenny and I. You should be proud of our boy, Martha, he's one hard bargainer. But we came to a solid agreement—Kenny's going to stay in Los Angeles, he's going to resume his studies at the University of the West, and he's going to follow his own road. And hey, he even convinced me to give him my Cadillac for the journey." Carl looked at Kenny and winked. "After all, I never did get him a high school graduation gift."

"You're applying to West?" Annabelle asked Kenny with a glint in her eye. "Well, I'm sure they'll take you. You'll immediately destroy the curve for everyone."

Carl looked over at Officer Torres and gestured toward the cell door. "I think there was a misunderstanding between my son and me, officer. He thought I had given him permission to use the car. There was no malice aforethought."

Officer Torres nodded conspiratorially, then he stepped to the cell and unlocked the door. Kenny walked out of the cell and into the arms of Annabelle, who put a hand to her nose and offered him only a half-hug. "God, Ken, you smell terrible," she said. "We need to find you a bathroom. Martha, could we find Ken someplace to wash up?"

But Martha didn't acknowledge her. Kenny's mother was still glaring at her husband, and her body was stiffening at the sight of the man. Carl tried to smile at her.

"Hi, honey," he said, holding out his arms. "Isn't this a surprise."

Martha's eyes narrowed.

"Sorry I never called."

Martha growled.

"Did you miss me?"

Martha didn't miss him. She connected her fist with his jaw on the first try. Then she hit him on the ear. The cheek. The temple. The chin. And on the mouth, over and over.

Martha flailed at him, pounding Carl Kernick in every spot not protected by quivering arms and hands.

"Don't! You! Ever! Put! Your! Wife! Or! Child! Through! This! Stupid! Shit! Again!"

It took Kenny and Annabelle three minutes, and the help of four police officers, to pull her off him.

CHAPTER 52

★ ★

Although he had once been the most powerful man in the world—at one time more omniscient and well-informed than any other human being on the planet—former president Charles Bentley Kidd found himself spending all of Wednesday morning and most of the afternoon on a desperate, fruitless search for his daughter.

He started with the streets around Santa Monica, walking them up and down with his eyes tuned for a tall, pretty girl with auburn hair. By midmorning, he was searching the Third Street Promenade but saw no sign of her in the shops and eateries. His only lead came at a sushi restaurant, where a manager told him that Annabelle had been in the night before and used the phone. Where she called, the manager didn't know, but he told Kidd that she had left right after the call and had not been back. When Kidd asked what kind of mood Annabelle was in, the manager described her as "distracted." Then he eyed Kidd with no hint of irony. Kidd thanked him and moved on.

Thinking Annabelle might have called her mother, Kidd returned to the Mendelssohn. He hunted down a phone number for Margaret in Chicago and placed a call to her. It turned out to be a pathetic endeavor. The call lasted twenty seconds, just long enough for Margaret to ask what he wanted, surmise the situation, and curse him out viciously for being a piss-ass father of unparalleled fuck-up proportion.

She needn't have reminded him. Ever since he had watched Annabelle charge from the Mendelssohn and disappear down Ocean Avenue, Kidd had felt like a pile of dog shit. What had he done to his precious little girl? Why had he interfered? Kenny wasn't bad for her. Of all the boys to take an interest in Annabelle over the years, Kidd actually thought Kenny the best. Why hadn't Kidd seen that potential through all the jealousy? Why had he been clouded in his judgment by possessiveness? How could he make things right?

The first step toward resolution was to find Annabelle—everything else flowed from there. Thwarted by Margaret, he hung up and called a rental car company that delivered the vehicles to their clients. When the deliveryman arrived an hour later with a minivan, Kidd signed for it and, for the first time since his inauguration as the governor of Ohio, drove himself.

It was an awkward experience, this renewed acclimation to gauges, shifts and pedals. He jerked the car at starts and often forgot to use his turn signals, and driving on the freeway caused him fits of anxiety. But he felt rewarded by the experience, as if he were reclaiming some forgotten part of his life, making himself independent once more.

He drove to the University of the West and surveyed the campus, but he never slowed the minivan to anything less than ten miles per hour. He found Annabelle's dorm dark and the campus vacant. Off campus, he parked on Soltavega Boulevard and searched the coffee houses and restaurants that ringed the university grounds. Annabelle was nowhere to be seen. He couldn't even locate a girl who resembled Annabelle—a girl from whom he might get a single, soothing jolt of recognition before he discovered his mistake.

As three o'clock approached and the sun sunk lower in the sky, Kidd realized he was at a dead end. With evening coming on, he decided to play his last card—locating Kenny. Kidd was beginning to think that wherever Kenny was, Annabelle would also be.

Kidd stopped at a bar called Slobberchops and made his way to a payphone. Pumping in some change, he rang Miguel, who was spending the day at home recuperating from an acute case of bruised gonads. Kidd intended to ask Miguel to provide him with a contact number for Officer Enrique Torres, but when Miguel answered, the chief of staff had other news.

"He's out," Miguel said, still cringing from the soreness in his testicles.

"Did his father put the screws to him?" Kidd asked.

"No charges were filed, if that's what you're asking," Miguel said. "But I don't think the old man got what he was looking for. Whatever progress he might have been making in there was cut short when his *mujer* showed up."

"*Mujer?*" Kidd asked. "I don't understand."

"His *mujer*," Miguel said. "His woman."

"Whose woman?"

"Carl's woman," Miguel said.

"You mean his wife?" Kidd asked. "You mean Martha?"

"I don't know what they call her, boss, but you wouldn't want to mess with this chiquita." Miguel laughed through his pain. "From what I heard, she beat the shit out of him. They almost arrested her, too, but Enrique let it go. He figured it was between the family."

Martha Kernick is in Los Angeles, Kidd thought. How the hell did that happen? "What time did this all go down?" he asked Miguel.

Miguel told him the events had occurred around noon. Then he told Kidd something else. "Your daughter was with her."

Kidd shook his head, trying to reconcile how Annabelle and Kenny's mom became connected. He decided he didn't care. He needed to find out where they went.

"Call me back in a few minutes," Miguel said. "I'll ask my cousin."

Kidd hung up the phone and waited, agonizingly, until he had counted to three hundred. Then he pumped more change into the slot and dialed Miguel.

"Enrique said he doesn't know where they went," Miguel stated. "But the old man did leave a cell number last night so Enrique could tell him when to come and get the boy."

"It's my best shot," Kidd said, although he didn't relish the idea of speaking with Carl Kernick again. Everything about what they had conspired to put Kenny through felt dirty. Kidd took the number on the back of a cocktail napkin, then he thanked Miguel. "And give my best to your swollen *cojones*," he added. "On behalf on my daughter, I apologize."

"Thanks, boss," Miguel said. "And I was thinking—" But Kidd hung up.

More change. Kidd dialed the number he had scribbled on the back of the cocktail napkin. The receiver felt cold against his ear. His heart started to race, and his skin went clammy. What if Carl hung up on him?

"Hello?"

The voice over Carl's cell phone wasn't Carl's. It was female—soft and fluffy, like a cattail swaying in the summer breeze. It was a voice from Kidd's past, although it wasn't a past very long in the making.

"Mrs. Kernick?" Kidd asked.

There was a tittering chuckle on the other end of the line, followed by a contented sigh.

"Oh, Bent," the voice said. Then it lowered to a whisper. "We've had sex. I think you can call me Martha."

In the end, it was Martha Kernick who once again stepped forward to save Charles Bentley Kidd during a time of despair.

After exchanging pleasantries, Martha informed Kidd that Annabelle was staying with the Kernicks at the Rostoff Hotel Sunset, which was located in the eleven-hundred section of Sunset Boulevard. From the bar in Westwood, Kidd was only a few miles away. He thanked Martha and told her he would be right over.

"Would you like me to tell Annabelle you're coming?" Martha asked.

Kidd pondered the idea briefly. "I'll leave that to your maternal judgment."

Martha thought for a second. "Just come over," she said. "We'll make it another of our little secrets."

Kidd hung up the phone feeling a tad guilty. He wondered how many days, months or years it would be before Martha learned that their "little secret"—the torrid affair between them—was no longer a secret, and to Kenny it certainly wasn't little. He tried to give Kenny some credit. Maybe the boy will understand why things like that can happen between two people, Kidd thought. Maybe he'll let his mother retain the memory of that exotic time in her life unburdened by the rancor of an angry child. Kidd certainly hoped so. He knew he would always look upon his experiences with Martha as the beginning of his rebirth into the realm of feeling and emotion, and he hoped Martha would forever cherish their time together as well.

Thirty minutes later, through a heavy rush of traffic, Kidd stood before the door to Room 627 at the Rostoff. His insides tightened as he tapped a set of shaking knuckles against the muntin. It took Martha Kernick all of three seconds to open up.

"Hello, Bent," she said, spreading the door wide.

She looked prettier than Kidd had even remembered—in fashion and in face. Gone were the houndstooth slacks and bulky pullover tops that had always made her appear so dowdy. Now she wore a pink wing collar shirt, black wide-leg pants with a bit of shimmy at the ankles, mule pumps, and a string of pearls looped twice around her neck. She had dyed the gray out of her hair and lost some weight, which showed up most noticeably in the reduced padding of her cheeks and chin. She had even waxed her eyebrows down to thin, neat strips—not that he would have ever said anything, but they had been a touch gnarly before.

But for all her beauty, Kidd felt only a fleeting surge for her in his loins. Their time had come and gone, and she had been the one to end it. He was thankful that she had. Otherwise, in the screaming intensity of their bodily conflagration, Kidd might not have experienced enough quiet time to hear what his heart truly desired—times like when he was traveling over the vast rolling prairies of Iowa and Nebraska on a Sunday, or crossing through the pristine solitude of the Rockies, where the lighter air pressure made noise less caustic.

"Thanks for having me, Martha," Kidd said.

"My pleasure," said Martha. "It's so good to see you again, Bent." She leaned forward and kissed him on the cheek. "Come in. Please."

Martha led Kidd into the hotel room, which was a bigger suite than Kidd's accommodations at the CandyLand. Kidd glanced around the sitting room, but saw no sign of anyone else.

"Where's Kenny?" he asked, removing his jacket.

"He and Carl went to Santa Monica to look at real estate," Martha replied. She took Kidd's jacket and hung it in the closet. "Kenny said he wants something near the ocean but close enough to campus. Honestly, I don't know what they're going to see at this time of day. It's almost dark outside."

He's staying here, Kidd realized. Kenny is staying in Los Angeles. How the hell had he pulled that off? Kidd's plan was foolproof. How could Carl possibly have screwed it up?

But Kidd didn't want to fight anymore. He tried to remember his thoughts from earlier in the day—good thoughts of Kenny as a person; great thoughts of the special qualities the boy brought to the world. As for any relationship between Kenny and Annabelle, Kidd would step aside and watch their parts fall where they may.

"I'm glad for him," Kidd said, forcing a smile. "He needed to get out of Connecticut."

"We all needed to get out of Connecticut," Martha added wryly. She pointed at the minibar. "Would you like something to drink?"

Kidd waved her off. "Those things are always so over-priced."

"Nonsense," Martha said with a laugh. "It's on Carl. Everything is on Carl. Take a bathrobe home if you'd like. Or that flat-screen television. He'll cover it."

Kidd declined politely with a raised palm. "I really just want to see Annabelle," he said.

"Certainly," said Martha. "She's right over here."

Martha led Kidd to a bedroom down the hall. She knocked, waited for permission to enter, then pushed the door open to reveal Annabelle sitting on the bed. Kidd's daughter was wrapped under the covers and had a paperback in her lap. Annabelle looked up as the door opened. She went pale at the sight of her father.

"I'll leave the two of you alone," Martha said. Kenny's mother turned to leave.

"Martha?" Annabelle called after her.

"Yes, dear," Martha said, turning back.

"We're still going shopping in a few minutes, right?" Annabelle's eyes were eager with anticipation. Or was it fear over her father's unexpected presence? Kidd couldn't tell.

"That's right, dear," Martha said. "Dinner and shopping in Beverly Hills. I've still got plenty to burn on the MasterCard." Martha let loose a wicked laugh and shut the door.

In Martha's absence, an awkward silence filled the room. Annabelle closed the paperback and placed it against her chest.

"May I come in?" Kidd asked.

"It's a free country," Annabelle said. "You of all people should know that."

Kidd entered the room and sat on the edge of her bed. He eyed the book she was hiding behind.

"What are you reading?" he asked.

"Just a detective story," Annabelle said. "Do you know how many ways there are to kill someone in this world? I've learned a few things."

Kidd cleared his throat, trying to sway his mind away from the unpleasant image of being murdered by his daughter to the beautiful image of a daughter found. "I looked for you," he said. "A sushi restaurant told me you'd been there and left. I didn't know what had happened to you."

"You needn't have worried," Annabelle said. "I slept at the Happy Traveler near the pier. Which, thanks to Martha, was better than on the pier. Or under it."

"Annabelle, there's something I need to tell you."

Annabelle held up a palm. "We are way past that point, Daddy. You kidnapped me, then you locked me into a hotel room with some jackass who likes to watch Mexican soap operas, then you almost got Ken killed."

"I did it for your own good," Kidd said. "I did it for both your goods."

Annabelle clenched her jaw. "You know, I don't think I can take anymore of your spin, Daddy. The past year of it was hard enough."

Kidd let out a dejected sigh. "Annabelle," he said, "regardless of what went on this past year, don't ever think that I've never wanted anything but the best for you."

"You've wanted the best for me?" Annabelle said. "Is that what you really wanted?"

"It is," Kidd said.

"Is that what you still want, even now?" Annabelle asked.

"Wholeheartedly," Kidd said.

"Then stop lying to me," Annabelle said. "Stop lying to me, stop lying to Mom, stop lying to everybody. All you do is lie. That's the problem."

Kidd sat limply on the edge of the bed and dropped his chin to his chest. There was nothing he could say. Annabelle was right. Kidd had been lying to everybody his whole life. To speak the truth—who his father really was, what he really wanted out of life and love, why he did the things he did—might mean to subject himself to obliteration at the hands of repulsion, or worse, apathy. That was a fear with which Charles Bentley Kidd had lived consummately—the fear that nobody would love him. And yet, that fear had led him into actions which had actually caused him to be unloved by the majority of Americans, which had destroyed the love from his wife, and which had placed in jeopardy the affections of his beautiful child.

"The most horrendous day of my life, Daddy," Annabelle said, "was the day I learned that everything you were telling me was fiction. That what I believed about you was one big charade. And the worst thing is, most people create lies by their silence, by what they don't say, by letting false impressions stand. But you created them with your mouth. And that shows malice aforethought."

Malice a-what? Kidd thought. Christ, the way his daughter was phrasing it, Kidd felt guiltier than he ever believed possible. But he also felt pride. He seriously considered calling the Justice Department and recommending Annabelle as the next special prosecutor. President Russell was sure to fuck up sooner or later, and Annabelle was just the pit bull to sic on his skinny ass.

"My life has always been complicated, 'Belles," Kidd told her. "My relationship with your mother even more so. Complications lead to things, things you aren't always proud of. Maybe someday you'll understand."

"Right now, Daddy," Annabelle said, her eyes locking onto his, "all I want to understand is how not to marry a man like you."

Kidd felt a sharp pain at his sternum, as if Annabelle had just pressed a carving knife to his chest, sliced deep, and delivered up his beating heart for Thanksgiving dinner. "You can't mean that, 'Belles," he said.

"I do mean it, Daddy," she said, "because it's the truth."

"That's an ugly truth," Kidd said.

"The truth may be ugly, Daddy, but it's a beautiful ugly. It's a respectful ugly, too." Annabelle tossed the paperback to the nightstand, then she threw off the covers and slid out of bed on the side opposite her father. "Now, if you'll excuse me," she said, "Martha and I have a date to go shopping."

Kidd stood up and watched Annabelle slip on a pair of clogs. She was wearing low-rider jeans with an orange halter top. Over the halter, she tossed a leather jacket and cinched it at the waist. Not the most refined clothing to flaunt on a trip to the boutiques of Beverly Hills, but then again, Annabelle had changed. She wasn't the same girl she had been in Washington. Now she was letting her personality create her style.

Annabelle grabbed her bag from a chair near the desk. She turned and stood tall, eyeing her father in the same dismissive way the U.S. Secretary of State might eye a visiting diplomat from some scrawny island shithole. "Anything else?" she asked.

Kidd pursed his lips. He didn't want her to go. If she went, he was certain he would never see her again. He proposed a compromise. "I don't know what your plans are tomorrow," he said, "but I'd like to see you on Thanksgiving."

Annabelle folded her arms. "The Kernicks are taking Ken and me up to El Tocón for dinner. We have reservations for mid-afternoon. That was Ken's and my plan before you made your grand entrance last night."

"Yes, okay," Kidd said, remembering what Night and Day had told him about Annabelle's plans, and what shithead means he had taken to thwart them. "But I was hoping you might be willing to join me for church in the morning."

Annabelle raised an eyebrow. "Church?" she asked. She chuckled in disbelief. "Honestly, Daddy, when was the last time you were in a church?"

"It's not as long as you think, Annabelle," Kidd said. "There's a nice Baptist congregation in Santa Monica that has a service tomorrow at ten. You could meet me there and still make your dinner in El Tocón with time to spare."

Annabelle shook her head. "Why do you want to go to a Baptist service, Daddy? We're Catholic."

"No, 'Belles," Kidd said, "you're Catholic—you and your mother. But I'm a Baptist. All of me. Right down to my blood." He tapped his chest with shaking fingers.

Annabelle crossed her eyes at her father. "I'm sorry, Daddy, but I don't know what the hell you're talking about."

"Come to church with me tomorrow, 'Belles," Kidd said, "and you'll understand exactly what I'm talking about." Kidd held her in a genuine gaze. "And it will all be the truth."

"The truth?" Annabelle said. "Do you mean that?"

"I'll take an oath," Kidd said, raising his right hand. "I, Charles Bentley Kidd, do solemnly swear that I will faithfully execute the honesty which I am about to undertake, and will, to the best of my ability, preserve, protect and defend the dignity of my precious Annabelle."

"So help you God?" Annabelle asked.

"So help me God," her father said.

"He better," Annabelle said.

Thus, it was arranged. Annabelle would meet her father at the First Baptist Church of Santa Monica tomorrow morning at 9:30, and she would extend an invitation for Kenny and the

Kernicks to join her. At the service, Kidd would make peace with his daughter, and he would also mend fences with the boy he considered a son. But most important, he would come to terms with himself. It was an opportunity he couldn't pass up, no matter how uncomfortable its execution might be.

Kidd walked Annabelle out of the bedroom, then he escorted her and Martha down to the Rostoff's valet. Outside, he kissed Annabelle goodbye and hugged Martha, whispering "Thank you" into the ear of Kenny's mother for a host of reasons she probably would never understand. Then he got back into his rental minivan and drove to Santa Monica as fast as he could manage without getting pulled over for speeding. He had had enough of the LAPD, after all.

But his need for speed was sincere. There was only one way Charles Bentley Kidd could make good on the promise to Annabelle, and there was only one man in Southern California who could make that way a reality. Kidd needed to contact Reverend Harland Stubbs. And quickly.

CHAPTER 53

★ ★

Annabelle arrived at the First Baptist Church of Santa Monica a full forty-five minutes before the start of the Thanksgiving Day service. She was already sweating on the cool morning over the exact reason why her father had asked her to join him there, and wondering nervously about what she would be in for once she found out.

He's not going to embarrass me again, she kept telling herself, more of a prayer than a declaration. I don't think I can handle it if he embarrasses me. I'll get up and walk out, I swear to God.

For support, she had not come alone to the church. Ken was with her, and she adored him for it. Not only had he not put up a fuss on the previous evening when she asked him to escort her, but he had read her nervousness over the whole affair, anxiety she tried hard to conceal. Maybe he read it in the fact that Martha said Annabelle had barely eaten at dinner, or maybe because she had tossed and turned when she tried to sleep, but, regardless, sometime in the night, after an indeterminable amount of restlessness, she heard Ken get off the couch at the other end of the room, walk over to her, sit on the corner of the bed, and hold her hand. His hand felt warm and soothing to her, and she easily let her fingers melt into his own. She fell asleep almost immediately and didn't open her eyes until the alarm clock went off. When she rolled over to say good morning to Ken on the couch, he was already up. She heard water cascading from their private shower. Behind the door, Ken was humming what sounded like an Elvis Presley tune—"Viva Las Vegas," she thought. Annabelle smiled. Ken would always have Las Vegas, particularly the memory of a splendid night with Darby Duvall, and she was glad for him.

They drove over from the Rostoff Sunset in Ken's newly-bequeathed Cadillac—a gift from his father, who, along with Martha, was joining Annabelle and Ken for the service. Ken may not have had a driver's license, but he was behind the wheel nonetheless, much to the protest of Carl, who stated from the backseat that a boy without a valid permit had no business being on the road. Martha told him that if Ken could drive cross-country without crashing his vehicle upside-down in a ditch (which Carl had apparently done), then Ken had certainly earned the right to drive them to church, laws or no laws. When Carl complained openly that his gift to Ken now left him without a car, Martha stepped in to defend her son again.

"Oh, stop fretting about it, Carl," she said. "Just go buy yourself one of those new Porsche Magnet SUVs. When you left me without a vehicle, that's what I did." Whereupon Carl Kernick made a sucking sound like he was choking on his tongue. Ken wanted to pull off the freeway to get his father something to drink, but Martha bade her son onward. "He'll be fine, Kenny," she said. "It's after he sees his credit card bills that I'm afraid of. You best make sure you have your will in order, Carl." She laughed wickedly and slapped her choking husband on the back. He was still choking twenty minutes later when they pulled into the parking lot for the First Baptist Church.

As Annabelle and the Kernick family walked to the church's front entrance, Carl got his lungs in order, but Annabelle felt her own lungs stiffen. Among all the parishioners gathering on the steps to greet one another, her father was nowhere to be seen. She stopped in the middle of the crowd, squinting through bright sunlight, and looked around for him, but he wasn't there. Carl Kernick grew visibly impatient with the delay. Annabelle had deduced early on that Ken's father wasn't a man who liked to stop for anything.

"Maybe he's inside," Carl huffed.

"I don't know," Annabelle said, standing on her toes to get a better view. "He didn't really say where he wanted to meet, only to be here."

"Let's go inside," Carl said, more like an order than an option.

Before they could turn for the doors, Annabelle was approached by a smiling African-American woman in a gorgeous periwinkle dress. "Are you Annabelle?" the woman asked, placing a hand on Annabelle's back.

"I am," Annabelle said.

The woman held out her other hand. "I'm Tabitha Stubbs, Pastor Stubbs's wife. I assume you're looking for your father."

"We are," Carl said curtly. Martha slapped him in the stomach.

"You'll see him shortly," Tabitha Stubbs said to Annabelle. "I'm one of the greeters today, so why don't I see you to your seats?"

"We have seats?" Carl Kernick said.

But Tabitha Stubbs ignored him. She guided Annabelle and her guests through a door and into the foyer of the church. "You're down front," she told Annabelle. "Although, if there are four of you, we'll have to make room."

Tabitha Stubbs led Annabelle and the Kernick family down the aisle of a white-walled church that was already full with worshipers. Chatter filled the hall as they walked in, but when they made their way down the aisle, escorted by the pastor's wife, the chatter muted with stutters of recognition. Annabelle hoped that people were simply recognizing Ken from the *Los Angeles Post-Tribune* photo of him in Las Vegas with Darby Duvall, but she knew it was a pointless wish when a twentysomething woman to her left said to a companion, and not quietly, "What's Annabelle Kidd doing here?" Annabelle smiled politely. But at that moment, the former first daughter realized how much she preferred those mute-but-pithy moments of identification instead.

They were led to the third row of seats on the left, which was reserved. Half the seats were occupied by an attractive African-American family which Tabitha Stubbs introduced as her father, sister, brother-in-law and her three nieces, all teenage girls. She also introduced her own five children—three boys and two girls—who were sitting in the row in front of them, along with a graying Asian gentleman she identified as the mayor of Santa Monica. After greetings were exchanged, Tabitha handed the guests their bulletins, then she asked her family to move down one seat, indicating with an extended arm for Annabelle and the Kernicks to squeeze into the three available chairs. Martha sat first, then Annabelle and Ken shared a seat. Carl Kernick took the aisle.

"What's going on?" Ken asked as they settled in. He was staring stone straight at the empty chancel, trying not to draw attention to himself with the slightest movement.

"I have no idea," Annabelle said. She patted his thigh, which was practically in her lap.

Minutes passed and her father still hadn't made an appearance, and even if he had shown up, Annabelle didn't know where he would sit. Eventually, a piano player stepped out from a room in the back and the crowd quieted. The player sat at his Steinway and hit the keys. Everyone stood. A choir, robed in cobalt blue garments and carrying folders of sheet music, appeared at the back of the church and began to make the procession down the aisle, all while belting out a rousing rendition of "'Tis So Sweet to Trust in Jesus." The church erupted in voices—some good, some not so good. Ken glanced at Annabelle, who reached down, took a hymnal from the holder attached to the back of the chair in front of them, and turned to the psalm indicated in the bulletin. She tried to sing, but her tones were off and she was embarrassed. Ken tried as well, but when he turned around to look at the procession, he suddenly clammed up.

Annabelle felt him grip her forearm. Then she heard him say, "I found your father."

Annabelle stopped singing. She turned and followed Ken's gaze to the back of the procession, and her mouth dropped. Her father was bringing up the rear of the procession, walking side by side with a limping man she assumed to be Pastor Stubbs. And he was doing something she had never seen him do in a church before—he was singing. To the heavens.

"Oh, no," Annabelle said, cupping a palm to her face to conceal her growing terror. "Oh, God."

She and Ken watched the procession slink down the aisle. The twelve-member choir passed her row, their throats exploding in song. Then the choir master and assistant pastor passed by. Then Pastor Stubbs and Charles Bentley Kidd. Her father found her in the crowd and winked at her, then he belted out a verse of hymn and followed the procession to the chancel.

The choir and choir director took up position on a set of risers near the back of the chancel. The pastor, assistant pastor and her father stood next to them but had cushioned seats. All turned to face the congregation. The piano player crushed the chords for the last verse of the hymn and the voices of the parish swelled in harmony. Then the song ended and a peaceful calm spread over the hall. Pastor Stubbs hobbled forward to the podium and switched on a microphone.

"Thank you, friends," he said, his voice as lush and soothing as honey. "Thank you for coming out this morning to give thanks and praise to our Heavenly Father for the many blessings He has bestowed upon us this year. Please be seated."

There was a rustle as the congregation sat. Annabelle watched her father take to his chair with an eager smile on his face.

As Annabelle struggled to get comfortable in the reduced confines of her shared seat, and against the grist of what her father was up to, she felt Martha Kernick lean into her from her left.

"You didn't tell me Bent was going to be part of the service," Martha whispered.

"I didn't know," Annabelle whispered back.

"Well, he looks absolutely wonderful," Martha said. Annabelle scrutinized Ken's mother knowingly. Martha flashed a guilty, confessional smile, and Annabelle couldn't help but smile back. Of all the women her father had cheated with, she liked Martha Kernick the best.

Annabelle stared at her father on the chancel and felt her bile rise on a crest of impending doom. Instinctively, she reached out for the one thing she knew would calm her—Ken's hand. She weaved her fingers into his and immediately felt better.

In her newfound serenity, she was able to formulate a clear, concise and rational plan of action for the rest of the service— in case of embarrassment, grab Ken and run. With his Cadillac and a lead foot, they could be in Mexico in two hours.

CHAPTER 54

★ ★

Annabelle squeezed Kenny's hand so hard he thought she was going to snap his fingers in half.

"Are you all right?" he whispered into her ear. The smell of her skin had become more intense over the last few minutes, and it wasn't moisturizing lotion she smelled of, or bath soap. It was a far more ominous scent—the blunt burst of fear.

But Annabelle never turned her head. She kept her eyes locked squarely on her father as the pastor stepped forward to greet the congregation. When the pastor glanced down in silence before offering up a prayer, Annabelle nodded to Kenny, indicating she was fine. But Kenny could tell that she was merely putting on a brave face. Kidd's unexpected presence in the procession had rattled Annabelle to her bones, especially after Kidd had implied to her that they would be sitting together—father and daughter—sharing a pleasant Thanksgiving morning at church. Kenny could only imagine what Annabelle was thinking at that moment, as she watched her disgraced father hobnob among the officiates of a church where he had never worshiped, with an expression of piety on his mug that seemed wholly out of place given his history. Kenny wanted to ask Annabelle if she was okay again, but he knew she would just agree. For the truth, he would have to let her fingers tell her story.

Those fingers stayed forceful throughout the pastor's prayer, and they didn't let up through a set of announcements which were delivered like miniature sermons from various members of the parish about all the things the congregation had to be thankful for during the past year. They eased off briefly for a rocking rendition of "How Shall I Follow Him I Serve" which accompanied a passing of the collection plate, and they even managed a playful tug when the plate arrived at their row and Martha made Carl give a donation of all the big bills in his wallet, approximately four hundred dollars' worth, which caused Carl to growl.

But Annabelle's fingers went right back to their stiffness after the hymn when she and Kenny saw the pastor give Kidd an anticipatory tap on the leg with his hand. The pastor stood, smoothed the flaps of his suit coat, and walked limp-legged to the podium.

A metallic thump echoed across the hall as the pastor adjusted the microphone on the podium. Once the microphone was set, the pastor let the echo fade, then he cleared his throat and looked solemnly upon the congregation. "Friends," he said, his voice flowing over his flock, "today on this great day of celebration, it is my pleasure to introduce a special guest—"

"Oh no," Annabelle said. Her fingers curled, and she dug her nails into Kenny's dress pants.

The pastor continued, "Last Sunday, I had the honor of meeting this man for the first time, although I, like you, thought I knew him already." The pastor shook his head dramatically. "On the contrary, the man I found sitting in this parish that morning was nothing like I expected. In fact, I found him to be warm, kind, respectful, and honest. I hope you'll accept him today as he offers us his special message of faith. Please welcome as our guest sermonizer, the former president of the United States, Mr. Charles Bentley Kidd."

The pastor turned and held out a stumped wrist to Kidd. The ex-president rose cautiously and walked to the podium. The congregation gave their one-time leader a hesitant smattering of applause. It was clear that they were as confused by his presence on the chancel as Kenny and Annabelle.

Kidd reached the podium and shook the pastor's hand. The pastor turned and walked back to his seat near the choir. Kidd faced the congregation and adjusted the microphone. He smoothed his tie, took a sip of water from a glass, and coughed to clear his throat.

He's scared, Kenny thought. The man who had once commanded the full force of the most powerful nation on earth is standing in front of a few hundred Baptist churchgoers, and he's scared. For the first time since they had met, and through all they had experienced together, Kenny thought he had finally gotten a glimpse of the real Charles Bentley Kidd—vulnerable, devoid of airs, with a fear that seemed steeped in rationality instead of need. Kenny liked what he saw, this truth. But Annabelle didn't. Her nails dug deeper into Kenny's pants.

Kidd began, "Pastor Stubbs, Assistant Pastor Clyde, Choir Director Phelps, members of the First Baptist Church of Santa Monica, thank you for having me here today as part of your celebration. You should all know, however, that Pastor Stubbs did not ask me to speak to you. Last night, I imposed myself on him with this request, and during a very late-night phone call at that. Regardless, he was gracious enough not to turn me down. So thank you, Pastor Stubbs."

Kidd turned and nodded to him. The pastor smiled and nodded back. Somebody two rows behind Kenny and Annabelle let out a churlish wheeze.

"I'll try to be brief," Kidd continued, ignoring the wheeze and setting his caramel voice firmly on the path of powerful elocution. "Many of you probably do not know this, but throughout my life, I've never been a person who tolerated weakness. All my life, from as far back as I can remember, I've sniffed out the weakness in others, pounced on it, ridiculed them for it, and gotten angry and self-righteous about it. I wanted everybody to be strong, you see. I wanted everybody to be tough. What I didn't want was to be burdened by somebody else's inability to perform at a time of maximum requirement, or to take care of themselves in general."

"Where the hell is this going?" Kenny asked Annabelle.

"I don't know," Annabelle said, exasperated. "But how do you feel about Mexico? We can be there by noon."

"Let's just sit tight," Kenny said. He patted Annabelle's thigh. To his surprise, Annabelle listened to him.

"What I never understood," Kidd said, "was that my disdain for weakness came from the fact that I was weak. Weaker, in fact, than anyone whose weakness I deplored."

Someone in the crowd let out a "Speak it, brother!"

"Last night," Kidd said, "after a conversation with my daughter, as that concept finally sank in, I asked myself, 'Charles Bentley Kidd, how does this weakness manifest itself in you? Through bravado? Arrogance? Self-centeredness?' While I am guilty of them all, those are just symptoms, too. Where my weakness really shows is in honesty. In being honest with myself. And while many of you may think that my indulgences were a way of being honest with my desires, the fact is that my pursuit of indulgences stemmed from not being honest with myself a long time ago."

Kidd wiped his brow with a palm, then he lifted a glass of water off the podium and took a sip. The sip's duration seemed interminable, as if Kidd might be contemplating exactly how deep he wanted to go with his next statement. Finally, he unlocked his lips from the rim and returned the glass to the podium.

"Let me go back to something I've been keeping hidden for a number of years," Kidd said. He cleared his throat and remained silent for a few moments. A look of pain overtook his face. "My mother," he said, "was an amazing woman. To say that I loved her would be a gross understatement. Anna Bunton Kidd raised me alone. She provided for me. She nurtured me. And although we were not well off financially, we were truly rich in love and respect. But growing up, I believed that my mother came from Oxford, West Virginia. I believed that at seventeen she had married a boy from the next town over—my father, Horace Kidd—and that he had died in the Nickleton Coal Works explosion shortly after I was conceived. I also believed that my mother was so devastated by his death that she fled West Virginia and relocated to Hawleyville, Ohio, to start a new life. I was born in Hawleyville, and you know the rest of that story. But you don't know the truth. Neither did I until I was sixteen years old. My mother did not come from Oxford, West Virginia, as she claimed. In fact, her name was not Anna Bunton. And she never married a boy named Horace Kidd. She couldn't have. Because Horace Kidd didn't exist. My mother's real name was Annabelle Earl. Her real hometown was Stampler, West Virginia. When she was seventeen years old, she went to work for, and subsequently fell in love with, the pastor at the Elm Street Baptist Church. His name was Charles Ray Laudermilk. He was married with a family at the time. He is my father."

With those words, a rumble of disbelief spread through the congregation. But the parishioners' reactions didn't matter to Kidd—he just forged ahead.

"My mother created and perpetuated the lie about the fictitious Horace Kidd to protect the man she really loved from certain disgrace. And I know she loved him, because she never loved another man for the rest of her life. Her love for Charles Ray Laudermilk was so strong that my mother was willing to give up her family to keep the pastor from scandal. In her later years, she often wondered how much she had destroyed her parents and siblings by abandoning them, and it chewed at her, it really did. But by then I was immersed in Ohio politics, probably destined to become governor, and she didn't think she could sully my name by revealing that I was, indeed, the bastard son of a preacher man."

Behind him, Kenny heard whispers. Lots of them. The rumble of disbelief had grown into a chant of denial.

"Love is strange like that," Kidd said, oblivious to anything but the flow of his words. "When love is fully present in our lives, it can make us do the craziest things. We all know that, and we've all been there. But I've also learned that when love isn't present in our lives—not in its truest sense—its absence can create a vacuum that also makes us do crazy things."

Kidd looked squarely at his daughter, and his eyes began to shine with moisture. Kenny felt Annabelle's hand clutch hard around his.

"When I met my wife Margaret, I was eighteen years old. What a surreal age that was. I was considered by the law to be an adult, but I didn't feel like one. I was also away from home for the first time, living in the biggest city I had ever seen, and I was forced every day to plot out my own direction, a skill for which I was never very good. But worst of all, I was empty inside, mostly because I was still reeling from the shock of finding out about my true parentage. That shock was made worse by the fact that I couldn't tell anybody about it. The personal shame of it was too great, but also I didn't want to hurt my mother. During my first few weeks at Jesuit University, I was a boy in search of himself, in search of some identity, and it was ultimately Margaret Huff who gave me those things. From the beginning, Margaret saw the best in me. She brought me confidence and strength. She made love to me so frequently and so passionately that I believed I had worth. In the force of her personality, I felt a thousand times larger than I had ever felt, and that sense of grandeur bore fruit. Through her, I became more popular, more charming, more attractive to other people, and most of all, more focused. In the process, she helped me to feel the way I wanted to feel— meaningful in the world. But while I did love Margaret, I loved her less for matters of the heart and more for the way she managed me."

Kidd took another sip of water and swallowed hard. When he put down the glass, he said, "I always knew that I didn't truly love Margaret the way a husband needed to love his wife. You good people know what I mean by that—loving her soul, loving her body, loving her mind and her flaws, loving her no matter what. But I married her anyway, because that's what she wanted. Now, don't get me wrong, I thought I could grow to love her truly. But ours was a marriage with a simple goal, and that goal was political ascension. The pursuit of power brought glue to our union. Years later, we had a beautiful daughter,

Annabelle, who is more of an adult at nineteen than I will ever be, and Margaret and I reveled in raising her. It would be another gross understatement to say that we both cherish her deeply. You don't just cherish a child; you love them with the purest form of love you can ever feel. But there's another side to that love—it can't fill you completely. Neither could my affection for Margaret. So I did what any politician would do—I buried myself in work, hoping that the climb of political power would sate me. For the most part it did. But love is love, and love yearns."

Kidd coughed uncomfortably, and with his next words, Kenny could see why. "I started cheating on Margaret when I was a state representative," Kidd said. "It happened slowly at first—a tryst here and there—always trying to be discreet, but always looking for love to soothe my emptiness, too. Even as new women came into and out of my life, I thought I could control my passions by constantly stepping up the political ladder to bigger and better offices, which I hoped would make me slow my philandering ways. Unfortunately, I ended up discovering the opposite. With each higher office, my desire for love only burned stronger. It became a vicious circle—a merry-go-round I could never get off, and one that kept spinning faster and faster with each step forward. When I was elected president, the merry-go-round finally spun out of control. I had achieved the ultimate office I could ever reach. There was nowhere to go but down. Then my mother died, and the restrictions I had always placed on myself for discretionary purposes, so that I didn't embarrass her, came off. That's when I spiraled into disaster. You all know the stories by now. If you don't, feel free to pick up a copy of the Special Prosecutor's Report—it's a hell of a read. Sorry, Pastor."

Pastor Stubbs grinned and waved off the curse with a good nature. The congregation, however, remained silent.

"With the death of my mother," Kidd said, "I plunged into the abyss in a frantic, desperate search to find true love. One day that search came to an end in Amanda Pacheco. I know that many of you think my affair with her was purely a sexual event, and that I didn't love her. That she was just a child through whom I could recapture my youth. Honestly, I've wondered about that myself at times. But all I can show you is this—"

Kidd reached into his breast pocket and pulled out a heart-shaped lollipop, still in its original plastic wrapping, with a red, white and blue bow tied around its stem. Kenny hadn't seen Kidd produce an Amanda Pacheco Twirly since Chicago, when he had given one to the concierge at the Millennium Tower for information on Margaret's whereabouts. The lollipops and the humidor had disappeared after that, and Kenny had forgotten about them until this moment. Kidd held up the lollipop for the congregation. Many snickered as they began to realize what it was.

"Yes, I know, go ahead and laugh," Kidd said. "I deserve it. This is indeed one of the infamous lollipops made for me by Amanda Pacheco. At one point, I had more than three hundred of them, which she had given me as a sign of her love. This one, though, is my last."

Kidd inspected the lollipop from front to back. "So why is it still here?" he asked. "You all know my appetites—why haven't I devoured it like I devoured the others? In a moment of want, or of nervousness, or depression, or fear? Moments when I always turn to an oral fixation to settle my nerves. Why? Why can't I bring myself to open this final wrapper? Rationally, I know that a lollipop is nothing more than a blend of sugar, food coloring and artificial flavor, but to me, this one is supremely special, a holy relic, because it's all I have left to remind me of her."

Kidd looked at Annabelle again, and even Kenny could tell that a whopper of an admission was about to pass his lips. "With all due respect to my wife," Kidd said, "and to my daughter, and with all due respect to you, the good people of First Baptist, I cannot hide the truth any longer. I love, and am still in love with, Amanda Pacheco. I knew I loved her the moment I set eyes on her in Boston that afternoon. While we've been through the wringer together, and while my love for her has not only affected our lives but also the life of the nation, I know I will love her forever. Like my mother's affection for Charles Ray Laudermilk, my affection for Amanda Pacheco will not die, and I don't think I'll ever be able to love another woman after her. She's ruined me for anybody else, although there are others who were very special to me in my time of solitude." Kenny saw Kidd smile warmly at Martha Kernick. He sure as hell hoped his father hadn't seen it. Then Kenny heard Carl's stuttered breathing and knew that the man had fallen asleep.

"But also like my mother," Kidd said, "my love for Amanda blinded me. It caused me to make gross errors in judgment, and it took my mental faculties away from the glorious job of being the leader of the free world—a job which requires at its every step a man undivided. I was divided. I was juvenile. I was not worthy, nor was I fit, to be your president. The people of this great land deserve a leader who can hear them, who can empathize with them, who can understand them, and in my search for love, and then in my bliss at finding it, I could do none of that. For those immense shortcomings, I apologize to you all. I apologize to this nation. I deserved to be removed from office. My focus was gone and the country suffered for it. You all suffered. If I could do it over again, I would pull a King Edward the Eighth and resign my position for the woman I loved. But ego and hubris have a tendency to cloud perspective. I didn't think I had done anything wrong. Now I know otherwise. And I ask your forgiveness for it."

An excited ripple spread over the congregation.

"But I need to be forgiven on so many levels," Kidd said. "I apologize most wholeheartedly to my wife. Margaret didn't deserve the humiliation I brought down on her, and she's rightfully angry. None of this mess was her fault. Margaret is what she is—she's a general; she leads. If I had had more fortitude in my younger years, or even more fortitude when I was thirty, before Annabelle was born, I may have been able to admit to her the things I needed to admit to make everything better for both of us."

Kidd looked at Annabelle.

"But I am so glad my daughter came along," he said, melting his moist eyes into Annabelle's beautiful green orbs. "I simply could not imagine life without my precious 'Belles, regardless of the dynamic between her mother and me. I apologize to her as well. Annabelle, I have embarrassed you to such a degree that I don't know how you can ever feel close to me again. That includes the way I acted this past week, after I tried to regain your trust. Please forgive me, 'Belles. I do stupid things, and if I were just by myself, that would be fine. But you're my daughter, and it crushes me to think that my stupidity reflects negatively on you. I am so sorry, Annabelle. I can only promise you that if you will continue to welcome me into your life, I'll try to make you proud again."

Kenny felt Annabelle's fingers freeze in his grip, as if she were stuck in contemplation of her father's offer.

"And I apologize to everyone who found themselves caught up in my madness," Kidd said, looking directly at Kenny. "Especially to those of you who treated me better than I deserved, yet did not get treated well by me in return, even after we had become friends." He threw Kenny a wink, then looked away. "But most of all," he continued, "I apologize to the people of America. I brought shame, disgrace and economic peril to you during my time in office. I embarrassed you in front of the world. What I have offered today is not meant to excuse me for my actions; it's only meant to help you understand. In a few short moments, I will step away from this podium, and when I do, I'll be stepping into history. It is my great hope, however, that my years after the presidency bring honor to the country. Please know that from this day forward I am a repentant man who will try to make it happen. Please know, also, that irrespective of my failures, I was, am, and always will be your grateful and humble servant. Thank you."

Kidd bowed his head, then he turned and walked back to his seat near the choir. There was silence in the hall. He sat and looked at Pastor Stubbs, who gave him a warm smile. Kidd blew out a relieved breath and looked down solemnly. When he looked up, the congregation erupted in applause.

To Kenny the sound was amazing. It was louder than any clapping he had ever heard. The roar of approval was soon made even greater by a standing ovation. Everyone in the congregation rose and cheered, including the Stubbs family, the choir, the piano player, Martha, Kenny and Annabelle, and the mayor of Santa Monica. Of all the people to stand, though, Kenny found Annabelle the most inscrutable.

Kenny could still not imagine what she was feeling at that moment. Her father had just admitted to an entire church of people all the things he had never admitted to the people closest to him—things, in fact, which he had gone to extraordinary lengths to deny: that he had never loved Margaret Huff Kidd the way a man needed to love his wife; that he had lied to her for years; cheated on her incessantly; used her for his own gain; misled her; and in the end, humiliated her to an extent that no woman ever deserved, Rhino or not. Such was a heavy load for any child to bear. How could Annabelle handle it?

As the applause died down, the piano player ran his fingers along the keys and struck a chord, and the choir jumped into another rocking hymn. The program identified the song as "It is Well with My Soul," and Kenny found it to be quite appropriate for the moment. He watched Kidd join in with the singing. The former president was smiling, raising his voice loudly. Kenny glanced over at Annabelle and saw that she too was smiling as she sang. When she noticed Kenny watching her, she reached down. Their hands joined, Annabelle once again weaving her fingers between his, and Kenny had his answer about how Annabelle was taking her father's confession—her fingers were pliant and soft; they were dry and welcoming; they blended with his instead of fighting against them.

He gave her hand a gentle squeeze. She looked at him inquisitively.

"Everything cool?" he asked her over the music.

"I'm fine with it," she said, gathering his meaning. She leaned into Kenny so he could hear her better. The fearful scent of sweat on her was gone. "For once," she said, "my father actually told me the truth." She jiggled Kenny's hand in her own, gave him a moment to gather her meaning, then she gazed forward with electric emerald eyes and set her voice to song.

The church swelled with the power of the hymn. Parishioners raised their harmonies in praise of their Heavenly Father. As Kenny sang, off-key but committed, he surveyed his surroundings on this bright, fresh morning.

He looked at his father, who had woken up and now seemed tense from his face to his feet. Kenny couldn't blame the man. It was a new world for Carl Kernick—a world in which his once-meek wife now ordered him around, his once-compliant son now demanded independence, and both of them now spent his hard-earned cash faster than water over Niagara Falls. In a few days, Carl, on behalf of his son, would make an offer on a twenty-five hundred square foot, three-bedroom condo in the same neighborhood as the Mendelssohn. The down payment on the condo alone would cost Carl Kernick five times what Martha had paid for her new Porsche, the recently-purchased vehicle whose revelation had sent Carl into a fit of choking earlier that morning. Once the necessary papers were signed, and the deal closed, and Kenny had moved in, Carl would then have to wish his son well, hop on a plane, and fly back to a life that, for all intents and purposes, no longer existed—all his hopes and dreams for Kenny evaporated; the dynamic with his wife topsy-turvy; no one to boss around anymore except for his employees. It would be tough on the man, this strange power shift, but Kenny didn't care. Carl had made life tough on his family for ages. Now he was going to get his karmic backlash. And it promised to suck.

The woman who would deliver the majority of that backlash was standing to Kenny's left and singing like a wounded meadowlark. Kenny shifted his gaze from his father to his mother, and he could only shake his head. He didn't know what to think of this alien life form who took the shape and appearance of Martha Kernick. As if she could read his mind, his mother turned, caught him looking at her, and blew him a kiss. Kenny could only nod back. His mother now seemed a completely different person than he had known all his life. Since arriving in Los Angeles, she had smiled more, worn makeup, and radiated an odd confidence. And she looked stunning in her new Beba Prax suit, which, Annabelle confided to him, cost more than seven thousand dollars on Rodeo Drive. In essence, his mother looked happy. Someday Kenny and Martha might discuss her affair with Kidd, but not today. Today was for celebration. He doubted he would bring up her indiscretions anytime soon, either. From what he had learned during his travels with Kidd, Kenny knew it was better if he first tried to understand his mother before passing judgment—to get a true knowledge of her relationship with Carl; to see what she was lacking in her life with him; and to weigh how much that lacking ate at her. Once he tried to understand, he was hopeful that he could accept her actions, then move on. But looking at her, he couldn't deny that the affair with Kidd had somehow unleashed the best in her. He had a serene sense that Martha Kernick, doormat for decades, would fight for what she wanted for the rest of her life. God help his father. The woman was unbound.

The third verse began and Kenny glanced once more at Annabelle. She was beaming, her whole face aglow, as she stared off at her father, gazing at her dad in the special way a daughter should. Kenny followed her gaze to Kidd. He could see why Annabelle was so happy.

At the chancel, Kidd appeared like a man transformed. He was standing tall, with his jaw set firmly and his shoulders loose. Even his face seemed smooth and youthful, devoid of the creases Kenny had first noticed on that day in the driveway, when Kidd had returned with the Secret Service from a Wal-Mart excursion. But it was his hair that struck Kenny as the most changed. Kidd's locks, once dull with burden, now cast a rich, mocha glint from the lights above. Kenny smiled at the difference. He started to think that Kidd looked like a president again, but then he corrected himself—Kidd, Kenny saw, looked like a human being again. Like a man who had traveled on a dark and perilous journey to a hell of his own making, but who had somehow managed to return to the world stronger, smarter, a lot more humble, and a lot more conscientious of his fallibility when faced with choices. That Charles Bentley Kidd had once been a president of the United States seemed incidental to Kenny. Kidd's pursuit of power had clouded him, forced him off track, made him settle for relationships for which he really had no heart; then to compensate, he had pursued relationships which almost destroyed him. Now that Kidd had traveled that perilous road and survived, Kenny held out hope for the man. Between verses, Kenny offered up a silent prayer that Kidd's life from this point forward would be, if nothing else, a joyfully contented one.

And finally, after sweeping his eyes over the multitude of faces in the congregation, and seeing relief in their eyes as well, Kenny looked at himself.

What he saw astonished him. In two weeks, he had gone from being a wandering college dropout to someone who possessed ironclad goals for the future; from being mousy to being bold; from being a slave whose life was determined for him to being a master of his own life's path; from being someone who hated himself for his meager physicality to someone who placed value on the overall package—brains, confidence, style, and most important, how much you showed respect to the people around you.

He had gone, ultimately, from being a boy to being a man.

And it had been Kidd who affected the transformation—a former president as catalyst. For all the times they had cursed each other out, or Kidd had insulted him by calling him names, or they had exchanged physical blows, Kenny could only love Charles Bentley Kidd like a father, brother and uncle all rolled into one. He could even forgive Kidd for having him arrested and incarcerated two nights before. After all, crazy things happened on the road. Passions were inflamed. Territory became sacred. You couldn't spend fourteen days in close quarters with someone and not have conflict.

Regardless of how they had butted heads, Kidd had helped Kenny make the first forays into adulthood. In the process, Kidd had grown up as well. Perhaps a little too late for some, like his wife, but better than never for the man as a whole. What the future held for both Kenny and Kidd was known only to that Heavenly Father to whom the congregation was singing its song of praise. But Kenny was certain of one thing—

Should Kidd ever find himself in trouble again, be it in two weeks, two years or two decades, he could always come back to Santa Monica. Kenny had a Cadillac, after all, and there were still a lot of highways in the nation that Kenny and Kidd had not traveled. Kenny would even take time off from school or work for the man. He would invite Kidd to sit in the passenger seat and tell him to kick back. If Kidd were old and frail, he would get the man an orthopedic cushion. Then he would use his legally-procured driver's license to take Charles Bentley Kidd on another journey. Where they would be going this time was anybody's guess. But in the end, Kenny knew for sure, they would find the exact place they were meant to be.

EPILOGUE

★ ★

It would seem to Charles Bentley Kidd, in later years, as he looked back on this day for its grander historical implications, just as scholars at the time were beginning to look back on his administration for its grander historical implications, that the Thanksgiving of his fifty-third year wasn't really like Thanksgiving at all, but more like Easter Sunday—a day of profound spiritual resurrection after enduring a brutal execution at the hands of the State

Kidd's transformation from obliterated politician to renascent member of society began when news of his confession started to spread across the nation that afternoon, fueled on by word-of-mouth accounts from several members of the parish who went home and, instead of sitting down to a Thanksgiving meal, logged onto the *Los Angeles Post-Tribune's* website to report the speech through the "NewsAngels" link. When those parish members finally did get around to eating, they found themselves the recipients of phone calls from the *Post-Tribune*, which was seeking interviews. At midday, with an abstract of the speech pieced together through attendant memory, a story was written up by an on-call obituary writer who hated Thanksgiving and had volunteered to man the "NewsAngels" desk. His story read like a death notice, but its style didn't matter. Like a whirlwind forming out of a single twist of breeze, what had originated in humble, obscure fashion in a Baptist church in Santa Monica quickly gathered momentum and mass as it spun ahead through the country. By Friday night, as the nation settled in for the remaining half of a holiday weekend, the whirlwind was so large, and the other holiday news so slow, that most people in America couldn't avoid it. Whether on the networks or cable channels, or even Telemundo, reports of Kidd's speech flowed across news tickers, headed hourly updates, became the hot topic on talking-head programs, and saturated the Internet.

But as much as America read or heard about the speech, and as much as the country sopped up Kidd's words of repentance, there was still something missing—the immediacy of video.

That's where Pastor Stubbs came in.

After taking Kidd's phone call from bed on Wednesday night, the Reverend Stubbs tossed on some clothes and rummaged through his den closet, looking for a camcorder. If the former president of the United States was going to speak to his congregation the next day, Pastor Stubbs was going to tape it, if only for himself or his family, or perhaps as a visual history for the church, if anybody even cared.

Once the stories of Kidd's confession began to appear, Harland Stubbs knew he was sitting on a cash cow. The tape turned out to be of fine quality, considering he had set up the camcorder in the balcony. It showed Kidd from a high angle, as if the camera itself were looking down on him for his misdeeds, and given Kidd's powerful voice, the audio was excellent. Pastor Stubbs wrestled with the idea of selling the tape for profit, of making money off another man's burden, but it wasn't until he talked it over with his wife on Friday evening that his mind was put at ease.

"Charles Bentley Kidd chose your house, Harland," Tabitha Stubbs said. "If he didn't want you to record him, he should have gone to the Mormons down the street. They would have run his sinful ass back to Ohio."

"But what do we do with the money?" the pastor asked.

"I don't know," his wife said. "Think of something the church needs. Maybe a new roof."

"Or better," Harland Stubbs said. He knew just the thing. But it wouldn't be cheap.

The public-service Channel U.S. came in with the first offer—two hundred fifty thousand dollars. Not wanting the appearance of greed, and securing through the transaction enough money to buy the item he coveted, Pastor Stubbs took the deal. Channel U.S. played the tape in primetime on Saturday, airing it in conjunction with in-studio commentary, analysis from a renowned psychologist, and the insights, via satellite from Las Vegas, of a member of Kidd's administration: Tom Prudell, the former chief of staff turned president of Nevada State University, who kept squirming in his chair as if he had reeled in something else lately—like a case of the crabs.

The impact of the broadcast was immediate. The airing became the most-watched program in Channel U.S. history, knocking out of the top spot the impeachment verdict for Charles Bentley Kidd the previous May. It even required encore presentations on Sunday morning and Monday night. And seven weeks later, after much construction and a significant chancel redesign, the First Baptist Church of Santa Monica had something its pastor had always envisioned for it—a dunk tank baptistery. Built into the back wall of the chancel just above the choir risers, it looked to the congregation like a giant fish bowl. Some parishioners called it an eyesore, but Harland Stubbs was proud of the addition. For his first baptism, he bought a pair of high-priced rubber waders and a new suit. Then, to much fanfare, including a glowing article in the *Post-Tribune* by the former obituary writer, recently promoted to lifestyle reporter, the first person he baptized was Annabelle Kidd.

Looking back some time later, Charles Bentley Kidd would view the Channel U.S. broadcasts as the point where his life became an impressionistic blur of activity and requests.

Not to be outdone by a public-service news organization, NBC contacted Kidd on the Monday night after Thanksgiving to line him up for an hour-long special on one of its primetime news programs.

"The taping will have to be done fast," some youthful producer jockey told him. "The brass wants it to air for November sweeps. They end on Wednesday, in case you didn't know."

Kidd didn't know, but he happily obliged. The producer set up an interview to be conducted in the banquet room of the Mendelssohn on Tuesday morning. When the producer's entourage arrived, Kidd discovered that NBC had flown out a disarmingly familiar face to handle the interview—White House correspondent Susan Fratz, the woman Kidd had surreptitiously propositioned on his way out of office. With her cinnamon hair and tight body, she still looked as delicious as ever, especially when she sat down across from him on the two-chair set wearing a high-cut miniskirt that would have made a hooker on Hollywood Boulevard blush. Was she trying to tell him something? Kidd wondered. Did she finally want him to "take a ride down?" But to Kidd, it didn't matter. He had moved beyond her delectable dainties. He answered every question she posed with nothing but respect and dignity for her as a reporter, and as a woman. He was the model of the perfect gentleman. He said exactly what he meant and meant exactly what he said; there was no subtle innuendo for the married Ms. Fratz this time around. After ten hours of taping, when she shook his hand, told him it was good to see him again and turned for the door, she looked back at Kidd with confused eyes. Kidd couldn't tell if her expression was one of shock that he hadn't hit on her—or disappointment.

The explosion of interest in reconciliation between a disgraced former president and his abused populace created something of a cottage industry for Charles Bentley Kidd. He found himself over the course of the following year garnering large speaking fees on college campuses across the country. Each event drew fantastic crowds and always brought out the local news crews. While the question-and-answer periods that followed his speeches could get quite heated at times—students almost invariably confronted him over a parent's lost job or his predatory treatment of women—Kidd found the experience cathartic, for both him and the audience. Corporate America wasn't blind to Kidd's growing charms, either. Some companies hired him for exorbitant fees to preach to their workers about the perils of interoffice romances, while others just wanted him to extrapolate on how to handle management issues in the heat of a crisis (mostly for what not to do). In short, Charles Bentley Kidd became retro. He became popular again. And cool.

But for all his renewed fame, and for all the wealth which was swelling the seams of his bank account on a weekly basis, Charles Bentley Kidd often found himself a lonely man in the few years after his re-emergence into public life.

He discovered that in the quiet times he missed Kenny, times like when he was driving with the radio off, and the rush of air and the hum of tires created a lulling rhythm which made his mind wander to the past. Kenny had saved Kidd from a life of complete obliteration—that fact was clear to Kidd now, and he fully appreciated it. While Martha Kernick had brought Kidd back to feeling, Kenny had put him on the road to redemption and pulled him like warm taffy until he was shaped into a more acceptable form. For that, Kidd would always be grateful to the boy. Sometimes he just wanted to pick up the phone and call Kenny in Santa Monica, but he always stopped himself. From what Kidd heard, Kenny had quite a life out there. He was the top student in his class at the University of the West, where he was majoring jointly in physics and philosophy, and his condo a few blocks down from the Mendelssohn had become party central on weekends. And he was in love. The object of his affection was reportedly an effervescent Asian girl named Tuggy, a friend of Annabelle's from the volleyball team who was built like a tightly-wrapped firecracker. Tuggy, in turn, was bringing out the best in Kenny. According to Annabelle, he had grown five inches in the past year, and he was working out with Tuggy to gain muscle and tone. Kidd wished him well. He would always think of Young Kernick as a son, and in some strange way, as a father, too, for what he had created in the boy, the boy had also created in him.

Kidd missed Annabelle as well. With their relationship saved by Kidd's confession at the church that Thanksgiving morning, Kidd found himself desiring her company to catastrophic degrees. Annabelle was about to graduate from the University of the West, and after that he didn't know where she would go. She had talked about ideas as diverse as graduate school, working in corporate America, playing professional volleyball, and joining a relief organization. Wherever she ended up, Kidd felt certain that her destination would mean the end of her life as his little girl. Annabelle was standing on the brink of emancipation. Once she crossed into it, Kidd knew he would only see his daughter for wisps of time. The realization dug a pit in him.

But as much as he missed Kenny and Annabelle, the person Kidd came to miss the most was Amanda Pacheco. After all, his longing for Kenny and his daughter arose from a parental affection, but his longing for Amanda grew straight from the heart.

He had hoped that, in the weeks after his confession, Amanda would come to him. That she would see coverage of the event and that she would call. She never did. And he didn't have the heart to call her. To Kidd, that would be forcing himself back into her life, and he had already forced her into a life of notoriety from which she had probably never recovered.

Then one day, she appeared.

He was at a book signing in Portland, Maine, at a small boutique in the Old Port near the water. As Kidd stood at the podium reading a chapter from his memoirs that dealt with the Pastrygate scandal, he glanced beyond the crowd and saw her standing toward the back of the room near a shelf. Even from a distance, he could tell that she hadn't changed in seven years. At thirty, she still looked beautiful, although she had cut her hair and lost a slight amount of weight. But the best thing was, she was smiling at him.

From that day on they were inseparable. She had never married, and told him point blank that she had waited for him, even if he never came. She told him she loved him and could never love another. Often she cried and asked if he could forgive her for testifying against him; he told her he would have done the same thing if faced with prosecution. And in time, as their relationship blossomed anew, she said she wanted to move to Simondale with him, where Kidd continued to maintain his house on Hoban Lane, although he was rarely there. Instead, he moved to Maine, where Amanda had retreated in the aftermath of Pastrygate to hide from the world. "People leave me alone up here," she told him. In the year after the scandal, and with relative anonymity, she had even opened her own patisserie on Forest Avenue.

They never married. Margaret Huff remained steadfast in her opposition to divorce to the very end, even at the frequent pleadings of her daughter to let the marriage go. "Not on your life!" Margaret would yell at Annabelle. "He'll rot in the ground before he marries that fucking whore!" From her mother's tone, Annabelle could tell that Margaret Huff intended to live to the age of two hundred just to see that promise through.

In the absence of a marriage, Amanda Pacheco became Charles Bentley Kidd's de facto wife. She made a nice home for him in Cape Elizabeth, just outside Portland, and to much fanfare, she accompanied him in triumphant return to the grand opening of his presidential library in Hawleyville, where Kidd finally made peace with the hometown he had humiliated by christening a museum that dealt honestly and from all points of view with his presidency, and which drew much-needed tourists to an area reeling from the recent closure of the soap factory. She also encouraged him to reconnect with his Earl family cousins, all nineteen of them, and even the Laudermilk sons, who were now in their seventies and each on their third or fourth wife, so that he could meet his long-lost relatives and half-siblings. And in time, she bore him a child, a son, whom they named Charles Kenneth Kidd.

But few things made Kidd happier in later years, or did more to solidify his redemption, than the honor bestowed upon him by President Katharine McQuade during Kidd's seventieth year, when his hair had turned gray and his step was slowing.

A war was brewing between two African nations over mining rights for newly discovered gold deposits along a border. Given the importance of mining to the Sub-Saharan economies, and considering the history of tribal genocide in the region, the war promised to be long, intense and bloody. Someone had to step in. That man was Charles Bentley Kidd.

President McQuade named him an envoy, and Kidd headed off to Africa with a small entourage, intent on making a deal. After two weeks of negotiations, war was averted at Kidd's gentle insistence. The parties struck a bargain and divided mining rights rationally. And upon returning to the United States, Kidd could hold his head high and rightly claim that he was, in fact, the bringer of peace to Angola and the Democratic Republic of Congo.

But more than anything else, Charles Bentley Kidd had evolved, over time, into the bringer of peace to himself. He had affected that transformation by becoming an honest father to his children, a trusted partner to the woman he loved, and a solid citizen to an America that eventually treasured him again. And those accomplishments, he believed to his last days, were the greatest he had ever achieved.

ACKNOWLEDGMENTS

★ ★

Unlike Kenny Kernick, I do not know everything. Never was that fact more in evidence than during the writing of *All-American Kidd*. I am indebted to the following people or organizations for their guidance over the course of this book's development, from concept to publication—

For research: James Fitton of the United States Department of the Treasury, Robert Nelson of Wrabacon, Inc., Christopher Serb in Chicago, Matthew Garth for all things Baptist, Harvard University, the David P. Ehrlich Co., C-SPAN, and the Bossard Memorial Library in Gallipolis, Ohio.

For their support and encouragement during the writing: Jacqueline Zinno, Michael Brandi, Kathryn Lasky, Jessica Holley, Sherrie Greenlaw, and the late Mary Conway.

I am particularly grateful to the team at Group Poulain—Andrea Alley, Lead Editor; Kristin Chavonelle, Editor; and Beth Schoeller, Lead Proofreader—for their tireless efforts on my behalf.

And finally, I wish to thank my parents—my father, the poet Robert Henry Poulin, for the writing genes, and my mother, Betty Culpovich Brier, for the determination and fortitude to put them to use.

The individuals or organizations listed above have honored me with their generosity. If any errors, omissions or flaws remain in *All-American Kidd*, they are purely my own.

ABOUT THE AUTHOR

Rob Poulin was born in Maine and spent his youth there before attending college in Massachusetts. After graduating from Holy Cross with a degree in economics, he settled in Boston and began the dual life of corporate American by day and writer by night. *All-American Kidd* is his first novel.

Made in the USA
Charleston, SC
21 March 2016